The Malone Brothers Boxed Set

S.L. STERLING

To all of those who have found their true love.

A Kiss Beneath the Stars

A Kiss Beneath the Stars

Copyright © 2018 by S.L. Sterling

ISBN: 978-1-7751087-3-3

Editor: Erica Russikoff of Erica Edits; www.ericaedits.com

Cover Design: Thunderstruck Cover Designs

Chapter One

I pulled up outside of the home I had known for the last five years. I was meeting with the real estate agent today. Finally, the house had sold and I had been asked to come and sign the deal. I let out a sigh when I saw that the driveway was empty. I should have known better; as usual, she was running behind. I'm not going to lie, I was thrilled to get rid of this place—the memories here too real for me to continue to stay. I've been living with my sister, Evelyn, and her husband, Derek, for the last six months anyway. I shut the car off and headed up to the front door.

I had gone through the whole house, walking from room to room. I knew I was just doing this once again to punish myself for everything that had transpired. When I decided that I'd had enough of memory lane, I headed to the kitchen to wait for her. I could have chosen any room in the entire house to wait for her; why I had chosen this room, I had no idea. The room that held the most vivid memory for me. I looked around. At one point, it had been my favorite room in this whole house. He'd had it designed exactly how I wanted it—my dream kitchen. Now, I hated everything about it.

I took a seat at the breakfast bar. The silence was deafening, and I wished I had insisted on going to her office as opposed to coming here. As I glanced around the room, my memory traveled back to that morning, that dreaded morning when my once perfect little life came to a screeching halt, ending everything that was left.

It was my day off and I was sitting eating my breakfast, drinking my tea and reading through the morning paper. Things were still strained between Jason and me. Dr. Plante, my therapist, had told me that until he would come to couple's therapy to talk through everything that had happened, things would only get worse. Now at times I wished I had been more adamant that he come with me instead of pretending like it didn't matter.

I sat reading the entertainment section when I heard papers rustle behind me. I glanced over my shoulder. Jason stood in the doorway. "Morning. I see that new action movie you wanted to see has gotten great reviews. Maybe we could go see it on Friday."

"I already saw it," Jason mumbled and then went quiet again.

I had figured he would be happy that I had suggested it; after all, he was always complaining that I never wanted to do anything. His words hit me like a slap in the face. I took another bite of my bagel and continued to read the paper, trying to pretend like I wasn't bothered by his admission.

After a few minutes, I turned back to Jason and noticed that he hadn't moved from the spot he was standing. "Is everything all right?"

"I want a divorce." His voice shook as the words fell from his lips. I studied him. I couldn't believe what I had heard, but his head hung low, and he avoided my eyes. The small bit of breakfast that I had consumed threatened to make its return. Looking around, suddenly everything that we had worked so hard to have seemed like a waste, and all it had taken was those four little words.

I didn't know what to say. I had barely left the house in the past six months, and I had just returned to work and now this. I could feel the anxiety and depression creeping their way slowly back into me, despite all the medication Dr. Plante had me on. I dropped my bagel onto the plate that sat in front of me and glanced at the envelope he held in his hands. I looked at the man who stood before me. We used to be so in love; now I barely recognized him. How had things come to this?

"I take it you're wondering what's in the envelope?"

"What do you mean you want a divorce? Why?"

"I can't do this with you anymore. I've watched you deteriorate for months, ever since...well, ever since..." His eyes stayed down, and his lip quivered. "Well, it's just you're not the same person I fell in love with. I've been in contact with a lawyer, and the divorce agreement has already been drawn up."

"Ever since what, Jason? Why don't you just say it—ever since I lost our baby. I know you blame me, so just say it!" I glared at him. I would never forget the look in his eyes on that horrible day when he had come to the hospital and found out

the news. He blamed me for the loss and blamed me for the fact that I wouldn't be able to get pregnant again, and now he would add the divorce to that list as well.

He placed the envelope he was holding on the table in front of me. "I want it to be clean and easy. No stress for you or me. I've given you everything, including the house. All you need to do is sign the papers. Don't make this harder than it needs to be." He pulled his hand away from the envelope, and that was when I noticed he no longer wore his wedding ring, and by the looks of it, he hadn't for some time. It was gone, discarded as if it had meant nothing. I started to wonder exactly how long he hadn't been wearing it. "Did you hear me?"

"Don't make this harder than it needs to be," I mumbled as I stared at the envelope in front of me. Truthfully, this past year had been awful, but I had tried to pick myself back up, really, I had. Losing a baby wasn't easy, but being told that you wouldn't be able to have another was like having your heart ripped out and shredded into a million pieces. We knew that there were other options available, but our relationship had fallen into a state of total disrepair. We hadn't slept in the same bed in months, and he was never home; when he was, we ignored one another. We had spoken more in the last five minutes than we had in the past five months. I said nothing. I just kept my eyes locked on the envelope, fighting back tears. I jumped when the back door slammed shut. I hadn't even seen him leave. Just like that, he was gone.

When my stomach stopped threatening to release its contents, I finally picked up the envelope and opened it. I had nothing left in me. At this point, even if he had taken it all, I wouldn't have fought him, so it really didn't matter what that envelope contained. I tried to focus, tried to read what lay on the white paper, but all I saw was a jumbled-up mess of words.

After he had left me those documents and had walked out that door, he never did come back home. It was almost as if all that had happened didn't really matter to him and he had washed his hands of me completely. All his clothes hung in the closet, never to be worn again.

It was almost a month before I had my brother-in-law Derek check over the documents. I knew that if Jason had lied to me about what those documents contained, it could be much worse for me once those papers were signed.

When I finally got the green light from Derek, I signed the paperwork and dropped the envelope back at Jason's office, leaving it with the secretary. He might have given me everything, but I was the one who lost. Along with those documents, I handed him whatever was left of me. I didn't know who I was anymore, and what was worse, I didn't care. Every little bit of the person I once was had died that day.

The sound of footsteps in the hallway pulled me out of my memory. I sat, holding my breath, waiting for the person who belonged to those footsteps to come around the corner.

"There you are. Sorry I am late; I had another offer to close. Let's get these papers signed," Rachel sang as she dropped a folder on the counter. Again, that dreaded envelope flashed before my eyes. I blinked the memory out of my head and wiped away the stray tear that floated down my cheek. I took her pen and signed away the home I had once loved. Unfortunately, I couldn't sign away the memories that went with it, and no matter how hard I tried, I knew they would never leave.

After everything was completed, I drove back to my

sister's in silence. Everything was gone of the relationship that had once shown so much promise. I pulled into the driveway of my "new home" and sat staring at the house. Soon the front door opened, and Evelyn stood on the front porch waiting for me to get out of the car. I closed my eyes, leaned my head against the headrest, and took a deep breath. It was finally over.

Suddenly, my door was pulled open and Derek stuck his hand inside the car. "Come on, sis. Let's get you inside." Evelyn still stood on the front porch, watching me. I took hold of Derek's hand and climbed out of the car. But as soon as he wrapped his arms around my shoulders, I couldn't hold back my tears any longer.

Chapter Two

Autumn – Six Months Later

I lay in bed, totally engrossed in the latest release from my favorite romance author, when I heard a quiet knock on my bedroom door. Setting the e-reader down on the bed beside me, I looked up to see Evelyn peek her head in. "What are you doing?"

"Just reading. What's up?"

"I want to talk to you about something." She made her way into the room and flopped down across the foot of the bed, just like she used to do when we were kids.

"I know, I know, I've overstayed my welcome. Just give me a couple of months to find a place. Dr. Plante says that I should be able to return to work in the new year."

"No no no, it's not that. Don't be ridiculous. You can stay as long as you want. Derek and I already told you that."

I sat back and relaxed a bit. I felt like I was imposing on

them. I had been there for almost a year and felt like they were ready to get their own lives back in order. "Okay, then what did you want to talk to me about?"

"Honey, Derek and I have been talking. We think you need to get out, start doing things again, maybe start dating again."

"But this is where I am happy, Evelyn. My God, you sound just like Dr. Plante." I sighed. I wasn't in the mood to listen to this again. I had already heard it today at my appointment. None of them would ever understand what I had been through, especially not Evelyn. She was in a happy, wonderful relationship with a man who worshiped everything about her. I had been burned and didn't even see it coming. The rug had been pulled out from underneath me at a time when I was already broken, and just broke me more in the process. I had absolutely no desire to meet anyone.

"Derek has a friend that we think might be a good fit for you. We thought you might be interested in meeting him."

"Let me stop you right there. I don't think that this is a good idea, Evelyn. I'm not ready to date."

"Autumn, you've spent months locked up in this room. You go to the store, doctors' appointments, and the occasional trip to the mall with me—that's it. Other than that, you spend your nights lost in the pages of these books with your fantasy men. You've got to get back to normal things. We want you to get better. I'm just suggesting a single date. I am not asking you to marry the guy."

She wasn't going to let this go. I knew her. I also knew there was no point at all in arguing with her. "What's his name?"

Evelyn jumped off the bed and started dancing around the room. "His name? You'll find out at dinner."

"I'm not going out with a guy whose name I don't know, Evelyn."

"Derek has known him forever. You have a date with him this Friday night, dinner at The Whisperwind Inn at eight."

"A date at The Whisperwind Inn—a really expensive restaurant—with a guy whose name I don't know? Sounds stellar." I rolled my eyes.

"He told Derek The Whisperwind Inn. He wanted to pick you up, but I figured that might be too much for you."

"Geez, Evelyn, thanks for thinking of me." The nerve of her. It would be too much for me to have him pick me up. How about the fact that they had both been plotting this fix up for who knows how long, or the fact she wouldn't even tell me his name?

"I'll even loan you my black dress," she said, practically flying out the door. "You'll look amazing," she yelled as she ran down the hall, leaving me in the room with my book. I lay back on my pillow and looked up at the ceiling. I knew nothing about this guy, and as the thought of going out with a stranger flipped around in my mind, my stomach started to turn. I was about to go downstairs and give them both a piece of my mind when the door to my room sprung open and Evelyn came in carrying her dress bag.

"Here you go. It should fit. I know you have lost some weight since your divorce. If it doesn't fit, then we will go shopping." I was reminded of old times; we always shared clothes from the time we were in our teens. Being the same size had its advantages. She came over, pulled me off the bed, and opened the bag. "Try it on."

Evelyn

Derek was sprawled out on the couch, watching the news, when I returned to the living room. "Well, how'd it go?"

"It took a little convincing, but it's a go. I even got her to try on my dress. I think I even saw a glimpse of happiness in her eyes when she saw herself in the mirror. At least, I think it was happiness. Could have been pure hatred directed straight at me too." I sat down on the edge of the couch and shrugged my shoulders.

"You're absolutely sure this is a good idea?"

"Yeah, why wouldn't it be? She needs to start getting out."

"Yes, I know, but Hunter, really?"

"How many other single guy friends do you have? Two, maybe three? I just think he is the most suitable choice."

"I know, it's just he's been in more pants than the whole lot of us guys combined. He's also just gotten out of a relationship and if I know him, which I do, he's just going to be looking for his next conquest. He may be too much for her."

"You're talking about him as though he is only after sex, Derek. He's a decent guy."

"Yes, he's a decent guy. I am not saying he isn't. But

whenever Hunter breaks up with someone, sex is generally all he is after, Evelyn. Remember, I've known him a long time."

"Whatever, I don't believe it. I've known him a long time too, Derek. He has never given me that impression." I went to stand, but Derek grabbed me by the hand.

"Let me ask, how many times do you ever remember seeing him with the same girl twice, aside from Jocelyn and Brandi?" I thought back through all the times we had dated as couples. Shaking my head, I looked at Derek. "My point exactly."

"Great. She'll never forgive me," I said, looking to Derek, tears filling my eyes.

"Don't worry, I'll talk to him. I'll tell him to just take her out and show her a good time."

I frowned and met Derek's eyes.

"Don't worry. Not like that."

Chapter Three

Autumn

The Whisperwind Inn was in the old courthouse and looked out over the bay of Kings Cove. It had been renovated to accommodate the restaurant. I had wanted to go there for years, but Jason always complained, saying it was far too expensive. It basically boiled down to the fact that I just wasn't worth it. I walked up the front steps of the restaurant, and the doorman held the door open for me. I stepped inside. Everything was bathed in candlelight, and soft violin music floated through the air.

"Do you have a reservation, miss?" a young woman asked.

"Yes, I think so. I'm here to meet someone. I'm not sure if he is here yet or not."

"Do you have a name the reservation is under?"

I hesitated. Since Evelyn never gave me a name, I hadn't a

clue what the reservation could be under. I could feel the heat rise in my face. "This is going to sound silly, but I'm here on a *blind* blind date. I don't even know his name," I whispered. I was going to kill my sister.

"Ahh yes, you're the secret blind date." The young lady smiled at me and grabbed two menus. "Right this way, miss. The other party hasn't arrived yet, but I can show you to your table if you like."

I nodded and followed her into the restaurant. She took me right to the back and sat me at a table that was overlooking the bay and marina. The view was amazing. As I sat waiting, I watched out the window. Snow had started to fall gently. I opened my menu and started reading, the smell of food causing my stomach to grumble.

"Could I get you something to drink while you wait for the other member of your party, miss?" a young waiter asked.

Looking down at the drink menu, I quickly read over each item. "I'll have a glass of water for now please." The waiter walked away as I glanced over to the door. I had no idea what he even looked like. If I had to endure this nightmare of a blind date, my sister best hope that he was at least good-looking. Soon, the waiter brought over my water and set it in front of me.

My phone suddenly pinged with a message. Glancing down at my screen, I saw a message from Evelyn asking me if he had arrived yet. It was after eight-thirty. I went to type out a message when I heard a familiar voice behind me. I turned slowly, praying it wasn't who I thought it was. I couldn't believe my eyes. Jason. Jason was here—on a date! He sat at a table slightly diagonally across from me with Anna, my best friend. Funny, she had been ignoring my calls, and now I see the reason why. A fiery rage came over me. I picked up my cell phone and dialed Evelyn.

"Hello there, beautiful," Evelyn sang over the phone.

"Is this guy showing up or what?" I demanded.

"What's wrong? You sound upset."

Upset wasn't even the word. I swallowed hard, trying to fight back the tears. "That's because he hasn't shown up yet, Evelyn. I have been sitting here alone for forty-five minutes."

"Just calm down. Derek spoke to him today. I know he is on his way, Autumn. That can't be the only reason you're upset."

"Don't tell me to calm down! It isn't the only reason. Jason is here."

"As in *your* Jason?"

"Yes, Evelyn, as in *my* Jason. He's sitting here having dinner with my best friend. The same Jason who always told me this restaurant was too fucking expensive. I don't want him to see me, Evelyn. Especially not here alone," I whispered into the phone in a high-pitched voice, not even taking a breath.

"Oh, honey, relax. Your date is on his way."

I glanced over my shoulder to see that Jason had disappeared from the table. I was just about to turn around when my eyes locked with Anna's. She quickly pretended to be looking at her dessert menu. I began to panic, my eyes darting around the room trying to locate him. "Whatever, Evelyn. I've got to go." I hung up my phone, got up from the table, gathered my things, and ran out of the restaurant.

I made a mad dash down the front steps of the restaurant, almost colliding with a man who was on his way in.

Ripping open my car door, I collapsed into the front seat, out of breath and with tears falling. I had just been stood up on the first date that I've had. To boot, I ran into the only man I'd never cared to lay my eyes on again—with my best friend, no less. There was no way I was going home right away. I wanted to be alone. I didn't want to see or talk to Evelyn. None of this would have happened if she had just minded her own business. I was perfectly happy being alone in my room with the fantasy men in my books. Once I had calmed down, I drove for a bit, finally parking the car at the side of the water. I needed to find a way to get over everything that had happened, and I wasn't going home until I figured out how to do it.

Glancing down at the clock on my dash, I saw it was almost one in the morning. I pulled into the driveway and shut the car off. Evelyn probably had a small fit when I didn't come straight home. The light in the front room was the only one on in the house. I silently prayed that no one was up; I just wanted to go to bed. I didn't want to hear Evelyn's crap. The tears had stopped long ago. Now, I had the greatest urge to just get out of this town for a while. Maybe Dr. Plante was right, maybe a change of scenery was what I needed. I of course had been adamant that he didn't know what he was talking about, but after tonight, after seeing Jason and Anna together, I was beginning to think he might be more right than I cared at the time to admit.

I opened the door and tiptoed into the entryway. When I was almost certain they were both in bed, I slowly released the breath I hadn't realized I'd been holding.

"Well, how did it go?" Evelyn peeked her head around the corner, a grin on her face.

"Fuck, Evelyn, you scared the shit out of me." It took me a minute to catch my breath before shutting the door behind me. I stood with my eyes closed against the door for a second and took in a deep breath before I answered her. What was she supposed to think? It was after midnight. She didn't know that I had run out of the restaurant after I had spoken to her. She would have thought that he would have shown up, and we would have had our date.

"He didn't show up, Evelyn, so I left. I agreed to this date and I got stood up. What does that tell you?" I kicked my shoes off and hung my coat up.

"But, it's after midnight. Where have you been?"

"Does it really matter? Do me a favor, Evelyn. Don't ever ask me to go on another date, okay? I can't handle it, and I told you that. So next time, just respect my answer instead of shoving your opinion down my throat." I left Evelyn standing in the foyer and headed up to the safety of my room. Once I was behind closed doors, I got changed, grabbed my computer, and flopped onto my bed.

Chapter Four

Hunter

The alarm woke me from a deep sleep. Rolling over, I slammed my hand down on the clock. It was only five; I had been asleep less than four hours. I lay in bed with my arm over my face taking in the quiet, debating getting up for a couple of minutes. I had gone back to the office last night after my supposed date had left the restaurant. Throwing myself into work, I finally left the office around twelve-thirty. I had wanted to get the files closed for a couple of the cases I had finally finished. But now I had to be back at six-thirty as I had clients coming in this morning at eight, and I wanted to familiarize myself with the documents my paralegal had completed.

My phone suddenly chimed with a message. So much for my few minutes of quiet this morning—surely it was either Bryce or Chase. Carter knew better than to message me this early in the morning. Grabbing my phone off my nightstand, I saw a couple texts from Derek and my appointment reminder for this morning. Frowning, I clicked open the messages. They must have been delayed from being delivered. The first message was Derek asking when I would be arriving at the restaurant, and the second was demanding to know why I had stood up Evelyn's sister, which told me it was Evelyn, not Derek, who had sent the message. I threw the phone down on the bed and ran my hand over my face. I didn't have time to worry about it. I'd call him later and sort it all out. Right now, I had no choice. I had to get my ass ready and into the office.

I grabbed my usual breakfast on my way: a coffee and bagel from the Starbucks drive-thru. When I got to the office, I was surprised to see I was the first one there. It wasn't a bad thing. It would give me a chance to finish preparing for my meetings. I went in, got comfortable at my desk, and threw myself into my work. My coffee and bagel would soon grow cold just like they had done every morning these days.

"Morning, big guy," I heard Bryce call from the hallway.

"Hey." I looked up from my desk. I was just doing one final check over and watched as Bryce and Chase came strolling into my office with coffees in hand and made themselves comfortable on the couch. "What's up?"

"Hard at work already?"

"Well, some of us have to work. Someone must keep money coming into the company. Don't worry, though, you'll thank Carter and me in about thirty years."

"Yeah, yeah. So, did you get laid last night or what?" Chase laughed.

I rolled my eyes. It was too early for their shit this morning. I was tired, and I felt bad. I had never not made a date on time. "No, fuck, I got stuck in traffic on my way. I was really late, and by the time I had gotten there, she had already left. So, I came back here and continued working."

"Ah well, next week. Don't worry, Hunter, you can get your dick wet then." Bryce chuckled to himself.

"Fuck off, Bryce."

Oh, by the way, Carter won't be joining us this year," Chase said as he took a sip of his coffee.

"What? Why isn't he going with us?" It was our annual brothers' vacation. Every year the four of us ventured off and went to a vacation spot in the Caribbean. This year we were off to Jamaica, to the Pacific Jewel Resort. I couldn't wait to get away. I needed this much-deserved vacation time after the long hours I had been logging in this office.

"Hope wants to work on some home renovations," Bryce and Chase said in unison.

"Yeah, well, that's what happens when you get married. Your life is no longer your own. Listen, guys, I have an appointment coming in in about thirty minutes, and I have to make a private phone call." They looked at me, then at one another, and finally stood and headed to their offices.

As soon as they were gone, I got up and closed my office door. I didn't need those two listening in on my call. I dialed Derek and waited while his phone rang.

"Hey, Hunter. What the fuck happened to you last night? Evelyn was freaking the fuck out all night, in case you couldn't tell." Derek's voice came over the phone.

"Hey, Derek. Man, traffic was insane when I left the office to head home to change, so I was already running late by the time I left home. I was buried deeper in traffic on my way to the restaurant due to a couple of bad accidents, and by the time I finally got to the restaurant, it was almost nine. She'd already left. I'm sorry. I feel horrible, man. I hope we aren't in too much shit with Evelyn."

"She was pretty pissed. Especially once her sister came home. She thought you stood her up."

"Man, you know me better than that. I don't stand up women. Listen, I'll make it up to her. We can reschedule for tonight. I'll come pick her up."

"No, it's okay. Evelyn says not to worry about it."

"You sure? It would make me feel better."

"Yeah, I'm sure. She says it's fine."

"All right, well, as long as you know the truth, and you pass it on to Evelyn that I didn't stand her up. Let Evelyn know I'll make it up to her. I gotta run."

"For sure, man, I'll pass on the message. We'll get together for drinks soon."

"Yep, once I'm back from vacation. Have a good one!"

I ended the call, grabbed my cold coffee, and headed off to the boardroom to wait for my clients. I couldn't wait—in a couple of days I'd be lying on the beach in the hot sun, looking for my next piece of ass.

My cell phone rang just as I was about to walk into the boardroom. I hoped it was Carter. I was hoping to run a couple things by him before my meeting, but he was late.

"Hunter, it's me, baby. I need to see you." I rolled my eyes as I heard the familiar voice over the phone.

"Jocelyn, this isn't a good time," I barked. Jocelyn and I had dated for the past couple of years, but when she became super possessive, it had ended quickly for me, and I cut her loose. Unfortunately, I couldn't say the same for her.

"I need you. I want us to try again," she begged over the phone, practically crying.

"Jocelyn, begging and crying isn't going to get you what you want. I told you it's over." I slammed the files down on the boardroom table. *Fuck, why did I answer this call?* She was the exact reason why I had call display. I should have checked it. This woman was severely unhinged. Looking up, I saw Cynthia, our receptionist, walking down the hall toward the boardroom, no doubt to tell me my clients were here. I held up a finger, signifying I needed another minute. She nodded and headed back to the front.

"Please, baby. I miss you so. Maybe we could take a vacation together—you know, rekindle the flame."

"Jocelyn, there are no flames to rekindle. There isn't even a match. Now I'm going to hang up, and I don't want to hear from you again. I have to go." The last thing I heard was her uncontrollable sob into the phone as I ended the call. I took a minute to compose myself. This case was too important to fuck up. I glanced at my watch, inhaled deeply, and pressed the call button on the intercom. I needed this vacation more than ever now.

Chapter Five

Autumn

I poured the hot coffee into my favorite mug. I had barely slept all night; it was going to be a long day. Removing the eggs and bread from the fridge, I started to make myself some breakfast. I figured after I ate maybe I would go crawl back into bed for a couple of hours.

"Morning," Evelyn sang as she walked into the kitchen.

Why was she always in such a good mood? *Oh yeah, because her life hasn't fallen apart*, I reminded myself. "Morning," I mumbled.

"Listen, I want to apologize. I should have listened to you, but you need to know that you weren't stood up; he got delayed with traffic. So that is good news. He would like to make it up to you. He said he would come pick you up tonight."

I put my hand up in front of her face. "Evelyn, please. I told you last night, I don't want to talk about it."

"I'm sorry, Autumn."

"Don't be sorry. Whether he stood me up or not, it doesn't matter. I told you I am not ready to date right now." I cracked two eggs into a bowl and started whisking them before dropping them into the hot pan.

"I know. I just thought it would do you good. I care about you."

I took a sip of my coffee. I felt bad for being so hard on Evelyn, but she needed to understand. "If you care about me then please just listen to me. Even if it was only dinner as friends, I'm not ready to be out in public dating. I'm not ready to get involved with anyone, especially when it isn't on my terms."

Evelyn sat down at the table and started reading the paper. The silence, combined with the tension in the room, was starting to make me feel like a caged animal. I really needed to remember that Evelyn was only trying to help me; she only wanted what was best for me. I also knew it wasn't really Evelyn that was making me so edgy, but the fact that I had seen Jason at that restaurant.

I cleared my throat and took a sip of coffee. *I may as well drop the bomb on her now*, I thought to myself. "You'll be happy to know that I booked a trip."

Evelyn immediately stopped flipping the pages of the paper and looked up at me. "What? Where are you going?"

"Jamaica, to the Pacific Jewel Resort. Dr. Plante thought it would be a good idea for me to get away. So, I booked it last night after I got home. It was the last straw when I saw

Jason last night at the restaurant. It's just me and my e-reader on the beach for one week."

"By yourself? You're going all the way to Jamaica alone?"

"Yes, Evelyn, by myself. Don't worry. I am perfectly happy going away alone. I need this." I sat down at the table with my breakfast. "It's all good, really," I said, taking in her surprised expression.

"Okay. If you're sure. When do you leave?"

"I'm sure. I leave in two days. Now, onto the fun part. I know you love to shop. We need to go out and get some shopping done for my trip. I need a few new things."

Evelyn's eyes lit up and she rubbed her hands together in excitement. She loved to shop, and now with that project, she would hopefully drop the dating crap. "All right, yes, we can hit the mall tonight after I finish work. I want to make sure you're the sexiest thing on that island. Maybe you'll meet a tall, dark, handsome stranger who will rock your socks off there."

I dropped my head into my hand. She wasn't going to let it go. Instead of arguing with her, I just ignored the comment and continued eating breakfast, making plans to shop.

"I don't know about this bathing suit either, Evelyn," I called from inside the dressing room. I was beginning to feel very insecure. I hadn't bought a bathing suit in close to five years, and from what I remembered, they had way more material to them than they did now.

"For the fifth time, just open the door and let me see. I'm sure it's all in your head."

I unlatched the door and came walking out in the multi-colored bikini Evelyn had forced me to try on. "I don't know, Evelyn. This is basically string holding three scraps of material together. I think I like the black bikini instead; it at least has more material to it than this one."

"Girl, you look amazing. Don't be stupid. You have to have this!"

"I don't know."

"I'm telling you. You look hot."

"You have said that about every suit I've put on. And I am sorry, but how you kept a straight face with some of them, I will never know."

"Yep I have, because it's true. You're a beautiful woman, Autumn, whether you choose to believe it or not. You're going to look even more amazing after you get your hair cut, colored, and styled too. I've booked us at the salon tomorrow for that, plus a mani and pedi as a surprise."

"You what?"

"Well, I am not letting you go away without some pampering. It's my treat."

I rolled my eyes and turned to go back into the dressing room. Once I was changed, I grabbed both suits and came walking out. Evelyn stood and watched as I set the multicolored bikini on the table in the back room with all the other discarded suits.

"What are you doing?"

"I'm just going to go with the black one." I walked out

and grabbed a white knit cover-up off the shelf and headed to the front cash register. While I was waiting my turn to check out, I watched Evelyn grab the suit off the table and come up to the counter. "What are you doing?"

"If you're not going to buy it, I'm going to buy it for you. If you don't believe me that you look hot in it, then put the suit on when we get back to the house and let Derek tell you."

I looked at Evelyn like she had lost her mind. "That's just plain weird, Evelyn—having Derek give me an opinion on how I look as I stand before him half naked. No thanks."

I ripped the suit from her hands and placed everything on the counter. I'd buy the suit just to shut her up, and if I didn't wear it, I would just return it when I got back. That way Evelyn would be happy, and I wouldn't need to listen to her complain.

Chapter Six

Autumn

I had landed less than an hour ago and was already feeling more relaxed. Evelyn had wanted to drop me off at the airport, but I wouldn't let her. As I was leaving, she once again brought up meeting someone. "Go have a good time, and for goodness' sake, if someone shows some interest in you, don't be a bitch." Those were her wise words. Sure, it would be nice to have someone in my life again, but I was so afraid of getting hurt that it was almost impossible to let my guard down.

The bus pulled up outside of the resort entrance. As I exited the vehicle, the warm breeze washed over my face. Within minutes the driver had all the luggage unloaded, and I grabbed my bags and walked over to stand in the line that was forming at the front desk, so I could check in. It had to be 90 degrees, and it was ten o'clock at night. I shrugged out of my light jacket and tied it around my waist.

As I was waiting, one of the staff members approached with a tray of champagne. "Miss? A welcome drink for you."

I smiled and took one of the glasses. "Thank you." I took a sip, loving the way that the bubbles exploded on my tongue.

I glanced around. The lobby was lined on both sides with little stores and a couple of restaurants. There was a lobby bar off to the left that was surrounded by other guests. Laughter and music floated through the air.

"Welcome to the Pacific Jewel Resort, miss." I stepped up to the desk and handed them my booking information. "Thank you. It will just be a couple of minutes."

While I was waiting, I grabbed my cell phone and connected to the resort's Wi-Fi. I typed out a quick email to Evelyn and Derek, letting them know I had arrived and that I was shutting off my phone until I returned. I had promised that I would contact them, but that was all. I wanted no interruptions on this trip, no reminders of home. Hitting send, I shut the phone off, just in time for the girl to return with my key. "Ah, miss, you're staying in room 4432. I will have someone bring you to your room."

The bellman pulled the cart up beside the walkway to my room. It was a little bungalow-type building that housed only two rooms. I hoped my neighbors were quiet. He pulled my bags off the cart and headed up the walkway in front of me. He opened the door and turned the lights on. "Your room, miss," he said, leading the way in and placing my suitcase down.

While he busied himself, I glanced around the room. It was decorated in beautiful, bright tropical colors. I looked to my right and saw a little galley way that had a sink on one side and the closet on the other, which led to the bathroom. Walking in, I looked around. There was a shower tub to my right and another door to my left that led to the outside, to a small walled-in courtyard that held an outdoor shower. A bench seat was surrounded by two tropical plants, one on each side, and a bamboo ladder held two white towels. I had already decided that this was the first place I was heading in the morning. Walking back in, I went into the bedroom. A king-size bed filled the upper part of the room and a flat screen TV was facing the bedroom, and there was a small sitting area below, which contained a couch and a couple of chairs. The bellhop pulled open the sliding glass doors, letting the room fill with a warm breeze and the smell of hibiscus. "This way to your private sun deck, miss." I peeked out the door, and sure enough, there was a little balcony with two Adirondack chairs and two sun loungers.

"Is everything all right, miss?"

It was more than all right. I was here, and now I could relax. Turning, I gave him a smile and a tip. "It's perfect."

"All right, miss, if you need anything, just ring the front desk. Also, room service is available twenty-four hours if you would like something to eat. Oh, and I almost forgot, you do have a fully stocked mini bar as well. No extra charges will be applied." He pointed to the small fridge in the room.

I nodded and walked him to the door. "Thank you." I watched as he made his way back to his cart, and then I shut the door. I looked around the room again. I could feel more of the tension I'd been holding leave my body, and my muscles were starting to ache in response. Opening my suitcase, I took a few minutes to hang up some of my dresses and then changed into a wrap so I could head to the lobby for a drink.

Fighting my way through a crowd of people, I finally made my way up to the lobby bar. A pianist played soft music off to the side while some couples danced. The laughter from the crowd was, at times, louder than the music. I spotted a single chair off to the side at the bar and took a seat. It felt good to get out and be around this type of energy.

"What can I get for you, miss?" I looked up and saw a young bartender smiling down at me.

"Gin and tonic with lime, please."

"Is that everything?"

I nodded and sat back, taking in my surroundings. I saw a young bride and groom with their wedding party, older couples sitting on couches along the walkway to the lobby bar, and staff running everywhere making drinks and taking orders. "Your drink, miss." The bartender set the drink down on a napkin and slid it in front of me.

"Thank you." Taking a sip of the drink, I glanced across the bar, and that was when I saw him for the first time, standing and talking with two other men who closely resembled him. He was insanely good-looking. He wore white linen pants that hugged him just tight enough. The black shirt he wore was perfectly pressed, and even though it hung loose on him, it didn't take away from his powerfully built chest, back, and bulging biceps. I watched as his forearms flexed as he held a glass in his large, strong hand.

When he stepped up to the bar, I couldn't help but study him. His icy-blue eyes stood out against his deeply tanned skin and black hair. His chiseled jaw flexed as he ordered his drinks. He was easily the best-looking man I had ever laid my eyes on. When our eyes finally met, I felt a funny feeling in the pit of my stomach causing me to quickly look away.

I took a long gulp of my drink, emptying the glass. Just then the bartender dropped another drink down in front of me. Taking another long gulp, I couldn't help but look back over to him. As our eyes connected again, he flashed a soft, sexy smile and winked at me. I glanced away. I could feel the heat in my face, as well as the long-lost ache throbbing between my legs. Taking a deep breath, I locked eyes with him again. I stood, drank down the last of my drink, and made my way back to my room.

Hunter

"Three of the same, please."

I stood at the bar while I waited for the bartender to finish making our order. The night had been kind of boring until she walked up to the lobby bar. I had barely been able to take my eyes off her. It wasn't my style to gawk, but she was so damn cute. She had been watching me for a bit, but I pretended like I hadn't noticed. I was waiting to see if anyone joined her, but when she sat down by herself in the corner and ordered one drink, I knew she was here alone.

It didn't stop her from looking over her shoulder from time to time, looking for someone to talk to her, when she had made eye contact with me. Her grey-blue eyes were stunning against her flawless skin. Her dark, windblown hair hung just past her shoulders, and I wondered what it would be like to run my fingers through it. When we finally locked eyes for a third time, I felt my dick twitch in my pants. I was going to head over to talk with her, but she downed her drink and headed toward the rooms.

"What the fuck is taking so long?" Bryce said, coming up behind me. Chase pushed his way through the crowd on the other side of me and leaned against the bar. I had barely heard them; hell, I had barely heard anything going on around me for the last five minutes, I was so taken with her. My eyes followed her as she walked through the lobby, my gaze firmly planted on her ass.

"You find something, Hunter?" Chase jabbed me in the ribs, trying to get my attention.

The bartender set down our three drinks and went on to his next customer. I couldn't even dignify them with an answer. Picking up my drink, I continued watching as she disappeared into the darkness. I walked away from the bar and sat down at an empty table, waiting for my brothers to join me.

"Fuck, you got it bad already?" Bryce asked, sitting down next to me.

"She is cute!" Chase chimed in.

"If you don't want her, I'll have a go at her," they both said in unison, laughing.

I ignored their comments. I didn't have to tell them to stay away. We had an unwritten rule.

"How about we go hang back at my room," I suggested. It had been a long day of traveling and I was done. I wanted to be on my game tomorrow for whatever or whomever presented itself to me. I wasn't going to lie, I was silently hoping it would be her.

Chapter Seven

AUTUMN

The green lights screamed two o'clock. I rolled over. Two in the morning and the music was still going, and the laughter was getting louder on the other side of the wall. This was going to be a nightmare if I had to listen to this every night for the rest of the week. I flicked on the TV, hoping that it would drown out some of the noise, but it just kept getting louder. I had placed a call to the front desk over forty-five minutes ago, requesting they send security, but clearly, they were not coming.

A large bang against the wall, followed by more raucous laughter, caused me to jump. That was it; I couldn't take any more. I jumped out of bed, threw on my shoes, grabbed my key, and darted out the door. Walking to the other side of the building, I pounded on the door. They probably couldn't even hear me with all the noise they were creating. I pounded again. I was getting angrier by the second. I went to pound a third time when the door was abruptly opened.

I was ready to bawl out whomever was on the other side of the door, but as soon as I saw who it was, I choked on my words. It was him, the guy from the bar. Instead of saying anything, I stood there, taking in the sight that was before me. He was shirtless, and I couldn't keep my eyes from traveling from his bulky muscular chest to his very solid eight pack. His pants hung just low enough to give me a peek at that deeply carved "v."

"Can I help you?" His eyes trailed down my body, and I could feel myself heat up under his gaze. At that moment, the realization hit that I was standing there half naked, braless, wearing nothing but a short white T-shirt that barely covered my pink silk panties. I watched as his eyes once again trailed down my body.

"Hey, eyes up here!" I demanded, raising my voice. The music that had poured out of the room stopped suddenly, and I saw two heads peek around the corner.

"Not that you care, but I've been trying to sleep for the last three hours! Could you please keep it down?" I swallowed hard, trying to cover up myself the best I could from his gaze.

"Sorry, beautiful. My brothers can be pretty loud when they get drinking." His deep, sexy voice sent a quiver right to my center. The corner of his mouth quirked up as his eyes traveled my body again.

"I said, eyes up here!"

"Don't blame us, Hunter," his brothers shouted in unison. "You were the one who wanted to party back here." Hearty laughter fell from inside the room. I couldn't help the smile that came to my lips. As soon as I looked back up at him and saw him watching me, my smile quickly vanished.

"They were just getting ready to leave. I promise, no more noise." He gave me a wink.

I nodded and turned to walk away, pulling my shirt down to try to cover myself from his gaze.

"I'm sorry, I didn't catch your name?"

"That's because I didn't give it to you," I said, glancing over my shoulder at what I was now sure was the sexiest man I'd ever seen, his eyes scanning over me once again as I continued to walk back to my room.

"Good night then, beautiful."

I ignored him, walking back toward my room, trying to calm my heavily beating heart. Once inside, I leaned up against the cold door. I could still hear the murmur of deep voices followed by laughter on the other side of the wall, but I ignored them. I went to the sink and ran cold water and splashed it on my face, trying to calm the heat that was running through me. Never in all the time I had been with Jason had he ever looked at me like that, nor had he made my center throb the way mine was throbbing right now from just being near him.

Once I had cooled down, I crawled into bed, my thoughts quickly traveling to the man on the other side of the wall. I squeezed my thighs together. I would never get any sleep if the hot, heavy pulse between my legs didn't calm.

The voices carried on for another five minutes, and then I heard the door slam on the other side. Finally, it was quiet.

Chapter Eight

HUNTER

I glanced at my watch. It was almost noon, and I still hadn't seen Bryce or Chase. After leaving my room last night, they more than likely headed back to the bar to cap the night off. I on the other hand couldn't get that brown-haired beauty off my mind. The way that T-shirt had ridden up over that perfect ass as she walked away from me, giving me a peek at those pink silk panties—that image had permanently imprinted itself on my brain. After the guys left, I jerked myself off twice to thoughts of what it would be like to have my hands gripping that ass while I planted my tongue in her hot pussy.

I adjusted myself. I needed to cool off, so I grabbed my towel and took off toward the pool.

The sun was hot as I scoured the pool deck looking for a

spot, any spot, to relax. Most of the chairs had been taken, but I finally found an empty palapa. I kicked my sandals off, placed my towel down, and headed over to the bar to grab a drink. As I waited to be served, I glanced around, trying to see if my brothers were around. Then I spotted her.

She lay sprawled out on a lounge chair, e-reader in hand. Her dark hair was pulled into a loose ponytail, her black bikini leaving very little to my imagination. I couldn't help but take in the rise and fall of her perfect, full breasts and the soft curves of her body. She looked so sexy. I kept my eyes firmly planted on her, adjusting myself once again to hide my arousal.

"What can I get you, sir?"

"I'll have a beer, please."

He set the beer down on the bar in front of me within seconds and went on to the next guest, but I held my hand out, signaling for him to stay.

"Do you have a server around?"

"Yes, sir."

"I was wondering if I could have a drink delivered to someone, please."

"Yes, sir."

"Great, I want you to make this, all equal parts: vodka, peach schnapps, and cranberry juice." He quickly busied himself, making the drink I had requested. As I was waiting, the waiter came back behind the bar. I grabbed the pen off his tray and a napkin and quickly wrote a note and folded it. The bartender set the drink in front of me, and I signaled to the waiter. "See that brunette in the black bikini lying over there?" I asked, pointing to her. "Could you deliver this drink and note to her for me, please?" I placed a twenty into his hand and took a drink of my beer before heading back over to my palapa.

Autumn

Music was blaring in my ears as I lay in my lounge chair. I set my e-reader beside me and stood up to reapply more sunscreen. It was hot today, and I didn't want to burn. I glanced around the pool area. I hadn't seen him today. Maybe he had left already. Well, at least I could hope he had. I adjusted the back of my chair before sitting down to continue reading.

I was completely engrossed in a scene when I felt someone tap my shoulder. Shading my eyes with my hand and looking up, I saw a waiter standing before me. Figuring he was taking drink orders, I shook my head no. I didn't want to be bothered, so I went right back to reading when he tapped my shoulder again. This time, I removed one of my earbuds and smiled up at him. "Yes?"

"Miss, I have a drink for you." He smiled and held out a glass filled with pink liquid.

I gave him a soft smile. "I'm sorry, you must have the wrong person. I haven't ordered anything."

"No, miss, I don't believe I do," he continued, holding the glass in front of me.

I could see he wasn't going to let up, so I politely took

the drink from him and set it under my chair. I had no idea who the drink was from, so there was no way I was going to drink it.

"And this as well, miss." He held out a napkin with something written on it. Once I had taken that from him, he continued on his way.

Looking around, I saw no one watching, so I unfolded the napkin and stared at the words that were sprawled across it.

"Hope you enjoy your pink silk panties. I know I sure did." I could feel the blush rise to my cheeks. As I stared down at the note, I couldn't help but smile.

Folding the note, I placed it inside the cover of my e-reader. I tried to get back into the book I was reading, but my mind just kept drifting back to that note. I took another peek around the pool, looking for him, but I still couldn't see him anywhere. Glancing at my watch, I figured I had another hour in the sun before I had to get ready for dinner. I grabbed the drink, took a small sip, and tried to get back into the story.

Hunter

I had kept my eyes on her while the server delivered the drink. The look of confusion on her face at first was priceless as she glanced around the pool trying to figure out where the drink had come from. But I absolutely loved the look on her face when she received the note.

"There you are, you fucker!" Bryce called out from behind me, causing me to look away from her. Chase and Bryce both approached with two women following.

"Yes, I'm here!" I turned back to watch her as she read the note, but I had missed it. In that two seconds that I had taken to glance at my brothers, I had missed the look on her face, the realization it was from me. How was I supposed to know if it was safe to talk to her after last night?

"Hunter, meet Alyssa and Julia," Bryce said, introducing the ladies to me. I nodded at them both, turning my attention back to what was in front of me.

"They have a friend for you, Hunter," Chase said, sitting down beside me, pulling one of the two women onto his lap. I said nothing; I just kept my focus on my brown-haired beauty.

"Hunter? Did you hear what I said?" Bryce asked and then followed my gaze in the direction I was looking.

"Ahhh. Girls, I don't think Hunter is interested in meeting your friend, sadly," Chase said, looking in the same direction. I could then feel their eyes on me.

"No, I'm sorry, I'm not," I answered. "I'm headed to get ready for dinner. Where are we eating tonight, boys?"

"Just the buffet. Drinks afterward?" Chase asked, putting his arm around Julia and pulling her into him.

"Sounds good, see you in an hour." Taking my towel, I headed back toward my room to get ready for dinner, but not before I stole one more glance in the direction of her.

She had the drink I had sent her in her hand. I watched as she took a tiny sip, and I could tell from the expression on her face that she enjoyed it.

Chapter Nine

Autumn

Soft music floated through the air of the small restaurant. I put the last piece of chocolate cake in my mouth, savoring the final bite; it practically melted. I had been happy to spend a quiet evening alone. My waiter returned to my table with a hot cup of coffee and removed my empty dessert plate.

Sipping on my coffee, I couldn't help but watch another couple across the room. He listened attentively to whatever she was saying, then they both laughed. They looked at each other with such adoration. I tried to remember when Jason had looked at me that way—like I was his world—but I couldn't remember a single time. I thought we had been in love, but it was becoming apparent to me that maybe, just maybe I had been more in love with him. Suddenly, a heavy feeling came over me. Would I ever find that? Would I ever find a man who would look at me like that? Would every man now reject me, just like Jason had, when they found out I couldn't have children? We had taken vows, for better or for worse, and when things had gotten worse, he took the easy road, never looking back.

"Miss, you all right?" I felt a hand touch my shoulder, shaking me out of my thoughts. I could feel tears running down my cheeks, and people were staring.

"How embarrassing. Yes, I am fine, thanks." I sniffled, wiping the tears away. I finished off the coffee, composed myself, tipped the young gentleman who had served me dinner, and headed out for the rest of the evening.

The first stop I made was the restroom. I was sure my makeup was a mess after that ridiculous outburst. I looked in the mirror—yep, a mess. I opened my little clutch bag to re-apply my eyeliner.

The lobby was still relatively quiet when I returned; people were still eating dinner. They were having a lounge singer at nine. I was looking forward to a relaxing evening. I walked up and took a seat at the bar, ordering a gin and tonic with lime. A piano player played a few classical pieces off to the side. I recognized the song he was playing immediately as one that had been played at my wedding. While it brought tears to my eyes, it also made my stomach turn. As soon as he finished playing that piece, I took a sip of my drink to stop those random tears from falling. It was then I heard a familiar deep voice. I looked over to the buffet door. Hunter, at least that was what his brothers called him, wore black dress pants that were perfectly tailored to his size. His cream-colored linen shirt hung open, a quarter of the way down, giving me another glimpse at his bulky build.

I watched as he was finally joined by his two brothers, with three women trailing behind them. So, he was here with his wife. What a pig, looking at me like that last night when I practically banged down his door, half naked. Wonder where she was while all that nonsense was going on. I could feel myself getting angry and agitated. I hated men like that. Then for him to be all cute today and send me that drink. I wonder if she knew what type of man she was married to. Bet she didn't. Most of the time, women are oblivious to it all. I picked up the drink in front of me and drank it down while nodding to the bartender for another one.

I kept my watch on him. The group of them sat down at a table all together while he made his way up to the bar. As he stood there, waiting to be served, our eyes finally met. The corner of his mouth turned up as he took notice of me. I looked away from his gaze. I would have welcomed that sexy gaze if he weren't married. Ignoring him for a few minutes had done the trick. He was already back sitting with his brothers. Maybe now I could relax, now that he wasn't watching me.

One of the bartenders suddenly slid a shot in front of me. I jumped and looked up at his smiling face. "Wet Pussy!" He winked and sexily leaned against the bar.

"Excuse me?" I'm sure the look of shock and horror on my face said it all.

"Wet Pussy—a shot from your friend sitting over there at the table, miss." He pointed over to the group of them.

A fiery rage overtook me. That was it, I couldn't take any more. This wasn't cute; it was disgusting. Getting up from my seat, I abandoned my drinks and marched over to him.

"You," I demanded, pointing my finger at him. "I'm sure your wife here would be interested in knowing what you just sent me, and possibly about the lovely little note you sent over to me with that waiter this afternoon, as well. I'm not some whore, just so you know. So, if this is your attempt at trying to get into my pants while she isn't around, it's not going to work." I stopped speaking and looked at them all. The women just sat there looking at me as if I had lost my mind. The guys, on the other hand, sat there with smirks across their faces. "The three of you think this is funny, do you?"

"Told you not to do it, Hunter. You've pissed her off now. She's a little too uptight for your liking, bro."

"I'm not uptight," I gasped. "I just don't appreciate a married man behaving in that manner."

They both burst into laughter again, this time the women joining with them. "Sweetheart, he isn't married."

I could feel myself getting defensive. "Don't call me 'sweetheart.'" The heat rose to my face.

Hunter stood up and walked over to me, closing the space between us. He was so close I could feel the heat radiating from his body. The scent of his cologne was intoxicating. I swallowed hard as I looked up into those blue eyes. He seriously was one of the most attractive men I had seen from a distance, but up close, he was breathtaking.

He grabbed both of my hands in his, his touch sending shivers down my body. "No, beautiful, I'm not married." His soft and sexy voice washed over me. "I just happen to find you severely attractive, and I was trying to have some fun with you, put a smile on that beautiful face. Now please quiet down. You're creating somewhat of a scene, and I don't like unnecessary negative attention brought upon me."

Our eyes were locked. I felt as though my face were on fire. I glanced over to the rest of the group, and then I saw the crowd gathering. Suddenly, the open-aired lobby didn't seem so open, and I felt like I was suffocating. I had to get out of there. I shoved myself off Hunter's chest and darted through the crowd of people, praying I never laid eyes on him again.

As soon as I was out of the lobby and halfway back to my room, I slowed my pace. I glanced over my shoulder, to make sure he wasn't following, before I stopped to take a breath and remove my shoes from my aching feet, walking my way back to my room.

I dropped my shoes on the tile floor, changed, and cracked open the mini bar fridge, making myself a gin and tonic. I took the drink out to the back patio and sat in the quiet, listening to the tree frogs chirp.

My mind kept running back to him. I kept thinking of the way he had looked at me last night as I stood outside his door—his eyes trailing over my body. The look in his eyes had told me everything he wanted to do to me, same as tonight, but at the same time, it made me feel uncomfortable.

What was going on with me?

I could still smell the captivating scent of his cologne,

and it was driving me insane. The way his hands felt in mine when he grabbed hold of them, and the heat radiating off his body as he drew closer to me. I had wanted him to take me in his protective arms right at that moment and kiss me, make me forget everything that had happened over the last couple of years. I had wanted to feel his powerful, large hands make their way over my body. I wanted to know what it would feel like to be held while he kissed me, to know how the weight of his body felt as I lay underneath him.

I had to stop these thoughts, but the more I tried, the more they continued to invade my mind. I rubbed the middle of my forehead, closed my eyes, and gave myself a minute to contemplate an idea. What if...just what if I let my guard down like Evelyn suggested? What if just for one night, or hell even this week, I did something completely spontaneous? What would it hurt? It wasn't like I would ever see this man again. I'm twenty-nine years old and I have needs too. Needs that hadn't been satisfied by anything other than a piece of vibrating plastic for the last three years. Yes, it had been three years since I had felt the touch of a man.

I took another sip of my drink when I heard the sliding door to his patio open, accompanied by male voices. They were back, no doubt to party it up and keep me up half the night. I didn't want to be seen out here, so I quietly headed back into my room, shutting the door and pulling the curtains across.

Chapter Ten

AUTUMN

I woke up bright and early with a pounding headache. I drank way too much last night, finally crashing into bed at an ungodly hour, drunk. I lay in bed waiting for the room to stop spinning. Finally I rolled out of bed and went out to the outdoor shower. I could hear the shower running next door, and immediately my thoughts went to him naked on the other side of the wall. I waited until the water stopped and I heard the door to his bathroom close before I started mine.

I decided to put on the bathing suit that Evelyn had forced me to purchase and ordered room service instead of going to the buffet for breakfast. I didn't want to chance running into him this morning.

After breakfast, I headed down to the pool. It was a little later than I liked to get down there, but I was hoping it was still early enough to get a good spot. I grabbed a chair by the edge of the pool and set down my towel and e-reader. It was already a beautiful, clear, sunny morning. I removed my cover-up, almost instantly feeling self-conscious in this little ball of string that Evelyn had called a suit. Doing my best to ignore that feeling, I grabbed my sunscreen and poured a generous amount into my hand. I was just about done applying the lotion to my legs when I heard the same deep, sexy voice from the night before. "Morning, beautiful!"

I could feel the embarrassment from the way I had acted the night before climbing through my body. I closed my eyes, drew in a deep breath, and murmured, "Morning."

"How are you this morning?"

I lay down on the lounge chair and tried to get settled into my book. "I'm fine." I was trying to ignore him, hoping he would take the hint and go away, but he just stood there. "What is it?"

"It's just I couldn't help but notice that you didn't put any sunscreen on your back. I would hate to see you get burnt, and the sun is pretty strong down here. If you'd like, I can put some on your back and then I promise I will leave."

I apprehensively handed him the sunscreen from my bag and put my e-reader down. "If it's the only way to get you to leave me alone, then fine." As he took the bottle from my hand, his fingers grazed mine, sending a jolt through me. I lay on my stomach, thinking what a mistake this was. I heard the snap of the lid and the squirt of the lotion, and then felt the rubbing of his hands together. *Please don't be good with your hands, please don't be good with your hands.* I hoped that if I prayed for that long enough, it would come true, but somehow, I already knew that my prayers were going to go unanswered.

As soon as his large, strong hands started to massage the lotion into my shoulders, I knew I was in deep trouble. As he worked his way down to my lower back, I could feel the heat pool between my legs. I tried hard to relax, but the lower he got, the more tense I became. His hands felt amazing, and I wasn't sure, but there was a moment when I thought a slight moan had escaped my lips.

"Did you say something, beautiful?"

Fuck, I had moaned, how embarrassing. I closed my eyes and quickly rolled onto my side to stop him from continuing, his hand resting on my waist. "Nope, nothing. Thank you. I'm good."

"You sure? It's not all rubbed in yet."

"It's fine. It will soak in." I avoided his eyes and threw my sunglasses on. "I need to get back to my book."

His eyes never left mine as he wiped the lotion that was left on his hands onto the towel he was carrying. I rolled back onto my stomach and picked up my e-reader as he walked away. "One more thing..." He turned back to me. "What's your name?"

I wasn't sure I wanted him to know my name. I still felt like an ass after last night, but clearly what had happened hadn't stopped him from speaking to me. I dropped my e-reader down in front of me. "It's Autumn."

"Autumn, well, you have a wonderful day. I'm going to go and get some sun." I watched as he walked away and found a chair across the pool deck with his brothers.

Later that afternoon, I rested my head on my arms.

Hiding behind my sunglasses, I pretended to be asleep, but truthfully, I couldn't take my eyes off him. It had been almost three hours since his hands had been on me, and I could still feel how good they had felt. I could just imagine how amazing they would feel doing other things to my body.

Chapter Eleven

It was noon by the time the entertainment started, reggae music blaring. I'd kept my eyes on her all morning. She almost knocked me to my knees when that soft, sexy moan left her lips as I rubbed her back. She had finally flipped from back to front, sadly hiding that perfect ass from me. This girl desperately needed to have fun. She was too pretty not to smile. Whatever it was that had made her so uptight, I was becoming damn determined to wipe it from her memory, at least for one night.

Just as Bryce and Chase joined me by the pool bar, a roaring male voice boomed over the loud speaker. I watched as Autumn jumped and buried her face behind her e-reader, as if she were trying to hide.

"All right, everyone, it's time for some fun! It's BODY SHOT TIME! Participants, grab your partners!" The music started up as the entertainment crew walked over to the bar and grabbed lime wedges, salt, shot glasses, and a few bottles of tequila.

"We've got our girls, Hunter. You should go get yours," Bryce said, nodding in Autumn's direction.

"Yeah, Hunter, go get her," Chase chimed in.

I looked at them and shook my head. "No, I promised her I'd leave her be, and that is what I am going to do."

Bryce and Chase looked at one another, then back to me, and with shit-eating grins, they both took off in Autumn's direction. She was completely oblivious to the actions going on around her. I watched from a distance as they both approached her. She looked annoyed, and when they pointed in my direction, the look of panic and horror that came over her face said it all. If I'd ever had any type of a chance with her, it was gone now.

"Ladies, please accompany your men up on the stage and have a seat!" the member of the entertainment crew shouted into the microphone.

I watched as Autumn put her hands up in front of her, trying to push them away, as she shook her head adamantly. I knew Bryce and Chase weren't going to take no for an answer, and I was right. In one swift motion, Bryce picked her up, threw her over his shoulder, and carried her up to the stage.

Once Bryce had her up there, Chase came running over to me and pulled me off the barstool. "Come on, dumb ass."

Chase dragged me up on the stage and placed me across from Autumn. She looked irritated as hell, and to be honest, I wasn't that happy with either of them myself.

"Everyone, can I have your attention on the main stage?

It's body-shot time. Three shots per couple. You guys vote for your favorite couple. Winning couple gets a bottle of rum! The crowed roared, and the music started blaring.

The entertainment staff walked across the stage, one staff member for every woman. They stood behind them armed with a bottle of liquor. The music started, and I locked eyes with Autumn. I couldn't read what was going on in that head of hers, but the look of fear and anger that was painted across her face gave me a good idea. Bryce and Alyssa went first, followed by Chase and Julia.

We were up next. I watched as they put a lime wedge in her mouth, poured the shot of tequila, placing the shot glass between her breasts, and sprinkled salt along the crook of her neck. I walked up to her, placing one arm behind her back and the other on her hip. I leaned into her and whispered, "Don't be scared. Just relax. But, I can't promise I won't bite." Giving her a wink, I placed my mouth on her neck and slowly licked the salt. Then I buried my face into her chest and took the shot glass between my lips, drinking down the clear liquid. Finally, I leaned into her and took the lime wedge from between her lips. I stood back up and looked down at her. She was biting her lower lip, and her eyes were closed tightly.

"Next one. Ladies, lean back." Again, I watched as they sprinkled salt across her upper abs, filled the glass, sitting it on her navel, and placed the lime wedge between her breasts.

"Men, have at it!" The music started again as the crowd started cheering.

As soon as my hand went around to cradle her, she tensed at my touch. My eyes met hers. Her pupils were dilating, and she was breathing faster than before. I bent down and alternated between licking and sucking the salt off her, giving her a gentle love bite as I finished. Downing the shot, I took the lime into my mouth, making sure my lips grazed the soft flesh of her breasts. I felt her shudder in my arms.

"Time for a third and final shot! This one is a little more risqué! Ladies, lean all the way back."

I watched once again as they shook salt just below her navel, and repeated the placement of the shot and lime.

"Men!"

I stepped forward and took in the light blush on her cheeks.

"Ready?" I whispered as she bit her lower lip and nodded.

Gripping her hips, I ran my tongue across her lower abdomen, softly and gently making sure I got all the salt. Then I moved to the shot and again to the lime wedge that sat between her breasts. As I closed my mouth over the lime and my lips grazed her skin, she let out a low, soft moan.

Keeping my hands firmly planted on her hips I stood up, her heavy-lidded eyes looking at me. "Wasn't so bad, was it, beautiful?"

Autumn

Hunter stood firmly planted between my legs as we waited for the other three couples to complete their shots. I couldn't peel my eyes from his; they were killer. How this man wasn't married from that reason alone was beyond me. He held my hands in his, interlocking our fingers together, his stare just as intense as mine. I didn't have an answer for him. Was it that bad? Hell no. I'd kill to see what else he could do with that mouth.

We had no choice but to sit there until everyone was finished. I hated crowds, and to be honest, this was the most mortifying thing that had ever happened to me. I hadn't always been shy like this, but Jason had always been so reserved. He would never have done anything like this, and over time, I had grown into that reserved person as well.

The roar of the crowd became silent. While my eyes were still locked with his, he started to move into me, and just before his lips grazed mine, the crowd erupted in a chant of couple number three. He abruptly backed off as they brought over our bottle of rum.

Bryce and Chase bolted as soon as we were handed our rum, taking off with their lady friends toward the beach. Hunter helped me off the stage, and with my hand in his, he walked me back over to my seat.

"Enjoy, Autumn." He set the bottle of rum down beside me as I relaxed back on the lounge chair. "I'll see you around." He turned to walk away. I suddenly didn't want him to leave. I had decided to take Evelyn's advice—*just have fun*—even if only for one day.

"I take it that was your brothers' idea?" I murmured.

He looked over his shoulder at me, turned back around, and walked back over. "Yes, I'm just going to apologize for that now. I told them not to, but they don't listen. It sometimes amazes me that they've come as far in life as they have."

I couldn't help but laugh.

"Listen, would you like to join me for dinner tonight?"

I bit my bottom lip and thought about what he had asked. I really wanted to just say yes. I didn't want to spend the rest of my vacation all alone, which was completely different from the way I had felt when I left. He seemed nice enough, but I was still hesitant.

"Just dinner. I promise you, I'm not the asshole you think I am."

"I never thought that."

"Sure you did. I could read it on your face. I was just having some fun with you the other night; I meant no harm. I wanted to see you smile. You looked so sad."

When I saw the look in his eyes, I knew he was being sincere and not just saying what he thought I wanted to hear. "Okay. Dinner."

"Great, I have reservations at the Thai Rose tonight. I'll tell those two fucks to take off for the night. How about I pick you up at six? We can have a drink or two before dinner."

"Sounds great. I look forward to it."

"Okay, well, I'll let you get back to your sun and your book and I will see you at six."

<h1 style="text-align:center">Chapter Twelve</h1>

I couldn't keep my mind on anything, no matter how hard I tried. My thoughts jumped from the feel of his hands against my bare skin to the look in his eyes when he finished each shot. *Just stop*, I murmured to myself as I finished applying the last coat of mascara. Walking to the closet, I pulled out my black V-neck wrap dress and my favorite pair of black heels. I had no idea why I had even agreed to this and wasn't sure if I had it in me to be carefree. The man had infuriated me only a night ago, but there was a part of me that thought there was no way he could be as bad as he seemed. As soon as I was dressed I checked myself out in the full-length mirror, pulling off a random piece of lint and straightening any flaw I could see in the material. I didn't know why I cared if I looked good or not; I certainly wasn't trying to impress him.

I spritzed a little more body spray over myself and gave

myself another once-over. Never had I been so nervous or had fussed over myself so much when I went on a date with Jason. I grabbed my key and clutch from the counter. My stomach was suddenly in knots. I took a deep breath and let it out slowly, trying to calm my nerves. I opened the door and let the fresh night air wash over my face. It was just starting to get dark. The pathways were all gently lit with dim lights, and couples were already walking hand in hand toward the main lobby area. I walked down the front steps, wishing the sick feeling would leave my stomach.

The minute I rounded the corner and caught a glimpse of his large frame, my stomach instantly felt at ease. He was dressed in all black, which made his skin look much darker than it had earlier today. He must have been checking his email, but as soon as I cleared my throat, he put his phone in his pocket and looked in my direction. I watched as his eyes trailed over my body. At first, I felt a little self-conscious. "Hello there! You look amazing." I swallowed hard and gave him a smile. I wasn't used to compliments. The most I would have ever gotten out of Jason was *you're wearing that? I guess it will do.*

"You ready for dinner?" He held his arm out to me, and I placed my arm through his, resting my hand on his forearm, as we headed up to the lobby.

We chose a table for two off to the side of the courtyard near the bar. He pulled my chair out and placed his hand on my lower back as he guided me to sit down. "What can I get you to drink?"

"Gin and tonic, please."

"Lemon or lime?"

"Lime, please." I watched him as he walked over to the

bar and stood there waiting for the bartender to take his order. Once he had placed our order, he turned to watch me, never taking those sexy blue eyes from me while he waited. With drinks in hand, he came back over and sat across from me.

"Thank you," I said, taking a sip. I needed something to take the edge off.

I suddenly felt uneasy sitting there with him. My heart began pounding in my chest. I really didn't know what to talk about and was thankful when I spotted both of his brothers walking toward us.

They both stopped at our table wearing shit-eating grins. "Hunter, what time is dinner at?" Bryce questioned, smiling at me. The pair of them were still dressed in their swimming attire.

"Didn't you guys get my messages? I called both of your rooms earlier." Bryce and Chase looked from me to Hunter and smiled.

"So, you finally asked her out, did you, big guy?" Chase grabbed Hunter's large shoulders. I watched as his jaw flexed. Even though I didn't know him, I could tell he was irritated.

He gave me a tight smile and stood. "Excuse us for a minute." He led both his brothers away from the table and had a few words. He looked so intense and irritated, but sexy as hell, as they both laughed at whatever he was saying. I smiled inwardly to myself.

When he was finished, he turned and walked back to join me at the table. "Sorry about that."

I looked over at both Bryce and Chase and smiled as they

both waved before heading back to their rooms. "That's okay. I take it they are your younger brothers?"

"How did you guess?" He smiled.

"I have an older sister. I know I've irritated her like that in the past. We have a way of getting under your skin without even knowing it."

"Yes, like earlier today." He winked.

I blushed at the memory of his mouth on me.

"I'm sorry about that, by the way. I hope you can forgive them and me. I don't want you to be upset. I was trying to calm you down up there. I could tell you were on edge."

I took a sip of my drink and smiled. "It's okay. It was kind of fun." Again, I could feel that familiar heat crawl up my face.

A sexy smile lit up his face. Clearing his throat, he glanced at his watch. "We need to get going. Dinner is in fifteen minutes."

We walked out of the restaurant and into the warm night air, his large hand resting on the small of my back. I couldn't remember the last time I had laughed so hard, and I had realized he was right—he wasn't the asshole I'd thought he was.

"Care to take a walk with me, beautiful?"

I didn't want to be bombarded by looks from his brothers, so I nodded. I was enjoying my time with him alone. We walked down the pathway and to the other side of the resort, which edged against the ocean. As we walked, he grabbed my hand and interlocked his fingers with mine. We walked in total silence. About ten minutes into our walk we found a little covered gazebo with couches that went out over the ocean. Hunter nodded in the direction of the little hut. "Would you like to sit for a bit?"

"Sure," I answered softly.

While he took a seat on one of the couches, I walked to the edge of the hut and looked out over the water. The full moon illuminated the ocean, making it look like millions of glittering diamonds. I could see lights from a cruise ship out in the distance. "It's so beautiful out here."

"Yes, it is, in more ways than one." I turned and smiled at Hunter. He was watching me intently.

A cool breeze blew, causing a chill to run through me. I rubbed both my arms, trying to warm up. "I wish I'd brought my jacket," I said, sitting down opposite Hunter.

"There's plenty of room over here beside me. I'll keep you warm." He gently patted the empty spot beside him.

A funny feeling rose in the pit of my stomach. It took me a minute before I went and sat down next to him. Three years was a long time to not have leaned my body against a man's, and judging from the way my body responded to the activities this afternoon, there was no denying I was extremely attracted to him. Removing my shoes, I slid back onto the couch as he wrapped his arm around my small frame, pulling me against his muscular body. As the warmth from him seeped into me, I slowly started to relax.

"Comfortable?" he whispered.

"This is nice," I said softly. It felt good to be held by someone again, even if it was someone I barely knew.

Closing my eyes, I laid my head against his shoulder, breathing in his masculine scent.

"So, what brings you here?" he asked softly.

I was quiet. I wasn't sure I wanted to tell him the truth—that I was trying to get over the loss of my baby and a divorce. "I just needed a break from some things going on at home right now. What about you?"

"Vacation with my brothers. We do this every year. My older brother, Carter, didn't make it down this time. It's a good thing, however. That way we didn't need to close up the firm for a week."

"What do you do?" I asked while interlocking my fingers with his.

"My brothers and I have our own law firm. Carter practices Family Law, Chase is Contract Law, Bryce practices Estate Planning, and I'm in Corporate Law."

"Those two are lawyers? I never would have guessed," I said, laughing.

"Yeah, I know. They definitely let loose outside of the office. But really, I can assure you that they are all very professional. What about you? What do you do?"

"I'm kind of in between jobs right now. I had to take some time off of work due to illness, and when my benefits ran out, they told me I had no choice but to return; however, my doctor said I wasn't able to return yet, so they let me go." I swallowed hard. I raised my head off his chest and looked into his eyes. He gently brushed the hair away from my face and rested his hand on my cheek.

"Is everything all right, Autumn? I don't like the sadness I see in your eyes. Looks like you have the weight of the world on those shoulders."

"It will be in time." I smiled, but I turned my eyes downward and sat up, pulling away from him. He was right; I did hold the weight of the world on my shoulders—my world and the mess it had become.

As soon as my body was away from him, I longed for his touch. As if he knew, his hand caressed my back. "Hey, don't hide those beautiful eyes from me." I met his eyes again. This time, desire radiated through them. He reached out and placed his hand behind my neck, pulling me toward him. Slowly leaning forward, with his eyes moving from mine to my mouth and back, he placed a gentle kiss on my lips. Heat pulsed through me as he sucked my bottom lip into his mouth. In that moment, it was like we were the only two in the world.

He gently guided me back into the cushions and continued his assault on my mouth. At first, I was paralyzed, not knowing really what to do, but he was gentle and tender, and soon I had wrapped my arms around his neck and welcomed his lips. He coaxed my lips apart with his tongue, sweeping my mouth. I let out a soft moan as he ran his fingers through my hair.

Suddenly, he pulled back, looking over my shoulder. Off in the distance we heard his name being called. "Fuck, those two drunk asses are on their way. What do you say we head back to our rooms?" I didn't want the moment to end, but I also didn't want it interrupted. Placing my shoes back on, I stood, and we walked arm in arm back to our rooms.

Chapter Thirteen

Autumn

The stars twinkled above us. We stood at the end of the walkway to our rooms, Hunter looking deep into my eyes. His hand caressed my cheek, and he leaned in and kissed me like I had never been kissed before, his tongue exploring every part of my mouth. Wrapping me in his arms, he kissed me deeper, the kiss becoming stronger and more forceful. I placed my hand on his chest, stopping him.

"What is it?" he asked breathlessly as he studied my face.

"Hunter, please. Go slow." I didn't know exactly why I had stopped him, but I could feel the throbbing heat between my legs and was afraid I might erupt right there on the walkway. My panties were completely soaked. It had been so long since I had felt this way, and the intensity was overwhelming me.

He closed his eyes and pressed his forehead against mine, gently kissing me again.

"Please go slow. It's been a while for me." I wanted to take that comment back, but the words had already fallen from my mouth.

Hunter looked into my eyes and smiled. "Would you like to come in for a nightcap? I promise we'll go slow." He held both his hands up in surrender while studying my face.

Chewing on my bottom lip, I tried to decide, but my head was already nodding in a yes motion. A large part of me was curious to see where the night would go. I wanted to see what it was like to be with another man. Jason had been the only one. The sensible part of my brain was screaming *no, you barely know him,* and I'd never even considered having a one-night stand in my life until this moment.

Placing his hand on the small of my back, he guided me to his door and opened it.

He placed the do-not-disturb sign on the handle and shut the door behind him, turning toward me and taking me in. I stood looking around the room, clutching my little purse in my sweaty hands, afraid to let it go. It felt as if it was my only lifeline, and if I let it go, all hell would break loose. Walking toward me, he took hold of my hands in his. "Relax, sweetheart." I slowly let go of my clutch, dropping it into his hands. He set it down on top of the bedside table.

As he looked up at me, I could see the heat in his eyes. It was the same heat he had been looking at me with this afternoon and just a few minutes ago out front. I took a step back and leaned against the cool wall. I was so hot, I needed some sort of relief.

"As I said before, it's been a while since...I'm just a little nervous."

He stepped toward me, running his hands up and down my arms.

"There's no reason to be nervous. I'm not going to hurt you." His eyes washed over my face, his stare getting more intense.

"I can't stop thinking about what it felt like to hold you in my arms and run my tongue over your body," he whispered. "How you tensed at my touch. How you shuddered when my lips met yours to take that lime."

I closed my eyes, vividly remembering the way it had felt.

"How your skin pebbled." A shiver left my body, despite the heat that was radiating from him as his lips grazed the side of my neck.

"And when you let out that sexy little moan, I wished it had been more than my tongue causing that," he whispered in my ear, sucking my earlobe in his mouth.

He pulled back and looked me in the eyes, studying me, before his lips gently grazed over mine, softly sucking my bottom lip gently into his mouth.

I couldn't take it anymore. My center was painfully throbbing, and I was soaked. My nipples were hard, and if he had run his hands over them, I was sure I would come on the spot. Wrapping both arms around his neck, I attacked his mouth, kissing him hard. Fuck taking it slow; it had been three long years of feeling dead. It was refreshing to feel totally alive, and my body was crying with need.

Pulling me away from the wall, he wrapped his arms around me and ran his hands down my back, cupping my ass and pulling me into him for an even deeper kiss. I could feel his hardness pressing into me as he pushed me up against the wall. Suddenly, he hoisted me up and wrapped both my legs around his waist, carrying me over to the bed. He sat down and lay back. As I straddled his lap, I could feel him fully straining against his pants. I ground down on him, a hard moan escaping his lips. His hands grabbed hold of my breasts. As he sat up, he bit my nipples through my dress. Dropping my head back, I let out a loud groan at the feel of his mouth on me. He reached behind me, un-tying my dress. I stilled as he pulled the dress off my body. He unhooked my bra, slowly sliding it off me, so my breasts were exposed to him. He looked at my face and then down to them. Holding them in his hands, he alternated between them, first gently licking and then sucking each nipple into his mouth. All the while he looked me directly in the eyes. I let out another loud groan as he continued. With one swift, fluid move-ment, he flipped me down onto the bed and stood between my legs as he looked down at me longingly. He pulled his shirt over his head as I took in his strong chest and shoulders.

He placed his hand under my ass, lifting and pulling me down to the edge of the bed. I lay before him in my panties as he stood and studied me. He unzipped his pants, letting them fall to the floor, and then pulled his boxers down, springing himself free. He was much bigger than Jason—in both length and width. So big in fact I wasn't sure if I would be able to handle him. I tried not to show the fear in my eyes when I saw him, but he had already taken notice at my gaping jaw, lifting the corner of his mouth in a half smile. "What is it, Autumn?"

I averted my eyes, "It's..." I could feel the blush rise to my face. "It's just I'm afraid you're not going to fit."

He chuckled lightly as more heat crept into my cheeks. "No worries, beautiful, I'll go slow." He placed one hand on each of my knees and slowly spread my legs open. He didn't hesitate. He leaned down and kissed the inside of each of my thighs, then placed his mouth on the crotch of my panties. A low groan escaped his mouth again as he pressed his tongue against me. "My God, you're so wet. I can't wait to taste you." He moaned into me.

"Hunter, stop. What are you doing?" I squeezed my thighs together almost trapping his head.

"Relax, beautiful, I'm just going to have a little snack."

"No."

"Don't tell me you've never..."

I blushed, shaking my head. No, I had never done that. Jason had always been all about his satisfaction.

"Someone has been doing you a great disservice. Just relax. I've been told I am very good with my tongue." He ran his hands over my breasts, my legs falling apart. He leaned down and kissed me just above my panty line.

He squeezed my thighs with his hands and then, in a quick, swift pull, ripped my favorite pair of lace panties off me. Burying his face into me, he licked and sucked at my clit. I couldn't help the moan that escaped my mouth as my back lifted off the mattress. If he kept that up, I would come on the spot. Inserting a finger into me, he continued. I could feel myself start to tighten as he inserted another finger, pumping them in and out slowly while he continued sucking my clit into his mouth.

"Hunter, please stop. I'm going to come," I cried out as my fingers gripped his hair.

"Then come for me, beautiful." There was no stopping

him. He continued pumping his fingers, finally curling them up to hit that special spot inside of me, as he continued sucking on my clit. It was like I forgot to breathe; my back arched off the mattress and I cried out.

He kissed the insides of my thighs again as he crawled up between my legs. I watched as he pulled a condom from the bedside drawer and slipped it on himself. He rubbed the head of his cock against my wetness and then I felt the pressure as he pushed himself at my opening. He took his time sliding into me, inch by inch, letting me adjust to him as he went. "Fuck, beautiful, you're so tight. You feel amazing," he whispered. My nails dug into his back as he pushed the rest of himself slowly into me all the way to the hilt. Once he was fully seated in me, he held himself there, letting me adjust to him. Raising my legs up onto his shoulders and leaning forward, he began drilling into me. Reaching down, he rubbed my clit as he thrust into me harder and faster. I could feel him start to swell as I tightened around him. His breathing became more erratic and he let out a deep groan. I felt his muscles start to tighten as he unloaded into me. He collapsed on top of me and stayed there holding me until we both caught our breath.

Reaching down between us, he held onto the top of the condom as he pulled himself out of me. "Stay here. I'll be right back." He got up off the bed as he walked into the bathroom, grabbed a warm cloth, and came back, cleaning me up. Throwing the cloth down on the floor, he laid down beside me, pulling me into him, placing my head on his chest. We were quiet as we laid there, him tracing light circles on my back as I listened intently to his heart beating wildly in his chest.

The room was dark. I had no idea where I was. The soreness between my legs quickly reminded me what had happened, and then I felt Hunter's arm tighten around my waist. I looked at the clock—three in the morning. I laid there for a moment, trying to calm the panic that was rising in me, but it was no use. I couldn't breathe. I needed to get out of there. I waited until he rolled over, his deep snore filling the room. I felt around the room, trying to find my clothing. I found everything on the floor in a pile, finally finding what was left of my shredded panties just under the edge of the bed. I dressed the best I could in the darkness, grabbed my shoes and clutch, and slipped out the front door.

As soon as I was in the safety of my own room, I dropped everything and let out an uncontrollable sob. What had I done? Sex with a complete stranger, not once, but three times? What had I been thinking? Taking a deep breath, I tried to stop the tears from falling, but it was no use. Every part of me shook as I removed my clothing, leaving my dress along with everything else in a heap on the floor. Heading out into my private outdoor shower, I turned the water on, letting the hot water hit my body. I sank to the ground, sitting and crying. I let the water wash the tears down the drain. I wasn't crying over what had just happened hours ago—it was amazing—but rather what had happened years ago, as the realization hit that Jason had never really been the one. When the water finally turned cold, I picked myself up off the ground, shut off the lights, and went into the bedroom, wrapped in a towel. I dried off, slipped into my T-shirt, and crawled into the cold bed.

It was almost eight in the morning when I woke up from a restless, broken sleep. The sun was streaming through the windows. I rolled over, the familiar ache I felt between my legs quickly reminding me that last night did in fact happen. I had never succumbed to a man's touch like that before, not that quickly anyway. Jason had never turned me on like that, with a deep need to be satisfied at an exact moment. The whole night had been like nothing I had ever felt or experienced. We couldn't seem to get enough of one another.

I pulled myself out of bed and ran a brush through my hair. I packed up my beach bag and got dressed in my bathing suit and wrap. Grabbing my bag, I opened the door. As I went to close it behind me, I found an envelope with my name scrawled across it taped to the door. I had no doubt in my mind who it was from, so I placed it inside my bag and headed up for breakfast. Once I had sat down with my food, I reached into my bag. Grabbing the note, I took a deep breath, my chest aching. I leaned back against the chair, and with shaky hands, opened the note, already dreading what was written inside.

Autumn, I'd hoped to wake up to your beautiful face this morning. I hope your leaving wasn't due to regret. I want you to know I thoroughly enjoyed last night, and it would probably break me to know you feel differently. I will be away from the resort today with my brothers on a scuba-diving/deep-sea fishing adventure. I've arranged for you to have a very relaxing day at the spa—on me. After all, I'm sure you are rather sore from last night. You're scheduled to be there at nine. I have arranged a special surprise for dinner tonight and hope that you will accompany me. Please meet me outside of Tranquility at seven. Until then, beautiful, I hope you enjoy your day. — Hunter

A tear ran down my cheek as I folded the note and placed it back in the envelope and into my bag. I checked my watch, eight-thirty. After finishing my breakfast, I made my way to the spa.

Chapter Fourteen

Hunter

The night air was cool coming off the ocean, as I stood outside of the restaurant waiting for her to arrive. I had reserved a private table on the beach for us for dinner. Everything was set. Now all I needed was her. I could feel my pulse start to race at the sound of heels approaching, but my hopes crashed quickly when the person came around the corner and I saw it wasn't her. I glanced at my watch. It was already twenty after seven. She probably wasn't coming, and the staff had already told me that they couldn't hold my reservation for much longer. I swallowed, fighting down my disappointment, and went to let the waitress know that the table needed to be canceled, when I heard a soft voice say my name.

I turned and saw her standing at the end of the walkway. She was stunning, her hair pulled up into a loose bun, which showed off her neck. Soft tendrils were falling around her face. The white dress she wore hugged her in all the right places. A soft smile came over her face as she approached me. Pulling her into me, I kissed her just below the ear. "Hello, beautiful. Ready for dinner?"

The waitress smiled at the pair of us and grabbed two menus. "This way, please." She turned and led us away from the door.

"Hunter, where are we going? The restaurant is right there."

My hand tightened around hers. "Trust me. You're going to love it." I winked at her and placed my hand on the small of her back, guiding her through the narrow path in front of me.

We stepped from the tight pathway out onto the beach. There, a table for two was set up on a small platform for us in the moonlight. I watched her expression as she saw what was in front of us. "Hunter, this is amazing." A smile lit up her face.

"A quiet dinner for two." I led her to the table, pulling out the chair for her, and then took my seat across from her. The waitress then poured us each a glass of white wine, leaving us to look at the menu.

I watched her as she studied the menu. I could barely take my eyes off her, and to be honest, I didn't want to. There was still something hidden in those eyes of hers; I just wish I knew what it was. The waitress returned a couple minutes later to take our order. Autumn ordered the roast chicken and I the lobster. As the waitress walked away, I made eye contact with her, her beautiful grey-blue eyes sparkling against the light of the moon. "What do you think?" I asked her.

"It's beautiful. I didn't know they offered dinners out here. Of course, a romantic dinner on the beach for one doesn't sound all that appealing, does it?" She let out an adorable little giggle as she looked at me.

"They don't normally do this. I had to put in a very special request. How did you enjoy your day at the spa?"

Her eyes turned down. "It was the most relaxing day I have had in a long time. Thank you. But I don't feel right about it, so if you could please tell me what all of that cost, I would like to repay you."

"No need, beautiful. It's on me."

I watched as she took a sip of wine, her eyes darting back to mine. "That's very kind of you, but I can't let you do that."

"It's already done. Now no more talk about it."

There were tears in her eyes as she sipped her wine, and now she was avoiding my gaze. I wasn't sure how to read her, but I could tell there was something weighing on her mind, and I knew it wasn't me. She wasn't the type of woman who had been spoiled previously, if at all, and I had a feeling that it made her extremely uncomfortable.

Autumn

. . .

I left the topic alone after that, trying to accept the fact that he had wanted to treat me, not that he was doing it because he wanted something in return. I finally relaxed, letting those thoughts leave my brain, and tried to enjoy dinner. Our conversation ranged from our favorite movies, drinks, and hobbies to Hunter's adventures for the day. We talked about his brothers and my sister. The conversation was fun, light, and filled with laughter, making the time pass quickly.

It had been the most romantic dinner I had ever shared with someone. Jason could never have touched this. He hadn't been the type to pull romance or to surprise me with a day at the spa. He always told me things like that were a waste of money, which I now equated to *I just hadn't been worth it*. But the thought or idea of a complete stranger spending that kind of money on me because he wanted to didn't sit well with me either.

The sound of the waves crashing into the shore and the soft music playing in the background had created a beautiful atmosphere. The staff had just finished clearing away our dessert dishes when Hunter stood and held his hand out to me. "Care to dance with me?"

Removing the napkin from my lap and setting my coffee cup down, I placed my hand into his. Taking me into his arms, he pulled me into his chest, our bodies swaying to "Perfect" by Ed Sheeran. We danced in the moonlight under the stars until the staff turned the music off and we were left on the beach in total quietness.

Slowly, we walked down the beach to one of the palapas. "Did you want to sit down with me for a bit?" he asked as he started pulling me toward the seat. We both sat on the edge of the mattress, looking out toward the ocean. The moonlight was shimmering off the peaks of the waves. "How did you enjoy dinner?"

"It was lovely. To be honest, I've never experienced anything like that before."

"You mean to tell me that the men in your past have never treated you to anything like that before?"

"I'm afraid not. The man in my past didn't believe in romance."

"I'm sorry to hear that."

"It is what it is, Hunter," I said a little harshly.

"Doesn't sound like the men you've been with know how to treat a woman like yourself."

I could feel the heat rushing to my cheeks, and I turned my head to look away from him and down the beach. I hadn't meant to snap at him. When I turned my attention back to him, I saw desire in his eyes.

He leaned in and pressed his mouth to mine, his tongue finding mine. He placed his hand on the back of my head, and his kiss deepened as a low moan left my throat. He trailed kisses from my mouth to my ear and down my neck, while his hands roamed my body. My thoughts traveled back to the night before, to the amazing way he had made me feel, and then the feelings of doubt poured into my mind. Jason and I were over, that was for sure. I had accepted that and tried to move on. That's what last night had been about.

I ran my hands over Hunter's bulging biceps and up to his chest. "Hunter." He continued kissing and sucking on my neck, ignoring my call. "Hunter, please," I choked out, tears starting to form in the corners of my eyes.

He pulled back and looked at me. "What is it,

Autumn?" he whispered while brushing my hair out of my face.

"I don't think I can do this." My voice was barely audible as tears slid down my cheeks.

He held me in his embrace but stilled his hands. "You can't do what?"

The pain that was building in my chest was almost too much to bear. I couldn't help but feel sad over the fact that I was finally facing and accepting the closure of the divorce that had happened two years ago. I was afraid that by telling him what was really bothering me that he would walk away from me in an instant. Who would want someone with this much baggage? What was worse was that standing in front of me was a sexy, sweet man, and even though I had only known him for a few hours, I could easily see myself falling totally head over heels in love with him. That revelation scared the shit out of me. I felt that by continuing down this current path, I was only going to end up really hurt, so it would be best to end things right now. You didn't fall in love with someone you barely knew; that's how I got into the mess with Jason.

Placing his thumb under my chin, he lifted my face to his. "Autumn? What is it, love?"

I fought at first to look him in the eye, but finally gave in. "I'm not just here for a fun vacation."

"Okay."

"I'm divorced—not recently or anything—but I'm struggling to try to put myself and my life back together again." As soon as those words left my mouth, the heaviest sob shook my body. Hunter didn't respond. He just kept his arms securely around me, holding me.

"That's what I needed the break from."

"It's okay, sweetheart. Divorce happens, and it's tough for some people."

"This is different."

"Tell me."

"You don't want to hear it, and I don't want to bore you with all the details."

"You aren't boring me, and I think maybe you need to talk about it. It's only you and me on this beach, so you're stuck with me. But you're in luck because I'm a really good listener."

I wasn't sure if I should share with him or not. This wasn't just cut and dry. I kept my head down, my eyes averted from him for what seemed like ages. "I have nowhere I need to be, baby, except right here with you. So, no matter how long it takes, I'll wait for you to talk to me," he whispered.

I finally let out the breath I had been holding and decided to just lay it all out, letting the cards fall where they may. "We'd been married for two years. Things were going well except we both wanted children, but I was having trouble conceiving. He had been putting so much pressure on me, but when it eventually happened, he didn't seem to be as excited as I thought he would be. Things were going okay. I was healthy, and things were progressing normally. One morning I woke up. I was about three months into my pregnancy, but I wasn't feeling very well. I chalked it up to just being pregnant and went to work anyway. A couple hours later I found myself being rushed to the hospital, cramping and bleeding badly. By the time I got there, I had already lost the baby. When he arrived, the doctor came in just in time to tell us that I wouldn't be able to have any chil-dren. I could tell from the second he heard that news that he blamed me for everything; it showed in every one of his actions. From that day forward he became distant. He started working long hours, some nights not coming home at all. I was battling depression, which kept getting worse not better. It took a year before I finally returned to work. I'd been back a couple of months when one morning he met me in the kitchen. He announced that he wanted a divorce. He told me he couldn't live with the fact that I would never be able to give him children and that he was tired of watching me deteriorate. For him, it was basically over. He already had all the papers drawn up that I just needed to sign. He wanted it quick, easy, and with as little stress as possible on both of us, so he just handed over everything to me. After he walked out that door, I never saw him again. He never came back. He was just gone. I finally dropped off the divorce papers to his office and the rest has led me here."

Hunter

I didn't know what to say. I certainly wasn't expecting to hear what she had shared with me. I watched as the tears rolled down her cheeks, her body shaking. What kind of an asshole would do that to this angel? He was acting as if he was the only one who'd lost anything, when really it was her who had lost everything. Her life had been totally affected, and she had absolutely no support system whatsoever. It's no wonder she always looks sad. She has every right to be sad. "Please, Hunter, I don't want to hurt you, but I fear last night was a mistake," she cried, her red eyes meeting mine.

Watching the tears fall from those beautiful eyes was literally killing me. She had already suffered so much, and it wasn't fair that she still was. I didn't know what was happening to me. I let her go from my hold, took a couple of steps away from her, and turned to look out at the ocean. My mind screamed at me to just walk away, not to get involved, but my heart—for some reason, my heart told me not to let her go. As I stood there listening to her cry, and even fighting back tears myself, I heard her faintly whisper behind me. "Please, Hunter, please just leave."

I felt a very unfamiliar feeling building in my gut. I couldn't describe it, but it didn't calm until I had pulled her back into me and kissed her hard, holding her tightly in my arms. When the kiss broke, I sucked in a deep breath. "I'm not going anywhere, Autumn. So, you cry, cry until your heart is content, and then together we'll move on." I pulled her tightly against me and held her. I'd lost track of how long we'd been standing there like that, but she had finally quieted down and was just resting her head on my chest.

Sitting down on the palapa mattress, I pulled her down beside me. She shivered as the cool night air blew off the ocean. I moved myself back onto the mattress and guided her up to lay beside me, my body blocking the cool night breeze from her. She curled her body into me and lay there. Rolling onto my side with her in my arms, I kissed her lips. "I want to take away all your pain, baby," I whispered to her as I kissed her again.

"Please," she moaned as she placed her hand on the back of my head and pulled me into her, pushing her body against mine.

She was so small in my arms. I loved listening to the sounds she made as I kissed her.

Chapter Fifteen

Hunter

Morning rain tapping on the window woke me. I felt her body against mine and looked down at the sleeping angel laying beside me. I glanced at the clock. It was already eleven. My flight left at eight, which meant I had to leave the resort no later than five.

Rolling onto my side, I pulled her body into me, a gentle, soft moan coming from her lips. I placed a kiss on her bare shoulder. I didn't want to leave her. I didn't want to move. I wanted to stay in this moment forever. After she had poured her heart out to me the other night, she became a different person, not afraid to express herself or have fun. It was like she had washed away all the guilt that she had been holding onto.

We had spent the last three days together—getting a couple's massage, having dinner, laying in the sun, taking a tour through Shaw Gardens, and going horseback riding on the beach. It had been amazing getting to know her. But today was the last day I would be with her, and I secretly wished that I could stop time forever. We hadn't had a chance to talk about what would happen after this week. As a matter of fact, neither of us had even shared where we lived. I just knew that no matter where it was, I was willing to give everything I had to make it work.

I brushed the hair away from her neck and started kissing her slowly. She let out a soft moan as she stretched and rolled herself against me. Running my hand down the flat of her stomach and into her panties, I started rubbing her clit, dipping my finger into her wetness and back up over the small bundle of nerves. A soft moan escaped her lips. I rubbed her until she was begging me to stop, gripping my bicep, digging her nails into me. I kept going until an orgasm finally ripped through her. Then I placed a strong, deep kiss on her lips.

"Hunter, you ready for lunch, man?" Chase shouted from outside the door, causing us both to jump.

"Come on, man!" Bryce shouted, pounding on the door. "It's our last day. Get out here and join us, you ass."

I placed another kiss on Autumn's lips and crawled out of bed, throwing on a pair of jeans. Covering her up, I went to open the door. Bryce and Chase stood there looking at me. "Well, it's about fucking time, man." They pushed their way through the door. I put my hand out to stop them both from entering. "What?" Bryce looked at me in surprise. I shook my head at the pair of them.

"What? Oh, she's here?" Bryce and Chase laughed, both trying to peek around the corner.

"Yes, now give us a few minutes and we'll meet you down by the pool restaurant for some lunch."

Chase looked at me and smiled. "Well, is she any good?" he mouthed.

I gave them both an annoyed look and pushed them both back out the door, shutting it behind them. I laughed to myself as I made my way back to the other room. "I swear, for two grown-ass men, they sure can act like children occasionally." As I rounded the corner, Autumn was already out of bed, throwing on one of my T-shirts, laughing at what I had said.

"Let me just run next door and get dressed and then we can meet your brothers for some lunch." She kissed me deeply before heading out the back door and into her room to get ready for the day.

Autumn

The day had gone relatively fast, and before I knew it, I was standing with Bryce and Chase in the lobby as Hunter turned in his room keys. I had a half hour left with him and then he would be gone. When Hunter returned, Bryce and Chase took off to say goodbye to their lady friends, leaving us to one another.

"Listen, Autumn, the past few days have been wonderful. I've given it some thought; I'm not sure where you live, and to be honest, it really doesn't matter because I would like to stay in touch, see where things may go between us." He grabbed both my hands in his and smiled at me.

"I'd like that," I said, meeting his eyes.

He reached into his pocket and handed me a business card. I took it from his hand and read what was printed on it, a large smile spreading across my face. "What is it, beautiful?"

"It shouldn't be as hard as you think. You work about an hour away from where I live," I whispered, reaching up and placing a kiss on his lips.

He kissed me hard, sweeping his tongue through my mouth. Then he looked deep into my eyes, not hiding how he felt. "You have no idea how happy this makes me, beautiful. Now what is your number?" He pulled his phone from his pocket, opened up his contacts, and typed me into his phone while I rattled off my number for him. He shoved his phone back into his pocket and led me over to an empty seat in the lobby, pulling me down onto his lap. Wrapping his arms around me, he kissed me again, sucking my bottom lip into his mouth.

I rested my head against his. "Don't you dare start something we can't finish. We don't have time."

"Want to bet?" He wagged his eyebrows at me. I leaned in and met his lips again. "Come with me," he whispered between kisses.

At first, I protested, but he kept pulling me through the crowd of people that were waiting for the bus. We walked quickly along the front of the resort and stopped just outside of the men's bathroom.

"Hunter, I can't go in there."

"Yes, you can." He winked at me and looked back over his shoulder to make sure no one was watching as he pulled me through the men's bathroom door. I felt my heart start to pound, but the bathroom was empty. As soon as we were inside, he pushed me up against the door and locked it. His mouth was instantly on mine, his hands gripping my ass, lifting me and wrapping my legs around his hips. His kiss deepened as he carried me over to the counter and sat me on the edge of it.

"Take your panties off and lift your skirt," he whispered, his breath tickling my ear. "I'm going to make you moan so loud, the whole lobby will know what just happened."

A chill ran through me at the thought as I wiggled out of my panties. Wrapping his arms around me, he held me on the edge of the counter, knelt down, and placed my legs over his shoulders. His eyes met mine before he buried his face between my legs, licking and sucking at my center. I had to bite my lower lip to keep from moaning. I could feel myself just about to come when he pushed my legs off his shoulders and stood up. "I want to hear you one more time as I bury myself in you." I heard his zipper lower.

I parted my legs to make room for him. Reaching down between us, I held him in my hand and stroked his thick cock.

"Fuck, I can't wait to feel you," he moaned as I continued to stroke him.

"Do you have a condom?" I asked.

A look came over his face. "FUCK!"

I bit my bottom lip. *It would be nice to feel a man inside of me again without something between us,* I thought. I knew

I was going way too fast with all of this, but honestly, we really hadn't gone slow with anything else.

"What is it, beautiful?" he asked as he studied my face.

"I want to feel you inside me. Just you with nothing between us," I whispered, my eyes begging him.

I placed him at my entrance and rubbed his hard cock through my wetness. He groaned loudly as he slid himself deep inside of me. His hands gripping my hips, he held me against him as he pumped into me hard, fast, and deep. Small whimpers escaped my lips the harder he thrust. I could feel him start to swell as I tightened around him. He let out a deep groan when he slammed into me. As he filled me, I wrapped my arms around his neck and buried my face into his shoulder, screaming his name through clenched teeth as I came.

He met my lips as he pulled himself out of me and zipped his pants back up. I straightened my skirt and bent to pick my panties up off the floor. "Give those to me, beautiful." He smiled at me as he held his hand out. "I want a reminder of you until I see you again." I handed them to him and watched as he put them in his pocket. As he looked at me, I could feel the blush rising onto my face.

The bus pulled up to the front of the lobby. I closed my eyes and tried to fight down the lump that was forming in my throat.

The bellhops were already organizing the luggage and

had started to load it into the bus. "I guess this is it," I whispered, my eyes burning.

"Just for now. I'll be in touch with you soon. I promise," he said, looking toward the back of the lobby, signaling over my shoulder to both Chase and Bryce to get to the bus.

I blinked. I could feel a hot tear slip down my cheek. Hunter looked down at me, a loving smile on his face. "Don't cry. I promise, before you know it, you'll be in my arms again." He wiped away the lone tear and leaned down, pressing his lips to mine, wrapping me in his arms. I nodded, inhaling his scent.

It wasn't long before they were boarding the bus. I stood watching as it pulled away from the lobby, taking him from me. Once they were no longer in sight, I walked back to my room and started to pack my things. I was halfway through when a funny feeling came over me. Suddenly I was afraid that he wouldn't call, that maybe this was all there was supposed to be between us. When we got away from this island, life would return to normal, and it was possible that he would forget about me and everything we had shared. As I was packing my carry-on bag, I found the letter he had taped to the door for me. I re-read his words, a warm feeling crawling through my body. Meeting him had been a big deal for me. Trusting again, opening up, and sharing the things I had shared with him hadn't been easy, and I just prayed that he knew that. I was looking forward to seeing where things could go, but at this moment, I felt completely exposed and extremely vulnerable.

Chapter Sixteen

AUTUMN – TWO WEEKS LATER

I'd been home now for a couple of weeks and had settled back into my routine. I missed Jamaica—the sun, the music, but most of all, I missed Hunter. I hadn't heard from him since the night he left the resort except for a text that let me know he had gotten home safe. I of course had responded when I landed, but after that, there had been no communication. The only person I had told about him was Dr. Plante, mainly because the day I went to see him I was having serious doubts that I would ever hear from him again. He told me that I might need to prepare myself to accept the fact that it could have been nothing more than a fling. He had wanted me to text or call Hunter during my appointment with him to try to ease my mind, but I was too afraid. Instead, I found myself in his office in tears convinced that if he hadn't already called me then that was all the proof I needed, and I didn't need to make a fool of myself any more than I already had.

I rolled over in bed. It was Thursday morning. Evelyn was off today, and by the sound of things, she was tearing apart the downstairs. She was starting to decorate for Christmas.

I sat up in bed and checked my phone, just like I had done every morning for the past two weeks. My nerves were getting the best of me as I unlocked the phone to see the exact same thing: no message from Hunter. I grabbed the glass of water from my nightstand, taking a drink to get rid of the lump that was forming in my throat.

I finally got up, got dressed, and headed downstairs for some food. Walking into the kitchen, I grabbed a mug from the cupboard and poured myself a cup of coffee.

"Good morning!" Evelyn sang as she came walking into the kitchen with another box of decorations.

"Morning."

"So, now that Derek finally isn't around, are you going to tell me what really happened on your trip?" She dropped the box on the floor and poured herself a cup of coffee. Derek had been on vacation for the last two weeks, and we hadn't really had any time to talk.

"What do you mean?"

"I don't know... Did you meet anyone?" I smiled to myself as the memory of Hunter flew into my mind. I took a sip of coffee. "You did! I knew it. I could tell from the look on your face the minute you stepped off that plane!" she sang as she flopped down on the chair beside me.

I went quiet. "I did. I met someone."

"Well, you have to tell me about him. First, let's start with his name."

"His name is Hunter." I began searching through my phone for a picture.

"Are you going to see him again?" she pressed.

"We were going to try to stay in touch, but it's obviously not going to work. I haven't heard from him since I came back."

"I'm sure he just got busy. Did you message him?"

"No." I continued my search through my pictures until I came upon the one I was looking for. It was the night of our candlelit dinner. I handed the phone to Evelyn. "This is Hunter. That night he set up a private candlelit dinner on the beach for us. We shared wonderful conversation, ate fantastic food, and danced under the moonlight. I think it was the most romantic night we spent together."

Evelyn took the phone from me and looked down at the screen. "This is him?"

"Yes, you know, it's really a small world. He works an hour away from here. We never spoke of where one another lived until the night he left. He suggested keeping in touch, and that was when I found out where he worked."

I looked at the expression on Evelyn's face as she looked at the photo. I could tell she was hiding something. "What is it, Evelyn?"

She looked up at me and smiled. "Nothing. He's very handsome. So, how far did it go between the two of you?" I could feel the heat rising in my cheeks. I wasn't sure I wanted to share that with Evelyn. I didn't want to hear the lecture that I was sure would be coming from following her advice. However, it was too late. She already knew. "You didn't!"

"Yes, we did." I couldn't help the smile that formed on my lips, thinking back to those nights.

"Must have been good to make you smile like that." Evelyn nudged me with her shoulder. "Well, as long as you used protection."

"Okay, Mom." I swallowed hard, thinking about the last time we had been together, unprotected.

"I'm sure he'll contact you. Now drink up and help me put this stuff up." Evelyn dug into a box of decorations and handed me a bunch of garland. "These are for the railing. Let's go."

Chapter Seventeen

EVELYN

Derek was late coming home from his first day back at the office, so Autumn and I had eaten dinner without him. Autumn had already gone to bed. I on the other hand couldn't even think about sleeping. It wasn't that I wasn't tired, because I was exhausted. Autumn was weighing on my mind, and without Derek home to talk to, I knew it would just keep nagging at me.

Listening to her talk about Hunter had nearly broken my heart. I didn't want this bastard to do this to her. I felt the strong need to protect her, even though she would insist she was fine. It's just she had had her heart broken enough in the past couple years. She didn't need this. Once I got her talking, she had continued telling me about her trip and about all the time she had spent with him. I listened painfully for hours as she shared everything with me—from how he tried to get her attention to how they ended up in bed together.

I couldn't believe my eyes when I looked at that picture. There she sat on his lap, his arms wrapped around her. It was Hunter—Derek's friend—the same guy I had tried to set her up with on that blind date. Hunter—the same guy my husband had warned me of being a player. I prayed she didn't notice the look on my face. I was afraid that my sister had just been on the receiving end of a guy who was just looking for a good fuck.

Listening to her go on and on and seeing the look on her face just about broke my heart. I had a good mind to call him up and let him have it for not calling her. To think that I had thought they would make a good couple. She didn't need this. After all that had gone on with her in the past couple of years, she needed a real man, not one who was just going to play her. I prayed Derek was wrong about him, but the cards certainly weren't stacking up in Hunter's favor.

Finally, I heard the key in the door. I jumped out of the chair and basically attacked Derek in the front hall. "It's Hunter," I whispered.

"Who's Hunter?" Derek looked at me like I'd lost my mind.

"The guy."

"What guy? Evelyn, what are you talking about?" Derek dropped his briefcase down on the floor and hung his coat in the closet.

"The guy she met on vacation. I told you there was a guy; it's him! She showed me a picture. I'm going to tell you, if he is pulling one over on my sister, I will..."

"What are you going to do, Evelyn? I'll tell you, you're

not going to get involved." Derek kissed me on the cheek and headed into the kitchen. "I'm starving," he called over his shoulder.

"Derek, you said yourself he's a player." I followed him into the kitchen.

"Evelyn, you can't babysit her forever. She's a grown woman. And I never said he was a player."

"You have to call him," I said. I grabbed the phone from the base and held it out in front of him.

Derek looked at me like I was crazy. Putting the plate down on the counter, he walked over to me and took the phone from my hand. "Evelyn, love, calm down. Like I said, Autumn is an adult. She went away, she met someone, she had a good time. If he doesn't call, he doesn't call. I'm not going to call him, and you're not going to call him." He kissed me on the cheek and went back to preparing his dinner. "Did you tell her we know him?"

"Well...no...but..."

"Why not?"

"It doesn't matter."

"It doesn't matter that we know him? But you want me to call him to tell him to call her. Listen, whatever happens, happens. She'll have to deal with whatever it is. I've returned the RSVP to his firm's Christmas party, marked with three guests, so the worst thing, if he doesn't text her, they'll run into one another at the party. So, let's let it be. But for now, I want you to make a cup of tea and relax." He leaned in and kissed me.

Derek infuriated me sometimes. Why couldn't he see that she was going to get hurt and I had to protect her. "Derek?"

"What?"

"She can't get hurt again. It'll be the end of her."

"You cannot protect her forever. What happened between Autumn and Jason was horrible. It shouldn't have happened, but sometimes I think it was for the best. I never liked him anyway, and she is too good for a guy like that. She is going to have to learn to date again, and she will go through more assholes than she will nice guys before she finds one to settle down with. I know Hunter from both sides. He can be a total asshole, as we all can be, or he can be an amazing guy. He has a lot going for him. Now, I've had a long day, so I'm going to eat my dinner, relax, and watch some TV. I want you to make your tea and leave it be." Derek sat down to eat his meal, leaving me to sit in the kitchen to brood. It took me a few minutes, but I finally put the kettle on, made a cup of chamomile tea, and did my best to calm down.

Chapter Eighteen

HUNTER

I sat behind my desk, staring at my computer screen. It had been hell since I had returned. Shit had hit the fan with two of the biggest cases I had been working on before I left, and I'd been locked behind closed doors in meetings with these clients since I had returned. Days had been long, and I was tired.

I ran my hands over my face. I needed a fucking break from all of this. Picking up my mug, I took the last gulp of my cold coffee. I'd been working around the clock since I had returned home. The office was quiet—Carter had left over two hours ago—and I was alone. I needed to turn my attention to something other than these case files for a bit. I got up out of my chair, grabbed my phone, and lay down on the couch. Once I was comfortable, I scrolled through the pictures from my vacation.

There she was with me the day we had gone horseback riding, my arms wrapped around her waist as she sat in front of me on my horse. Her grey-blue eyes stood out against her deeply tanned skin. I could feel myself getting hard at the memory of her body pressed up against mine, her ass sitting between my legs. I felt awful; I hadn't even had a chance to send her a text since we got back, but honestly, I hadn't had even a second to myself except to sleep and shower. Still, whenever I had a spare second, she was all that had been on my mind.

My finger hovered over her number. I wanted to call, but what if enough time had passed and she had decided she didn't want anything to do with me? *Where the fuck did that thought come from?* I wasn't an insecure man by any means. I went after what I wanted, in all parts of my life. Fuck it. I pressed her number and waited for it to connect. I needed a weekend out of here anyway, and tomorrow was Friday. Whether Carter liked it or not, I was taking the weekend off, and I wanted and needed to spend it with her.

As soon as it started ringing, I felt my pulse pick up. I was hot. Fuck, I was sweating, and I could hear my pulse whooshing in my ears. I had never felt this way when I had called a woman before. I must be coming down with something. Good thing I was lying down. I was beginning to feel lightheaded.

I was just about to hang up when finally, on the fifth ring, a very sexy, out of breath Autumn answered. "Hello?" The sound of her voice went straight to my cock.

Autumn

"Hey, beautiful." I heard his deep, sexy voice come over the phone.

"Hunter?" I could feel my pulse pick up.

"Yes, it's me. Before we get talking, I want to apologize for not calling you sooner. Work has been crazy since we returned, and I've spent pretty much every waking moment behind my desk at home or at the office. I hope you can forgive me."

"Of course. How have you been?" I could hear the shake in my voice. I felt like my heart was going to beat right out of my chest, I was so nervous. I'd been checking my phone for the past two weeks, waiting to hear from him, and finally he had called.

"Aside from busy, missing you." His voice was so deep and sexy, it was making my center throb. "What about you? How have you been?"

"I'm doing okay."

"Any second thoughts about what happened between us?"

The only regret that I was feeling now was thinking that he wouldn't call, that I'd only been a notch in his belt. "No. I hope there aren't any with you either."

"Not one on this end either. Listen, I'm not going to

keep you; it's late, and I'm just heading out of the office for the night."

"You're just leaving now?" I asked as I glanced at the clock. It was almost ten-thirty.

"Yes. It's been a long freaking week. The reason for my call..." I could feel my throat getting tighter, and my chest was starting to hurt at what was coming next. I was trying to fight back the threat of tears when his question took me by surprise. "What are you doing this weekend?"

"Pardon?" I swallowed hard. I wanted to make sure he asked what I had thought he had.

"This weekend, do you have plans?"

"As in tomorrow?"

"Yes."

"Nothing pressing."

"Well, I was wondering if you would like to come spend the weekend with me."

"As in stay at your place?"

A deep chuckle came over the phone. "Yes, beautiful, unless of course you want me to make you scream my name at your place. Somehow, I don't think your sister would approve though."

A warm chill ran through my body, my center pulsing at the thought. "I'd love to."

"Great. Did you want me to pick you up?"

"No, I can drive. Where do you live?" I searched around my nightstand for a pen and piece of paper as he rattled off his address.

"I'm taking the day off tomorrow, so how about you be at my place at noon."

"Sounds good, I'll see you then."

We said our goodbyes, and as I went to hang up, I heard him call my name. "Oh, and Autumn?"

"Yes, Hunter?"

"Be well rested. There won't be much sleep once I get you in my bed." I was instantly wet at the thought and could feel myself blush. "Good night, Autumn," he said with a deep laugh.

"Good night, Hunter."

I set the phone down on the nightstand. I could already feel the excitement building in me. I couldn't keep myself from grinning like an idiot. When my pulse had finally calmed down, I got into my flannel pajamas and crawled into bed. I was extremely turned on and needed to divert my attention to something other than Hunter, his bed, and the memories that were floating through my head. Turning on my e-reader and finding the book I was in the middle of, I tried to read. It was starting to help until both of my characters had a hot, passionate romp up against a wall in their apartment, which reminded me of the first time we had slept together. I had no choice but to put the e-reader down onto the nightstand. I shut the light off and lay back against the pillow. I clenched my thighs together to try to calm the hard throbbing, but it did little good.

I was just about to slip my hand into my pants when I heard a knock on my door. "Autumn, you still awake?"

"Yes. Come in." I sat up and turned on the bedside lamp. Evelyn pushed the door open and came into my room.

"I'm sorry to disturb you. I hope you weren't almost asleep, but I need to talk to you."

"Okay." She walked hesitantly over and sat down on the

edge of the bed. The look on her face said it all: there was something wrong.

"It's about Hunter... I'm worried about..."

I put my hand up to stop her. "He called. I'm spending the weekend with him. I hope you'll be okay to finish the decorating alone. I really want to go." I smiled. "I'm really excited to see him."

A huge grin lit up her face. "Absolutely! Go! Have a fantastic time!" She jumped off the bed and walked to the door.

Her demeanor had turned one hundred and eighty degrees. There was something that she wasn't telling me, and I wanted to know what it was. "Evelyn, what was it you wanted to say?"

"Oh, it's nothing really. Have a great time. I'll see you in the morning." Pulling the door shut behind her, she left the room. I shut the light off, flopped back on my pillow, closed my eyes, and tried to get some sleep.

Chapter Nineteen

Hunter

Sunday morning was here already. It had been the quickest weekend I think I'd had in a long time. I opened my eyes; the room was still dark. I could feel the soft puff of her breath against my neck. I loved holding her in my arms, her body pressed into me, her head on my chest. I wrapped my arms around her tighter. At this point, I wasn't sure I really wanted to let her go. This weekend had been nothing short of amazing. We'd had a wonderful dinner Friday night at one of her favorite restaurants; we took in a play at the local theater on Saturday; we went skating at the park yesterday afternoon; and we topped the night off with dinner that we cooked together, curling up on the couch and watching a couple movies afterward. It felt like we had known one another all our lives. I hadn't been this happy in a long time. None of the women I'd been with could even begin to hold a candle to this girl. In the little time we'd spent together, my feelings ran deep for her. I felt as if I were falling in love.

She began to stir as I placed a gentle kiss on her forehead. She adjusted herself closer to me and threw her leg over mine. "Morning," she murmured.

"Shhh, baby, it's not time to get up yet."

"Then why are you awake?"

"I was just lying here thinking how great it feels to have you in my arms."

"I'm glad because I think it may be my new favorite place." She placed a light kiss on my neck.

I rolled her onto her back and found her mouth easily. "I'm glad, but I think you might like this a bit more." Biting on her bottom lip gently, I continued the assault of kisses down her neck to the top of her breasts. Rolling her nipple in between my fingers, I gently sucked the other one into my mouth, grazing it with my teeth. She arched her back and let out the most beautiful sleepy moan I think I'd ever heard.

Inching down her body, I continued trailing kisses over her stomach and thighs. I placed my hands in between her legs, gently forcing them apart. "I'm craving to taste you again." I couldn't help myself. I had her there so willing and wanting; I had to have her again.

Her legs fell open, and I kissed the insides of her thighs. She let out a little laugh as my facial hair tickled her soft skin. Laying myself between her legs, I locked her legs around my arms, spreading her open. I didn't want her to have the chance to get away from me. "Hunter?"

"Yeah, baby?" I lightly blew over her wetness. I could feel her body quiver.

"I want you." Her voice shook with need.

"I'm here, baby. All you need to do is ask." She hardly ever told me what she wanted and was hardly ever vocal, but I loved it when she was. I was so hard I could barely stand it; the throbbing was beginning to hurt. I continued blowing over her wetness, my hands finding her breasts, gently pinching and rolling her nipples between my fingers.

"Hunter. Please." I kissed the insides of her thighs again.

"What do you want, beautiful?" She reached down and ran her fingers through my hair.

"Lick me."

I almost came on the spot, hearing her ask me to do that. I wasted no time. I buried my face into her sweet center. As soon as my mouth connected with her, she let out a deep, throaty moan and bucked her hips up into me. I sucked her clit into my mouth, running my tongue down to her entrance and back up to her clit.

"I want you inside me," she cried out as I relentlessly continued licking her clit in small but firm strokes.

"You do?"

"Yes, please, Hunter. Put your cock inside me."

I released her legs and crawled up in between them. Taking my cock in my hand, I gave it a couple of pumps as she watched before placing it at her opening. "You sure you want it?"

"Yes, all of you, please."

I couldn't wait to get inside her. I pressed the head of my cock into her wetness and buried myself in her. I stilled once I was seated in her, letting her adjust to me. "Happy now, baby?"

I cradled her in my arms and gently pumped into her. Her moans were my reassurance. I watched her face in the early morning light, her eyes closed. She was biting her bottom lip, and she was breathtaking. I could feel myself start to throb; I couldn't take much more. I even tried slowing my pace, but it wasn't doing any good. I could feel my balls start to tighten and knew it was only a matter of seconds. A couple more pumps and I felt her tighten around me. As she buried her face into my neck I heard her breathlessly whisper, "I'm coming." I held her tightly in my arms as I pumped deeply into her one final time, unloading myself into her.

Autumn

I opened my eyes and was greeted by bright sunlight. I must have fallen back asleep this morning while we were cuddling. Rolling over, I noticed the bed was empty. I could hear music playing, so I crawled out of bed and threw on Hunter's T-shirt. I entered the kitchen. Hunter stood shirtless in lounge pants, his back to me, pouring two cups of coffee. I loved the sight of his strong back and broad chest. "Morning, beautiful. How did you sleep this morning?"

"Really good." I smiled. Hunter handed me a mug of coffee, took my hand in his, and led me over to the couch.

"What about you?"

"I did, considering all the interruptions." He winked at me and took a sip of his coffee.

I curled my feet underneath my legs and looked down at the mug I held in my hands. I was starting to think things that I shouldn't be. This weekend had been perfect in every way. We got along amazingly well. Everything with him was so comfortable, but for some reason, I just kept waiting for the bubble to burst.

"Why the sad face? What is it?"

"Nothing. It's silly really."

"When it comes to you, nothing is silly." Hunter placed his hand under my chin and lifted my face to meet his eyes.

I was afraid to tell him. Jason had never liked it when I shared my feelings about anything. He always dismissed how I felt, in the end never caring about how that made me feel. I could feel him observing me. I sat there, staring down at the mug in my hands. He reached over and placed his hand on top of mine, trying to get my attention. When I didn't look at him, he took my mug from my hand and set it on the table, placing his mug down beside mine. He then took both of my hands into his. "Autumn, you can talk to me. What is it, love?"

"Hunter, I..." I was so afraid of uttering my concerns that it was almost paralyzing.

"I'm going to sit right here until you tell me what's going on in that pretty head of yours. I'm a good listener—remember—and I'm not going to move, no matter how long it takes."

"Hunter, I'm scared."

"Of what?"

"What's going to happen with us after this weekend? It took you so long to contact me again after Jamaica. I can't be left wondering."

"Well, I'm hoping that you're going to want to see me again. I really like you, Autumn. I know I waited after returning to call you, which was a mistake." I looked into his eyes. "I certainly don't plan on making that mistake again." He leaned in, brushing his lips over mine. "Just so you know, you don't ever need to be afraid of talking to me."

I met his lips for another kiss. As our lips parted, he reached over and grabbed my mug, handing it to me.

"Listen, I wanted to ask you something." Hunter got up from the couch and grabbed a card off the counter. "I have a corporate Christmas party to attend. Would you be interested in being my plus one?" I took the card from his hand and looked down at it. I frowned. It looked very familiar. It took me no more than a few seconds to figure out where I had seen it before. I read the inside of the invite. Evelyn and Derek had received one just like it in the mail. "What is it?"

"That's funny. My sister's husband, Derek, received one of these," I said, examining both sides of the invitation.

"Derek Dasse?"

"Yes! How do you know Evelyn and Derek?" I questioned.

"I've been friends with Derek for years. We went to law school together. We refer clients to one another as well. Before I left for vacation, they tried..."

A look of realization came over Hunter's face as he stopped mid-sentence.

"Hunter, what is it?"

"You were my date."

"What? What are you talking about?"

"This is going to be weird, but did they try to set you up

on a date with one of Derek's friends just before you went away? With a guy who never showed up?"

"How did you know that?" I said, wiping away a tear at that memory. It was impossible for me not to cry about that. I had been so upset that night.

"Because I was your date. I was late. I arrived shortly after 9:00 that night, but you'd already left. I'm sorry about that, Autumn."

It sure was a small world. I stood there not really knowing how to respond to that. I swallowed hard and decided without really thinking about it that maybe it was better that we hadn't met that night. It might not have turned out the same way, especially with seeing Jason with Anna that night. I couldn't figure out why Evelyn didn't say anything to me when I showed her his picture though after I returned from my trip, but that was something I'd have to take up with her. I handed him back the card. "Yes, I'll be your plus one." I stood up and kissed him on the lips, wrapping my arms around his neck.

"Okay, beautiful, I'm going to go grab a quick shower. You okay out here for a few, or do you want to join me?" He stepped closer, wrapping his arms around me and pulling me into him.

"I'll be okay out here. Go have your shower. I'm just going to relax and have my coffee." Kissing me one more time, he headed off down the hall.

I had just gotten dressed and set my bag at the front door. Hunter was still in the shower when I sat down to read the paper. I was halfway through an article when I heard a knock on the door.

I walked over to the door and pulled it open. On the other side stood this petite blonde. Her eyes raked over my body with disgust. "Who are you?" she demanded, practically pushing me over as she walked into the condo. "Where's Hunter?"

"I'm Autumn," I answered, holding my hand out to her. "Hunter's in the shower. And you are?"

"Jocelyn."

"Maybe I can help you with something, Jocelyn?"

"I doubt it. I need to see Hunter. I have news for him." She walked further into the condo, dropping her purse and coat down on the couch. Without even knowing who she was, I could already say I wasn't a fan.

"What do you think you're doing answering his door?" she asked, taking me in again. "Who did you say you were?" Jocelyn asked as she walked over to the counter and started snooping through Hunter's mail. I didn't feel right letting her continue her search through his private things.

"I don't think you should be doing that."

"Why shouldn't I be, Autumn? That is your name, right? You're wondering who I am, and here you are answering his door at eleven on a Sunday morning? I am his girlfriend, after all!"

The room suddenly got very small, and I felt weak in the knees. I had just spent the weekend with him—not to mention all that time in Jamaica—and he was involved with someone. So, he had been lying to me all along. My stomach started to turn at an alarming rate. I didn't know what to say. What could I say? He had just been inside of me not six hours ago. I walked slowly to the front door and put my shoes on. I was just getting my coat from the closet when Hunter called my name from down the hall.

I couldn't answer him. My throat was so tight, and my eyes were burning. He came around the corner in nothing but a towel.

"Jocelyn?" I could hear the shock in his voice.

"Hunter, baby, I don't know who this woman is or what she is doing here, but she was kind enough to let me in. I forgot my key. I need to talk to you, baby."

"Cut the crap. You don't have a key, and you don't belong here. Now, I've got nothing to say to you, Jocelyn."

Hunter pushed past her and walked over to me, placing his hand on my shoulder. "Autumn, wait, what did she say to you?" Shrugging out of his touch, I grabbed my bag and opened the door.

"Hunter, baby, let her leave. I have some news I want to share with you, and you need to hear it alone," Jocelyn called from the living room.

Turning, I looked at Hunter with tears in my eyes. As soon as I blinked, they streamed down my face, and there was nothing I could have done to stop them. I was gutted. He lied to me, and now I had nothing to say to him. He grabbed my arm with his hand, but I pulled out of his grasp. "Goodbye, Hunter."

I ran down the hall and hit the button for the elevator. I could feel his stare from the doorway. I kept my stare ahead as I held my hand over my mouth, hoping to stop the threat of being sick. It seemed like hours for that elevator door to open. I glanced back one final time. He stood there, his eyes to the floor, running his hands through his hair, still wrapped in the white towel. I heard her call his name from inside the condo, and that was when he looked up at me through teary blue eyes. I was just about to turn to run back to him when the elevator doors opened. I stood for a moment, debating going back and letting him explain, but when she called his name for a third time, I decided to step into the elevator and go home.

Chapter Twenty

Hunter

My heart broke as I watched her get into that elevator. I didn't want to create any more of a scene than what had already been done. I certainly didn't want to deal with the situation with Autumn while Jocelyn was here. I walked back into my condo, slamming the door behind me. I stared at Jocelyn who was sprawled out on my couch, trying her best to look sexy. "What the fuck are you doing here, Jocelyn? What did you say to her?" I demanded through clenched teeth.

"Why, nothing, love." She got up off the couch and walked over to me, running her hands along the edge of the towel that hung loosely at my waist.

I tensed, pulling away from her. "Jocelyn, I'm warning you. Get your hands off me. Now, what did you say to her?"

"She asked me who I was, so I told her."

"What exactly did you tell her?"

"The truth, Hunter. I'm your girlfriend."

I felt the anger begin to pulse through my veins. This woman was unhinged. "Why the fuck would you do that?"

"Because, Hunter, it's true."

"Jocelyn, how many more times do I need to tell you? We are over, finished. There is and never will be any more us," I fumed, slamming my fist down on the counter.

I watched as a smile came to her lips. "Hunter, don't be ridiculous. We can't be over."

"Jocelyn, what the fuck is wrong with you? Listen, I'm not doing this with you again. Now, get out."

"Hunter, please, you have to listen to me."

"I don't have to listen to you. Now, go. There's the door!"

"I'm pregnant, Hunter."

"Whatever trouble you have gotten yourself into this time has nothing to do with me. Get out!" I stalked down the hall and slammed my bedroom door shut.

I listened to the endless sound of a ringing line as I pulled into the empty parking lot. I slammed my hand down on the wheel; I was so fucking pissed. After Jocelyn had left, I decided to head to the office. I needed to do something to calm myself down, and normally throwing myself into work did it. However, I had thought about Autumn all the way to the office. I needed to explain, and I wasn't going to give up until she let me. The phone rang another half-dozen times before I finally ended the call and headed up to the office.

Jocelyn was insane. That's all there was to it. I wasn't sure how dumb she thought I was, but it had been seven months since the last time we had been together, so even if she was pregnant, it definitely wasn't mine.

Once inside, I turned on my laptop and tried burying myself into work, but the only thing that was occupying my mind was those teary beautiful grey-blue eyes as Autumn had stepped onto that elevator. I'd wanted to go after her, but I had been frozen in shock. I picked up my phone and tried her again. Again, the same thing—the line just rang. Running my hand through my hair, I threw my phone down on my desk and headed to the lunchroom to make a coffee. I was convinced it was going to be a long night.

As I headed down the hall, I saw the light on in Carter's office and decided to go there instead. He was sitting behind his desk, working away on his computer. "Hey, you got a minute?" I asked, standing just outside his door.

"Hunter! What are you doing here? I thought you were taking the weekend off to bang that broad you met down south? At least that's what our brothers told me." He laughed, looking up from his paperwork.

"Carter, she's not some broad. I need to talk." His demeanor changed the second he looked at my face. This was serious. I needed guidance, advice—something—and Carter was always my go-to.

"Come in and sit." I caught the worried look on his face. "Is everything okay?"

I sat down across from him. "Jocelyn showed up at my place this morning," I said, deadpan.

"Oh, for fuck's sake." Carter put his pen down and sat back. "I thought you got rid of that crazy bitch."

"Yep, so did I. Autumn let her in while I was in the shower."

"What happened?"

"Jocelyn is Jocelyn. She started lying to her, and Autumn left in tears. She wouldn't give me a minute to explain—nothing. Autumn has been through a really tough time, so I know this was a big blow to her. After she left, Jocelyn told me she is pregnant and it's mine."

"Well, you know it's not. Hope and I saw Jocelyn while you were away in Jamaica. She was out with another guy."

"I know it's not mine. And I don't care whose it is."

"Why don't you go see Autumn—explain it in person as opposed to over the phone?"

"I'm afraid to."

"Why is that? You've never been afraid of talking to a woman before." He was right. Nothing had ever stopped me from getting what I wanted. I sat there for a few minutes, staring at my hands, lost in thought.

"Hunter, what's going on?"

"I really like this girl."

"Then what is the problem?"

"She's Derek's sister-in-law."

Carter looked at me. "I see. You're one of Derek's best friends. I can't see that being the issue. So why don't you tell me what the real problem is?" Suddenly, I felt very cornered. Why was he pushing me? I leaned back in the chair and rubbed my face with my hands.

"Fuck, Carter, I don't know."

"I think you do. I just don't think you're ready to fully

admit it to yourself." He sat back, putting his feet up on his desk and his hands behind his head. For a minute I thought he enjoyed seeing me squirm.

"Ready to admit what?"

"Hunter, let's look at this situation for a second. Since you have been back from this trip, I've seen a difference in you. You've barely even looked at another woman since you've been back. You know, Bryce and Chase told me all about this trip, about your behavior. They both admit that you're different too. Christ, Chase told me the other night you guys went out for a beer after work and the hottest woman he's ever laid eyes on out and out hit on you and you brushed her off completely."

"So, what of it?"

"What of it?"

"Yeah, so what, I just didn't want to be bothered that night."

"No, No, I know you. Never in your entire life have you turned down willing pussy, especially after a breakup."

"What are you saying, Carter?"

"If you ask me, I think you're in love with her."

I couldn't believe my ears. There was no way. I swallowed hard, shaking my head. "No, Carter, it's not that. I'm afraid Derek is going to kick my ass." It was a lame excuse, but I would say anything to hide what I already knew was true.

"It has nothing to do with Derek. You're in love with this girl, and it's freaking you the fuck out."

"No, Carter, that's not it."

"I've been there, remember? I remember what it was like."

I ran my hands over my face. He was right. I was having such a hard time trying to explain my feelings. All I knew was that when I was with her I was happier than I had been in a long time and it was scaring the hell out of me.

"How is this even possible, Carter? I barely know her."

"Hunter, man, love hits you when you aren't even looking. It's not up to us to decide when or with whom or how long it takes."

"I don't know, Carter."

"I do. You're acting the same way I did when I met Hope. It just took me a lot longer to figure out what I was feeling. Let me ask you, is it different with Autumn than it was with any of the other girls?"

"Is what different?"

"Sex, everything? Is it different with her?"

I sat there trying to sort out exactly how I felt. "Fuck yes, it's different, Carter, and she is all I can think about."

"Then I guess you have your answer. Now get out of here right now and go see her."

<h1 style="text-align:center">Chapter Twenty-One</h1>

Autumn

The tears fell as I drove toward home, soft Christmas music playing on the radio. I knew he was too good to be true. I had stopped on my way home at a bookstore, grabbed a coffee, and looked around for a bit. Books were always my go-to when I was feeling down. It did me good, plus I didn't want to drive while I was as upset as I was.

Putting the car in park, I turned the engine off and grabbed my suitcase and the full bag of books I had purchased. I carried everything into the house. The snow was really starting to fall now. It was quiet as I entered. Derek and Evelyn still weren't home, which was probably a good thing. I was angry at them both for not coming clean about knowing Hunter, and I wanted time to calm down before I confronted them.

I carried my stuff up to my bedroom and decided to take a hot shower before getting changed. I knew Evelyn would need some more help decorating tonight, which might be a good thing for me to keep my mind off everything that had happened. The only thing plaguing my mind all the way home was Hunter. While waiting for the shower to warm up, I turned on my cell phone and plugged it in. I had a bunch of missed calls—all from him. I threw my phone onto the bedside table. I wanted to call him back, but I also didn't know what to say. I was so hurt, and I didn't want to listen to a bunch of excuses. I didn't even know how to deal with this.

I was in the kitchen, grabbing a bite to eat, when both Evelyn and Derek came walking through the door. "Hey, Autumn! How was your weekend?" Evelyn sang, dropping the bags she was carrying onto the counter.

"Well, first, I'd like to know why you never told me you guys knew Hunter," I demanded without turning around. I wasn't wasting any time.

Neither of them said anything. I could feel them both just staring at me. I slammed the knife down on the counter and turned to face them. "Well?"

Evelyn looked to Derek and back to me but said nothing. "Derek, what about you?" I questioned. "Hunter told me that you're one of his best friends."

"Don't talk to me about this. It was all your sister's idea to not tell you that we knew him. Honestly, I thought you should know. So, Evelyn, while I put some of this stuff away, why don't you talk to her about that."

"Way to sell me out, Derek," Evelyn cried.

"Evelyn?"

"Autumn, it's just you looked so happy the other night when you had finally heard from him. I just wanted to let you enjoy that."

"I don't buy it, Evelyn. Maybe you didn't want to tell me because you knew he had another girlfriend?"

Derek stopped putting groceries away and turned to face us. "Autumn, why would think that?" Derek questioned, holding a can of soup in his hands.

"Oh, I don't know, because she showed up this morning at his condo while he was in the shower, barged in, and made herself very much at home while I was still there." Evelyn looked to Derek and then back to me. She had nothing to say and I knew it. I grabbed my plate from the counter and was just about out of the kitchen when I heard Evelyn call my name.

"Autumn, he isn't seeing anyone."

"How would you know that? How can I even trust that anything that comes out of your mouth is going to be the truth?"

"The reason I didn't say anything to you the other night was because he was the man I actually set you up with before you went away. When he didn't show that night, I was pissed with him and forced Derek to call him and tell him. He wanted to take you out the next night, but you were so upset with me and the whole situation, I had Derek tell him not to worry about it. Then you booked your trip and left. I never gave it much thought after that. When you returned from vacation and I saw that was who you had met, I didn't want you to think I had sent him there. So, I kept my mouth shut.

It was a complete surprise to me that he was the one you had met. Thursday night, when I came into your room to talk with you, I was going to tell you. You had been so distraught that he hadn't called so I thought it might be best to come clean. However, when I saw how happy you were that he had called, I decided against it. I know that he isn't seeing anyone and hasn't been seeing anybody for about seven months or so. And you should know that the Christmas party that we are attending is at his law firm. I've already sent in our RSVP to include you as well."

I closed my eyes. She was telling me the truth. When she brought up news of the Christmas party, however, I felt myself get a little dizzy. How did I forget? I had agreed to be his date just this morning before all of this happened. "Well, don't count me. I won't be attending."

"Autumn, you're being ridiculous."

"No, Evelyn, you don't understand. I agreed to be his date. He asked me to go and be his date to the Christmas party."

"And you said yes?"

I nodded my head and then the tears started to fall. "I mean, I agreed before she came back and announced who she was. Evelyn, I can't. I just can't. I can't put myself out there again." I ran from the kitchen and up the stairs, slamming my door behind me. I flopped down on the bed, lay in the dark, and cried.

Evelyn

"I told you." That was all Derek said to me after Autumn had run from the room, and then he turned his back and went back to putting away the things we had bought.

"What is that supposed to mean, Derek?"

"Exactly what I said. She deserved to know the truth long before now. You should have told her as soon as you saw it was him."

"Well, I certainly didn't expect it to end up this way. Could you call him?"

"Evelyn, at this point, I'm not getting involved. This is between them. It's a total misunderstanding—I already know that. If it was Jocelyn that was at his apartment, I can understand why Autumn is as upset as she is. That woman is a lunatic. She is completely unstable, and she's been after Hunter to get back together since they broke up."

"I'm not asking you to get involved. I just was hoping you could call him and maybe invite him over, so they could talk."

"Seriously?" Derek turned and looked at me. "You're serious? That's enough, Evelyn. Just leave it be. Let them come to terms with things on their own."

"But..."

Derek took a step forward and placed his hands on my shoulders. "But nothing. Please just put your concentration into other things like finishing the decorating, talking Autumn into going to the Christmas party and being Hunter's date, and trying to mend things with her. Other than that, don't worry about things between them. If it's meant to be, it will be."

I sat down on the stool at the counter and put my head into my hands. I felt horrible for her. All I wanted for her was to be happy. I never meant to hurt her through all of this.

Chapter Twenty-Two

Hunter

After I had talked to Carter last night, I'd headed back to my condo. I needed to set Jocelyn straight before I even attempted to work things out with Autumn. I didn't want her interfering anymore, so I called her. After that nightmare ended, I spent the remainder of the night trying to sort through how I truly felt, trying to accept the fact that I was indeed in love with Autumn and that she might just be the one, even though she may not know it yet.

The pile of paperwork that sat in front of me this morning needed my immediate attention, and even though I had been here since five, there wasn't even a dent in it. Late last night I had sent Autumn a text inviting her to lunch with me today. I had just finished sending out a few emails and was about to grab myself another cup of coffee when my phone pinged with a message. My heart skipped a beat as I saw her name pop up across my screen.

AUTUMN: NOT FEELING VERY WELL TODAY. I WILL SEE YOU AT THE PARTY ON SATURDAY. UNTIL THEN.

I sat there reading and re-reading her words. That was it. She had turned down my lunch date. I shut my office door and planted my ass down on the couch. Checking my calendar quickly, I saw I had no appointments booked for the rest of the day, which at this point, I was glad for. As I lay there with my arm over my face, I could feel a headache coming on. I knew I needed to get the fuck out of here.

"You not feeling well?" I heard Carter say from the doorway.

"Hey, not really."

Carter took a couple steps into my office and shut the door behind him. He sat down in the chair. "Have you talked to her?"

"When I went home last night, I dealt with Jocelyn first. I wanted her completely out of the way before I even attempted speaking with Autumn. Once I was truly convinced you were right, I invited Autumn to Willows Landing for lunch today."

"And?"

"She turned me down. She said she would see me at the party Saturday night."

"Well, at least it isn't a *no, I never want to see you again.* Why don't you come by the house tonight? Hope is making prime rib. Join us for dinner. The girls would be happy to see you."

"It's okay. Thanks for the invite, but I am not feeling very sociable right now. I think I will just finish up here and head home. First, I am just going to go and get some air. I've been here since five."

Carter glanced at his watch. "You've already been here for four hours?"

"Couldn't sleep." I gave him a half smile.

"It's not a wonder you're not feeling the greatest. Go get some coffee and breakfast. Come back in a couple hours. And if you change your mind about tonight, our door is open. I've got to get ready for my appointment."

I grabbed my keys off my desk and decided he was right —some air and time to myself might do me good. As I was headed toward my car, I noticed the florist across the street. I had to get this woman to speak to me other than the text I had received. I couldn't just sit and wait for Saturday. I needed her to know I wanted her. I headed across the street to start winning her back.

Autumn

We had just finished placing the garland on the banister and over the doorways to the living room and kitchen. We only had the finishing touches to put on the living room and then the tree. I was headed to the kitchen to refill our coffee when the doorbell rang.

"Autumn, can you get that, please, and I'll get us coffee?" Evelyn asked as she walked by me, grabbing our mugs from my hands.

"Yep, I'm on it."

Pulling open the door, I was greeted by a man in a white uniform holding a clipboard. "I have a special delivery for Autumn Taylor."

"I'm Autumn." I smiled at the man.

"Please sign here." He passed me the clipboard, pointed to the spot I needed to sign, and headed back to his truck. I quickly signed the paper. I watched as he walked back up the walkway, carrying a large white box.

Evelyn had just finished pouring us some coffee when I entered the kitchen carrying the box. "Who's that from?" she asked, glancing over her shoulder.

I set the box down and shrugged. Opening it, I was greeted with two dozen lavender roses mixed with baby's breath. A card was propped between the flowers.

"Well, who are they from?" Evelyn was at my side just in time for me to the open the card.

I stared down at the card in my hand as tears came to my eyes. Who knew four little words could mean so much.

With you, it's different. — Hunter

I felt Evelyn squeeze my shoulder, and then she pulled me toward her for a quick hug. "Why don't you call him, meet him for lunch? I can finish the living room. Just be home in time to help me bake some cookies. I'll put these up in your room for you."

I smiled at her and wiped the tears from my eyes. A wave of nausea rolled through me as I climbed up the stairs to get my purse. I stopped and took a breath, waiting for it to pass, then I grabbed my cell phone, purse, and keys. I would call him on my way into the city.

Chapter Twenty-Three

Hunter

I had just been seated at the table at Willows Landing when my phone pinged.

AUTUMN: ALMOST THERE, JUST PARKING.

I smiled to myself as I read her message. I was just about to hit reply when I saw her walk into the restaurant. As soon as she spotted me, she waved and made her way over.

"I guess I'm a little under-dressed," she said, looking around the restaurant and then down at her jeans and sweater.

"No, as always you're perfect, beautiful." My eyes skimmed her body. "This is just a great place for business people to meet for lunch. To be honest, the food sucks, but they're quick and close."

I stood and pulled her into me. "Thank you for coming," I whispered into her ear.

We both slid into our seats. I could barely take my eyes off her. "I want to start off by saying I'm sorry for what happened Sunday morning. You have now met the worst decision of my life."

"Hunter." Her soft voice hit me right in the gut as my name rolled off her lips.

"No, Autumn, please, there is no one in my life. Jocelyn is my ex. She just can't seem to get it through her head, but I assure you that we are over, and after a few hours of debate, she now understands that. I'm sorry that this happened. I tried to have you hear me out, but you were so upset. I figured it was best to just let you go. I really hope it's not too late to repair things with you." I sat there holding my breath, watching her expression, and waiting for her to answer me.

"No, Hunter, it's not. I should have given you a chance to explain. I wasn't being fair to you. I'm the one who should be sorry."

"Well, you're forgiven, beautiful. Now, let's eat." I could finally start to relax.

It wasn't long before we were both in the swing of the same relaxed momentum that we had always experienced around one another. I watched as she put the last mouthful of the lemon cheesecake she had ordered for dessert in her mouth and closed her eyes, savoring that last bite. The waitress had dropped the bill off at the table, and I placed cash into the folder and glanced at my watch.

"I take it you need to get back to the office?"

"Unfortunately, I do. I'm still piled under paperwork."

I stood and grabbed her coat off the hook and held it

open for her. She slid into it and grabbed her purse, and we walked hand in hand out of the restaurant. "Where did you park?"

"Across the street."

I kept hold of her hand as we crossed to her car. She threw her purse into the back seat and that was when I took my opportunity to block the driver's door. As she turned around, she was right against me. "Thank you for joining me." I looked down into her face. Pushing the stray piece of hair from her forehead, I cupped her cheek with my hand. Leaning down, I placed my lips on hers. I felt her place her hands on my chest and grip my shirt as I kissed her deeper. When we parted, I looked into her eyes. "As much as I'd rather take you back to my place and ravish you, I really do have to get my ass back to work."

"That sounds like way more fun than having to get back home to help Evelyn finish making Christmas cookies.

"Message me later. I guess I will see you Saturday?"

"I'll be there." She slid into the driver's seat, and I shut her door. Heading back across the street to my own car, I watched as she drove away.

Chapter Twenty-Four

Autumn

It had been four days since I met Hunter for lunch. We had spent late nights talking on the phone, and those late nights were finally catching up to me. I was exhausted. To top it off, the last four mornings I had woken up feeling nauseous, and some of the days that feeling lasted into the early afternoon. I had even been sick two of the mornings. I was supposed to go out today and shop for a dress for the party, but I was dragging my ass.

When I finally started to feel better, I headed off to the mall. Since I was already going out, I called my doctor's office and booked an early afternoon appointment. If I had the stomach flu, I didn't want to make everyone sick and, therefore, would have to cancel for Saturday.

I sat waiting for the doctor to come into the exam room.

I had just picked up my phone and started reading through my Facebook feed when the door finally opened. "Hello, Autumn. How have you been?"

"Hi, Dr. Morgan."

"How are things going with Dr. Plante?"

"Good. I'm finally down to a once-a-month visit. We've decided that I'll be good to return to work in the new year. He wanted me to get through Christmas first."

"That's great to hear and a very wise idea. Get through this stressful time of the year. So, Autumn, what brings you in today?" He sat down at his desk and pulled up my chart, reading it over.

"Well, I think I may have the stomach flu. I've been feeling pretty tired, and the last four days I've had really bad nausea throughout different times of the day. A couple of the days I've been sick, and I've had a few mornings of really bad abdominal cramps."

"I see." He started typing notes into the computer. "Anything else? Chills, sweats, aches?"

"No."

"Autumn, when was the date of your last period?"

I thought for a moment. "Maybe five weeks ago? Should be here any day now. What does that have to do with anything?"

"Well, your symptoms line up more with pregnancy than the stomach flu."

"That's impossible. I had a miscarriage. I was told by you that it would be impossible for me to get pregnant again." I could feel tears building behind my eyes as panic set in.

"Well, Autumn, doctors can be wrong. I think we will do some blood work and rule it out."

I watched as the doctor filled out a requisition for blood work. I could feel the tension building in my chest. He scribbled on the form and held the paper out for me to take. I reached out with a shaky hand and sat there staring down at the form that had been presented to me. "Autumn, what is it?"

"This isn't supposed to happen. I'm not supposed to be able to get pregnant."

"Autumn, I'm not saying you are. I'm just saying that we should check. As I said, doctors can make mistakes. Of course, if it makes you feel better, we will make sure that you are on our high-risk list for the term of your pregnancy. If you are indeed pregnant, that is."

"Why is that? Because I already lost a baby?"

"Yes. But let's not jump to conclusions without knowing for sure that you are pregnant. If you get the blood work done today, the results should be here tomorrow, or at the latest, Monday. I can call you as soon as I see the results, and we will go from there. If you really want to know, you can go to the drugstore and purchase a pregnancy test. Now the lab is still open, so if you head on up to the second floor and get that blood work taken care of, there is a good chance it will be back tomorrow before I leave for the day."

I walked with my head down out of the doctor's office. Once I was away from the office door, I leaned up against the wall. My insides felt like they were quivering. I closed my eyes and tried to take a deep breath when my cell phone vibrated in my pocket. I wiped the tears from my face and grabbed my phone. Hunter's name flashed across my screen, and that was when a wave of nausea came over me again, this time sending me running for the bathroom.

I hung the dress bag up in my closet. I still hadn't responded to Hunter. Truth be told, I hadn't even read the texts he had sent. Since leaving the doctor's office, I felt that this whole relationship was now up in the air, and I was sinking faster into the same black hole that had taken me two years to crawl out of. I didn't want to hurt Hunter the way I'd hurt Jason. I'd failed him, and I feared I would fail Hunter as well.

I could feel the contents of my stomach threaten to rise every time I thought about it. I didn't even know if Hunter wanted children, which was a ridiculous thought—of course I didn't know; we'd just started seeing one another. Not that it mattered. If I was pregnant, I was afraid it would end in the same manner that the last pregnancy did. Plus, after being told that I couldn't have children, I had come to accept it, but now, to be faced with the possibility that it had been a mistaken diagnosis, well, I just couldn't go through another heartbreak again.

I went into the bathroom and splashed my face with cool water. Looking at myself in the mirror, I made a promise I wouldn't mention it to him, or anyone for that matter, until I knew for sure. And if I did decide to tell Hunter, which I probably wouldn't, I would give him the choice of being involved in the baby's life, but as for us, I would just end things with him. That way if I lost the baby, it would be me who must deal with the consequences, not him. I didn't want to hurt him. It wasn't fair.

We'd only had unprotected sex a couple of times. I still thought there was no way the doctor was right. It had to be the stomach flu; it just had to be. I threw another handful of cold water on my face and grabbed the towel next to the sink. As I looked at myself in the mirror, a funny realization came over me. I grabbed my phone from the nightstand and scrolled back through my calendar, carefully counting the weeks again and again. I'd been wrong. It had been seven almost eight weeks since my last period, not five.

My phone rang in my hand as I recounted for what seemed like the fiftieth time. I absentmindedly answered, my voice shaking. "Hello?"

"There's my beautiful girl. I was just thinking about you."

I shut my eyes tightly at the sound of the deep, sexy voice on the other end of the line, and suddenly, I just wanted to be wrapped in his arms. "You were?" My voice continued to shake while I smiled through my tears.

"Is everything okay, Autumn?"

"Mmm...yes, yes, it's fine." I sniffled.

He was quiet for a few moments. If I couldn't hear him breathing, I would have thought he had hung up. "Are you sure?"

"Yes, I'm good. What's up?"

"I was just about to leave the office and was thinking how nice it would be to have you come spend the weekend me. I was hoping that you would come tonight and maybe bring your attire for the party. That way we could show up together."

I wiped the tears from my face and cleared my throat.

"Sounds wonderful." I glanced down at my watch. It was already six. "I can be there around eight."

"Okay, baby, sounds good. I can't wait to see you."

"Me too. I'll see you soon."

Chapter Twenty-Five

Hunter

The winter storm the forecasters had been predicting started shortly after I got home. The roads had turned into a horrible icy mess, causing the city to start closing some of them. I had left work as soon as I had called her, stopping at the store to pick up some items for dinner. I then came home and started preparing us dinner. Autumn finally arrived shortly after nine. I was never so glad to hear that knock on my door. After dinner, I suggested we crack open a bottle of wine, but Autumn wanted tea instead, so tea it was. We curled up on the couch and watched *It's A Wonderful Life*. The credits had just started rolling when I pulled her closer to me and wrapped my arm around her. "You tired, baby?"

"A little."

"Want to go crawl into bed?"

She turned and met my lips, kissing me ever so softly. As I pulled away, she nodded and sat up. I got up and grabbed our mugs from the table as she turned off the TV and shut the lights off on the tree.

"I'll be there in a minute, babe. Go crawl in."

I watched as she walked down the hall. I needed to tell her how I felt. I wasn't sure how she was going to react, but I needed to get this off my chest. Carter was right. I put the mugs into the dishwasher and quickly cleaned up what mess was left in the kitchen. I closed the blinds, shut the fireplace off, and headed down to the bedroom.

As soon as I entered the room and my eyes hit the bed, everything that had been running through my mind completely disappeared. I had to do a double take. Autumn was sprawled out before me, in a very sexy black lace bra and panties that were sprinkled with hints of soft pink. I could feel myself hardening at the sight of her.

"It's about time you got here," she purred, twirling a strand of hair through her fingers. "I've been thinking about you doing very naughty things to me all night, especially when we were lying on the couch out there. I could feel you pressed into me."

I walked over and crawled onto the bed, running my hand up her body. "Fuck, Autumn, you look fucking amazing." I could barely stand the tightness in my pants I was feeling right now.

She raised herself up onto her elbow and ran her fingers along the waist of my jeans before reaching down and gripping my cock through them. "I want you. All of you, in me," she whispered.

I leaned down and kissed her as she unzipped my jeans. "Then take me, baby."

I lay down onto my back and slipped out of my jeans and boxers. Just as I was about to get back on top of her, she placed her hands on my chest, pushed me down, and straddled me. Sitting up, I wrapped my arms around her, kissing her. With a quick flick of my fingers, her bra came undone. Slowly running the straps down her shoulders, I was finally face to face with her perfect tits. Her nipples were already hard and were calling to me. I sucked one into my mouth, while running my fingers over the other, gently pinching it between my fingers. She jumped as soon as I had done that.

"What is it, baby?"

"Just sensitive is all. Be gentle and go slow with me," she whispered into my ear.

As I kissed her neck, she dropped her head to the side and let out a loud moan. I couldn't wait any longer. I needed to bury myself in her. "Hold on, baby, let me grab a condom from the drawer." I leaned over and went to open the drawer, when she placed her hand on my chest.

"Hunter?"

"Yeah, beautiful?"

"No condom. I like it better with nothing between us."

She reached down with her fingers and started rubbing the small bead of wetness that had formed on the head of my cock. I really couldn't take it anymore. I quickly ripped the sides of her lace panties, pulling them off her. As soon as she was exposed, I ran the pad of my thumb over her clit. She was already wet and wanting. I wanted to watch her come undone, but she grabbed my hand, stopping me.

She raised herself up onto her knees and took my cock in

her hand. She ran the tip of it through her wetness and then placed it at her opening, sliding down until I was fully inside of her. I felt her body shudder and watched as her eyes closed and she bit her bottom lip. "Fuck, Autumn, you are so tight." I sucked her bottom lip into my mouth.

Once she was used to having me this way, I lay back and reached down to start rubbing her clit with my thumb. I could feel her tighten around my cock as she rode me. Gripping her hips, I thrust up into her as she finally let go, letting out the loudest, sexiest moan I had ever heard her make. I could feel my release building so I thrust into her tight pussy a couple more times before I emptied myself into her. She collapsed on my body, breathing hard.

I took her in my arms and slowly laid her down, rolling her onto her back. I pulled out of her and headed to the bathroom to clean myself off. Returning with a cool cloth, I cleaned her as well. Slipping into bed beside her, I pulled her into my arms, resting her head on my chest. It wasn't long before she fell asleep, but I lay wide awake, watching her sleep, thinking of how I needed to tell her tomorrow.

Chapter Twenty-Six

I woke to an empty bed. Reaching over, I placed my hand on the cold sheets beside me. I could tell Hunter had been up for a while. I could hear soft music floating from the other room. I got up and put my T-shirt and yoga pants on and picked up the remnants of another pair of ruined panties off the floor. I really needed to stop buying lace panties for him. He loved ripping them off me. I found my bra flung over the headboard.

I took my time getting ready to go out to see him. I wasn't sure if I was going to be sick and wanted to wait for the feeling to pass. By the time I had washed my face, brushed my teeth, and pulled my hair back into a ponytail, the feeling had somewhat passed. I walked down the hall and peeked around the corner. Hunter sat at the breakfast bar, shirtless, reading the paper and sipping on a hot cup of coffee. He was deeply engrossed in whatever article he was reading, so I leaned up against the wall and just watched him. I fought the tears building. I didn't want to leave him, but I felt it would be for the best. I wanted to burn the image of him in my brain, so I would never forget the way he looked. I stood there for what felt like hours, studying everything about him, before I finally cleared my throat, letting him know I was there.

He looked up and smiled. "Good morning."

I walked over, stood behind him, and wrapped my arms around his waist, placing a kiss on his bare shoulder. "Morning."

"Let me grab you a coffee."

"I can do it. Relax. Enjoy your paper. You looked deeply engrossed in that article."

"Yeah, I was."

"Well, sit down, relax, and read. It's okay, I'm good. Let me refill yours." After I grabbed his mug, he gave me a smile and put his head back into the paper.

Hunter had seemed off the rest of the morning. He was rather jumpy around me and oddly quiet all through breakfast and into the afternoon. "Are you coming down with a cold? You seem off today."

"Nope, I feel fine. How about we take a walk before we get ready to head to the party?"

I was starting to feel alarmed at the change in his behavior. "Sure, okay."

We headed out into the snow and across the city street to the park. The snow that had fallen overnight had amounted to more than I thought from looking out his condo window. Of course, everything looked different from the twenty-sixth floor. As we started walking, Hunter grabbed my hand and placed it through his arm. It was only four-thirty and already dark. The trees of the park were lined with white lights that glistened off the snow, creating a magical feel.

"Wow, it's beautiful. I've never actually taken the time to ever walk through this park at this time of year." Jason had never been a fan of Christmas. He was always focused on the cost instead of the experience. For me, that sucked the fun and magic out of the whole season, but like everything else, I had just grown used to it.

"It is. I love walking through here this time of year. Good place for me to unwind and calm my nerves," he answered then grew quiet again.

"What's on your mind?" I asked, gripping his forearm.

We had just walked by a city bench, and Hunter pulled me over and sat down. He brushed the snow off the spot next to him and patted the bench. As soon as I sat down, he angled his body toward me and took both my hands into his.

"I want to talk to you about something that's been on my mind." His eyes wandered down to our clasped hands, his thumb gently rubbing my hand.

I could feel a knot form in the pit of my stomach. I wasn't sure what was coming, but I was beginning to think from how he had been acting today, it wasn't good. I hoped I was wrong as we had the party to attend in a couple of hours. How could I face all those people if we had just broken up?

"Okay." I swallowed hard. I really wasn't sure I wanted to hear the words, but when his eyes met mine, all I saw was a warmth and happiness glowing in them.

"Autumn, this isn't easy for me to say, so I'm just going to say it."

"Okay." I smiled. I could tell that this was hard for him.

"I know we haven't been together long, and my intention isn't to scare you off, but the time we have spent together has been amazing, utterly amazing. I feel so at ease with you and have since that first night we spent together. I honestly feel as if I have known you all my life. Autumn, I'm falling in love with you."

His words frightened me and surprised me at the same time. Considering the circumstances of what I was going to be finding out, I knew for sure that I would crush him. Since I was expecting the complete opposite of what was just said, I tried hard not to come off as shocked, but I couldn't help it. "What?" I gasped.

"What did you think I was going to say?"

"I don't know. You have just been acting funny today. I was worried something might be wrong." I laughed more to myself, tears falling from my eyes.

"Nothing is wrong. I was just nervous." He leaned in and gave me a kiss, pulling me into him.

I could feel the reassurance in his kiss as I kissed him back and rested my head on his shoulder. We sat there for a bit, watching the snow lightly fall. He just held me in his arms, occasionally placing a kiss on my forehead. We were just about to head back to the condo when my cell phone rang. My stomach fell as I glanced at the screen. I prayed silently to myself that the answer I was waiting for was the one I wanted to hear. "Give me a minute, will you? I have to take this."

"Sure, go ahead. I can always use more time out here."
He smiled at me and sat back down on the bench.

I got up and stepped out of earshot from Hunter to take the call. I kept glancing over my shoulder at him, his eyes following me the whole time as if he were afraid I would disappear.

Hunter

I couldn't take my eyes off her. I had felt so much anxiety, waiting to tell her how I felt. I was glad that it was out in the open now, but the fact that she didn't say anything back was bothering me. I wasn't going to rush her, and I certainly didn't want to show her that it upset me. I knew she probably just needed time. She walked over to the tree across the walkway and stood there with her back to me, turning to look over her shoulder every once in a while to meet my gaze. My brow furrowed at the look on her face—a look of shock with lots of sadness. Then she would just shake her head like she was silently agreeing to something.

I wished I could hear what was being said on the other end of the phone. I watched as she covered her mouth with her hand, like she was trying to stop from being sick. When she turned to look at me this time, I could see tears in her eyes. Whatever was being said, it couldn't have been good news. I silently prayed it wasn't her ex. I would kill him if I ever laid eyes on him. He had hurt her so much, and all I wanted to do was repair her heart.

When she finally hung up, she didn't turn around. Instead, she stood staring down at the screen. I could tell she was shaking. I wasn't sure if I should go to her or wait for her to come to me, but when she put her hands over her face and the sobs shook her body, I immediately got up and went to her.

"Autumn? What is it?" I placed my hands on her shoulders, waiting for her to talk.

She kept her back to me for a bit, then finally turned and buried her face into my chest. Wrapping her in my arms, I held her tightly, assuring her I was there when she wanted to talk. She said nothing—just cried, her hands gripping my shirt.

When she finally calmed, I was still holding her, afraid that she might crumble if I let her go. "Autumn, I don't want to pry, but is there something you need or want to talk about?" I whispered into her ear.

"Yes, but not right now," was all she murmured.

"Okay, but I am here when you are ready, okay?" I kissed her forehead.

"I know that." She laid her head against my chest. "We need to get ready for the party." She glanced down at her watch. "I don't want you to be late to your own event."

"If I'm late, I'm late. You are what matters right now."

With her head on my shoulder and her hand in mine, we walked back to my condo and got ready for the party.

Chapter Twenty-Seven

"Jingle Bells" was playing as I stood by the fireplace in the hall, waiting for Hunter to return. By the time we had arrived, the event was already packed. There must have easily been over two hundred people. Hunter had introduced me to a bunch of his clients and had headed over to grab us a drink. I still wasn't feeling very well after the phone call I had received, and I'd spent twenty minutes in the bathroom getting sick before we left. After that, he really wanted me to talk about it with him, but I refused. This wasn't the kind of thing I could dump on him when he had an important event to go to.

"Hey, Autumn," I heard behind me. I turned and spotted Evelyn approaching with Derek.

"How are you enjoying the party?" Derek asked.

"It's okay, a little boring. I can't believe you guys do this every year."

"It's a little dry, I will admit, but it's a matter of business." He laughed. "Where's Hunter? I wanted to talk to him about something."

"He went to grab us a drink. He probably ran into someone. He's been gone for a bit." I glanced around, trying to spot him.

"Is everything okay? You look a little stressed, Autumn." Evelyn rubbed my back with her hand.

"Yeah, I'm okay. Just tired, I guess." She could read me like a book. She just gave me a look. I knew I wasn't fooling her. I looked away. I certainly wasn't telling her here, and I didn't want to start crying again. She could break me easier than anyone.

I quickly changed the subject to Christmas shopping, and soon she was going off on what malls we should hit. Evelyn's best friend Alyssa appeared. She was married to a lawyer at Derek's firm. "Hey, Evelyn, Autumn, how are you enjoying the party?"

"Just another boring mix and mingle like last year," Evelyn answered, and they both laughed.

"Autumn, it's nice to see you. I haven't seen you in a couple of years, but I wanted to say I'm sorry to hear what happened between you and Jason. How have you been?"

"Thanks, I'm doing okay now." After the day I had, hearing Jason's name was the last thing I'd wanted. I had more than come to grips with how things had ended with him, and I wasn't sorry, so why should anyone else be? It wasn't her fault. She didn't know what a bastard he really was.

"You better get used to life with a lawyer, Autumn. At least we won't ever be alone at these parties anymore, right Alyssa?" Evelyn said, doing her best to change the subject. "I'll be right back. I have to use the little girls' room."

"Oh wonderful! Are you dating someone from Derek's firm?" Alyssa asked as I watched Evelyn make her way through the crowd.

I shook my head and gave a small smile. "Not from Derek's firm. I'm dating Hunter Malone."

"Ohhh, one of the Malone brothers! The best one of them all too. Lucky girl!" A funny look came over her face.

"Alyssa, is something wrong?" I questioned, her eyes firmly planted ahead on the crowd.

"I'm glad to hear that you are finally dating again. I don't want you to look now, but I think I just saw Jason." Just as she said it, Evelyn came back over, immediately noticing the look on her face.

I couldn't believe my ears. "Please tell me he isn't here."

"Yep, it's him." Alyssa turned and looked toward the bar, my eyes following hers in the direction she was looking. "See the tall hunk over there by the bar in the white shirt? He is talking with him right now."

There Jason stood talking with Carter, both with their backs to us. They both laughed at something that was said and went back to the conversation they were having.

I felt the contents of my stomach flip. My worst nightmare was right in front of me.

"I've got to run. Charlie was just about ready to go when I saw you guys. Evelyn, I'll call you tomorrow." Alyssa left Evelyn and me there.

Evelyn was trying hard to calm me down before Hunter

returned. "Autumn, don't worry. You don't have to talk to him. Chances are he'll leave before he even sees you."

"But what is he doing here, Evelyn?"

"Well, it is a client appreciation Christmas party. Perhaps he is a client of one of the other lawyers here."

She was right. "Just don't leave me until Hunter is back, please."

"I wouldn't do that. You don't even need to ask."

I turned my attention back to the bar. Carter and Jason were both gone. My beating heart seemed to calm, knowing he was gone. "Here you go, beautiful!" I turned and saw Hunter approaching. He smiled and handed me my drink, Evelyn excusing herself to go find Derek.

I took the drink from his hand and took a sip of ginger ale, letting the cold liquid roll down my throat. "Are you feeling any better?" he asked as he wrapped his arm around me, resting it on my waist, holding me against him.

"I'm starting to, yes," I lied. I had been starting to feel better until I saw Jason.

"Good, I'm glad. I hope you're not coming down with the flu." He kissed the back of my neck.

Hunter and I went back to mingling. Anything to keep my mind focused on something other than Jason. We were standing, talking to two very lovely couples, when I heard his voice behind me. Turning away from the group, I saw Jason speaking with Carter. I stood, staring, pouring all the hate from my body directly at him, when I faintly heard my name. Hunter placed his hand on my shoulder, pulling my attention back toward the conversation.

I was trying to focus all my attention on what everyone was saying so I could calm down. Just as I started to maintain my calm, Carter came over with Jason and introduced him to Hunter. This was turning out worse than I had imagined. Sure, okay, he was here. That didn't mean I wanted anything to do with him. Just as Carter was about to introduce me, Jason addressed me.

"You guys know one another?" Hunter asked, rubbing my shoulder.

"You could say that," I whispered. I could feel Hunter stiffen at the realization of just exactly who Jason was. He placed his arm possessively and protectively around me and stood behind me like a rock, letting me know he was right there and wasn't going to let anything happen to me.

"How are you, Autumn?" Jason's cold eyes hit mine.

"What are you doing here?"

"I'm a client. What are you doing here? Lord knows you could never afford these guys."

Hunter wrapped his arm tighter around my waist, resting his hand on my stomach.

"Wait a minute, are you actually dating my ex-wife? I'd say that could be considered a conflict of interest."

Hunter stood firm against me, never faltering. "How so? You have no business with me personally," he answered. Carter stood, taking it all in. He didn't look pleased.

"All right, Jason, that's enough. Let's go over and mingle with some other people." Carter went to walk away, but Jason kept his feet firmly planted, staring at us as Hunter was trying to keep me calm.

"Hunter? That is your name, isn't it? You know, on second thought, you can have her. I'm sure you'll find out all about her and her psychosis. Let me give you fair warning now: After she lost our baby, she couldn't get her shit together—probably still doesn't have it together—but at least she's a great fuck." He glared at me, a smug smile forming on his lips. "Just forewarning you, big guy." Jason smacked Hunter on the shoulder.

Hunter stepped around me, sheltering me from Jason. "Don't touch me again. And if you ever insult her the way you just did, I swear to God it will be the last insult you ever make, you fucker."

People were already starting to stare, and I didn't want Hunter to create a scene. I placed my hand on his shoulder and whispered for him to calm down, but it did little use. He kept his focus trained on Jason. Evelyn came rushing over, pulled me back away from Hunter, and tried to get me to the nearest bathroom. Jason must have opened his mouth again to Hunter once I was out of earshot because the next thing I knew, Hunter and his brothers, along with Derek and security, were escorting Jason to the door.

"Evelyn, I want to go home now."

"I know, sweetie. As soon as Derek is finished helping the guys, we will head home."

"No, please now, I can't possibly face any more people tonight. I don't want to see Hunter. This was humiliating."

"I promise, sweetie, as soon as Derek is back, we will go."

Evelyn had gotten our coats from the coat check, and we left to go outside to wait by the car. Evelyn quickly sent a text to Derek to let him know to meet us at the car and to tell Hunter where we had gone. Within twenty minutes, we were headed back to the house.

Chapter Twenty-Eight

I shut the car off and walked up the steps to the front door. I had never thought I would see the day when I would have to escort one of our clients out of an event. It was all Carter and Derek could do to hold me back once I got him outside, and they both forced me back inside, leaving Chase and Bryce to deal with him and security. Once inside, I was disappointed to learn that Autumn didn't want to see me, and Derek had told me he was taking the girls home. But, it was probably for the best. I knocked on the front door and waited. Evelyn finally opened the front door with a sad smile on her face.

"Morning, Hunter."

"How is she?" I wanted to skip the small talk. I needed to know how my girl was.

"She hasn't been down since we got home last night." I

glanced at my watch and saw that it was almost eleven. She'd been locked up in that room for almost thirteen hours. "I can't promise that she'll talk to you or want to see you, but you're welcome to try. She wouldn't answer Derek or me this morning."

Evelyn told me how to get to Autumn's room. I climbed the stairs and came to a stop outside of her door. I gently knocked and waited.

"Go away, Evelyn," I heard her sob.

"Autumn, it's me. Can I come in?"

I stood waiting, but there was no answer. After a few minutes of waiting, I opened the door and peeked my head into the bedroom. The blinds were closed, leaving the room in darkness. I saw Autumn's outline on the bed. She lay with her back to the door, her shoulders shaking. I walked into the room and shut the door behind me, the click of the latch sounding through the room.

"Go away, Hunter, please."

I climbed into the bed and lay behind her. "No way, I'm not going away." I went to put my arm under her head, but she jumped off the bed.

"Hunter, I told you to go away. I don't want to see anyone."

"Autumn, it's okay."

"It's not okay, Hunter. You've now met my worst regret, and he's right—I'm totally fucked up. You don't deserve to be with that. You're a good man. Give yourself to someone who can give you what you need."

"You are what I need, and you're what I want. I don't care what he says or what he thinks. It's my opinion that matters."

I sat watching her as deep, guttural sobs escaped her throat. Her eyes were red from crying, and her face was streaked with tears. I walked to her. I had to comfort her. Watching her like this was killing me. I put my hands on her shoulders to pull her into me, but she pushed me away with both of her fists.

"Hunter, just leave. You will anyway." She turned away from me and walked into the bathroom, slamming the door.

I sat down on the end of her bed and put my head in my hands. She wouldn't even give me a chance to talk to her. I didn't know what to do or how to handle this. I waited at the end of the bed for a half hour, listening to her cry in the bathroom, until I absolutely couldn't take it anymore.

I walked down the stairs feeling defeated, frustrated, and totally pissed off. I should have beaten the fuck out of Jason when I had the chance. I didn't know how to get her to talk to me. I hoped she just needed some time. As I walked to the front door, I heard Derek's voice behind me. "Any luck?"

"No, she went into the bathroom and told me to go away. I waited, but I can't take the sound of her crying any longer."

"Evelyn and I will come pick up her car this afternoon. Give her a few days; she'll bounce back."

I nodded, said goodbye to Evelyn, and headed out to my car. I drove around the city for a couple of hours and took a walk through the park before heading back home. I hit the gym in the condo and then spent the rest of the night watching a hockey game. I didn't even feel like working, which was a first for me. Normally it was my go-to when trouble struck. I had just gotten comfortable in bed when I heard a knock on the door. I contemplated not answering, but when another knock rang out, I decided to get up.

I was surprised to find Autumn standing in front of me. She didn't say anything. She just fell into my arms, crying and shaking from the cold. I pulled her inside, helped her out of her coat, locked the door, picked her up, and carried her down the hall and into the bedroom. I laid her in the bed, climbed in beside her, pulling the covers over us, and held her close to me. We didn't need to say anything. I knew she needed me, and I couldn't be happier to have her in my arms.

Chapter Twenty-Nine

AUTUMN

It was three in the morning. I had spent the last two hours tossing and turning, listening to Hunter snore. My stomach ached and my head hurt from crying. A deep chill had set into my body, and no matter how much heat was radiating off Hunter, I couldn't get warm. My body's stress response had kicked in. I knew the feeling well. I crawled out of bed, trying not to disturb him, and grabbed his bathrobe off the hook on the bedroom door, wrapping myself in his scent.

I plugged the tree in and turned on the fireplace in the living room. I lay down on the couch and covered myself with the blanket that lay over the back of the couch. I was still frozen. I lay watching the lights twinkle on the tree, thinking over everything. I jumped when I heard Hunter clear his throat.

"Baby, what are you doing out here?" His voice was thick and sleepy.

"I couldn't sleep. I'm okay, go back to bed, I'll be in soon."

He didn't return to the bedroom. Instead, he came over and sat down on the edge of the couch. "I'm not going anywhere, not until you talk to me."

When I didn't immediately start talking, he pushed his arm under my body and lay down in front of me, boxing me in on the couch and throwing the blanket over his half-naked body.

"Baby, you're shivering."

As I met his eyes, I knew this man was there for me. It didn't matter what I had to tell him; he would always be there. Whether I was insecure about something, whether I had good or bad news or a good or bad day—he would always be by my side. No problem would be too big for us to handle. I had nothing to fear in telling him what I had learned earlier this weekend, nothing. But it didn't matter. There was a part of me that was afraid that if something happened, he would walk out of my life just as Jason had, without warning.

"It has to do with that phone call I received yesterday," I whispered.

"Bad news?"

"Depends. Some might say that." I looked away from his eyes. How was I going to tell him what I had found out and how I felt about it? I couldn't tell him while those blue eyes were staring back at me. I swallowed hard and closed my eyes.

I felt his warm hand graze my cheek, which made a tear fall.

"Are you okay?" he whispered.

I shook my head yes, wiping away the tears. "I'm pregnant."

He stilled, his hand falling from my cheek. He didn't need to say anything because the look on his face said it all.

<h1 style="text-align:center">Chapter Thirty</h1>

Hunter

The office was still empty. My brothers would be arriving within the hour. It was going to be a day from hell for me—meetings upon meetings—and already I was so exhausted, I could barely concentrate on anything other than Autumn and the news she had shared with me. I took a sip of the cold coffee sitting on my desk and rubbed the back of my head. I closed the file in front of me. There was no point; I had read and re-read it. I should know this case like the back of my hand, yet here I sit, completely lost. I sat back and closed my eyes, trying to get a grip on myself.

When I had seen her that day at the resort, all I had wanted was fun—nothing more—especially after only getting out of a relationship seven months earlier. I hadn't been looking for anything serious, and now, things had changed in a big way. I was so in love with her, it hurt, and not only that, I was going to be a father.

She had left in tears shortly after she had told me, mumbling something about how she shouldn't have told me and now that she had, she did not want to be a disappointment to me. Granted, I admit, I didn't take the news well. I could barely speak, it shocked me so. I knew her reaction was because of her past relationship with that ass, but what I couldn't figure out was how she could ever think she would become a disappointment to me. I had tried to call her this morning on my way into the office, but once again, she wasn't answering my calls. I had even called Derek this morning, but he had already left for the office. I was still waiting for a call back.

I got up from my chair and lay down on the couch in my office. Today was the last day of work before we shut down for Christmas, and normally we all came in early, so we could leave as early as possible. I placed my arm over my eyes. My head was pounding, and the tension in my back and shoulders was killing me.

"Hunter? What are you doing here already?"

I looked up to see Carter standing in my doorway. So much for peace and quiet. I sat up but said nothing.

"Hunter?"

I wasn't a weak man by any means, but this whole situation was bringing me to my knees. I put my head in my hands.

"Come with me."

I got up off the couch and followed Carter down the hall to his office. "Take a seat." He placed his briefcase on the floor and hung his coat up. He headed out and came back with two steaming cups of coffee, handing me one.

"Now, talk to me. What is going on?"

"Fuck, Carter, it's a mess. She's pregnant."

The look on Carter's face almost scared me. "Jocelyn? It is yours?"

"No, fuck, Autumn. She's pregnant, and this one is for sure mine."

"It's okay, Hunter."

"It's not. She told me early this morning and left the condo mumbling that she shouldn't have told me, and she didn't want to be a disappointment to me. Now she won't answer my calls, nothing. She could never be a disappointment to me."

"Did you tell her that?"

"If I had been given the chance I would have, but she practically bolted from the place before I could even grasp what she had told me. I know that those words have something to with her ex—that asshole, Jason—the one that created the scene at the party the other night."

Carter walked around to his desk and turned on his computer. "First thing is first, her address."

"15 Logan Circle."

Carter started typing on his computer.

"What are you doing?"

"Clearly, my brother is a mess and has totally forgotten how to win back a woman, so I am starting off by sending her flowers. That is the first step. Give me your credit card."

"I just sent her fucking flowers. This is going to take more than flowers."

"Credit card." He just sat there staring at me until I pulled out my wallet and handed him my card.

As soon as he was finished with the purchase, he sat back and looked at me. "What exactly did Jason say to her the other night?"

"It wasn't what he said to her, but more what he said to me. He basically said that I should wash my hands of her."

Carter sat for a minute, thinking about what I had just said. "I probably shouldn't tell you this, but what the hell. He's pissed me off, acting out like that. He hired me for their divorce. It was back before we had this firm, so she probably hasn't put two and two together yet."

"I kind of guessed that. You are the best family lawyer in town."

"I don't know how much you know about their separation, but he wanted her to have everything. I thought it was rather strange at first. Most people fight for whatever they can get. Not him, he was very clear in his direction: just give her everything."

I sat, frowning, waiting for my brother to continue.

"The day I gave him his bill, he got up and closed my office door. He wanted to know if he could confide in me. Of course, I nodded. After all, he was a client. He asked that what I was about to tell him stay between us and the four walls, no matter what. That was when he told me the real reason for the divorce and the reason behind giving up everything."

"Why did he leave her?" My heart went into my throat.

"He'd been having an affair with her best friend for the entire duration of their relationship, including the time they dated. When she lost the baby and headed into depression, I guess things got bad between them. She didn't want much to do with him, and he started spending more time with her friend. People had started to notice—everyone but Autumn. He wanted an out. Her best friend was pregnant with his baby, and they were very much in love. When Autumn was starting to get better, I guess she started asking him why he was never around. He just blamed work, saying that they were working on large projects that required his time. To keep her from figuring things out, he came to me and had the papers drawn up. He gave her everything because he figured it was easier for her. That way, there would be no reason to fight to keep anything, and given her recent state, she would more than likely just sign. Sure enough, within a month of receiving the divorce papers, she signed. He had his out, and she was none the wiser."

I sat in shock. This poor woman had been traumatized by this douche—made to believe that she wouldn't be any good to anyone because of what had happened.

"Now, he is working with Chase on a bunch of stuff for his new business. So, he is still a client of this firm, Hunter."

"No-not anymore! Tell Chase to sever the relationship."

"We can't do that."

I slammed my fist down on his desk. "We can, and we will. If I see Jason step foot in here again, I won't be held responsible for what I may do or say. So, it's best, given the circumstances, that this firm severs all ties with him."

Carter thought for a moment. He would be in deep shit if this guy found out he had broken client confidentiality. "All right, Hunter, you're right. I will have Chase immediately end things with him after the new year."

"No, he will sever this relationship this morning."

"Okay, this morning."

I got up to head back to my office. I wanted to try to call Autumn again before we opened the doors. "Hunter?"

I turned back to face my brother.

"Everything will be okay. You'll see."

I sat behind my desk, filing away the last piece of paper before I headed out for the day. It was five, and like usual, I was the last one here. Carter had gone home to be with Hope and the girls, and Chase and Bryce were headed out of town to see the women that they had met down south. Me? I was headed home to an empty condo. Carter had invited me to dinner again, but I thought it best just to go home. I didn't feel like being around anyone, but I had assured him I would be at his place bright and early on Christmas morning. Grabbing my coat and briefcase, I locked my office door and was headed down the hall when my phone rang.

I prayed it would be Autumn and answered quickly. She should have gotten the delivery by now.

"Hunter."

"It's Derek. You called? Sorry, I've been in meetings all day. What's up?"

"Hey, Derek, you able to meet me for a drink somewhere?"

"Yeah, I'm still in the city. Let me call Evelyn and let her know I'll be late. How about we meet at Joe's Place in twenty?"

"Sounds good. See you soon."

I had been sitting in a booth at the back of the bar for almost twenty minutes, when Derek finally walked in. Traffic was heavy out there with it being only two days until Christmas, so it wasn't a surprise that he was late. He stopped at the bar before heading back to where I was seated.

"Just ordered us a Scotch." He sat down across from me after taking his coat off.

"Thanks."

"What's going on?"

"Derek, I have something I want to ask you, so I'm just going to get straight to the point. Plus, I'm sure you want to get home."

"Okay, shoot."

"It's about Autumn. What happened with her marriage? She's given me little snippets, but not the full story. After what happened at the party the other night, I just want to know the whole truth."

"Geez, Hunter, I'm not sure I should say anything. It's not really my place."

"Derek, you're my best friend. I need your help, please. I'm begging you."

"What's going on, Hunter? You don't normally beg for anything." He laughed.

I took a deep breath as the waitress dropped off our drinks and smiled. I drank down the amber liquid and nodded at the waitress for another two to be delivered. As soon as she walked away, I mumbled, "Yes, I am begging you because she won't let me help her."

"It's not going to matter what I say, Hunter. That's Autumn. She is very stubborn, and she won't take help from anyone. I'm honestly surprised she has let Evelyn and me help her as much as she has."

"She's carrying my baby, Derek, so whatever you know, you've got to tell me." I continued telling him about what happened with her the night before at my condo. Derek picked up his glass and sipped his Scotch. He met my gaze as he put his glass down on the table, the look on his face saying it all. "So, please, tell me."

Derek sat there pondering for a minute, deciding whether or not to tell me. I was sure he was afraid Evelyn would have him by the balls if she found out he told me. Taking a deep breath, he began, "All right, but fuck, you didn't hear it from me. They'd been married a couple years. They tried basically right away to have a baby, but they had trouble conceiving at first. Jason wasn't a patient man, so that put more stress on her. Finally, after about a year, she finally got pregnant, but three months into her pregnancy, she ended up losing the baby. This put a tremendous strain on their relationship, even more when they were told that the chances of her being able to conceive were nil. She became severely depressed after finding out that news. She went on medical leave, barely getting out of bed most weeks. Jason, he just buried himself in work, or at least that's what he claimed. Personally, I think he was buried in someone else, but that's just my opinion. Anyway, soon their relationship began to suffer. She always felt as if he blamed her for what happened. One morning, he came downstairs to break-fast and dropped the bomb that he wanted a divorce. She had nothing left in her to fight. Basically, she asked me to read over the documents, and when I gave her the go, she signed. It took her about six months after the divorce before she sold everything and finally moved in with us."

"Fuck me, what a dick. So, his behavior the other night wasn't out of character then?"

"Not really. What was he even doing there?"

"I found out today that Carter was hired to do his divorce papers before we had the firm. He hired him back when he was working for that other family law firm. That's probably why you never put the two together. He's now hired Chase to do some contract work for him. Well, up until today anyway."

"Did Jason sever the contract with him after the other night?"

"No, I forced Chase to sever the relationship with him."

"Why?"

"Carter shared a little tidbit of information that he tech-nically shouldn't have, and I told him that I wanted the firm to have nothing to do with Jason, especially after the display the other night."

"What did he tell you?"

"It's not good, Derek."

"Doesn't surprise me, to be honest."

"I believe Autumn should know the truth. I just have to figure out how to tell her. He confided in Carter. Appar-ently, from the time they got together, Jason was screwing around with Autumn's best friend. When things got hot and heavy between the two of them, he wanted out and didn't know how to tell Autumn, so the loss of the baby was the perfect time and excuse to get out. He used that as a reason to leave her and made her believe that it was because she could no longer have children."

"To be honest with you, Hunter, none of this really surprises me."

I looked at Derek and finished the third glass of Scotch that had been delivered to the table.

"Why is that?"

"I figured he was always putting on a show for the family. I had seen him around the city with a few other women shortly before and after she got pregnant. At one point, I pulled him aside and mentioned it to him, but he said they were just business lunches. He doesn't know that I was at a restaurant for lunch one day and he was there with another woman. After watching them for a while, I determined it wasn't business—let's put it that way."

"Was it her friend?"

"No, some woman I'd never seen before."

"Does Autumn not speak with her friend anymore?"

"When they divorced, Autumn basically shut everyone out of her life except for Evelyn and me. She stopped doing anything with anyone. She was a shell of the person she once was when she moved in, and to be honest, the first time I have seen the real Autumn in the last two or three years was after she met you. You're good for her; she just needs to realize it."

"Why didn't you say anything about what you had seen that day at lunch?"

"I mentioned it to Evelyn, but she said I must have been mistaken, that Jason wouldn't do that."

"Why didn't you say anything to Autumn directly?"

"I should have, but shortly after I saw him, she lost the baby and then with the divorce, I just figured it was best to let sleeping dogs lie. If I had told her, it would have crushed her more to add that information into the mix. She really thought he was her everything. If you had seen the way she crumbled when she pulled up to the house the day she moved in, you would have wanted to do whatever you could have to protect her too."

"No doubt."

"Now, she at least hates him, which is a far cry from how she felt when she first came to stay with us. It might be easier for her to hear that truth now if you really think she should."

"I just don't like that she thinks the whole relationship breakdown is her fault, because it isn't. He was never truly dedicated to her. She needs to know the truth."

Derek called over to the waitress for a couple more drinks. "I couldn't agree with you more, Hunter."

Chapter Thirty-One

I sat in the living room wrapped in a blanket with Christmas movies on TV. I had barely been paying attention to anything going on in the movie; I was exhausted. I hadn't slept all night. I hadn't returned home right away. I wanted to make sure both Evelyn and Derek were already gone for work before I returned. When I got home, I had tried to get some rest, but the same images played through my mind like a bad movie. First, it was the look on his face after I had told him I was pregnant—the fact that he said absolutely nothing but sat up and pulled away from me after he found out. There had been no need for me to stay there. I now knew how he felt, so I threw on my clothes, boots, and coat and ran from his condo, not even giving him a minute to be able to digest the information, let alone say anything. Running was something I had become very good at doing when things got even the slightest bit tough. I had placed a call to Dr. Plante, but he still hadn't returned my call. I couldn't blame him. It was Christmastime, after all.

I got up off the couch and headed toward the kitchen to make a cup of tea when the doorbell rang. I was greeted by the same delivery man who had brought the roses the other day. He was carrying a large vase of stargazer lilies mixed with deep pink roses, baby's breath, and greenery. Attached to the side of the vase were two teddy bears. It was so beautiful. "Autumn?"

"Yes."

"I have a delivery for you. Two deliveries for you in a rather short time? Someone must find you really special."

I smiled as he handed the vase to me; he nodded and wished me a good day. I carried the flowers inside and placed them on the kitchen table. I had just found a card neatly tucked inside the flowers with my name sprawled on it, not that I had to guess who they were from. Just as I went to open it, Evelyn came through the kitchen door carrying a pile of grocery bags. "Autumn! You're home! Great! Can you help me bring in the rest of the bags, please? Derek's going to be late."

I set the envelope down onto the table, slipped my shoes on, and headed out the door to bring in the last of the bags.

"What did you do? Buy out the entire grocery store? It's only the three of us for Christmas dinner!" I asked as I came through the back door, my arms full of bags.

"Where did these come from?" Evelyn asked, ignoring my question. She was standing in front of the flowers, looking them over, as I dropped the last of the bags onto the floor.

"I was just about to open the envelope when you came in." I walked over and picked up the little notecard.

FORGIVE ME, I GOT STUCK. LOVE, HUNTER

"Hunter sent them."

"I see. They are beautiful. You guys have a fight?"

I decided at that moment to just tell her. "No, we didn't have a fight. I've decided not to see him anymore."

"What? Why on earth not?"

I could tell from the tone of her voice that she wasn't impressed with me. Marching over, she ripped the card from my hand and read it.

"So, you did have an argument. It obviously couldn't have been that bad. You were just there last night, for goodness' sake. Autumn, this man is good for you. Both Derek and I have seen changes in you for the better. Give the man a chance, and for the love of God, stop making him spend outrageous amounts of money on flowers for you."

"I'm pregnant."

I heard nothing, not even the sharp inhale of her breath. As I turned to face her, her eyes locked on me.

"You heard me, Evelyn. It's not Hunter's fault. It's mine."

"But I thought..."

"Yes, so did I, so you can imagine my shock when I found out. But the doctor has confirmed it, and I for once am choosing to look after it myself. He didn't ask for this. And if the same thing happens like before, he won't have to deal with the hurt. I couldn't protect Jason from this, but I can protect Hunter."

"Autumn, why are you doing this? You're going to need him. That baby is going to need him."

"What am I going to need, Evelyn—another man to pick up the pieces after things go south, just to destroy our relationship in the process? No, thank you, I'm not going to be responsible for another broken relationship after another failed pregnancy." My eyes were burning, and I could feel the tears begin to fall. I took a deep breath and was about to lash out at her again when Derek came walking through the back door.

Derek looked at Evelyn and then directly at me with a knowing look. He knew too. Hunter had called Derek; that was why he was late.

"You need to talk to him, Autumn. You're not being fair." They were the only words Derek uttered as he set his briefcase on the floor.

A sob escaped my lips. "You know, if you guys are so keen on speaking to him about me behind my back, you tell him for me that we're over."

"Believe me, I didn't want to get involved, but I'm not going to watch you destroy one of the best things that has ever happened to you. He loves you, so be an adult and talk to him." Derek slammed the door behind him and walked into the kitchen to grab some coffee.

I couldn't take it anymore. I ran from the kitchen, up the stairs, and into my bedroom, throwing myself face down on the bed and sobbing. I didn't mean a word of what I had said. I loved the man, and I wanted so badly to be with him. Another Christmas was about to fall upon me, and once again I found myself in the same situation I had been in for the last two years—utterly alone. Only this year I was more alone than I'd ever been.

Snow was falling heavily outside. It was Christmas Eve. I had finally spoken to Dr. Plante, which was a good thing because I seriously felt as though I was falling apart. He assured me that things would be okay, but he suggested I at least be fair and call Hunter. He told me hiding and running weren't the answer. I knew I had to face things; there was no denying that. He told me he would be calling me on Boxing Day to see how things went.

I lay in bed watching the end of *Scrooge*. It was almost midnight. I sat up, grabbed my cell phone, and scrolled through my missed calls. Hunter had called numerous times throughout today. *You must be honest with him. Let him know how you feel. You must be fair.* Dr. Plante's words cycled through my head.

I dialed his number, pressing that lone green button, and waited for the call to connect. I knew it was late; he was more than likely already in bed. I held my finger over the end button, half praying that he wouldn't answer, but on the second ring, I heard his voice.

"Autumn, baby, is that you?"

"Hi. It's me."

"Thank God. I'm sorry for the way I reacted to the news. I was just..."

"Shocked? I think that is the word you are looking for." I softly laughed.

"You could say that."

"Me too. I wasn't supposed to be able to have children after what happened, so you can imagine my surprise."

"And then I go and act like a total dick when you tell me. I'm sorry I wasn't very supportive."

"It's okay, Hunter. I'm not angry; I was more hurt. Our relationship has been very fast and intense for me, and then to find this out, well, it was the icing on the cake."

"I understand, but you know I'm here for you, right? That I'm here for us? That I do want there to be an us?"

"Yes, I know. I think I just need time. Time to sort things out myself, to be sure—"

He didn't let me finish. "To be sure of what? That I'm really going to be there for us, provide for you and the baby? You should know I mean what I say."

"Hunter, that's not what I'm worried about."

"Then what? Because when I tell you something, and I commit to something, I follow through one hundred percent. I wouldn't have gotten where I am today if I didn't have that drive or commitment."

"I need to be sure that I..." I could feel myself start to cry.

"This would be easier if we were together, so we can sit down and talk. I'm coming over."

"No, Hunter, please." I could hear his deep exhale on the phone.

"That you what? Just tell me."

"That I won't lose this baby, that I won't end up without you." The line went silent. I sat there, not even hearing him breathe. "Hunter, are you still there?" Tears were now flowing down my face.

"I'm here," he answered weakly. "Autumn, you don't

ever need to worry about being without me. If you lost that baby, it's something we would deal with together. Jason—he wasn't fair to you. You need to know something. Fuck, I wanted to tell you in person, but now is just a good a time as any. He didn't leave you for the reason you think."

"What are you saying?"

"Autumn, he was having an affair with your best friend, from the time you guys started dating. She apparently got pregnant, and they wanted to get married. He needed a reason to leave you, so he could be with her. When you lost the baby, he used that as the perfect excuse. He made all that shit up."

"How...how do you know all this?"

"He hired Carter to do your divorce. Carter told me everything."

I didn't know how to respond to this. I sat quietly for a few moments, letting what he had told me sink in. Jason hadn't left me for the reason I had thought. Anna's face the night at The Whisperwind Inn flashed before me. It wasn't a wonder she couldn't look me in the eyes. A sudden surge of anger came over me, followed by pure hatred. I had spent all this time thinking that the reason he left was because I was broken, and because of that, I had been running from this wonderful man.

"Are you okay?"

I hadn't realized how long I had been sitting there without saying anything.

"Autumn?"

"Hunter, would it be okay if I just took some time?"

"Of course, baby, whatever you need. Just know that I love you."

"Thank you."

"How much time do you think you need?"

"I don't know, Hunter. I'll let you know. I love you too."

I hung up the phone and lay back against my pillow. That was the first time those words had left my mouth. As sobs racked my body, I tried hard to digest what he had told me. I think I hated Jason more than I ever could now—and Anna? I had a good mind to call that bitch up. I wasn't sure how much time it would take before I knew what I wanted to do, but I knew that time was what I needed. I just hoped that Hunter would wait for me.

Chapter Thirty-Two

Hunter – Four Months Later

I sat at the breakfast bar in my condo, reading the Saturday morning paper. It had been four very long months. I'd heard from Autumn on and off, but she refused to meet me. At least she was talking to me. I'd been secretly giving Derek money every couple of weeks for Autumn and the baby. I told him not to tell her, and he vowed he would hold onto it until the baby was born or until Autumn started needing things. The last time I had met with him, he had assured me that I would hear from her, as he would sometimes drop my name in casual conversation.

I had spent so many hours talking to Carter about everything, I was sure he was sick of me. But like any good older brother, Carter listened and told me the best thing I could do now was continue to give her the space she had asked for, but still let her know I was there and waiting for her when she was ready.

I glanced at the clock. I had a lunch meeting with Carter and a potential client who would be needing both of our services eventually. Even though I didn't feel like going, I knew I had to get ready, so I put my coffee mug in the sink and headed to get showered and dressed.

I stood waiting to be seated at the Trademark Restaurant, reading over the menu that had been sitting on the podium. I kept glancing out the window for Carter, who still hadn't arrived but had sent a text letting me know he was on his way.

"Can I help you?" My stomach did a flip at the sound of the voice that greeted me. I didn't even need to look at who it was; I already knew.

I was greeted by those grey-blue eyes. "Autumn." I smiled as my eyes met hers.

"Hunter." Her cheeks turned that pretty blush pink as she took me in.

"How have you been?"

"I'm doing okay. You?" I could tell from the sound of her voice that things probably weren't okay.

"I'm okay."

A guy in a suit walked up behind her and whispered something into her ear. The expression on her face changed and she looked up at me. She cleared her throat and her voice took on a more professional sound. "Do you have a reservation, sir?"

I could tell from the change of her tone that the guy behind her was her boss, and I didn't want to get her in trouble, so I played along. "I do, under Malone."

She ran her finger down the list of reservations, looked at me, and smiled. "This way, please, sir."

As I walked behind her, I couldn't help myself, my eyes traveled down her body, taking in her curves from behind. I couldn't help but get aroused. I missed her terribly, in more ways than one. She finally stopped at a table and placed the three menus down. "Enjoy your lunch." That was all she said as I took a seat. I watched as she walked away from me.

All through the lunch meeting, I couldn't take my eyes away from the front door or the podium she stood behind. I kept catching her glance over my way, a soft smile on her lips. When she walked over and sat another couple near our table, I took in her profile. A small but noticeable baby bump was there, and it was in that moment that I longed to run my hands over it. I was missing out on something I didn't even know I wanted or would want. I mean, I had nieces, and I was thrilled with them, but this? It wasn't fair what she was denying me. That was the second I decided I needed to fight harder for what I wanted and for her.

Throwing my mail down on the counter, I poured myself a Scotch. I needed to relax. Seeing Autumn at lunch today had thrown me into a major funk. I'd heard it from Carter after the client had left. I was so distant and distracted that I had barely heard two words the whole meeting, and I guess it showed. I knew he was pissed.

I had been the last one to leave the restaurant because I

had wanted to find Autumn. When I had first seen her, I wanted nothing more than to wrap her in my arms, pull her into me, and not let her go. When I went to leave, I checked for her, my eyes scanning the restaurant, but she was nowhere to be found.

I sat down on the couch and flipped on the news, trying to rid my mind of her, but no luck. I picked up my phone and sent a text to Carter. Seconds later, he sent back a message.

CARTER: BUSY, CAN'T TALK RIGHT NOW. CALL YOU IN A BIT.

Seconds later, my phone rang.

"That was a quick bit, Carter."

"It's not Carter." The sound of her voice hit me right in the gut. "I hope it's okay that I called you."

"Of course it is, baby. I looked for you after lunch today, but you were gone."

"Yes, I'm sorry. I had to go for my lunch. Doctor's orders."

Doctor's orders? What had she not been telling me? "How have you been, Autumn?"

"Okay."

"And the baby?"

"Everything is going okay." I wasn't sure if it was sadness or nervousness I was hearing in her voice.

"What's with the doctor's orders? Are you sure everything is okay? Where are you?"

"They are just watching me closely, Hunter. I am fine. I'm sitting in the parking lot of the restaurant. I'm just on my way home. I was going to stop by before I left the city, but figured it might be best if I didn't. I thought it might be just as awkward as today. So, I decided to call instead. I wanted to ask for your help."

At this point, I would have given her whatever she needed if it meant her coming back to me. "I'll do anything. What do you need?" If this was the only way she was going to let me close, then dammit, I would be there for her.

"Well, with the baby coming, I think it's time I found my own place. I don't want to be a bother to Derek and Evelyn. Would you be willing to look at some places with me? If I tell Evelyn, she will get upset, and I don't want to hear it from her."

I frowned. I wanted her here with me, dammit, but I didn't dare tell her that for fear I scared her away again. "Yes, of course, beautiful. Look at some places on the Internet, and next week I'll come pick you up and we will go look at them. Sound good?"

"Thanks, Hunter."

"Anything you need, don't be afraid to ask." The line went quiet. I could tell she was still on the other end because I could hear her breathing, and then the lightest whimper escaped her lips. "Autumn? Are you sure you're okay?"

"I have to go now. Evelyn will be upset if I am late for dinner. I'll see you next week."

And she was gone. She sounded so lost, and when she gave me that light whimper, I knew she was crying. I got up from the couch and headed into my office. I needed a plan and I needed one fast. I dialed Carter. I wasn't taking *I'm busy* for a fucking answer this time.

Chapter Thirty-Three

AUTUMN

It was already eight in the morning. I had the next three days off, and I really didn't feel like getting out of bed, but I was supposed to be going to see apartments today. I grabbed the remote off the bedside table and turned the TV on. I was tired, my body exhausted. I had cried myself to sleep last night; I missed him so. Seeing him at the restaurant last week had confirmed that.

As I lay there watching TV, my phone pinged with a message.

HUNTER: GOOD MORNING, BEAUTIFUL. GET UP AND GET READY, I'M COMING TO PICK YOU UP.

I tucked my head back under the blankets and shut my

eyes. I placed my hand on my growing belly. "You deserve a daddy too, don't you? I have to remember it's not just about me," I whispered. As if in response to my statement, I felt a slight movement and smiled to myself. I quickly typed out a response to Hunter, crawled out of bed, and headed for the shower. I only had a small list of places, the problem being there wasn't that much listed for rent that I could afford on the little I was making. I knew he had said if I needed anything just to ask, but I just couldn't do that.

I was ready and waiting by the front door when Hunter finally arrived. "Good morning." He stepped in and gave me a kiss on the cheek. "I have something for you. Close your eyes." I was hesitant at first, but when I opened them, he stood holding a large gift basket full of baby items. I could feel myself getting choked up. I didn't know what to say.

"You think a guy could come in or what?"

"Oh yes, please. I placed my hand on his arm and guided him into the kitchen, where he placed the basket on the table.

"Wow, Hunter, this is amazing, but you didn't have to do that. I've been buying things as I go."

"Whether I had to or not isn't the point. I wanted to." His hand went to the small of my back, and he placed another kiss on my cheek.

"Thank you for this." Glancing in the basket, I saw there were things that I would need that I wouldn't have been able to afford right away.

"I hope you like it. Carter and Hope helped me pick everything out."

"I do. Thank you." I could feel tears start to burn my

eyes and that telltale lump in my throat, so I grabbed my water and took a sip.

"Well, are you ready to go, beautiful, or are we going to be late?"

We pulled out of the parking lot of the last apartment I had on my list. We had seen them all. I was beginning to get discouraged. Every time I thought I had found the one I would take, Hunter quickly found something wrong with it. The first was too drafty, the second he didn't like the neighborhood, the third would need renovations, and this last one he didn't care for the shady characters in the hallways. This elimination left me with only two other apartments in the classifieds that I could afford, but if Hunter didn't like any of the ones we had already seen, there wasn't any point in looking at the others.

"How about a bite to eat? You hungry?" he asked as he put his hand over mine.

"Starving."

Hunter stopped the car outside of a little Italian sandwich shop, and we headed inside and placed our order. We took a seat in a booth at the back of the restaurant and waited for the waitress to bring over our water.

"So, out of all the apartments we saw today, which one did you like best?" Hunter asked. "You already know my take on all of them."

"Probably the one on Main if I had to choose. It was not too big, and really, it was the nicest building out of them all."

"I see. Well I have a place to show you. We have an appointment next week on Friday. So, don't accept anything before then. I think you might like this one better."

I didn't want to wait and risk losing the apartment. "Well, what if I called and just put a small deposit down on it? That way I won't risk losing it if the other place doesn't work out."

"You could, but I have a feeling you might like this other place a little better than the one on Main. I would wait, but if you insist, call and ask if they would hold the apartment with a small deposit, but make sure it's refundable. Honestly, if they ask for more than a couple hundred dollars, I wouldn't do it."

Resting his hands on the table, he held them out to me, and I placed my own in his, his large, strong hands enveloping mine. As soon as our skin touched, I felt a familiar tingle between my legs and a tremor run through my body.

"I've missed you." The heat in his eyes gave away everything he was feeling.

"I've missed you too, Hunter. Thank you for spending today with me and giving me a hand with this. You have no idea how much this means to me."

Bringing my hand to his lips, he pressed a soft kiss to the back of my hand. "I'm glad you asked me." The waitress brought over our food. Once we had eaten, Hunter drove me back to the house and walked me to the door.

"Did you want to come in, maybe catch a movie?"

"I would love to, but you were falling asleep on the drive

back. I think you need your rest, beautiful. Plus, I don't want to overstay my welcome. I'll see you next week, okay?"

I was unsure how to read his decline and felt a little disappointed, but I tried my best not to show it. "Sure. I do need my rest." He kissed my cheek, and once he knew I was inside, he headed back to his car and drove away.

Chapter Thirty-Four

After spending the day with Autumn, I was even more determined to win her over. There was no way I was letting her live in those shitholes we had looked at. She was expecting an apartment viewing on Friday, and that was what I was going to give her. Chase and Bryce arrived early Sunday morning. Today we were getting the nursery somewhat set up, and I needed all the help I could get. I had decided to move my office into the smaller of the two spare bedrooms and use the larger for a nursery. This was my last and only chance to win her back. It had to be done right. I had just made a fresh pot of coffee and took two mugs to Bryce and Chase, who were already on the floor disassembling my desk.

"If we don't have to take the full thing apart, let's not. It will be easier to reassemble that way."

"Great plan. That will save on time too."

I carried another drawer full of office supplies into the other room and set it against the wall as they carried in one section of the desk.

The boys had the whole office, including the desk, completely down, removed, and reassembled by the time the carpet company had arrived. They came in and lay down the thick, plush white carpet. The carpet installers were just leaving as Carter came walking in.

"Paint is here. Hope finally settled on the color out of the choices you gave her."

"Great! Bryce and Chase are in taping and covering the new carpet. We should get started right away." With the four of us working on it, the room had three coats of paint by the early afternoon.

"When does the furniture arrive?" Bryce asked, shoving the last of his food in his face.

"Tomorrow night after work. I think they said they'd be here by seven." I placed my empty container down on the table. We had just finished eating the Thai food I had ordered and were now all relaxing in the living room.

"Anyone want a beer?" I asked, gathering up the now empty food cartons and beer bottles that were scattered all over the table.

"No, man, I got to get back home to Hope and the girls." Carter stretched. "Dinner with the in-laws tonight."

"Yeah, we got to bolt too. We have a couple big appointments tomorrow and want to get prepped."

"All right, guys, well, I can't thank you enough."

"No problem. Glad we could help."

Chase and Bryce were the first ones gone. Carter turned

to me before he left. "This is going to work, Hunter. No doubt in my mind. Things will be fine. She is going to love it."

"Thanks. I sure as hell hope so. I can't have her living in one of those apartments we saw, I just can't."

"All right, I'll see you in the morning."

"Have fun tonight," I called as he headed down the hall toward the elevator. Just as the door closed, my cell phone rang. I ran to grab it off the table, glancing at the screen, and noticed Autumn's number.

"Hello, beautiful."

The other end of the line was empty. I could faintly hear crying. "Autumn?"

"Hunter, I need your help. Please tell me you can help me."

My heart was in my throat. "What's wrong?" I didn't like the panic in her voice, so I got up and headed to the door, throwing on my shoes and grabbing my keys while waiting for a response.

"Derek and Evelyn are both out; I can't get a hold of either of them. I don't know what to do."

"It's okay. Calm down and take a deep breath. Tell me what's going on."

"I woke up feeling really crampy. I just stayed in bed, but when I went to get up, there was blood all over. I'm bleeding really bad, and I am in pain. Please, Hunter, hurry." She sobbed.

"Sit tight, I'm on my way."

I bolted out the door, with my heart in my throat, and raced to get to her.

Chapter Thirty-Five

AUTUMN

As soon as we had gone through the registration at the hospital, they sent me up to Labor & Delivery. Hunter had quickly run back down to the car to pick up my bag that I had brought. I wasn't sure what was going on and didn't want to be without some of my own stuff.

I was resting in bed, waiting for the nurse to come do an ultrasound, when Hunter came back into the room. He placed my bag on the bench seat and sat down beside me on the edge of the bed.

"How are you feeling?" he asked, taking my hand in his.

"Okay, just a little crampy. The nurse was in just a couple minutes before you came back. They are going to do an ultrasound to make sure everything is okay. I'm scared, Hunter." I had been fighting back tears and couldn't hold them back any longer.

He squeezed my hand in his, letting me know he was there. "Just relax. You're safe and in good hands here." Just as he got comfortable, the nurse wheeled in the portable ultrasound machine, followed by a doctor.

"Autumn, we're going to do an ultrasound to make sure everything is all right. Sir, if you wouldn't mind leaving the room until we are finished?" The doctor asked as the nurse went about getting everything ready.

Hunter stood and walked to the door. He was just about to step outside when I looked up. His head was down, and his shoulders were hunched over. I couldn't bear to see him look so down. "No, doctor, that's not necessary. I want him to stay."

He turned and looked at me, a small smile coming to his lips, as I waved at him to come back.

"He should be here; after all, he is the father."

He walked back over, sat on the edge of the bed, and took hold of my hand. As soon as the wand was on my stomach, we heard a heartbeat. Relief washed over me. I looked at Hunter and our eyes met, his eyes dancing with happiness.

"Well, everything looks good." The doctor put the wand down. "I'd like to keep you overnight for observation, that way we can keep an eye on the baby's heartbeat and you—make sure you're not having any contractions."

"Is everything going to be okay?" I asked, tears in my eyes.

"I can't see any reason why not right now, but I want to be sure. Have you been under any stress?"

"Some. I lost my first baby. I've been very worried about this pregnancy."

"Yes, I saw that in the nurse's report. I don't want you to

worry. You're in good hands. Now, tonight, I want you to get some rest."

After the doctor left the room to carry on with his rounds, the nurse stayed and hooked me up to the cardiotocograph to monitor the baby's heartbeat and any contractions I might be having. Hunter had headed down to the food court for a bite to eat while I took the time to get some rest.

Hunter

I walked from the food court, stopping into the gift shop just before I got to the elevator. I grabbed a vase of roses from the flower fridge and a purple teddy bear off the shelf. I paid for my purchases, adding in a TV card and a bottle of juice, and made my way back up to the fourth floor. If she was going to be here overnight, I wanted to make sure she had something to do in case she couldn't sleep.

The elevator ride gave me time alone with my thoughts. I had never been so worried about anything before as I was tonight when I drove to her place. My heart had been in my throat the entire time. I didn't quite understand how much something I couldn't even hold yet could mean so much to me. I wanted to be a part of this relationship. I wanted to see my baby born, and I wanted to be a part of their lives. I just wished she would let me get closer to her.

I walked down the hall and peeked into her room. She lay there with her eyes closed, her head resting against the pillow. The gentle beeping sound of the monitors she was hooked up to was soothing. I placed the small vase of roses on her bedside table and sat at the end of her bed. Her eyes opened, and a slight smile formed on her lips.

"I think I'm going to get going, let you get some rest."

"Please don't leave just yet. I don't want to be alone."

I got up, leaned down, and gave her a kiss as she shuffled over and made room for me. I crawled up beside her, being careful of all the wires she was hooked up to, and put the TV on. Finally, we found a movie and started watching that while she relaxed in my arms.

Autumn

He whispered in my ear as we watched the credits for the movie: "Did you want me to stay with you, beautiful?"

It was so nice having him here with me. Just knowing that he wanted to be here had taken away a lot of the stress I had been feeling. When I had been in the hospital last time, Jason wouldn't even stay with me to eat a meal; it was as if he was afraid he would catch something being here. I took a deep breath. I didn't want Hunter to leave, but I knew he must be tired. I grabbed his arm, wrapping it around my body, and I buried my face into his strong chest, breathing in his scent.

"Thank you."

"For what?"

"For being here and staying with me. You have no idea how much that means to me."

"Don't be silly."

"No, Hunter, you don't understand. I didn't want to bring it up but, before, Jason never stayed. He would come see me, but that was it. He never stayed. You came, and you stayed. It means the world to me."

"Autumn, please don't think about him anymore. That's so over."

"It still hurts, Hunter, knowing that someone could be that careless."

"I know, baby, but he's gone. It's time to focus on what's in front of you."

Just as he said that, a nurse came into the room. "What's going on in here? Are you feeling okay, Autumn?"

"Yes, why?"

"Your heart alarm was going off. I told you there was to be no unnecessary stress. Now, love, you need to calm down." She came over and grabbed my wrist, quickly checking my pulse.

"I'm sorry, nurse, that would be my fault."

"You should probably consider heading home, sir. She needs her rest."

"I can assure you I was just getting ready to leave."

"Good idea." She pressed a couple buttons on a couple of the machines and headed out the door.

I looked at Hunter. Tears were building in my eyes. "I

know you work tomorrow, and I really want you to get some rest, but do you think you could stay with me a bit longer? I really don't want to be alone right now."

"I can go in late. Remember, I'm one of the owners of the company." He smiled and cupped my cheek. "And remember, you're more important to me than anything. So, if you want me to stay with you, I'm here. As long as Nurse Ratched doesn't come back in and force me out." I smiled and laid the bed back. Hunter climbed in beside me, adjusting his arm so it was under my neck, pulling me into him. I curled my body into his and closed my eyes. Hunter reached up and shut the light off over the bed. Then he pulled up the blanket around us and held me until I drifted off to sleep.

Chapter Thirty-Six

Breakfast was delivered bright and early the next morning. Hunter had stayed well into the middle of the night, leaving around four to get showered and dressed for work. He had already been back to check on me before heading to the office for the day. I had promised him that once I saw the doctor, I would call him right away.

I had just finished my breakfast when Evelyn walked into the room at a frantic pace. "My God, are you okay?"

"I'm fine, Evelyn, just waiting for the doctor to see if I can go home."

"I was so worried when I got your note. What happened?"

"I woke up, not feeling very well, to cramps. I wasn't too worried until I got out of bed and saw that I had started bleeding."

"Why didn't you call us? How did you get here? Your car was still at home. Did you call an ambulance?" She was frantic and rambling, pacing around the room.

"Calm down. I called Hunter. He came, picked me up, and brought me here."

Evelyn finally started to calm down once she found out everything was all right. She sat on the end of the bed, talking with me, when the doctor came flying in. "Well, how are you feeling today, Autumn?"

"Better, thanks."

"I see you had a bit of an elevated heart rate last night." Evelyn squinted at me. The last thing I wanted was for her to think I was lying to her.

"Yes, I just got a little upset at something."

"I hope everything is okay?"

"It is now." I smiled.

"Well, the good news is everything looks to be normal," he said while glancing through my chart. "I'm glad to say you can head home today if you like. I'll be sending over a copy of my report for your doctor. I would like you to take it easy for the next few days—lots of bed rest and no stress either. I will include a note for your employer as well. I want you to take a few days off. It will be up to your doctor if he wants you off for good. Do you have any questions?"

"Time off? But I just started this job, and I need the money."

"What you need is rest. It's extremely important to look after yourself right now. Like I said, it will be up to your doctor if he wants you off any longer than a few days. Now, are there any other questions?"

I felt like I had just been scolded. Evelyn sat there with

an *I told you so* face. She had been on me to take care of myself for the last couple months. "I don't think so."

"All right then, I'll send the nurse in to unhook you from all the monitors, and you can be on your way." He smiled and headed out of the room.

"So what was wrong last night?"

"What do you mean?"

"Your heart rate? What got you upset?"

I told Evelyn everything that Hunter had told me back on Christmas Eve. The fact Jason had cheated on me from the start, the way he used the loss of the baby to divorce me. When he had first told me, it upset me, but now it felt like a huge weight had been lifted from my shoulders. I had wasted so much time not living my life and believing something that wasn't true. That belief almost had me throwing away the best thing that had happened in my life.

Just as I wiped a tear from my cheek, a nurse came into the room and went directly to the monitors. "Are you having any pain, Autumn?"

"No, why?"

"Your heart rate monitor is going off again. I told you last night before I left that you needed to stay calm."

"I'm sorry. It was my fault. She's okay, really," Evelyn spoke up.

The nurse looked at us both. We could tell she was annoyed. "Well, she's allowed to go home today, and we really don't want to see her back here until it's time for that baby to be born." She scribbled down something on my chart and headed out the door.

"I'm just glad you are okay. Now we won't talk about all that until we are on our way home, okay?" Evelyn winked at me. I smiled back, and we sat watching TV while we waited for the nurses to come in and unhook me from all the machines.

Hunter

My watch read eleven-thirty. I was tired, and work was proving to be impossible today. No matter how much I tried to concentrate, my mind just swung back around to Autumn, the baby, and what could possibly be taking her so long to call me with an update. It had been like that for months now, and I felt that my work was starting to suffer because of it.

Carter strolled by my office. "Hey! I noticed you came in later than normal this morning. Everything okay with Autumn?"

I had called Carter on my way to her place last night. I was so panicked, I didn't know what to do.

"I wasn't going to come in today. I spent the night at the hospital with her. As far as I know, all is good. She was waiting to see the doctor this morning when I left."

"It was probably stress. Same thing happened to Hope when she was pregnant with Haley. Have you told her what you did with your condo yet?"

"I hope you're right. No, I haven't told her yet. I was planning to show her on Friday, but I think I may do it sooner—all things considered. I called to see if I could bump up the delivery of the furniture today. They said it shouldn't be a problem."

"Good idea. When does it arrive?"

"Hopefully in an hour or two, which means I have to be on my way. I've rescheduled all my appointments for next week. I'm going to work from home the rest of this week. What are you up to?"

"I was just going to see if you wanted to head out for lunch. I guess I'll go see what those other two jackasses are doing." We both laughed, and Carter walked away in search of Bryce and Chase.

Just as I got up from my desk and was heading out the door my cell phone rang.

"Hello?"

"I'm finally back home. Everything is fine." My heartbeat accelerated at the sound of her voice.

"Great, what did the doctor say?" I shut my door and sat back down behind my desk, glancing at my watch. I had forty-five minutes to get back to my condo.

"It was a threatened miscarriage. The doctor took me off work for a few days and wants me to rest and stress less. I'm supposed to make an appointment with my own doctor this week. He will be the one to take over and advise on further instruction."

"Okay, love. I'm glad everything is okay. Listen, I wish I had time to talk with you, but I have an appointment, and I have to get going. What are you doing Wednesday night and for the rest of the week?"

"Well, Evelyn has locked me in my room and is waiting on me hand and foot. She is already driving me bananas and

I've only been home for twenty minutes. By then I'll be ready to get out of here." She laughed into the phone.

It was good to hear her laugh. "All right, well, I'll come pick you up. I'm taking some time off this week, so if you need out of there before then, just call, okay sweetie?"

"Okay. Thank you."

"Okay, beautiful, I gotta run. I'll talk to you soon. Take it easy and look after yourself and our baby."

Chapter Thirty-Seven

Autumn

I was feeling better with each day that passed. It was already six, and I was patiently sitting in the living room, waiting for Hunter to arrive. He had called and said he was running a bit late because he had to grab some groceries and stop by the office, and now traffic was bad. I had packed my bag and was waiting for Evelyn to bring it down. She hadn't let me lift a finger all week; I was getting restless. I picked up the paper and started flipping through ads for apartments.

"I don't know if it's a good idea that you go away already. The doctor did say bed rest," Evelyn stated as she threw my bag down by the front door.

"I know, Evelyn, but I will either rest here or there. What's the difference?" Evelyn shrugged her shoulders.

"Exactly. There isn't one, except you can watch over

every move I make if I'm here." I stopped at the classifieds and began reading over apartment listings.

"What are you doing?" Evelyn asked, looking over my shoulder at the newspaper.

"I'm looking for apartments while I wait for Hunter to pick me up. I already searched the web for a few in an area nearby. Just thought I'd see what I could find in the paper as well."

"What do you mean apartments? You're not moving." She took the paper from my hands. "Derek and I have already talked about it, and we've decided that you are staying here."

"Evelyn, please, not this again. You and Derek don't make my decisions. I need to get back on my feet. I'd like to have my independence and my privacy. Plus, now that I'm starting to see Hunter again, it would be nice to be able to have him over, cook him dinner, and watch a movie instead of me always going there."

"Well, you will have to fight Derek and me on this, and you're not going to win. You can have Hunter over anytime you want," she said, sticking her tongue out at me, causing me to laugh.

"You're impossible." Whether she liked it or not, I was still going to look.

The doorbell rang, and I went to get up, but Evelyn had already jumped up and run to the door. "Hey, Hunter."

I sighed and headed to the door. I was looking forward to seeing him. "Hey, beautiful, you ready?"

Evelyn turned to me and smiled. "Look after her, Hunter. Don't let anything happen to her."

I rolled my eyes at Hunter and mouthed, "Get me out of here," to him behind Evelyn's back. "I plan to, Evelyn. You don't need to worry." He chuckled to himself and grabbed my bag from the floor.

Hunter held his hand out to me. I placed mine in his, and he led me out to the car.

Hunter

I was quiet on the drive back into the city. I had listened to her tell me about her conversation with Evelyn and then about not being able to find a place. She admitted that she lost the other apartment to another family who was able to put the full amount down. When she finally quieted down, I placed my hand on her thigh.

"Autumn, love, you're not supposed to be stressing. We'll find you a place. Plus, we still have the one I found to look at, remember? I think you're going to like it."

"I know, I'm sorry. It's just that Evelyn is driving me crazy. She won't let me do anything. She already deemed that I would be staying with them."

"Well, at least you know you have a place. Now, I want you to relax. We are going to have nothing but stress-less fun over the next few days."

I pulled into the parking lot of the condo and took a

breath. My stomach was in knots. I was praying that she would take me up on my offer. Everything that had happened over the last few months had shown me that I wanted to be with her more than anything, especially after this past weekend. Seeing her in pain and so scared, I was glad she had turned to me for help and that I had been able to calm her, even if, at the time, I felt completely and totally helpless.

After we got in and settled, I poured us a couple glasses of water and sat down in the living room. Autumn looked tired. I watched as she sat back and closed her eyes. "Are you feeling okay, baby?"

"Yes, just tired."

I relaxed back into the sofa and patted the spot between my legs. "Come lay with me."

She looked at me and smiled and then turned and leaned her back against my chest, resting her hands on her growing belly. "Give me your hand," she said softly.

She took my hands and placed them on her belly. "Feel that?"

I could feel slight movement under my hand. I smiled to myself. This was the first time I had felt my baby. We sat that way for a while, her relaxing against me, my hand feeling my baby move around. I placed gentle kisses on her neck, and she giggled.

"Hunter, I want to thank you."

"For what?"

"For sharing the truth with me about Jason. I was so angry when you first told me, but I guess a part of me always knew something wasn't right between us."

"You're welcome. To be honest with you, I'm kind of glad he threw you away."

"Well, that's a lovely thing to say! Why is that?"

"Well, because without him doing that, I'd never have had that chance to meet you and fall in love with you." I kissed the side of her neck.

"I love you too, Hunter."

<h1 style="text-align:center">Chapter Thirty-Eight</h1>

Hunter

I opened my eyes; the room was still in darkness. It must have been early. I rolled over, careful not to wake her, so I could see the clock. It was only four. I tried to go back to sleep, but instead, I just kept thinking about showing her what I had done with the condo. When my mind simply wouldn't shut off, I crawled out of bed without disturbing her and made my way into the kitchen.

I set the coffeemaker to brew and tried hard to relax. I knew she wanted out of Derek and Evelyn's place, and I couldn't say I blamed her, but I didn't want her living on her own or in some slum. The apartments that we had seen were just that. I saw in the paper last week that one of them had been raided by the police. There was no way in hell that my baby or the mother of my child was going to live in that. Not after all that she had been through. I was determined to support her fully even if she wouldn't let me. That was the kicker, though. Autumn was so determined she didn't need help that it was frustrating.

While waiting for my coffee to brew, I quietly opened the door to my old office and peeked inside. If she said yes, she would have everything she could ask for. She wouldn't want for anything. If she said no, well, I would have to find another way to win her heart. I simply wasn't giving up. She had no idea what I was capable of when I set my mind to something.

I jumped when I heard the water run and quietly shut the door and headed out into the living room. I grabbed a mug and poured the hot coffee into it, taking a sip. My nerves were getting the best of me. Coffee probably wasn't a wise choice. I flipped through the morning paper, waiting for her to appear. Finally, I heard the door of the bedroom click open. She looked stunning wrapped in my oversized bathrobe, hair tousled to the side. "Good morning. Sleep well?"

"Good morning. I did. It's so much quieter here. You're up early. Is everything okay?"

"Yes, of course. I'm just an early riser, you know that." As she walked toward me, I patted a spot on my lap for her to sit. She carefully sat, and I leaned back into the couch, pulling her into me, wrapping my arms around her, and giving her a deep kiss.

Autumn

I hadn't stopped talking about seeing this apartment all through breakfast. Hunter kept trying to change the subject, but I would quickly weave the conversation back to the apartment. I really wanted to be on my own again.

"What time are we leaving to see the apartment? Did they happen to say if it was available already?"

"It's pretty much available right now," Hunter answered as he loaded the last of the breakfast dishes into the dishwasher.

"Has it been empty long?"

"Not too long."

"How much work needs to be done to it?"

"Not much from what my friend told me."

I took a sip of my tea. "Do they require a deposit plus first and last month's rent?"

I was worried about money. I hadn't been working that long, and the restaurant didn't pay that well. The money I had received from the divorce and the sale of the house was pretty much gone. Therapy hadn't been cheap.

"Autumn, you're not supposed to be stressing. Now, there is no need to worry. You know I'll make sure you have all that you need."

Before I could protest, Hunter walked over to me, wrapped his arms around me, and kissed me. "Now, go get yourself dressed, and let's go see what we think of this place."

"Is it far from here?"

"Not too far. Now go." He smacked me gently on the butt as I walked past him into the bedroom.

I was ready in twenty-five minutes. Hunter was still seated at the breakfast bar, his head buried in the newspaper.

"Okay, Hunter, I'm ready."

A nervous smile appeared on his lips as he walked around toward me. "Okay, give me two minutes. Have a seat," he said, pointing to the couch.

He headed down the hall to the bedroom while I made myself comfortable. I'd been waiting for five minutes when I finally stood up and looked out the window. The city was beautiful from up here—so quiet and peaceful while all the little people scurried around. I turned to sit back down when I heard Hunter call my name.

"Coming." As I made my way down toward the bedroom, I saw that he was standing just outside his office door. "What is it?"

"Close your eyes."

"What? I thought we were going?"

"We are, just close your eyes. This will only take a minute. I have something I want to show you."

I let out a breath and closed my eyes tightly. I felt him place his hand on my lower back, his other hand brushing against my growing belly. When I heard the door opening, Hunter whispered in my ear to take a step forward. "I've got you, beautiful. I won't let you fall." Both of his hands gripped my hips.

Carefully stepping forward, he removed one hand from my waist and up to my arm and whispered, "Okay, open your eyes."

As my eyes adjusted, I was taken aback by what I saw. He had turned his office into a warm and cozy nursery. The hardwood floors were replaced with plush, white carpet. A white crib sat underneath the window, the matching white change table to the left and the dresser to the right. In the one corner sat the biggest teddy bear I think I had ever seen in my life. A glider rocker sat in the corner between the crib and change table, an afghan laying over the back.

"I hope you like it. I did it for you, for us, for our baby. I would love it if you would move in here with me. No more searching for apartments, no more fearing that I won't be there. I want to be there. I don't want to miss any more time than what I have already."

Everything was so beautiful. I took a few steps toward the crib and peeked inside. A crib quilt covered in teddy bears lay inside.

"The crib will also change into a regular bed once the crib is no longer needed."

He had thought of everything. As I listened to him go on telling me about things, tears flooded my eyes, and once I blinked, they were rolling down my cheeks. Everything was so perfect and well thought out. I looked at Hunter. The smile he was wearing slowly began to vanish.

"What is it? Do you not like it?"

I looked around the room at all he had done, all he had given up. There was nothing I didn't like. How could he ever think that? "It's not that. You...you gave up your office?"

"Really, I just downsized into the smaller room across the hall. To be honest, I don't even really need it here. I work too much as it is."

I didn't know what to say. I just kept looking around, every time seeing something that I hadn't seen before. The pictures on the wall, the growth chart against the closet door, the mobile that hung over the crib—it was all there. I felt Hunter step up behind me, placing his hands on my shoulders. "Can I be honest with you?"

When I looked at him, his eyes held no lies, and I knew whatever was coming next was going to solidify everything that he had already said through the reveal of this surprise. I nodded my head because I didn't trust my voice at this point.

"I've never been more scared of losing something in my entire life than I was the other night. I was actually afraid of losing something that not eight months ago, I had never even contemplated having, wasn't even sure if I ever wanted or would ever have. You came into my life at a time I wasn't looking for anything except for a little fun, but now I'm so in love with you and in love with everything that can be, I don't think it's possible to ever let you go. Please say something."

I turned and looked at Hunter. He stood there, his eyes watery. I had never seen him look as vulnerable as he did in this moment. I walked over to him and placed my hands on his chest. Reaching up, I placed my hand behind his head and pulled him forward, kissing him. It only took a second before I was wrapped in his arms.

When we broke from the kiss, he looked into my eyes. "Is that a yes?"

"Yes."

Chapter Thirty-Nine

Autumn

After breaking the news to Evelyn, who was surprisingly happy for me, we moved my stuff into Hunter's that weekend. Evelyn made sure that I knew I would always have a place if I needed, which I already knew, but she still felt better telling me.

"We'll still shop, right?" Evelyn cried as she hugged me for the hundredth time.

"Would you get control of your wife, Derek?" Hunter joked as he stood by the door, waiting for Evelyn to finish smothering me.

"Yes, Evelyn, we will still shop. You're acting like I am moving across the country." I laughed.

"You're absolutely sure about this, right? This is the right thing for you to do?"

Nothing like calling me out on the red carpet in front of

Hunter or anything. But I was completely sure of my choice. "Yes, I'm sure."

I thought back to that moment as I unpacked the last of my clothes and placed them in one of the dresser drawers Hunter had cleared for me. As I stood back up, I met his reflection in the mirror. "How's everything going in here?"

I smiled. "Good. Almost done."

Wrapping his arms around me, he nuzzled his face into my neck, kissing my shoulder. "Good, because I want you."

He continued kissing my shoulder and up the back of my neck. I closed my eyes, reveling in the feeling. As his hands ran over my breasts, I stopped him. "Not now."

I felt bad denying him, because as much as he wanted to, I wanted to. However, I was petrified of having any other complications. We had come this far. He gripped my hips and pulled me tighter into him. I could feel his arousal pressing into me.

"But the doctor said it was okay."

"Yes, I know. You made sure to ask him three times at our last appointment." Rolling my eyes, I looked at Hunter who let out a low chuckle at my annoyance.

"Sorry, I can't help it. You have no idea how sexy I find you right now." He nipped at my earlobe, sucking it into his mouth.

"If what's poking into me is any indication, then I may have a slight idea!" I reached behind me, gripping him through his pants, and squeezed, making him groan deeply.

I guided him over to the bed, forcing him to sit down on the edge, and pushed him backwards so he was lying down. I ran my hands down his chest and slowly unbuckled his belt. I couldn't stand to see him beg anymore. As soon as the belt was undone, his cock was already peeking out of the waist of his jeans. As I bent and licked the bead of precum off the head of his cock, he sucked in a breath. Unzipping his pants, I held the weight of him in my hand and stroked his length, teasing the head every once in a while with my mouth. It wasn't long before he came, letting go of months of pent-up frustration.

Chapter Forty

Hunter returned to work the following Monday. He had a full day of appointments, but he had blocked out from noon until two for some personal time. I was going to the mall to buy some baby clothes, and he was going to come have some lunch and spend some time helping me pick things out. We had found out we were going to have a baby girl, which I think scared the shit out of him more than he cared to admit. Even though he claimed that it didn't matter, I knew he had been secretly praying for a boy. Seemed that girls ran in the Malone family. I pulled the car into the mall parking lot and finally found a spot. I sent Hunter a quick text, letting him know I was at the mall and would be inside.

I was on my way to the Baby Boutique when I heard my name. I stopped, turning in time to see Jason walking toward me. I was surprised he didn't stop dead in his tracks from the look I had given. Instead, he just kept approaching. I could feel the panic rising in me, but then I remembered the words Hunter had told me. I no longer had anything to fear; whatever Jason spewed at me would just be words.

"Autumn."

I turned abruptly, making sure that Jason had full view of my very pregnant belly.

"What do you want, Jason?" He basically stopped in his tracks. "Wow, you're um...you're um..."

"*Pregnant* is the word, Jason. Yes, I'm pregnant."

"But..."

"But what?" I glared at him.

He didn't know what to say as his eyes met mine. But I certainly wasn't going to back down from him either.

"I know everything, Jason. I know the reason you left me was because you were having an affair with Anna. How dare you! You put the blame on me for all those years, making me think I was completely worthless and would never be wanted by anyone. You're sick."

I rubbed my hand over my belly as I felt the baby shift. The look on his face said it all. It was true, and for once, he had no rebuttal.

"You have anything to say for yourself?"

"I'll sue them."

"You'll sue who?"

"Your boyfriend and his precious brothers. That bastard betrayed my trust."

"Save your money, Jason. It wasn't my boyfriend or his brothers. My brother-in-law told me. He saw you over the years throughout the city with various women all while you were dating me and while we were married. You're a pig,

Jason, and you'll get exactly what you deserve. Now, leave me be."

"Autumn! Hi, it's been so long." I turned to see Anna rushing over to me, a grin on her face. "I saw you a few months ago at the restaurant. I was going to come over and say hi, but you were gone before I had the chance. How have you been?"

I stiffened when she placed a hand on my shoulder.

Jason wasn't budging. He just stood glaring at me while Anna was all smiles. Did they honestly think I was this stupid? I was suddenly feeling very cornered and confused when I felt a strong hand grip my shoulder. "Everything okay here, baby?" Hunter leaned in and kissed my cheek. I relaxed almost instantly.

"Don't play it up, Anna. Some friend you turned out to be. You two totally deserve one another. I hope you'll both be very happy together."

Jason and Anna both looked to Hunter and back to me, probably deciding to stay and argue or move on and be done with us both. Luckily for Jason, he took the smarter of the two paths. Taking Anna's hand in his, they made their way away from us.

"Are you okay?" Hunter whispered.

"Honestly, I couldn't be better. Let's go get some stuff and eat lunch." I reached up on my toes, kissing him on the lips, as he wrapped his arm around me, leading me toward the store.

Chapter Forty-One

I was in the office trying to get a bit more work done when Autumn appeared in the doorway with a cup of hot coffee.

"I thought you'd like this."

"That's perfect, babe, thank you."

"I'm going to go lie down now, maybe finish the book I am reading. I'm tired. Will you be working long?"

I glanced at what I needed to get through. Lately, she hated going to bed without me.

"Maybe another hour or so. You go rest and read. I'll be in as soon as I can." She leaned down, kissing me hard. As her tongue found its way into my mouth, I felt my cock stiffen. I was horny as hell. "Baby, I need to concentrate to get this work done."

"I know, just giving you a little preview of what's to

come in the future." She ran her hand down my chest stopping at the bulge in my pants.

I let out a deep groan and playfully swatted her ass as she walked away from me.

Once I had finally calmed myself down, I buried myself back in my work. I had just finished the last bit of paperwork, saving and printing the documents, and was about to shut down my laptop, when I heard Autumn call my name. I took my time at first, just trying to tidy the mess that sat on my desk when she called my name again—this time, a little more frantic. I stopped what I was doing and headed into the bedroom.

"What is it? What do you need?"

"I think it's time."

"Time for what?"

"Hunter, it's time. Get the bag from the closet."

A few hours later, I sat holding this perfect, little, sleeping bundle in my arms. Her little fists were held up by her mouth as she lay in my arms. She was so tiny and so perfect, wrapped in her little pink blanket.

I looked over at Autumn when I was able to finally peel my eyes off her. She was resting, her eyes closed as she lay against the pillow. We knew the whole family was out in the waiting area, ready and waiting to meet the newest addition to the family, but we had asked the nurse for a few minutes of private time.

"How are you feeling, baby?" I asked her in a hushed tone, not wanting to startle her.

"Tired."

"Do you want to hold her?"

She smiled and nodded her head. As soon as I placed her in her arms, Autumn started to cry. "I can't believe she is here and she's mine."

Sitting down on the edge of the bed beside her, I placed my arm around her. She rested her head into me as we both sat and looked down in awe at our little baby girl.

The nurse walked in to check and make sure everything was okay. "You know, you two have a room full of family members that are driving me crazy. They are waiting to meet this little angel."

"We know," Autumn said, smiling up at her. "Just a few more minutes."

"Five more minutes and I'm letting them in. Your sister is rather persistent." She winked at me, pressed a couple buttons on Autumn's IV, and left the room.

We took those few minutes to just be a little family, relishing in the blessing that had been given to us.

Chapter Forty-Two

Autumn – Eight Weeks Later

Evelyn pulled the car into the driveway and put it in park. "Thank you so much for coming and spending the day with me. I've missed you."

I smiled. I had missed my sister, and I truthfully needed the break. "Thank you for making it so enjoyable. It's been an adjustment with Kaylee."

"I'm sure. Are you coming in? Surely you can stay for another half hour for a coffee."

"Actually, I should be going. I'm sure Hunter is climbing the walls with Kaylee by now."

"He's a big boy. I'm sure he can handle her."

Something was going on. Evelyn was only persistent like this when she was hiding something. I squinted my eyes at her. "What's going on, Evelyn?"

"Nothing. I just want to have a coffee with you before you run away again."

"No, I lived with you long enough to know that something is going on. You're being weird."

Ignoring me, she reached into the back of the car, grabbed my purse along with the few bags I had sitting back there, and ran into the house. Rolling my eyes and laughing to myself, I went after her. My jaw dropped as I walked through the door and was greeted by Hunter. He stood in the foyer wearing my favorite black suit, and in his hands he held a dozen deep-red roses. I glanced from Evelyn to Derek, who was holding Kaylee in his arms.

"What's going on?" I glanced at all of them in turn.

"Autumn, we're going on a date tonight. Evelyn and Derek are going to look after Kaylee."

"No, they're not. Besides, I can't go on a date; I have nothing here to wear."

"But you do, my dear. Upstairs in your old room is a dress that I picked out for you to wear tonight."

They all stood, grinning at me. "We'll be fine with Kaylee. It's not a big deal. She can't be that difficult to look after," Evelyn said, forcing me up the stairs. "Now let's get you ready for your date."

Thirty minutes later, I descended the stairs wearing a form-fitting white V-neck dress. As soon as Hunter laid his eyes on me, I knew where I would end up before this night was over. The desire and want that was radiating from them sent a shiver down my back. He took me in his arms at the bottom of the stairs, placing a firm, telling kiss on my lips. "Ready?" His eyes searched mine for my answer before kissing me again.

I kissed Kaylee as we walked out the door, spouting instructions to both Derek and Evelyn. "I already went over everything with them. They have everything they need, so there is no need to worry," Hunter said as he wrapped his arm securely around my body.

As soon as we were seated in the car, I turned to Hunter. "So, how did you get here, and where are we going?" I could barely contain my excitement.

"Derek came and picked us up. Where are we going? That is a surprise." He winked at me and placed his hand on my upper thigh. "But I can promise you that you are going to love it."

We drove for about a half hour, when Hunter pulled into the parking lot of The Whisperwind Inn. I looked at him and smiled.

"So, a while ago, traffic held me up from a date that would have led me to the most amazing woman I have ever met. Instead, I had to travel over a thousand miles to get to her, so tonight I thought it might be fun to relive the date that never was."

Taking my hand, we headed into the restaurant where we were immediately taken to the back. All the tables surrounding us were empty. "I reserved the same table that I reserved that night, but I also asked that they keep the back half of the restaurant empty."

"You reserved the whole back of the restaurant?" I whispered.

"I did. The owner is a client of mine, so he's doing me a favor."

He nodded as the hostess stopped at the table. A bottle of my favorite wine sat chilling on the table. As we took our seats, a waitress poured us each a glass of wine. After we had both perused the menu and made our choices, Hunter reached across and grabbed hold of my hand. "My beautiful girl."

Soft music played in the background as Hunter watched me take a sip of my wine. We sat staring at one another. I loved looking into his eyes; so many unsaid things were flowing between us.

"Do you remember this song?" I was so lost in his eyes that I hadn't even heard the music playing. I listened to the melody, remembering the song so vividly, I could almost feel the breeze blowing off the ocean. "Care to dance with me?"

Taking his hand, he walked me out into the middle of the room and held me while we danced to the same song that we had danced to in Jamaica that night on the beach, where he had kissed me under the stars. I rested my head on his chest, getting lost in his arms.

When the song ended, I went to walk back to the table when I felt a slight tug on my hand. I turned. Hunter was down on one knee, holding out a small black box, my hand in his other. My breath hitched.

"You already know I've completely fallen for you. You're my first thought in the morning and my last thought before I fall asleep, and you consume almost every one of my thoughts in between. You've given me the most perfect, precious gift I could have ever asked for, and nothing in my life has ever meant so much to me as the pair of you. I broke my own rules when it came to you, and I felt my world flip the first time I laid eyes on you. Only once in a lifetime will you meet that person who will change everything, and you did, you did change everything. I'm so glad that someone threw you away, so I had the chance to pick you up and love you. I choose you. Spend the rest of your life with me."

As I looked at Hunter through teary eyes, I saw tears in his own eyes. I knew at that moment that without a doubt there was nothing that he wouldn't do for us. How could I say anything but yes? "Yes, Hunter, yes."

He stood, grabbing hold of me and pulling me into him. Taking the ring from the box, he slowly slipped it on my finger, pressing his lips to mine.

We had just returned home from picking up Kaylee. It was late, and thankfully she slept almost all the way home. Hunter had taken her in to put her to bed while I got changed. It had been an amazing evening, and it was now time to relax. I walked out into the kitchen in my silk bathrobe and turned the kettle on. I flipped the radio on and let the music dance through the air. I had just placed my mug on the counter in order to grab a mug for Hunter when I felt strong hands grip my hips.

"There you are." His voice was deep with passion, as he placed a kiss on the back of my neck, sending waves of heat through my body. He spun me around and pulled me firmly into his hard chest.

He was still semi-dressed. His suit jacket had been flung over the half wall in the entryway. His white dress shirt hung open exposing his chiseled chest and abs, and his suit pants hung low enough to expose my favorite part of him, the "v."

My hands found their way inside his shirt. I ran my hands down his bulky chest, over his tight abs, stopping and resting on the waistband of his pants.

Pushing me against the counter, he kissed me hard, sucking my bottom lip, his tongue finding its way into my mouth. He trailed a string of kisses to my ear, sucking my earlobe into his mouth. "Kaylee is sound asleep," he whispered into my ear, his breath causing me to giggle.

"She is?" My fingers skirted along the waist of his pants.

His hands traveled down to my ass, which he firmly gripped, lifting me up and setting me on the counter. "You're playing with fire, beautiful," he growled as my fingers grazed against his hot skin. I slid my hand down the front of his pants and felt him, hard and ready for me.

"You sure she is asleep?" I teased as I continued to rub him, sucking on his bottom lip.

"Sound asleep," he moaned as he slowly undid the tie to my robe exposing me to him. He kissed the tops of my breasts and ran his hands over my nipples, making them hard. "I'd love a little private time with you, but you have to keep quiet so we don't wake her up."

"I don't know if I can. You know what you do to me."

He went to push me back on the counter, but I pushed his hands away and sat up. "Not here. Let's go to the bedroom."

"No, baby, right here."

He pushed himself between my legs, gently cupping my breasts in his hands, rubbing his thumbs over my sensitive nipples.

He laid me back on the breakfast island and started kissing the insides of my thighs, the stubble on his cheeks tickling me. I was already quivering in anticipation as he inched his way toward my center. "Lace panties... You know what happens when you wear lace panties," he growled, quickly ripping them off me.

He ran his finger through my wet folds, making me quiver, as he watched my expression. He started circling my clit with his thumb, kissing the insides of my thighs again. He placed my legs over his shoulders and pulled me to the edge of the island. "Are you ready, baby? Cause I'm going to devour you."

I let out a loud giggle, which quickly turned into a deep inhale, as his mouth found my clit. He was alternating between sucking and licking; it wasn't long before I was screaming his name.

As I came down from my orgasm, Hunter picked me up and carried me into the bedroom, throwing me onto the bed. He quickly shed his shirt and suit pants and crawled in between my legs.

"Now this time, you have to be quiet." He laughed while showering me in light kisses all over my body.

I loved the look on his face as he ran himself through my wetness, teasing my already sensitive clit with the head of his cock and making me squirm. "Tell me you want it."

I had barely gotten the words out of my mouth; the next thing I knew, he was fully seated in me.

Epilogue

HUNTER – FOURTEEN MONTHS LATER

"Here's your coffee." I sat down beside her. "Flight's been delayed again." I sighed, we were headed to Bora Bora for ten days, and we were both anxious to get going. To be honest, I was probably more afraid that she would change her mind before the plane got a chance to take off.

"Okay, well, let me give Evelyn a call and make sure everything is okay with Kaylee." I handed her my cell phone and watched as she walked to a quieter area—if there was such a thing—to call her sister.

I turned to Carter and Hope. "Will it always be this hard to get her to leave her?"

"Hunter, she is doing remarkable considering this is your first child. Kaylee is just a little over the age of one. Don't be hard on her. I didn't leave the girls for a couple years after they were both born," Hope answered.

"It's true, I didn't have a vacation alone with my wife for over six years, Hunter. I wasn't even allowed to talk dirty to her in our own bedroom while fucking her for fear the girls heard."

Hope slapped Carter on the arm and started to laugh. "You're such a pig." We all laughed, Carter and I a little harder than Hope.

"Yeah, but you love it." He winked at her and put his arm around her.

"Did you finalize all the plans, Hope?"

"I did. Everything is set for the second day we are there. You have no worries; my capable little hands have been busy over the last month. I have a live video feed set for Evelyn, Derek, and Kaylee to watch as well, along with Bryce and Chase. Autumn still has no clue?" Hope and Carter looked over toward her and smiled at me, waiting for my answer.

"None."

"She's on her way back over," Carter spoke up, clearing his throat.

Autumn sat down, looking a little stressed, and handed me my phone. "Everything okay?"

"Evelyn sounds stressed." She bit her bottom lip. "I don't know if we should go, Hunter. Maybe this is a bad idea."

I looked at Carter and Hope. Hope nodded at me and grabbed Carter's hand. "Honey, let's go through the duty free and see if we can find something for the girls." At Hope's hint, Carter got up and winked at Autumn.

Once they were out of earshot, I turned to her, taking both of her hands in mine. "Baby, Kaylee will be fine. She loves staying with them. Your sister can handle it."

"I know, I've just never left her with them for longer than a night."

"She'll be fine. I promise you. We can email and check in from the resort every day if we need to."

"I don't know. What if she gets sick?"

"You've arranged everything with the doctor; it'll be okay. Plus, if Evelyn has kept Derek alive this long, there's hope for Kaylee." I grinned as I placed a kiss on her cheek.

Autumn relaxed herself into me and entwined her hand in mine. We'd been sitting there about a half hour when Hope and Carter finally came back to join us. "Everything good?" Hope asked.

"Just had a moment of panic, all is good." She smiled.

"Flight T878 to Bora Bora, departing Gate B54 is set to board."

"That's us!" Hope said, grinning.

Grabbing our bags, we slowly made our way over to the gate and got in line. All this planning for our first vacation had finally come to an end, most of it kept secret from Autumn, because little did she know that by the time we returned to this very airport, we would be Mr. & Mrs. Hunter Malone.

In Your Arms

In Your Arms

Copyright © 2018 by S.L. Sterling

ISBN: 978-1-7751087-9-5

Editor: Erica Russikoff of Erica Edits; www.ericaedits.com

Cover Design: Thunderstruck Cover Designs

Prologue

HOPE — FOUR WEEKS EARLIER

I could hear the girls playing down the hall while waiting for Carter to come home. The life we had built with one another had been nothing short of amazing, but lately our relationship was feeling strained. He had been secretive about everything including work, and work was one thing he never held back from me. I had always enjoyed hearing what he and his brothers were working on—minus the names of course; client confidentiality wouldn't allow him to break that. It wasn't just being secretive, though. We had spent the better part of the last two months arguing over EVERY-THING, which wasn't normal for either of us. I could count on one hand the amount of times we had argued over the years.

"Mom…" Kendall screamed, banging on the door and pulling me out of the memory of last night's argument.

"Mackenzie wants to pack now to go to Grandpa's. She has her suitcase out."

I sucked in a breath, staring at myself in the mirror. "Kendall, tell your sister I will talk to her in a few minutes. Read her a book until I get there."

"Okay, Mommy." I listened for her little feet to go off running down the hall. I let out another breath and brushed the hair from my face.

"Please please please, don't let this be happening," I whispered to myself as I glanced at my watch. We had gone over this topic a few times over the last year; our family was complete and there was no need for any more babies.

A sick feeling came over me as I waited. *What would I tell him? How would I tell him?* I glanced at my watch again; it was time. "Hope, I'm home!" I heard Carter's voice from the hallway.

I closed my eyes. He shouted my name again and then he started yelling at the girls for whatever mess they had gotten into. I looked down at the little white stick that sat on the counter, and staring back at me were two dark, perfect little pink lines.

CARTER

I sat behind my desk Wednesday night, typing away on my keyboard. It was after eleven, the house was quiet, Hope and the girls had already gone to bed, and I sat waiting for an update from Hunter on the case he was working on. I was leaving next week for a business trip, so I wanted to know exactly where things stood with his case. With both of us away and out of the office, that meant Bryce and Chase had control, and neither of us felt quite comfortable with that yet.

I sent off an email to confirm my reservation at the hotel I would be staying at next week and dove back into the paperwork that my paralegal had done. There were a few things she would need to change before Monday's meeting, so I finished noting my changes for her, so she could work on it tomorrow.

My phone vibrated against the desktop, taking my attention away from what I was reading. Grabbing it I answered the call.

"Hey, man, it's done, it's over. He's going to prison."

"Wow. I'm surprised that it hasn't hit the news yet. Thanks for the update. When do you figure you'll be back?"

"In a couple weeks. There are a few loose ends that need to be wrapped up here, and then once those are done, the remainder should be able to be done at the office."

"Sounds good. I leave on Monday, so I'll tell Anna to have everything wait for your approval business-wise until you are back."

"Sure thing. Have you mentioned anything to Hope about this case?"

I looked toward my office door and picked up my glass of Scotch from the desk, swirling the liquid around. "No, not yet."

"I see." He went quiet. I should have told her. I mean, after all, it was her ex-boyfriend whom our firm was representing. "What else is going on?" Hunter asked, pulling me back to the conversation.

I swallowed hard. "I received a message from Felice the other day."

"Wow, that's a blast from the past. How is she?"

"Good, she and Mike need some legal advice and asked that I stop in while I'm in town next week. Mike had been in touch with me last year; they are going to adopt a child and just want me to look over things."

"Is Hope okay with that?"

I went quiet, taking a sip of Scotch. "I'm not exactly sure."

"You haven't told her?"

"Not exactly. I don't want to spend our ten-year anniversary in a fight."

"Carter, you need to tell her—you do know that—before you go."

"I know, I just don't want her to worry."

The line went silent. I talked to my brother about lots of things, but never my relationship or any of the troubles we were having; however, the truth was I had to talk to someone. I was afraid that both issues may just be the push our relationship needed to end it all.

"Is everything okay between you two?" Hunter questioned.

I twirled my pen between my fingers. After he had confided in me last year about things with Autumn, I knew without a doubt he would listen. I drew in a deep breath. "I'm not sure. Things been different lately. I feel like I am losing her."

"What do you mean?"

"It's almost like we don't know each other anymore. She's short with me, barely looks at me, and we have been arguing a lot."

"I think you guys just need some time alone. This weekend away is going to be good for both of you. You need to find your way back to each other. I've noticed a difference since Kaylee was born, I won't lie. But, man, if things aren't feeling right between you, don't let something so innocent and work related get between you. Tell her the truth about what has been going on. Let her know you are seeing Felice and Mike while you are away. She may not like it, but at least your conscience is clean."

My younger brother seemed to finally have his shit all together. I had aided him in getting there, maybe I should listen to him now. Maybe it was my turn. "I'll tell her. Listen, I got to go and get into bed. Early morning."

"No problem, I have to call Autumn anyway. I promised I would when I finished tonight. I'll be in touch tomorrow. Oh and if she isn't too receptive to what you have to tell her, you do know that you have a place on my couch, right?" he chuckled.

I let out a small laugh. "Sounds good, thanks. Talk to you soon."

"Yep, oh and Carter?"

"Yeah?"

"For fuck's sake, shut the damn computer off and go make love to your wife."

He was gone after that. I hung up the phone and sat back against my chair, laughing at what he had just said. That was my brother, always about the pussy. I looked down to my wedding picture that had sat on my desk for the past ten years. Hope was so beautiful that day, and still to this day, there was no doubt in my mind that I was in love with her. Maybe Hunter was right—we just needed to take the time and find one another again.

I set my phone down and went to get up when it vibrated again. Felice's name flashed across the screen: "Let me know when you arrive. Dinner might be a good idea, just to get um reacquainted."

I frowned. I didn't need dinner to look over fucking adoption documents. I deleted the message without responding and left my office. As I walked down the hall I stopped and checked on both the girls, covering both, and then made my way down to our bedroom.

The bedside light was still on, casting a warm glow over the room; the TV was playing a repeat of *Friends*. Hope was on her side, facing away from me, uncovered. I shut the television off and looked over at Hope. She lay there, her little white tank top short enough to show off her perfect ass in my favorite black thong. I felt my cock stiffen at the sight as I stripped out of my shirt and pants. I crawled in and inched my way up behind her, placing a single kiss on her shoulder. I ran my hand over her hip and down her soft, silky leg.

"I tried to wait up," she murmured in the sleepiest, sexiest voice I had heard in a while.

My fingers traveled back up her leg, over her thigh, and hooked in under the edge of her panties. Pulling them down, I placed a kiss on her hip. I was throbbing, I was so hard, and I was growing harder with each second that passed. It had been almost five weeks since I felt myself buried deep in her, her legs wrapped around me, moaning as I pounded into her. My fingers dug into her skin as I gripped her hip, pulling her closer to me. She rolled over onto her back, running her fingers through my hair and shattered any hopes that I had of repeating that night. "Not tonight, baby. It's late and I have to be up early to take Mackenzie for her dance photographs."

She placed a soft kiss on my cheek and rolled back over, pulling the blankets over her body. I lay back against my pillow, Hunter's words running through my mind. I wanted to make love to her, but every single time I had tried over the past four weeks, I had gotten shot down. I was seriously starting to doubt my confidence. She never turned me away this often. I lay there, letting her take her beautiful body and eyes away from me, and I tried to rid my mind of those dirty thoughts.

Chapter Two

HOPE

I had been planning our ten-year anniversary weekend for months, and it was finally here. We were headed to Briar's Vineyard for dinner, a new upscale restaurant and winery that only served the finest foods. Then we were off to spend two nights at Everland Hotel and Spa, the newest hotel in King's Cove Harbour. This weekend needed to be special; I needed it to be special. I planned to tell Carter about the baby, and I prayed he would be happy and that it wouldn't ruin our weekend, but I feared it would. I stood at the bottom of the stairs, glancing at my watch. It was already three. Dad would be here any minute to pick up the girls.

"Let's go, girls. Grandpa will be here soon." Just as the words left my lips, I turned to see my father's car pull into the driveway.

I pulled their little suitcases over to the door and opened it just before Dad rang the bell. "Hello there, how's my girl?" Dad said, pulling me in for a hug.

"Good, Dad. Sorry, I'm trying to get those granddaughters of yours ready." I wrapped my arms around him, taking in the hug he gave, which was always so warm. There was something about a hug from your father when things were bothering you that could always calm your soul, and mine needed calming.

"It's okay, I don't mind visiting with my girl for a bit." He stepped inside and removed his shoes, and together we walked into the kitchen. I grabbed the juice from the fridge and poured us both a glass as my father took a seat at the breakfast bar.

"Mom! Mom! Is it okay if we take a bunch of our dolls to Grandpa's?"

I shook my head at my dad and smiled. "Girls, we have gone over this already—coloring books, crayons, and one stuffy each, along with one bedtime story. Now Grandpa is here, and you do have a bit of a way to travel, so you better go and get your things ready."

"Okay." They both walked away in a pout. "I told you she would say no," Mackenzie whimpered.

I looked to my Dad and laughed. "Sorry, I swear they should be ready. They have been planning this overnight trip as soon as they found out they were going. I think they've had everything packed three or four times by now."

"No need to apologize. I remember a little girl who was the exact same way when she was their age."

I smiled and took a drink. "How's Mom?"

"Good, she is home baking, getting ready for the weekend. Maybe I'll finally get that pie I have been asking for."

"Maybe." I smiled. "Although you do know you shouldn't be eating that stuff with your heart the way it is. Mom told me about your last checkup."

My father waved a hand in front of his face, dismissing my comment, and changed the subject. "How is Carter?" Dad asked, his face getting serious.

"Good. He isn't home from work yet. He called this morning, said he might be a little late tonight; there was something going on that he needed to finish," I said, looking down at my hands, the simple gold band catching my eye.

"He should be working late with all that has gone on."

I frowned. I had no idea what he was speaking of. "Carter always works late, Dad. It's our anniversary, though. I would have figured he could have let work go for a bit this weekend."

"He hasn't mentioned anything to you?"

"About work? Nothing lately."

"So, you don't know what is going on?"

I shook my head, a funny feeling rising into the pit of my stomach. "Dad, you're scaring me."

"Trent King is going to prison. It has been all over the news today." I didn't know what to say, I hadn't heard or thought about Trent in almost thirteen years. "His father is probably rolling over in his grave. I'm so glad you had your senses about you and decided to marry Carter."

"That wasn't always the case, if you remember correctly, so don't tell me it was a good thing I came to my senses. You used to hate Carter, Daddy. Besides, what does Trent going to prison have to do with Carter?" I got up off the stool and put my empty glass in the dishwasher.

"Well, it's his firm that is representing him. I believe Hunter has the case."

I was just about to ask Dad more about what he had heard when the girls came running into the kitchen carrying their little backpacks.

"We're ready, Grandpa," they both sang in unison.

"All right then, let's get you in the car," he said, picking up Mackenzie and taking Kendall by the hand.

"Okay, girls, you be good for Grandpa and Grandma. We'll see you Monday morning."

"I want to say goodbye to Daddy," Kendall started crying.

"Well, Daddy isn't home yet." As I put her coat on, she started screaming at the top of her lungs and kicking her feet, demanding to see her father. One thing was for sure—she had her father's temper.

"Daddy wants to say goodbye to you too, Kendall." I heard Carter's deep voice behind me. "You think you were going to go away for the weekend and Daddy wasn't going to be here in time to say goodbye?" I turned to see Carter standing in the doorway, looking as handsome as ever.

Kendall and Mackenzie both ran to Carter, and he swooped down and wrapped his arms around them both. "All right, you girls be good for Grandpa and Grandma, and Mom and I will see you Monday." He kissed them both and stood to shake my Dad's hand. "Brian, how are you doing?"

"Good, Carter. Good to see you. Have fun this weekend, kids," Dad said and turned, taking both girls by the hands.

We watched him walk both the girls to the car and get them situated.

"You all packed and ready to go?" he whispered into my ear as he wrapped his arms around me from behind.

"I am. Figured you might like to shower first, but I've confirmed our reservations."

"All right, baby. Give me half an hour."

I was sitting in the living room, dressed, a glass of sparkling grape juice in my hand, waiting for Carter to get out of the shower. I shut the TV off, slowly wandered into his office, and sat down at his desk. It was a room I very rarely wandered into anymore, except to dust and vacuum. When we were first married, I couldn't keep count of how many nights I had found myself on top of this desk, my legs over his shoulders, his face buried in my center. I smiled at the memories as I ran my hand along the smooth, cold desktop. His wallet and cell phone sat in a neat little pile just above his keyboard and beside that his keys.

I flipped the screen of the computer on and went straight to MSN. My curiosity had gotten the best of me and I needed to see if what my dad had said was true. As soon as the page loaded, it was the first article I saw. "CEO of King Enterprises found Guilty for Embezzlement" was right there in black and white. It was true; Trent was going to prison.

I clicked further through the article. Hunter Malone, one of the senior partners of Malone Law—the lawyer hired by King Enterprises—declined an interview. No wonder Carter hadn't mentioned anything to me. I sat in deep thought, staring at the words on the computer screen, until I heard the shower shut off. He had been so argumentative and distracted lately, working so late into the night, I felt like I barely saw him. Now I knew why: Trent King. Carter had always done what he could to protect me from things, and I could understand his not wanting to tell me about Trent. I shut the screen off and went to stand up when Carter's cell phone screen lit up. I hadn't meant to look and wished I hadn't, but when the name flashed across the screen, I couldn't help myself.

FELICE: RESERVATIONS BOOKED AT SILVER MEADOWS RESTAURANT. LOOKING FORWARD TO SEEING YOU.

I frowned, my eyes burning while trying to fight back tears from my eyes. Why was Felice messaging him dinner reservations? As far as I knew, they hadn't spoken in years. A funny feeling hit my stomach, thinking about Carter's business trip next week to meet with clients over a custody battle. I tried to take a deep breath. Felice was a damn nightmare, to say the least—a name from his past, our past, and a name I had never cared to hear again in my life.

I drank down the remainder of my sparkling grape juice, wishing now I could have a glass of wine. I slowly ran my hand over my flat stomach. I had been trying to find the perfect moment to tell him the news, but lately there didn't seem to be a right time, and possibly tonight or this weekend wasn't the right time either. However, I felt more disturbed than ever now after seeing Felice's name on his phone. Perhaps she had finally won him, and I was the fool all along. Maybe I had finally lost him to her. I got up from his chair, walked to the door, and shut the lights off in his office, returning to the living room to wait for him.

Chapter Three

HOPE

I was quiet all the way to the hotel. I wanted so badly to bring up the message I had seen on his phone; however, I also didn't want to spend the night or the weekend arguing. "Everything okay, love?" he asked as he pulled the car into the parking lot.

"Yes, of course, why?" I smiled, swallowing hard.

"You just seem quiet, but as long as you're sure." He reached over and grabbed my hand, taking mine into his.

"Dad told me about Trent. Is that the reason you have been so quiet about work?"

"Yes, it's been tough. Since we weren't sure what was going to happen, I didn't think there was any point to mention it. Hunter has been working like crazy on this case. He did what he could, but the evidence doesn't lie. Are you okay?"

"Of course, it's just you normally share things with me, so I was surprised you didn't tell me."

"I didn't want you to worry. It certainly wasn't on purpose, Hope. This was a big case."

He ran his thumb over the back of my hand. "Let's get settled, shall we?"

We checked in and then we made our way to our room. Carter wheeled the suitcase in and set it up on the luggage rack. I followed behind him. Immediately, my eyes went straight to a large vase of red roses on the desk. I noticed a small envelope tucked between the roses, and a bottle of wine sat beside them in a chiller.

I walked over to the desk and stuck my face into the roses, taking a deep breath, and then I tugged at the little envelope and opened it.

"Congratulations on ten years. Love, Mackenzie, Kendall, Grandma, and Grandpa."

I let out a small laugh. "The girls sent us flowers," I said, looking over to where Carter was standing. Instead of paying attention to me, his face was buried in his phone as he typed back a response to whomever had contacted him, a look of annoyance and frustration on his face.

"Great," he grumbled. I knew that tone too well; he had barely heard a word I had said.

"What time is dinner?" he asked again, furiously typing away.

"Seven. We have a couple hours," I said. Walking over to him, I reached up, my hands shaking, and opened the top two buttons on his dress shirt, slowly making my way for the third as he continued typing away. "We could always use that time to...you know...spend a little private time together." My fingers danced in circles across his chest before running down the front of his shirt and gripping his cock through his dress pants.

He stopped, turning his attention away from his phone to my eyes. He smiled down at me. "I could probably be persuaded to release some tension." His large hand took my face and held it gently. Leaning down, he met my lips. His kiss felt like fire, and as his tongue swept through my mouth, I started to get that familiar ache in between my legs. As it built and as his hands started to travel my body, we were interrupted once again by his phone pinging numerous times in a row. He pulled away, my lips feeling a void that I wasn't quite ready to feel just yet. "Give me a minute."

As he read the messages on his phone, his brows drew together in an agonized expression. His expression said it all. "You have to respond, don't you?"

"I do. It's a client." His eyes met mine despairingly. I wanted to say no, put it away, spend time with me, but the look in his eyes told me it was important.

I held back tears and gave him a weak smile instead. "Go ahead."

I expected him to sit down at the desk and take the call that was going to come in, but instead, he took his phone and headed out the hotel room door, leaving me in the room, alone.

I busied myself while waiting for him to return by starting to unpack our bags. Once I had everything hung up, I sat down on the bed, arranged the pillows behind my head, and started thumbing through a magazine that I had found on the desk. Half an hour later the door to our room opened and Carter came in.

"That didn't take too long. We should get ready and head out to the restaurant," I said, laying the magazine beside me. When he didn't say anything, I looked up at him. He was just standing in the doorway looking at me. "What is it? What's wrong?"

He shook his head regretfully. "Honey, I don't know how to tell you this. The clients that I am seeing in New York...they need me to come now."

The smile that had been on my face when he had come back had slowly diminished. "But this weekend..."

"I know. I know. It's not what I want either, but unfortunately, I must go. There have been some new developments in their custody battle, and well, they are counting on me to help them." He walked over and placed his hands on my shoulders, trying to pull me into him.

I didn't know what to say, so it was best I said nothing at all, and I didn't want to cry either, so I pulled out of his touch and started packing things up. As I went to walk past Carter to get to the suitcase, he reached for me, grabbing me by the arm. Again, I shook out of his hold and continued grabbing the few things I had unpacked. "It's best if we just get going, Carter. I don't want you to be traveling too late."

Chapter Four

HOPE

I sat in the car, watching the houses go by as we drove home. Once it had started to rain, I kept my mind focused on the droning hum of the windshield wipers. It kept me from crying and focusing on disappointment. We hadn't said anything to one another since we had left the hotel. He was visibly upset; he had never missed our anniversary weekend, no matter what he had been working on, so I knew this night was just as important to him as it was to me. However, this specific anniversary felt a little more important to me.

I continued looking out the window while Carter was on the phone with his secretary and assistant. "Text me the flight information and see if you can get the hotel to extend my reservation, even if I have to switch the room I have, oh and tell Alicia to have my files ready before she leaves the office tonight. I'll swing by in an hour or so to pick them up on my way to the airport."

He ended the call just as we pulled into the driveway. I didn't wait; I got out of the car and headed toward the door. Once we were inside, Carter dropped his phone and keys by the door and carried our suitcase up the stairs to the bedroom. I followed quietly. "Why don't you come with me? I'll call Alicia and have her purchase another ticket. Call your mom and dad and ask them to keep the girls for a few days extra. We'll go into New York, see a show, have dinner. During the day you can shop, take in some sights, and relax at the spa while I am working."

"No, it's okay. You're going to be busy. The last thing you will need is me there in the way." I grabbed my T-shirt and sweatpants off the end of the bed and took them into the bathroom to get changed.

"Why would you say something like that? You are exactly what I need." Carter stopped undressing and looked at me.

"Don't worry about it, Carter. It's fine." I walked toward the bedroom door, and without looking back, I mumbled, "I'll go down and make you something to eat before you leave. Don't be too long or you will miss your flight."

When I hit the bottom of the stairs, Carter's phone was going off like crazy. I picked it up and swiped the screen to see Felice's name again—this time it wasn't just text messages; there were two missed calls from her as well. I felt a rush of saliva to my mouth and threw his phone down. I didn't want to know what they said. I had never wanted to see her name plastered over his phone screen ever again after the summer we had gotten back together, and I certainly didn't want him to meet with her for any reason. She was the only reason that we had never seen Mike again after their wedding.

I stormed my way to the kitchen, slapped together a sandwich, and went to the living room to lie down and wait for him to come down. As I lay there, I listened to the familiar sound of his footsteps above me, and my thoughts went to the unborn child I was carrying—our unborn child. I still didn't know how to tell him. We had decided that two was enough. He was so busy with the firm, and in the next few years, he wanted to pull back the reins and travel more. Now with this business trip and seeing her name splashed across his phone, along with the messages from earlier, I was doubting our relationship and his reasons for not wanting any more babies. He had been so withdrawn lately.

Tears were streaming down my face as I watched him carry his suitcase, briefcase, and suit bag to the door. "Princess, you sure you don't want to come with me? I'm sure your parents would jump at the chance to watch the girls a little bit longer. Or even Autumn and Hunter. Let me call Alicia." He reached for his phone.

"It's fine, Carter, please," I said, wiping the tears from my face. I wanted to pretend that I was fine, but my hormones had gotten the best of me, and honestly, I was crushed.

"It's not fine, look at you." He reached out, placed his hand on my waist, and pulled me against his strong chest. "Aside from me having to leave and ruin this weekend, what has gotten you so upset? This isn't like you."

I shrugged. Instead of telling him the truth, I mumbled,

"I was just really looking forward to some private time with you. I miss you."

"Then come with me." He smiled, pressing his forehead to mine. "Don't make me beg."

Kissing the tip of his nose, I pulled away from the comfort of his arms and together we walked into the kitchen. "Just come eat, you're going to be late." I placed the sandwich I had made for him in front of him and poured him a glass of milk. I sat beside him while he ate.

Soon we stood together at the front door, and as he stepped out of the house, he turned, setting everything down on the stoop, and quickly grabbed me, wrapping his arms around me. "You do know I love you, right? That you and the girls are my world, and I really wish you would get on this plane with me?" I nodded, he was going to make me cry if he kept this up. "I love you, Hope. I'll be back as soon as I can. We will celebrate this anniversary." He leaned in, his lips crashing down onto mine, consuming every inch of my body. I was lost in his kiss, in his arms, but then all that flashed before my closed eyes was her, waiting for him in that damn restaurant. I wrapped my arms tighter around his neck, whispering "I love you" into his ear. He kissed me harder and then he pulled away, leaving me wanting more.

I watched as he climbed into his car and reversed out of the driveway. I did my best to hold it all together as I waved goodbye. I locked the door and went back to the couch, flipping on the television. Soon I found myself in tears; my stomach hurt, my eyes burned, and I wondered at that moment why I had let him go without bringing up my concerns about the texts I had seen. Instead, I was going to torture myself until he came back. Suddenly, my cell phone rang. I grabbed it from the table, my parents' number flashing on the screen. I sucked in a deep breath and answered. "Hello?"

"Mommy!" I heard the girls shout. "Happy Anniversary!"

"Thank you, my loves. Why aren't you both in bed?" I glanced at the clock; it was almost eight-thirty.

"Grandma made pie, and we had some. We aren't tired." I laughed.

"Are you being good?"

"Yes, Mommy, we called to say good night to you and Daddy." I looked around the room. "Can we say 'night to him?"

"Sorry, girls, Daddy had to run to the store. How about if I wish you a good night from both of us?"

"Okay, Mommy." I knew the girls were disappointed. I could hear it in their little voices, but I would have to do.

"Girls, can you put Grandpa or Grandma on the phone?"

I heard the girls run away laughing and yelling for my Dad. Finally, he picked up. "Hey, Angel."

"Hi, Dad. Listen, if need be, could the girls stay with you for a couple extra days?"

The silence on the phone was deafening. "Hope, is everything all right? You sound funny."

"Everything is fine, Dad. I'm just asking."

"Of course, they can stay anytime, you know that."

"Thanks, Dad. I'll check in with you tomorrow."

"No need. Go and enjoy yourself."

We said our goodbyes, and I hung up the phone. I looked around the room and then down to the ring on my hand. It felt like yesterday that I was in this same position. I'd already lost him three times, and now here I was again. We'd been having troubles; every marriage does, but I never thought in a million years he would give up so easily and run back to her. I took a deep breath and tried my best to calm down. *They were only messages.*

I sat up and dialed his number. I wanted to hear his voice, but it went straight to his voicemail. I thought about leaving him a message but knew he probably wouldn't get it until his plane landed, and I didn't want to do that to him. I got up, shut the TV off, and grabbed my purse, keys, and shoes. Within minutes I was in my car on my way to Autumn and Hunter's. I decided that I would spend the night there and, come morning, I would try to book a flight to go and reclaim what was mine.

Chapter Five

Autumn

I had just finished putting Kaylee to bed and had finally sat down with a hot cup of tea. I let out a deep breath. I was tired and was looking forward to Hunter returning from his business trip. I glanced at the clock—almost ten. I switched the fireplace on and turned the TV on low to watch my favorite show, *The Affair*. I needed something to keep me awake until Hunter called. I needed to hear his voice.

A light knock on the door startled me. We lived in a secure building, and no one had called up. Hunter didn't like me to answer the door this late when I was home alone, but I still felt like I should see who it was; it could have been Sylvia, a little elderly lady down the hall. Getting up from the couch, I peeked out the peephole; Hope was standing there. I unlocked the chain and deadbolt and pulled the door open.

"Autumn, I'm sorry. I know it's late, but I didn't want to be alone, and I had nowhere to go." The tears streamed down her face.

"What happened? Come in. Are you all right? Where is Carter?" I was a little worried. They were supposed to be celebrating their anniversary this weekend.

"Carter had to leave for the airport tonight; he was called away on business. He took me home before he left."

"Oh, hun, come on in. He must have been so upset to have to leave you tonight."

Suddenly she burst into tears. "I think Carter is seeing another woman." As soon as the words had left her mouth, she flew into my arms, her body shaking. I held her, stroking her hair as she cried on my shoulder.

"Hope, honey, I'm sure it's nothing like that. Come in, love, and sit down. I'll get you some tea." I took her coat from her and hung it along with her purse just inside the door. "Now tell me, what's happened?"

"I don't know. Tonight, when my dad came to pick up the girls, he told me about Trent, my ex—he's gone to prison. Carter normally talks to me about work and he never mentioned anything about that case. I mean, sure, Hunter is the one who is working on it."

"Well, maybe he didn't tell you because he didn't want to upset you."

"Trent is old news, and it's not the fact that he didn't tell me about it; he's just been so distant. But it was what I saw while I was in his office reading the article on the internet that's really upset me."

"What did you see?" I asked as I filled the kettle with fresh water.

"Well, Carter received a text message, and I accidentally looked and saw that it was from his ex-girlfriend Felice. She told him she can't wait to see him next week."

"Hope, just because she messaged him, doesn't mean he is cheating on you."

Hope let out a heavy sigh. "No, I agree, but he's been so secretive. We've been fighting a lot, and he never mentioned Felice at all. If you knew her, you would understand, and from the looks of things, she's been messaging him for a while. He has been very withdrawn... I'm just worried that my marriage is over," she said, sobbing into her hands.

"Give me a minute, I'm just going to check on Kaylee. I'll be right back." I turned the kettle on, handed her the box of Kleenex, and went down the hall to Hunter's office.

I picked up Hunter's private line and quickly dialed his number. "Hello, beautiful, I was just about to call you. I can't wait to get home to you tomorrow. I get as hard as a rock just thinking about it."

"I can't wait to see you too." I smiled. "Listen, Hope is here. She is rather upset."

"What do you mean? It's their anniversary; they're supposed to be away together."

"I know. She showed up about ten minutes ago, in tears. She says she's worried their marriage is over."

"What?" I could hear the tension in his voice, and I knew when he was tense, he knew something.

"She says she saw a text on Carter's phone from a Felice. Do you know anything about this person?"

I heard him blow out a breath. Whenever he did that, I knew he for sure knew what was going on. "Fuck me. I told him to tell her," I heard him mumble.

"You told him to tell her what?"

"Felice is his ex-girlfriend, if you could even call her that. She's married now to Mike, the man who used to own the bar we hung out at when we were in school. They are looking to adopt a baby, and they needed a lawyer to look over the paperwork. Mike originally contacted the firm. Since Carter is the family law specialist, the case was handed to him."

"Oh my God. So, it's all a misunderstanding?"

"Yes, but so was most of the issues with their relationship from early on."

"What should I do, Hunter? She's really upset."

"Listen, keep her there. Get her talking about something, and I'll try to get a hold of my brother."

"Okay, I'll do my best," I sighed into the phone. "I can't wait to see you."

"Me too, baby, me too. I'll be there before you know it— probably before you wake up Sunday morning. My flight is scheduled for late tomorrow night. Make sure Kaylee isn't in our bed, and make sure you are naked." I giggled.

"I love you," I whispered into the phone.

"Love you too, beautiful." I hung up the phone and headed back out into the living room. "Is everything okay?" she asked through tears.

"Yes, she's been really fussy today. She was stirring when I went in, but she's now sound asleep. Why don't I make us some popcorn?"

"That would be great. Let me help, I'll get the tea." Hope got up, bringing over my now cold tea to the counter, and together we made tea and popcorn. I got Hope a pair of my pajama pants and one of Hunters T-shirts, and once she was changed, we settled onto the floor of the living room with blankets and pillows and put on HGTV.

"Why don't you tell me the story of how you guys met?" I asked. I needed to get her talking, and if she shared that with me, I hoped maybe she would see how silly she was being.

She looked at me and smiled. "You have all night?" she asked, shoving a couple pieces of popcorn into her mouth.

"Well, Hunter won't be back until early Sunday morning, and I've had nothing but conversations with a two-year-old lately, so yes, I have as much time as it takes." We both started to laugh.

"All right, but don't say I didn't warn you. It started the night things ended between Trent and me...three years after Carter had left for university."

Chapter Six

The movie droned on in the background as Trent's tongue danced over mine. His hands reached up my shirt, his fingers running over my breasts. I could feel his hardened ridge as he ground into me. His lips left mine and he continued kissing down my neck. As soon as his hand reached the button on my jeans, a funny feeling rose in the pit of my stomach.

"Trent, no, please," I cried out, reaching down and placing my hand on his, stopping him from going any further.

He blew out a frustrated breath and raised himself off me, running his free hand through his hair.

"For fuck's sake, Hope. We've been dating for almost three years and our engagement is going to be announced in two weeks. Are you ever going to let me in there? You're tighter than Fort Knox."

I couldn't help it. Something didn't feel right; I wasn't ready. My mother always told me to wait and make sure I was with "the one." I wished she had never instilled that in me; somehow, I felt it would have been easier. "I'm sorry, Trent, it's just your roommates are right down the hall," I whispered.

"Ah, so it would be better if we were in my room. You're afraid of someone catching us?" He stood, adjusted himself, and held out his hand for me to take. He was a good-looking guy, with brown hair, brown eyes, and deeply tanned skin from spending the winter with his parents down south. He was set to take over his father's multibillion-dollar company. Daddy said I would be silly to walk away from Trent, that I would be set for life, but to be honest, I wasn't sure if being with Trent was a life I truly wanted for myself.

I looked at him, unsure of what to say. "It's not that. I would just prefer that my first time, be, well, not in a shared apartment with three other guys."

"Fuck, honestly, what are you so afraid of?"

I was a shy girl; I didn't want anyone to hear us. I looked down to the floor, away from his piercing eyes.

"Seriously, Hope, just shove your face into a damn pillow."

I felt like I could cry. I stood up from the couch, grabbed my purse, and walked over to the door. "Trent, please take me home."

My father originally suggested that I give Trent a chance. Trent's parents, the Kings, were good friends with my parents. After Carter, my ex, had left a message on our answering machine and broken up with me, I had been crushed. To this day, I had never actually heard the message he had left. My father had gotten to the message first and had deleted it before I had gotten home, and Carter had never called or come around again. It wasn't long afterward that my father became tired of seeing me so depressed, and within a couple of weeks, he arranged for me to meet Trent. So, after a few meetings with the Kings and Trent, Trent and I went on our first date. In the beginning, we had fun, and soon we had been dating for a couple of years. It was just in the last year I had started to learn things about Trent that I didn't like. First, Trent was a guy who very rarely, if ever, heard the word no in anything he did, and because of that, he was very controlling.

He sat there looking me in the eye, stunned that I would turn him down.

"Come on, Hope, don't be like that. Just come over here. I promise, I'll be as gentle as I can."

"No, Trent. Please take me home."

He stood up from the couch and whipped the remote across the room. "Take yourself home, Hope. The night's over. I'm done with being teased to the point that I'm at now. We're through, so take your cock-teasing ass home."

"What do you mean 'we're through'?" I questioned.

He turned and glared at me. "I'm tired of trying to get my girlfriend of almost three years to sleep with me. I've been as patient as I can be, but as soon as I go to touch you, you stop me. I can't take it anymore. We are over, done. I can't be married to someone who won't spread their legs for me, Hope. My parents expect grandchildren and I'll be dammed if I don't give them what they want. If I can't with you then, well, I would just have to find someone else, and that is frowned upon in my family. So instead, I am breaking up with you. I want to keep my options open for now. If you change your mind, we will talk." I sat there furious as hell as I watched him get up from the couch and stride down the hall like the cock-swinging asshole he really was. This was the side of Trent King that my parents had never seen.

I looked down at my watch; it was already close to eleven, which meant I would miss my curfew, and I'd already been told if I were late one more time, I would have to find another place to live. To have a curfew at twenty years old was a bit ridiculous, in my opinion, but my parents were very strict, and I still lived under their roof.

I grabbed my jacket from the back of the chair, swung my purse over my shoulder, and left his apartment. Once I was out in the street, I reached into my purse and pulled out my wallet. Only two dollars—that would never get me a cab ride home; I was thirty minutes away. I grabbed my cell and thought of whom I could call. Mom was out of town. The only person left to call was Dad or my friend Carly.

I quickly dialed Carly. On the fifth ring, she picked up. "Hello?" she said, clearing her sleepy voice.

"Carly, it's me. Are you able to come pick me up and take me home? I'm stuck outside of Trent's."

"Really, Hope? You need to get a car. Why can't he drive you home?"

"We're over. We had a fight, Carly, please. I don't want to have to call my dad. He's angry enough with me for not getting into school, and now I'm going to miss my curfew."

I could hear whispering through the phone and knew right away she wasn't alone. I rolled my eyes and then I heard her voice. "Fine. But you owe me."

I hung up the phone and sat down on the steps of

Trent's apartment building. Carly finally pulled up an hour later with Josh in tow. Figures. I had probably interrupted their "awesome sex"—as she put it—and they had to finish before they came to get me. I didn't care, and as long as Dad was in bed when I got home, he probably wouldn't even know I was late. I climbed into the back of her car, and she pulled away from the curb.

My prayers that Dad would be in bed were snuffed out when Carly pulled onto my street. I could see the house from the corner. It was lit up like a Christmas tree, and there were police cars lining the street and in the driveway. "Didn't you call home?" Carly asked.

"Nope. I was hoping he would be in bed."

"Looks like you might be in a little trouble, Hope," Josh said, laughing from the front seat. "Looks like every police officer in the city is in your driveway."

"Yeah thanks, Josh," I whispered. Grabbing my purse and jacket, I climbed out of the back of the car and walked slowly up the front steps. I flinched when I heard my dad screaming from inside the house at whatever poor cop he had called.

I opened the door as quietly as I could and walked toward the kitchen. I stopped just inside the doorway. The room was filled with six officers and my father. My father was barking orders when he took notice of me. "What do you have to say for yourself, young lady?" my father demanded.

All eyes turned and were on me. "I'm sorry."

"You're sorry? You're sorry?" my father chuckled, but the enraged look on his face said it all. He glanced to the men who stood in the kitchen; their notebooks sat open in their hands, pens poised ready to take down notes. "I called Trent an hour ago. He said you had some sort of childish fit and you left. I thought you were dead in a ditch somewhere."

That was just like Trent, lying to make me look bad. No doubt he would now claim that I no longer wanted to see him and that I was the one who broke it off with him. He would never tell his parents or mine the truth. "Daddy, I'm sorry..."

"Men, as you can see, my daughter is alive and well. You may return to your duties." Being a high-powered CEO of one of the largest corporations in the city, he had a lot of pull. I watched as each officer walked from the kitchen, nodding their heads at me. I wanted to scream at them not to leave me alone with him, but I stood there, nodding back, and kept my mouth shut. Once they were gone, I turned toward my father. His angry eyes glared at me.

Did I dare tell him that the "amazing" man he was making me marry had told me to get out and find my own way home at nearly eleven at night, because I wouldn't sleep with him yet, or did I just take the blame? "I'm sorry, Daddy."

"No. There is going to be no more of this. This is the last time, Hope. Your mother and I, we have tried to get through to you so many times. We have introduced you to one of the most prominent young men in the city, who stands to inherit his father's multibillion-dollar corporation."

"Oh, here we go," I mumbled, rolling my eyes.

"You realize that you will be set for life, especially since you don't care to go to school. I have basically handed you the world, Hope. This is how you thank us? I find myself at almost one in the morning with a kitchen full of officers, thinking the worst, and your mother, well, she is beside herself on her retreat. She is supposed to be relaxing and enjoying herself; instead, she's spent the last hour in tears worrying about you. Now go to bed. We will talk about everything in the morning."

"We broke up." Tears came to my eyes, and I ran up the stairs to my room and flopped on my bed. It wasn't long before I heard Dad's solid footsteps stomping up the stairs and stopping right outside of my room.

"What do you mean you broke up?" He threw the door open and stood staring at me.

"Just what I said, Daddy. We broke up. Didn't Trent say anything?"

"No, Hope, he didn't. You realize your engagement announcement is going out in a month, and it will be formally announced at our anniversary party a month after that. You've just got cold feet. So, whatever is going on between the two of you, it best be fixed in that time. Your mother and Mrs. King have all the formal invites announcing your engagement ready, and they have already ordered your wedding invitations. They've rented Wolf-marsh Country Club for the wedding, and the menu has been decided."

When did they do all this, I asked myself. "I didn't ask you to do that. Besides, how can everything be ordered already? There isn't even a set date."

"Yes there is. Together the Kings and your mother and I set the date for exactly six months after the engagement."

My stomach rolled. I didn't want to marry him. I looked around my room, pondering what to do. Did I tell him the truth? Would it even matter? I could feel him staring at me.

"Get your shit figured out, Hope. Life isn't always about getting what you want. It wasn't for me, and it's not going to be for you. You have exactly four weeks." The door slammed shut, and I lay in bed staring up at the ceiling, trying to calm the anger that was growing inside me by the second.

I heard a car door slam outside and got up to look out the window. I saw him across the street. Dark hair, broad shoulders, six feet of pure bulky muscle. The man who had broken my heart, Carter Malone, got into his car and drove away. I had watched him for years from this window, crushed on him, and dreamt of what it would be like in his arms, for most of my teen years. Finally, he asked me out, and we dated throughout the last summer he was home. It had been an amazing summer. We were in love, or maybe I was in love and had been fooled easily. He had to leave to go to King's Cove Harbour to visit the university he would be attending, and that trip was the end of us. In one summer, I had fallen in love and had my heart broken, and that is how I found myself in this mess.

I had been out with my mother shopping, and when I came home, my father told me Carter had left a message for me—he no longer wanted to see me. I had cried for days. My father had deleted the message without letting me hear it. Thinking of that message that had been left three years ago, that I had so desperately wanted to hear, finally made me snap.

I jumped off my bed and pulled my bedroom door open in time to see my father walk into his bedroom. "I'm not marrying Trent, that is all there is to it. Honestly, I guess I should have just gone after Carter like I wanted to three years ago." I slammed my bedroom door and flew to my bed, flopping face first onto the mattress. I expected my father to storm into my bedroom and argue with me more, but when I heard his bedroom door slam shut, I just cried into my pillow.

After the tears had stopped, I lay and look at the ceiling, fighting back more tears, while the anger building inside of me reached explosive levels. It was an anger unlike I had ever felt before. I couldn't stay here anymore. I got up, went to my closet, pulled out the largest backpack I had, and started packing up the items that I would need. I pulled open my nightstand drawer and reached in the back. I pulled out a small pile of cash I had been saving. I quickly counted—I had about eight hundred dollars and whatever room was left on the Visa my father had gotten me. It wasn't going to go far, but I shoved that money into my wallet, placing it in my purse.

After I was packed, I grabbed my laptop and went directly to the bus station, purchasing a one-way ticket to King's Cove Harbour. I grabbed my bag and snuck down the stairs to wait for the cab. While I waited, I pulled out my phone and went straight to Facebook, right to Carter's profile. The first picture that popped up caught my attention. There he stood in front of King's Cove Harbour University, with three other guys—one I recognized as his brother Hunter. I typed out a quick message to him and had just hit send in time for the cab to pull up in front of me. I looked back at the house I had grown up in, then climbed into the back of the cab, praying that by the time I arrived in the city, Carter would respond back to me.

Chapter Seven

Carter – Present Day

I plugged my phone into the charger and reversed out of the driveway. She was still standing in the doorway, my princess gave me a small wave, and then shut the door, separating my eyes from the view of her.

I called the office to let them know I was on my way and asked them to hold any and all messages until I got there. Then I shut my phone off and turned up the radio. I needed to think about what had happened tonight.

I knew Hope had worked so hard to organize this weekend, with little help from me. I had been very busy and I felt terrible about that. Family time with her and the girls meant so much to me, but I had been so preoccupied with work. When the call came in tonight from my clients, they were desperately worried, and even though I should have told them I would have to see them on our scheduled date, Hope also knew it wasn't like me to abandon my clients when they needed me. But somehow, I knew deep inside that me having to leave wasn't the reason she was truly upset.

I played our conversation over in my mind from when we had first gotten back home. I felt so awful about having to leave that I had thought of the perfect solution on the drive home. She rarely turned down a trip with me to New York, but this time she wouldn't hear of it. When she said, that she was the last thing I would need I felt my heart break a little. For some reason she didn't realize that I needed her, that I always had. I hadn't given her any reason for her to doubt that, but why she was thinking differently was beyond me.

Bothering me the most out of anything wasn't the fact that I had to leave, or the fact that she thought she would be in the way, it was the way she clung to me when I was walking out the door. It was the same way she clung to me the night I finally won her back all those years ago. I knew that hug all to well—it wasn't one of happiness, but one of fear. She was afraid she was losing me, and in her mind, I was already walking away. Whatever had caused this fear, I wished she had told me. And after all these years and all we had gone through, it broke my heart knowing she was afraid to bring up what was really bothering her.

Thinking of that brought tears to my eyes and I blinked hard and tried to focus on something else. I stopped at the light and looked out the window. I saw a couple of kids on the sidewalk. He was walking away from her and she was standing calling to him, begging him to stop. Watching this brought me back to the day that Hope had finally come back to me. I smiled to myself at the memory of that night and continued on my way to the office.

<h1 style="text-align:center">Chapter Eight</h1>

I lay with my hands behind my head, my eyes closed, my mind drifting, wondering what her mouth would feel like wrapped around my cock. I reached down and ran my hand through her silky blonde hair; she turned her head to face me, those beautiful blue eyes staring back at me as her head rested on my chest. She smiled that beautiful sleepy smile I remembered so well. I jumped, the sound of the door opening pulling me from my dream state. The girl I had picked up last night stood there looking at me with a smile, her dark curly hair framing her face.

"Hi." She sauntered over to the edge of the bed and sat down beside me, running her hand down my chest.

"Hey." She started rubbing her fingers in tiny circles over my chest just like the girl from my dreams used to; I grabbed her hand to stop her. After her, I stopped any woman from doing that to me. That was her thing, and her touching me that way brought back too many memories of Hope.

"Want to go for round three?" she asked, placing a few light kisses over my abs. I felt my half-stiff cock start to harden at the thought. She continued to kiss her way down my abs, her hands running back up and over my chest and back down again. She was just about to pull the covers down over my now painfully hard cock when I stopped her.

"Something wrong?" she asked, her devilish brown eyes looking up at me.

"Nope, just tired."

"He doesn't look too tired." She grinned.

"I just need to get some sleep."

She stood up from the bed and looked around my room in search of her clothes. I couldn't help but take in her perfect form. She was an attractive girl, as were all the girls I brought home, but they were nothing more to me. They were here merely to fill a void that I had felt for the past three years.

"Are you taking off?" I asked.

"I think so. Maybe I'll see you tonight?" she asked, avoiding eye contact with me.

"I doubt it, babe. Got to study." It didn't really matter, I didn't normally hang out at the bar I had met her at, and I was always careful not to divulge my local hangout. I normally didn't bring girls back to my apartment either. I may have slipped up on that one. Chances of running into her again were slim to none unless she came back here, which I prayed she didn't.

"What about over the weekend?" I watched as she

covered up her beautiful legs in jeans; not too long ago they had been wrapped around my neck.

"I work most of it, and I have to finish off a few assignments," I said, stretching.

She threw her shirt on and grabbed her coat from the back of my desk chair. "You going to walk me out?" she asked, batting her eyelashes at me.

I sat up and pulled my sweats on.

"Perhaps dinner?" she asked quietly as we got to the door. I was going to be in trouble with this one. Three times in the last five minutes she has asked to see me again. I guess it was time to lower the bomb. It wasn't the first time; I'm sure it wouldn't be the last time that I had to do this either.

"Honey, I'm not really looking for anything serious right now."

I watched her eyes drop to the ground. She turned away and slipped her shoes on. "I had a good time," I whispered in her ear, before sucking her lobe into my mouth.

"Me too," she mumbled, stepping out into the hall.

"I've got your number. Maybe I'll call you sometime. You suck dick like a fucking champ," I said, winking at her. I'd become a total asshole when it came to women, and it wasn't something I was proud of. My mother would have slapped the smile I wore right off my face if she'd heard me say something like that. Regardless, it had to be done.

"Don't bother," she called back as I watched her perfect ass walk away from the apartment door before heading back inside my apartment to study.

Chapter Nine

Hope - 13 Years Earlier

I had been in the city a little over two days and hadn't heard a thing from Carter. In fact, he hadn't even read my message. I had gotten myself a dingy little hotel room for the week. It was a dump. There were stains on the sheets, and the room smelled of urine, but it was cheap; it would have to do. I had barely slept. I had listened to two people fight on one side of my room and two other people fucking on the other. My dad would go haywire knowing this was where I was staying.

I opened the door to my room and sucked in a deep breath of fresh air. Pieces of garbage lined the outside wall of the building, and dirt was caked on the windows so thick, it looked like they hadn't been washed in years. As I shut the door to my room and turned to walk toward the stairs that would take me to the parking lot, two men sat outside of their rooms. They both looked at me and smiled. Both were missing teeth, and a heavy BO smell poured off them. They probably hadn't washed in months. I hurried past them both as they whistled and catcalled after me. Once I was down to the street, I headed off in the direction opposite to the one I had come from two days ago. First thing I needed was to find some type of a job. I certainly wasn't planning on ever going back home, but there was no way I could stay in this place any longer than necessary.

Soon, I was in a better part of the neighborhood and I walked past a bunch of restaurants and storefronts hoping that one of them had a sign stating help wanted. I was feeling defeated as I came to the end of the buildings—there was nothing. I was just about to turn around when I saw a sign for Joe's Bar and Grill. The place looked like a hole in the wall. It was in the basement of this building, but they had a help wanted sign out front. As I approached the stairwell, I was greeted by a bunch of bikers. Most of them ignored me, but one of them stopped me before I went in.

"Look at what we have here..." he said, eyes raking over me. "Sweetheart, you look good enough to eat."

I felt a funny feeling in the pit of my stomach, but I ignored him and pushed past him into the pub. I looked back over my shoulder to see his face pressed up to the glass, continuing to watch me from outside.

The place was empty inside. One or two people sat in booths against the far wall sharing some food. I walked over to speak to the girls behind the bar. "I'm here to inquire about the job?"

She looked me over. "One moment, darling," she purred. "I'll get the manager."

I sat down while I waited. Within minutes, this guy

walked around to where I was sitting. "Hey, I'm Mike. Holly said you were here to inquire about the help wanted sign."

"I am."

"Well, it's a waitressing position. You ever waited tables before?"

I shook my head. "I can learn. I'm sort of in a desperate position."

He thought for a moment. I was pretty sure he was going to turn me down. "I'm a fast learner and a hard worker. I don't have any references, but if I don't turn out to be any good, you can just let me go."

"Whoa, hang on. I can tell you need this job badly and you are the first person to inquire in over two weeks. I guess maybe we could give you a shot."

"Really?"

"Yeah, when are you able to start?"

"Anytime. Right now."

He grabbed his phone from his back pocket, checking something quickly. "All right well, you're in luck. One of the girls called in sick; I need someone tonight. We will see how tonight goes, and if you work out, your hours will be four until close, three days a week, at least for now, summer may change that though. Days will be determined depending on the needs of the business."

"What does it pay?"

"Four dollars an hour plus tips."

How the hell does one live on that, I thought to myself. I didn't have the right to be choosy though. The hotel room I had rented for the week had already cost me two hundred dollars. "Okay." I smiled.

He looked me over. "I know it doesn't sound like much,

but we do split tips in here, so you should be fine. Uniform is black skirt or pants and black tank top, nothing too revealing. If you can be here today at two, we can go over the basics, and I'll have one of the girls help you out tonight."

I glanced at my watch. It was already eleven and I would need to find a place to get what I needed to wear. "One question: I'm new in town, where is the closest mall?"

"About three blocks away. I'll see you at two."

Chapter Ten

CARTER - 13 YEARS EARLIER

I sat staring at my calendar. It was clear—I needed no distractions over the next three months; I was getting ready to take my last set of exams this month and then I would be taking the BAR exam in September. Carson was getting ready to go to Europe for the next three months before going on to study his specialty, and I was going to have the place all to myself. It couldn't have come at a better time, to be honest. My future lay in my hands, and there was no doubt, I had to pass.

My phone vibrated against the desk. I finished penciling in my study schedule for the week and then grabbed my phone, checking to see who it was. I knew Carson was standing over my shoulder and I prayed he didn't look at my phone. As soon as I saw the name, I excused myself and headed into my room.

FELICE: HAS HE LEFT YET?

ME: NOT YET, HE'S JUST FINISHING PACKING.

FELICE: I CAN'T WAIT TO SPEND SOME ALONE
TIME WITH YOU.

I didn't respond to that message. I wasn't going to lead her on.

"Carter, have you seen my spare charger?" Carson stuck his head in the room. I dropped my phone beside me.

"I thought I saw it in the kitchen."

He took off again in search of the last few things he needed for his trip. My phone vibrated again.

FELICE: WHAT TIME IS HE LEAVING?

ME: I TAKE HIM TO THE AIRPORT AT SEVEN.

FELICE: OH WELL. I PROBABLY WON'T BE
AROUND TONIGHT, BUT I AM FREE
TOMORROW.

ME: NO PROBLEM.

Just then a picture message came through. Clicking the message open, I was faced with a picture of her perfect tits on the screen. Fuck me! I could feel myself grow hard.

"Carter, do you have an extra bag I can borrow?" I shut the screen off, dropped my phone down beside me, and pulled my spare pillow over my lap.

"Yeah, in my closet."

My phone vibrated again. I didn't dare look at it while Carson was in the room. As he dug through the closet, looking for my duffel bag, my phone went off again and again. "Fuck, man, are you going to get that?" He stopped, turning to look at me.

"It's just one of the guys at work."

Then my phone rang. I lay there ignoring it, knowing exactly who was calling. "What the fuck, Carter, are you going to answer that?"

I peeked at my phone, Felice's name and picture covering my screen. "It's the wrong number."

He stopped what he was doing, turned to me, and held out his hand. "Give me the phone. You know how I love those wrong numbers."

"Na, never mind, man, you'll be late." I took my phone and buried it deep in my pocket. If he saw who was on the phone, I would be a dead man. Carson had been after our neighbor Felice for the past year, but lately she was more interested in me. She had just suffered a bad breakup and, like me, wasn't looking for anything too serious. She just wanted to have fun, but I'd been down the Felice road already and wasn't too keen on doing it again. "It's all good, man, they'll stop calling."

"You're acting strange. Are you having a bad day or what?"

"No, man, just tired and stressed." Carson shrugged and finally went back to searching for my bag, which he finally found at the bottom of my closet.

"Okay, I just have to pack this, and we can be on our way to the airport."

I nodded. "I'm just going to rest. Let me know when you are ready."

As soon as he was out of the room, I picked up my phone again, this time opening up the chat window. Three more pictures lay across my screen—Felice in all her glory. I looked over the pictures once again, taking in the round curve of her ass and her perky, full breasts. I adjusted myself, and then another message came through.

FELICE: I SAW HER LEAVE THIS MORNING. WAS SHE FUN AT LEAST?

ME: SUCKED DICK LIKE A CHAMP.

FELICE: DID SHE NOW?

ME: YEP, FELT DAMN GOOD TOO. IT'S BEEN A WHILE.

FELICE: THAT'S TOO BAD. YOU KNOW THERE IS A WILLING GIRL RIGHT ACROSS THE HALL. NO NEED TO GO SO LONG. YOU HAVEN'T HAD ME SUCK YOU OFF IN A WHILE.

ME: WON'T HAPPEN. AS ATTRACTIVE AS YOU ARE, I REFUSE TO MIX THAT WITH OUR FRIENDSHIP AGAIN.

I had made up my mind after the last time I had made that mistake, for the second time. The first time was right after I moved here, after seeing Hope when I returned home with the infamous Trent King. The girl who ultimately took my heart and broke it into a million pieces in only a few weeks' time. The second time with Felice, well that had just been a lonely night and a drunken mistake. I knew she was just seeking comfort because she had just broken up with the man she had been seeing. I shut my phone off and closed my eyes. I guess she wasn't going to respond to me, which was a good thing; these types of conversations with her had to stop.

"I'm ready, man," Carson yelled.

I got up off the bed, quickly changed into dark blue jeans and a white button-down shirt, shoved my phone in my pocket, and left to take Carson to the airport.

Chapter Eleven

CARTER

I walked into Joe's place, the smell of stale beer and fried foods hitting me hard. I grabbed a seat at the bar, while waiting for my brother Hunter and a couple other guys from school. I should have been studying, but I needed to unwind, and I was hungry. I looked up from the menu and saw my buddy Mike approach from the far end of the bar.

"Hey, man! What can I get you?"

"Hey, Mike! Grab me a pint of whatever you have on tap tonight." Joe's Bar and Grill was a small neighborhood bar and restaurant. I had spent many nights here throughout my years at school; it was my home away from home. The best thing for me was it was close enough to home that I could walk if things got out of hand.

"Here." He slid the glass across the bar to me. "You're in here earlier than usual tonight."

"Yeah, I just got back from taking Carson to the airport. I still have about three hours of studying to do tonight when I get home."

Mike chuckled to himself while pouring a couple beers for the two men who had just walked in. "Yeah, so you decided to come down here and drown your sorrows instead."

"Yeah, the sorrows of having an apartment all to myself for the next three months." I let out a deep laugh.

"Hey, how'd that chick turn out, the one you took home from the dance club last night? She was all over you."

"Fuck, she stayed the night. She was at least good for some tension release."

I took another mouthful of beer, emptying the glass. "Can I get another one, and a couple pounds of wings while you're at it?"

"Sure thing. You going to be here for a bit tonight?"

"Probably, the guys are coming, why?"

"Just want you to check out the new waitress I hired. She is hot as fuck and sweet too. I think she might be good for you. She's a cute little blonde with gorgeous blue eyes. Suddenly I'm upset at myself for instilling the 'I don't date my waitresses' rule," he chuckled.

"Sweet, but you know I don't tend to mix with any of your girls. Too close to home."

Mike let out a laugh. "You really don't want any attachment, eh?"

I shook my head and took a drink, not with a blonde-haired blue-eyed girl I didn't. "Nope. The broad I had last night, I probably shouldn't have taken home. She was persistent this morning. I had to lower the bomb."

Mike let out a laugh. "All right, man, you guys going to grab a table?"

"Probably, just put us in a good section."

"No problem. Why don't you just take your usual spot?" I nodded. I knew the guys would be here soon, so I walked over to our usual table and took a seat.

I glanced at my watch; it was almost midnight. I stood in the bathroom, my head against the wall, more to hold me up than anything, while I emptied my bladder. I heard the door open and the bathroom fill with loud music, getting quieter as the door shut, and then I heard my brother's voice behind me. "Carter?"

"What is it, bro?"

"How many drinks have you had tonight?"

"The usual. Why?"

"No reason."

"If there is no reason then why ask? It's not like I am driving home."

"I was just wondering because I fear we may have a slight problem on our hands."

I zipped up my pants. I'd had way too much to drink, but I wasn't letting him know that. I dragged my sorry ass over to the sink and washed my hands before turning to face my brother. "Don't tell me that chick I picked up last night is here?" That was the first thought that entered my mind, and I laughed it off.

"No, no, but you may wish she were here. I think this may be a little worse."

"Worse? What, let me guess, she is here with her big burly boyfriend and he's waiting to kick my ass because of the mind-blowing orgasms I gave her," I chuckled.

"I wish that were the problem," he mumbled. He continued saying something under his breath that I couldn't quite make out.

"What did you just say?"

"I said you'd wish it was that, but it's not."

"Just spill it, Hunter. What's the problem?"

"Hope is here."

I felt the blood drain from my face, and suddenly the effects from all the alcohol I had consumed had left me. Hope, a name I had wished I could have forgotten in the three years we'd been apart. The girl who almost cost me my passion to become a lawyer when she broke my heart three days before I left for law school. We lived down the road from one another all our lives, and if truth be told, I'd always had a crush on her, and it had taken me years to finally grow the balls to go after her. Her parents had always disliked me, never thought I would amount to anything because we didn't come from money. My father had worked hard, building his law practice one client at a time. We certainly weren't poor, but nothing was given to us kids except our education.

I had planned to take Hope with me when I moved away for school, but while I was away looking at apartments for us, her parents had introduced her to Trent King, the only son of one of the richest families in town, and my best friend. He had been gone that summer, the summer I had finally gotten up the nerve to ask her out. I had to leave for three weeks to get organized and find us an apartment. As soon as I had found us a place, I called and left her a message, and put down first and last months' rent. Even though I could barely afford the rent, I figured with three jobs and the little money I had set aside, we would be just fine. When I returned from the city, I went over to surprise her with the news, and that was when I saw her with him in the park. At first, they were just walking, and I didn't think anything of it, but then he leaned in and kissed her. I watched her pull away at first and look down to the ground, shaking her head, but then he whispered something in her ear and she threw her arms around his neck, throwing her body against him and kissing him, the same way she kissed me.

I was devastated as I drove home. For days I lay in my room, debating writing my resignation letter to the university, but I didn't want to stay at home near her either. So, I packed my bags and headed off to school early to throw myself into my studies, and aside from birthdays and Christmas, I hadn't been home since.

"What do you mean Hope is here?"

"She's working here. I think maybe you should go home."

The new waitress Mike had been talking about was the girl I had never gotten over. "I'm good, Hunter. There are no hard feelings between us. I let that shit go a long time ago, so there really isn't a problem. Now if you tell me Trent King is out there somewhere then we may just have a slight problem." I pushed past my brother and stepped out into

the loud bar. Glancing over at the table, I saw Felice talking
with the guys, so I walked back to the table, sat down beside
Felice, and ordered another beer.

Chapter Twelve

HOPE

I had just returned from my break and was going to be following one of the girls on the floor for the rest of the night. She had already gone over things with me in the back and told me just to stick close to her. We stopped at the end of the bar waiting for Mike to give us our section, and that was when I saw him. All six feet of hard muscle. One look at him and I instantly knew I had made a mistake. I had left him on the word of my father—no other reason. Honestly all I knew was what my father had told me the dreaded message said, but I hadn't heard it for myself, hadn't heard how he sounded. I had seen that he had come back home, but he wouldn't even look in the direction of my house. I had gone to see him, but he refused to come to the door, and after he had left, I had tried calling him for weeks with no answer. Occasionally, our home phone would ring, my father claiming it was the wrong number. I was beginning to wonder if the last three years hadn't been a punishment of sorts, for leaving him without speaking to him, leaving me in a horrid relationship only to now find myself single and no further ahead.

While I was waiting for Ashley, I kept watch on him. He looked so good, dressed in dark jeans and a white button-down shirt, the sleeves rolled up showing off his muscular forearms. I wondered if he still wore the same Calvin Klein cologne that he wore when we had dated. The scent of that cologne had been firmly imprinted in my brain. The bubble I was in burst in my face as I watched a brunette walk over to the table and sit down beside him, Carter placing his arm around her and pulling her into him.

I couldn't help the jealousy that coursed through me. I looked her over from head to toe. She was dressed in busi-ness attire, her buttons down her shirt open enough that you could see just the top of her black bra, her breasts spilling over the edge, her black dress pants fitting snuggly. She was full-figured, and she fit right against Carter, who seemed to really like her; he had wrapped her in his arms and hadn't let her go yet. I couldn't peel my eyes away from them. When he finally released his hold on her, he leaned in and gave her a lingering kiss on the cheek and then she got up and walked away.

"Hope, are you paying attention?" Mike's voice rang out. I jumped and tore my eyes away from Carter. Both Mike and Ashley were standing in front of me, a little annoy-ance written on their faces.

"Sorry. Yes." I shrugged my shoulders and gave him a small smile. "I thought I saw someone I knew for a minute."

Mike continued. This time he had my attention for another whole five or six minutes, and as his voice started to drone on and on, I found myself looking over his shoulder, my eyes locking on Carter. His blue eyes seemed to dance against the lights of the bar. Soon that same girl was back; she placed her hand on his shoulder, whispering something in his ear. I was struck with another pang of jealousy when he wrapped his arms around her and pulled her into him to allow her to lean between his legs. I thought I was going to implode.

As the night went on, the guys who had been there with Carter eventually left, one by one. Then he moved and sat in front of the bar talking with Mike, the girl planted between his legs. I did my best to keep out of his sight. I wasn't sure what I was even doing here now. I guess I figured we would see one another, and things would go back to the way they had been. At least that was what I had been hoping for. However, now I didn't even want him to know I was working here.

As the night went on, I threw myself into my work. We were stationed in a different area than the one Carter was in, and I had done my best to forget that he was even there. After we had finished our last break, I went to grab a glass of water from behind the bar, and that was when I noticed Carter and that women had left. I breathed out a sigh of relief, but not without a couple of tears escaping too.

Carter

. . .

Hunter had been right; it was Hope. Even though I had wanted to get her attention, I knew she was completely off limits. So instead I turned my attention to the woman who had been hanging off me all night. The more I had to drink, the better Felice was beginning to look, and at least I wouldn't be walking out of here alone. That was the last thing I would want Hope to see. I had let Felice sit nestled between my legs all night, her scent eventually driving me crazy, as my hand sat on the flat of her stomach and her ass rested against my cock.

"Come on, man, I'm taking you home." Hunter had stood beside me, his coat on, waiting for me to hop to.

"Man, I'm fine. I'll get home."

"Have you forgotten that you have an exam tomorrow? Let's go."

"Fuck, Dad, I said I'm fine." I gave him a shove.

"I'll take him home, Hunter, it's fine." Felice stood and placed her hand on the side of his face, standing up on her tiptoes to give him a kiss. My brother glared at me as he said good night to Felice.

After Hunter had left, she turned to me and ran her hand over my cheek. "What do you say, big boy, how about we get you home?" She leaned in and teased my lips with hers.

"May be a good idea," I said, sucking her bottom lip into my mouth.

As we walked home, all I could think of was running my fingers through that soft blonde hair, looking into those blue eyes, and holding on to that perfect little body that should have been mine. Regret, of not banging on her front door and speaking with her the night I returned, was starting to eat at me again.

"Carter, this way, babe." Having walked right past our building, I smiled and turned back, heading up the front stairs. We took the elevator and walked down the hall toward our apartments. I waited while she got her key from her purse. She slid the key into the lock and turned toward me. "Why don't you come in for a while?" She ran her hand down my chest. "Have a nightcap," she whispered in my ear.

"You do know that nothing is going to happen between us, right?" I said, reading her eyes.

"I do." She swallowed hard, a look of disappointment coming over her face.

I followed her inside her apartment and watched her walk down the hall. "Help yourself. There is beer in the fridge," she said, throwing her purse and coat down on the table.

I took a beer from the fridge, opened it, wandered into her living room, and sat down on her couch, leaning my head back. As I closed my eyes, the only thing I saw was Hope. I was pretty sure she was going to haunt me forever, just like she had for the past three years. I replayed over and over in my mind exactly how I felt when I had seen her that night with him. I had wanted to approach her tonight, wanted to pull her in my arms and get one more chance to hold her tight.

"Open your eyes, big boy," I heard Felice's voice drawl.

She finally came into focus. She was wearing a long silk bathrobe that hung open, and to my surprise, she was completely naked underneath. I felt myself harden at the sight before me. She walked over, the silk bathrobe teasing me as she walked with the occasional peek at her breasts. She didn't wait. She straddled my lap, pulling the bathrobe open and sitting with her tits in my face. "Someone's a little excited," she mewed, grinding down on me.

"Felice, did you not hear..." she held her finger up to my lips, shushing me.

"I think you need this, Carter. We both need this." She started unbuttoning my shirt until it was completely open. She raked her nails down my chest and popped the button on my jeans. She then grabbed my hand and placed it on her breast. "Touch me."

In that moment, with my hand on her breast, my cock throbbing, my mind drew a blank as to why this was a bad idea. I wrapped my other arm around her and kissed her deeply, cupping her breast, feeling the weight of it in my hand. My phone rang, bringing me back to where I was. I stopped and looked into Felice's eyes. I moved out from under Felice and stood, pulling my phone out of my pocket. My brother had saved my ass from making a huge mistake.

When I got off the phone, I looked down to Felice. "Thanks for the nightcap, but I've got to go." I didn't look back. I just walked to the door, stepped into the hall, and went across the way to my apartment. I shut and locked the door behind me and headed straight for the shower.

I wrapped the towel around my waist and made my way to my bed. Flopping down on it, I pulled my phone from my pocket and started scrolling through Facebook. A few minutes later a message popped up on my screen from Hope. I read through the message, quickly going to Hope's profile, and saw her most recent status update: "Starting a new life."

I clicked on her profile picture. She was so beautiful, and I knew where she was. *Fuck it*. I quickly jumped off the bed, got dressed, and headed back to Joe's place. Screw studying for my exam, I was going to get my girl back.

Chapter Thirteen

HOPE

The last songs of the night were finally playing. I was exhausted and happy to see that the bar was almost empty. We had been instructed to start our cleanup, so while I cleaned tables, Ashley went to grab the broom from the back. I had just emptied the tables against the far wall and started wiping them down when I felt a hand grab my ass. "Hey, baby, you're a cute little thing. What time you finish up tonight?"

I turned around abruptly and came face to face with one of the bikers that had been eying me most of the night. It was the same biker who had been outside earlier today. He was rough, dirty, and at closer look, about twice my age. He wore a black bandanna, and his beard was grey and straggly. His breath smelled of booze mixed with cigarettes. I looked over his shoulder toward the bar to see if Mike or one of the bartenders were there, but everyone was gone. "Fuck," I mumbled under my breath.

"Yeah, baby, that's exactly what I want to do to you," he whispered, running his dirty finger down the side of my cheek.

I could feel panic rising in me now. There were few patrons left in the bar, who wouldn't even make good witnesses, never mind help me. Since I was new, I wasn't sure how much I was allowed to defend myself, and Mike was nowhere to be found. I looked around for Ashley or one of the other girls, but they must have all been in the back.

I swallowed hard. "I'm not interested, thanks."

"You're not interested? But, baby, I would give you the ride of your fucking life. You should reconsider," he chuckled as he ran his finger down between my breasts and leaned into me. I backed up, banging into the edge of the table. I was as far as I could go, and I closed my eyes as his stale breath washed over my face. "You smell fucking delicious—good enough to eat anyway—and I promise I would eat this all night long." He winked at me and placed his hand between my legs, kissing me on the cheek. I knew the tears were going to start to fall any minute now.

"Pete, I believe the lady said she wasn't interested." A loud booming voice came out of nowhere, causing me to jump. I blinked hard and opened my eyes, not sure what direction the voice came from, but saw no one. The guy spun around and that was when I saw Carter, standing tall and threatening behind him, through the watery film on my eyes. Our eyes locked. "Hope, go into the back."

The dingy man turned his attention away from me and onto Carter. My eyes still locked on him. I would have figured he had forgotten about me, but the way his eyes washed over me as he stood there told me different. "Hope, go now, love."

Carter

"Carter," her soft voice called. I had always loved hearing the sound of my name on her lips, apparently still did judging from my body's response, but right now I would prefer she just left. I'd had the pleasure of helping Mike out with this asshole once; things had the potential to get nasty with Pete.

"Go to the back, Hope. Get your stuff. We're going home."

"Hope? Is that your name? Beautiful name for a beautiful girl."

"Now, Hope," I demanded.

She looked from him to me and ran to the back, leaving the tray on the table. "Pete, I'm not going to tell you again, leave her alone."

I watched as his eyes trailed after her, raking over her body, and I felt myself getting rather territorial. "You banging that sweet little ass?"

I grabbed him by the collar and pulled him closer, looking into his tired eyes. It wouldn't take much for me to wipe the floor with him. I was bigger, stronger, and now somewhat sober. "Nope, she's just a friend, but I take it you didn't hear what I said."

"Don't tell me you wouldn't love to have those sweet little legs wrapped around your head there, boy. You aren't a saint; I've seen the piece of trash you've taken home from here." The anger that was coursing through me wasn't going to do him any favors. I had just fisted my hand and was pulling back to give it to him when a voice I recognized boomed from behind me.

"Carter, that's enough! Pete, get out of here! I've had enough," Mike yelled. Suddenly, I felt Mike grab hold of my hand, and I reluctantly let the man go.

"Fuck, Mike, I'm just trying to get myself a piece of ass. A gorgeous one at that."

"That's my staff, Pete. You know you don't touch my girls. Now, take your ass home and sober yourself up."

Pete looked to Mike and then at me. Knowing he was defeated he started to stagger toward the front door. He kept looking over his shoulder for any sign of Hope, taking his time until he finally couldn't fuck around anymore. As soon as the door was shut, and he was gone, I sat my ass down in a chair. I could feel Mike studying me in the way he always did, trying to figure out what had gone on. "No, I don't want to talk about it. What time is she finished, Mike?" I wasn't in the mood to be fucked with now.

"Two-thirty."

"Mind if I wait for her?"

"I don't care. But I think you need to talk about it." Mike turned and started tidying up behind the bar.

"I don't."

When Hope came back out, her eyes were red. She had

been crying, that I was sure. I watched her from across the room while I was pretending to be on my phone. She pulled her hair free from the clip that was holding it in a messy bun and allowed her blonde hair to fall down her back and into her face.

I looked up and saw Mike studying me. "So, care to tell me how you know her?"

I couldn't take my eyes from her. I remembered everything about her. "Well, that my friend is the girl who broke my heart," I mumbled.

I didn't need to say any more. Mike nodded and broke his cardinal rule by pouring me a Scotch after closing and setting it in front of me. "Drink up, man. Cheers."

"Cheers." I grabbed the glass that sat in front of me and raised it to my mouth, letting the warm liquid pour down my throat.

Chapter Fourteen

I grabbed my purse from the employees-only area in the kitchen. "Good night, Mike," I called as I went to go back out to the front door.

"Good shift tonight. Here you go." He held out a wad of cash for me to take.

"What's this?" I asked, taking the money from him and putting it in my purse. There must have been close to three hundred dollars there.

"That is your share of the tips. Be here tomorrow night at four. You've earned yourself a job."

I smiled. "See you then."

I stepped out into the quiet room. The first thing I saw was Carter, his head down resting on his arms, his eyes closed. He looked so peaceful as he slept. I approached him slowly, and just as I went to place my hand on his shoulder, his sleepy blue eyes opened. "You ready?" he asked.

I nodded. He stood, grabbed his jacket, and walked behind me, holding the door open for me to go through.

Nothing was said between us. We started walking for a bit in the direction of my hotel. It had been ten minutes when he finally asked where I was staying.

"I have a room over at The Knights Inn," I said, clearing my throat. I could feel my face getting warm. He had lived here for three years; surely, he knew what type of shithole I was living in.

He frowned. "How long have you been staying there?"

I swallowed hard, ignoring his question, and kept walking.

"Are you living there?"

I didn't answer him. I couldn't because I couldn't look at him. Finally, he grabbed my arm, stopping me, and pulled me around to face him. As soon as our eyes met, I crumbled. "I have nowhere else to go. I left home. I only have a few hundred dollars to my name. My credit card was canceled." I really didn't want to cry in front of him, but the tears were already pouring. I spun around and started walking again. I was almost at the corner when I noticed Carter wasn't with me. I turned to look behind me and watched as he turned and started heading in the opposite direction.

"Where are you going? I thought you were walking me home?"

"Home? Fuck, that isn't your home, Hope. It's a soon-to-be-condemned shithole filled with prostitutes, druggies, and guys like your friend Pete. We're going to my place. We can get your stuff in the morning. At least there I know you will be safe."

I stood there, looking after him.

"Are you coming, Hope? Girls like you don't stay at places like that. Come on, my roommate's gone for the summer. You can have his room until you find something better."

I didn't know what to do. He was right, I didn't belong there, and I knew that. He slowed his stride as I stood there looking after him. I glanced in the direction of my hotel. The streets were dark, and to be honest, I didn't want to spend another night in that dump. A light rain started to fall as I watched him slowly walk farther away from me. I glanced back down the dark road to the scummy hotel and thought about just heading back there, but then I looked back to Carter. I shivered a bit and changed my mind, running to catch up with him. As I walked beside him, shivering, I wrapped my arms around myself and rubbed both arms to try to warm up.

"Here, take my jacket," he said, taking it off.

"No, no, I'm fine."

"You're not fine, you're cold. When did you become so stubborn?" He pulled the jacket around me and wrapped it over my shoulders, the warmth from his body still lingering inside the coat. I breathed in the familiar smell of him; it hit me right in the center. He smelled the same as he had three years ago.

We walked in silence the rest of the way to his place, just the sound of rain hitting the pavement and the occasional car driving by, but being with him, I felt safer than I had since coming to this city.

I followed him into a clean apartment building and got in the elevator. As soon as the doors closed, I leaned up against the wall, fighting to keep my eyes open. "Tired?"

"Hmmm...yes. I haven't had much sleep in the past week." I closed my eyes for a moment, and when I opened them, Carter was staring at me, a soft smile on his lips.

"What?" I murmured.

"You're cute when you're tired. You always were." I couldn't help but blush as his eyes locked with mine.

The elevator finally opened on his floor, and Carter tore his eyes away from mine. I trailed behind him as we headed down the hall toward his apartment. My eyes were firmly planted on his ass. He had always looked incredible in jeans. "Here we go." My eyes flew from his ass, and I watched as he slipped his key into the lock.

He stepped aside and held the door open for me. "After you." His voice was soft. As I walked by him, I accidentally brushed up against him, that touch sending a shiver through me.

Carter

She had scooted past me and I took a quick second to check her out before I walked through the door, locking it behind me. She removed her shoes and slipped out of my coat, holding it in her hands. I took it from her and hung it up in the closet. "Let me give you a quick tour. The place isn't very big, but it's clean and safe." I pointed out where my bedroom was and where she would be staying, the bathroom and the rest she could figure out. Just as I finished showing her around, something struck me: she was finally standing in the apartment I had originally rented for us. She looked up at me and smiled, and then a funny look came over her face. "What is it?"

"I just realized I don't have anything to sleep in. All of my things are back in the hotel," she said, looking at me with innocent eyes.

"It's okay, I'll grab you something." I wandered into my room and sorted through my dresser, pulling out a T-shirt for her. I quickly took my clothes off and put on a pair of shorts. When I emerged from my room, I caught her eyes wandering over my bare chest. I had bulked up considerably since she had seen me last. She took the shirt from me, her hand shaking as she reached out. "Thanks, Carter. You're sure it's okay that I stay in here?"

"I'd rather you be here than there, so yes, I'm sure. Tomorrow we'll head over to the hell hotel and get your stuff, and as I said, until you find something other than that shithole, you can stay here with me."

"Thank you," she whispered. Taking the shirt, she wandered into the bathroom, shutting the door behind her. I grabbed my keys from the counter and hung them on the hook by the door. Within minutes, the bathroom door opened, and I watched as she walked into Carson's room and shut the door behind her.

Fuck, I wanted her. The want had never diminished even the slightest bit over three years, and tonight just proved exactly how much. I had just buried that want behind my studies and behind the wall that I had built over my heart. When I saw Pete touch her, I felt like I could have torn him from limb to limb. My overprotectiveness came out, and then when I found out where she was staying it was out in full force.

I went out to the kitchen and grabbed a bottle of water from the fridge. I looked at the time. It was almost four. I was going to be useless to take my exam in the morning. I lay down on the couch, after lighting a couple candles on the living room table, and closed my eyes. I turned the stereo on low and put on soft music; I needed to unwind. It had been a long day and I was exhausted. I lay with my arm over my eyes just listening to the light jazz pouring from the speakers. I found it almost impossible to relax knowing that she was only on the other side of a flimsy wooden door. All that kept running through my mind was that tight ass and how close to within reach she really was. Hunter had been right; she wasn't healthy for me. It had taken me so long to get her out of my mind. For the first year, the few times I had gone home, I would find myself watching for her to come home from wherever she had gone, and almost every night it would end in anger, because I would find her with him.

I grabbed my cell and texted my brother. He was the only one with whom I could share this. My cell phone lit up almost right away.

HUNTER: PLEASE TELL ME YOU DIDN'T BRING HER HOME.

ME: WHY?

HUNTER: IS SHE AT YOUR APARTMENT
RIGHT NOW?

ME: MAYBE.

HUNTER: GO TO BED, CARTER. YOU DON'T
WANT TO GET YOURSELF INVOLVED WITH HER
AGAIN.

I stared at my screen. He was right—what did I know about her? She had shown up out of the blue working at the bar I hung out at and living in some shithole. I knew nothing more. I didn't know if she was single, married, pregnant—anything. The little I knew was that she had left home. But I did know that the feeling growing in me wasn't good, because I had an overwhelming desire to take her and make her mine again.

HUNTER: PLEASE, CARTER. DON'T DO THIS TO
YOURSELF AGAIN.

I threw my phone on the table. He was right. I couldn't allow myself to get involved with her in any way whatsoever. I had come too far, and this summer was far too important to the rest of my life. I couldn't throw it away over a girl; I couldn't throw it away over her. I shut the stereo off and blew out the candles, took one last look at the door she was behind, and wandered into my room, shutting the door behind me.

Hope

I lay in bed staring at the red numbers on the clock. It was almost five. I kicked the covers off, I was so hot. I got up, opened the bedroom door, and peered out into the darkness. Carter must be in bed; there was no light spilling from his bedroom. I took my chances, running in my T-shirt and panties to use the washroom and then returned to the safety of my room.

I crawled back into bed and lay there staring at the ceiling, thinking back to earlier tonight. The memory of him standing in front of me shirtless kept playing like a movie in my mind. I had wanted so badly to run my hands over his chest, to pull myself into him and nuzzle at his neck.

I hadn't been touched by a real man since him, and I had forgotten how his large, strong hands felt as they ran over my body. I closed my eyes and tried to imagine them running up my bare leg, gripping my ass as he kissed my neck. I could feel myself starting to get wet from the thought of him. I had often felt this way when thinking of him, but I was afraid to quench that ache. Slowly, I slipped my hands inside my panties, gliding my fingers over my clit. The more I imagined his mouth licking and sucking on my nipples, kissing his way down my stomach and the feel of his strong hands slipping under my ass, gripping me tightly as he finally buried his face between my legs, the more the throbbing ache needed to be quenched. As I ran my fingers over my clit again, I was sure a moan escaped my lips.

I stilled when I heard the loud click of his door opening. I was suddenly pulled back into reality. Ripping my hand from my panties, I fought hard to calm my beating heart. I listened hard, hearing nothing. I decided to grab a bottle of cold water from the fridge. When I stepped out of my bedroom door, I was knocked to the side as Carter collided with me. He reached and grabbed me before I fell to the ground, wrapping me securely in his arms, his hand landing on my almost bare ass and my one hip. I gripped his shoulders as he steadied me on my feet.

"I wasn't expecting you to be there. Are you okay?" he asked.

I couldn't speak. All I could feel was the fire building in me again, this time at the feel of his hand on my ass. I looked into his eyes and slowly moved my hands from his shoulders, resting them on his chest, which was even more of a mistake. He felt more amazing than he looked. My eyes finally traveled from where my hands rested, taking in the contour of his neck to his lips, and finally meeting his beautiful blue eyes. He really was a stunning man. He looked down at me, his hands still firmly gripping me, not saying anything.

"Are you okay?" he repeated softer this time. I shook my head, afraid my voice would give away what I was thinking.

"Sorry, I needed some water and had to use the washroom. I wasn't expecting you to come right out of the bedroom door at that exact moment." He smiled as his hands dug into my skin.

Almost as if I had burned him, he ripped his hands off

me. "Sorry, I didn't mean to grab you like that," he mumbled. "I didn't want you to fall."

I wanted to scream that it was okay and to take his hands and put them back on me where they had been, but instead I stepped back inside my bedroom door and let him pass, watching after him as he walked into the bathroom, shutting the door behind him. I stood staring at that door for a few moments and then went to the kitchen and grabbed a water from the fridge. Instead of opening the cold bottle, I placed it on the back of my neck. It wasn't just the heat from the early summer night that was making me hot anymore.

Carter

I ran cool water into the sink and filled my hands, splashing it over my face. I hadn't meant to grab her, but now I couldn't get the thought of running my hands over that tight round ass out of my mind. She had fit against me so perfectly then and still, but when she ran her hands over my chest, it felt like she trailed a burning match across my skin. I fucking wanted her, and no matter what anyone said, I was going to make her mine again. I had to.

I pulled the towel off the rack, dried my face, and left the bathroom to go and grab a cold water. I needed to get back to bed. If she was still up, I didn't know if I could trust myself around her. I stepped out of the bathroom and came around the corner to see her standing with her back toward me, that perfect ass peeking out from under the T-shirt she wore.

My eyes skimmed over her, my thoughts running a mile a minute, my favorite one being her kneeling on all fours before me, her hair wrapped around my hand, while I took her from behind. I felt my dick twitch. I needed to control my thoughts. I was only in boxers; it would be hard to hide what I was thinking from her if she turned around.

"Are you feeling okay?" I couldn't help but ask her. She had a water bottle pressed up against the back of her neck.

I saw her jump a little and turn to look at me. Her eyes trailed down my body. They seemed to almost jump out of her head. There was no hiding it now; I was well endowed, and in the light that cast from the bathroom, I knew she could see I was as hard as a rock.

"Yep, just warm in here. I'm going to head back to bed." She swallowed hard, her eyes trailing over me once more before she buzzed past me and into Carson's room. Before she shut the door, she turned and ran her eyes over me a third time, a soft smile coming to her lips. "Good night," she whimpered as she shut the door, leaving me standing with a raging hard-on alone in the living room.

Chapter Fifteen

Hope

A knock on the apartment door finally woke me from my sleep. I lay in bed, waiting for Carter to answer, but when I didn't hear him and the knocking kept up, I got up and headed to the door.

"Carter, love, open the door."

I frowned to myself and pulled the door open. It was the woman from the bar last night. Upon closer look, I realized I knew her from somewhere else, but my memory failed me.

"Can I help you?" I watched as her eyes skimmed my body. I looked down at myself, realizing that I was only in the T-shirt Carter had loaned me.

"Who are you? Where is Carter?" she asked, looking over my shoulder into the apartment.

"I guess he isn't home. I'm Hope." I held my hand out

to her, but she didn't shake it. Instead, she continued to look over my shoulder. "...and you are?"

"Felice, from across the hall. What time do you expect him?"

"To be honest, I haven't a clue where he even went, so I can't even guess when he will be home."

"I see, well, can you give these to him? He left them in my apartment last night," she said, holding out a pair of black boxers. I couldn't help but blush.

As I took the boxers from her hand, I looked up at her and noticed she was studying me, as if she knew me from somewhere as well. "Where do I know you from?" she asked.

"I work at Joe's."

"Sure, yes, that's it." She was still studying me intently.

"Is there anything else you need?" I asked. I was getting a little freaked out.

"Just tell Carter I stopped by."

"Sure thing."

I shut the door and locked it, walked to Carter's room, and threw the boxers on his bed.

Chapter Sixteen

Carter

Hope had still been asleep when I had left this morning. I needed to work off this frustration I was carrying. After returning to my room after our encounter, I had spent a copious amount of time with my hand and the remainder of the early morning tossing and turning. At seven, I decided to pack my gym bag and head off to the university to get in a workout before I had to take one of my final exams.

As the elevator opened to our floor, all I could think of was my pillow, but the closer I got to my apartment, all I could hear was music. I had one hell of a headache from being up all night, and when I stopped outside the door, I realized the music was coming from inside my apartment.

My head pounded. The music was even louder when I opened the door. Dropping my gym bag on the floor, I glanced around the corner and saw the sexiest pair of fucking legs I had seen in a while. They were smooth and well defined and were flung over the back of my couch, and for a moment I thought about what they would be like wrapped around my neck as I buried my face between her creamy thighs. However, I didn't need a repeat of what happened this morning, so I did my best to stop those thoughts. I had no right to think of her that way anymore anyway. She wasn't mine, but fuck it, there was nothing wrong with looking, so I leaned up against the wall and just took in the sight before me. I noticed the remote for the stereo lay on the table beside me. I smiled to myself, grabbed the remote, and shut the godawful noise off.

"What the..."

"You're finally awake," I chuckled.

The legs disappeared, and Hope popped her head up and looked in my direction. "Good morning, Carter! Hope it's okay that I was listening to your stereo. I felt like some music."

Her blonde hair was tied up in a messy bun, and she wore a thin, little, black tank top that left nothing to my imagination, a hot-pink bra on underneath. It was hard enough to draw my eyes away from her beautiful breasts that were almost spilling out of her tank top. She wore snug little jean shorts, and when she turned around to set her drink down on the table, the cheeks of her tight, round ass hung out the bottom of those short shorts, which just led back to her damn legs. I could feel myself getting hard and had to avert my eyes away from her and concentrate on something else, but it did little good, my dick was already throbbing.

"Sorry about the noise, Carter. I wasn't sure when you'd be home. I got up and had a quick shower. I had this in my bag from work last night, so I got dressed and made myself comfortable while waiting for you to come back."

She came around and flung that hot little body at me, giving me a hug. I prayed that she wouldn't be able to feel my growing excitement. As she wrapped her arms around me, I noticed that she still wore the same damn body lotion; a light fresh mix of citrus invaded my senses. She smelled good enough to fucking eat.

"I see that," I said, wrapping my arm around her and pulling her against me for a quick hug. "So, you comfortable here? You're going to stay here until you find something, right?"

"Well, I really don't want to impose on you and I do have that hotel room."

"Hope, give it a rest. I told you you're not the kind of girl that stays there. So, unless you found something else, I won't have it any other way. You'll stay here with me. I'll be busy with work and studying anyway, so if you're worried about seeing me often, I can assure you that we probably won't even cross paths. You have free rein, and you can have what's-his-name here if you want."

I averted my eyes. I knew his damn name—it felt like poison on my tongue, but I wanted to know if she was still involved with Trent, and this was the easiest way to find out. It would be better this way, instead of coming home to find them together.

"It's okay. No need to have Trent here. I'll find a place as soon as I can." Well, that blew up in my face. I didn't get the answer I needed, and I watched as she walked back around the couch to grab her water. Her phone suddenly pinged with a message. She grabbed it from the table, and I could see the tension roll through her body as she read whatever was on the screen. She rapidly typed out a message but still sat there, a frown on her face, staring at the screen, finally tearing her eyes away and looking back at me. "So, what's going on?"

She threw her phone back down on the table and sat down on the couch. I grabbed a bottle of water and then joined her. "I'm not going to lie to you, Hope. I find it odd that you are in the city working at Joe's. So, are you at least going to tell me what you are doing here?"

"I told you, I left home. I thought maybe I might look into going back to school."

"I see." I took a drink, emptying the water bottle. "Why? Isn't what's-his-face going to take care of you?"

She hung her head. "Carter, you know what his name is, and I don't want to be kept by him. I want to do this for me, to prove to my parents that I can."

I frowned. "Are things not so good in paradise, Hope? I mean, that is why you left me, because things would be easier, right? That way you didn't have to go to school or work."

A deep pink color rose to her cheeks, and she looked away. "I have to go get my things. I don't want to have to pay for another week." She got up from the couch, leaving me sitting there, water bottle in hand.

"I asked you a question. That is why you left me, isn't it?" I needed to know, and it couldn't wait. "You left me because I was never good enough for your father...or for you. With me, you would have to work for what we needed. It wasn't going to be handed to you on a silver platter." I followed her into my roommate's room—her room for now.

She had her little backpack that she was using as a purse sitting on the bed, and her head was in her hands. "That's why, isn't it?"

"I never left you, Carter. You came here to look at apartments, and you never came back."

"I did too. I spent a couple weeks here, and after I found this place I came right back. I called and left you a message. I wanted you to come with me. I wanted to surprise you, but it seems you were already...preoccupied."

"What are you talking about?" The look on her face scared me; it told me she really didn't know what I was talking about.

"I left you a message. I told you I was through here, that I'd found us a place. You never returned my call and when I returned, I saw you in the park. I watched as you kissed him. I thought maybe I was mistaken, so I watched you for a bit. You walked home with my best friend, hand in hand, and there on your front porch he kissed you again."

"What park?"

"The park by your house."

She blinked hard. "Carter, no, you left the message that you were through with me. You didn't even have the decency to tell me to my face. Instead, you left a message on my family's answering machine. I was totally devastated, Carter."

I stopped. Had she not gotten my message? "Did you not get my message?"

"No, my dad told me. He didn't want me to hear it. I cried for days, Carter. It felt like my world had ended." She wiped tears from her cheeks. "I have to go and get my stuff, although I have no idea why I should even bother." She got up and pushed past me, slipped her shoes on, and walked to the door. "Oh, and before I forget, your neighbor returned your boxers." She walked out the door, slamming it behind her.

I stood there in a daze. She had never gotten my message. Her father had lied to her. Lied to her to take her away from me. He really didn't think I was good enough for her. I stood there, letting that sink in for a moment. Once the realization hit, I headed out the apartment door and across the hall, and knocked on Felice's door, for a totally different reason than finding out why she showed up at my apartment door with another man's boxers.

Chapter Seventeen

CARTER

I had felt better after talking things through with Felice. She may be a bit of a tease, but she was my best female friend, and she knew a lot about my past relationship with Hope and what had happened. Just like my brother though, she had told me to tread lightly, not to let myself get involved with Hope, and I was doing my best to follow that advice. I had spent most of the following week out of the apartment either working or studying. But the nights we were both home proved to be the hard ones as I watched her prance around the apartment half-naked, in those tiny little shorts and tank tops. I was at the point that I couldn't take it much more. I wanted her, and if I was in the apartment while she was still up, I could barely concentrate on anything else.

I sat at the library table. I was supposed to be studying, but instead I was stuck on her Facebook profile. I had friended her again, and now I was checking to see if I could find out her relationship status. Since the last post before her status update was one of her and Trent at the movie theatre a little over three weeks ago, I took that as she was still involved. I huffed out my disappointment, threw my phone on the table, and opened my textbook, trying to bury myself in studying. My last exam was tomorrow, and I needed to pass it in order to take the BAR exam at the end of summer. I had just gotten into the material, finally being able to shut my head off, when someone gripped my shoulder.

Hunter walked around the other side of the table, spun the chair around, and straddled it. "What are you doing here?"

"What's it look like?"

"It's just, you normally study at home, not here. You always complain that it's too noisy."

"Yeah well, it is noisy, but my apartment hasn't exactly been quiet lately either, so I came here."

"Is everything okay? Sounds to me you're avoiding being at home."

I ran my hand over my face and leaned back in my chair. If only he knew. "There may be a good possibility that I am."

"Why?" he asked hesitantly. I looked up at him, and from the look on his face, he already knew what the problem was. "You invited her to stay, didn't you?"

"I couldn't help it. I went back the other night to make sure she would be okay to walk home. That was the only reason, I swear. When I got there, ole Pete was making advances, so I waited for her. I was just going to walk her home, Hunter, that is all, but then I found out where she was staying, and I couldn't let her go back there."

"That's why you sent me a text at four in the morning. Carter, she is in the past for a reason. You don't deserve to have this shit happen to you again."

"Hunter, please, spare me the lecture and just hear me out."

He crossed his arms in front of him. "Go ahead then."

"She was staying in that hell hole over on Clifford. Everything inside of me screamed not to let her stay there, so I brought her to the apartment and offered her Carson's room until she finds something else."

Hunter closed his eyes and kept them closed, taking in a deep breath. "Awesome, Carter, just awesome. So basically, you're planning to torture yourself all summer long, perhaps something will happen between the two of you, perhaps it won't, but then Mr. Big Balls will come walking back into her life, and you'll be left holding your heart again. Let me ask you, have you ever really gotten over her?"

"Yes, Hunter, I've gotten over her. There have been other women, many women."

"Yes, I know, Carter. There have been many women, but none that you have been overly happy with and none that you have dated. I just think you're making a mistake. I mean, I support you with whatever you decide. You're my brother; I love you and I want to see you happy. Just be careful."

One thing about my brother—he may be cocky, arrogant, and full of himself, but he always cared about me. "Look, I've got to study. My exam is on Friday."

"All right, man, I have to get to class anyway. You are coming tomorrow night?"

I nodded and watched as Hunter walked away. He was right, I knew he was. She was in my past for a reason. When I had seen her that night with Trent, it was like someone had plunged a hot knife right into my heart and twisted it. We had only spent a summer together—that was it. We had never slept together, only fooled around a little. She had wanted to wait, and I respected that of her. But, no matter how much I tried to fight it, my heart was telling me it was time for us to give it another try, and sometimes you must listen, because lord knows you don't get second chances too often.

Chapter Eighteen

"Time, pencils down." I placed my pencil on the desk. I stretched and looked up at the time. Four hours felt like they had flown by. I was exhausted. I had barely had enough sleep last night trying to get caught up on my studies. I let out a deep breath; I could feel the tension starting to leave my body already.

"Bring your exams up and drop them in the box on the table. Final grades will be posted in four weeks." My stomach grumbled and flipped. I felt like I was going to be sick. If I failed this exam, I would be finished.

As I stepped out into the fresh air and made my way to the car, I turned my cell on and dialed Mike. I wanted to see if he could get out. The phone rang three times before he picked up. "Hey, buddy, are you doing anything right now?"

"Working. Training more new staff."

"I see. If I pop by, would you have time to grab a drink with me? I need to unwind. Just finished my final."

"Sure thing."

I dropped my bag into the backseat of the car. I was just about to back out of the parking spot when my phone pinged again. Pulling it from my pocket, I saw Hope's name flash across the screen.

HOPE: HOW WAS YOUR EXAM? WONDERING IF YOU WANTED TO GRAB DINNER TONIGHT. I HAVE THE NIGHT OFF.

I was just about to answer, but I stopped. Maybe Hunter was right, maybe this wasn't the smartest choice I had made. Instead of replying, I threw my phone down on the console and reversed out of the parking lot.

The apartment was empty and dark when I got there. "I guess she must have gotten tired of waiting for my reply," I mumbled to myself. I grabbed a quick shower and then dressed into a pair of jeans and a black button-down shirt, threw on a splash of cologne, and made my way over to the pub.

The place seems more packed than usual, I thought, as I fought my way through the crowd to the only empty bar stool. Mike was behind the bar, so I grabbed the empty seat and ordered a beer.

"Hey, Carter, how was the exam?" he asked.

"Not too bad. You guys are busy."

"Of course, and short staffed, as always."

"So, care to tell me what's going on between the two of you?"

I glanced around through the crowd, ignoring the question Mike had asked. If I myself had known what I was doing, it would be fine. I spotted my brother and then the rest of the guys. "Mike, I'm headed over to the guys. They're here already."

"You got it. I'll bring the refills."

As I approached the table, I watched Hunter punch Phil in the arm and give him a serious look.

"Well, if it isn't the man of the hour. Have you fucked her yet?" Phil called while downing another shot. I rolled my eyes, ignoring him, and glared at my brother before I took a seat. He was the only one who knew Hope was staying with me; how dare he betray me and breathe a word of it to the guys.

"Hello to you too," I responded back. "How much of that shit has he had?" I asked Hunter.

"Maybe a little bit too much. Want a beer?"

"Already ordered. Just started myself a tab. Mike's bringing over another round, but I think Phil here needs to be cut off."

I looked through the crowd again and then turned my direction back to the guys. They all sat there staring at me with shit-eating grins on their faces. "What?" I shrugged.

"Nothing, man, we were just hoping for some details."

"Details?" I played stupid, pretending to not know what

they were talking about and praying that they really didn't know the situation.

"Yeah, you left with Felice last night, but then you came back in here for that new chick. We had just left the other bar across the road and saw you come back in here." I gave Hunter the I'll-kill-you look. He new better than to tell the guys anything.

"It was nothing. I forgot something here, and then I helped Mike with something in the back," I lied.

"We're sure you did," Phil slurred. I glared at my brother, and Hunter quickly changed the subject. Soon they started with their usual banter back and forth, cutting one another up and looking for their next piece of ass, which took the heat off me for a bit.

A while later, Hunter made his way back from the washroom and sat back down at the table, smacking me on the back. While the other guys were locked into a deep conversation with a bunch of women at the next table, Hunter leaned over toward me. "Don't look too hard, bro, but she's here."

"Who's here?"

"Your woman. She's in the back booth over there with a guy that very much resembles Trent King," he answered, nodding in the direction of where they were sitting. I looked over Hunter's shoulder, a surge of jealousy running through me as I kept my eyes on them. Their conversation seemed to be intense, and it looked like she was getting uncomfortable.

"Not my problem," I answered and grabbed some nachos from the plate in front of me. I turned my attention to our group, but I couldn't help my eyes wandering over to her and their table. I was fine until I witnessed him slamming his fist down on the table, causing her to jump, then he stood up and walked toward the washroom. Everything about her screamed she was on edge, and once he left, she placed her face in both her hands, her body starting to shake. Soon, he returned, sitting down across from her, and their argument continued. When she started to cry harder, I got up from my seat and went to walk over there, but Hunter grabbed my arm before I could get away.

I looked down to his hand resting on my forearm. "Don't get involved, Carter."

I glanced back over to them, watching. "She's in trouble, Hunter."

"This isn't your place, Carter, remember."

I took my brother's advice. Sitting back down, I tried hard to turn my attention to what the guys were talking about, but my mind and focus were only on her. I watched her walk into the washroom, her eyes red and her face streaked with tears. I kept my eyes on him: Trent King. We had grown up together, but now he was just a conceited, rich boy instead of my best friend.

"Carter? Carter? Are you going to join the people at this table tonight?" Derek said, snapping his fingers in my face.

I turned my attention back to the guys and smiled. "Sorry, guys. I guess I have other things on my mind tonight."

Derek and Phil looked at one another and smiled then excused themselves from the table to go and talk to a couple of women at the bar. Hunter sat there staring at me. "Carter, don't do this to yourself, man."

"Do what?"

"I can see it written all over you. You want her."

"Nope, you're wrong, but I'm not going to sit by and watch her be treated like shit either."

"Just admit it to yourself. Stop fighting it. If you want her, go get her."

I looked over and saw that Trent was now standing. He said something and then slammed his fist on the table again, but this time he took off toward the door, leaving her there crying.

Hunter looked in the direction of her table and then back at me. I watched Trent as he shoved his way through a few people that were in his way and pushed the door open, shoving two more girls to the side who were on their way in.

"Are you going to go make sure she is okay?"

I looked over. Tears were streaming down her beautiful face. "You guys good?" I heard Mike ask.

"Bring me two beers, please." I kept my eyes on her. She wiped her cheeks and looked around the room, one of the waitresses stopping to check on her and make sure she was okay. I watched as Hope nodded, grabbing her hand and giving a weak smile, the waitress finally leaving her. Mike set both beers in front of me, clearing off the few empties we had accumulated already. I excused myself, taking both beers with me. "I'll be back."

As I approached her table, I tried to blow off the anger that was inside of me. I stopped beside her table. She had kept her head down so she hadn't seen me coming. "Want a beer?"

She didn't look up. "No, thank you," she mumbled.

"I think it may be needed." I sat down across from her and held the bottle in front of her, waiting for her to take it.

She looked up. Her blue eyes were bloodshot. "Carter?"

"You all right?" I asked.

She slowly reached across the table and took the bottle from my hand, her fingers grazing mine. "Thank you. I'll be fine."

"Care to tell me what that was all about?"

"It was nothing. Don't worry about it."

"It didn't look like nothing." I took a drink of my beer, watching her.

"He's an asshole," she mumbled, and I watched as the bottle met her lips. "Thank you for the beer."

"I'm going to agree with you on that. What happened?"

"We broke up before I moved here. He wanted me to go back with him to speak with my parents. I have nothing to say to them or to him, so he got angry."

Relief washed over me now that she had verified they had split. "I see, well since you aren't going to follow him, how about you stay and spend some time with me and my friends tonight?" I nodded in their direction. I already knew they were watching us. I could feel their eyes on the back of my head. I glanced at my watch; it was already seven. "We'll grab some food and then we can spend the night dancing. Could be a fun night." I winked at her.

"I guess." She smiled.

"All right, well wipe those tears away. Let's go. I'm not going to dance with a mess. You're much prettier when you smile." We stood, and I placed my hand on her lower back, guiding her over to where the guys were sitting.

Hope

It was nearing two. Most of the guys had already left, leaving Carter, Hunter, and me at the bar. I had excused myself to use the washroom, and when I returned, I saw Carter and Hunter having what looked like an intense conversation. I stayed near the bar watching from afar, and soon Carter patted Hunter on the back. Hunter grabbed the girl he had picked up earlier, and together they walked out of the bar, hand in hand. Carter then made his way over to where I was sitting. "Would you like anything else?" he asked.

I went to answer when Mike came around and let us know it was last call.

"Just a water." I smiled back.

"Two waters please, Mike." As Mike walked away, Carter kissed me on the forehead. "I'm just going to go and settle up the bill." He winked, and I watched as he walked over toward the opposite end of the bar where Mike was. I sat back down at the table until he came back over. I was getting tired. We had drunk, danced, and laughed the night away. It was honestly the most fun I had had in three years, and a far better way to end the night than the way it had begun. Soon the music changed and one of the first slow songs of the night played. I sat there getting lost in the music, my body swaying. When I opened my eyes, I was surprised to find

Carter sitting across from me watching me. He didn't smile; he just sat there studying me, finally passing me the bottle of water. The next song they played was one of my favorites, "Say You Love Me" by Jessie Ware. A few people ran out to the floor and started dancing. I smiled as I watched them. "You probably want to go. I know you have to study tomorrow," I said, grabbing my water from the table. Throwing on my light jacket, I bent to grab my purse when I felt his hand on my arm, stopping me.

I turned and looked at him. His eyes had a burning, faraway look in them. Stepping closer, he brought his mouth to my ear. "Dance with me?" he whispered.

I placed my hand on his forearm and silently nodded. He guided us over to an empty spot on the dance floor where he pulled me into his arms, and together, we started gently swaying to the music. At first, I had a hard time catching my breath, but the longer his arms were around me, the safer I was beginning to feel. Soon my head rested on his chest and I felt at home. We stayed this way until the last song of the night finished playing and the bar had closed, and it was at that time that I realized these arms, his arms, were right where I had always wanted to be.

Chapter Nineteen

I lay in bed staring at the ceiling. I hadn't been able to sleep since we had parted ways after coming home. When we had shared the elevator back to the apartment, I couldn't keep my eyes off her, those baby blues staring up at me, full of want. I was glad when we had come into the apartment and she finally went to her room. If she had kept looking at me like that, biting her bottom lip and playing with the corner of her shirt, it wouldn't have been very long before I had pushed her up against the wall and devoured her.

For two hours I tossed and turned thinking about the end of the night—dancing with her, feeling her against me as I held her in my arms, wishing that last song would play forever so I didn't have to let her go. I let out a sigh as I glanced at the clock. There was no point in lying here anymore. I was never going to fall asleep, so I grabbed my textbook and my book light from my desk and went out to the living room. I glanced at her door; it was closed. I let out the breath I was holding. I didn't want to disturb her, but at the same time, I wanted her to come out here. I sat on the couch, turned the small light on, and started to read. I was finally deep into a case study that I found fascinating when I heard my name faintly behind me.

"Carter."

I raised my head and looked around behind me. The moonlight was pouring out of Carson's bedroom door. "I didn't wake you, did I?" I swallowed hard as my eyes ran over her body. She was wearing a tiny white tank top and panties, nothing else, and my cock instantly noticed and stood at attention.

"No. I want to thank you for tonight."

"You're welcome. What else are friends for?"

She reached out and laced her fingers with her own. "How did you know I was there?"

"You don't think guys talk?" I heard a little giggle come from her. "Hunter told me." I turned back toward my textbook. She needed to go back to bed; I needed her to go back to bed. When she didn't respond, I glanced around behind me and saw her standing there, her hands behind her back. I cleared my throat and patted the seat beside me. "Come, sit."

She walked over, and once she was in the light, I could see the outline of her nipples and knew she was bra-less. As her eyes followed mine, she blushed. She grabbed a pillow and placed it in front of her, blocking my view. I remembered how she loved it when I would suck on them. I could almost bring her to orgasm without even touching her anywhere else, and I found myself wondering if she still loved it. My cock throbbed at the memory.

She sat down close beside me and placed her tiny hand on my leg as she leaned over to see what I was reading, her breast brushing against my arm. I inhaled deeply, that familiar scent of fresh citrus invading my nose. "Looks interesting." She giggled.

"I'm sure the normal person would find it dry and boring. It would probably put you to sleep quickly," I mumbled. At times these cases were even boring me, especially compared to what I was thinking of doing to her right now.

She looked down to where her hand rested on my thigh, her soft blonde hair falling into her face. I wanted to brush the hair away from those beautiful eyes, like I used to do.

Instead, I placed my book on the table and sat back against the couch, resting my arm behind her. Without notice, she moved over closer to me, leaned in, rested her head on my shoulder, and deeply inhaled. "You always smelled so good, and I always felt so safe in your arms. I missed them; I've missed you, Carter." When the words fell from her lips, I was done. I turned slightly and brushed the hair back from her face, my hand resting on her cheek.

Her face was pink with eagerness, and her eyes were filled with a curious, deep longing. I hesitated at first, but then I leaned in and gently brushed my lips against hers. She tasted exactly like I remembered. I pulled away, her lips still moist from where I had kissed her. "I hope it's okay that I did that?" I asked, swallowing hard, studying the look in her eyes. My hand rested on the side of her neck, and I could feel her pulse beating quickly.

She could barely tear her eyes from mine. "Yes." Her voice was shaking, like she was nervous, or possibly wasn't entirely sure it was okay, so I leaned in again and brushed her lips, this time my mouth covering hers hungrily. When we parted, she whispered, "I am so glad you were there tonight." She hastily turned her head away from me, biting her bottom lip.

I placed my thumb and index finger under her chin and lifted her head, so her eyes met mine. She was so warm. She looked into my eyes, desire and want pouring from them. I leaned forward and kissed her, forcing her lips open with my tongue.

She didn't fight. Instead she quickly pushed the pillow aside, pulled herself around, and straddled my lap. She rested her hands on my shoulders at first, then as the kiss progressed, I felt her wrap her arms around my neck. With her eyes closed, she kissed me harder and deeper, a soft moan coming from her when I rested my hands on her hips and ran my tongue, once again, through her mouth. I was as hard as a rock now and knew she could feel me through my shorts as she ground down on me, another moan escaping her lips.

My hands on her hips, I gripped her tighter. My lips parting from hers, I continued to explore the soft skin of her neck. She let out another moan, and I felt my cock jump. "Don't do that, Hope."

"Don't do what?" she asked breathlessly against my ear.

"Don't fucking moan like that."

"Or what?"

I wrapped my hands under her ass, stood up, and carried her into my bedroom, her arms wrapped securely around my neck as she kissed me deeply. I sat down on my bed, placing her back on my lap. With her in my arms, I pulled her forward as I lay down. Soon she lay beside me and rolled onto her back. I raised up on one arm, looking down into her face. My mouth slowly met hers, slowing the eagerness of my kiss. My hand rested on her flat stomach, and soon her hand moved mine onto her breast. My thumb brushed her nipple through her shirt, and she let out another soft moan as she arched her back, pressing her breast into my hand.

"I remember how sensitive these were," I mumbled, placing my mouth over her breast, gently biting her through her shirt. "I could almost make you come just from that, do you remember?"

"Yes." She giggled breathlessly as I reached behind her and grabbed her ass, my hand traveling down to lift one leg up, so it could rest on my hip. She was so tiny and felt so good in my arms; it was taking everything I had not to rip those white panties off and bury myself in her. She wanted to moan? I'd make her moan.

"I loved it when you did that," she answered shyly.

"Do you still?" I felt an unfamiliar surge in my stomach as I looked down at her, waiting for her to answer the question.

"Why don't you find out?" she whispered in my ear, running her fingers through the hair on the back of my head.

I met her lips again, running my hand over her ass. Taking my free hand she pushed it between her legs. With her hand on top of mine, she ran my fingers over the wetness of her panties.

I was so turned on, I had to have her. I pushed myself up and flipped her, so she was completely on her back. She lay against my pillow looking up at me, unsure of what was coming next. I grabbed her by the knees, pulling her down toward me and placed my hands on her waist. I slipped my fingers into the waistband of her panties. She lifted her ass just enough, so I could slowly pull them off her. As I lowered them down her body, I made sure my fingers roughly grazed the skin of her thighs. Her eyes closed as I continued raking my fingers down her legs. When I had removed her panties and had finally torn my gaze from her body to look at her face, I saw that she was innocently biting her finger, a light blush on her cheeks.

Throwing her panties on the floor, I gently pushed her knees open wide, exposing her to me. She was shaved bare and glistening. "You want me to touch you?"

She nodded her head.

As soon as she did that, I ripped off the tiny top she was wearing. Meeting her lips with mine, I felt her tug at my T-shirt. I reached back and pulled the shirt off me, sitting back up between her legs. "Are you finished with him, Hope?"

She slowly nodded her head. I had to know before I got involved with her like this. We had never had sex, and there was no way I could open myself up like that to find out she was still involved with him. I knew that once I had a taste of her, there was no way I could go back to anything else. I wasn't taking a shake of her head for an answer; I wanted to hear the words. "Are you finished with him, Hope?" I asked again.

"It's over, Carter. You're who I want. You were always who I wanted." As soon as the words were past her lips, I ran my fingers over the inside of her thigh, coming close to but not touching her center.

"Touch me, Carter. Please touch me." She closed her

eyes, arched her back, and bit her lip. I loved listening to her beg, and if I had to, I would keep making her beg all night because every time my name escaped those lips, my cock got harder.

I bent down and took her nipple in my mouth, running my tongue over it and biting it gently. With her head arched back, she kept pushing those beautiful breasts into the air. She was about to come undone already, I could tell. I released her nipple and ran my fingers through her wetness. I heard her suck in a breath, a deep moan coming from her throat as my fingers danced softly over her clit.

I couldn't wait to bury myself in her. "Are you still a virgin?" I asked, whispering in her ear as I continued circling her clit.

I pulled my hand away from her, waiting for her answer. She looked at me. Her cheeks and chest were flushed, those innocent eyes of hers peering back at me. She slowly nodded her head. She had waited. It was something I respected about her more than anything. "Are you sure you want…"

She put her finger to my lips, her face becoming serious, and nodded. "Yes, Carter, I want it to be you."

I kissed her slower and deeper than earlier. I needed to take my time with her, let her know that what we were about to do meant something to me as well. It was the only way I could do this. All the feelings I had felt for her before came rushing back and hit me harder than I had expected, my heart pounding hard. To be honest, I knew they had never really left; they had just been buried behind lots of women, studying, and many booze-filled nights.

Hope

I closed my eyes, letting myself get lost in his kiss. In that one single moment that I had said yes to him, all the feelings I still held for him floated through my head. It had been three years, but those feelings had never died.

His eyes raked boldly over me as he removed his pants and whipped them into the corner. My heart jolted, and my pulse pounded as his fingers danced down my arm to my hand. He took my hand in his, placing it on his hard cock. My heart hammered in my chest as I noticed that my hand barely even closed around him.

He brushed his fingers over my clit and then I felt his finger at my entrance. He met my lips, and as he forced my lips open with his tongue, he slowly pushed one finger inside of me. I gasped as he slid another finger into me, his thumb continuing to brush over my clit. He pulled his lips away and placed his hot mouth on my nipple, lightly sucking it with his mouth.

I let out a loud moan; I could feel myself starting to tighten around his fingers. "Not yet, don't come yet," he whispered, pulling his fingers from me, leaving me feeling empty. Kneeling between my legs, he pushed them open again and looked down at me. I was so open and on display to him. He reached over and opened his nightstand drawer, pulling out a condom. I watched as he tore the package and rolled the condom over himself. "You ready?"

I nodded, swallowing hard. "Just be gentle, Carter, please."

"You don't need to tell me that. Just be still and try to relax." I felt him at my entrance, and then he started to slowly push against me. I could already feel him stretching me. The burning sensation took my breath away; it was almost too much, and he was barely even in me. He stopped, letting me adjust before he pushed further in. "Relax, baby, just relax and breathe."

I hadn't even been aware I had been holding my breath until he had said something. As soon as I exhaled, he pushed in a little more, stretching me even further. I bit my lip to keep from crying out as he wrapped his arms around me and pushed himself all the way in. "Relax, baby." His hot breath brushed over my ear as he whispered the words.

He started easing himself in and out of me, and the more I relaxed, the less painful it became. Soon he was deeply planted inside of me, moving slowly and deeply. A few short pumps and I could already feel myself tightening more around him. He reached under me, holding my waist, his fingers finding my clit. I couldn't fight the sensation building in me as he continued stroking over my clit. He pumped a couple more times, and I finally felt myself let go, calling out his name. I gripped his biceps as he continued pumping into me, and soon I felt his muscles tighten, and he too finally let go.

He crashed on top of me, breathing hard, and held me tight. A few minutes later I watched as he held the top of the condom and pulled himself from me. He got up from the bed and headed to the bathroom. I scooted over to the back of the bed and was horrified to see a few drops of blood on his crisp white sheets. I didn't have time to hide it. He was already standing in the doorway, holding a cloth in his hand, looking down at me. I could feel the tears building behind my eyes.

"It's all right, it's normal. Don't worry about it. Just lie back and relax."

I did as he said, trying to let myself relax. He gently opened my legs and eased the warm cloth between them, cleaning me. He said nothing, just watched me as I closed my eyes. He lay down on the bed beside me and pulled me against him, holding me in his comforting embrace. "Are you okay? I didn't hurt you, did I?"

"I'm okay. It hurt a little."

He pulled me closer, our bodies melding together, and met my lips. After we parted, I rested my head on his shoulder. I closed my eyes, letting myself fall asleep to the feel of his fingers dancing along my hip.

Chapter Twenty

HOPE

We'd had an amazing day together. We went to the zoo, wandered through the stores downtown, and then ate lunch. We stood hand in hand as we waited for the elevator to lift us to our floor, then we both wandered down the hall to the apartment door. I watched Carter slide the key in the lock, then he held the door open for me to walk through, coming in behind me.

"I'm going to go change," I said, giving his hand a squeeze and heading to my room.

"All right, I'll order the pizza."

We parted ways, and by the time I had changed and made it to the couch, Carter was already relaxing with his feet up on the coffee table. He wore black sweatpants and no shirt; my eyes trailed over his hard muscles. I grabbed two bottles of water from the fridge and pulled a fifty from my purse. He had paid for the entire day; there was no way he was paying for dinner too. I set the water on the table and held the money out for him to take. "What's this for?" he asked, looking up from the magazine he was reading.

"Dinner. Please take it." I shook it, waiting for him to accept it.

He ignored me, burying his face back in the magazine.

"If you don't take it, I'll have to force you to take it. Please, Carter."

He chuckled to himself. "How are you going to do that?" He continued reading and ignoring me.

I sat down beside him, not saying anything, studying his face. "Carter, come on."

"Hmm." I scooted over closer to him, holding the crinkled fifty-dollar bill, and rested my hand on his abs.

"What are you doing?" He continued reading. I slipped my hand into his pants, dropping the fifty there, and went to remove my hand, but he was faster. He dropped the magazine and placed his hand over the top of mine. I looked down to where our hands met. His other hand coming up to my chin, he tilted my head back so I was looking at him. While his eyes studied mine, he leaned down and brushed my lips with his. "Don't start, cause if we start, I can't promise I'll be able to stop."

Looking up into his eyes I whispered, "Maybe I don't want you to stop."

A loud knock interrupted the moment. I felt his hand loosen around mine, and I pulled my hand from his pants. "Get the door," he said under his breath, sitting back against the couch.

"I, um, need the money," I said, biting my lower lip.

He gave me a sexy smirk. "Go ahead," he said, holding his hands up in front of him in an innocent gesture. I looked down to his lap, where I could see the firm outline of his hard cock through his sweats. "What's wrong?"

"Nothing." I got up from the couch and went to my purse before heading to the door. With pizza in hand I returned to the living room and set the box on the table. I went to sit down and that was when I saw a white envelope with my name on it laying where I had been sitting on the couch. "What is that?" I asked.

"It's for you, open it," he said while grabbing a slice of pizza from the box.

I studied him for a moment and then I carefully picked up the envelope. Peeking inside, I saw a single slip of paper. I pulled it out carefully and gasped at what sat there. A boarding pass in my name to the Dominican Republic. "What is this?"

"We are heading to the Dominican Republic for the weekend. I wanted you to come, so I purchased you a ticket."

"Carter, I can't go. I have to work," I said, looking down at the ticket in my hand. "Plus, I can't afford to pay you back for this. There's no way," I said, shaking my head and holding the ticket out to him.

"What if I told you I'm paying for it and that I got you the weekend off?"

I couldn't look at him for fear I'd cry, so I just kept my focus on the ticket in my hand. "I don't know what to say."

He stood and walked over to me. He reached out, his hand caressing my cheek. "Say yes," he said, looking into my eyes. "Just say yes." He stepped away from me and walked into the kitchen.

I looked again at the ticket, then stood and went to follow him, but he returned holding two napkins in his hands. I looked up at him and into his eyes, thinking for a moment. "Yes, but on one condition."

"What's that?"

"That you let me pay you back when I can."

He leaned down, his mouth covering mine hungrily. "Okay. Let's eat and then I'll help you get packed." He kissed me again and then we sat down and ate.

Chapter Twenty-One

"Sir...Sir?" I felt a hand shake my shoulder, pulling me from my memories. The flight attendant stood in front of me. "I'm sorry, sir, but we are going to be landing soon. You need to secure your laptop and place your seat in the upright position."

I nodded and looked down to my screen. I was supposed to be working on some documents, but instead I had spent the last couple of hours remembering the past.

After I had passed through customs, I turned my phone on while waiting for my cab. Almost instantly it started to ring. I pulled it from my suit pocket, glanced at the screen, and frowned. Hunter's name flashed across the screen. "Hello?"

"Carter, it's me. There is a bit of a problem. I just got a call from Autumn. Hope is over at our place."

"What is she doing there? I left her at home. She said she was going to pick up the girls from her parents. Is everything okay? There isn't anything wrong with her or the girls, is there?" I could feel panic rising in my chest at the thought of being so far away and them needing me.

"Did you tell her where you were going?"

"Yeah, she knows the situation with these clients. I really wanted her to come with me when I had to leave early, but she refused."

"Autumn says she told her that she thinks you are seeing someone. She said she saw a message on your phone earlier tonight from Felice."

"Hold on." A funny feeling came over me. There had been no messages from anyone when I had left.

I quickly checked my texts and, sure enough, there sat a string of messages from Felice that I hadn't seen, probably because Hope had gotten to them first. It was very much unlike her to check my phone.

"Fuck. Mike contacted me a bit ago. They want to adopt a child and asked that the next time I was in town I look over the paperwork while I was here. She's been messaging me over the past two weeks, asking what documents I needed, and apparently, she messaged me sometime tonight and said she was looking forward to seeing me. Hope must have seen the message while I was in the shower."

"So you didn't tell her you were going to be seeing them while you were away?"

I was silent. It had been wrong not to tell her, but I didn't want Hope to worry. I should have told her, but I didn't want to fight with her tonight or ever over something and someone who meant nothing to me. "Fuck no, I didn't."

Hunter was silent and then he cleared his throat and asked me a question I never in a million years thought he would ever ask me. "Carter, is something going on?"

"Are you serious? Are you seriously asking me this right now?"

"All I know is Autumn told me she is really upset, Carter. She says she thinks your marriage is over."

"Are you at home?"

"No, my flight heads out in a couple of hours. I got things wrapped up early."

"Call Autumn back and tell her not to let Hope leave. Fuck the meeting, I'm coming home."

"What about the clients?"

"My marriage is more important than some fucking clients, Hunter. I'll tell them an emergency arose back home and that I will be back here for the original scheduled date. Tell Autumn to keep her there and to not tell her I'm coming."

"No problem."

As soon as I was off the phone with my brother, I turned back around to return to the ticket agent. I needed to get home to my wife.

Chapter Twenty-Two

"Were you really done with Trent at this time?" Autumn asked, taking the last gulp of her tea.

"I was. I was so completely in love with Carter; it had just taken me that long to fully realize it."

"So, the day Trent showed up at the bar, what did he come to say?"

"Well, he was sent by my father to bring me home. He wanted me to go with him, to sit down together and tell our parents that the marriage wasn't going to happen, but I refused. I had nothing to say to my father."

"And so he left, just like that."

"Yes, he too had other plans for his future. He had apparently already met someone else, but what I didn't know was that my father had other ideas."

"Want more tea?" She stood up from the floor and grabbed my mug.

"Yes, please." I got up from the floor and went over to refill the popcorn bowl.

"You said that your dad never liked Carter. What caused that?

"Well, it was all because of a business deal between my father and his. He blamed Carter's father for the loss of the sale of his company. So really it wasn't Carter he didn't like. He just needed to get to know him. Plus, my father ended up finding out that it was really Trent's father that made the original deal fall through, not Carter's father. King Enterprises wanted to own my father's business at any cost. Once my father found out the truth, he started hating Trent." Autumn and I started to laugh.

The phone rang, startling us both. I glanced at the time; it was almost midnight. I frowned at Autumn, but she shrugged her shoulders. "It might be Hunter. Sometimes he calls this late." She smiled, grabbing the phone. "I'll be right back."

"Hello?"

"Hey, baby, it's me. I spoke with Carter. He is on the next flight out. He said to keep Hope there. He asked that you don't tell her."

"Okay, she's spending the night. It's too late and she was too upset for me to let her drive home."

"How is she doing now?"

"Better. I've got her talking."

"About?"

"I asked her to tell me how they met."

The line went quiet. "Hunter?"

"Yeah, well, no judging. I wasn't always how I am now."

I started to laugh at him; he sounded nervous. "I already guessed that."

"Great, I'll see you soon, beautiful."

"Before you go, how many women have you been with?" I asked seriously and then giggled into the phone.

"One. You're the only one who matters, so you're the only one I count."

I laughed into the phone, and after we said our goodbyes again, I hung up and headed back out to the kitchen. "It was Hunter calling to say good night."

A look of sadness came over Hope's face. "That is sweet that he does that. I remember Carter used to do that when the girls were really young. Lately though he hasn't bothered."

"All right, none of that. So he bought you a ticket to the Dominican Republic. What happened next?"

We grabbed our mugs of tea and the bowl of popcorn and sat back down on the floor together, and I listened once again.

Chapter Twenty-Three

CARTER — THIRTEEN YEARS EARLIER

I walked back to our lounge chairs. Felice had decided to join the group at the last minute and so she and the guys were all off playing beach volleyball with a bunch of people they had met earlier that morning when we had arrived at the resort. I set our drinks on the table between our chairs, and I peeked at Hope, who was lounging with her eyes closed.

My eyes rolled up her body. She wore a white bikini that set off the tan of her skin. I took in the soft curves of her body, and when my eyes hit her breasts, I could see the outline of her nipples through the top. We hadn't had time to be with one another again before leaving, and I was dying to feel her again. I had loved hearing her moan my name as I sunk into her.

She rolled onto her front, propping her cute little ass into the air. I couldn't help but look. I wished we were the only ones by the pool. I wanted to run my hands over that cute ass. "I'm just going to jump in the pool to cool off," I said and took off toward the edge. I wasn't even hot, but I needed to calm my throbbing cock, and the more I stood watching her, the worse it was getting.

After dinner we had grabbed a couple late drinks at the bar. A bunch of us were still sitting in the lobby, laughing and talking. I was in the middle of a story when I felt Hope's hand dance along the back of my neck. I looked down into her eyes. They were filled with a longing that needed to be satisfied.

"Guys, I think you'll have to excuse us. We're going to turn in," I said to the group, winking at Hope. I caught a look of jealousy from Felice as I grabbed Hope's hand, pulling her with me.

The warm air blew over us as we walked hand in hand in silence to our room. I slid the key card into the lock. Once inside, I leaned against the corner of the wall and watched as Hope went around to the end of the bed and slipped out of the little white sweater she wore. She ran her hand along the bottom of the king size bed and looked up at me innocently.

"Something wrong?" I questioned.

"There's only one bed. I meant to mention it to you earlier."

"Is that a problem? You don't want to sleep with me?" I asked, watching as a soft smile formed on her lips. "What is it?"

She shook her head, not saying anything. She turned that beautiful face away from me and opened her bag, pulling out her shorts and a tank top. I pushed off the wall and walked up behind her, wrapping my arms around her and pulling her against me. "What are you doing?"

"Getting ready for bed," she answered, running her hands along my forearms.

"I don't think you'll be needing these," I whispered in her ear, taking the clothes from her hands as I ran my tongue along the rim of her ear and took her lobe in between my lips. She inhaled deeply, closing her eyes and tilting her head to the side. I studied the creamy flesh of her neck before I placed my lips on her skin. "You sure you want to go to sleep?"

She shrugged her shoulder. I didn't expect her to answer. We had only been together once, and to be honest, I had gone so easy on her, I didn't expect her to want to do it again. Keeping her in my arms, I walked around in front of her and pressed my lips against hers. "Lie back."

Hope

I slowly backed up until the backs of my knees hit the edge of the bed. I could see a burning in his eyes and this take-charge look. I sat down on the bed, placing my hands at my sides, and looked up at him.

"Lie back, Hope." This time the command was stronger than before.

A funny flutter hit my stomach. I could feel the sex

pouring off him already. He pushed me back, and I had no choice but to lie down. His hands left my shoulders and ran down my chest, his forefingers and thumbs lightly pinching my nipples through my top. I closed my eyes and bit my bottom lip as his hands continued to trail down to my waist. "Take this off," he commanded, tugging on my shirt.

I reached up and opened the buttons down the front, slipping out of the shirt and letting it lay beneath me. "And the bra." His eyes were piercing into me, demanding. This was a Carter I didn't know, but the feelings my body was giving off told me that I liked this side of him.

I watched as he pulled his shirt off and I lay staring up at his hard chest, muscles rippling. "Can we shut the light off?"

He chuckled, "Nope, I want to see every inch of you. Take it off."

My face went red as I brought my hand up to the clasp between my breasts. Anytime we had fooled around in the past, when we dated, it had always been in the dark. Even a few nights ago, it had been dark. He had never seen me in the light, and suddenly I was afraid he wouldn't like me. He leaned over me, his hands on either side of my head, and studied my eyes. "Take it off," he growled.

I pinched the clasp between my fingers and felt a cold rush of air against my breasts as the material from my bra fell away. My face was on fire as his eyes left mine and traveled down my chest. He leaned down and ran his tongue over my hardened nipple, his eyes meeting mine again.

His hand reached down between my legs, his fingers dancing over the material of my jeans. "Take these off."

He stood up and let his shorts drop to the floor. I could see the outline of his hard cock through his boxers. I undid the button on my pants and slid them off. Then I lay back against the bed and again he leaned over me, giving both of my nipples a little lick but not taking them into his mouth as I secretly hoped he would. He kissed his way down my stomach. Every kiss I felt myself flinch. I was throbbing and was already soaked, and he had barely touched me. He knelt onto the floor and threw my legs over his shoulders.

"Do you want to feel what it's like to be kissed here?" His fingers danced over my wet panties.

I closed my eyes and arched my back as he continued to tease me through my panties.

"Answer me. Tell me what you want," he said, pressing his thumb onto my throbbing clit.

"Yes."

"Yes what? You want to know what it feels like to be licked and sucked?"

"Yes." My breathing was becoming erratic. When he pulled my panties to the side, I could feel the cold air hitting my wet skin.

I felt him spread me open, and finally his warm tongue gave my clit a little lick. I sucked my breath in, waiting for him to do it again. He pinched my clit between his fingers and then I felt his hot mouth on me again, this time sucking. "Oh fuck, Carter," I cried out.

I started to push away and tried to move up the bed. I could feel myself starting to lose control, but instead of letting me get away, his hands gripped my waist, pulling me back down to him, his mouth leaving me. "Stay right here. Come on my tongue."

He gave my clit a little lick and then slowly licked my slit from opening back up to my clit before taking it in his mouth again. I gripped the blankets beneath me, arching my back off the mattress, trying to fight my orgasm. Again, he slowly licked from bottom to top. I let out a loud moan, pulling my hand up to my mouth and biting on my hand to keep quiet. "Let it out, baby. Let me hear you come."

He continued running two fingers on either side of my clit, rolling it between his fingers before sealing his mouth over the top of me, sucking and licking until I couldn't hold it back anymore.

"Carter...please..." I ran my fingers through his hair, gripping while screaming his name as I let myself go, his lips never leaving my center until my orgasm finished ripping through me.

Once I had regained control of myself, I noticed he stood up at the end of the bed looking down at me, a sexy grin on his face. I was sure I was a mess, but the look in his eyes told me he was totally turned on. He reached into his bag and grabbed a condom from inside. I watched as he ripped it open and sheathed himself. He pushed me up on the bed and kneeled between my legs.

He rolled his forearms under my knees and tugged my body closer to him. I felt him run his cock through my wetness, coating himself in my juices. Within seconds, I felt him pushing at my entrance.

"Don't hold back, Hope, and don't fight me. I'm not going to be gentle with you. I can't."

His words sent chills through me, but I had never been so turned on.

Carter

I pushed my cock into her, sinking into her warmth. She let out a little cry once I was buried in her. I didn't give her time to adjust to me this time. I pumped hard into her, her fingers gripping my hands tightly. I wanted to be buried in her as far as I could, so I pulled out of her. "On your hands and knees, baby."

At first, she was hesitant, but when she saw the look in my eyes, she quickly repositioned herself. I wasn't giving her a choice; I would move her myself if I had to. I took in the sight of her cute ass and gave it a smack. I came up behind her, taking my cock in my hand and positioning myself at her entrance, and pushed into her, deeper this time.

She called out my name as I pulled back and buried myself into her again and again. "You're so fucking tight," I whispered before taking her earlobe in my mouth.

I didn't take my time with her, and I wasn't gentle. As I pounded into her, I rested one hand on her hip and placed the other on her shoulder, so I could hold her in place. I wanted her to feel every single inch of me, and I could tell she was by every moan she let out. When I felt her start to tighten around me, I knew I was running out of time. I slowed my pace a bit and pushed into her even deeper, which I didn't think was possible. "Rub your clit," I demanded.

I knew she had reached down between her legs to rub her clit because every once in a while, she spread her fingers and wrapped them around my cock so she could feel me pumping in and out of her. I could feel my orgasm building in me at the mere thought that she was rubbing herself while I was buried in her, and I wished she was on her back, so I could watch. "Harder, Carter." She surprised me at this demand, but the sound of those words leaving her lips sent a wave of excitement through me, and I pushed into her harder, faster, and deeper. Making sure she could feel every inch and every muscle, I soon heard her cry out and felt a rush of heat as she came. I couldn't hold back any longer. I finally let myself go, pouring myself into her.

As soon as I had come down, I slowly slid myself out of her, pulled off the condom, and tied it. Once I had cleaned myself off, I came out with a cloth and cleaned her, holding the warm cloth against her.

I pulled her against me under the covers and shut the light off. She was asleep before me, and as I held her, I realized that I really was in trouble. I was falling completely in love with her. My heart belonged to her, and I prayed that she was ready to be with me—completely this time.

Chapter Twenty-Four

HOPE

I sat on the beach watching the waves as they crashed against the sand, my mind wandering back to last night. Carter had woken me in the middle of the night and had slowly made love to me. It was unlike anything I had ever felt before. Slowly, sweetly, and quietly our bodies moved together. There was no demanding, were no harsh words, just a connection so great I wasn't sure I even knew how to handle it. Afterwards we had fallen asleep wrapped against each other, and we had stayed in bed late into the morning, getting up at almost lunchtime to spend the day at the pool.

Just before dinner, I left Carter with the gang and told him I had forgotten something back at the room, but instead, I had come down to the water to gather my thoughts. There was no doubt how I felt about him. I was in love with him, but I hadn't exactly been honest with him, and after last night, it was eating at me. Trent and I had broken up, but my father had other ideas, and I knew he was still pushing for what he wanted. Trent had offered to take me home and together we would tell them that the wedding wasn't happening, but I didn't want to return. I didn't want to see my father just yet. I knew I would have to find a way to show Daddy I was in love with Carter. Even if he disapproved, it was my life, not his.

I was lost in my thoughts, watching the waves crash into the shore, thinking about the problem at hand, when I heard my name being called. I looked over my shoulder and saw Felice approaching.

"Hey, Felice."

"What are you doing all the way down here?" she asked, smiling. "I thought you were getting something from your room."

"Just taking a minute. Would you like to sit down?" I said, moving over.

"Thanks." She sat down, looked out at the water, and cleared her throat. "Hope, do you mind if I talk to you for a moment?"

I shook my head and smiled. "Of course not. Is something up?"

"No, I wouldn't say that. I was just wondering how things are going? Are you enjoying the trip so far?"

"Yes, it's been wonderful."

"Good. So, tell me how are things between you and Carter?"

I softly smiled and looked out at the water, thinking back to last night. "They are good. At least I think so."

She was quiet for a moment. "So, I can't help it, but this whole sudden relationship is sort of surprising to me."

I sat staring out at the ocean. "Why is that?"

"We have been neighbors since he moved across the hall. I know all about what happened between the two of you. I was the one whose shoulder he cried on, it was my body he took out his frustrations on after you and since then, and the string of women that parade in and out of his apartment on a weekly basis has been unbelievable. I've wanted him for a long time, Hope. There was one point not too long ago when I figured for sure we were going to get together. It was the night you showed up. We had gone home together, and things were getting hot and heavy, and then suddenly he stopped and left and you showed up. I don't like people who get in the way of things I want, Hope."

My stomach started to turn at her words. *He'd been with Felice?* The thought sickened me in every way possible, but I wasn't going to let that part phase me. "He's been with other women?" I choked out.

"Yes, the door to his apartment is like a turnstile. One leaves, another enters. He loves to talk about the women he's been with too. At first when he started talking to me about them, I figured it was to make me jealous, but then I wondered if it might be best to stay away from him. But let's face it, he is hot. It's been somewhat of a challenge. He will be quite the catch for someone."

I bit my lip, fighting back tears. "Has he...has he said anything about me?"

"Not to me yet, but I'm sure he is up there right now talking with the guys about you or one of his other conquests."

I didn't know what to say. I just sat there, her words swimming around in my head. I watched a couple stroll down the beach, holding hands, and a couple of kids playing in the sand. Her words were killing me. *He had strings of women and her?* She finally broke the silence by clearing her throat.

"Listen, Hope, I don't want to come off sounding like a jealous friend, but just be careful with him, okay? Whatever it is that is going on between the two of you, make sure you really want it."

"What is that supposed to mean, Felice?"

"Exactly what I said. Don't play games with him."

I looked at her, not knowing what to say. She was acting as though Carter had been the only one to get hurt in our past.

"Felice..." She cut me off before I could say anything else.

"Seriously, Hope, you didn't see him. Just be careful with him. Whatever hold he has on you has the potential to break him for anyone else."

I stared out into the water, wondering why she and I were even having this conversation. "Felice, I would never hurt him on purpose." I wasn't about to admit to her that I was afraid this time I may be the one to get hurt. *Parades of women.* Those words stuck in my head like they had been glued there.

"Never said you would, but remember he's a great guy who has a lot going for him. I would give anything to have a guy like him."

I frowned. "You'd give anything to be with a guy who had a parade of women coming in and out of his apartment? What kind of a girl are you, Felice?" I spat back.

She bit her lip. "Okay, maybe it's not quite as bad as I explained. I'm just saying..."

"What are you saying, Felice?" I glared at her.

"You know, I have wracked my brain trying to figure out where I know you from and it finally came to me last night while I was watching you pour yourself all over him. Two years ago, at my uncle's Christmas party, you were dating my cousin, Trent."

"So what? That is no secret, Felice."

"No, it's not. I guess what I am saying is you better tell Carter the truth before someone else does."

I didn't know how to react to what she had just told me. "I see. Well thank you for your concern, Felice, but it's none of your business."

"Carter is a friend of mine. It is my business."

I stood and turned my back away from her and continued looking out at the water. Felice continued to sit there, and I could feel the tension between us when I heard Carter's voice calling my name in the distance.

"That's my cue."

I said nothing. I didn't want her anywhere near me, and with Carter fast approaching, I needed to turn my mood around and fast. I looked over my shoulder in the direction from which I had heard him call my name and saw him walking across the beach toward us. Felice ran off in the other direction, and I stood there looking out over the water, fighting back tears. It was seconds later that I felt Carter's hand run down my arm. I turned around and wrapped my arms around his neck, breathing in his scent.

We spent the rest of the night watching the entertainment that the resort put on. Felice had turned in early, and I couldn't have been more thankful. After the show was over we had a couple more drinks and then we all turned in.

After we returned to the room and made love, I rested my head on his chest, listening to his rapidly beating heart. A shiver ran through my sweat-covered body. "You cold?" he asked, pulling the blanket up over my bare shoulder and pulling me tighter against him.

"A little," I said quietly.

He placed a kiss on my forehead and then lay back against the pillows. "You were pretty quiet tonight after we got back from the beach. Everything okay?"

Of course I had been quiet. After Felice had spoken to me on the beach, I didn't really have much to say. "Yep, I'm good." I placed a soft kiss on his cheek, taking in the scent of his skin.

I rested my head back on his shoulder and thought about the words she had said. I knew no matter what that Carter was going to find everything out. It was no secret that when I went back for the anniversary dinner, Daddy would be announcing the engagement, pushing me to get back with Trent anyway.

"Can I ask you something?" I knew that after having sex with him, it probably wasn't the best time to be discussing Felice, but my curiosity was getting the best of me.

"Anything," he murmured.

"Felice? She is just your friend and neighbor, right?"

"Friend and neighbor, that is all." He took a deep breath. "But there was a time a while ago that I was involved with her, but it was over before it started for me. Why do you ask?"

"No reason, just wondering."

"Did she say something to you, Hope?"

"Nope. Nothing, I was just wondering." I leaned up on one elbow and looked at the clock. It was almost midnight and we had to be ready to leave the resort at five. "We should get some sleep."

I turned my body away from Carter and felt him wrap his arms around me from behind. We had fallen asleep this way every night since we had been here. Only tonight, with the words of Felice looming in my mind and the upcoming anniversary dinner only a few days away, I had a hard time letting the ease of his breathing and the comfort of his arms lull me to sleep.

Chapter Twenty-Five

HOPE

We had been home a little over five hours when Carter was called into the law firm where he had been interning. I still had tonight off, so I ordered in takeout from a restaurant that Carter recommended and had just finished eating in front of the TV.

When my show was over, I got up and threw out the empty container in the garbage. I quickly washed the plate and glass I had used and set it in the drain pan. Locking the apartment door, I grabbed my mug of hot tea and headed to the bathroom. I needed to unwind. I had been feeling super stressed since Felice had confronted me, and a hot bath was the perfect solution. I squirted a generous amount of my favorite body wash into the tub and started the water, making sure it was the right temperature. As soon as the tub had filled, I stepped in and slowly sunk into the hot water. I leaned back and rested my head against the back of the tub. As my body started to relax, I realized just how much tension I had been holding onto.

As the heat sunk into my body, comforting me, my mind drifted straight to Carter. The last night in the Dominican Republic—how he stood talking with the guys, watching me across the way, that sexy smile on his face. The way he put his arm around me while we were walking back to the room, the way he had kissed me, his large hand on my cheek, pulling me toward him and devouring my mouth. How he had slowly undressed me, his eyes following his hands as they trailed over my body. I remembered how his hands felt as he gently touched me, dancing over my skin. Just thinking about it had my center start throbbing. Suddenly my phone pinged with a message, interrupting and pulling me away from my solitude and my dream state. I picked up the phone, hoping it was Carter, but as soon as I saw the message, my stomach sank.

MOM: WHERE ARE YOU STAYING, SWEETIE?

ME: DOES IT REALLY MATTER, MOM?

MOM: YES, IT MATTERS. I WANT TO KNOW YOU ARE SAFE. DAD TOLD ME WHAT HAPPENED.

ME: I'M FINE, MOM.

MOM: PLEASE TELL ME YOU'VE COME TO YOUR SENSES AND ARE AT TRENT'S.

ME: YOU MEAN HE HASN'T SPOKEN TO YOU?

I held my breath, waiting for her response.

MOM: NO, HE HASN'T RETURNED OUR CALLS.

ME: I'M IN THE CITY, MOM. I'M NOT WITH TRENT.

I had figured that her reply would be instant, but instead the phone was quiet. I waited and waited to hear what she had to say. Finally her message came through.

MOM: IN THE CITY? WHERE? WHERE ARE YOU STAYING?

ME: IT DOESN'T MATTER. I AM SAFE.

Really, that was what she was worried about? They were forcing me into a relationship with the biggest dick on the planet and she is worried about me living in the city alone. I rolled my eyes. I could take care of myself. As much as I didn't want to tell her, I figured it would just be for the best.

ME: DON'T TELL DAD, MOM, BUT I AM WITH CARTER.

MOM: CARTER?

ME: YES, MOM. CARTER, MY EX, THE BOY FROM OUR NEIGHBORHOOD.

MOM: NEITHER YOUR FATHER NOR TRENT WOULD WANT TO KNOW YOU'RE STAYING WITH ANOTHER MAN. I THINK YOU SHOULD COME HOME.

ME: I'M NOT COMING HOME. I'M TAKING SOME TIME, MOM. END OF STORY.

MOM: YOU ARE COMING TO THE ANNIVERSARY DINNER, AREN'T YOU?

My heart sank. I hadn't asked Carter to join me for this dinner, and I wasn't sure if he would say yes, but I had to ask him.

ME: YES, I WILL BE THERE.

I could only imagine the look on their faces when I showed up with Carter. I laughed as I imagined her sitting there with my dad, his head about to pop off. I would make a trip home before the dinner and speak with my father. I lay my phone down on the side of the tub. I didn't want to read any more from her.

When my phone pinged again, I decided I'd had enough of relaxing. I shut my phone off, got out of the tub, dried myself off, and wrapped the plush black towel around me. I grabbed my phone and my tea, opened the bathroom door, and went to the small kitchen to drop my mug in the sink. I grabbed an apple from the fridge and turned to head into the living room when I came face to chest with a man.

I let out a loud scream, dropping my apple and phone onto the floor.

"Princess, relax, it's only me. I didn't mean to scare you."

"Fuck, Carter." I took in a deep breath, trying to calm my rapidly beating heart. I watched as his eyes skimmed my body from the floor up.

"I'm...I'm sorry. I didn't think you would be home already," I mumbled and looked down at myself. "I'm not very appropriately dressed to be running around the apartment, am I?"

"To be honest, I think you might be a little overdressed." As the words fell from his lips, a rush of warmth filled my body. He wore that sexy smirk I had grown to love.

He reached behind his head, and in one swift motion, peeled the shirt from his body. I couldn't help but look at the perfectly chiseled body that stood before me: broad shoulders, defined pecs, and an eight-pack of abs I was suddenly dying to lick. He put Trent to shame. Honestly, he put most men to shame. God, I had to get a hold of myself.

As he came closer, I stepped back until the counter was firmly planted in my back. I could feel the heat from his body pouring off him as my face met his chest. He placed two fingers under my chin so that his eyes never left mine. Once our eyes locked, his fingers left my chin and slid down to the edge of the towel that was wrapped around me. His fingers traced along the edge of the towel, his fingers grazing my skin occasionally, before he finally gave a little tug and the towel fell away from my body. "Whoops," he chuckled. I could feel my face going red as his eyes trailed down my body. I still wasn't used to him seeing me naked. "That's better." He winked, his lips meeting mine.

His hands wrapped around me, squeezing my ass as he pulled me closer to him. He picked me up and started carrying me to his room when a knock on the door stopped us. We both looked to the door. "Fuck," he mumbled, placing me back on the ground. "I'm going to get that, just in case it's my brother. He has a key. I don't want him barging in here interrupting us. Go get into bed. I'll be right there," he growled.

I nodded and made my way to his room, crawling under the covers. I lay there listening, and that was when I heard Felice's voice saying something about next weekend and needing a date. My heart sank at first, but then I heard him mumble something about being busy that weekend, and seconds later, he stood in the doorway, smiling at me.

"Sorry about that," he said as he entered the bedroom. "It was Felice."

"I thought so. Listen, before we get into anything, do you have plans next weekend?"

"Nope, I'm all yours."

I smiled. "Good. My parents are having an anniversary party, and I really don't want to go alone."

He sat down and let out a breath. "I don't know, Hope. They've never really liked me."

"I don't care, I like you. That should be enough." I got up and straddled his lap, placing little kisses on his lips.

"All right then, I'm all yours." Wrapping his arms around me, he assaulted my mouth with his tongue, deeply kissing me.

Chapter Twenty-Six

HOPE

I had borrowed Carter's vehicle on Wednesday to go see my parents. I drove in silence, thinking of what I was going to say to my father. I pulled into the driveway, shut the car off, and looked up at the house I had known since childhood.

I finally got out of the car and walked up the front steps. The door suddenly pulled open, and my father stood there.

"Well, well, well. Look at who has finally come home."

"I'm not here to stay, Daddy. I came to talk to you."

"Well, come on in then."

I walked into his office and sat in the chair across from my father's chair. My insides were shaking with nerves. My father walked around and sat down across from me, resting his arms on the desk in front of him. "I take it you came to talk about the engagement announcement."

"Yes. It's not going to happen. I am extremely happy where I am right now. So, please, I am begging you…"

"Fine, you're happy. That is fantastic, but have you ever thought how much happier you will be with Trent?" He sat back in his chair and looked at me.

"No, Dad, you don't understand. I'm not happy with Trent, and he isn't happy either. We don't want to be married. Daddy, I beg you, please, don't force me into this. It's not what I want."

"And you have spoken to Trent about this?" he questioned, tapping his pen against the edge of his desk.

"Yes."

My father sat there looking me directly in the eyes. He didn't say anything for a long while and then he cleared his throat.

"Fine. I will call and speak with the Kings and call the engagement off."

"Really?"

"Yes, really. You say you are happy where you are, then fine, but if I do this, you need to move back home."

I felt lighter than ever after having Daddy agree to end this silliness. "I have already spoken to Trent," I said, getting up to hug my father.

He wrapped his arms around me. "So we will see you on the weekend?"

"Yes, Daddy. It will still be a plus two; I am bringing Carter." I smiled.

"Fine."

"Where is Mom?"

"She is having lunch with one of the ladies from the

country club. She will be upset she missed you, but I will tell her that you will be here this weekend. Afterwards we can discuss you moving back home."

Chapter Twenty-Seven

H OPE

The rest of the week had flown by, with the looming party hanging in the distance. After visiting my father, my parents had wanted me to come and stay at home for the weekend, but I had refused. It had been slow that week at the bar—tips had been minimal—but I still managed to have enough to pay for two nights at a little motel just on the outskirts of town. Carter had offered to pay, but I refused. He had, after all, just paid for my flight to the Dominican Republic.

"So, you did tell your parents I was your date, correct?" he asked, setting our bags on the bed.

"Yes, of course."

"Okay. I just don't want this to be an issue. We've been over this a million times this week; your father never liked me, Hope."

"Relax. To be honest, it's none of their business who I bring."

"So, does this mean you are finally going to stand up to them about us?"

I stood and walked over to him, placing my hands on his face and pulling him in for a kiss. "No need to worry. I will handle my father."

My hands slowly danced down to the top button of his dress shirt and started to undo the buttons, one by one. Once his shirt was completely open, I pushed it off his shoulders and ran my hands over his chest. I locked eyes with him. His were hungry with need as I rested my fingers in the belt loops of his jeans.

"What is it you want?"

I let out a little nervous giggle, not saying anything, my fingers moving to the button of his jeans. He grabbed my hand, moving it to his cock. He was already hard, and I had barely touched him. When my hand cupped him, he sucked in a deep breath. "This. I want this," I said shyly.

He grabbed me, picking me up and taking me over to the bed where he threw me down, his hand running down the front of my body. I could feel my body start to tremble at the simple touch. He lay beside me, placing his hands behind his head, a glint of playfulness in his eyes. I sat up and gently tugged at the button of his jeans, sliding the zipper down tooth by tooth. His cock peeked out of the top of his boxers. I kept my eyes locked with his as I bent down and licked the head of his cock. His sharp inhale sent chills through me. I wanted to hear him do that again, so I once again licked the head.

"You're such a tease." He reached down and ran his fingers through my hair.

I pulled him out of his boxers, holding the weight of him in my hand. He raised up and pushed his pants the rest of the way down, kicking them off. I kneeled between his legs and took him in my hand, running my hands over his cock.

"I want to feel your mouth wrapped around me," he growled.

I ran my tongue from the base of his cock to the tip and then placed my mouth over him. Running my tongue around him, I listened as his breathing increased. I pulled him from my mouth, holding him in my hand and slowly stroking him, running my tongue around the head and finally tasting the bead of precum at the tip.

He reached down and placed his hand on my cheek. "Come here," he quietly demanded.

I crawled up beside him and met his mouth harshly with need. He pushed my open shirt from my shoulders, throwing it across the room. He pulled my skirt and panties down and threw them in the opposite corner of the room. His hands quickly found their way between my legs, and he ran his fingers through my wetness, making me shiver at the touch.

The harshness of his kiss finally slowed, and he began to take his time.

Carter

. . .

Her body squirmed beneath me as I continued running my fingers over her swollen clit. I watched as she bit her lip, trying to stifle her moans. She was beautiful. I leaned down and placed my lips over hers, sucking her lower lip into my mouth, as I slid two fingers inside of her while continuing to rub her clit with my thumb. She was so tight around my fingers, and I knew she was close, so I continued, her fingers clawing at my back. Finally, she cried out. I removed my fingers from her and looked down into her eyes. "I love you."

A look of surprise came over her face as she looked into my eyes. I couldn't hold back how I felt for her anymore. I was determined that I was not going to lose her this time. She had to know. "I love you, Hope. I never fully realized just how much until I finally saw you again."

"Carter, I love you too." Her voice was weak, but the tears that built in her eyes told me she was serious. I held her in my arms, pulling her tightly against my chest, and together we lay there entwined in one another.

Chapter Twenty-Eight

Carter looked amazing in his perfectly tailored black suit. I stood beside him in my new black cocktail dress, and together we walked hand in hand up the front steps of the banquet hall. As soon as we entered, we were greeted by a waitress carrying a tray of champagne. "Could I interest either of you in a drink?" she asked with a smile, holding the tray out to us.

We both took a glass and continued into the room. I quickly glanced around. Many of my parents' friends looked my way, whispering to each other when they saw a different man with me. I felt Carter's hand at the small of my back, which gave me the confidence boost I needed as we made our way through the crowd to look for our seats.

"Hope, thank God, there you are. Your parents are looking for you." I turned and saw my aunt coming toward me. "Who is this handsome man?" she said, eying him up and down. Aunt Tess was a divorced, highly attractive, middle-aged woman and was always looking for her next conquest.

"Aunt Tess, this is Carter. Carter, my aunt Tess."

"Hello. Nice to meet you, handsome."

"Hope, I was just speaking with your mother. She says your father is looking for you. He wants to see you. He's angry, Hope," she said, whispering in my ear as she pulled me away from Carter.

"I'll be right back."

"Go ahead. I'll be here." Carter gave my hand a squeeze before my aunt dragged me away from him.

"Your mother wants to see you before he gets hold of you. Let's hope that we find her first."

"What else is new, Aunt Tess? He is always angry at me," I moaned. She was practically dragging me behind her, when my father came into view. She tried to hide from his line of sight, but it was too late.

"Brian, I found her." My father turned around, his gaze fierce.

"It's about damn time you arrived, Hope. I saw you came with someone."

"Yes, I did. That's Carter, Daddy. I told you."

"Ah yes, Carter. Well, I'm sorry to say that you are not going down that path again. It took me long enough the first time to get you away from him. Don't make me do it again."

"Yes, and exactly why did you do that?"

"He's a loser and he isn't good for you."

"He isn't a loser, Dad. He's a very smart man and a hard worker."

My mother came walking over, smiling at me. "Hope, love, there you are. You ready for the big announcement tonight?" she said, wrapping her arm around my shoulder. "You really should have gotten a new dress," she whispered in my ear, pushing me away from her and looking me over.

"This is brand new."

"Well, it will have to do. It's just not what I would have chosen for you to wear for such an announcement," she said, her eyes running over me again in a judging way.

"That's okay, because there isn't going to be an announcement after all. Didn't Daddy tell you?"

My mother looked from me to my father with a confused look on her face. "Beverly, Hope came home and shed some light on how ungrateful she is that we have put this marriage together."

"Oh." My mother turned and looked at me, "Hope?"

"Mom, please..." I begged. "I explained to Daddy that I'm with Carter, and he agreed to cancel everything."

My mother let out a loud laugh. "Not that boy. He is nice and all, but honestly, Hope, grow up."

"No. I would rather be with someone who loves me back than be with a domineering man. I would rather live in squalor than live with that!"

People started to look our way, including Trent's parents. "Hope, you will stop this behavior right now," my father demanded, gripping my arm.

"No, Daddy, I won't."

I turned to head back to our table when I saw Carter walking over our way. He walked right over, holding his hand out to my father. "Sir, good to see you again. Carter Malone."

"Carter, nice to see you. How's school?"

"Good, sir. I just received my final marks. Top two percent in my class. I take the BAR at the end of the summer."

"I'm sure you'll do very well. Then you will screw people just like your old man." My mouth hung open as he dismissed Carter, as if he were nothing more than the dirt on the bottom of his shoe, then turned away with my mother to go speak with Trent's parents.

"Dad, you are going to apologize to him right now," I said, stomping my foot hard on the floor.

My father turned, glaring at me. "I've had enough. Now before you make any more of a scene and ruin the whole evening, I suggest you get to your seat and sit down."

Carter grabbed my hand and pulled me away from my parents, making our way back to the table. All eyes followed, and murmurs and whispers floated through the air. I could feel my blood start to boil at the way both my parents had just treated Carter, and something in the bottom of my gut told me my father had lied to me and that another surprise was just around the corner.

"I'm sorry my father is such an asshole, Carter. This was a bad idea. I think maybe we should just go."

Carter pulled the chair out for me and waited for me to sit down. I looked around the room and noticed Trent staring at us as Carter handed me my glass of champagne. "Just calm down, Hope. Tell me what happened."

I was just about to start telling him the whole truth when out of nowhere came a very familiar voice calling to Carter. We both turned in the direction that it came from and saw Felice walking over to us.

"Felice," Carter's deep voice called out. I fought back the tears coming to my eyes when I saw her coming toward us. This night was getting worse by the second.

"Felice, what are you doing here?" he asked, placing his arm around my shoulders.

"My aunt and uncle are here. They sent the invite. My cousin apparently has an important announcement to make; I couldn't miss it. I believe you know my cousin, Hope, Trent King," she said, glaring at me, a smug smile coming across her face.

I stared back at her.

"Such a small world. I grew up with Trent. I never knew you were his cousin," Carter said, moving behind me.

I went still and felt a funny kind of heat pour over me. Carter's hand gripped my shoulder tighter. Felice went to say something, but my father cleared his throat into the microphone and started to speak. "I'll see you later, Carter. It will be exciting to hear the announcement," she drawled. "Hope, it was nice seeing you too. I can't wait to see your reaction to the news." She smiled, turned, and walked away.

"What did she mean by that?" Carter asked, sitting back down beside me.

I had nothing to say. The sick feeling in my stomach started to get worse. It was like she had known all along. I took a sip of my water as my father's speech droned on. All the while I continued to try to get Carter to leave, but he refused. He said I should be there to help my parents celebrate. As soon as my father had completed his speech and toast, dinner was served. Carter was involved in a conversation with a lawyer friend of my father's, and I sat there quietly picking at my dinner, not really eating anything because my stomach was turning. I excused myself to use the washroom just before dessert was to be served.

"Are you feeling okay?" Carter whispered, grabbing my hand as I got up. "You're awfully flushed."

"I'm fine. I'll be right back." I squeezed his hand and headed toward the washroom.

As I entered the room, I was happy to see that it was empty. I walked over to the counter and looked at myself in the mirror. I could barely breathe, knowing what was coming. I had to get us out of there before Mr. King made his announcement; I just didn't know how. I didn't want to lose Carter again.

The bathroom door swung open and I glanced in the mirror to see Felice walk in. She gave me the cat-ate-the-canary smile and glared at me as she walked over to the sink and stood beside me. She placed her clutch down on the counter and searched through it. She pulled out her compact and dusted her face. "So, does he know?" I stood still, not knowing what to say. "I take it from your silence that he doesn't. He's going to be crushed, Hope, and it's going to be all your fault. I told you to be careful."

"I'll take care of it."

"Oh, I'm sure you will, just like you already have." She threw her compact back into her bag, zipped it up, and grabbed her clutch, walking back over to the door. "Don't worry, I'll pick up the pieces, just like I did the last time. You know, I never thought I would say this to any woman, but you deserve my cousin." She opened the door and headed back out to the party.

I looked at myself in the mirror, wiping the tears from my eyes. I grabbed my lip gloss and coated my lips before throwing it back into my bag. I quickly left the washroom. I had every intention of getting back to the table and telling Carter I had been sick and that I needed to go home. As I was walking across the room looking at Carter, I suddenly heard my name called. I stopped dead as the words that followed next literally shattered my heart in two. "Tonight, I'm happy to announce the engagement of my son, Trent King, to Hope Heathcote."

Everyone stood up and started clapping, everyone except the person with whom I had locked eyes. He sat there staring at me, a look of confusion mixed with a completely gutted look on his face. Tears filled my eyes as he stood, nodded his head, turned, and walked away from me. A woman I barely recognized came over to me, took my hand, and walked me over to where Trent stood. I kept my eyes locked on Carter, constantly wiping the tears from my eyes. I watched him walk up the stairs we had come down. I had no time to chase after him because soon Trent and I were enveloped with people congratulating us and our parents.

Finally, after all the congratulating had been done, I fought to get away. I needed to find Carter. This was all a misunderstanding that I needed to sort out. I searched through the crowd for him, but I couldn't see him. I pulled my phone from my purse and texted him as I continued to search through the sea of people, but there was no answer. I called him as I quickly headed to the front of the banquet hall, hoping and praying he was outside, thinking surely he would give me time to explain.

With the phone ringing in my ear, I ran out the front door looking to my left and then to my right. There were so many people out there that I had to slow down to scan over them once again. Finally, I saw him over against his car, his head hung low, staring at the ground. Tears filled my eyes. There was no way I was letting him get away from me this time; he had to believe that I didn't want this. I went to call out to him, but my throat was so tight from fighting back tears, I knew there was no way he would hear me. I started running in his direction, but then I saw Felice walk up to him and throw her arms around his neck. He hugged her back, pulling her against him tightly. In that moment, everything stopped. I couldn't breathe. I stood there watching as she placed a kiss on his cheek, and then he grabbed her tightly. She whispered something into his ear and then he kissed her, like he had kissed me not twelve hours ago. I was finished, my heart broken. I wasn't sure what to do. I was angry at her, angry at him, and livid with my parents. I couldn't keep my eyes off them; it was like I was punishing myself. Again, she whispered something in his ear, kissed him again, and then they both got into his car and drove away.

I crumbled onto the steps outside of the front door, my head in my hands. I let out an uncontrollable sob. In a matter of minutes, I had just lost the only thing I ever wanted. The fire burning in my gut told me that now was the time I needed to stand up to my father and find my way back to Carter.

Chapter Twenty-Nine

CARTER

We drove back to the hotel in silence. Felice waited in the car for me to run inside, change, and grab my bag. When I walked into the room, the first thing I saw was the messy bed, where Hope and I had made love and said I love you for the very first time, not more than six hours ago. I tried not to look, but when you don't want to see something, it's like you are blinded by it. I gathered my things, shoving everything into my bag, and headed back out to the car. Felice was silent all the way back to the city, holding my hand the whole way home. I had nothing to say, and even if I did, I wouldn't even know where to begin. I switched the radio on and thought about the girl I had always been in love with, and how she had burned me good this time, making me look like a fool. The first time had been a misunderstanding on both our parts, but this—this had been a blatant lie.

The drive home seemed to take forever, and I was exhausted by the time I pulled the car into my parking spot and shut the engine off. I leaned my head back against the headrest and shut my eyes, letting out a deep breath. I just sat there listening to the sounds of the traffic passing by. "Carter, we should go inside. It's late." I felt her hand slide onto my leg.

I left my bag in the car, and we walked into the apartment. After taking the elevator in silence, we walked down the hall toward our apartments. I planned to go in and go to bed; however, Felice had other ideas, and instead of her going into her apartment, she came into mine. I didn't care. I didn't have the energy to fight, and I was undecided as to whether I would rather have company or be alone right now. Kicking my shoes off, I headed for the fridge. "Want something to drink?"

"Sure."

I reached in the fridge, pulling out two beers, opening hers and handing it to her before opening mine. Felice followed me into the living room. I flopped down onto the couch, putting my feet up on the table, and then turned on the TV. Felice sat beside me. I could feel her watching me as I flipped through the channels, trying to find something to watch.

"Are you going to be okay?" she asked quietly.

"Fine. I'll be fine." I had no choice but to be fine. I would bury myself in my studies for the rest of the summer and forget all about Hope. What choice did I really have? I had done it once before; I could do it again. I glanced over to the chair and saw her grey sweatshirt flung over the arm. She had been wearing it the other morning when she got out of bed, and that was where it lay after I peeled her clothes off her and took her up against the wall. An overwhelming surge of hurt mixed with anger flowed through me, and I got up and walked over to where the shirt lay, grabbing it and whipping it into Carson's room. All her shit was still here, which meant she would either have to come back or I would have to take it to her. I slammed his door shut, as if shutting it would erase everything that had happened.

"Carter," Felice called.

"Felice, I said I would be fine." I downed the remainder of my beer and went to the fridge for another one, taking it back into the living room and sitting back down beside her.

"Maybe you just need your mind redirected for a while," she said, her fingers trailing along my collarbone.

I closed my eyes and let my head lie back, taking in the feel of her hand on my skin. I felt her switch positions and then felt her lips graze my ear. "I can make you forget her, Carter. Just give me a chance."

I opened my eyes and looked at her, turning my head to meet her lips. I pulled her over onto me, so she was straddling my lap, my tongue sweeping through her mouth. Running my fingers through her hair, I started kissing down her neck. I could feel her hands running down my chest, and then she gripped my cock through my pants. "Give it to me, Carter. Fuck me hard."

I opened my eyes, my hands falling away from her body. "Felice, I can't do this."

"Sure, you can, baby. Let me make you forget," she begged, rubbing my cock through my jeans.

I reached down, pulling her hand off me. "Get off me. I can't do this."

"What's wrong?"

"I can't do this with you. You're not her, and I'm not going to pretend for one night to use you, just to bury my feelings like I did before."

"It's okay, Carter. One night would be enough for me."

I shoved her off me and stood. Grabbing my beer, I drank the rest of it down. There was no way this was going to happen. I couldn't do this, nor did I want to. The only one I wanted in my arms was Hope, regardless of what had happened tonight.

"I told her, you know. I told her if she wasn't serious about you, not to play games."

I walked to the door and opened it, not looking at her, but waiting for her to leave.

She continued mumbling away, but I ignored her. Finally she got up off the couch and walked toward me. At some point she had removed her shirt and bra and stood before me, taunting me. "You don't want me?"

I couldn't even look at her, and I'm a man; I love tits, and I had always thought she had a great set, but it didn't matter. I grabbed her shirt from her hand and covered her. "Good night, Felice." She walked across the hall digging in her purse for her keys. I shut my door and locked it before she had a chance to turn around. Then I shut off the lights and headed into my bedroom. I stripped down to nothing and crawled into bed. As soon as I buried my face into the pillow, I smelled her—that light, fresh citrus scent all over my pillow and my sheets—and as the scent continued to invade me, my thoughts flew to the memories we had made over the last few weeks. I knew without a doubt that she was supposed to be mine. I lay there as long as I could, punishing myself in my mind, until I couldn't take it any longer. I got up, got dressed, and headed down to Joe's place.

Chapter Thirty

Hope

I sat out front the banquet hall, taking in the silence and fresh air. My eyes were swollen, and my throat and chest hurt from crying. The doors to the hall opened, and Trent came out. Everyone had pretty much left. The only people still here were my parents, Trent's family, and the odd family members. I sat against the wall, my legs pulled up to my chest, my head resting on my arms.

Trent came over and sat down beside me. "I'm not too thrilled about what happened tonight either, Hope." He was quiet as he said the words, not looking in my direction.

I had nothing to say, so I just listened.

"It's no secret, Hope, that we aren't right for each other. I'm not in love with you, and I've met someone, someone at my father's company. I've been seeing her since we broke up."

"That's great, Trent. I'm happy for you." I swallowed hard, my heartbeat accelerating.

"I don't love you; I don't think I ever have. I don't want this marriage any more than you do."

"Have you told your parents that?"

"I did, tonight, after the announcement."

"Why not before?" I asked, swallowing hard.

"I wanted you to come back with me to talk to them, but you wouldn't, and I get why—you thought your father sent me to get you. But after I thought about it and after I watched you tonight, I realized how happy you were when you were with Carter, possibly how happy you always were with him. I realized it was wrong of me to want you and to try to take you from him because I see now that you were never that happy with me, Hope. Someone would have to be blind not to see that you are in love with him."

Our eyes met, and I gave him a soft smile. "I am. I came back and talked with my dad. He said he would talk to your parents, that he would call this whole thing off, but he lied."

"It's okay. I will talk to my father, and if worst comes to worst, I will talk with them both. Okay? I'm sorry for the trouble I have caused; I will fix it."

I smiled at him. "How about I drive you home?" he asked, holding his hand out for me to take. I placed my hand in his and he pulled me up.

"I'm staying at a motel not far from here. I need to get my things, but before you take me to the hotel and to my parents, would you mind driving me into the city? I want to see Carter. Mom and Dad are going to be here for a while by the looks of things."

"Sure, come on," he said, wrapping his arm around my shoulder. "Don't worry. Everything will work out."

Together we walked down the front stairs and over to Trent's car. He opened the door for me and helped me in and then walked around to the other side. We drove in silence back to the hotel and once I had my things, he drove me to the city.

The house was quiet as I lay in my room, staring up at the ceiling. My small bedside light was on; my head was pounding. The trip to the city had been uneventful. Since I had gone with Carter, I had left my keys inside the apartment, so I couldn't get in. I had banged on the door until finally Felice had come to her door, and within minutes, she had me in tears and running for the elevator.

After Trent dropped me off at my parents', I had tried to text Carter, and then call, but he had shut his phone off. I didn't want to believe that Felice was right, that he was in bed in her apartment, but I was beginning to wonder. I was staring at my cell phone praying for a reply when I heard the front door slam and my father's elevated voice in the entryway below. He was yelling at my mother. I closed my eyes and let out a breath; I just wanted to be left alone. I had thought about asking Trent to drop me at one of the girls' houses that I worked with, but I was exhausted and upset and couldn't remember how to get there.

"Hope, get your ass down here now!" My father's voice bellowed up the stairs.

I closed my eyes, wishing he would just leave me be.

"Hope! I said now!"

I clenched my fists and flung my legs off the side of my bed. I glanced at my cell phone and thought about trying to call Carter one more time before heading downstairs, but my father had different ideas.

"Young lady, if you don't get down here in two seconds, I swear you're on your own!"

Seriously, the idea was tempting and appealing as hell, and I had planned to leave in the morning anyway to head back to the city.

"What?!" I screamed as I pulled the door open and stomped down the stairs.

"Hope, it's come to our understanding that neither you nor Trent want to marry."

"No, we don't. I tried to tell you that. We don't love each other, Daddy."

"Let me guess...because you love Carter." My father rolled his eyes as he sat down in his chair and put his feet up on the ottoman in front of him.

"Yes! What is wrong with that?"

"Hope...where do you think you are going to be with him in five or ten years?"

"Definitely not divorced. He is going to be a lawyer, Daddy. He will be able to provide a good home and life for me."

"But you'll have everything you could ever want with Trent."

"Sure, everything but love. I would rather have that,

then all the money and belongings in the world. You should give Carter a chance, get to know him."

"Hope, I don't need to get to know him. He is just like his father, and you, young lady, don't know what you are talking about. So, this man can provide love, but what else is he going to provide?" My father looked at me, drumming his fingers on the edge of his chair, waiting for me to answer.

"Carter is a good person. He is smart and hard-working. You heard him tonight; he is at the top of his class."

"Great, good. Top of his class, so he has book smarts."

"Well, that's more than I can say for Trent. Did you know that your prize choice dropped out of university last year and his parents don't even know yet?"

I turned away from my father and grabbed my purse from where I had left it on the chair when I had come through the door.

"Hope, I'm afraid to say it, but if you aren't going to marry Trent then I am going to have to ask you to move out."

"Brian, that is enough. You heard it straight from Trent tonight. Neither of them want to marry, and this is your daughter. It's time you start listening. I want her to be happy, so just because she doesn't agree with your views, doesn't mean you kick her out," my mother said, resting her hands on my father's shoulders.

"No, end of the week, Hope. Let's see how well you do with your choice."

I looked at my father, then at my mother, tears coming to my eyes. I could see by the look on his face that he meant every single word. I stared at my father. I didn't have anything to say. Carter was where my heart lay.

"You'll see, Daddy, you'll see."

"Yes, we will."

I walked out of the room and up the stairs. My mother's voice droned on in the background, begging my father to reconsider. I swear in moments like these, they too must have had an arranged marriage. As soon as I got to my room, I grabbed my cell phone, dialing Carter. It rang and rang, and just as before, there was no answer. I tried not to read into it, leaving a short and brief message, begging him to call me back. I looked around my room at all of the things that were there—the clothes that hung in the closet, the books that sat on the shelf, my laptop, pictures of my parents and me over the years in frames on the shelves that held other things. I walked to the closet and started packing up all the things I wanted to take. Then I called Mike, letting him know I would accept the full-time position that he had offered me before I had left for the anniversary party.

Chapter Thirty-One

Carter — Present Day

I sat in my seat on the plane, waiting for the crew to open the doors. I could only get an indirect flight home and was glad that the first leg was done. I rubbed my eyes. My heart ached thinking back to all that had happened when we were younger, and I couldn't wait to get my hands on my wife. I had notified the office as soon as we landed to call my clients and tell them there was an emergency at home and I would be there first thing on Wednesday morning. There was nothing more I could do; I needed to get home. I needed to get home to my wife. I knew I should have told her, but I wasn't sure how she would react at the mention of Felice's name.

I quickly sent a text to Mike instead of Felice, letting him know that something came up back home and I would have to cancel our dinner meeting. I told him I would still look over the paperwork and asked him to kindly send it via email. I didn't plan to return alone on Wednesday; my wife was coming with me.

I glanced at my watch. It was already two. I would have to run through the airport if I was going to make my connecting flight. I stopped quickly at the information desk to make sure I had the correct gate, and nothing had been changed. The attendant tapped on the keys and frowned as she waited for the information. "Sir, it looks like that flight has been delayed by two hours. You have plenty of time." The airport attendant looked up at me and smiled.

"Great, thanks." My gut sank, I'm not going to lie. I just wanted to get home to my baby. I slowly walked toward the gate I was supposed to board at, stopping on the way to grab a coffee. It was going to be a long night if I didn't get some caffeine in me.

Once I had found my gate, I sat down at a table in the small lounge and opened my briefcase. I figured I may as well do some work while I wait. I opened my laptop, and before starting, I booked two tickets for Tuesday evening. She was going with me; I didn't want to hear any more about it. We needed quality time. If our parents couldn't take the girls, one of my brothers could.

I sat there, sipping my coffee, working away, when my phone pinged. Glancing down at the screen I was surprised to see Mike's name; after all, it was the middle of the night. The message was simple enough: "Call me."

I dialed and waited, finally hearing his voice. "Hey, Carter."

"Mike, I'm sorry to have to cancel on you guys on such

short notice; there's been an issue at home that I have to tend to."

"I hope it's not the girls?"

"No, no, everyone is fine. I received a call when I landed, but I had no choice; I had to turn around. I won't be back until Wednesday morning, and I can only stay in town for a couple nights. I have to be back home for court on Friday afternoon."

"It's understandable, but I didn't even know you were coming into town."

"What do you mean? Felice messaged me. She set up a dinner meeting to go over adoption papers."

"Seriously, Carter, I had no idea. But there is something I would like you to see."

"All right, email over what you want me to look at."

"I just did before you called." He sounded down and a little strange to me.

"Everything okay, Mike? You don't sound like yourself."

"I've been better. I think it's best you just open the email, Carter."

"All right. Let me just take a quick peek and make sure I got it." I opened my email on my laptop, connected to the Wi-Fi, and waited for emails to download, finally seeing Mike's name. I opened the attachment and almost choked on my mouthful of coffee. I was no stranger to seeing these documents. I dealt with them more than I dealt with anything else, and I was suddenly grateful for everything I had in my life.

"Mike, are you sure this is what you wanted me to look at?"

"Yep." He cleared his throat. "You are someone I trust."

"I'm sorry, man. I'm shocked. Felice's message said she wanted me to look over adoption papers."

He let out a deep laugh. "How long have you been in touch with her?"

"She messaged me a couple weeks ago. Now that you mention it, her texts came across as desperate." Then as I sat there thinking back, she had never once mentioned Mike in any of them.

"Desperate, that's funny. She's been fucking everything with a dick. Maybe her candy has finally run out and she's looking now to revisit old flames. Anyway, we're through. So if you wouldn't mind looking over the paperwork, I would appreciate it."

"Yeah, no problem. Why aren't you trusting your lawyer?"

He cleared his throat. "I don't have one. I was planning to represent myself with one of those DIY kits. She bled me dry, and I'm hanging on by my fingernails. I have the bar still, but she emptied all of our accounts."

"Mike, you cannot represent yourself with a kit you bought off Amazon," I chuckled. "Don't worry and don't submit those papers. We will get things together. You've got a lawyer now. I'll be in touch with you on Monday morning. We'll go over everything, and I'll get proper documents drawn up."

"Thanks, Carter. I just don't know how I will pay you."

"No need to worry about it. I do a certain amount of pro-bono work per year, and I haven't hit my quota yet."

"Thanks, Carter."

We hung up, and I texted Felice letting her know I was cancelling, and then I buried myself into work until I heard the call for my flight. I packed everything up and got into line with my boarding pass. I felt my phone vibrate in my pocket and looked at the screen.

"What do you mean you have to cancel? You're going to cancel on this?"

I scrolled down and saw a naked picture on my phone of the one and only Felice. I hit delete and blocked her number. If she thought for one second that that was going to entice me or that there could be anything between us ever again, she would have other thoughts once she received Mike's divorce papers with my name signed on the bottom.

I relaxed into my seat on the plane and closed my eyes. Once the plane was in the air my mind went back to the night that Hope walked back into my life.

Chapter Thirty-Two

The anniversary dinner had been two weeks ago—two weeks since I had seen Hope. She had left a couple messages on my phone, but I had been too hurt to return her calls. In those two weeks, I had fended off Felice more than I cared to count. I had also called in sick more than I had in the past three years, I hadn't been to the gym, and I had barely left my apartment.

I was sitting on the couch, looking for something to watch, when someone pounded on the door. "It's open," I called from the couch.

I heard the door open and close and then Hunter's voice behind me. "Man, what the hell has happened to you?" My brother walked in and looked around my destroyed apartment. "You do realize that Carson is going to be back soon. He's going to flip," Hunter said as he looked around at the mess of dirty clothes, pizza boxes, and old takeout food containers that were strewn all over my apartment.

"So what, I'll clean it," I grumbled.

"Good. Are you coming home to Mom and Dad's with me? They are expecting us around six."

I glanced at my watch; it was almost three. "What day is it?"

"Carter, man, it's Friday. We're going home this weekend...Mom's birthday dinner...ring any bells?" Hunter cleared the dirty clothes off the chair and sat down.

I ran my hand over my face. I couldn't remember the last time I had showered or done laundry, and I had run out of clean dishes at the beginning of the week.

"Fuck, man, you better get your act together. Mom will be hurt if you don't come home."

"Just tell her I'm working."

"No damn way. I'm not going to lie to her. Pick yourself up, have a shower, and let's go. What the fuck happened to you anyway? Where's Hope?"

I took a deep breath. "She decided that marrying Trent King was a better idea than being with me."

"I don't want to say 'I told you so,' but I told you, man."

"I don't need to hear it, Hunter."

Someone pounded on the front door. I closed my eyes and looked at Hunter, and then the voice that rang out gave it away. "Oh Carter, baby, open the door."

I squeezed the bridge of my nose and looked to my brother. "Fucking Felice. She hasn't given up. Last night she showed up at my door dressed in a trench coat with nothing underneath but red lace pantics."

"Sweet ass! You should totally get with her."

"Here you go. Here is the show she put on for me the night before last." I handed him my phone after opening the chat conversation she'd had with me. He scrolled through picture upon picture of nude photos of her.

"Let me get it. If you aren't going to tap it, I will." I watched as my brother jumped up off the chair and ran to the door. "Get your ass showered and ready. I'll be back in twenty minutes."

I chuckled to myself, got up, and headed to the bathroom.

We'd been on the road for just over an hour and I had listened begrudgingly to Hunter drone on and on about his adventure with Felice. "Fuck, man, you should have done it. She would make you forget all about Hope."

That was the last line I needed to hear, because I didn't want to forget all about her. I wanted her, every ounce of her, right now and forever.

"Have you been to Joe's?" I casually asked.

"Yep. We called you, but you must have been wallowing."

"Was she there?"

"Nope. How about, this weekend, you concentrate on nothing but getting the next piece of ass and letting Hope go."

I threw my phone down into the center console and rested my head back against the headrest. I didn't want to forget about her. My phone pinged with a message a little while later. Grabbing my phone, I checked my messages, praying that Hunter had taken care of Felice and that she would leave me alone, at least for a while. But as soon as I saw the name that crossed my screen, I threw my phone down and fought the urge to be sick. I couldn't...I couldn't even bear to read what she had to say.

I cranked the tunes on the radio the rest of the drive home. As Hunter turned the car down the old familiar street, an overwhelming feeling rose in the pit of my stomach. What if I saw her while I was at home? I mean, she did live right across the road from my parents. After my brother pulled into the driveway, I climbed out of the car. The first eyes I locked on were hers. She stood on her parents' front porch looking at me, her eyes dark. She raised her hand in a little wave. I turned my back away from her and demanded my brother bring the bags in.

Carter

After dinner I sat in my father's den, sipping on Scotch, and reading through the evening's newspaper. Hunter had gone out with Chase and Bryce to see a movie. After they had left, I had finally taken a few minutes to read through the texts that Hope had sent. She was asking to meet me for a coffee. I was sure she just wanted to get her things, but she would have to wait until I was ready. I let out a breath, threw the paper down, grabbed my glass, and sat back in my father's leather armchair.

"Well, son, how is the studying coming?" My father came into his office and sat down behind his desk, rooting through one of his drawers, looking for something.

"As well as can be, Dad."

My father took one look at me, got up from his chair, and shut his office door. "Son, what is it?"

"What is what, Dad?"

"Who do you think you are fooling? You look like shit. What's going on?"

I was quiet, downing the last bit of Scotch from my glass. I made my way over to my father's cabinet and poured myself another glass. "Want some?" I asked, holding the bottle up.

He nodded. I filled the two glasses and set the bottle down. When I turned, my father took the two glasses from my hand, a worried expression coming over his face. "Are you in some sort of trouble, son?" I said nothing, just sat down and sipped another mouthful of the golden liquid, savoring the burn as I let it slowly roll down my throat. My father sat there in silence, waiting for me to talk. I wasn't sure how much I wanted to tell him. "Son, if you are in trouble, just talk to me. We can figure it out."

"I'm not in trouble, Dad." I sat there, tapping the glass with the ring I wore, listening to the clink of the metal against the glass. "Have you ever wanted something so badly, but knew there was no way you could have it?"

"You know what I have always told you: work hard and you can have whatever you want."

I rested my head back. "I know, but sometimes those things are just out of reach."

"No, nothing is out of reach if you want it badly enough. As soon as you are done with this final exam, my friend has an opening at his firm; he needs a fresh family lawyer. He's already told me to have you forward your grades and resume. A couple of months working there, and you should be able to get whatever it is you want."

Oh God, he thought I was talking about a physical item. "No, Dad, this isn't something I can acquire with money. It's just this girl."

"Your future holds so much promise, Carter. Any woman should be happy to have you. You shouldn't waste your time on those who aren't. If this is what all this moping is about then I suggest you straighten yourself up." I looked at my Dad; the serious expression on his face told me he thought I was being ridiculous. "You know, Hunter told me what mess he found you in."

"I'm in love with her, Dad," I blurted.

"Did you tell her that?"

"Yes, or I thought I did."

"You thought you did? It's either you did or you didn't."

I looked at the glass in my hand and shrugged. "She's in love with someone else."

"Are you sure about that?"

"She's engaged, Dad."

"May I ask who this girl is?" My father tapped his ring on the edge of his glass, waiting for my response.

"It's Hope." I closed my eyes. My father had represented her father's company in a legal battle a few years ago, and after that, our parents didn't get along. I had no idea what had really happened except that it was a bad business deal gone wrong, but I had always been friends with her. "I know what you're going to say, Dad—just to stay away and find someone else..."

My father held his hand up to shush me; it was something he had always done to stop anyone from putting words in his mouth. I looked at him and stopped speaking. "Carter, first, don't put words in my mouth. Second, if you feel that strongly for her, then talk to her. It's not my place to tell you whom you can and can't love. I know she's been home at her parents'. I've seen her around town. We have always liked Hope. Her parents? Well, that is another story. But don't be foolish; we want to see you boys happy in your lives, and right now I can tell you aren't happy. So, buck up, be a man, and go after what it is you want, not just in your personal life, but your business life as well."

My father stood, grabbing his glass, and headed toward the door to his office. "Oh, and Carter, take it easy on the Scotch. It's five hundred dollars a bottle."

"No problem, Dad. I'll replace it with my next paycheck."

"No need. I love you, son."

"Love you too, Dad." I sat back in the chair and finished off the glass in my hand. Once I had gathered the courage, I pulled my phone from my pocket and sent Hope a text asking her to meet me at the local coffee shop.

Chapter Thirty-Three

HOPE

It was close to six. I was supposed to meet Carter at the coffee shop at seven. I was nervous and trying to calm my nerves as I searched through my closet, trying to figure out what to wear. I had pretty much packed everything for my move this weekend. Things with my move had been delayed because the apartment I had rented needed repainting and new carpet. As I searched I became upset the dress that Carter loved on me was already in the city, in his apartment. I glanced at the time, my stomach rolling. Only half an hour to go. I had just showered and put on lotion, vanilla invading my senses. I finally settled on my white sundress and pulled it from the hanger.

I grabbed my purse from the bed and headed downstairs, taking my keys off the hook by the door. I pulled the door open when I heard my father clear his throat behind me.

"Good to see you've finally gotten dressed. Mr. and Mrs. King are bringing Trent over to sit down and talk. This nonsense has to stop, Hope."

I closed my eyes, a shake running through my body. "Dad, I've already told you, there is nothing else to talk about. He and I are no more."

I turned to walk out the front door but stopped. Mr. King was walking up the front steps, his wife and Trent trailing behind. I glanced at my watch. Carter would probably already be at the coffee shop, and I desperately needed to meet him.

"Dad, this is so not fair. There is nothing for us to talk about."

"Hope, it's for your own good." He pushed me aside and welcomed the three of them into the house. Trent looked to me and shrugged his shoulders.

After all the fake pleasantries were exchanged, my father guided all of us into his study. I felt my phone buzz in my pocket and knew it was Carter. I pulled my phone from my pocket, and just as I went to type my password in, my father ripped the phone from my hand and placed it in his desk drawer. "You're not sitting here with your face in your phone all night." He slammed the drawer shut and that was when I felt my heart sink. He was going to ruin the best thing for me all over again.

"Hope, sit down," my father barked, closing the door and nodding toward Trent. "Trent, you too."

Carter

I glanced at my watch. I had been waiting for forty-five minutes. It was starting to get dark. I was still sitting at the little table inside the shop, continuing to wait. With each passing minute, the excitement I had had at the thought of putting my hands on her again was diminishing.

After another twenty minutes, I pulled my phone out of my pocket to see if there were any messages from her —nothing.

I typed out a couple texts and waited, but she never responded.

I ordered another coffee and sat back down. I waited there for another half hour, and when I still hadn't heard from her, I decided to get in my car and drive home. Fuck this, she was mine; that was all there was to it, and I was going to claim her.

I pulled into my parents' driveway and inhaled deeply as I shut the engine off and climbed out of the car. I needed to figure out what to say now. The longer the words I had planned to say ran through my head, the more ridiculous they sounded.

I stood by my car for a few minutes and then started walking toward her house. I rounded the corner, and she came into sight. Standing on the porch in a white sundress, tears pouring down her cheeks, my perfect love looked off into the distance. I was just about to call out to her when the front door opened and out stepped Trent fucking King. He placed his hands on her shoulders, then she turned and stepped into him, letting his arms envelop her. In that moment, all the courage and confidence I had had that I could win her back was gone. Watching this unfold before my eyes, I realized that the days we had shared over this summer were all I would ever have with her. It was the end of us.

Hope

I watched as Mr. and Mrs. King walked down the front porch steps. "Trent, let's go. You'll fire that bastard, Trent, that is all there is to it. End of story. He was the one who signed the contract."

Trent stayed behind, not saying anything to his father as he continued to bark all the way to the car. Trent walked over to me. "Shhhh. Don't cry. I've settled everything. It's done, Hope." I looked up into Trent's brown eyes.

"You did?" I whispered.

"When you came out here to get some air, I told them. Your father is pissed; my father is pissed."

"What was that about Daddy's job?"

"No need to worry about it. I've already taken over King Enterprises. Your father's job is safe."

"Yeah, but what contract did my father sign?"

"I have no idea, but I promise you his job is safe." He placed a finger under my chin, forcing me to look him in the eyes. "I promise."

"Thank you." I smiled through my tears.

"Go message your man. If you need anything, just text."

I ran into the house and poked my head into my father's study. He was gone, so I went to grab my phone from the drawer. On the desk sat a mess of papers, and the only thing that caught my eyes was the King Enterprises logo. I picked up the sheets of paper and read over the words: Purchase Agreement. I browsed through it, not really understanding what I was reading until I came to a clause that made my skin crawl. "Upon the marriage of my son, Trent King, to your daughter, Hope Heathcote, a single check in the amount of 2.5 million dollars will be cut to Brian Heathcote for the purchase of your business, Heathcote Incorporated." I felt the blood drain from my face. It looked like my father had sold me. The rage I felt got stronger when I heard my father start yelling at my mother in the kitchen. I took the contract into the kitchen with me and stood in the doorway, watching both my parents argue. "Hope?" my mother asked. "What is it?"

"Did you know about this?" I asked, holding up the document in front of her.

"What is that?"

"It's nothing!" my father shouted.

"It's nothing? Mom, maybe you'd care to read it, especially clause thirteen. It's an agreement between Dad and Mr. King."

My father walked over, ripping it from my hands. "Brian, let me see that." My mother reached for the paper, but he tore it away from her.

"Actually, I can tell you what it says. Father made an agreement that upon my marriage to Trent, Mr. King would pay Dad for his business."

My mother turned, glaring at him. "Brian, please tell me that isn't true."

With both our eyes on his, he suddenly didn't seem like that powerful man that he had always seemed to be in my eyes. He looked little and pale and weak.

"I...I didn't want to agree. It was business. I needed the money; my company is bankrupt. I had a good deal set up. Malone Law was the client's lawyer, but something happened and that fell through, and then King showed up. It was more money than the other company had offered, and I got to keep my job." My father broke out in a sweat. "I'm sorry. You need to believe me, I'm sorry."

"How could you?!" I screamed. "Is that what I am worth to you? You would rather see me miserable, so you can have your precious money? I hate you."

"Hope, please, it wasn't like that." My father started breathing heavily, clutching at his chest, and just before he got the next words out, he collapsed on the kitchen floor, right before our eyes.

"BRIAN!" my mother screamed and ran to him. "Hope, call 911 now."

Chapter Thirty-Four

Hope – Twelve Years Earlier

Carter had sent my things back to my parents' house with Hunter. Carter refused to talk to me except to tell me that we were over. At this news I threw myself into things at home, never looking back, just concentrating on getting Dad healthy.

I had spent the last four months at home helping my mother after almost losing my father. Throughout that process, I finally found it in me to forgive him. He had been so desperate to keep our household and lives afloat from debt collectors, he saw it as the only way. He never thought that Mr. King would actually force him to make the deal. After Dad had gotten out of the hospital, I called Trent and explained everything. He assured me that everything would be taken care of and my father would be paid what was owed to him.

I had finally moved into the apartment in the city. I couldn't stay at home, even though I had forgiven my father, so I enrolled in school for business and was starting back at Joe's for my first night shift. Mike and the girls had helped me move into the apartment, and due to the circumstances, Mike had held my full-time position until I returned. I had been back in the city a week and wanted badly to drop by and see Carter—to explain everything to him—but decided it was best just to let him go. I knew it would only be a matter of time before I saw him again anyway. I glanced at the date on my phone. He would be taking the BAR exam tomorrow. Hunter had told me that after everything had happened, Carter had postponed taking it until now. For a brief moment I thought about texting him to wish him good luck, but I was already running behind, and I couldn't be late tonight of all nights. I grabbed a muffin from the pack on the counter and a bottle of water from the fridge and headed out the door.

By six the place was packed and the music was blaring. Once I got going, I had forgotten all about everything that had been plaguing me for weeks. It was good to be back at work with everyone. I had just gotten off break and was about to stock some of the coolers before heading back out to the bar when Mike came into the back.

"Hope, I need you to take over Mary's section. She had to leave; her daughter is ill. I'll have one of the guys back here fill the coolers."

"No problem." I walked around to the end of the bar and out to the section I had been assigned and stopped dead in my tracks. The first table in my section had to be a joke. I looked over my shoulder and saw Christie. Grabbing her arm just as she passed me, I asked, "Where was Mary working again?"

"Section #1. Are you looking after her tables?"

I nodded, glancing back at table #3.

"Great, table #1 wants two waters with ice, table #6 wants two white wines, and table #3 wants a rye and ginger..."

"...and a Scotch on the rocks," I answered and finished taking in the man before me.

"How did you know that?" she asked, smiling.

I shrugged. "He looks like a Scotch drinker." I waited at the bar to order the drinks. As I stood there, I kept glancing back over to the table. Felice sat there playing with her curly brown hair that fell softly over her shoulders, perfectly framing the open neck of her shirt that was showing off way more than it should have been. She kept smiling and laughing and reaching across the table to touch Carter's arm. I could feel the jealousy building in my gut, and the more she touched him, the more I wanted to spit in her drink.

"Here you go, Hope," Mike said, sliding the tray of drinks over to me.

"Thanks."

I picked up the tray and delivered the waters first. Then I went over and dropped off the two glasses of wine, getting an earful about how late their food was. After I asked them to let me check on their order, I started to make my way over to the last table—a table I really didn't want to serve. I glanced over and once again saw Felice running her hand down Carter's arm as she excused herself to head to the washroom. I let out the breath I was holding and made my way over to the table after she had already left.

I said nothing, just set the rye and ginger where Felice had been sitting and the Scotch down in front of Carter. He didn't look up. He kept his face buried in his cell phone, perhaps writing an email. "Can I get you anything else?" At the sound of my voice, he stopped and slowly lifted his head from his phone.

"Hope. What are you doing here?" he asked, a look of shock coming over his face.

"Working. I wasn't supposed to be in this section, but Mary had to go home."

"No, I just mean here in general. I figured that being back with Trent, he would take care of everything, and you wouldn't have to work anymore."

I was just about to start explaining when I heard her dreaded voice behind me. "Well, well, well. Look what trash the cat dragged in."

"I could say the same thing about you." I smirked.

She picked up her drink and took a sip. "This is not what I ordered. I want a new waitress. Carter, get Mike to get us a new waitress."

Carter looked at Felice and then back to me, rolling his eyes. "There is no need to get a new waitress. Mike makes all the drinks." He reached across and picked up the glass and took a sip. "It's exactly what you ordered."

"No, it's not." She turned toward the bar and waved at Mike. Carter shrugged his shoulders and mouthed an apology.

"Is there a problem here?" Mike asked, coming up behind me.

"No..." Carter tried to speak, but Felice spoke over him.

"Mike, we have a slight problem. We need a new waitress, and this drink isn't what I ordered."

"It's a rye and ginger. I poured it myself, and that is what you always drink, Felice."

"Nope, you've made a mistake then. And, please, get us a new waitress."

Mike nodded and looked at Carter who looked annoyed and totally pissed off. "Okay, no problem."

As Mike walked away, I stood there, my eyes locked with Carter. I just wanted to tell him everything, but Felice wouldn't have it. "Run away, little one. Leave me to my date."

I could feel the tears burn my eyes. As the words fell from her lips, he looked away from me. I slowly backed away from the table and went over to where Mike was standing at the end of the bar. "Mike, can I go back to what I was doing tonight? Give the girls the three tables I had, please."

I couldn't deal with this tonight; there was no way. Mike took one look at my tear-filled eyes and nodded. "Sure thing, Hope. Go on."

Carter

Dropping Felice off at her apartment door had been the best part of this whole date. I watched her as she slid the key into the lock and turned it slowly, then she turned and leaned seductively against the door frame. Like maybe if she fucked me with her eyes I would come in.

"You want to come in for a little nightcap?" She winked, running her hand down my cheek.

"No, I really need to get studying. You know I take my exam tomorrow."

"Well, it may do you good to get your mind on something else for a little while," she said, running her finger along the collar of my shirt.

"I don't think it will. Good night, Felice." I stepped across the hall and opened my apartment door. Not looking back, I shut the door, leaving her in the hallway.

I sat down and tried to study, but all I could think about was Hope. She had looked so beautiful, and I wanted so badly to be able to talk to her. I pulled out my phone and scrolled to her name. I'd deleted every text she had ever sent me after reading the first two words of her last text: "I'm sorry." That was all I had needed to see to know that it was over between us, and so I had sent her a goodbye text and sent her things with Hunter.

Finally throwing my phone down, I went into my bedroom and quickly changed into a pair of sweats and a T-shirt. I continued to try to focus on studying. I had less than twelve hours. In more ways than one, I felt like I was drowning. Once I got into the material, three hours had seemed to fly by, but I realized I hadn't even made it halfway through the the first section of my notes. Hope just kept invading my thoughts.

I leaned back, closing my eyes. "Don't do this to yourself, Carter. You can't do this," I murmured aloud to myself. I tried again to bury myself in my studies, but there was no way I could get into it. I glanced at the clock. If I hurried, I could make it to the bar before Mike locked up for the night.

I got up and ran to the door, quickly throwing my running shoes on, grabbed my keys, locked up, and ran to the elevator.

In my rush to get there, I almost ran right past the bar. I ran down the steps to the entrance and went to pull the door open, but the lock stopped me. I put my face to the window. A couple girls were sweeping up the floor. I knocked, but they just ignored me just as they had been taught to do. I thought for a second and then I pulled my phone out of my pocket and messaged Mike. Soon he appeared and opened the door. "Sorry, man, the girls have been told not to answer the door after it's been locked. New policy."

"I understand. Is she still here?"

Mike nodded. "Go on, have a seat. She's cleaning the floor tonight."

I took a seat at the bar. No sooner had Mike disappeared than she walked out dragging a garbage bin behind her and a couple beer cases to put empties in. She stopped at the first table and began clearing it. She looked a little thin to me. As she leaned over, I couldn't help but check her out. I longed to feel her tight ass pushed up against me in bed while I pulled her into me. I watched as she walked back to the bar and turned on the music. Nick Santino's "I Just Wanted You to Know" filled the bar. The only song in the world at this time that made me think of her. I watched as she swayed to the music, mouthing along with the words. I watched her for as long as I could and then I stood and walked up behind her.

"Hope," I said as softly as my deep voice would allow.

She turned abruptly. "What are you doing here?" she asked, her eyes all watery.

"I came for you."

"What about Felice?" she asked, wiping at her cheeks, freeing them of tears with the palm of her hand.

"What about her?" I asked.

She looked at me, almost as if she wasn't sure what to think. Was I with her or wasn't I?

"Hope, just listen."

"I'm sorry, Carter. I'm sorry I didn't meet you that night."

"I get it. You may be with him, but if I don't say exactly what I came here to say, then I'm going to lose the last shot I may have to be with you—forever this time. I owe it to myself to tell you even if I'm not the one who ends up walking away with you. I'm not about to carry around the regret of 'what if' with me for the rest of my life, never knowing what could have been."

She stood there looking at me, giving me time to put the words together. I couldn't help it; I was nervous. There had been nothing in my life up to this point that made me as nervous as this moment. I gripped her by the waist, pulling her into me. She came willingly, pressing her little body up against mine, where she fit perfectly.

"These eyes, those lips, and this body...I want you forever. It's taken me a long time to figure it out, but I don't think I can live my life without you. You're the one meant for me, Hope. I know I have only ever said it once, but I'm in love with you. I can't fight it any longer. I know you are with Trent, and I want you to be happy, but I can't..."

"I love you too." Her soft voice rang out.

I stopped and looked at her, tears in the corner of her eyes. "What?"

"I love you too. I'm not with Trent. That was what I was trying to tell you months ago. All of this is my father's fault. When he sold his business, he agreed that I would marry Trent and that was when he would be paid for his company."

I looked down into those beautiful eyes. She looked heartbroken. "Seriously?"

"Yes, I found the contract. He almost died, Carter, and for the four months that I spent by his side, helping my mother, I fought with myself. It took me a long time, but I have forgiven him. He didn't do it to be mean; he did it to save us. I guess he was in a lot of financial trouble, and he doesn't actually hate you."

I didn't give her another chance to say anything more. My lips just crashed down on hers, my tongue sweeping through her mouth.

Chapter Thirty-Five

Hope — Present Day

"I honestly don't think you have anything to worry about, Hope. These boys are a different breed. Carter loves you so," Autumn said, shoving a couple more pieces of popcorn into her mouth.

"Deep down I know that, but I also know just how persuasive Felice can be."

"Seriously, I don't think you need to worry about her. So, whatever happened to Trent?" Autumn asked, drinking down the last of her tea.

"He ended up marrying my friend Carly, and five years later, they were divorced. He turned out to be quite the play-er," I laughed. "However, now he is going to prison."

"Did Carter ever speak with him again? You did say they had been best friends."

"Yeah, one night we ran into him at Joe's place. I guess

Trent had always been jealous of Carter. He had seen how happy we were together when he had come home at the end of the summer, and so he demanded his father add that into the contract when they purchased my father's business."

"Wow. Just wow."

"Yep, that ended in a fight."

We both got quiet for a minute. "So, Felice can't be the only reason you are upset, Hope. I think you know he would never cheat on you. So, what is it?"

I looked down to where my hands rested on my belly. "About two months ago we had been talking about having another baby, or I had been talking about it. Carter told me he was happy with how things are, and he just wanted to put his focus into the firm. So, we agreed no more kids. Four weeks ago, I found out I am pregnant."

Autumn squealed with delight. "Oh my God, that is awesome! Congratulations!"

"Yeah but knowing that he doesn't want any more children doesn't make it so awesome."

"Honey, be serious. You have two wonderful girls who Carter loves to death. Do you honestly think that after all this time he is going to throw everything away including another child and go have a fling with another woman?"

I started to laugh. "Well, since you put it that way, I guess I am being sort of silly."

"Yes, I think so."

Autumn grabbed her phone from the table. "You know, I think that once Hunter gets home, we should go pick up your girls, and you should meet Carter in New York. The girls can stay with us. I can use the help around here."

"Really?"

"Yes, really. You need to spend some time with Carter. So, tomorrow that is what we will do, okay? There is a straight flight I see that leaves at seven in the evening. If we can't make that one, there is another one at ten."

I leaned over and hugged Autumn. "Thank you so much for tonight."

"You are welcome. Now, I must get some sleep. Morning comes early! Let me grab you a pillow and a couple blankets for the couch."

Chapter Thirty-Six

CARTER

I had finally landed and cleared customs. I was thrilled when I got to my car. I had just finished loading my bag in the trunk when my cell phone rang.

"Hello," I answered, my voice cracking. Not only was I tired, but the stress had finally caught up to me. It wasn't every day that I received a call from my brother saying my wife was going to leave me.

"Carter, it's me. I just got back to my condo. Your wife is sound asleep on my couch. I'm going to leave the door open, so just come on in when you get here. I'm going to go make love to my wife."

I chuckled. That was my brother; he hadn't changed. "All right, thanks. I'll be there shortly, and for the love of God, keep it down. I don't want to listen to your heavy breathing or her screaming your name when I get there."

I hung up the phone and climbed into my car, started the engine, and drove to my brother's place. The elevator ride seemed to take forever, and I was once again reminded of our earlier days, me rushing up the elevator to get home to the girl I loved. A smile came to my lips as the door opened and I got off the elevator. I walked to his door and took a breath before opening the door slowly, poking my head in and seeing my love sound asleep on the couch, one leg on top of the covers, just how she had always slept.

I slipped out of my coat and shoes and walked over to where she lay, looking down at her angelic face. I had fallen for her so long ago and couldn't for even one second ever imagine my life without her. I slipped out of my suit jacket, laying it on the arm of the chair, and lifted the blanket that she slept under. I crawled in behind her, pulling her against me, just like I had done countless times over the years.

I pushed my arm under her head, and as though she sensed my touch, she quietly moaned my name.

"Yeah, baby, it's just me."

"What...what are you doing here?" she asked, sleepily rubbing her eyes.

"Well, a little birdie told me that my love was upset, so I put everything on hold and rushed back here."

She rolled over and looked up at me, her eyes hazy. "Who told you?"

"My brother called. What's going on, princess?"

She buried her face in my chest, her body starting to shake as all the pent-up emotion that she had been carrying came pouring out.

I didn't know what to do, so I just held her close to me, tears starting to flood my eyes too. I too had felt like I was losing her, and I had missed feeling her near to me. "Shhhh, baby, don't cry."

"I can't help it. I feel like I'm losing you, like I'm losing us."

"What makes you think that?" I swallowed hard.

She grew quiet, burying her face into me. "It's her."

"Who?"

"I saw a text from her on your phone. You were going to meet her for dinner while you were away."

I let out the breath I was holding. I knew immediately that she was talking about Felice. From the start, that woman had been nothing but trouble for us. "Yes, I did. I was going to see her and Mike on business, not just her. It turns out she was up to her old tricks; she and Mike are divorcing. I talked to Mike. She lied, but no worries, I know that once she gets the divorce agreement with my name signed on the bottom, I can guarantee she won't ever call me again. Not to mention, her number has been blocked."

"You were going to see her on business?"

"Why else would I see her?" I asked, looking down into her eyes—those eyes. "I have everything I could ever want right here in my arms."

"Really?"

"Yes, really. Do you realize that when I look at you every morning, it's like I am seeing you for the first time? I know I am not perfect, and lately things haven't been great between us, but through all the hard times and the hiccups in the road, the one thing I never ever doubted was my love for you."

I pushed the hair out of her face, placing my hand on her cheek, and met her lips, sweeping my tongue through her mouth. "What do you say we head home? I don't want to make love to you on my brother's couch."

She let out a little giggle.

After we drove home, I carried her up the stairs, placing her down on the floor inside our bedroom. I pushed her up against the wall, taking her mouth with mine, my hands busy with the buttons on her shirt. My hands ran over her breasts, cupping them, while I sucked her earlobe into my mouth. I ripped my shirt from my body and felt her small hands tug at my belt.

I kissed her deeply and then slid the cups of her bra down under her breasts. Slowly kissing my way down her neck, I bent and took one of her hardened nipples into my mouth. Then I moved over to the other, causing her to let out a loud moan. As I kneeled in front of her, I slowly kissed my way down her stomach. I looked up and took note of her watching me. I grinned up at her and flicked the button on her jeans open, inching her jeans and panties down until they were pooled at her feet.

She reached behind her, unhooking her bra. She went to step around me, but I placed my hand on the flat of her stomach and pushed her back against the wall. I pulled one of her legs up and placed it on my shoulder. I buried my face between her legs, first running my tongue through her wetness and then sucking her clit into my mouth. I felt her hands grip my hair as I continued licking and sucking her. I could feel her starting to tremble.

"Carter, stop. I'm going to come," she moaned, gripping my hair tighter.

There was no way I was stopping. "No, baby, I got you. Let yourself go."

I continued flicking my tongue over her swollen clit until she was trembling so much, I was afraid she might fall, so I grabbed her and carried her over to the bed, laying her down. "On your hands and knees now," I growled in her ear.

She looked at me and bit her lip, shaking her head no.

"Now, princess. You're going to feel all of me pounding into you."

She placed her hand on my chest, kissing me. "Make love to me, Carter," she cried in between kisses. "Let me know I'm yours."

"You are mine, always." I pulled her into my arms, kissing her deeply. She wrapped her legs around my waist and I slid into her, thrusting slowly but deeply.

Hope

There was something about the way it felt to be held by him as he thrust inside of me that made me know he was mine. I loved listening to his harsh breath in my ear as he got closer to the edge. I could feel his love in everything he did: the way his hands caressed my body, the sweet words he whispered into my ear, the way he kissed me. I never should have doubted anything. There was no possible way anyone could fake that.

After we climaxed, we lay together, my body perfectly molded to his, another indication that we were meant to be together. His fingers danced along my shoulder. When I looked up into his face, I saw that he had his eyes closed. He was gently breathing as I traced tiny circles on his chest.

"I love you," he whispered. "Don't ever forget that."

"Deep down, I know that. I guess I just got scared," I whispered.

We fell asleep in each other's arms; it was the most comfort I had felt with him in months.

Chapter Thirty-Seven

HOPE

We dropped the girls off at Hunter and Autumn's for the two days we would be gone, and I called them as soon as we were settled into the hotel. I had spent the day shopping and was now on my way to meet Carter in Central Park. He requested that I meet him at Bethesda Fountain. I watched the buildings pass by as the cab drove down the road. I glanced at my watch when finally, the driver pulled to the side of the road. "Miss, your stop." I paid the fare and climbed out of the back seat.

I made my way into the park and over to Bethesda Fountain and started looking for Carter amongst the groups of people that were there. When I didn't see him, I took a seat on a park bench and listened to the sounds of the people surrounding me. I heard my cell phone ping. A message from Carter populated on my screen, letting me know he should be here shortly; he was stuck in traffic.

I smiled and quickly texted a response, letting him know where I was sitting.

While waiting, I watched some performers around the fountain entertaining some people. I took in the pretty colors of fall that were surrounding me. The fact that this little piece of heaven could exist in such a busy city always amazed me. I felt a tap on my shoulder and turned to see these three musicians standing behind me holding their instruments. "May we play for you, miss?"

I wasn't sure what to say. I thought it was a little strange that out of all the people here, they chose me. I looked around the park for Carter. When I didn't see him, I smiled and nodded. "Sure."

"Do you have any requests, miss?"

"No. Play whatever you would like." I smiled.

As they started to play, I realized the song sounded very familiar to me, but I couldn't remember where I had heard it. I sat and listened, letting the music flow through me just like I used to do. I felt a strong hand grip my shoulder. It was a touch that I would know anywhere, and I looked up only to see his handsome, chiseled face looking down on me.

"Good evening, princess." He leaned in and brushed his lips over mine. "Not sure if you remember this song or not. I watched you sway to this song that night in Joe's, the night you came back to me for good."

I listened harder and realized it was that Nick Santino song. I hadn't heard it in years.

"You don't know this, but this song holds a very special place in my heart, Hope, because the words are exactly how I felt for those dreaded three years that you weren't with me." He kneeled onto one knee in front of me and pulled my hands into his. "I never want to feel that way ever again."

"Me neither."

He reached into his jacket pocket and pulled out a little black box, popping it open. Inside, nestled between two little black velvet cushions, sat a beautiful princess-cut diamond solitaire.

"I couldn't afford this when we got engaged the first time, but thirteen years later I can, so I was hoping you would do me the honor of renewing our vows."

I felt the tears slip from my eyes and trail down my cheeks. He reached up and ran the pad of his thumb over my cheek as the music continued to play in the background. "No more tears."

"Yes," I cried, wrapping my arms around him. He stood up, pulling me with him, holding me against him. In front of all the people in the park, we started dancing together to the same song we danced to that night years ago.

Chapter Thirty-Eight

We had been back from New York for a month, and things between Carter and I couldn't have been better. Having decided to wait to tell Carter the news until I had received confirmation, I visited my doctor's office.

I checked the clock—it was almost eight. Carter was working late and had called earlier to let me know he would be home around nine.

"Come on, girls. It's time for bed," I said, shutting off the TV.

"Ah, Mom, we want to wait up for Daddy."

"Not tonight, girls. You both have school in the morning. Now let's go upstairs and brush our teeth."

I walked behind them both as they slowly made the climb to the second floor and went to the bathroom. It took ten minutes before they were both ready to climb into bed. I sat down on Mackenzie's bed, pulling the covers up and over her and kissing her good night on the cheek. Then I made my way to Kendall's bed. Picking up and placing her favorite teddy bear in her arms, I kissed her good night.

I walked over to the door, shut the light off, and stood and watched them. They were both almost asleep by the time I left. I had just shut the door to their room when I heard the door open and close downstairs.

I ran into our bathroom and ran a brush through my hair before making my way downstairs. "Welcome home," I said as I stepped off the last step. "You hungry?"

"Starving. I'll be right there, just going to drop this stuff in my office."

I nodded and made my way to the kitchen to heat up his dinner. My stomach rolled with nerves as I waited for him, the smell of roast beef upsetting my stomach as I set the hot plate on the table.

"Smells great." He walked into the kitchen and sat down. I watched as he removed his tie and set it on the table beside his plate. "Are you feeling okay?"

"Yeah, why?" I set the glass I had been sipping water from on the counter and turned to look at him.

"Last time you had that look on your face around roast beef you were pregnant with Mackenzie and Kendall," he chuckled to himself and stabbed into the meal that sat before him.

I turned away to hide the look on my face and then I heard the clink of the fork on the edge of the plate. "Hope?"

"Yeah," I said, turning around to face him.

"Are...Are you pregnant?"

I shook my head in a yes motion, unsure of what he was

going to say. "I know you didn't want to have any more kids, but I did make sure. I checked with the doctor today, and I am a little over two months."

Instead of the reaction that I expected, a smile floated to his lips, and he stood up from his chair and walked over, taking me in his arms. "Over all the years we've been together, you've given me the most fulfilling relationship, two beautiful girls who I love with all my heart, and now this."

"You're not angry?"

"Angry? Why would I be angry? Hope, I am over the moon with this news, and I can't wait for the next few months to be over so that we can hold this little guy in our arms."

Epilogue

"And one more push, Hope."

I felt Carter grab my hand tighter as I gave one final push. I heard the cry of a newborn baby fill the room.

"And we have a boy," the doctor sang out as he placed the warm body on my belly.

Carter sat at the head of the bed, holding my hand, his other arm wrapped around me. "You did it, baby. You did it—another healthy baby." He placed a kiss on my forehead.

A few hours later I was dosing peacefully in the quiet hospital room. The door opened and Kendall and Mackenzie came running in, Carter walking in behind them.

"Mommy, Mommy, Mommy!"

"Girls, I explained to you both, you need to be quiet," Carter sternly scolded.

Kendall looked to Carter and started whispering, calling

for me. I smiled as they both climbed onto the bed beside me.

"Hello, my lovelies. Please tell me you were good for Uncle Hunter and Aunt Autumn today."

Mackenzie nodded. "Kendall was bad, Mommy. Uncle Hunter got angry." I laughed. Hunter's equivalent of getting angry generally involved apologizing to the girls first and then giving them ice cream.

"No. I was good, I swear. It was Mackenzie."

"Okay, girls, that's enough now. Mommy needs her rest."

The nurse returned to the room, pushing a bassinet carrying our newest member of the family. Both the girls smiled to each other and looked over the edge of the bassinet at the sleeping baby.

"Girls, this is your baby brother, Carl."

We had chosen the name after Carter's father, who had passed away shortly after we had gotten married. Carter sat the girls down in a chair beside me and picked up the baby, first setting him in Mackenzie's lap. She looked down into his sleeping face.

"Mommy, he is sleeping."

I smiled as I watched the amazement on their little faces. Carter then placed Carl onto Kendall's lap.

"He's so little. Were we ever this little, Daddy?" Kendall asked.

"You were, maybe even a bit smaller," Carter whispered.

Carter brought Carl over to me and placed him in my arms, leaning down and kissing me on the forehead. "I'll be right back, princess. I am just going to take the girls out to your parents."

Once they were gone, I looked down into Carl's face. I could see Carter in him. He had a lot of Carter's features.

Carter walked back into the room and shut the door behind him quietly. He sat on the edge of the bed and pulled me into him. I could feel the panic rising in me at the sheer thought of ever doubting him.

"Hope, you have made me happier than I ever imagined. Look at all we have accomplished and brought into this world. Thank you."

"What for?"

"For not marrying Trent King, and coming back to me."

"Thank you for leaving Felice that night and coming back to me."

He leaned down and kissed me deeply, sweeping his tongue through my mouth. He crawled in the bed beside me and rested against the mattress, pulling me against him. Carl lay in my lap, looking back at both of us.

"No doubt about it, he looks like you," I whispered.

"Funny, I thought he looked like Trent." I started to laugh and rested my head on his shoulder. "I love you so."

"I love you too, princess."

His To Hold

His to Hold

Copyright © 2019 by S.L. Sterling

All rights reserved. Without limiting the rights under copyright reserved about, no part of this publication may be reproduced, stored in, or introduced into a retrieval system, or transmitted in any form or by any means (mechanical, electronic, photocopying, recording, or otherwise) without the prior written permission of both the copyright owner and the above publisher of the book. This is a work of fiction. Any references to historical events, real people, or real places are used fictitiously. Other names, characters, places, and events are products of the author's imagination, and any resemblance to actual events or places or persons, living or dead, is entirely coincidental. Disclaimer: This book contains mature content not suitable for those under the age of 18. It involves strong language and sexual situations. All parties portrayed in sexual situations are consenting adults over the age of 18.

ISBN: 978-1-9995736-6-9

Editor: Brandi Aquino, Editing Done Write

Cover Design: Thunderstruck Cover Designs

Chapter One

BRYCE

I walked into the office Friday morning and, having gotten only three hours of sleep the night before, knew I looked like shit. Staying up arguing with your ex because she doesn't feel the need to leave your condo takes its toll. We had broken up months ago, and I had taken pity because she had nowhere to go, but now she was just being an unreasonable bitch.

I probably wouldn't have even come in today, but Hunter and Carter had called a last-minute meeting with Chase and me. I had no choice but to go in. I was hoping to sign on as junior partner this year and it would look bad if I hadn't shown up. My brothers had gotten nothing handed to them, and they believed in making me work for what I wanted.

Chase and I had been working with one of our top clients on a corporate merger. They were looking at buying a smaller local company, but upon thorough review of the books, things weren't looking consistent. Our client wanted a second opinion, and I couldn't say I blamed him.

I entered the office carrying a hot cup of coffee and a bag containing a breakfast sandwich from the coffee shop around the corner from my place. I didn't have the time or desire to eat at home. Alyssa wasn't even up out of bed when I left, and I knew if I hung around and took my time, she would start on me as soon as she was awake.

I glanced at my watch. I was on limited time, and as soon as this meeting was finished, I needed to start preparing for my own upcoming meetings today. My phone hadn't stopped going off all morning, starting as soon as I had turned it on. I greeted Josie and Kim and entered through the doors of our boardroom. I took a seat beside Carter, who had his head down in the client file.

"Morning," I mumbled, sitting down and unwrapping my breakfast, running my hand over my face.

"About time you got here." He chuckled. "I see you got the breakfast of champions this morning."

"Yeah, I know. Sorry I'm late. Alyssa still hasn't left. She is making my life a living hell."

"You really should deal with that, instead of hoping she just goes away."

"It's not like I haven't tried," I said, taking a bite of my sandwich and ignoring what my brother said. He knew the troubles I had been and still was having with her, and he knew how hard I had tried to get rid of her. I took another bite and downed it with a mouthful of coffee as Chase walked in carrying a cup of coffee and sat on the other side of Carter.

"Jesus, you're just as bad as Bryce," Carter said, closing the client file and looking to Chase.

"Yeah, well, it was a late night, if you catch my drift." Chase smiled smugly.

"We don't want to hear about your latest conquest. It's a business day. Save that for guys' night," Carter said, clearing his throat and diving right in. "Hunter had an early appointment this morning, so he won't be here."

Carter cleared his throat again and jumped into all of the company business as usual. "All right, so I did manage to get a minute to look over some of the case files you two are working on, especially the one you asked me to look over, and I know you want a second opinion," he said, shuffling some papers around.

"So, here's the problem: There is something definitely up with the new documents your client was given. Your client is right to think something is going on. Things are not consistent. So, you guys are going to advise your client to request a meeting with TexCorp. You are both going to go over those documents firsthand at that meeting and request any other documents that you see fit that will support the documents here. Chase, according to your email, the meeting has been set for four weeks from Monday, is that correct?"

Chase nodded.

I pulled my phone out of my pocket and pulled up my calendar. "The tenth of February?" I questioned.

"Yep, eight in the morning."

I updated my calendar with the meeting details.

"Chase, send over the details to Bryce," Carter ordered. "Bottom line, your client feels that they are lying about something, and I agree, so it's up to the two of you to figure it out. He wants a second set of eyes on everything before he enters into the contract."

"Fair enough." I stood. "If that is everything, I need to get to my office."

"Yes, that's it. Have a good day, boys," Carter said as we both left the boardroom.

Chase and I parted ways, him going into his office just around the corner from the boardroom. I continued down the hall, and as soon as I rounded the corner to my office, I was immediately attacked with questions. I wasn't in the mood this morning for this, and I barked out orders and answers left and right a lot harsher than I normally would.

I had just gotten into my office, shut the door, and sat down, when Kim, my legal assistant, came in and handed me the file that she had been working on for a meeting I was to have on Friday. She didn't say anything. She laid the file on my desk and left quietly, while I listened to my voice mail.

Of course, the first message I had was from Alyssa. I rolled my eyes as I listened to her whine, and by the time I hit that last message and her voice came over the speaker again, it pissed me off more than I already was. I let out a breath as I hung up the phone, trying to regain my composure.

Once I had calmed down enough, I opened the file that Kim had left for me and began going through all the paperwork she had completed. Every page I looked at was nothing but a half-assed attempt at putting together information for me. Everything about it was wrong. I pressed the intercom, calling her into my office. I waited, drumming my pen on the edge of the desk.

"Mr. Malone, you wanted to see me?" she meekly

announced as I sat behind my desk, highly agitated and pissed off.

"I did. Please, come in and sit down." I nodded to the chair across from me. My eyes followed her as she shyly walked in and took a seat in the chair. She folded her shaking hands in her lap and looked at me.

"In regard to these documents. What the fuck are you thinking? I can't go into a meeting with these clients with this type of drivel," I said, throwing the paperwork around.

I could see the tears welling in her eyes, but I didn't care.

"Sir, I completed everything as—"

I held my hand up to stop her. "If you dare say you completed everything as I would want it, you may collect your things and head home right now.".

Her lip started to tremble. I glanced out my office door and saw Josie walk by my office, glaring at me, at my behavior and utter lack of professionalism.

I got up and slammed my office door shut. I had already had it out with Josie today as well, before I had even come into the office this morning. I had zero professionalism today, along with zero patience, and I knew it.

I collected the mass of paperwork, shoving it back into the file, and handed it to Kim. "Fix it," I barked out, and turned my attention to another file sitting on my desk.

She stood there looking at me, not knowing what to say or do.

"I suggest you get to work. You have many hours of it to do, and you aren't going to get it done by standing there staring at me," I barked.

She hid it well, but I could see a tremble in her lower lip before she quickly turned and left my office. I was sure I would have a complaint filed to Carter and Hunter in a matter of minutes for how I had just treated her. If that happened, I was sure my shot at junior partner would be put in jeopardy, and it would be just one more thing I could blame Alyssa for. After all, she was the reason behind my delightful attitude.

Before I opened my next file, I went to take a sip of my coffee, finding it had gone cold, which set me off even more. Mug in hand, I walked down to the coffee room. Employees were stepping out of my way, whispering to one another, as I walked down the hall, most turning their faces away from me, but no one dared speak to me with the way I was behaving.

As soon as I walked in, I saw Kim in the corner with Josie. She took one look at me, wiped her eyes with her thumb, and left the room, along with every employee in there, except one—Josie. She had been my personal assistant since I became a lawyer here. She knew me better than most of the staff, aside from my brothers. She, like them, was not afraid to call me on my shit.

"Bryce, may I have a few words with you in your office when you are finished here." She didn't give me a chance to reply. She turned on her heal and marched out of the room, no doubt, heading down the hall to my office.

With a fresh cup of hot coffee in hand, I made my way back to my office. When I entered, Josie sat in the chair across from me, drumming her fingers on my desk.

"What is it?" I barked.

"Bryce, I have just spoken to Kim. I have talked her out of reporting you to HR and to your brothers, so essentially I just saved your ass. What is wrong with you? You don't act this way."

"Nothing."

She looked at me in disbelief. I knew it because she was right. I never acted this way.

"Bryce, you better get your shit together. I looked at Kim's work before she submitted it to you. There was absolutely nothing wrong with it. Now, if this is a personal issue between yourself and her, then I suggest you have a talk with Carter or Hunter and get her transferred. You cannot and will not be abusive to staff. I won't allow it. Do I make myself clear?"

One thing about Josie that I had always admired was she never cared if she stepped out of turn. She was right. She was saving my ass, and for that I was thankful.

"I mean it, Bryce, and if it's a personal issue outside of this building, then you best go home and straighten it out before you get yourself into trouble."

"Send Kim in," I grumbled.

"Are you going to be rational?" she asked.

"I said, send her in."

Josie looked at me, shook her head, and left without another word.

Ten minutes later, Kim appeared at my door, file in hand. She was just about to sit down when my phone buzzed on my desk.

"Put the file on my desk and I will review it once again."

"Mr. Malone, if I have done something wrong, please tell me."

"It's not you, Kim. Leave the file. I am giving you the rest of the day off with pay to make up for my behavior. Go to this address." I quickly scribbled the address of the day spa Hunter and Carter sent their wives, Autumn and Hope, to and handed it to her. "Have whatever treatments you would like and send the bill to me."

I'd probably be up shit creek for doing this, but I handed her the slip of paper anyway. She quickly took the paper from my hand and left my office without another word.

It was 10 p.m. by the time I had decided to head back to Chase's apartment. I had decided to stay there going forward, until Alyssa vacated my condo. I entered his condo to find all the lights off. No doubt Chase was either out or had some broad over.

I kicked my shoes off and loosened my tie and threw my suit jacket down over the back of the couch. I made my way into the kitchen. I needed something to eat.

Pulling the fridge open, I grabbed the veggie tray and quickly made up a plate. After I ate, I made my way down to the spare bedroom. I changed and crawled into bed, then laid there with my arm over my face, letting the tensions of the day leave my body.

I had just about drifted off to sleep when I heard a woman moan Chase's name, and then the rhythmic sound of his headboard banging on the wall above my head. Last thing I wanted to listen to was my brother banging some broad.

I closed my eyes, trying to ignore the sound, but it just

kept getting louder. I got up and pounded on the wall. "Trying to sleep in here, fuckface!" I shouted. I didn't care. If I couldn't be happy, why should he?

The rhythmic sound stopped, only to start again a few seconds later, and kept going until she was moaning and screaming his name even louder than before.

I rolled my eyes. I was irritated as hell, not to mention horny. With every bang of the headboard, I too wished I could sink myself into someone. I lay there for a few more minutes, and when I couldn't take it anymore, I got up out of bed and slid my suit pants back on, grabbed my shirt and jacket, and went back to the office.

Chapter Two

Bryce - A week later

"Bryce. Wake the fuck up."

I felt someone shove my shoulder. I opened my eyes, squinting at the light that was already pouring in through the windows of my office. What time was it, and what had happened last night?

As soon as I moved, I felt a searing pain run through my head. I blinked hard, Hunter and Carter coming into focus, both standing above me, frowning. What the hell were they doing here?

"What...what time is it?" I yawned, sitting up, rubbing my temples.

"It's seven-thirty. What the fuck is going on in here? This office is a disaster," Hunter said as Carter took a minute to pick up the plastic food containers that were strewn about on the floor.

"Have you been living here?" Carter asked, looking annoyed.

I saw him looking at the clothes that hung in the corner of my office. I ran my hand over my face, trying to sit my sorry ass up. I had tied one on last night, getting too drunk to be able to drive back to Chase's condo.

"Yeah that is what Josie suspects," Hunter answered.

I'd had enough. Alyssa still wouldn't leave the condo, and all Chase was interested in was fucking women all hours of the night. I didn't know what the fuck was going on. I also didn't know what I had done wrong. It wasn't like either of them hadn't lived at the office at one point in their careers.

"You know Kim came to my office the other day to complain, right?" Carter told Hunter.

"Yeah, she called my office, but I was in with a client and had to leave right after that meeting. What was all that about?"

"Apparently, he gave her shit, and then paid her to take the day off. He then sent her to the spa, some form of bribe perhaps."

They were talking amongst themselves as if I wasn't even in the room.

"Fuck, it's enough!" I shouted, rubbing my hand over my face and sitting up, my head still pounding, the room spinning.

"Bryce, what the fuck is going on?"

Both of my brothers stood looking at me. Thank God I had put my pants back on before passing out last night or this would have looked way worse than what it already did.

I cracked my neck, sat up, and looked toward the door. Josie walked by my office door on her way to her desk. She looked in quickly, and when she saw Hunter and Carter standing there, and then me staring back at her, she picked up her pace.

"Bryce, are you going to answer us?"

I really had nothing to say, except that I hated everything about my life at this exact moment. I looked to the garbage can filled with takeout containers, the empty bottle of booze that lay sideways on my desk, and the clothes that hung on hangers on the corner of my bookcase. "It's nothing."

My brothers looked at one another and then sat down. "We don't think so, Bryce. Spill it."

As more people began to pour into the office, Hunter got up and shut my office door and pulled the blinds on the windows that were open toward the hallway to give us more privacy.

"For God's sake, throw a shirt on, would you? Have some sort of respect for yourself," Carter demanded and threw a dirty, balled-up shirt at me that had been thrown in the corner earlier in the week.

"Surely you have not had clients in this office?" Carter asked.

I shook my head and threw my shirt on. "No, no clients."

"Did you actually bribe Kim?" Hunter asked, looking at me, waiting for my response.

I put my head in my hands. "Kind of," I whispered, running my hands over my face again.

"I don't think I need to tell you how against our policy that is, do I?" Carter barked.

"No, I already know. It was a mistake."

"Are you sleeping with her?" Hunter asked, picking up

another container off the floor and throwing it into the garbage.

"What?" I gasped. "Are you serious?" Where the fuck did that thought come from? Who did he think I was, my brother?

"Are you sleeping with your paralegal? Because that is even more against our policies than I care to admit," Carter barked.

"Lord no. Fuck, I made a mistake, but I am not stupid enough to stick my dick into one of our employees."

"Bryce, this is warning number one."

Carter was never one to fuck around. He was always all business, and seriously, I knew better.

"I'm aiming for junior partner here. You actually think I would sleep with my paralegal? I don't fucking believe it." I jumped up off the couch and paced around my office.

"I wouldn't have thought you would bribe an employee either, to be honest," Carter answered.

"Look, I'd had a shitty day. I looked over the documents she had prepared and took shit out on her that had nothing to do with her. She bitched at Josie, who fucking told me, so I gave her the day off, treated her to a spa treatment. I didn't think I did anything wrong. I certainly didn't think she would lodge a fucking complaint," I said, throwing the almost empty bottle of liquor into the bottom drawer of my desk.

"As I said, that is warning number one," Carter repeated.

"Shove your fucking warning, Carter." I took a step toward him, but Hunter stepped between us. "All right, Bryce, calm the fuck down." He placed a firm hand on my chest and looked me in the eyes, reading what was there.

"Carter, how about you go and grab us some coffees and muffins from the bakery downstairs. Let me talk to Bryce for a second," he said, not taking his eyes from mine.

Carter didn't argue. I could tell he was fed up, which he should be. He was the one who started this firm and decided to pull each one of us in. He got up and left my office, shutting the door behind him, not once making eye contact with me. I looked at Hunter, him at me.

"Now you are going to sit down and tell me what is going on?"

"It's nothing."

"Oh no, no way. You think because I get rid of Carter, I'm letting you off the hook? Now sit down and explain yourself."

I was just about to start telling him when Josie knocked on my door. Hunter got up and walked over, pulling the door open. She looked over his shoulder directly at me and shook her head before turning her attention back to Hunter. "Carter called. He said you have an appointment downstairs, Hunter."

"Thanks, Josie."

Josie walked away and Hunter turned to me.

"I already know this has to do with Alyssa and you. I know things aren't good, Bryce. I also understand how hard it is to get your shit together after you've broken it off with someone you were planning to marry. Has she left your condo yet?"

It was like my brother was a mind reader. I leaned back against the couch and let out a breath. "No. I've been staying with Chase, but I am tired of listening to him bang anything with a heartbeat."

Hunter looked at me and chuckled. He glanced around the room and back to me, a look of pity coming to his eyes. "Get your office cleaned up, take the rest of today off, and effective immediately, you are on vacation. Two weeks," he said, pointing to me. "Get your clothes out of here too. Tell Alyssa she has two weeks to move or you will have her legally removed. Go up to the lake house, alone, and sort your shit out. You hear me."

"I can't. I have appointments this afternoon."

"No, you don't, not anymore. I'll have Josie reschedule them. I am doing this for your own good, and if I find out that you don't leave, I will have her change your passwords too so you can't access anything."

I rolled my eyes and watched Hunter leave my office. As irritated as I was, he was right. I needed a break. The last six months had gotten to me. I couldn't say I was sad over my breakup. Just more frustrated at the fact that she was torturing me because I had taken pity on her the night she started to cry when I told her she had to leave. Feeling sorry for her had gotten me to the point I was at.

I started gathering my things and cleaning my office. I didn't waste any time. I packed up all of my clothes, piled the garbage neatly in the bin, grabbed my laptop, and shut the lights off, heading down to the parking lot to my car.

The condo was quiet when I entered.

"Hello?" I called out. Silence was the only thing that greeted me.

I noticed a few boxes sat partially packed up on the dining room table. Thank goodness. That meant Alyssa was packing her shit.

I dropped the mess of clothes I carried in my arms into

the laundry hamper and walked over to the couch and flopped down. I leaned my head back against the cushions and pinched the bridge of my nose. The tension of the morning sat firmly planted in my neck and upper back.

I only sat for a few minutes before getting up and going down to the bedroom. I pulled my suitcase from the closet and quickly packed two weeks worth of clothes, then booked myself a late-afternoon flight. I went into my office and pulled a sheet of paper off one of my legal pads and quickly wrote: Alyssa, you have two weeks to get out. I'm done.

I dropped the sheet of paper on the table by her boxes, grabbed my bags, and locked the door.

Chapter Three

I sat behind my desk dreaming of the ocean as I hit print on my computer. I had spent the last two weeks preparing for today. It was so close I could taste it. I could already feel the heat from the sun on my skin, if I thought about it hard enough. I was anxious and excited, and I seriously couldn't wait until tonight. Not only was I going on vacation, but I got to spend the whole week with Don.

After five long years together and doing our best to make the long-distance relationship work between us, I was sure that this trip would be the one. He was going to pop the question; I just knew it. I could feel it. Sure, we had been having problems with the distance thing, as anyone would, and he had kept asking me to move down with him, but I kept putting him off.

One night, Don expressed his feelings about the issues

we had been having. He felt neglected, so we began planning this trip and working on us. We hoped it would help our relationship, and so six months ago I had put in for this time off. It had been fifteen years since my last vacation, and I seriously didn't think it would get approved. Mark, my boss, never allowed me time off. Don had told me that I should just take it to him, so that was what I did. He finally granted it—begrudgingly, of course.

The printer rang out the telltale beeps that it was finally finished printing the documents, and I grabbed the reports for Mark. I bundled them together, securing them with a clip, and carried them down the hall to his office, stopping outside to take a breath. With the pending merger, I was petrified that at any given moment, he would take back the approval on my vacation.

I knocked and pushed the door open, entering the room. He was seated behind his desk, typing away.

"Here you go. Just what you asked for." I set the stack of data on his desk.

He picked them up and flipped through them, nodding his head. "Yes...yes, these look so much better, Mia. See, I told you a few simple tweaks would be all it would take, not to mention it would make all the difference."

"Uh huh," I gritted out. I hated being bullied into doing something that was wrong. Last night when Mark called me at home, after I had already given him all the data, he told me I would need to make things "look better," so he asked me to make a few adjustments. The conversation had ended with the threat of, "You don't want to lose your job, do you?" So to avoid a huge argument, I had just done what he had asked instead.

"Yes, this is exactly what I am talking about. See, you even put the company back in the black. This couldn't be more perfect, Mia."

"Uh huh, that is what you essentially wanted, wasn't it?"

Mark looked up from the reports and studied me.

"Mia, is there a problem?"

"No, nothing at all. Let me know if you need anything else before I leave," I answered, turning on my heel and walking out of his office.

While on my way back to my office, I stopped in the staff room and grabbed a cup of coffee, and my empty lunch bag from the fridge. I just wanted to be able to grab everything and go once 5:00 p.m. hit.

"Looking forward to vacation, Mia?" Janet asked.

"I am. I can't wait. I can't wait to sit under palm trees, put my feet in the hot sand, and drink margaritas."

"You deserve it, putting up with Mark and his demanding ways every day for the past five years. I'm surprised you have lasted this long. The girl before you only made it six months, and the one before her only three."

I smiled and added a little sugar to my coffee. I was over-worked. A company this size should have had eight people in my department. Instead everything fell onto my shoulders.

"I'll see you later, Janet. I got to get some things finished before I leave." I didn't want to hear from someone else how much of a sucker I was. I already knew.

I took my coffee and made my way to my office, shutting the door behind me. I sat down and stuck the USB drive into my computer and began copying all the original files I had handed to Mark — the ones that were showing the nega-tive returns, the ones that he demanded be altered. Bottom line was the company was in major trouble and this pending merger would be the only thing to save it, so it had everyone in a tizzy.

I had put in a ton of overtime hours in the last few weeks, which I already knew I wouldn't get paid for, just like all the other overtime hours. I seriously couldn't wait to get out of here.

I sipped on my coffee and then hit the print button, printing out all the original files I had done as well. I didn't want to solely rely on a digital copy.

My cell phone rang, and a smile came to my lips when I saw Don's name on the screen. "Hey, babe," I answered.

"You sure you are going to be on that flight?"

"Yes, why wouldn't I be? I'm just tying up a few things here at the office, and as soon as I am done, I'm running to grab my bags and getting on that plane. I'll see you at the airport at ten."

"Yeah, uh huh. You're sure it won't be like the last time? I sit waiting for you and you call me fifteen minutes after your flight was supposed to land and profusely apologize?"

"Don, I said I would be there."

"Yeah sure. I'll believe it when I see you step through those doors."

"Babe, seriously, I will be there. Everything is packed."

"Sure, yep, just like last time right," he barked.

"Don that was different, and you know it. It was a damn emergency."

"Yeah, and what about the time before that?"

"Don, I'll be there. I've got to go and finish so I'm not late. I'll see you at our usual meeting spot."

"Yep." He was gone before I had a chance to say good-bye.

I hung up my phone. That call had struck a nerve, but I didn't have time to think about it. I knew that once we were together, everything would be fine. I just wanted to get what I needed printed and copied before I left. I turned my attention back to the file and began printing off my payroll reports when Mark came striding into my office.

"So, Mia, about this vacation."

"What about it?"

"You aren't really leaving, are you? I mean I could really use your help here this week."

I couldn't believe what I was hearing. "I'm leaving in a few minutes, Mark."

He chuckled as he looked around my office. "I really thought you were kidding when you handed me the notification of vacation. Unfortunately, I'm afraid that I need you to do some work for me, either here or while you are away."

"No way. Absolutely not." I ignored the fact that he was standing there in front of me.

"I just need a couple of hours of your time this weekend, and perhaps five- or ten-hours next week."

"Mark do I really need to remind you that I haven't had a vacation in fifteen years. I have two thousand and twenty-six-point-seven hours in my vacation bank. That is like a full year of time I could take off and you would have to pay me. Also, did you know that I have somewhere in the ballpark of almost thirty-five hundred hours of overtime that hasn't been paid out, since you stopped paying me my overtime three years ago?"

"Yeah, so what of it."

"What of it? It's illegal, Mark. It would take one phone call to a lawyer, just one." I looked at him as if he were completely stupid.

He ignored everything I had said as if I hadn't even spoken. "Monday morning. I'll see you at eight. I will email you the list of what I need you to do this weekend, and I want to go over a bunch of things before the meetings with the lawyers in a few weeks. Just so we are on the same page."

"Yeah, right, Monday. Uh huh. I won't be here, Mark."

"I know you, Mia. You'll be here before I am. We've gone over this so many times. I will see you then." He left my office and carried on down the hall, whistling as he went.

I had created this, by always being so accommodating, always doing everything that he had asked. I had canceled plans with friends, family dinners, I had even gone into work the afternoon of my mother's funeral, all because I had been too stupid to stand up for myself. Now Mark was asking me to put my integrity on the line by fudging reports just so this merger would go through. All of his demands had finally pushed me over the edge, and I'd had enough.

I drank down the remainder of my coffee and pulled the reports from the printer, shoving them into my briefcase.

I wasted no time. I reached into my drawer and gathered my paystubs from the past year and shoved them into my bag, along with the USB from my computer. I wanted to make sure there was nothing left for the temp that was coming in to fill my spot. If there even was a temp, which there more than likely wasn't, since Mark hadn't even taken me seriously.

I glanced at the clock. It was almost 6:00 p.m. I would

have just enough time to get home, drop my stuff off, and be on my way.

I got up from my desk and looked around my office, my second home, and smiled. I had everything I needed in case this backfired on me. I shut the lights off and was on my way to a week of freedom and the hope of a future husband.

Chapter Four

MIA

I had gotten off the plane and made my way over to our usual meeting place, just underneath the large bagel sign in the middle of the airport. I dropped my bags on the ground and looked through all of the people to see if I could spot Don. I didn't see him yet, and I glanced at my watch. We had agreed to meet at 10:00 sharp, and it was already 10:30. My plane had been a bit delayed, but he would have been able to see that. Perhaps he had run to the washroom.

I took a seat on a nearby bench and pulled out my phone to text him. I waited patiently for the phone to boot up, and once it had, I noticed I had a voice mail waiting for me. I already had a good guess who it was from, but I decided to listen to it anyway.

Only it wasn't Mark. My pulse pounded wildly in my ears as I listened to the message. It was Don. He wasn't coming. He was breaking up with me! My pulse hammered wildly in my ears.

"A fucking voice mail! Unbelievable!" I gritted under my breath, shutting my phone off and throwing it into my purse. "I flew halfway across the country to have him break up with me through a fucking voice mail. He could have saved me the trouble," I said out loud as I sat bouncing my foot impatiently.

A lady turned my way and smirked. I could tell she was trying not to laugh at my outburst.

My first vacation in fifteen years, and this was how it was going to start. I should have known from the signs that were presented to me earlier today that this whole thing was a bad idea. This upcoming merger had stressed me out so bad, and the fact that my boss was an inconsiderate prick who demanded more and more all the time had burned me completely out, and now this.

I had started to notice the burnout a few weeks ago when I couldn't get up out of bed on a Monday morning to go to our usual business meeting. I had been having trouble concentrating as well. Don had been my rock throughout most of it, trying to be supportive, but then he started expressing that he was beginning to feel ignored. I tried to pretend that what he was saying wasn't true, but every time we had been together over the last few months, I had spent almost all my time working and ignoring him. I had hoped we had fixed our relationship enough; however, I guess we hadn't. I thought he would be getting down on bended knee professing his love for me sometime over the next week, but instead I sat here alone, feeling foolish. I probably would have been better off if I had just gone to the Dominican alone. Just one more mistake to add to my ever-growing list, and I had TexCorp to thank for that.

I dragged my bags behind me to the closest ladies room. Once inside, I slammed the stall door closed and leaned up against the cold brick wall. I took a couple of deep breaths and pulled out my phone. In those few breaths I decided that Don should tell me himself, not be a coward through a voice mail.

I dialed his number, expecting him to answer, but three rings later, his voice mail picked up. I hung up and pressed redial a couple more times, both yielding the same response.

"Okay so you don't want to answer. That figures. So I'll text instead," I mumbled to myself.

ME: I'm here, waiting at our normal meeting spot, under the bagel sign in case you've forgotten. Are you stuck in traffic?

I quickly used the facilities and had just finished drying my hands when my phone buzzed in my pocket. I pulled my phone out and looked down at the screen.

DON: Nope, check your voice mail

My stomach sank. What a bastard. I dragged my suitcase behind me and went to sit down near the gate I would be flying out of. I had hours to wait for my connecting flight. We had planned it that way so we could spend a little time having a few drinks and dinner prior to taking off.

I shut my phone off and threw it in my purse. "I won't be needing you, that is for sure," I mumbled and sat back against the chair. The tension in my shoulders was incredible, and now I couldn't wait to hit that beach. I debated grabbing a room at a nearby hotel for the six-hour wait, that way I could get some sleep, but decided against it.

"What to do for six hours?" I questioned as I looked around, and then I saw it—Take me Away Bar and Grill.

I studied the sign. A gin and tonic would be great right about now, but like always, I decided against enjoying myself and pulled my book from my bag. Besides, I didn't want to get drunk before I flew.

I opened my book to the last chapter I had read and tried to ignore the craving for a cold beverage. Minutes later, I shoved my book back into my bag and shrugged my shoulders. "Fuck it, you're on vacation. You deserve a fucking drink," I said to myself, then grabbed my bags and headed over to the little bar.

As I entered, I looked around for an empty table. The place was busy, couples and families sitting, eating, laughing away. I had no one to sit and laugh away with, so I looked around for an empty seat. I finally spotted one at the bar and wandered over. I sat down and the bartender immediately took my order.

Within minutes, I took my first sip of the perfectly mixed gin and tonic, that first mouthful going down as smooth and as easy as water.

I fished around in my bag for my phone and headphones, finally pulling them out and untangling the messed-up cord. I was going to sit here, drink my drinks, and listen to some music, maybe do a crossword or play a game on my phone, something, anything to help take away the fact that I was indeed sitting here alone, until I had to go.

I had powered up my phone and was just about to plug my earphones in when my phone rang. I frowned. Perhaps Don had realized he had made a mistake and changed his mind. Perhaps he was waiting for me.

"Hello," I answered.

"Mia," Mark's voice poured over the phone, causing me to roll my eyes, "about those reports. You missed one of them, my dear. Can you bring it in with you on Monday please?"

Of course, I had missed one. He would always find a reason to keep me where he wanted me.

"I told you, I won't be there Monday. I'm on vacation."

"Yeah sure, sure." He laughed.

That was it, I couldn't take it anymore, and just like that, I snapped.

Chapter Five

BRYCE

"I'm not a greedy bastard, Chase. I am one of the most giving people there is. Alyssa, she doesn't see it that way," I mumbled into the phone as the cab drove up the hill toward the airport. "It really bothers me that she thinks of me that way, you know." I looked out the window, watching the snow start to fall.

"She's just pissed off that you won't let her stay in the condo anymore," Chase mumbled into the phone.

I was sure he was tired of listening to my whiny antics by now. I had decided to end my two weeks off a little bit early. Well, a lot early. A full week early. I had been inundated with calls from clients, and frankly, I was bored being here alone.

Alyssa normally came with me to the lake house. She would go off shopping or to the spa, and I would work, and then we would meet up in town and go for dinner. Some days we would both head up to one of the ski resorts and spend the day. Scratch that, she would take advantage of what I had to offer and end up calling me a greedy bastard in the end.

"You're better off, bro. Believe me."

I rested my head against the headrest, listening to the radio playing, the song making me think of Alyssa and the night we had broken up. She had called me a greedy bastard and made her way out the front door to her mother's because she hadn't gotten her way. That had been my breaking point.

I had given her every single thing she had ever wanted, no matter the cost. I knew my brothers thought I was crazy, but I was in love with her and I wanted her to be happy. Of course, my brothers had expressed their concerns many times, telling me how one-sided they felt the relationship was. The last family dinner we had together, Autumn, Hunter's wife, had even made a comment to Alyssa about the fact that she didn't seem to want to be there. Of course, then Hope jumped on her as well, resulting in a huge argument between all three women that ended when Alyssa stormed out of the house and waited in the car for me. It had been a disaster, and after that, she didn't bother coming to family dinners anymore, and every time I went, she felt the need to express her displeasure.

"Deep down I know you are right, Chase. Guess it's just a little hard for me to believe right now."

Alyssa was missing me. I had heard from her three times today alone, each call getting a little more desperate as the night went on. Finally, she admitted she had made a mistake and wanted me back, that she couldn't make it on her own. I didn't bother calling her back. Instead, I called my brother.

"I can't forgive her, Chase. Not knowing what she really thinks of me. I gave her three years, man."

"Forgive her? There is no way you should forgive her. She fucked another man in your bed. Besides, don't forget, you were treated like shit for those three years. So grow a pair and tell her to fuck off."

I laughed into the phone. This was my brother!

"I'll make someone happy one day, won't I, Chase?" I asked, interrupting whatever it was my brother was droning on about.

"Yes, of course you will. She isn't the last woman on earth, Bryce. Now stop sounding like a big pussy and reattach your dick. Do you think you are ready to return to work, because I seriously don't think you are ready to come back yet."

"Chase, I am fine. Seriously, there is so much work to do, so I am coming back. I just arrived at the airport."

"Well you best have a better handle on things. I'm not going to argue. I am drowning with this merger and could use you to go over the reports, but I know Carter and Hunter were pissed with you. If you don't feel you can come back yet, you best stay there."

"I'm good, honestly. I will be there and help you get everything in order. Listen, I got to run. Just arrived at my drop-off."

"All right. Talk to you later, bro. Safe flight."

"Thanks, see you soon."

Minutes later, I had paid my cab driver and found myself fighting my way through the crowds of people in the airport.

I had come early. The lines were crazy long, so I wandered over to the window and watched the snow continuing to fall. As the flakes danced down to the ground, I wondered if perhaps I wasn't being ridiculous and probably should have had the taxi just turn around and return to the lake house. If this storm that they were promising started before my flight left, I'd have wasted my time.

Chase was right, I didn't need to be back in the city for another week, and to be honest, I truly didn't feel as if I were ready to go back. Instead the stubborn streak in me had insisted I get to the airport and head back home to the office and my new life. However, the ground was now covered with snow, getting deeper by the second. I looked up to see if my flight was still on time, and of course, it had been delayed and now wasn't scheduled to leave for another eight hours.

I wasn't going to waste my time worrying about it. I made my way over to the 'Take me Away' bar, deciding to drown my sorrows in a few drinks before my flight took off. I stepped up to the bar, signaling to the bartender, who held up his finger to let me know he would be with me in a minute.

I relaxed, glancing around the bar at all its patrons...and that was when I saw her. Mia, my best friend's little sister, was sitting on the opposite side of the bar on the phone, looking frustrated as hell.

I had to do a double take to make sure it was her, before I casually made my way over to an open stool beside her and took a seat. She hadn't noticed me yet. She was still talking with someone on the phone, determination, anger, and irritation lining her voice as she spoke.

She certainly hadn't changed, from what I remembered.

Brown hair, cute button nose, still sexy as hell when she was angry. I listened to what she was saying, something about it being fifteen years and vacation and "I'm not working on that right now." Whatever it was, it didn't sound very good, and she certainly didn't look happy.

She stopped speaking, listened for half a minute more, and then hung up, slamming her phone onto the bar so hard I was afraid it may shatter. She picked up her drink and mumbled, "What an asshole," before almost emptying her glass.

"What will you have to drink, sir?" the bartender asked, pulling a clean glass from the stack.

"Double scotch on the rocks please, and another one for the lady please." I nodded toward Mia and handed the bartender my credit card. "Just start a tab please." I was going to be here for a while.

"Listen, asshole, there is no need to buy me a drink. I am perfectly capable of getting my own," Mia barked back.

"Mia, is that any way to treat an old friend?" I practically whispered in her ear.

Those big, chocolate-brown eyes of hers landed on mine. She blinked hard as she looked at me, a smile forming on her perfectly bowed lips. "Bryce? Is it really you?" she asked, her soft voice barely heard over the loud crowd. Her eyes swept over my body, taking in my large, muscular frame.

"Yes, Mia, it's me."

She was as beautiful as she had been all those years ago. Her long, soft, dark hair was pulled back in its signature ponytail, just like I remembered.

"It's so good to see you." She smiled, reaching up to give me a hug.

"You too." I wrapped my arms around her and pulled her close, breathing in her scent. "Is it okay if this asshole buys you a drink now?" I chuckled.

"My God, I am so sorry about that." She buried her face in her hands to hide her embarrassment.

"It's all right. No offense. How's that idiot brother of yours?"

Grant had been my best friend growing up. Of course, after college we went our separate ways—me to law school, him to medical school, and now we only saw and spoke to one another online.

"He's doing well. He's up for promotion at his hospital. Him and June just had their second baby as well." She smiled.

Second baby. Here I was still single, having stupid arguments and ending serious relationships with the women I dated, and my best friend was a father.

"Wow! That is great. I'm so happy for him. So what are you doing here and where you headed?" I asked, looking down at the luggage that sat in between her feet and the bar.

"Dominican." She picked up her drink and drank the rest just in time for the fresh ones to arrive.

"Visiting our old stomping grounds, I see. Although it was much safer when we went. Now people only go there to get murdered." We both laughed.

I had often vacationed with Grant and his family growing up. We had spent two winters in the Dominican chasing girls and having fun. Well, he spent the time chasing girls; I spent my time dreaming of his sister.

She rolled her eyes at me and let out a little laugh. "I

suppose I would have been. Figured it would be nice to go back to a familiar place."

"So where are you living now?"

"Oh, I still live just outside of Kings Cove Harbor. I never ventured very far."

I felt my heart race a little. She still lived near me. What a small world it was.

"Small world. I didn't travel far either. I work in the city still. So how did you end up in Vermont, if you are going to Dominican?" I questioned. They didn't normally re-route planes going to the Dominican here.

"Ugh, don't ask. As Grant would put it, it's just another one of my many stupid, stupid mistakes."

I let out a laugh. "That doesn't sound very good."

"Ugh, just my life lately. What about you? What are you doing here?"

I could tell she was frustrated, not just by the tone of her voice and body language but by the way she was fidgeting. Mia only ever used to fidget when she was agitated.

"I'm on my way back home. I came up to my lake house here for a little rest and relaxation." I placed my arm on the back of her chair.

"Nice. Well, I hope at least one of us had a good vacation."

She blinked hard and turned her face from me for a second, and that was when I saw one lone little tear slide down her cheek. I frowned.

"I'm sorry," she mumbled, quickly wiping her cheek. "I guess I am a little more upset than I first thought."

When we were younger, I had hated seeing her upset and always strove to make sure she never felt that way for any reason whenever she was around me, and tonight wasn't going to be any different.

"That's it, no tears!" I said, slapping the bar counter. Mia looked at me. "Tears are only going to call for many, many more drinks!" I signaled to the bartender for another round as Mia began to laugh. "And food," I said, reaching for a menu and handing it to her.

An hour later, it was just like old times again. We had caught up, and we sat with drinks in hand, the plate of fully loaded nachos gone, only a few crumbs left.

"That was so good," Mia said, relaxing back against her seat.

"That it was. Looks like you need another drink there." I signaled to her empty glass, then to the bartender for two more.

"I don't know. This is more than I've had to drink in a long time." She giggled.

I glanced up to the TV above our table and saw the current weather report. "Shit, that doesn't look very good." I tapped Mia's shoulder to get her to look at the TV. Snow had pretty much blanketed the area. The city was closing roads, and flight cancelations were now in progress.

"Well, that is just fantastic. Tops off a completely shitty day with yet another complication," she said as she threw her napkin down on the empty plate. "Now what?" She got up from her chair and began rustling through her purse.

"Calm down, Mia. We don't know for a fact that our planes are the ones that are canceled." She ignored me, continuing to search her purse. "What are you looking for?"

"My credit card. I need to pay my bill and get out there before—"

Before she could even finish what she was going to say, a voice came over the loudspeaker, quieting the whole restaurant.

"Unfortunately, due to extreme weather, all outbound and inbound flights have been canceled. I repeat, all flights currently reporting as delayed and on time have now been canceled."

That announcement stopped her in her tracks, and she sat back down on her chair looking defeated.

"Now what am I going to do?"

"Mia, it's not that big of a deal. We just come up with a Plan B," I announced, swirling my scotch and taking a drink.

She smirked. "It's no big deal? I pretty much had to sell a kidney to get my boss to approve this time off. Besides, I don't have a Plan B. I barely had a Plan A, and we can already see how that turned out."

"Well how about we come up with a Plan B together and we will go from there. If that one fails, then we come up with another one. Where is your sense of adventure? In case you've forgotten, my plans were always fun. You can't deny that."

I reached for the food menu and wiggled my eyebrows. "But first we need dessert. All good plans are derived over something sinfully sweet. Isn't that what you always said?"

I caught a glimpse of a smile, and together we looked over the menu and settled on a slice of cheesecake. I went with chocolate and she went with cherry and another round of drinks to wash it down.

Once the cheesecake was placed in front of us, she didn't hesitate. She sunk her fork in and then took a sip of her drink and let out a breath. I watched as she took another forkful and closed her eyes as she savored the rich flavor.

"So, tell me what Plan A was."

"If you really want to know, I came here to meet my boyfriend of five years. We'd been planning this trip for the last six months. I was pretty sure at the time we booked he was going to propose."

I looked around in a frantic search.

"Bryce, what is it?" she asked.

"Don't tell me I am sitting in his seat, hitting on his girl?"

She let out a laugh. "He's not here. As soon as the trip was booked, we started having...issues. He claimed that I don't try hard enough in our relationship, and that work takes a ton of my attention. I won't lie, it does take a ton of my attention, but never all of it. Anyways, he isn't here because that no-good son of a bitch broke up with me while I was flying here."

"He broke up with you after telling you that you don't try hard enough?"

"He did! Through a damn voice mail of all things."

"Through a voice mail? So, he blames you for all the trouble and then he does that. I'm sorry, Mia, but he sounds like a dick. I'd say you at least deserve a better breakup than that. I'd at least have the heart to call you before you traveled all the way here."

She let out a laugh. "Thanks, but honestly, it really doesn't surprise me. Somehow, deep down, I figured he would end up being like that. Honestly, I'm not really all that torn up about it either. Funny thing is, since that voice mail, I feel as if a thousand-pound weight has been lifted off me."

I cleared my throat and took a sip of my drink. I certainly wasn't one to be giving relationship advice after everything I had gone through. I did, however, know how she felt because I had felt the same way after Alyssa walked out the door. I wasn't upset at the loss of her, more the idea of what she thought of me. I looked at Mia. She looked exhausted.

"All right! Well we can't stay here forever, so what did you want to do for Plan B? Any ideas?" she mumbled, swirling her fork around her plate, picking up little bits of cheesecake.

"Well, we can always head to my lake house. It's only ten minutes or so from here. It's got everything we need: a fireplace, hot tub, food, comfort."

She looked at me, a hint of playfulness in her eyes. "Really?"

"Yep. We can stay the week if you want. Let the storm pass over."

"That sort of sounds wonderful. Better than a beach vacation, to be honest."

That was the Mia I remembered. Even though she liked the beach, she always used to be more about comfort, and apparently, she hadn't changed. "All right, let me take care of the tab, and then we'll grab a cab."

"No, Bryce, really, I insist, let me."

"Mia, I'll take care of it," I said, placing my hand over hers to stop her from digging any farther into her purse. She turned those large brown eyes on me. I had expected her to argue, but she stopped and smiled.

I pulled my hand from hers and stood up from my seat. "Get your stuff together. I will be right back," I said winking.

I tapped my card on the debit machine and stepped off

to the side to wait for the receipt. I looked over at Mia while I waited. She was your typical girl next door. Down to earth, no nonsense, attractive, and one girl I had always wanted but never had. Grant had told me the first time he brought me to his house when we were fifteen that his sister was off-limits. When I saw her, I instantly knew why. Of course, I did what most best friends would do—I kept my hands to myself and pined over her for a few years.

After we all parted ways, time separated us. I went on, and over the years, we lost touch, until I had forgotten about her completely...or I thought I had. However, the instant she appeared tonight, it was like I had been transported back in time.

I watched as she pushed her dark hair behind her ear and licked her lips as she typed out something on her phone then shoved it back into her purse. I studied her closer. She looked tired and stressed, and I wondered when the last time was that she had any fun. It was that moment that I decided I was going to show her a fun, carefree week at my lake house. I had to, because judging from my body's response to touching her hand, I would be in trouble if anything else happened.

Chapter Six

Bryce stepped out from the curb and waved his hand in the air, signaling the next cab over. The car pulled up and the driver got out. "You again?" He chuckled.

Bryce started to laugh. "Yep, me again. Should have stayed at the lake house I guess."

"Going back, I take it." The man laughed as he came around and grabbed our bags.

Bryce opened the back door for me to get in the cab and slid in beside me. I sat back against the seat and watched out the window as we began the drive toward Bryce's lake house, the heat from the seats sinking into my body quickly relaxing me. It had been such a long day, and with all the stress, I had been put into a state of fight or flight, something I had long ago promised myself I would never get into again.

I closed my eyes, the smell of Bryce's cologne invading

my senses. It was musky and manly and smelled so good I just wanted to bury my face in his neck.

"Would you both like to listen to some music?" the driver asked.

"Yes please," Bryce answered, and soon the cabin of the vehicle was filled with soft music. Within minutes, the song had changed on the radio to one that I remembered from my teen years. It instantly reminded me of a memory I hadn't thought of in a long while: the night of Mary McGuire's party.

It was the last party of the summer. Grant and Bryce had both graduated two months earlier and were packed and ready to leave for their respective schools. The following week, they would be gone. My brother was supposed to have gone to the party alone, but when I found out Bryce was going to be there too, I begged him to taking me. I knew this would be one of the last times I would have to hang with Bryce, and that was the only reason I had wanted to go. I'd had a huge crush on him since my brother brought him home in the tenth grade. Bryce never looked at me in the way I had hoped he would, even though I had tried so hard to get his attention.

Over the years, he spent many overnights at our house, and I would parade around him in my short shorts and tiny tank tops, praying for a glance, a look, anything. I would conveniently put myself beside him when he and my brother were watching a movie or beg to go to the theater with them, but Bryce never gave me a hint that he was remotely interested in me. In fact, he rarely if ever even noticed me.

During the summer before graduation, Grant, Bryce, and Chase did nothing but hang out around our pool. I had quickly gone from a one-piece suit that summer to a two-piece, and I would lie around and sun myself, reading books or magazines, while the boys played in the water.

At first, I received no attention, and just when I was about to give up, I started to notice Bryce watching me when no one was looking, his eyes skimming over my body.

The past school year, Bryce's interest continued. He would occasionally bump into me in the hallway between classes and sit and study with me during his spare in the library, claiming that none of his friends had a spare at the same time. Then, about halfway through the school year, Grant and Bryce had some sort of falling out, and he didn't come around to the house often. Almost instantly, he stopped sitting with me during spare. They had just started hanging out again at the end of summer, and once again he was back to ignoring me.

Grant and I had arrived a little after 9:00 p.m. The party was already in full force. "Really, Mia, I don't know why you even want to be here. You don't know anyone!" he said as he walked in front of me.

"That's not true. A few of my friends are here. I'll be fine. Just go and find your friends," I said, pushing him away.

Just like I wanted, Grant went off to find the boys, and I went to get a drink, quickly losing sight of my brother in the sea of people.

I wandered aimlessly for a couple of hours, looking for anyone I may know, getting new drinks along the way, until I finally spotted Bryce heading up the stairs. With my heart in my throat, I fought my way through the people, careful not to trip as I made my way upstairs.

I planned to make Bryce mine once and for all tonight. After all, I had seen the way he had looked at me.

As soon as I got up there, I noticed that most of the bedroom doors were shut. Lots of people lined the hallway, but Bryce was gone. I slowly opened each door in search of him.

The first door I opened, I interrupted a couple who were almost having sex. Behind the second door the couple were making out on the bed. I knew he had come up here, so I shut the door and continued my way down the hall. Finally, I got to one of the last bedroom doors. It was cracked open and the light beside the bed was on, so I peeked through and saw Bryce standing there with his eyes closed.

I swallowed hard and finally, after I got up the courage, I pushed the door open a little and was just about to say "There you are" when he stepped forward and grabbed two hands. He pulled the owner of those two hands close to him, and that was when my breath caught in my throat. He was holding my best friend.

She stepped toward Bryce, and their lips slowly met. My eyes burned as I stood there. I didn't know what to do, except watch as every dream I ever had of kissing him shattered right before my eyes. I was frozen to the spot, so I couldn't move, and that was when Bryce opened his eyes and saw me standing there in the doorway. The look in his eyes was forever burned into my memory. That was when Kate turned and saw me as well. She had shouted something to me about being sorry and to wait, but I tore myself from that spot and ran with tears burning in my eyes. Halfway down the stairs, I felt my stomach start to turn, and I was now not only fighting the tears but also trying to stop the contents of my stomach from spewing everywhere.

I ran down those stairs, bumping people and getting dirty looks as I went. I just needed to get away. I didn't want to hear Kate's excuses. She knew how I felt about Bryce. How dare she do that to me?

I continued fighting my way through the crowd until I ran into someone's chest. I felt a firm hand grip my shoulders, stopping me. I blinked and looked up to see my brother standing there, and that was when the tears started to spill down my face.

"Mia, what happened?"

"Nothing, Grant. Just take me home please."

I ripped from his grip and bolted out the front door, running toward our parked the car. I pulled open the back door and crawled in, curled up into a ball, and waited for what felt like ever for my brother. He wasn't too far behind, and he drove me home, asking me repeatedly what had happened and whose ass he and his friends needed to kick. I never said a word, and I never said anything to him about that night, and I never mentioned Bryce again to anyone. I had never even thought about him...until now.

That night had absolutely gutted me, and now just thinking about it, I realized that I still held onto that anger. The months that followed that night had been spent with my face down in the pillow. I ended my friendship with Kate and shut myself away from everyone else. I couldn't have a friendship with someone who would betray me like that, and I just wanted to be left alone anyway.

Grant and Bryce went off to school, and I was left to heal my broken heart. It was for the best.

I was yanked from my memory when I felt the car come to a stop and felt a light tap on my thigh.

"Wake up. We're here."

I looked at Bryce, and then out the window, and saw a dark house sitting at the end of a walkway.

A blast of cold air flew into my face as Bryce pushed the car door open, snow swirling inside. I shivered, pulling my coat around me.

"Let's go." He held out his hand out for me to take.

I grabbed my purse and climbed out of the back of the car with his help. He dug into his pocket and pulled a crisp bill from his billfold and handed it to the driver, who had already placed our bags onto the sidewalk. I took hold of my things, and together we walked down the walkway toward the front door.

"Careful, don't slip."

"I'm not five. I'm all right."

"Don't yell at me. I remember how accident prone you are."

Just as those words fell from his mouth, I felt my foot slip on some ice. I screamed as I felt myself start to fall backward, but he dropped his bags and grabbed my arms before I went down.

"You all right there?" he asked, steadying me.

"Yeah, thanks," I said as I regained my balance.

Once we were up and inside the covered porch, Bryce pulled his keys from his pocket and quickly unlocked the door. "I turned the heat down before I left, so you may want to leave your jacket on until I get a fire built. It's gotten much colder since then," he said, reaching inside and turning on a light. "Come on in and make yourself at home." He ushered me inside and shut and locked the door behind us.

Leaving our bags in the entryway, we removed our shoes and stepped into the living room. In the darkness I could see that this room looked out over the lake, lights of the other houses off in the distance twinkling like stars against the water.

Within seconds, that view disappeared when Bryce turned the lights on, and I saw our reflection in the glass. Bryce stood behind me, watching me. A funny feeling came over me, and it flashed through my mind for one minute that this was how it should have been—us together.

"Give me a few minutes to get a fire going," he said, and I turned, taking in the room while he bent down and started setting the wood up for a fire.

The large windows spanned from the floor to the ceiling, and I imagined that in the morning I would have a clear view of the storm we had just driven through. Maybe it wasn't such a bad idea I had come here. By the looks of things, I wouldn't be going anywhere for days and would have been spending my time in a hotel room instead.

I turned around, taking in more of the room. It was decorated in dark greens and beige. An over-sized couch sat in front of the fireplace holding many large cushions and a couple of large fleece blankets that looked inviting. Two over-sized armchairs also looked comfortable enough to curl up into. The gigantic fireplace was gorgeous, the face of it appearing to be natural stone, and the wooden mantle was lined with photographs.

"Are those your nieces?" I asked, pointing to the

photographs over the fire as I walked over to get a closer look.

"Yep those three are Carter's, and the other two munchkins are Hunter's."

I could see signs of both of his brothers in their kids. Backing away, I noticed a large TV that hung over the fireplace. I could easily see myself sitting down with a glass of wine and watching my favorite shows.

Returning my attention to the fireplace, I sat down on the arm of the couch and watched Bryce. He was squatted down, assembling some kindling in the fireplace, the sleeves of his dress shirt rolled up to expose his muscular forearms. I could see the strength in his back now that he had removed his suit jacket, as he reached for a larger piece of wood.

"As soon as I am done here, I'll show you around the place, then we'll get comfortable and grab something to drink."

It was only a few more minutes before the fire was roaring away and the heat was pouring into the room.

"Come, let's take a look around. It's only a one-bedroom house, so you can take the bedroom, and I'll take the couch," he offered as I followed him down the hall.

He opened the door and behind it was the most luxurious bedroom I had ever seen. It was almost bigger than my house, and again beautifully decorated and furnished with a king-sized bed, large sitting area in front of the large window, and another large fireplace.

"The bathroom," he said, opening another door and flipping on a light.

I poked my head in and saw a large soaker tub that could

easily hold two, if not three, people and a massive walk-in shower.

"Wow, this is beautiful. You own all this?"

"I do," he answered as he pushed the closet door open and began shoving clothes to the back. "In case you want to hang some things up, go ahead. I'm going to go and grab us some drinks from the kitchen. Make yourself at home." He walked to the dresser and pulled open a drawer, removing his T-shirt and sweatpants. "Do you need anything warm to wear?" he asked.

"No, I should be fine. I did bring a couple warm things."

He nodded. "Well if you need anything, help yourself." He took his clothes and left the room.

I walked over and sat on the edge of the bed, my body sinking down into the soft mattress. I sat there for a couple of seconds, and then I opened my bag and pulled out my lounge pants and T-shirt, changing into them quickly before making my way back to the front room. I sank into the couch, relaxing as I felt the heat from the fire.

"Gin and tonic for you, scotch on the rocks for me." Bryce held the glass in front of me, and I reached up and took it. He placed his glass down on the table and sat next to me, pulling the blankets off the back of the couch and spreading them over us.

Chapter Seven

BRYCE

I relaxed back and took a sip of my scotch, the ice clinking against the glass. I was just about to ask Mia more about her ex when my phone started to vibrate in my pocket.

"Give me one minute," I said, and pulled my phone from my pocket and answered it. Instantly, I regretted it. I should have known better. It was too late for any of my brothers to call.

"Bryce, there you are." Alyssa's voice poured over the phone, and I closed my eyes and clenched my fists.

"What do you want?" I barked.

She was the absolute last person on the planet I wanted to talk to right now...or ever again, for that matter.

"Have you gotten a place yet or should I just leave your shit at your brother's?"

I rolled my eyes and pinched the bridge of my nose with my fingers. She was like an instant headache.

"Alyssa. What on earth are you talking about?"

"I've been packing your things. I just wondered where you wanted me to drop everything. I know you have been staying with Chase over the last few weeks, so I wanted to make sure that's where you wanted everything before I drop it off."

I didn't give her another second. "Have you gone mad? It's my place! It's my condo, as in I pay the mortgage and the bills. It's your shit that has to go, not mine," I gritted into the phone. "It's been five months. I took pity on your sorry ass and I gave you three. It's now been two more past that."

"Chase..." she whined, the sniffles starting. I was sure she was pouring fake tears at this point. "You try finding a place in this city. It's not as easy as it looks, you know. Can't I just pay you rent and stay here?"

"No, Alyssa, I don't need a roommate. Now get off your ass and find somewhere to live. At this point, I really don't care if you live in a cardboard box. I am finished. I am not finding, nor am I paying for, you to find a new place to live, and you aren't staying there. Just get your shit together and go."

I frowned, squeezing the bridge of my nose with my thumb and forefinger. I was so glad to be done with her and couldn't wait for her to leave. I had no idea what I ever even saw in her to begin with.

"Bryce?" she mewed.

"What?" I gritted into the phone.

"What about my ticket to Paris?" she questioned, and then grew quiet.

I couldn't believe my ears. "What ticket?" I gritted.

"The one you promised me."

I dropped my head back and took in a breath. It was taking all I had not to lose my composure. "When on earth did I promise you a ticket to Paris?"

"Seven months ago. It's just, I was thinking. Perhaps I could leave my things here and head over to Paris for a while to, you know, heal and find myself."

I let out a deep, hearty laugh, and then I felt the anger emerge and my chest start to ache. My head was pounding. She seemed to have a way of doing that to me lately.

"Alyssa, you have one more week, not a second, minute, or day more. Go to Paris, Italy, Australia for all I care. It's not going to be on my fucking dime. Now, I've got to go."

I hung up the phone and squeezed my fists tight. The woman absolutely infuriated me. I stood there letting the anger seep from my body before turning back to face Mia.

Maybe this storm was for the best. Perhaps I did need another week before I went back to everything. After all, I would have gotten home, found her still there, and been back in the exact same position I had been in when I had left. I knew my brothers would be happy I took the time. After all, they were the ones who had forced me here.

"Bryce, is everything all right?" I heard Mia's soft voice ask behind me, and then I felt her small hand on my shoulder.

Ignoring her question, I turned and grabbed her hand. "Come with me." I pulled her down the hall as she followed behind me, laughing. I raced to the kitchen and down the set of stairs that led into my wine cellar. "All right, pick a bottle, any bottle, but make it a good one."

She looked at me as if I were crazy, but then turned and looked at the wall full of wine, finally reaching up and pulling one out. She handed it to me, and I looked down at the label.

"This couldn't be more perfect!" I said, looking in her eyes. I knew she was questioning what the hell had gone on over the phone, but instead of asking she just smiled at me and went with it.

I pulled another bottle from the wall and tucked it under my arm. "For later." I winked at her.

Within an hour, we were halfway through the second bottle while watching the storm unfold on TV. Mia's foot was casually draped over my leg, just like old times.

"So, tell me, that call you had..."

"Yeah, that call. Let's just say that call is part—no, that call is the entire reason why I am here."

She bit her lip, her eyes growing sad as she took another sip of wine. I could tell the alcohol was getting to her now because her eyes were bloodshot, and her cheeks carried a rosy hue.

"Bad?" she asked.

"You could say that. It's been a very stressful few months, to say the least. I've been helping with this huge merger that Chase is working on. The case is a disaster. Our clients think the company is holding back or lying about some information."

"Ah Chase. How is he?"

"Good, crazy as ever." I laughed.

She let out a little laugh that went straight to my cock, just like it used to do when we were younger.

"Oh and then my ex—oh my wonderful ex—decided to

tell me one night that I'm nothing but a greedy bastard, so I broke up with her." I paused for a moment. "Well, that's not true. She broke up with me." I smiled at her and watched as she brought the wine glass to her lips, a smirk settling on them.

"A greedy bastard eh? I'm surprised someone would think that of you." She looked away from me, then cleared her throat. I knew exactly what she was referring to.

"All right, well, maybe when I was younger, but age changes people." I winked.

"Well something must have set her off. What did your boneheaded self do this time?"

She knew me well. Well enough to remember almost every breakup I had had.

"She got pissed off one night when I choose work over her. But really it wasn't like that. A client needed help. It was important, and I had to cancel our date. It wasn't the first time, but I always tried to choose her over work, and when I couldn't, I always made it up to her. She always said she understood, but for whatever reason, this time was different.

You know she told me that money meant more to me than she did. How ridiculous is that? At the time, she meant everything to me. She didn't understand I was only doing that to keep her happy, to be able to do the things that we both wanted to do, and to be able to go on the trips that she wanted to go on. It all takes money.

"You know what else took money? That two-carat diamond engagement ring I had custom ordered, that I was planning to surprise her with on our trip to Venice. All I can say is, it was a good thing I never gave it to her. When I had returned a couple nights later, after that argument, I found her riding another man in my bed."

Mia let out a little whistle. Perhaps I had divulged too much about the whole thing. I wasn't upset anymore, so I couldn't blame that. I was just angry now, and I feared that maybe I wasn't enough for any woman.

"I'm sorry to hear that, Bryce. No one should have to deal with that."

"It's okay. I was dealing with everything fine, until she wouldn't leave and started making me feel bad for asking her to. Then things started falling apart at work, and, well, here I am. Carter and Hunter had been watching it unfold, and when they figured I couldn't cope anymore, Carter decided to send me on a forced vacation!"

"Maybe it's all for the better? The breakup, the vacation, everything. The universe works in mysterious ways." Mia placed her hand on mine and smiled at me, her eyes glassy from all the alcohol we had consumed.

"You're probably right; it would never have worked anyways. I shouldn't have been so stupid. The writing was on the wall months and months ago."

We both sat there taking a moment to watch more of the storm on the television. It was coming down harder than before, and I was glad that we had this safe place to be.

When the silence became too uncomfortable to me, I sat forward and cleared my throat. "I want to make a toast," I announced.

"Oh yeah, to what?" She giggled.

"Here's to breakups and canceled plans!"

We clinked our glasses together and drank back the

remainder of the wine, Mia reaching for the bottle and topping us off.

I had stopped drinking an hour earlier, and now we were sitting watching an episode of *The Big Bang Theory* when I looked over at Mia. She was slouched down on the couch, almost asleep, the wine glass half-empty in her hand and almost falling to the floor.

I reached over and took the glass from her, placing it quietly on the table. I got up and sat next to her. "Mia?" I whispered. She didn't respond, so I placed my hand on her shoulder and rubbed her arm this time. "Mia?" I said a little louder.

"Hmmm?" she moaned, keeping her eyes closed.

"Come on, let's get you to bed." I put my arm around her back and sat her up.

"What? Where are we going?"

"To bed. Come on."

She grabbed hold of my arm, and once she was up, she leaned into me. I placed my arm around her to keep her steady, allowing her to rest herself up against me. I shut the TV off and slowly walked her down to the bedroom, occasionally stopping so she could regain her balance. "Are you trying to take advantage of me?" She giggled between hiccups.

"No, just helping you to bed." I had my arm fully around her waist guiding her into the bedroom. Once we were at the bedside, I pulled the blankets back and sat her down first before laying her down. I swung her legs up and placed them on the bed, pulling the covers over her.

"Don't go," she whimpered as she rolled onto her side and grabbed my hand. "Stay with me."

"Mia, you're dreaming. Get some rest. I'll be in the living room."

She didn't make another sound and eased the grip she had on my hand.

I was just about to the door when she called my name again. I stopped with my hand on the door handle.

"Bryce, please stay with me. I want you to kiss me, like you kissed her..."

Mia started to snore as I stood there looking over my shoulder at her.

"The universe works in mysterious ways, buttercup," I mumbled, repeating her words from earlier as I looked back at her.

I shut the hall light off and the overhead light in the bedroom and turned on the bedside light. I sat down and placed my head in my hands. There was no way she could have remembered that night. It had been a shitty end to the year that summer. I had finally confessed my feelings for Mia to her brother and asked for his permission to start seeing her, and he flipped on me and told me to do what was best for everyone and leave her alone.

I had done just that.

I stopped everything, including my friendship with Grant, only seeing him when we all went out as a group. We had all planned on going to that party that summer, and I had heard from Kate, Mia's best friend, that Mia was trying to convince Grant to bring her. I knew how persistent she could be, and so I showed up at the party. If all else failed, at least I would hang with the guys for the last time before I left for school.

I had arrived early and was a few beers in, when I was

approached by another one of Mia's friends and told that Mia was waiting for me upstairs. I couldn't wait. I had seen Grant, so I knew she must be there.

I excused myself from the group and went in search of the girl I wanted so bad. I found my way up the stairs and wandered down the hall to the room I was told she would meet me in. When I walked in, the room was empty, but I heard her in the bathroom. She called out for me to close my eyes, so I did, and shortly after I felt her hands in mine, and then I felt her lips on mine, and when I opened my eyes, it was like the floor fell out from under me.

Mia was standing in the doorway, watching everything unfold before her eyes. I had kissed Kate, not Mia. I had been tricked. I could remember the look in Mia's eyes as she backed out of the doorway, running from me.

I had run after her, but when I saw her speaking with Grant, I decided I'd better let sleeping dogs lie. If she told him, I knew he would kill me.

I left the party shortly after Grant did to take Mia home. I had gone by their place the next day when no one was home. I wanted to talk to Mia and explain what had happened, but no one answered the door. I tried one more time before I left for school. I knew she was no longer speaking to Kate; Grant had told me they had had some falling out before he had left for school. Once again, there was no answer, and I had no choice but to head on my way out of town for school. It had really been a horrible way to end the summer, considering it could have turned out so different.

Mia let out a soft moan behind me and rolled onto her back. I let out a breath and pulled my shirt off over my head and threw it over on the chair. Leaving my house pants on, I kicked my feet up on the bed and lay back, placing both arms behind my head. I turned and looked at Mia, who was now sound asleep on her side, her hands placed under her head.

"I wished I had a chance to make up to you for that night," I whispered. "Perhaps this week will be my chance."

Chapter Eight

Mia

I woke with a start to the sound of a phone ringing somewhere in the distance, the noise drilling into my head, and then I felt someone shove me. I was cold and uncovered, so I reached for the blankets, ignoring the noise, praying it would go away. I tried pulling a handful of the blankets I held, but nothing moved. Then I felt an annoying tap against my back again. I rolled over and looked through squinted eyes. I could see an outline of a form lying next to me.

"Mia, answer your damn phone," a husky, dry voice called out.

I blinked again and wiped my eyes. Bryce was sprawled out beside me. I quickly turned my head away, breathing hard. What the hell was he doing in bed beside me?

I took a second to compose myself and then peeked

again, still ignoring the ringing phone. He lay there shirtless, one hand over his eyes, the other resting on his solid eight pack of abs. I glanced farther down to see his foot rested on top of my leg, and I could make out the outline of his semi-hard cock through his pajama pants. We were both clothed, which was a good thing, but what the hell had happened last night?

I bit my lip and closed my eyes, trying hard to remember. Gin and tonics at the airport, wine, wine, and way too much wine. The very last thing I remembered was turning the TV to an episode of *The Big Bang Theory*.

"Mia, hell, answer your cell phone, my head is pounding." Bryce murmured, pulling the pillow over his face.

I reached around in my purse until I finally found my cell phone. "Hello." I waited, but no one responded. "Hello?" I repeated, rubbing my tired, dry eyes. When no one answered me this time, I hung up and rolled onto my back, looking up at the ceiling. I rested my arm over my eyes, still worried about what had happened between us.

I felt the bed move and shifted my arm just enough to peek over at Bryce. He was sitting up on the edge of the bed, his back to me. The absence of clothing allowed me to see more of him. His back muscles flexed as he stretched. He stood up and turned to me, his low-slung house pants accentuating his abs and that deeply carved V I had always loved.

He cleared his throat, pulling me from my thoughts. I didn't need to wonder what it would be like to run my tongue across those abs. I could feel the heat rising to my cheeks. I really needed a distraction.

"Nothing happened, just so you know."

I felt a sense of relief and disappointment run through

me at the same time, but to be honest, it would have been a shame to have spent a night with him and not remember it.

"You were really drunk, so I brought you in here and helped you to bed. I guess I must have dozed off. I'm going to hit the shower. We should get up and have some breakfast."

Lying on the bed, I watched after him as he wandered into the bathroom and shut the door behind him. I wished I was part of what was going on behind that closed door.

I opened my eyes and looked around the room. It was quiet and I could see light coming in through the sides of the drawn curtains. I must have fallen back asleep while Bryce was in the shower.

I glanced at the clock on the table. It was 11:00 a.m. I stretched and went to the window, pulling back the curtains to look out. The dark gray skies were still threatening snow after all that had fallen last night, but the snow-covered land-scape was beautiful.

I dropped the curtain, shutting the brightness out, and wandered into the bathroom, wet a cloth, and ran it over my face. I stepped back into the room, debating getting dressed, but my aching body had other ideas, and since I was still tired, I went and crawled back into bed. I was just about asleep again when my cell phone rang.

I ran my hand over my face and reached out from under the covers to dig my hand into my bag. I wiped my eyes and looked at the screen. "Seriously?" I huffed. I dropped the phone onto the bed and let it go to voice mail. Tara should know better than to call me while I was on vacation.

I rolled onto my back, rested my arm on my forehead, and stared up at the ceiling. I had just closed my eyes when my phone vibrated.

"Why," I cried. "Why are you doing this to me, universe," I asked and grabbed for my phone again.

I had three text messages and four emails all from Tara. I swallowed hard and read the emails, finding that she had a whole list of reports that Mark needed for Monday morning.

I quickly messaged her back asking if it could wait. Then I reminded her that I was on my first vacation in fifteen years and threw my phone back down on the bed. Within seconds, I felt the phone vibrate on top of the blankets and one simple word appeared on the screen. According to Mark the answer was "no."

I could already feel the stress seeping back into my body at her response, but I tried to shake it off. He wasn't getting them.

Wandering into the bathroom, I quickly showered, brushed my teeth, then flung my hair up into a wet ponytail because, well, I could, and then I dressed in a loose-fitting pair of jeans and T-shirt. I was glad I had packed a couple of warm things to wear. Grabbing my gray sweatshirt and my laptop, I made my way to the kitchen. It never mattered how much I didn't want to do anything for work, they always won, even now, because I could already feel the guilt of not doing it pour in.

I smelled the freshly brewed coffee the minute I emerged from the bedroom and followed that aroma to the kitchen. I rounded the corner, expecting to find Bryce, but instead I found plates of food spread across the island in the center of the kitchen. There was a little of everything, most of it having gone cold now, but nothing a microwave couldn't fix. Eggs, bacon, fresh fruit, dry cereal, pancakes, and oatmeal, everything looked great.

"Well, good morning. As you can see, breakfast awaits. Help yourself to anything you want. You may need to warm some of it up in the microwave. Also, there is yogurt in the fridge in case you want any, and fresh coffee. Would you like a mug?" I heard Bryce's deep voice behind me.

I shook my head in a yes motion and slowly walked into the kitchen, placing my laptop on the counter. I sat down at the island, opened my computer, and logged in. Bryce set the cup of coffee beside me, looking between me and the laptop.

"Is there Wi-Fi here?" I asked, taking a sip of the hot coffee.

"There is. Here." He came around to stand behind me, wrapping his arms around me, and quickly typed in the password and hit save. "There are plates right here when you are ready." Without another word, he pushed off the counter and left the kitchen.

The smell of pancakes and bacon made my stomach growl. I normally didn't have time to eat breakfast, unless I grabbed it from the coffee shop around the corner from the office—when I wasn't running late. I quickly fixed myself a plate of fruit, bacon, and pancakes and set it beside me while I logged into my remote office.

I had just popped a piece of bacon into my mouth and started working on the first report when Bryce entered the kitchen wearing running shoes and low-slung workout shorts, a green towel slung over his strong bare shoulder.

I looked up from my computer, slowly chewing. The first thing I noticed was his clear blue eyes. They stood out against his deeply tanned skin. His defined chest held a light sheen of sweat, and as my eyes traveled lower, I swore I could see the outline of his cock.

He looked down at the mess of papers I had scattered all over the counter and back up to me. "What you got going on here?"

I quickly piled the papers and took a sip of my coffee. "Nothing."

"Doesn't look like nothing to me. Looks like you might be doing work?"

"Nope," I said, taking a drink of my coffee.

"You're on vacation! It's time to shut things down." He picked up the papers I'd just piled, taking a strawberry from my plate and popping it into his mouth while winking at me. "Am I going to have to take these away from you?" he teased.

I let out a breath and smiled. Those blue eyes peered into mine, and a sexy smile was plastered on his face.

"No, and I know I shouldn't be working. It's just they are relentless, you know?"

"I get it." He stuck his tongue out at me, and I let out a little giggle. "All right, you have thirty minutes, then you are going to put this away. Then you should join me for a workout."

I took the paper from his hand. "All right. Go work out. I'm going to finish my breakfast."

Bryce smiled. "I'll be in here. Just going to do my run first. I know you aren't much of a runner."

"I'll be along shortly." I smiled and let out a laugh. "But you should know I'm not much of anything when it comes to physical activity."

"Gee, Mia, that is a shame." He winked as he walked by me and tapped me under the chin. "Thirty minutes. I'll be waiting."

I felt a surge of heat as I inhaled his scent and watched his ass in those low-slung gym shorts walk away from me and into a room off the kitchen. I cleared my mind, continued eating, and started working away. I got up to refill my coffee when I noticed Bryce had left the door open just enough that I could see him as he ran on the treadmill.

I couldn't tear my eyes away from him. I leaned against the counter and stood there drinking my coffee, watching him. A half hour later, I had long forgotten about the reports I was supposed to be working on, when he turned and looked into the kitchen. I still stood in the exact same spot watching him. I had only moved to grab more fruit. He gave me a sexy smile before shutting the treadmill off and grabbed his towel to wipe the sweat from his forehead and chest. He walked back into the kitchen and leaned against the counter, popping a piece of cantaloupe into his mouth.

"Like what you see, do you?"

I felt the heat rise to my cheeks. How was I going to hide this? I mean, I had literally been standing here drooling into my cup of coffee while watching the man run. There was no hiding it, he had caught me. What the hell was wrong with me?

I said nothing. Instead I drank down the last of my

coffee, rinsed the mug in the sink, and placed it into the dishwasher. When I turned, he stood there watching me, a look in his eyes that I had never seen before.

"I thought you were going to join me?"

"I was," I said, straightening myself up from leaning on the kitchen counter, avoiding eye contact with him.

"Well, how about this. Since you made me run for an hour and I am done with my workout, why don't we go out and sit in the hot tub?" He stood there with a sexy smirk on his face. I felt like all the air had been sucked out of the room at his proposition. "Don't try to hide it, Mia. You know the idea sounds good." He winked. "And I am pretty sure you brought a bathing suit, since you were going to be in sun and sand, so you're not getting out of it. It's time to relax." He shut my laptop down and stood, leaning against the counter, looking at me.

Did I want to join him in the hot tub? Hell yes, I did. The room was getting warmer by the second as we stood there staring at one another. I could barely breathe, so instead of saying anything, I grabbed my laptop and papers and looked over my shoulder at him as I quickly left the kitchen, shaking my head as I went.

"I hope you are getting changed!" I heard him shout behind me. "I'll be out back."

"I am! Meet you out there," I yelled back as I wandered down the hall as fast as I could and opened the bedroom door. I dumped everything onto the desk in the corner and turned to look over my shoulder out into the hallway. I thought for a second and then went over to my suitcase, lifting it up onto the bed. Unzipping the bag, I reached inside, pulling out a little white bikini, and let out a breath. Why the hell hadn't I packed a one-piece?

I went into the bathroom and changed, then looked at myself in the mirror. I played with the ties on my bathing suit for a second, and then grabbed one of the black towels and wrapped it around my body. I looked back at my reflection in the mirror one more time, trying to gather some form of courage of being almost naked in front of Bryce, and then shut the light off. I grabbed my flip-flops from my bag and made my way out to the back of the house.

I looked out the door and saw Bryce was already seated in the steaming water. He was facing away from the house and looking out onto the lake. I slipped my feet into my sandals and let out a breath as I stepped out the back door, the cold instantly hitting my bare skin. I clutched my towel, shivering, and ran to the hot tub and was just about to stop when my foot slipped on a patch of ice. I dropped the towel as I went down, letting out a scream. "Bryce, help!" I landed on my back with a *thud*.

Bryce jumped up and looked down to the ground. "My God, Mia, are you all right?" He jumped out of the tub and came rushing to my side. "Did you hit your head, anything broken?" he asked, placing his hand under my head to check for bumps.

"No, I think I'm okay." I reached for the towel and groaned as I tried to sit up.

"Don't move." He picked me up off the ground with ease and sat me on the edge of the hot tub. He took the towel from me and I slowly lowered myself into the hot water, embarrassment reeling through me.

"Get in. You're going to get cold." He set my towel on the stairs and then climbed back into the tub.

Once he was seated beside me, I began to laugh at how embarrassing that was.

"What's so funny?"

"I am just embarrassed is all, about the fall."

"Don't be. I remember how accident prone you are. Do you remember the time you went into the house to grab a drink for yourself and came back out to the pool and tripped over Grant's pants? You went headfirst into the pool, your drink flying, and when you hit the water, your bikini top flew off." He laughed.

"Oh God, don't remind me. I wanted to die when I noticed it had come off," I said, laughing at the memory, my hands covering my face.

"All my sixteen-year-old brain wanted was a little flash, but you covered everything up so tight it was impossible to see anything." He winked and reached over the side of the tub, grabbed a wine cooler, opened it, and handed it over to me. "Here you go!"

My face flamed with embarrassment, but I did my best to brush it off and took the cold bottle from his hand and took a sip. "What's this for?"

"We are celebrating our breakups today!"

"What do you mean, celebrating?"

"Let's be honest with ourselves. Obviously neither of us were meant to date these douches that we were involved with, and we are totally better off without them, so we are going to celebrate, baby!"

I let out a loud laugh. He was right!

"So, aside from this breakup, which was your worst?"

"Well, I guess it would have been when I was in my early twenties. I was out with my friends when a group of guys my friends knew showed up. I didn't know it at the time, but it was a fix-up. Anyways, I was introduced to the quiet guy in the back, Brenden. You could tell he was the bad boy of the group, you know what I mean. I was instantly attracted to him. We started seeing one another, but I really wanted to play it cool just so he didn't know how much I liked him. It became more of a push-pull type of relationship. One week he would want me, the next I would want him. Anyways, things finally got serious once we were done playing that game, and he moved in with me. We survived Christmas and Valentine's Day, and then things kind of crashed and burned."

"What happened?"

"I came home from work one afternoon, and a voice mail—no surprise there—was waiting on the machine for him. He had apparently been seeing a girl on the side and she called to let him know she was three months pregnant. I was so crushed, my heart broken, I packed up his things before he got home and left them down on the sidewalk for him." I drank down more of my cooler, looking over to Bryce.

"Wow, maybe you should get rid of voice mail. There seems to be a pattern here."

I let out a laugh.

"Honestly, I don't even know what to say to that," Bryce said, drinking back his beer.

"Well, what about you?" I asked. "What is your worst story?"

Bryce looked up from the bottle he was holding. With one look I could tell he had something on his mind that he was holding back for some reason. "It was this one, to be honest," he said, getting quiet again.

I looked over at Bryce and cleared my throat before downing the remainder of my cooler. "You know what this calls, for don't you?"

"No," he answered, pulling himself up out of the tub to sit on the edge.

"Meatballs!"

"Meatballs?"

"Yeah meatballs! Let's go make some. They are the perfect comfort food, trust me!"

Bryce watched as I climbed out of the tub and wrapped myself up in the towel, obstructing his view. "You coming?"

"All right, let's go make meatballs!"

Chapter Nine

Bryce

"You mix while I add ingredients," Mia said, opening the pantry door and pulling out a bunch of dry ingredients, while the ground beef defrosted in the microwave.

She stopped and went over everything she had pulled out, mentally remembering the ingredients, her face lighting up when she recalled the one she was missing.

"Did you want some wine before we start?" I questioned while grabbing the bowl and measuring cups she handed me.

"Um yeah...that is just a silly question. I'll grab the glasses."

The microwave beeped and she pulled the ground beef out and dumped it into the bowl, while I went down and grabbed us two bottles of wine. I returned to the kitchen and opened and poured us our wine.

"When you're done, could you break up this ground beef? Do you have any oatmeal or breadcrumbs?" Mia asked while searching the cupboard.

"I can do that. Oatmeal is on the top shelf; breadcrumbs are in the green container," I answered as I dug my hand into the cold beef and began to break it up. I couldn't help but watch her bend and grab the breadcrumb container. She had the most perfect ass.

She set it on the counter and opened it, taking a couple of handfuls and dumping them into the bowl, along with an egg for me to mix. I dug my hands into the cold meat and watched as she carefully measured and added a bunch of spices into a separate bowl.

"Make sure you mix it all together really well, and then we will add in these spices. Where do you keep the baking sheets?"

"In the cupboard beside the stove."

Soon we were through with the first bottle of wine and onto the second when we began rolling meatballs and placing them one by one onto the pan while the oven was heating to the desired temperature.

"Just you wait, I'm telling you, these meatballs are the best comfort food in the world."

"Eat a lot of these do you?" I joked.

Mia stuck her tongue out at me before taking the tray and putting them in the oven.

"Now for more wine! You want to pick another bottle or shall I this time?"

"Go for it!" she said, and I walked over to the top of the stairs and turned to look back at Mia. She had already begun to clean up the kitchen. I hadn't realized it before, but I had really missed her and her brother in my life.

I watched as she danced around the kitchen, putting ingredients back where she had taken them from and placing things in the sink to quickly wash up and put away. I stood there for a few minutes continuing to watch her, wishing I could correct the lie that I had told her earlier. That the breakup I had just been through wasn't really the worst breakup. What was my worst breakup was the night she had seen me with her friend. That the worse part of it was having to say good-bye to her. However, I already knew there was no way that I could. So, pulling my gaze from her, I trudged down the stairs to pick our next bottle of wine.

While the meatballs cooked, we both showered and changed into some loungewear. As darkness fell, snow had started to fall again, and I had just built a roaring fire in the fireplace. I had soft music playing and two glasses of my favorite wine poured. I had just finished placing the bottle back into the chiller and dimming the lights when I saw Mia from the corner of my eye come into the room carrying a tray.

"Here they are!" she sang as she set the tray down, meatballs piled high on one plate and crackers and cheese on another.

I held out a glass of wine for her and she reached out and took it from me, looking around the room as realization came to her face.

"What is it?" I asked.

"Bryce, is this how you seduce women? I mean, look at it here. A beautiful lake house, hot tub, fire, dim lights, food and wine?" The light was dancing in her eyes as she looked at me.

I grinned. "No, the seducing part comes later—much, much later," I joked. "Just thought it would be nice to relax a little. Now let me taste these meatballs you rave about!"

She didn't hesitate. She grabbed one from the pile and brought it to my mouth.

"Be careful, it might be hot inside."

I took a bite, my teeth sinking into the soft inside. It was the best meatball I had ever tasted, and I closed my eyes as I chewed. When I opened my eyes, Mia was studying my face, a look in her eye I hadn't seen on her before.

The silence between us was becoming a little uncomfortable, so I took the remainder of the meatball that she held in her hand and put it to her perfect lips, watching as she parted them and took it from my hand. As soon as her teeth sank into the warm meat, she too closed her eyes.

She was fucking gorgeous.

I couldn't help myself. As soon as I knew she had swallowed, but before she opened her eyes, I leaned down and took her mouth with mine. She didn't move as I kissed her lips, her body stiffening at first, but I held her in my arms, and soon the plate of meatballs was forgotten, and she was a puddle in my arms.

We fell to the couch and curled up together, her in my arms as I continued the assault on her mouth, my tongue forcing her lips apart. I could already feel myself straining against my pants, and I gripped her ass while I kissed her deep. I pulled her closer to me so she could feel what she was doing to me, my mouth moving from hers down to her neck. I felt her place her hand between us, resting it on my chest, signaling me to give her a second.

As I pulled my lips away, I noticed her breathing was hard and erratic and she was having a hard time catching her breath. I gave her a couple of minutes, letting her calm down a bit before taking her hand in mine.

"Come with me," I said, sliding off the couch and helping her to stand.

Together we walked hand-in-hand down the hall toward the bedroom.

"Where are we going?" she asked innocently.

"You'll see. Just keep an open mind okay." I couldn't take it anymore. I wanted her naked, but at the same time, I didn't want to scare her away. I had spent half my teenage life thinking of her perfect pink lips wrapped around my cock as she looked up at me through that mane of messy, soft, thick brown beautiful hair. The more I thought of it, the more I could feel myself getting harder at the thought of her doing that to me.

I shut the bedroom door behind her. She stood there watching me as I wandered into the bathroom and turned on the shower. It didn't take long before the steam was rising over the shower door, the glass starting to fog up. I dropped my gear, glancing out the door to catch her watching me, and then I got into the shower, my heart speeding up at the thought that I might have taken things with her a little too far and that she may not join me. I knew she wanted me, I could see it in her eyes, but I was still worried.

I ran my hand over the length of my cock. If I couldn't get satisfaction out of burying myself inside her and listening to her moan, then I guess good old faithful would do.

I shut the shower door behind me, the steam now thick enough in the bathroom that I couldn't even see my own reflection in the mirror. I placed one hand on the wall to balance myself while the hot water ran over my body, and I slowly stroked my cock with the other. I was hard as a fucking rock, and it was such a shame to waste this, but it needed to be done.

I stroked myself another couple of times, relishing the sensation, but stopped when I thought I heard the bathroom door creak open. I gripped my cock, continuing to stroke it, when the shower door opened, letting in a rush of cool air, and a naked Mia stepped inside.

My heart nearly stopped as she shook her hair from the ponytail she had it in, her breasts on full display for me. Her eyes trailed down to the hand that was wrapped around my cock, a light flush on her cheeks as she bit her lip and shut the door behind her.

I let my eyes wash over her body, her perky breasts before me, her rosy pink buds calling to me, practically begging me to suck on them. I looked up and met her eyes. She looked a little unsure of herself, and for a second I was afraid she may just turn and run. She hid her eyes quickly and her cheeks turned a deeper shade of pink as her eyes wandered down my body, landing once again on my already hard cock.

"I don't even know what I am doing," she whispered, and once again, I was sure she was going to run if I didn't act fast.

I didn't give her words another thought. I reached out and wrapped my hands around her waist, pulling her against me and meeting her lips with a harsh, demanding kiss, my tongue exploring the inside of her mouth, while the hot water washed down overtop of us. I tore my lips from hers. "Just go with it. This week is about letting go, remember?"

I pushed her up against the wall of the shower and kissed her again, taking her hands and wrapping them around my waist. I ran my hands over her breasts gently, running the palms of my hands over her nipples. I cupped them in my hands, feeling the weight of them as they rested there. It was a matter of seconds before I rubbed the pads of my thumbs over her nipples again, and she sucked in air and let out a beautiful little moan that went straight to my cock.

I stifled her moan and kissed her lips again, while running my hands through her thick, soft hair. She placed her hands on my chest, stopping me. "What are we doing? What am I doing?" she mumbled between kisses.

She had always been a little uptight, I remembered that from years ago. "Shhh, just go with it," I whispered, taking her earlobe into my mouth. "Who would have thought I'd still want you after all this time? I've waited twelve years for you," I whispered, those words slipping out before I could stop them.

"Bryce?"

I kissed her hard and turned her around, pulling her back flush to my chest. I needed to distract her from what I had said. She wasn't supposed to know. I kissed her neck and ran my hand down between her legs, my fingers quickly sliding into her folds. She was already wet for me, and I groaned as my fingers slid over her, rubbing her clit in slow circles. She dropped her head back against my shoulder and sucked her lower lip between her teeth. "Feel good, baby?" I whispered in her ear.

She moaned her approval, so I kept going, my other

hand reaching up and taking her nipple and rolling it between my fingers. When I felt her start to shake, I stopped, pulling my hand from between her legs.

She let out a small whimper. "Don't stop."

"I'm not, but there is no way I'm letting you come that way," I said, spinning her around to face me. Pushing her up against the wall of the shower, I kneeled before her. Holding her in place, I raised one of her legs over my shoulder and buried my face between her legs, sucking and licking her clit, while I buried two fingers inside of her.

Within minutes, her fingers were entwined in my hair and she was trying to stifle every sexy moan that came from her mouth, while her body was pressed against the wall of the shower.

A few deep pumps, and I began to feel her tighten around my fingers, I sucked her clit into my mouth and ran my tongue over her. Her legs began to shake, but I didn't stop. I kept going until she exploded in my mouth, her screams getting louder and louder.

Chapter Ten

MIA

I could feel Bryce holding onto me as I stood against the shower door, my eyes closed, my body shaking from the orgasm he had just given me. I could feel his breath against my lips and opened my eyes.

"You let go," he whispered, his lips meeting mine.

His kiss was exactly how I imagined it would be, and as hard as it normally was for me to let go, for some reason, with him, it was easy. If I were being honest with myself, it had felt good to lose control and not think about anything for a few minutes.

"Come on, let's go." Bryce shut the water off and opened the shower door. He grabbed a large black towel and wrapped it around me, then secured one around his waist.

My legs were still shaking as I took a step forward, so

instead, Bryce picked up my sated body and carried me into his bedroom. The room was dark, and he lay me down gently on the bed, crawling in beside me.

"Your sheets are going to get all wet," I said, smiling up at him.

He bent down and met my lips. "Doesn't matter," he whispered, brushing strands of wet hair from my face. "Remember...letting go."

He tugged at my towel and unwrapped it from my body, his fingers grazing the soft skin of my tummy. "You are beautiful," he mumbled, placing little kisses along my collarbone.

I heard a loud grumble come from Bryce's stomach and began to laugh as he continued to trail kisses down my body. "Are you hungry?" I asked.

"A little," he said, placing another kiss on my lips. "Nothing you won't fix."

I traced his lips with my finger. "How about I go and get you something from the kitchen."

"No, it's okay." He kissed down my chest. He was just about to swirl his tongue around my nipple when his stomach gave another loud growl.

"No, let me grab you something," I insisted, sitting up and wrapping the towel around my body.

"Take my robe. I don't want you to get cold. It's hanging behind the bathroom door."

I grabbed the heavy terrycloth robe and wrapped it around me and made my way to the living room first to get the food we had left, and then I wandered to the kitchen. I quietly pulled out the plate of fresh fruit and searched the cupboards for another plate. My hands shook with every move. I couldn't believe what we had done. I was not a spontaneous person by any means, and I could feel panic setting in. I had dated Don for almost a year before falling into bed with him, and my relationships before that took two years. I had never just jumped into bed with someone before, let alone a friend. I couldn't figure out what made this different.

I took a deep breath, steadying my hand while I piled food onto the two plates I had just pulled out of the cupboard, when I heard a throat clearing behind me. I turned abruptly to find Bryce standing there leaning up against the doorframe in low-slung house pants, a sexy-ass smile plastered on his face as he watched me.

"I told you I was coming right back." I giggled and continued loading the plates.

"I was lonely," Bryce said, pushing off the wall and coming up behind me, wrapping his arms around my waist and kissing my neck.

I placed the two plates down onto the island and watched as he grabbed a strawberry from one. He bit into it, and then I felt him run the cold berry over my neck.

"What are you doing?"

"Having a snack," he whispered as his mouth met the trail of strawberry juice on my neck.

I couldn't help but close my eyes and just feel his lips trail over my skin. I could feel myself getting wet again and pulled out of his embrace. "You need to eat."

He pouted as I stepped away and pulled down two mugs from the cupboard. "Tea?" I asked, switching on the kettle.

"Please." He piled a few more meatballs and cheese onto his plate and sat on one of the stools that lined the island.

The roar of the kettle whistled behind me as I popped a strawberry into my mouth. I filled two mugs with hot water and placed one in front of Bryce.

"So, where do you practice?" I asked, munching on another strawberry. "You said you were still in Kings Cove."

"Yep. Once Hunter graduated, he and Carter opened up a small law firm. By the time I graduated, they had more on their plate than they could handle, so I joined them. Chase did as well, eventually. I am currently working towards making partner. We sort of each studied and specialized in different parts of law so that we could have our own fully functioning family law firm."

I walked around and sat down beside Bryce and ate a few more pieces of fruit, while he did the same.

"So you guys are still pretty close then."

"Very. Aside from working together every day, we have family dinners every week. A time to put work behind us and just spend quality time together. They also share this place with me. This was supposed to be Hunter and Autumn's vacation weeks, but they canceled. They are due to have their third baby any day now."

"That is great to hear. Congratulations to them. Actually, I never thought Hunter would ever get married. I remember Grant always idolizing him."

"Yeah, I remember. Hunter was always chasing tail."

"So were you," I muttered.

Bryce stopped, his hand halfway to his mouth. "What are you talking about? I never..."

"Please." I let out a laugh. "You were too. I used to..." I stopped before I let it all out. He couldn't know.

"You used to what?"

"Nothing, never mind."

"No, by all means, say it."

"I used to hear the rumors," I lied.

We both grew quiet. I couldn't believe I almost admitted that I was jealous of every girl he ever dated. There was no way I could let that slip, no way.

We both sat quietly munching away and sipping tea. Bryce glanced at me every now and again, meeting my eyes. "So, I don't have to worry about this voice mail heart-breaker showing up here and kicking my ass, do I?" he asked, studying my face.

"No." I laughed. "Seriously, we were never going to work out. I knew it, and he knew it. It just took us five years to figure it out, I guess."

"I see."

"What about you?"

"Did I know it wasn't going to work out between the two of you?" He chuckled.

I started to laugh. "No, do I have anything to worry about?"

He looked at me and smiled. "Why would you be worried?"

"Hey, if you give girls orgasms like that all the time, I just want to make sure she isn't going to come back and claim you." I could feel my cheeks heating. Claim was the wrong word. It sounded like I didn't want to lose him, when the truth was, I didn't have him, and I'd never had him. This was a week of letting go, nothing more, so I shook the thought from my head.

"She isn't coming back to claim me. She may think she could, but it's over for me. She gave up her right to me when she fell into bed with someone else and became a snarky bitch in the process."

The room got quiet as we both looked at one another.

"Have you had enough?" he asked, signaling to the plates of food that we had pretty much picked over.

"I'm good," I said, placing my hand on my full belly.

He busied himself cleaning up the dishes and condensing what was left over onto the same plates. As soon as the plates were covered and back in the fridge, Bryce looked at me, his blue eyes giving away his thoughts.

"What?"

"I want to show you something. Come with me." He held his hand out to me.

I placed my hand into his large, strong, warm hand and followed him out of the kitchen and down the hall. He stopped at the patio door and tied the robe I wore tight around me.

"Stay here for a minute. Just going to open the hot tub."

I watched him as he ran out, his arm and back muscles flexing as he opened the tub and then ran back to the door and took my hand. "I don't want you to fall again," he said as he carefully walked me over to the edge of the tub.

Without even thinking, I dropped the robe, exposing my naked body to him, and climbed in. He then ran back and shut the outside light off, so we were bathed in darkness with nothing but the stars twinkling above us.

"This is it isn't it? Now, after all we have been through, it's going to come to an end. You're going to drown me in the dark so that neighbors don't see." I giggled. "It's over."

Bryce let out a chuckle. "Not at all." He dropped his lounge pants and climbed into the tub, lying back in the reclining seat. "Come over here."

I moved from the seat I was sitting on and slid my body between his legs. He slipped his arm around me, and I leaned back against his chest.

"Just take a moment and look up."

I did as he asked, seeing thousands of twinkling stars lined the night sky. They looked like millions of diamonds on a black background.

"This is amazing," I whispered, seeing a shooting star travel across the sky.

"Yes, it is. Honestly, this is my favorite part about being up here, coming out here and looking at all this."

My body resting against his, he wrapped his arms around my waist and gently kissed my ear. I relaxed into his arms and studied the night sky with him.

"You see that?" he asked, pointing to a grouping of stars.

"Yes."

"That is the Gemini constellation, Castor and Pollux. And that one is Orion's Belt..."

"Where does this come from?" I asked, stopping him from what he was going to say next.

"What?"

"All this star talk?"

"As a kid I loved astronomy. I would sit with my telescope and study the sky for hours on end."

"Really? I don't remember you ever mentioning anything about that."

"My brothers used to make fun of me for it, and once I hit my teens, I realized how much of a geek I really was. Girls really didn't like that stuff anyways." He grew quiet, and I could tell he was a little uncomfortable sharing this stuff with me.

"You dated the wrong girls." Realizing what I had just said, I cleared my throat and waited for him to continue.

I could feel him looking at me, and I closed my eyes quickly, hoping that he'd just continue. "What is that one?" I asked, pointing in the direction, hoping to distract him.

I listened as he rattled off constellations and the stories behind them, reciting them as if he had written them himself. As I lay there, I couldn't help but feel things that I probably shouldn't be feeling. After a while, he went quiet and pulled me tighter into him.

I could feel something inside of me that I hadn't felt in a long time, if ever. As I closed my eyes and listened to the sound of his breathing, I thought about my future. I could actually see myself marrying this man. How someone could throw him away and he now be single was beyond me. Maybe the universe was trying to tell me something by stranding me in the airport and strategically placing him there as well, giving us a chance to meet again.

A little while later, I was standing on the deck, wrapped in Bryce's bathrobe, waiting for him to close the hot tub and go inside. It was late and we were both tired.

"All right, let's go," he whispered.

I took a step toward the house when he gripped my wrist from behind, stopping me from moving any farther. He pulled me tighter against him and we looked into one another's eyes. He said nothing; he just held my gaze. I was about to say something when he leaned down and took my mouth with his.

This kiss was different from the others we had shared today. It was slower, deeper, and contained a hint of emotion as opposed to the pure, lust-filled want the others had carried. My heart beat hard, as his lips meant mine, this kiss, his kiss taking my breath away.

Chapter Eleven

"Here's breakfast." Bryce placed a plate of waffles and fruit in front of me. Once we woke this morning, after an incredible night, we had just lounged in bed in one another's arms.

"This looks fantastic," I said, reaching for the syrup and pouring the sticky liquid over the fresh homemade waffles on my plate. Bryce sat down across from me and I handed him the syrup. He did the same.

"Okay, so, it has cleared up enough outside, and the roads are able to be traveled. How about we take a trip into town today? We can go to the market, visit some shops, have some lunch. What do you say?" he asked, digging his fork into the waffles.

"Sounds great. I just have an email to respond to before..."

Bryce looked up at me, his fork now halfway to his

mouth. "No, Mia. No responsibilities. Vacation remember? Letting go of everything." He reached across the table and picked up my cell phone, pocketing it. "This will stay here today in the bedroom, along with mine. You can have it back when we get back. I'm on a mission to teach you how to have fun and let go," he said, winking at me.

"I have fun!" I exclaimed, rolling my eyes and laughing.

"When? Sitting in your pajamas at midnight doing reports? That's not fun, Mia. That is work. Now, last night that was fun." He winked at me.

He had a point. Aside from the last couple of days, I couldn't remember the last time I'd had a day without some part of work in it.

"Don't you ever just go out and have fun with friends?" he asked.

Somehow, over the years, the girls I hung out with had stopped asking me to join them. They would call, I would tell them I was too busy, and before I knew it, they just stopped calling. Those calls never came in anymore, and to be honest, I couldn't remember the last time I had spoken to any of them. "Not anymore," I mumbled.

"Mia, life is way too short, babe. You got to have fun, so today, we are going to have fun! It will be like we're sixteen again."

I let out a laugh and dragged my fork around my plate while thinking of what he had said. Those fifteen years without a vacation went by in a blink. When Mom got sick, even though it felt as if time stood still, I think it went by even faster. Bryce was right.

"Okay, I won't argue. Let's eat and get ready."

We lounged around for the rest of the early morning,

cleaning the kitchen after the mess of breakfast, watching a little TV, our legs entwined together as we cuddled under a blanket and competed against one another while watching *The Price is Right*. After that, we had showers and got dressed. The taxi had just arrived when I emerged from the bedroom, and soon we were in the back of the cab driving through the downtown area. I looked out the window to see the area was bustling with people.

"Sir, if you could just drop us in front of Lake Champlain Chocolates, please," Bryce asked.

"Sure, thing, sir."

"What is that?" I asked, taking in his handsome, strong features.

"I guess you will have to wait and see, but I will give you a hint: they have the best hot chocolate in the world."

Before we new it, the cab had pulled up in front of this cute, cozy little shop, and we both got out of the car. My mouth began to water as soon as I stepped onto the sidewalk. I could already smell the chocolate.

I waited while Bryce paid the driver and looked around at the shops on the street. Bryce turned toward me and smiled.

"Can we go over to that store over there?" I asked, pointing to a cute little antique store across the street.

"Of course, anything you want, but first I am dying for some of this. Come on." He placed his hand at the small of my back and guided me through the door.

We stood in line, and I couldn't help but look at all the items in the display case. Everything looked so good.

"Okay, so you have to try those," Bryce said, pointing to

one of the desserts in the display case. "We will get those to go, for later tonight."

"What is that?"

"Heaven!" he stated, smiling at me, while pulling me close and kissing my cheek.

After we had been served, we chose a quiet corner in the back of the little shop, away from all the people. I took a sip of the hot, thick chocolate and let it sit in my mouth, my taste buds exploding. It was the perfect blend of bitter and sweet.

"Good isn't it?" Bryce asked.

I nodded my head and took another sip, once again savoring the mouthful. We sat across from one another, a plate of chocolates between us. Bryce picked up one of the chocolates and held it out in front of me. "Open up."

I opened my mouth and he slid the chocolate inside. I bit down, and a burst of orange mixed with the bitterness of dark chocolate rushed into my mouth, and I closed my eyes to savor the taste.

"Well?"

"It's like an orgasm in my mouth," I muttered, savoring the sweetness.

He chuckled at my response.

"Okay, your turn," I said as I picked one up and held it out for him to try. He took it from my fingers and bit down. I watched his expression light up as he swallowed.

"My God, Mia, amazing choice. A mix of peppermint and chocolate, my favorite.

We sat there, each of us going back and forth, taking turns feeding one another, trying the chocolates. I had just swallowed the last bite of my chocolate when an older woman sat down next to our table.

"All right, only two more. Which do you want?" Bryce asked, bringing me back to our table.

I hesitated, looking back over at her. I could see the woman was watching us, a slight smile on her lips. I did my best to ignore her and picked one of the chocolates, Bryce taking the other one. At the exact same time, we popped them into our mouths, our eyes lighting up at the taste, and we both broke out into laughter.

"Raspberry!" we both exclaimed at the exact same time, continuing to laugh.

"Excuse me," a soft voice broke into our laughter.

We both turned and looked at this older woman who sat alone in the corner opposite us.

"I couldn't help but watch the two of you. You remind me of me and my husband. We used to come here once a year and do the same thing."

I looked to Bryce and smiled.

"That is wonderful. Is your husband getting your chocolate selection?" Bryce asked. "He really needs to get you the raspberry one." We both laughed and she gave a thoughtful smile.

"No, I'm afraid he isn't. I am here alone. He passed away five years ago. I make the trip here once a year, only on our anniversary. It fills my heart with the memories we shared, but I fear this may be my last year. My health hasn't been very good." She smiled at me, tears in her eyes.

"I'm sorry to hear that."

The lady nodded and looked down at her cup. "How long have the two of you been married?" she asked.

"Oh no, we're not married. We're just old friends," I blurted out, looking over at Bryce.

"Could have fooled me. You two have a certain...something. I can see it. The way you look at one another, the way your body language speaks to one another, you are going to get married." We both looked at one another. "I can tell. You see, you look at one another like me and my Charlie looked at each other. Give it time."

I looked at Bryce and him at me, a soft smile coming to his lips.

"I'm sorry if I made you both uncomfortable. I didn't mean anything by it." She began gathering her things. "I must be going. Enjoy your afternoon."

We both sat in silence, looking at one another as we watched her stand up from the table and make her way to the front door, waving and calling out good-byes to some of the girls behind the counter.

"That was weird. What do you say we make our way over to the antique shop you wanted to check out?" Bryce said, clearing his throat.

"Yes, let's."

We spent the afternoon, holding hands, wandering around town, and going in and out of all kinds of little shops. I made a couple of small purchases at the local bookstore. We were just about to call for the cab when we passed by the grocery store.

"We should probably grab something for dinner tonight," I said, grabbing Bryce by the hand and pulling him into the store.

Chapter Twelve

BRYCE

When we arrived back at the house, Mia went to lie down after we put the groceries away, and I went to my office. I had been working away when I glanced at the clock on my desk. It was almost 6:00 p.m. I hadn't planned on working that long and hit send on one final email and shut my laptop down. While we had been out, Chase had called and needed a couple of documents I had stored on my computer so he could send them off to my clients. He had promised me he would take care of anything for me while he was at the office this weekend, so I could focus on relaxing.

I sat back in my office chair thinking about Mia, wondering if she was still sleeping. We had spent a wonderful afternoon together, and for some reason, after only a couple of hours apart, I was already aching to be back beside her.

I didn't want to bother her just yet, though. I wanted her to rest, so I figured that I could at least make us a good dinner before the movie we had agreed on watching tonight.

I wandered into the kitchen and pulled out the two sirloin steaks we had purchased in town and busied myself seasoning them to perfection. Then I began working on the accompanying side dishes: sautéed mushrooms and onions and garlic mashed potatoes. While everything was cooking, I set the table, pulled my favorite Cabernet Sauvignon from the wine rack, and grabbed the candles from the drawer.

As I set them on the table, I could hear my ex's words in the back of my mind from that night that felt like forever ago.

"You're a selfish bastard. You make us dinner just to break it to me that you must go to work. You always expect me to keep everything up, and the one time in the last few months that you cook dinner for us, you can't even take the time to sit down and eat it with me."

Those words still haunted me, but it was so far from the truth that I didn't even know why they bothered me as much as they did. Regardless, I never wanted another person to think that way of me again, especially Mia. I don't know why I was worried about that or even thinking that way. Whatever this was, it was in no way the same thing. Mia and I had only just gotten reacquainted, and to be honest, after this weekend was over, who even knew if I would ever see her again.

Once the table was set and the side dishes were well on their way to being cooked, I turned the oven on and put the steaks in. I had planned to barbecue, but since we had been back, more snow had started to fall.

It wasn't long before the timer had gone off and dinner was ready. I shut the oven off and yelled down the hall to Mia to let her know dinner was ready while I plated the food. I placed the plates in our respective spots and sat waiting before realizing I had forgotten music and quickly set my phone to play a romantic mix of music.

I kept thinking I heard her coming toward the kitchen, but after waiting for ten minutes, I realized she wasn't coming and perhaps she was still asleep.

I got up from my chair and wandered down the hall. The bedroom door was still shut tight, and wild thoughts passed threw my mind of ways I could slowly wake her up. I pressed my ear to the door and could hear her muted voice, sounding frustrated.

Frowning, I reached for the doorknob and opened the bedroom door to find her buried under a mountain of paperwork, her hair a frazzled mess, and she looked exhausted and stressed. Her cell phone was pressed to her ear and she wore a very frustrated look on her face.

"No, you are not looking at it right. Column B, Mark, check column B," she mumbled under her breath.

She was just about to say something else when she noticed me standing there, watching her shove her hair away from her face in a panic. She placed her hand over the mouthpiece and whispered, "Bryce it's not a good time. I need to get this done. I can't talk right now." She huffed and went back into her phone call, shoving more papers around on her desk and barking instructions into the phone.

Instead of leaving, I leaned up against the doorframe and continued to watch her. She was so stressed there was no way

I was leaving. There wasn't a job or career in the world that should get a person into a state like she was in right now.

She balled her fists and inhaled deeply, gritting her teeth at whoever or whatever was being said on the other end of the phone. Without another word, she hung up and threw her cell phone down on the desk. Gripping the back of the chair, she hung her head. There would be no more of this for her tonight. This vacation was not about this or whatever was going on back home at work for her.

I stepped into the room and placed both of my hands on her shoulders, gently massaging the tension she held there. I pressed my body against hers, inhaling the scent of her lotion, and closed my eyes while I continued to massage her shoulders. I wanted to bawl her out for not resting like she was supposed to have been. It looked like she had been working this entire time. Instead of saying what was on my mind I continued to massage her shoulders, until the tension in her body finally loosened.

"You know, I have this wonderful steak dinner ready in the kitchen for the two of us, a couple bottles of wine, and a rich chocolate cake from that bakery for dessert. I say you close everything down, shut off that cell phone, and come with me," I said, sucking her earlobe between my lips. "I promise to distract you from all of this."

I was more than prepared for an argument than I ever had been when she surprised me by doing exactly what I had suggested.

"You're right." That was all she murmured before she leaned back into me and took my hand in hers.

I reached and shut the light off and together we walked to the kitchen.

Two hours later, with full bellies, we were wrapped together in a blanket on the couch, with two empty wineglasses sitting on the table in front of us. We had shut the TV off long ago, and she lay beside me, wrapped in my arms, her leg over mine and her head on my chest while she traced tiny circles on my bare chest and watched the fire dance, the only sound in the room the crackle of the fire. I absolutely loved the feel of her fingers dancing over my skin.

"Feeling better?" I asked.

"Much. Thank you."

I kissed the top of her head and wrapped my arms around her tighter.

"Can I ask you a question?"

"Of course."

She went quiet, and I felt her swallow hard. She didn't lift her head to look at me. I just heard her tiny voice ask the question I had been praying she wouldn't ask.

"Earlier you said something about waiting for me. Why did you never..."

I closed my eyes. Those words had slipped out. She was never supposed to hear them. Me and my fucking alcohol.

"I mean, if you liked me, that is, then why did you never take a chance?"

I could feel the nerves creeping into my stomach as if I were still that sixteen-year-old boy standing in front of her, instead of the thirty-five-year-old man I now was. I let out a breath. "I wanted you from the first day I laid eyes on you. I remember it like it was yesterday. You came walking down the stairs in the hallway of your parents' house, you had on ripped jean shorts and a yellow tank top. You wore your hair up in this cute messy ponytail, pieces of hair falling in your face. Your brother introduced us, and I remember you walking into the kitchen and my eyes instantly flew to your ass, your shorts low enough that I could see the black thong you were wearing. I remember thinking how bad I wanted to sink my teeth into your ass in that moment. I went into your mom's bathroom five minutes later and snapped one off."

She let out a giggle. "No you did not."

"I did too. I couldn't contain it. My dick was harder than that coffee table. I think your brother new it, too, because before I left that night, he made it extremely clear to me that you were off-limits."

She grew quiet again. "So, basically, you didn't ever ask me out or anything because of him."

I scooted down on the couch, so we were eye level. I wanted to look into those beautiful brown eyes that had always so innocently stared up at me. As soon as our eyes met, I took her mouth, my hand resting on her cheek, and kissed her deep and slow. A wave of excitement ran through me as our tongues met. I gripped her ass and pulled her against me. She needed to feel me, feel what she was doing to me. As I pulled her close again, she let out a sexy groan that almost shook me to the core.

"Come with me."

"Where?" Mia asked, looking up at me as I stood up, bent down, and picked her up fireman style and headed toward the bedroom. "Bryce, put me down." She laughed all the way down the hall. I stepped into the bedroom and laid her on the bed.

"You stay there," I whispered, kissing her lips before I went and closed the bedroom door. I turned to see her sprawled across the mattress, looking sexy as hell. She was like a dream come true to me. My eyes swept over her body as I walked back to the bed and placed both of my hands on either side of her head and leaned down to meet her lips.

"Remember where we left off earlier?" I said quietly into her ear.

"Hmmm, yes."

I lay beside her, shutting off the bedside light so we were bathed in darkness. I pulled the covers over us and pulled her into me, kissing her. I felt her hand pull at the string on my house pants, loosening them enough so that she could slip her hand inside. She grabbed hold of my aching cock, and I felt her tiny hand start to jerk me, her thumb running through the bead of precum that sat so patiently waiting for her.

I closed my eyes and lay back against the pillow, and then I felt tiny kisses on my chest. I looked down and met her eyes as she continued trailing kisses down my abs. My hand ran through her hair as she continued her descent. She pulled on the waist of my pants, and I lifted just enough for her to pull them down, and then I felt her wet, warm mouth take my cock. She swirled her tongue around me and sucked with just enough pressure that I could already feel my keyed-up body threatening to explode.

"Baby, stop."

She pulled her mouth from me and looked up at me with lust-filled eyes. I reached over and ripped a condom from the drawer and laid back down on the bed. Within seconds, I had the condom on, and she sat there looking at me, a hint of mischief in her eyes.

I reached for her hands and pulled her over me. She straddled my lap as I lined my cock up with her entrance and she slid down onto it with ease. I could see the pleasure all over her face as I filled every inch of her. Her head fell back, and she bit her full bottom lip as she ground down on me.

"Bryce, I'm going to come."

It had only been a matter of seconds that her tight pussy had been wrapped around my cock, but I didn't wait. I reached down and started stroking her clit with my thumb, while I matched her rhythm.

"Stop, Bryce." She placed her hand on top of mine, trying to get me to stop rubbing her clit, but I kept going.

"No, Mia, come for me. Just let go," I bit out, fighting to hold back my own orgasm until she came.

She was so responsive, and for a little longer, I could tell she was trying to fight off her orgasm, but I could feel her tightening around me. I gripped her waist with my one hand while continuing to stroke her clit. She was soaked, and when she tightened around me this time, I was powerless to hold back and felt myself start to let go.

Her moans filled the room as the warm rush of heat escaped her. I pulsed inside of her, emptying myself, and she collapsed on top of me while those last few pulsing blows of my orgasm left my body. I held her in my arms, while we both caught our breath. I couldn't remember the last time that sex had felt like that for me.

My fingers stroked her back as she came down, and she finally eased off me and laid down on her side. I quickly got up and expelled the condom in the garbage and went and crawled back in beside her. Slipping my arm under her head, I pulled her body into mine and tugged the covers over us, and before I knew it, we both fell asleep.

<h1 style="text-align:center">Chapter Thirteen</h1>

MIA

I opened my eyes, the bright green numbers of the alarm clock staring at me. 10:45 a.m. I blinked hard and tried to remember what day it was. I sat up looking around the room, finding that Bryce was already up and gone. I grabbed my phone from the table. It was Monday. I had slept until almost 11:00 on a Monday morning, which was unheard of.

I slipped into my discarded clothing that was piled on the floor and left the room. The house was quiet, and I finally found Bryce in the kitchen. He had just poured himself a cup a coffee and grabbed another mug from the cupboard when I entered the kitchen.

"Good morning, sleepyhead," he said, bringing over the mug of hot coffee to me and kissing me on the cheek. "Sleep well?"

"Too well." I grinned.

"Great, that means you're starting to unwind. I'm going to help once again with that process. I'm taking you over to the spa. You have a mud wrap and massage in exactly one hour." He popped a piece of fruit into his mouth.

"That sounds amazing. What are you going to do while I am doing that?"

"No need to worry about me, but if you must know, I am going to enjoy the sauna while you are getting pampered. So, go get dressed," he said, handing me a bowl of fruit before leaving the kitchen." He slapped my ass as he walked by and winked at me.

I carried my mug, along with the fruit, with me down the hall, and just before I entered the room, I could already hear my cell phone ringing away. I set the mug and bowl on the table and grabbed my phone.

"It's 11:00! Where the hell are you? You were supposed to be here at 7:30."

"Who is this?"

"It's Mark, and it's Monday. Where are you?"

"I told you, I went on vacation."

"Mia stop joking around. This merger is everything, and you are supposed to be here now. I need you here," Mark barked into the phone.

Bryce walked into the bedroom and glanced at me, a worried expression on his face. He didn't say anything; he just walked over to the closet and began searching for some clothes.

"Listen, I told you already, I haven't had a vacation in fifteen years. I have thousands of vacation hours banked, not to mention all those unpaid overtime hours. You can't deny me."

As the words fell from my mouth, I noticed Bryce had stopped what he was doing and now sat down on the edge of the bed. I could feel him watching my every move and listening to every word I was saying.

"I do the work of probably five, if not six, people. My department shouldn't just be me, Mark. Remember what I told you before I left. I meant it."

I hung up the phone and threw it into my purse, my head pounding. I sat down on the edge of the bed beside Bryce and rested my head on his shoulder.

"Who was that?" Bryce asked, placing his arm around me.

"My boss." I rubbed my eyes. "He's in a tizzy because of the merger that is happening."

"He needs you to work?"

"Well, of course, but I have been doing this straight for fifteen years with no break, the work of probably six people. He didn't believe me when I said I was going on vacation."

"Wait a minute, you're serious? You really haven't had a vacation in fifteen years? You do realize that is against the law, right? You must have close to twenty-three, twenty-four hundred hours banked. That is like a year's salary."

I laid back onto the bed and stared up at the ceiling. "Yep, and I have a pay stub to prove it too, along with about three years of overtime that hasn't been paid to me."

"What? He hasn't been paying you for your overtime either?"

I shook my head and sat back up, running my fingers through my hair. "He said to bank them and that I could have time off when needed, only they have just sat there accumulating because I never get time off." I blew out a breath. Just when I had begun to relax, as always, that luxury had been ripped away from me.

"Sounds to me like you need a lawyer. It just so happens that I know someone who would be more than happy to take on that case."

"No, I don't need a lawyer," I barked.

"Mia, what he is doing is against the law."

"It's okay, Bryce. He will calm down once everything settles down there. He says I will get paid out everything and not to worry." I reached into my bag, pulling out a pair of clean underwear and a bra. I grabbed the clothes I had already decided to wear for the day and bundled everything in my arms. "I'm going to hop into the shower."

"All right, you have an hour," Bryce said, watching me with a worried expression on his face.

I walked over to the bathroom, stepped inside, and shut and locked the door behind me. I just needed a few minutes to myself.

Twenty minutes later, I emerged from the bathroom, my hair wrapped up in a towel, and I sat down on the bed. I was starting to feel better already, and I dug through my bag to find my hairdryer. I was almost back to the bathroom door when my phone rang. I hesitated to answer at first but decided to anyway. As soon as I had the phone to my ear, I could hear Mark's angry voice pouring over the phone. "I need things, Mia, please."

"Mark! I told you—"

"No! I need those reports in two hours or else you are fired!"

Instantly the fight-or-flight response kicked in, and all the stress I had lost over the last three days was now back and stronger than ever. I went to say something back to Mark, but he was already gone. I dropped the phone onto the bed and forgot what I had been doing. I went over to the small desk where everything had been left yesterday and sat down and began working, quickly forgetting all about Bryce and my day at the spa.

Half hour later, I heard a gentle knock at my door, followed by Bryce calling my name. I ignored him. My boss was pissed, and now I was on an even more serious deadline than before. I had struggled to hold onto this job, and I wasn't going to lose it now.

"Mia, we have to—" He stopped mid-sentence as he pushed the door open to find me still with a towel wrapped around my head. He stood in my doorway looking down at me. I didn't look at him. I couldn't. I hadn't even gotten dressed, still sitting in the bathrobe I had put on after my shower. Work, as always, won.

"Mia, we have to go," he repeated.

"I can't," I bit out, typing away on the keys of my laptop.

"Mia, I watched you last night nearly have a nervous breakdown over this job that has broken so many laws. Does your employer not care about your mental or physical health? Does he not know that this is actually a form of harassment?" he bit back, standing there with his hands on his hips. I could see the lawyer in him coming out.

"You don't understand, this is my job."

"No, I understand fully. I see an employer who is taking advantage of you and an employee who is so afraid of losing her job that she will do anything to prove to them she is worth keeping. Now you are going to put that laptop away after you write him and tell him you will get right on that paperwork when you return to the office at the end of your vacation and not a minute before."

"I can't!" I shouted, pushing the hair from my face.

"You can, it's simple."

"I will lose my job, Bryce."

"Mia, you are not going to lose your job."

"I will, he told me so. You aren't going to be the one to have to pick up the pieces, I am. So, I am sorry to disappoint you, but I can't continue on with this party."

I stood up and pushed him out the door, slamming it in his face. I sat down and put my head in my hands, sobs racking my body. I didn't need some guy I hadn't seen in years coming back into my life and telling me what was right or wrong. I let the crying continue for a couple of minutes before I sucked it up, wiped my eyes, and went back to my laptop.

I worked straight through the afternoon and most of the evening until everything was completed. I sent off the final email, my phone ringing as soon as I received the notification it had been delivered and read.

"Hello."

"Mia, I'm sorry, but I'm going to have to let you go," Mark's voice rang out over the phone.

"What? Why?" I asked, choking back tears.

"I wasn't kidding, Mia. You had a deadline. You missed it."

My heart sank. I had nothing to say, and even though I had just spent hours working away, pushing away the one person I so badly wanted to be with, it hadn't mattered. In the end, I still lost.

I didn't argue. I physically couldn't. I simply hung up

the phone and got up from my chair and looked around at the mess before me, papers scattered everywhere. I was so defeated, I flopped onto the bed. All of this had been for nothing. I had been fired anyway.

In that second, my life, up to this point, flashed before my eyes. My mom was gone, I hadn't seen my brother in seven years, I had never met my niece or nephew, I didn't have a significant other in my life, and I had lost every single friend I had ever had, and all for what?

I thought back to the last few days here. They had been the best days I'd had in a long time, and I had just pushed it all away too. I wiped at the tears that had started to form in my eyes. I needed another shower.

I turned the water on and climbed in, letting the heat soak into my aching muscles. I was frozen, and so I turned the hot water on, reducing the cold. As I sat on the floor, letting the hot water run over me, I heard Bryce's words in my mind. I felt awful for how I'd treated him. He had been nothing but kind, and I had treated him like shit. All he had really done was show me that he cared enough to try to help me, which had been more than anyone else had done for me in a long while.

When I was as warm as I was going to get, I shut the water off and dried off, quickly dressing and going in search of Bryce.

I poked my head out of the door and saw the light on in the front room, while the rest of the house was dark. At least I didn't have to look far, I thought as I made my way down to the doorway. The TV was off, soft music playing in the background, a single light on by the couch. Then I saw Bryce kick his foot up on the back of the couch. I wandered in and walked around to the face him. Bryce laid there reading a book.

"Hey." I sniffled.

"Leftovers are in the fridge, if you're hungry. Help your-self to whatever you want." He didn't look at me. He kept his face down in the pages of his book and said nothing more.

"Is everything okay?" I asked, sitting down on the edge of the couch beside him, resting my hand on his thigh, which he pulled away as soon as I touched him, as if I had burned him.

"No, not really, and I am not even going to try and pretend that it is."

A funny feeling crept into the pit of my stomach at the tone of his voice. I had been in this situation before. It was all too familiar to me. Don and I had these types of conversa-tions numerous times before, each of them ending in a fight.

"Bryce, why won't you look at me?"

He kept his face down in his book, not necessarily ignoring me but not acknowledging me either. I started to get a sick feeling in the pit of my stomach.

"I'm sorry. I felt that was important to take care of, but it really doesn't matter now."

He slammed his book shut and threw it on the table. "Yes, I noticed. You should have seen yourself, or maybe you should have seen yourself the night before, too, when you were on the verge of having a nervous breakdown. You barked at me to go, so I left." Bryce sat up and rested his arms on his knees. "You know, Mia, you once had a backbone and would never let anyone walk on you the way they are walking on you. Open your eyes."

"I have a backbone, and I do stand up for myself. You need to understand, what I do at times needs to be fully explained because if the other person doesn't understand then I have failed. And it's my job! Who is going to pick up my life if I don't have one? Who is going to provide for me if I can't provide for myself? For me to blow him off so I can go and spend the day with the guy I've shacked up with for some weekend fling is completely irresponsible and it's not going to happen."

I could see the hurt in his eyes immediately after the words fell from my mouth. I instantly wanted to take them all back.

He didn't say anything. Instead, he got up from the couch, picked his book up from the table, and was just about to leave the room when he stopped and turned to look at me. "One thing I have learned over my years as a lawyer, there are ways of getting your point across without losing control. You had no control. I really hope the hours you spent behind that computer today makes a difference for you."

"Why do you even care, Bryce? Why do you even care how I am being treated?"

"I care because I hate seeing people get taken advantage of and I hate wasting my time, which I can plainly see I have done nothing with you but that. I was trying to show you there is more to life than paper and offices and deadlines. I'll be spending the night in my office. Don't bother coming down there. I think it's best that we both be alone tonight."

I watched him make his way back around the couch and go to leave the room. I wanted to scream, "Stop, don't go," but I couldn't. Tears filled my eyes, and just as he was about to step around the corner, a sob escaped my throat.

"I got fired," I blurted out. We were standing here hurting one another for nothing. None of it mattered anymore.

Bryce stopped and slowly turned around, looking at me. "What did you just say?"

"I got fired. You know what though? It's okay. Everything you have said to me this weekend has been true. None of it has been worth it. It wasn't worth it for me to throw away every friend I had. It wasn't worth it to not see my brother or meet my niece and nephew, and it wasn't worth it for me not to take the time to mourn the loss of Mom when she passed away either."

I flopped down on the couch, tears pouring down my cheeks. It was only a matter of seconds before I felt Bryce's arms around me, holding me. He pulled me into his chest, and I rested my head on his shoulder, and he held me until the tears finally stopped pouring.

It had been two hours and I was still sitting beside him, leaning into his chest, his arms still wrapped around me, running his fingers through my hair. The fire was now nothing but a bunch of glowing embers, the TV was on, casting a glow over the room, the light having been shut off a while ago. My chest was tight, and every once in a while, when I would inhale, I could still feel the upset within me.

"You need to talk to my brother. We will get this all sorted out," he whispered in my ear.

I didn't answer, but I thought about what he was saying.

"For real, Mia. He will make sure you get your job back."

I sat there thinking about what he was saying. "What if I

told you I don't think I want it back." My voice was barely audible, even to me.

"Well, if you don't want it back, that is okay, but they still owe you a lot of money."

"What will I do though? It's all I have known."

"You will find another one, in time. There's no rush." He kissed my forehead, pulling me against him. "I think for now, though, we should get some sleep."

I nodded. Sleep sounded like a wonderful idea. The exhaustion from the last few hours was catching up to me.

He took my hand and pulled me up off the couch and we walked to the bedroom. I crawled into bed and pulled the covers over me. I just wanted to sleep everything away.

At first, I thought he had left the room, going to his office as he had said he would, but instead the light went off and I felt the opposite side of the bed sink. He pushed his arm under my head and wrapped his other arm around my waist, pulling me tightly against his chest and into the warmth and safety of his embrace.

Chapter Fourteen

When I woke the next morning, I found her face buried in my side, tears streaming down her cheeks. I had done the best I could to comfort her, but this was a battle she needed to take care of on her own.

We ate breakfast, and then Mia asked me if it was okay if she had some alone time. I understood completely and gave her some directions to a trail out back of the house, and off she went for a walk.

I knew this had been hard on her. We had decided on something easy for dinner tonight, so I took some time while she was out to surprise her with my mother's beef stew recipe. She and Grant used to love it when we were younger. I had also pulled out all the ingredients for us to bake chocolate chip cookies later.

After I got the stew slowly simmering on the stove, I

pulled out all the bowls and measuring cups from the cupboard for the cookies. I was expecting Mia to be back soon when something caught my eye out the back window. Mia was sitting down on top of the hot tub looking out toward the mountains. She looked lost in thought, and I was just about to go make my way out the back door when the phone rang.

I popped a handful of mixed nuts into my mouth and grabbed the phone, still watching Mia out the back window. "Hello."

"Bryce, how are things going?"

"Hey, Hunter. Doing much better, thanks," I said. I owed my brother a lot for sending me on this vacation. He had been right, as he normally always was.

"Good to hear. Are you doing okay with all the snow? We were getting a bit worried. We hadn't heard from you. Autumn forced me to check in with you."

I let out a laugh. "Good to know someone cares about me. Really there is no need to worry. Everything is just fine."

"Good to hear. You still planning on coming home this weekend? Autumn and Hope want to know if you will be here for family dinner."

"Yep, I'm coming home." I stood there debating telling him about Mia, my gut practically screaming at me to just go ahead and do it. "Listen, I ran into an old friend. Mia, Grant's sister. You remember her?"

Hunter chuckled into the phone. "Yeah, I remember. The looker who used to crush on you so bad it made my head spin."

I frowned. "She did not," I answered back.

"Yeah, whatever. The way she paraded around you?

Carter and I always laughed whenever you and Grant hung out. She was like static cling, man. In a good way, that is. Don't hate us, but we took bets on when you were finally going to wake up your cock and notice her. We seriously thought perhaps it didn't work properly." Hunter let out a loud laugh.

I didn't say anything as I looked out the back window at Mia. She was gorgeous sitting there, the sun bathing her in a orange hue. Thinking back to those days—something I had done a lot of this week—never had I thought she crushed on me.

"Listen, I went by your condo the other day. I stopped in to check on things. It looks like Alyssa is gone," Hunter said, pulling me away from my memories.

"Good to know. We'll be heading back tomorrow. Nice to know I can return to my home."

"We'll?" Hunter questioned.

"Yes, Mia and myself."

"She is there with you? As in you shacked up with her for the week?"

I cleared my throat, getting tired of his behavior. "No we didn't shack up, Hunter. She was stranded at the airport. I simply offered her a place to stay."

"Sure...I am sure you did. You probably parked your car in the garage too." He chuckled.

I guess I deserved his response, after all the years I picked on him.

"I have a favor to ask of you. Mia needs some legal help from you, if you are so inclined," I said, being as vague as I could be. It wasn't my place to tell him what this was about; it was hers.

"No problem. She can talk to me at family dinner?"

I frowned. "At family dinner? I wasn't planning on bringing her."

"Well, you are now. Autumn just added an extra seat. We will see you then."

I let out a breath. "Okay, we'll be there."

We said our good-bye, and then I hung up the phone. I grabbed another handful of nuts, turned the burner down on the stove, and headed out the back door.

"Hey." Mia turned to look at me, a smile lighting up her sad eyes. "Dinner is cooking. I also have everything out to make those chocolate chip cookies you have been talking about," I said as I walked around to face her, forcing her legs open so I could stand between them.

"Sounds good." She wrapped her arms around my neck and rested her head on my shoulder.

"I just got off the phone with my brother. He said he is willing to help you." She was quiet. "He also said you used to have a crush on me." She pulled away and looked me in the eyes, her face going red. "Did you used to have a crush on me?" I brushed a strand of stray hair away from her eyes.

She nodded her head, her cheeks on fire with embarrassment. "Maybe a little." She held her forefinger and thumb close together and let out a cute little giggle. "Well, until you broke my heart, that is," she said, getting serious.

"I have no idea what you are talking about," I said, playing dumb and putting my hand to my chest in an innocent gesture. I seriously didn't believe that she crushed on me that long anyway, and I certainly wasn't expecting the next words that fell from her mouth.

"Mary Maguire's party, do you remember that?"

My breath caught. She really had crushed on me. What I had seen in her eyes that night had been the truth.

"Yeah, you remember." She let out a laugh. "It's okay, though. I dropped my friend like a hot cake." She winked at me.

"Listen, I feel like I owe it to you to tell you this, even though it happened years ago. That night, I was really searching for you. Your friend only got me up there because she said you were waiting for me. It was a ploy, a trick played on me. Apparently, your friend had a crush on me as well." She looked at me with curiosity.

"When I saw you in the door that night and the hurt in your eyes, I tried to run after you, but the crowd of people kept getting in my way. Then I saw you with Grant, and well, you know how that would have turned out. I tried to come after you after Grant left, before I went to school as well, but you were either ignoring me or weren't home."

"It's okay, Bryce. I got over you. It took three months, but after that, I forgot about you."

"Geez, thanks. Way to make a guy feel special!"

"Okay, well maybe I didn't forget all about you."

"Let's get inside and get those cookies baked, and after that have some food," I said, wrapping my arms around her waist and throwing her over my shoulder in true caveman fashion. I loved listening to her laugh as I smacked her on the ass and carried her into the house.

Throughout the afternoon, we talked about the past. We had laughed and laughed, Mia telling me all the things she used to do to try and get my attention. It had probably been one of the best days we had had here together, and I was so thankful to have her back in my life. Even if all we would ever have together was this week, it was enough for me. It would have to be.

"Grab the eggs and crack two into that bowl."

I watched Mia carefully pick up and crack the eggs, carefully removing the few pieces of shell that had fallen in. She poured the eggs into the cookie batter and then grabbed the flour.

"You know they do say that the one you are supposed to be with is usually right under your nose the entire time, right?" I said, stirring the batter together as she continued to pour the flour into the bowl little by little.

"Let's hope not. I don't want to marry my boss." She laughed, missing the bowl completely and spilling flour on the counter.

"That makes two of us because I don't want to marry my secretary. She is almost old enough to be my grandmother."

Mia scrunched up her face, and we both laughed while she dumped in another cup of flour.

"Seriously, though, who is *they*? You always hear it, they say this, they say that, but no one ever knows who *they* are." Mia took a drink of her wine and giggled.

"Yeah, and I think you have had enough wine there," I said, reaching for her glass and trying to take it from her, but she pulled it away and took another sip.

"Is that all the ingredients?"

"I believe so." I placed my hands in the bowl to mix everything together. "Oh no, wait, the chocolate chips."

Mia grabbed the bag and dumped some into the bowl, laughing hysterically at my shocked expression. Soon the cookies were in the oven, the dishes in the dishwasher, and

Mia was sitting up on the counter, swinging her legs, drinking her wine, looking adorably cute.

"Tell me, the first night we were here, how did you really end up in the bed with me?"

I let out a chuckle and shook my head. "A man never tells."

"Oh no, Malone, spill it."

"You begged me." I smiled sexily at her. "You begged me to stay."

"I did not."

"Oh, I am sorry to say you did. I will admit it was rather sexy the way you pouted your lips." I winked.

She wasted no time hopping off the counter and approaching me, a soft smile on her lips. How I wanted to kiss her... I don't know what was stopping me.

I could see something in her eyes. She wanted to say something, do something. I was just about to take the plunge, but we were interrupted by the oven timer. Instead we both jumped and reached for the oven mitts at the same time.

"You open the door. I'll get the cookies," she announced, tipping to one side as she giggled, a hiccup surprising her.

"No, sweets, better let me." I grabbed the oven mitt from her hand.

We plated the cookies and carried them into the living room along with our wine. Soon we were sitting in front of the fire, the TV on, laptop in front of us, and we munched away on the cookies we had made while we searched together for a return flight home.

Chapter Fifteen

We sat on the plane watching the in-flight movie and sharing a pair of earbuds. I had taken the window seat. I was snuggled into Bryce's side, and even though he had loaned me one of his hoodies before we left, I was still cold.

"I hope you're not coming down with something," he whispered to me as he felt my cheek. "You feel warm to me."

"I'll be all right. I'm sure it's nothing serious." I pulled the hood up around my neck and rested my head on his shoulder. I really didn't want this to end. I didn't want to be without him or his warmth for even a second, but we hadn't spoken about what would happen after we returned home. Even though I was returning home to no job, I really wasn't all that upset. Overall, it had been the best week I'd had in a long time, and I had learned that work wasn't everything.

Two hours later, we had landed back in Kings Cove and

we made our way through the airport to the parking lot. We had both been quiet throughout the flight. I couldn't tell from the expression on his face if he was happy or sad that we were back.

We were approaching the first parking lot when Bryce stopped. "This is where I am parked," he gritted out. Maybe he did look a little sad.

"Oh, well, I guess this is it then," I said, looking down at the ground. A huge part of me didn't want him to go.

"You have my number, right?" I nodded. "All right, well, give me a call sometime, and make sure you get in touch with Hunter okay? He is expecting your call."

"I will." I swallowed hard. Why did this feel like the end to me?

Bryce didn't waste time. He dropped his one bag to the ground and pulled me against him for a hug. Then he grabbed his bag and started on his way to his car.

I watched him for a couple of minutes, he would turn around and come back, but he kept walking. When I could no longer see him, I turned the cart and pushed my luggage to where I had parked my car and made my way home.

The only thing on my mind was the same thing that had been on my mind since I had gotten home earlier today: Bryce. I had wanted to call him but was afraid that calling so soon would make me appear desperate. So instead of sitting and torturing myself, I did my laundry, made dinner, and by 10:30 p.m. I shut the TV off and made my way to my bedroom. I laid in the dark with the TV on, wrapped in my duvet, wishing it were his arms around me and not a stupid blanket. I was cold and had started to come down with a sore throat.

I stared at the green numbers on my alarm clock. It was almost 11:00. Mark had called and left a few messages apologizing and begging me to come back to work. I knew he was under a tremendous amount of pressure with the merger coming up, but he had fired me. I knew he was worried about his job and things didn't look good for the company nor for the company that was looking to acquire it. The meeting with the lawyers was set for the coming week, and I knew this made Mark extremely nervous. Before I called him back, I planned to have a conversation with Hunter as Bryce had suggested. I had already put a call in to him.

I thought long and hard while away about what direction I wanted to move in, especially after he had fired me. I was tired of being treated like garbage and tired of being taken advantage of by this company. Bryce had been right; it had just taken me this long to see it.

I let out a deep sigh, watching the little numbers turn on the clock, seconds feeling like minutes, minutes feeling like hours. It was going to be a long night. I wondered if Grant was working tonight. I hadn't spoken to him since before I had left for vacation.

I grabbed my cell phone and dialed my brother. I knew if he was busy it would go to voice mail, but I was happy that on the third ring a very sleepy voiced Grant answered.

"Hello."

"Grant, it's me. Did I wake you?"

"Mia?" His voice took on a questioning tone and he cleared his throat. "Is everything okay? I thought you were on vacation with what's his name. Give me a minute, will you?"

I heard the mumbled voice of June, his wife, in the background.

"No, it's not the hospital, baby, it's Mia. Go back to sleep," he said. "Yes, everything is fine with her. Go back to sleep."

I felt awful. I had probably woken up the whole house.

"Sorry, Mia. Is everything all right?" he asked, his voice taking on that worried tone again.

I couldn't blame him. I never called him this late at night, but I figured he would be at the hospital working.

"I'm so sorry, Grant. I didn't mean to wake you all up. I feel awful. How about I just call you in the morning?"

"No, Mia, it's fine. Everything is fine. I'm just coming off a very long fifteen-day stretch at the hospital. Are you back from vacation already?"

I figured I would be okay, but the second he had uttered those words, my throat got tight and I broke into tears. Everything that had happened over the past week had made me second guess everything in my life up to this point.

"It was awful. Don broke up with me, the snowstorm messed up all my plans." I went silent, wondering if I should tell him about Bryce. I sniffled, the build-up of pressure in my sinuses causing a bad headache.

"Oh, Mia, I am so sorry. Are you okay?"

That did it, I couldn't hold back anymore. The tears started to freely pour down my face. "I can't continue this pace in my everyday life. It's killing me. You were right, Grant, I'm a mess." I continued sobbing into the phone.

"Mia, I don't want to sound like an inconsiderate brother, but...do you want or need a referral to see someone? I have friends..."

He had friends all right. His so-called friend had put me into this state. I kept quiet because I knew that wasn't what he meant. He had begged me to seek help after Mom had passed and when I had told him I was having a tough time at work. He didn't persist. He just told me to let him know if I needed help.

"I'll be fine, Grant."

"It's not a problem, Mia. If you do need someone, let me know. It will only take me a second to process a referral."

"I know. I was calling because I wanted to let you know I got fired while I was away. I am seeking the help of a lawyer."

"Good. I told you, what this company is doing is illegal. Who are you going to talk to?"

"Hunter Malone."

"Ahh, the good old Malone boys! Great choice. What made you decide to go with him?"

I cleared my throat and looked up at the ceiling. "Bryce." I held my breath. I wasn't sure what my brother was going to say to that.

"I didn't know that you still spoke to Bryce. How is he?"

"He's good. I haven't kept in touch with him. I ran into him at the airport the night Don broke up with me. I spent the week at his lake house when the storm stranded us." I got quiet again, deciding if I should continue about everything that had happened. Grant must have sensed that.

"Is there anything else you wanted to talk about?"

I chewed my bottom lip, staring up at the ceiling. There were so many things I wanted to talk about: the kids, visiting him, and Bryce.

Grant didn't say anything. Instead he waited for me to continue.

I was quiet, the words almost burning my tongue at what I wanted to ask him. "If I told you that I had the best time of my life this week with Bryce, would you be okay with that?"

I heard him take a drink of something and swallow hard. "I would. Why wouldn't I be? I mean, I seriously can't think of anyone better to help you out and look after you than Bryce. We've kept in touch over the years. He is a good man. And you are right to get in touch with his brother. He's a damn good lawyer. I don't think any of them would ever steer you wrong."

"No, Grant, you are missing what I am asking?"

"What are you asking, Mia?"

"Well, it's just I had such a good time with him. I guess what I am asking is if you would be upset if I wanted to start seeing him?"

Grant was quiet. I could hear him breathing, so I knew he was still there. I didn't say anything else. I just waited for him to answer me.

"How much of a good time did you have while you were away?" he asked, chewing on something.

I let out a little giggle at his question. "I'm not sixteen, Grant, and what I did or didn't do with him is none of your concern. But your approval is important to me, that's all."

"I never said anything!" he exclaimed. "And I know you're not sixteen. Do whatever makes you happy, Mia. That's all I want to see."

I grew quiet. I missed my brother so much. "Grant?"
"Yeah?"
"If I wanted to come out and visit sometime in the next couple of months, would that be okay?"

"Mia, of course. We told you anytime. We would love nothing more than to have you here."

"Really?"

"Yes. Jeanna's birthday is coming up. She's going to be five. I know that both the kids would love to finally meet their aunt. If you can make it happen, how about you come out for that?"

I swallowed hard, fighting back the tears. "Okay, I think I can do that," I whispered, my throat getting tight.

"Sounds like a plan then. And honestly, if you had that great of a time with Bryce and something develops, I will be happy for you."

Grant and I talked for a little while longer. He shared with me what had been going on at the hospital and with the kids, and I shared a few highlights of my vacation with Bryce. Actually, I hadn't been able to keep his name from my tongue. I figured Grant would more that likely notice, and if he had, he never said anything. We finally got off the phone an hour later, and I could barely keep my eyes open and fell into a deep sleep.

Chapter Sixteen

I glanced down at my watch to see it was only 10:00 in the morning. I had been busy working away on the upcoming merger since I had gotten into the office this morning, but my stomach was already growling. I dialed Hunter's extension to see if he could get out for some lunch. Chase had already turned me down, saying he had a lunch date with his newest conquest.

"Hunter."

I could tell he was concentrating on something when he picked up; the tone of his voice told it all.

"Hey, you able to get out for lunch today. Thought maybe Willow's Landing might be a good place. I'm dying for the chicken salad."

"Wish I could. Autumn has a doctor's appointment this afternoon, and I promised her I would go with her. Plus, I have an appointment with Mia in the next forty minutes, and I already know she is going to have a ton of questions."

I perked up at Mia's name. I hadn't seen her since we parted ways at the airport. We had been in touch through text, but that was all.

"All right, man, I have to go. My next appointment is here anyways. Good luck with your doctor's appointment."

"Oh, before you go, Autumn just wants to confirm that you will both be there tomorrow night."

I rolled my eyes. I still hadn't asked Mia. I needed to get off my ass and talk to this girl and stop being a coward.

"Yes, of course, we will both be there," I answered him, clearing my throat. Once we hung up, I picked up my cell phone and quickly sent a text to Mia asking her to call me. My phone rang almost instantly, Mia's name flashing across my screen. "Hello," I answered.

"Hi, I am just on my way to see your brother. What's up?" her cheery voice came over the phone. I was glad to see she was in better spirits.

"Listen, how would you like to have lunch with me today?" I swallowed hard. Last week, I had been balls deep in this woman, and now suddenly I was nervous about asking her to lunch. This didn't make sense to me.

"Of course, I would love to. Where should we go?"

"How about I just meet you in the lobby after your meeting?"

"Sure thing. I guess I'll see you soon then." I could tell she was smiling. I could hear it in her words, and I couldn't wait to see her face.

I worked through the next fifty minutes with an extra spring in my step and couldn't help but keep glancing at the clock all through my appointment. I knew that I would be seeing my girl soon. Just knowing she was in the building was enough to have my heart beating wildly in my chest.

"Jon, I guess I will get all these documents drawn up and sent to you via email in the next couple of weeks. Sound good?" I said, walking my client to the door.

"Sounds great, Bryce." He reached out and shook my hand.

"If you have any questions, feel free to call or email me."

I turned and walked back to my desk, my phone vibrating across the wooden top. "Hello, Bryce," I said into the mouthpiece.

"I'm waiting. You said in the lobby, right?" I heard her soft, sexy voice ask, the sound of it going straight to my cock.

"I'm on my way."

I ran out of my office and to the elevator, Janice looking at me. "Bryce, slow down."

"Sorry, Janice, just on my way to meet a friend for lunch. I'll probably be a little late coming back, so please reschedule my one o'clock." At least, I hoped I would be late, I thought to myself as I stepped into the elevator and made my way down to my girl.

We took a seat at Willow's Landing, Mia sliding into the booth across from me. She wore this little black dress with knee-high boots and a bright-blue scarf around her neck that set off her eyes. The dress wrapped around her body, accentuating all the best parts of her.

"What did you want to eat?" I asked, studying her as she read the menu.

Those pretty eyes looked up from the menu, and she bit

her bottom lip—the same lip that not a week ago I had sucked on.

"Did you feel like sharing something? I haven't been very hungry lately."

"What did you have in mind?" I took a drink of my water and placed the glass back down on the table.

"I have a severe craving for nachos."

"You got it. Did you also want to split a chicken salad?" I asked, closing my menu and dropping it onto the table.

She nodded her head and smiled at me, setting her menu off to the side as well. Soon we had our salad and nachos and both of us dug in.

"So I have a question for you, and I hope it doesn't seem too forward. If it does, just tell me no, and we will move on." I was rambling and I knew it.

"Go for it. After all, how much more forward can we get? You have seen me naked." She laughed and popped a chip into her mouth.

"Would you like to be my date tomorrow night?" I asked, hoping to avoid telling her where we were going.

"Um, sure. What is it, a work function? What do I need to wear?" she asked, pulling out her phone. "Oh and time?"

"Ah, I will pick you up at say 5:00. Dress casual. Jeans and T-shirt are fine."

She looked at me and smiled, tilting her head. "Bryce, where are we going?"

"How did your meeting with Hunter go?"

"Oh no, no way. You aren't getting off that easy. Are you asking me out on a date? Where are we going?" she said, resting her hand on top of mine, and I was trying hard to ignore her question. "Bryce?"

"Okay, okay, it's just my family dinner. I made the mistake of telling Hunter when we were back at the lake house that I had run into you, and Autumn asked me if I would bring you. I told her yes without even thinking twice." I shrugged.

"I see." She wiped her hands on her napkin and looked down at them.

"If you don't want to go, it's okay. I will just make up something." I shrugged, taking a sip of my coke.

"It's not that, Bryce. I want to go. I'm just surprised it took you this long to ask me. That's all." She shrugged, picking up another chip.

"It's not because I didn't want to. I guess I was afraid of the answer I might get."

"Why? Did you think I would say no?"

I shrugged. I wasn't exactly sure what I thought she would say. "I guess I thought you might say no." I swallowed.

She looked at me, the light dancing in her eyes, and shook her head. "I don't think I could ever utter those words to you," she whispered.

Chapter Seventeen

I fiddled with my hair in the bathroom mirror. I never understood why it was that when you had somewhere important to go there was always one strand of hair that just wouldn't co-operate.

I took my round brush, trying to get it to curl the way I wanted it to, and finally giving up, I tucked it behind my ear. I checked my makeup, making sure that it looked perfect. I walked out of the bathroom and picked my favorite pair of jeans up off the bed, slid them on, and checked my ass out in the full-length mirror. Then I threw on a black top and gave myself a onceover, finally completing the outfit with my knee-high black boots. I gave myself another onceover in the mirror, letting out a breath to calm my nerves.

I was heading down the hall to the living room when I heard a knock on the door. I glanced at my watch: quarter to five. I grabbed my purse and keys from the table and my jacket and headed to the door, pulling it open to see Bryce standing on the porch.

He was dressed in blue jeans with a black sweater that hugged him in all the right places, his three-quarter length jacket hanging open. His eyes ran over me, taking in all my curves.

"Hey, gorgeous, you ready to go?" he asked, holding his hand out for me to take.

"Yep. Let me grab my jacket. Give me the rundown again of who will all be there."

He helped me with my coat, and we left the house, locking the door on the way out.

"All right, so, Carter and Hope and their kids, Kendall, Mackenzie, and Carl. Then there is Hunter and Autumn and their daughters, Kaylee and Paige. Then Chase. I don't know who he is dating today. Most of the time he shows up alone. Mom may be there. Hunter wasn't sure if she was coming or not. She normally plays bridge with her ladies club tonight."

I let out a breath and fiddled with the strap on my purse as Bryce drove us over to Carter's place. I kept seeing Bryce watching me out of the corner of my eye. Finally, he reached over and placed his hand on top of mine to stop me.

"Are you nervous?" He chuckled.

"Maybe." I shrugged. "It's been a long time since I have seen everyone."

"It will be good for you. And you have already seen Hunter, so it's like you have been reacquainted with two of us."

The car ride wasn't nearly as long as I had hoped for

when Bryce pulled into the driveway of a two-story home. The gardens were perfectly landscaped, not a thing out of place. He shut the engine off.

"You ready?"

I searched around frantically in the front seat, looking over my shoulder into the back seat.

"Mia, what are you looking for?"

"We can't go in. The cookies I baked for dessert aren't here. I must have left them on the counter at home."

"It's fine. Hope would kill you if you brought anything, and so would Autumn. I brought wine. You can give it to them. Sound good?" he said, rubbing the back of my hand, trying to calm me down.

I nodded. I had just shut the car door when the front door opened and four girls came bounding down the front steps screaming, "Uncle Bryce!" They all shouted, running around and crashing into him. He took a second and gave each one of them a huge hug. They were all talking, telling him something different or wanting him to look at this or that, and he acknowledged them all, never missing a beat.

I didn't know how he kept up. Then, just like that, they were gone, running back to the house screaming for their parents.

"Sorry about that. They get a little crazy." Bryce laughed, coming around to my side of the car. He held out the bottles of wine he had picked up and gave them to me. "Ready."

I let out the breath I was holding once again, and we walked up to the front of the house. I could already hear everyone inside, talking and laughing. The kids were screaming. It was overwhelming, considering I didn't come from a large family to start with.

"We're here," Bryce announced, stepping inside and removing his shoes, and I followed, slipping my boots off and tucking them neatly into the corner.

"'Bout fucking time, you shithead," Chase said, getting up from his seat and smacking Bryce on the back.

"Chase, your language," a very pretty and very pregnant brunette scolded.

"Sorry, Autumn. I forgot about little ears." He chuckled and went back to take his seat.

"I'm Autumn," she said, coming right over to me. "Hope is in the kitchen. You must be Mia." She wrapped her arms around me and hugged me. "It's so nice to meet you."

"We brought some wine," I said, handing her the two bottles.

"Oh, what I wouldn't give for a drink right now," she whispered more to me than anyone else. "After the baby comes, look out." She laughed.

"I heard that." Hunter laughed, coming in behind Autumn and resting his hands on her sides. "Good to see you again, Mia," he said, placing a kiss on his wife's neck. "Soon enough, baby, soon enough, you'll get to have a drink. At least, I hope anyways. I have been cut off until this little one arrives." Hunter winked at me and continued into the dining room.

Autumn rolled her eyes at me. "He sneaks into the office every night and has a glass of scotch. He thinks I don't know, but I do."

I couldn't help but let out a laugh. Autumn took the bottles and disappeared into the kitchen. Bryce placed his hands on my hips and guided me into the dining room. He went around to what must have been his usual seat and pulled the chair that was beside his out and waited for me to take a seat.

"How is that brother of yours?" Chase asked once we were both seated.

"He's good. He's married to a woman named June. They met in medical school, and they have two kids: a boy, Thomas, and a girl, Jennifer," I answered.

"Do you see them much? He moved out west, didn't he?"

"Yes, Sacramento. He works at the Shriners Hospital for Children." To be honest, I hadn't a clue what my brother really did at the hospital. All I knew was that his hours were long, and he was normally always busy.

"Ah, you must be Mia."

I turned my head to see a beautiful blonde woman coming toward me carrying a dish of something that smelled yummy. She placed the dish on the table, and then came around and hugged me.

"I'm Hope, Carter's wife. Welcome to our home. We are thrilled to have you join us tonight."

I hugged her back, swallowing hard. "Thank you so much for inviting me."

"Well, when Autumn heard the excitement in Bryce's voice when he spoke of you, we knew we had to."

I glanced over to Bryce, the hint of pink in his cheeks telling me that was the truth. He had been talking about me. A warm feeling settled in the pit of my stomach.

"All right, sis. That's enough. Let's get on with dinner," Bryce said, clearing his throat.

I sat back down. This was almost too much for me. I looked to Bryce for help, and when his eyes met mine, he winked and mouthed, "You're doing great," and placed his hand on my thigh, giving it a squeeze of reassurance. Then he joined in the conversations with his brothers as if that hadn't even happened.

I was quiet throughout dinner. Everyone was talking amongst themselves. Hunter and Carter tended to the girls and helped them all with their dinner so that Hope and Autumn could eat in peace. It was so nice to see families working together; it was something I had never had. This brought me back to when Grant and I were kids and would join the Malones for family dinner. We were always made to feel welcome and as if we were part of their family.

Hope and Autumn busied themselves cleaning up the table after everyone had eaten. I went to help by grabbing two of the dinner plates, but Hope stopped me.

"No way, Mia. First meal here. You are our guest, and I won't have you help with anything, so you sit down. Next time will be different," she said, smiling and reaching for the plates I had piled together.

Chase had excused himself to take a phone call, and Hunter and Carter were busy with the other kids for a second. I leaned into Bryce's shoulder.

"You okay?" he whispered.

I looked at him and saw the happiness dancing in his eyes. I nodded. He placed his arm around the back of my chair and kissed me on the cheek when he was sure no one was looking.

Soon we were all seated back at the table, a slice of chocolate cake sitting in front of each of us and a steaming hot cup of coffee to go with it. The kids were off playing in the living room. Next thing I knew, Kendall and Kaylee were standing beside Bryce, holding a picture from one of their coloring books in their little hands.

"What do you want, girls?" Autumn asked, taking a sip of her herbal tea.

They held the picture above Bryce's head—a picture of cupid. "It's almost Valentine's Day. Cupid came to visit. You have to kiss the girl next to you," they sang as Bryce looked above his head.

He wrapped his arms around the girls and kissed them on their cheeks. "Noooooo..." they squealed. "You have to kiss her," they sang, pointing to me.

I could feel my cheeks getting warm as Bryce looked to me. "What will happen if I don't?" he asked.

"No more kissing ever," Kaylee sang out.

"It's true," Autumn said, winking at the girls.

Bryce looked over at me. "You heard them. Can't have that happen." He winked and leaned in and kissed me on the cheek. I could feel everyone looking at us, the heat in my cheeks making me feel as if I were on fire.

"Nooooooo!" the girls shouted. "Like Mommy and Daddy!" Kaylee shouted.

Hunter let out a laugh. "Yeah, Bryce, that was pretty weak. Don't force me to show you up." He laughed, winking at me.

Bryce turned back to me and placed his hand on my cheek, pulling me into him. His lips met mine, and I felt his tongue sweep through my mouth. The kiss was interrupted by a bunch of cheering little girls. Bryce slowly pulled away from me. I could tell he wanted more just from the look in his eyes. I wanted more, too, the throbbing at my center letting me know that loud and clear. The girls quickly moved on to Chase holding the picture above his head.

"All right, girls, that's enough now. Go and play," Hope said to the pair of them.

Their little faces turned into pouts as they wandered into what must have been the living room.

"Thank God, you saved me," Chase said, wiping his brow. "I have no one to kiss. I can't lose that for the rest of my life."

We all laughed.

"You have more practice than the three of us combined." Hunter chuckled.

"You're lucky they left because it would have been your wife I kissed," Chase said, winking at Autumn and laughing. "She'd have left your sorry ass in a heartbeat once I got hold of her."

The table erupted into laughter.

The evening continued, and before I knew it, Bryce had looked down at his watch. I glanced over to see it was almost 10 p.m. The girls had finally settled down—Hunter had put a movie on for them in the other room—and we were just sitting around talking. It was as if I had always been a part of this family.

"What do you say we get going?" Bryce said, leaning in to me.

I nodded. I didn't want the night to end, but at the same time, I knew everyone was tired. Chase had left two hours earlier after he had gotten a call from what Bryce was sure was his next lay and had so expressed that to the dinner table.

"Guys, I think we are going to head out," Bryce announced, standing up and pulling my chair out for me.

Hunter and Carter looked to their brother, knowing smiles on their faces. "We know what that means," Hunter said. "Going to get yourself a little action."

Autumn reached over and smacked him on the shoulder. "Enough," she gritted out, smiling at him.

"What? What did I say?" he asked, playing innocent.

"Let's go before my brother has us doing the nasty on the dining room table here," Bryce said, placing his hand on the small of my back and guiding me to the door.

We said our good-byes, and I thanked Hope and Carter for having me at dinner tonight. We walked to the car, Bryce coming around my side to open the door for me. His hand on the handle, I turned into him and met his lips. He slowly let go of the car door, pinning me up against the car and wrapping his arms around me to grip my ass and pull me closer. We must have stood there for five minutes, Bryce kissing down my neck, before he finally whispered in my ear, "Your place or mine?"

Chapter Eighteen

MIA

We decided to go to Bryce's place. After all, it was closer. We stepped into the elevator, and as soon as the doors had closed, he pushed me up against the wall, undoing two of the buttons on my shirt, kissing the tops of my breasts as they spilled out of my bra. I let out a moan as his lips danced over them and up to my neck.

The ding of the elevator stopped us. He pulled me out of the elevator, and we quickly walked down the hall to his condo door. Pushing me up against the wall while fishing in his pocket for his keys, he continued to kiss me, sucking my bottom lip into his mouth.

Finally, he pulled his keys out and fiddled around, trying to get the key in the lock.

"You never had this problem before," I moaned.

"What problem?" he asked, kissing my neck.

"Getting it in," I whispered into his ear.

"Believe me, in a few minutes I won't."

I heard the key slide into the lock, and he opened the door, pulling me inside and locking it behind us. I could feel the tension building in me at the thought of feeling him inside of me again, this time without the influence of alcohol. We kicked our shoes off and dropped our jackets in a pile at our feet.

He pushed me up against the wall and took my mouth, running his tongue across mine, his hands coasting over my body. I felt him grip the bottom of my shirt and his fingers danced over my skin, sending shivers through my body as he lifted my shirt over my head and let it drop at our feet.

He ran his thumbs over my bra, my nipples getting instantly hard at his touch that sent a hard pulse right to my center. I closed my eyes, allowing my other senses to feel his touch. I watched as he pulled his sweater up over his head, exposing his chest to me, and I ran my hands over his abs. Once he dropped his shirt to the floor, he grabbed me and pulled me against him.

He hoisted me up and wrapped my legs around his waist as he carried me down a hallway while he continued to consume my mouth. Next thing I knew, he had dropped me down onto his bed and stood over me, looking down on me. His lust-filled eyes swept over my body, his hand reaching down and flicking the front clasp of my bra open. He bent down and licked my left nipple, taking it between his teeth and gently biting it. I arched my back up off the bed, begging for him to do it again as he stood back up and once again looked down on me.

He reached down and gripped his cock through his

jeans, and then quickly flicked the button open on his pants and let them drop to the floor, the buckle of his belt making a loud noise.

He stood over me, one hand on his thick, raging cock. I couldn't help but keep my eyes focused on his raging erection, thinking about what it would be like to take him in my hands, in my mouth, in my—

Before I could do anything, both of his hands were on my hips, his fingers tracing along the waist of my jeans, teasing me. He undid the button of my jeans and reached underneath me, and with one swift rough pull, he ripped them off me, along with my panties. He looked down at me longingly and placed one hand on each side of my head, bracing himself as he leaned over and teased my lips, first with his lips and then with his tongue.

Every part of this kiss was different—the way it felt, the way it made me feel, and the way it made my body hum. I couldn't recall ever being kissed like that before, and I felt a surge of wetness and hot, heavy throbbing at my center.

He grabbed my legs, bending them, so I was open to him. He held himself with one arm still bent over me, while his other hand found my center, and his fingers danced over my clit, stroking me with just the right amount of pressure.

"I'm a very selfless lover, Mia, and I will always make sure you are fully satisfied before you ever even think of touching me or pleasuring me," he said, almost moaning.

His eyes were hooded now, desire running through them. He dropped to his knees and pulled me closer to the edge of the bed and buried his face between my legs. I sat up on my elbows to watch him, but as soon as his tongue connected with me, my head dropped back, and I gripped handfuls of the blanket that was beneath me. I tried hard to stifle the moans he was causing, but I failed, and I began to scream his name out with every flick of his tongue against my clit.

With every stroke of his cock he took me higher and higher. As I moaned out my pleasure, he continued running his thumb rhythmically over my swollen and sensitive clit, gently coaxing my third orgasm of the night from my tired body. He kept going, burying himself deeper and deeper inside of me, my screams getting louder and louder, until he collapsed on top of me, emptying himself into the condom. Breathing hard, he rolled off me and collapsed onto the sheets beside me.

I felt the bed move and felt the absence of Bryce. I didn't have the strength to move. I could barely open my eyes and look around the room. We had spent the night in and out of sleep, and every once in a while, I would feel him wrap his arm around my waist and grind his hard cock into me, which would begin another bout of sex, this last one lasting almost forty minutes. The sun was just beginning to come up, casting a soft glow throughout the bedroom. I could see the blankets and sheets were somewhere on the floor and I giggled to myself. I hadn't been with a man like him before. Most of them were passed out after the first five minutes, never to wake until the sun was long up, leaving me to take care of myself.

"What's so funny?" Bryce asked, returning to the bed and picking up the extra pillows and blankets from the floor.

"It looks like we threw a party in here," I murmured, looking around at the mess of blankets on the floor.

"Don't worry about it," Bryce said, adjusting his pillows and placing his arm behind his head, his other hand resting on his delicious eight-pack as he lay back. I snuggled into his side, trying to fight off sleep.

"You certainly weren't kidding," I whispered.

"About?"

"About you not being a selfish lover."

He chuckled, and I felt the bed move and the heat of his body getting closer as he rolled onto his side. He lay there looking into my eyes, then pressed his lips to mine. I felt his fingers begin to trace little circles on the top of my leg, getting closer and closer to my center. They finally made their way, and I felt two of his fingers run through my wetness.

"Bryce, stop."

"Come on, one more time for good measure before I have to leave for the office." He leaned down and took my nipple into his mouth, causing me to let out a moan and my legs to relax enough that he could run his fingers through my wetness.

He kissed his way down my soft belly and crawled between my legs again, his hands forcing them apart. I studied the way he took me in. With his hands forcing me open, his mouth met my center, his tongue working my very sensitive clit, slowly and gently sucking and licking. I could already feel my orgasm starting to build. He slid two fingers gently inside of me, and I let out a loud moan as his tongue continued to lick repeatedly over my swollen clit.

My cell phone started ringing, and I placed my hands on his head, signaling for him to stop as I went to reach for it.

"No, Mia, don't you even think about answering that," he growled and buried his face back between my legs.

The ringing stopped for only a second and started again. I looked over to the nightstand and reached for the phone.

"If you answer that, I won't stop. I will make you come into that phone receiver screaming my name. I doubt whoever is on the other end of the line will want to hear that, unless it's your ex. Which maybe in that case you should answer it. He should know what you really sound like when you truly come."

I started to laugh, my head falling back onto the pillow as he continued torturing me, my legs trembling. I dropped my phone on the floor, quickly forgetting about it as I felt my orgasm building. As he coaxed the last bit of my orgasm out of me, he rolled onto his back and I collapsed against the mattress.

"Fuck, Mia, you are so fucking hot when you come. I can't get enough of you."

I looked over at him as he ran his fingers through his messy hair. I could see his hard cock once again straining under the sheets. I sat up and ripped the sheet off him, my eyes landing on his cock. I ran my tongue over his hard abs, alternating between little licks and kisses.

"Mia, what are you doing?"

I said nothing and continued making my way down, finally taking his cock in my hand, running my hand over his shaft. I couldn't help it, I loved watching his face, the way he sucked his bottom lip between his teeth, the sound of his breath as he inhaled when I ran my tongue over the head of his cock.

"Put your mouth on me." He moaned as I continued stroking him.

I did as he asked and took his whole cock in my mouth, running my lips and tongue over him. I could taste the saltiness of his precum as I took his cock in my mouth. I felt his hand run through my hair and I opened my eyes, looking up at him. He was watching me, studying my face while I had his cock in my mouth. I felt him start to pulse and kept my eyes locked with his, and before I knew it, I felt him pour his cum into my mouth.

Bryce walked into the kitchen dressed in suit pants and a white button-down shirt, his tie hanging loosely around his neck, and his suit jacket flung over his arm. I greeted him with a smile as he lay the jacket down on the back of the chair.

"All ready?" I asked.

"I wish I didn't have to go in this morning. We could have spent the morning in bed." He came up behind me and buried his face into my neck. I let out a little giggle as his breath tickled my neck.

"I don't think I could handle much more," I answered shyly.

"Want to bet? What do you have planned for today?" he

asked, taking the coffee from me while I went back to cooking us some eggs.

"Head home, shower. Look for a job."

"You can always shower here if you like."

"It's okay. I need to get some clean clothes anyways."

I placed the plates down in front of us and sat down beside Bryce. He took my hand in his and rubbed the back of it with his thumb.

"Listen, how about after I'm done working, I come home, get changed, and we go out for a romantic dinner, just the two of us."

"Sounds great. What did you have in mind?"

"It's a surprise."

"A surprise? How will I know what to wear?"

"All right, I will give you a hint: dress to kill." He winked at me, took a sip of coffee, and dug into his breakfast.

Chapter Nineteen

Bryce

I strode up the walkway to Mia's house. It was a cute little bungalow with great curb appeal and beautiful gardens. I held a dozen red roses in my hand and rang the bell. Seconds later, Mia appeared. She looked stunning, the black cocktail dress she wore hugging every curve, and the black heals she wore accentuating her legs perfectly. As my eyes danced over her, I couldn't help but hope for a repeat of last night. I held out the roses for her and she smiled as she took them from me and buried her nose into them.

"These are beautiful."

"They're okay. You're the beautiful one."

She smiled, holding the door open for me. "Let me put these into some water before we go."

I couldn't help but watch as she walked away from me, those curvy hips swaying.

"So where are we going?" she asked from the kitchen.

"The Cellar. We have reservations at 7:00."

"Sounds great," she said, walking back into the living room.

"Did you happen to pack an overnight bag?" I asked casually.

She blushed at my question and slightly nodded her head. "Is that okay?" she asked, crinkling her nose.

I pulled her into me, kissing her on the cheek. "Baby, it's more than okay." I grinned. "We should get going."

We were seated exactly at the table I had requested, the view overlooking the falls of Kings Cove the best in the entire restaurant. We had placed our orders and were waiting on our appetizer. Mia sipped her wine as she looked out over the water, a soft smile coming to her lips.

"It's beautiful here," she whispered to me.

"That it is." I studied her expression. She was gorgeous, and I was so lucky to have run into her again. I felt alive again. That part of me that had died when Alyssa and I split was now back.

A part of me was a little afraid to share how I really felt, but at the same time, I needed to. I had only spent a week and an amazing evening and night with this woman, but I couldn't deny how I felt. I wanted her with me, I wanted to come home to her, share things with her.

We made our way through dinner, talking and laughing. I shared my frustrations over the case I was working on, something I had never done with Alyssa. Somehow, I felt I could trust Mia, and she wouldn't judge me. She listened attentively, never offering her opinion, something my previous relationship lacked. She shared with me her challenges of trying to find a new job. She also shared with me what she and Hunter had spoken about. They had a damn good plan, and I couldn't wait to hear how it all went over.

"So, when is your big meeting?" I asked, as she brought the forkful of cheesecake to her lips.

"Tomorrow."

"Are you doubting yourself?"

"No, I just hope that we do the best we can for this client. That is all I ever want." I sipped on my espresso. "What about you?"

"Tomorrow as well. I'm meeting Hunter in the morning at the coffee shop around the corner from work."

"Okay, so I say that after the day we have a long, stress-free night. We can kick back, watch movies, and make some meatballs." I chuckled. "I'm actually dying to have those again, by the way."

"It's a plan." Mia ate the last forkful of her cheesecake and smiled at me. "Your place or mine?"

"Either, doesn't matter to me."

"All right, tomorrow night, it's my place then."

I put the key in the lock and held the door for Mia, letting her enter first. "I'm just going to put this in the bedroom." She held up her bag and toed off her heals.

"Did you want to get changed?"

She bit her bottom lip as she nodded, fighting back a smile, and wandered down the hall, closing the bedroom door behind her. I went into the kitchen and put on the kettle.

"Tea or coffee?" I called out.

"Coffee would be great," I heard her call out.

I had just set the coffees on the coffee table and stood up when Mia appeared, wearing my favorite little white boy shorts and a tank top. My total sex kitten had changed back into the girl next door, and she looked good enough to eat.

I turned the TV on and turned on the fireplace. "Have a seat. I'm just going to go and change quick." I couldn't help checking her out as she walked past me and took a seat on the couch.

I quickly ran down to the bedroom, changing as fast as I could, and stopped into my home office on the way back out. I grabbed the small box off the shelf and walked back into the living room.

"Happy Valentine's Day." I sat down on the couch beside her and held out a small white box wrapped with a red ribbon.

She looked at me hesitantly, then between me and the box that sat in my hand. "What is that?"

"A little something, nothing big." I met her eyes. "Open it." I held it in front of her, shaking it.

She reached out and took the box from my hand, the tips of her fingers brushing mine.

"You didn't need to do this. I mean the flowers, dinner, they were wonderful."

I smiled and nodded. "I know. Just open it."

She pulled at the ribbon, allowing it to drop into her lap, looked at me, and pulled the lid off the box. I felt the anxiety building in my chest at what lay inside. It had no monetary value, something I had never dared give to Alyssa, but Mia was different. I feared, however, that her answer would crush my heart in an instant. She pulled out the folded piece of paper and opened it, reading the words that I had scrawled on it. Her hand went to her mouth, tears filled her eyes, and she looked up at me.

"I love you too," she whispered, climbing into my lap and wrapping her body around mine.

I kissed her slow and deep, lying down beneath her on the couch and tucked her between me and the back of the couch. I ran my fingers through her hair while looking into her eyes, every now and then kissing her gently, my heart full at her answer.

Chapter Twenty

BRYCE

Eight in the morning, and I sat at the boardroom table across from Chase. The view was a far cry from what I had left at home in my bed this morning. I hadn't wanted to leave her as I glanced at her sprawled across my bed sound asleep. Her long, dark hair sprawled across her back, her sexy long leg peeking out of the blanket right up to her thigh, the soft moan that had escaped her lips as I kissed her good-bye. I had wrapped her in blankets and quietly snuck out of the condo with just enough time to spare to grab a coffee.

We had been sitting there for twenty minutes, our client sitting beside me glancing impatiently at his watch as we waited. The receptionist who had brought us to the room finally appeared, carrying a tray of hot coffee and a plate of muffins for everyone.

"I'm sorry for the delay. Mr. Bentley is just waiting on a phone call and he should be right in."

Chase nodded and met my eyes. "I told you something isn't right here."

Mr. Ward, our client, whispered to us both, "Bastard is hiding something."

I took a mug of coffee and a muffin. Even though I felt like a million bucks after spending the last two nights with Mia, I was tired, and I was running low on patience this morning. I wanted to get this meeting over with so that I could get home and spend the evening with her.

"It's okay. We agree with you. Just let us look over the rest of what is presented. There is nothing to worry about. We won't advise you to enter into an agreement if something is amiss," Chase answered, taking a muffin and coffee as well.

I glanced at my watch. We had been sitting there for almost thirty minutes when finally, Dollanger and his side-kick Bentley walked in.

"Gentlemen, good morning," Bentley said, dropping a stack of papers on the table. "Now I have some of the reports, but I'm just waiting for the rest. Apparently, there is a bit of traffic and the department head is running late."

I glanced to Chase who looked back at me.

Bentley didn't wait. He dug right into the files in front of him, handing them to Ward, who handed them over to Chase and me. We started going over things as Bentley droned on in the background, trying to explain things to us.

I made a mental note of the questions I wanted to ask as he continued spewing information at both of us. I pulled out my legal pad and pen and started marking things down as I went over the documents in front of me.

A knock at the door pulled my attention away from what I was writing. "Sorry to interrupt, Mark, Mr. Dollanger, sir, but there is someone here to see you."

She didn't have time to announce anything else before Hunter walked in, and when he stepped off to the side, Mia came in behind him. What the hell? This was where she worked? Her eyes fell to mine, and she quickly turned her face away from me, first in embarrassment, and then a flash of surprise, then hurt mixed with anger flooding it.

Please tell me Mia didn't work for this company. If so, there was way more amiss here than we thought.

"Mia, care to disclose what you have told me?" Hunter asked, waiting for her to take the floor. She kept her eyes on the floor, her cheeks going red every time her eyes would meet mine.

I kept my attention on her, my head held high. I hadn't been prouder of her than I was at this very moment, even if this was her employer. She had decided to take control and stand up for herself.

"Gentlemen," her soft voice called out, "before you pursue this agreement, you should know that these reports have been doctored."

Ward looked to me and Chase, his eyes giving away everything he had been wondering.

"Whoa, wait a minute, Mia, you shouldn't make such accusations," Mark said, placing his hand on his shoulder. "Please excuse us for a moment. Mia has been very stressed lately, and she has recently gone off on sick leave."

Mia started shaking her head, but he grabbed her by the shoulders and turned her away from us.

"Bentley, let the lady speak," I announced to the room.

"We are interested in whatever she has to say. Mia, is it? Please go ahead." I wasn't going to allow her to be shuffled off. I knew the things she had to say mattered.

She shrugged Mark off her. "The reports have been doctored by me, under the direction of Mark," she said, looking to Hunter. He stood back and nodded his head.

Bentley looked at her then to Hunter, clenching his jaw tight, his head about ready to explode. He let out a nervous laugh. "She doesn't know what she is talking about," he lied.

"I can prove it," she said, looking over to me, and once again quickly avoiding my eyes.

"Mark," Dollanger questioned, "what is she talking about?"

Mark looked at me, fire burning in his eyes. I knew he was buried. He couldn't get out of this.

"Here." She handed Chase a bunch of documents. "These are the real documents. You can see from the date on the bottom of them. I took copies before I left on vacation, and while I was gone, I ended up getting fired. He asked me to fudge the reports before I left and threatened my job. I did what he asked, but I took copies of the correct ones."

Chase opened the files and looked at all the statements. "Everything here is showing a major, major loss," he said, studying them.

Hunter stood back, his arms crossed over his chest, watching everything unfold. "My client also has some employment law issues as well. Dollanger, did you know that my client has not had a vacation in fifteen years until recently? That she has over two thousand hours of vacation time banked?"

"What? Bentley, is this true?"

"She has also put in countless amounts of overtime without compensation, often working weekends and weeknights from home as well."

"She's lying," Mark choked out.

Hunter stood back and looked at him. "I don't believe she is. I have every pay statement for the last three years, plus her most current. She has recorded down her hours in a calendar for the past three years. I have gone over her overtime hours and every paystub for the past three years, and they only show payments of a straight forty hours per week. Still care to tell me she is lying?" Hunter asked.

Ward stood up, clearing his throat and taking his jacket from the back of the chair. Chase, Bryce, I don't think we need to spend any more time on this. We are done. I refuse to purchase a company that would treat its employees this way, not to mention I have no idea what it is I am even buying at this point."

Ward nodded his head at Mia and Hunter and excused himself from the room. I could tell Mia didn't know what to say when Ward stepped back into the room.

"Mia, if you would like to come in for an interview, my company is hiring a specialist right in your field. I would be more than happy to employ someone so hard working and loyal as yourself. Here is my card. Call my secretary and set up a meeting." He nodded and left the room.

Mia stood there, her mouth open at what had just transpired.

"Mia, how dare you? You have stolen company property," Mark said, his expression contorting into rage.

"As a matter of fact, my client—"

Mia held her hand up and signaled for Hunter to give

her a second. She swallowed hard and took a deep breath before continuing.

"Actually, no, I didn't. I was doing what you always told me to do from the beginning, and that was cover my ass."

Hunter stepped in behind her. "My client expects to be paid out all two thousand hours of vacation, and we will also be sending in an offer to settle up all overtime hours owed. I will send over a fax of our offer later this week to you, Dollanger. We will expect it to be cleared up within the next couple of weeks. Don't make us drag you into court. Mia, after you." Hunter held his hand out to guide her through the door.

I watched them walk out, a part of me rejoicing inside and wishing I could wrap her in my arms and congratulate her. I had never been prouder of anyone, watching her take control and stand up for herself had turned me on.

"Excuse me for a moment," I said, leaving the room and following Mia and Hunter.

I took the elevator down to the main floor and made my way through the lobby, turning the corner to the front door where I saw Mia standing talking with Hunter. Her hand was over her mouth and she looked as if she was crying, his hand on her shoulder doing his best to comfort her.

Chapter Twenty-One

I had never been so glad to leave a room in my life. With my heart beating hard and fast in my chest the entire time, I had gone through that whole confrontation, all while Bryce sat across from me. What the hell was he even doing there? Was this the big meeting he had told me about?

Walking down the hall, I picked up my pace. I needed air. I had a million thoughts running through my mind and none of them were good. By the time I hit the lobby, I was almost running, Hunter picking up pace behind me.

"Mia, Mia..." His hand gripped my arm, stopping me. "Mia, what is wrong? Everything went exactly as we hoped it would." Hunter pulled me over to the side into a quiet little corner in the lobby.

"Hunter, I don't care about that." I sniffled.

"Then what is it?"

"Did he know?" I blurted out, looking him in the eyes.

"Did who know?"

"Did Bryce know I worked here? Is that why he picked me up in the airport, to gain insight into this failing company?"

"Mia, wait a minute."

I heard Bryce call out, and I glanced over my shoulder to see him approaching us.

"Don't walk away from him, Mia, talk to him. You need to tell him what you are thinking."

"I've got to go. I can't do this today." I turned and headed toward the main doors, leaving Hunter standing there. I didn't want to be put into a corner, especially one I certainly didn't want to be in. I didn't want to hear what he had to say. I didn't want it to be true, but somewhere in my gut, I was petrified that it was.

"Mia, wait." I felt Bryce grab hold of my arm and spin me around. "Why are you rushing away from me.

"Mia, I'm going to leave the two of you alone. You have a lot to talk about," Hunter said, rubbing my upper arm. "Call me this afternoon. I want to go over the offer before I send it, okay?" He nodded at Bryce and walked out of the building.

"Mia, what is wrong?" Bryce tried to take hold of my hands, but I pulled them away.

"First, I want to thank you for everything, Bryce. I really can't thank you enough." I sniffled and wiped the tears from under my eyes. I had to say good-bye in the fastest way possible. I couldn't stand to hear the truth, and if he just let me leave after this, then we would be good. I would do what I always did: disappear into my busy life. Only right now, there was no busy.

"You're welcome, but why the tears?"

"Did you seek me out?"

He frowned. "What? What are you talking about?"

I huffed, trying to regain control over my emotions. "I guess I'm supposed to believe that it's just a coincidence that you were dealing with the merger for the company that I worked for?"

"Of course, it is, Mia. I don't know what you are talking about."

"The airport, the week at the lake house, you sought me out. Why? Was it just to get information on this company that you didn't have? You needed more dirt, and you knew I worked here, so you sought me out? There is no way I can believe that it's just a coincidence that after all this time I just so happen to run into you."

"Mia, what are you saying?"

"You expect me to believe that all of this is something more?"

Bryce stood there, thinking through my accusations. "What, you think the only reason I got involved with you was to gain inside knowledge about this company? Mia, I'm in love with you."

The tears poured freely down my cheeks as I stood there looking at him, the hurt in his eyes literally ripping my heart from my chest.

"You think I was faking it with you?" he went on. "You think all of this has been some sort of game?"

I slowly nodded my head, wiping more tears from my cheeks. He stood there looking at me, not saying anything for quite a while. He didn't try to comfort me when I thought he would. Instead he came out with an accusation all his own. "Okay, you want to play it that way, then perhaps this is your way of getting back at me?" he stated.

"What?" I said, looking up at him through blurry eyes.

"For that night all those years ago? Maybe you are the one who is playing games with me, Mia. Perhaps you saw me in the airport and figured this would be as good a time as any to get back at me for that night at the party."

"You're serious right now?" I spat.

His eyes drilled into mine. I could see the hurt. I could see that he wasn't lying when he said what I assumed wasn't true. I could also see that what he was saying sounded just as ridiculous as what I was saying.

"Sounds pretty ridiculous, doesn't it?" His sharp look beat down on me.

"Don't bother coming by tonight. I don't want to see you." I looked up into those baby blues and turned and ran out the front door, jutting out into traffic, car tires screeching and horns blaring as I ran across the street to where I was parked. I jumped into my car and pulled away from the curb, another horn blaring from the car I cut off.

I drove aimlessly around the city for a while, not really knowing where to go. I finally stopped at the grocery store, wandering the aisles and throwing food I normally would never eat into the cart, then paid and made my way home. I lugged all the groceries into the house, dropping everything down onto the kitchen floor, when my cell phone rang. Don's name flashed across the screen.

What the hell does he want? I thought to myself. "What?" I barked into the phone.

"Mia, is that you?"

"Who else would it be?" I demanded, pulling some of the items from one of the bags and putting them into the fridge.

"I just thought I would call and let you know I just sent some of your things through FedEx. They were things that you had left here on your last visit. They should arrive sometime in the next couple of days. If not, let me know, and I will call FedEx."

I didn't say anything. I stopped what I was doing and slid down to the floor. My stomach hurt, my head pounded, and I just wanted everything and everyone to leave me alone. I didn't hang up. Instead I sat there, my hand over my eyes, and whispered, "Don, can I ask you something?"

The line was quiet. "Sure." Only I didn't say anything; I just sat there afraid of his answer. "Mia, is everything all right?"

Even though we may not have been right for one another, Don was always one who was able to tell me the truth, even when I didn't want to hear it for myself. He could always pick up on when I was off my game.

"What is so undesirable about me?"

"What do you mean? Nothing is undesirable about you. You're a beautiful person."

"Then why did you not want to be with me?"

I heard him let out a sigh. "Mia it's not that I didn't want to be with you. I did. I tried tirelessly to make things work between us, but you don't trust. You never let anyone close enough to you to ever possibly let someone love you. It took me two years to break down your walls, and if we were apart for more than six months at a time, then I had to do it all over again. It was exhausting. You were constantly finding reasons to push me away, just like you do with everyone."

He was right, he had pegged me perfectly. Thinking back, I had done it with every boyfriend, every friend, and even my own brother. I was the one pushing everyone away.

Even though Don was still talking, I hung up the phone, letting it fall to the floor. I had made a mess of things once again, only this time it was with someone that I truly wanted to have in my life.

I pulled my knees into my chest and wrapped my arms around my legs, burying my face into my lap, trying to figure out how the hell I was going to fix us.

Chapter Twenty-Two

Bryce

I had work that needed to be completed, so I returned to the office after my encounter with Mia. I worked until 6:00 p.m., for as long as I could, until my mind was fully consumed with thoughts of her and how I was going to fix this, how I was going to fix *us*.

I took a long shower when I got home, trying to let go of some of the stress I was carrying. I had planned on coming home, making dinner, having a few drinks, and going to bed, since she didn't want to see me. Those words had hurt, and for part of the afternoon, I considered just giving up and letting her go, but my heart had other ideas. I needed to see her, I needed to fix this with us, and truthfully, I didn't want to lose her.

It sounded ridiculous, even to me. It may have only been

a couple of weeks, but those couple of weeks had been the best of my life.

I changed into a pair of jeans and a sweater, grabbed a water from the fridge, and headed out the door.

I drove the long way through town, making one stop on my way: my buddy's jewelry store. I wasn't in a rush. I was sure she would be up late tonight making her favorite stress meal anyway: meatballs and cookies. I spent a good hour in the store with my friend trying to find the perfect item, and after finding the only thing that spoke to me, I left armed with the little white box wrapped in red ribbon.

I continued driving through town, thinking of what I was going to say, when I finally came face-to-face with her. Should I just give her the box? No that was what I would have done with Alyssa. Perhaps I should just talk to her first. Whichever way I decided to do it, I was sure she would find something wrong with it and probably kick me to the curb. I had been so unfair to her this afternoon with my accusations.

Twenty minutes later, I pulled into Mia's driveway. I cut the engine and sat there for ten minutes just staring at the house. The light was on in the living room, and I could see flashes of light from the TV reflecting against the curtains.

I sat there until I saw her through the curtains, carrying a plate in her hands across the front room where she must have sat down on the couch.

I couldn't sit out here forever, so I opened the car door and stepped out into the cold night, the remains of the last snowfall crunching under my feet.

I shoved the little box into my jacket pocket and knocked on the door. Seconds later, the outside light was turned on and my nerves went into overdrive. The inside door pulled open, and Mia stood there. She didn't move to open the inside door and invite me in. Instead she looked at me through the glass. How I wanted to wrap her in my arms and make everything go away.

"Could I come in?"

Surprisingly she didn't argue or tell me no. Instead she stepped to the side and opened the door for me. She shut and locked the door behind me and held her hand out for my coat, still not saying a word. After she hung that up, I followed her as she walked into the kitchen carrying her empty plate. There on the counter sat a tray of meatballs, and I could smell the sweetness of her chocolate chip cookies that must have been cooking in the oven.

A small smile came to my lips.

"What's so funny?" she asked, squinting at me, a serious expression on her face.

"Nothing, it's just I didn't rush over here because I figured this was what you would be doing," I said, pointing to the tray of meatballs.

"Want one?" she asked, holding the tray up to me.

I took one, the oven timer letting out a loud beep. She set the tray back down and opened the oven door, pulling out a tray of chocolate chip cookies.

She pulled another plate down from the cupboard and loaded some meatballs and cookies onto it then held it out for me to take. "Dinner?"

I smiled, taking the plate from her, only she didn't smile back. Instead she picked up her plate, shoved past me, and went into the living room.

I took in a deep breath. This was going to be a long

night. I followed her into the living room and sat down on the couch beside her. She adjusted herself so her body turned into mine. Bending off a piece of the warm cookie, she popped it into her mouth.

Nothing was said between the two of us while we ate, but I could feel the tension in the room. I finished my food first and set my empty plate on the table in front of us.

"I'm sorry..." We both said in unison.

I couldn't take it anymore. The thought of her being angry with me for saying something as stupid as I had was killing me.

"I wasn't being fair to you," she mumbled. "I thought about it once I left. I panicked when I saw you sitting there, staring back at me." A single tear escaped her eye. "I was so afraid that you were only after the information on the company and all we had shared wasn't real that it was all I could do to remain in the room."

"Wasn't real? You think I could fake that, fake any of it?"

"You're a guy. Of course, you can. Sex to you is all the same, whether it comes with feelings or not." She laughed and rolled her eyes.

"That isn't true Mia. Maybe once I could, but never more than that, and never in my entire life have I told a woman I loved them when I haven't. And if you seriously think I could do that, then you don't know me at all," I said pointedly.

"Bryce I—"

I stood up and went to grab my jacket from the closet.

"You're leaving? Fine, just go, Bryce," she choked out.

I pulled my coat off the hanger and searched the pockets,

finally pulling the little box out, and then hung my jacket on the handle. I walked back over and sat down beside her without saying a word.

"Mia I'm sorry too. I was out of line when I said what I said to you about you getting back at me. I was hurt and thought it was easiest to cover it up by lashing out at you." I held the box out to her, and her eyes traveled to my hands. "Take it," I whispered.

She cautiously reached out and took the box from my hand, her fingers grazing mine, instantly sending a wave of heat through me. I watched her tear-streaked face as she slowly pulled at the ribbon. Untying it, she lifted the lid off the box. The tears then started to pour, as soon as she looked at what was inside, and she put the lid back over top of it.

"What is it? Don't you like it?" I asked.

"It's not that. I love it."

"Then what is it?" I asked, placing two fingers under her chin and pulling her head in my direction so she would look at me.

"It's just, I was so unfair to you about that comment I made today. I'm a master at pushing people away. I spoke to Don today and asked him what was so undesirable about me. That was his answer. I'm scared. I don't want to lose you, but my instinct is telling me to push you away from me." She sniffled.

"Well, then I guess it's a good thing that us Malone boys don't give up that easy, isn't it? I'm not going anywhere, Mia. My heart belongs to you. You are my home." I moved closer to her and pulled her into my arms.

"How can you possibly know that? It's only been—"

"I know...it's only been a couple of weeks. Actually, that isn't true. It's been years, Mia. Years of wanting you," I said, the back of my hand brushing against her cheek. "It just took seeing you again to realize it. Out of sight, out of mind is true, but when your heart holds feelings for someone, it kindly reminds you not to give up so easily. So, I'm not going to stop until I get it."

She buried her face into my neck and let out a sob. We sat together for a while, her head resting on my shoulder. Once she had calmed down, I kissed her forehead and took the little box off her lap, opening it. I removed the white gold chain that held the little infinity charm.

"Sit forward and hold your hair up."

She did as I asked, and I placed the chain around her neck.

"This was the only thing there that spoke to me. It represents how long and how much I finally realized that I loved you," I whispered into her ear and kissed the side of her neck, inching toward the top of her shoulder.

She shut the TV off and took my hand in hers, pulling me up. The sexy playfulness in her eyes nearly sent me to my knees as she led me down the hall toward her bedroom. With each step, she shed an article of clothing—first her socks, then her pants, next her shirt, until she stood in front of her bedroom door in nothing but a black lace bra and panties and the necklace I had bought her. I went to step forward to kiss her, but she placed her hand on my chest and stepped into her bedroom.

Grabbing my sweater, I pulled it over my head and undid the button on my jeans, a loud clinking sound as my belt hit her hardwood floors. I took a step forward while she took a step back, until she had fallen back onto the bed.

I ripped the cups of her bra down, exposing her breasts to me, and sucked her one nipple into my mouth while rolling the other between my finger and thumb. Mia instantly inhaled and let out a moan as her back lifted off the bed. I left her breasts and ran my hand down the center of her stomach to the waist of her panties, and in once swift pull, I ripped them from her body. She let out a gasp.

"Bryce, those were my favorite..."

"Shhhh, I will get you more."

She giggled as I placed a hand on each of her knees, pushing her legs open. As I looked down, I could see she was already soaked. I looked back up to see her lust-filled eyes watching me. I kept watching her as I ran my fingers through her wetness and up over her clit. Her eyes closed and she let out a soft moan. I pushed my boxers down, my cock already hard and throbbing. I needed inside of her right now.

"Where do you keep the condoms?" I asked, praying that she had some.

She bit her lower lip and shook her head no. "No condom," she whispered. "I want to feel you."

"You sure?" I kneeled between her legs.

She nodded her head, her sex-filled eyes looking up at me. I leaned down, connecting with her lips, my tongue running through her mouth, tasting her. I grabbed my cock, giving it a couple of pumps, which was totally unnecessary, as hard as I was, and I ran it through her wetness. I pushed inside of her slowly, watching her face as I buried myself deep into her. She was fucking beautiful. I loved watching her as I pulled out and pushed all the way in again. Her hands reaching up behind her head, she gripped the pillow the harder I thrust into her, soft moans escaping her lips.

"Rub your clit for me," I demanded. "Show me how you make yourself come."

She shook her head, a soft blush coming over her already heated cheeks.

I sat back on my heels; my cock fully planted inside of her. "Show me." I took hold of her hand and placed it on her lower belly. "Rub yourself," I whispered.

I could tell she was hesitant at first, but then her hand slowly moved to her center and she started rubbing her clit. I felt like I could bust, watching her pleasure herself while my cock was buried inside of her. I was fighting to hold back my own orgasm just watching her, but then I felt her tighten around me, and the sound of her moans getting louder and louder the closer she came, it was almost impossible, and as soon as I felt the hot rush of heat from her, I too let myself go, filling her full.

We lay in bed, her head on my chest, her body wrapped around mine, fitting perfectly against me, as if it was the only one that belonged there. We were on the cusp of sleep after our third round. I pulled her closer and she let out a sleepy, sexy little moan.

"Don't push me away anymore," I whispered.

She opened her sleepy eyes and looked up at me. "I won't. Well, I will try not to." She placed a little kiss on my chest and put her head back down.

"Good, now I don't want to scare you but move in with me."

I could tell, as soon as those words were past my lips, that she was scared and almost ready to bolt right out of the bed the way her body stiffened. I started rubbing her arm, and I felt her start to relax.

"Move in with me," I repeated, kissing her forehead. "We'll take it slow."

She nodded her head against my chest, and I heard her sniffle.

Chapter Twenty-Three

It was almost 8:00 p.m. and I was still sitting behind my desk at the office. The day had been long, and I couldn't wait to get out of here tonight. Mia had finally agreed to move in with me, and she was finally settled into my condo. We were putting her house up on the market this weekend.

I sat back in my chair and opened my desk drawer. My eyes instantly fell to the little black velvet box that had been sitting there since last week. I couldn't put it off any longer. I needed to make that call before I left the office tonight.

I scrolled through my contact list in search of Grant's number. It had been about a year since I had last spoken to him, right when things with Alyssa had gone south. Before dialing, I pulled open my bottom drawer and picked up the bottle of scotch that was hidden there, pouring myself a shot. I had done the same thing before the last phone call, only this time it was for an entirely different reason. I downed that shot and poured a half shot more, knowing after this call I had to drive home, then I picked up the phone and dialed his number.

The phone rang and rang, and just when I thought I might be off the hook, I heard his voice. "Dr. Hollis."

"Grant?" I said into the phone.

"You've got him. Who's this?" he asked, sounding a little confused. No doubt he was busy and was probably still at the hospital.

"It's Bryce," I answered, rotating that little velvet box between my fingers.

"One second." I heard him ramble off a long list of orders to someone and then finally silence.

"Did I catch you at a bad time?" I asked, kind of praying he said yes.

"No, not at all. Sorry, just at the hospital. I was just about to head out on lunch anyways. How the fuck are you?" He chuckled into the phone.

"Good, great actually. Work has been steady, and I finally made partner."

"That's fantastic, man! Congratulations."

"Thanks! Yeah, my brothers always make Chase and I earn everything, those bastards." We both laughed.

"How's Mia doing? She told me you two finally moved in together."

"Yeah, she finally agreed. It took some convincing on my part. She moved in with me earlier this month finally, and we are putting her house on the market."

"I'm glad to hear that. She seems really happy, far cry from one of the last few times I spoke with her."

We spent the better half of the next fifteen minutes catching up. Grant told me about his wife and kids, sharing with me that he was up for another promotion at the hospital. He had worked hard and made a good life for himself.

"Listen, if you guys are able to soon, why don't you both make the trip out here. It would be great to see you both. It's been a while, and Mia still hasn't met the kids."

"Sounds like a great idea. Send me your holidays, and I will make sure we get out there."

I heard Grant being paged in the background.

"Shit, man, I've got to go. My hour is almost up."

I could hear him chug down whatever it was he was drinking.

I sat there, still turning the little black velvet box in my hand. The purpose for my call quickly coming back to me. "Listen, can I ask you something."

I heard the page go off again in the background.

"Give me one minute."

I sat there listening as he spoke to someone in the background. I drank down the mouthful of scotch I had poured myself, feeling that good old burning sensation as I swallowed the golden liquid.

He gave out orders, finally returning to our call. "Sorry about that. It's not an emergency, thank God, but I do need to get going. What's up?"

I kept turning that little black box between my fingers, trying to find the courage for my call. "Grant, I called because, well, you are Mia's only family, and I..."

"You want to ask her to marry you, don't you?" he said, taking the words right from my mouth that otherwise may never have made it out.

I let out the breath I was holding. "Yes, I do. I want to spend the rest of my life with her."

"Then go for it, man. Let me know how it goes, and I swear if she doesn't say yes, ship her out to me for a couple of weeks and I will change her mind for you."

We both laughed. It was good to know that after all these years, Grant still had my back.

"Thanks, man. I'll talk to you soon."

We hung up the phone and I sat there for a couple of minutes still twirling that little black box in my hands. Now I just needed to find the perfect time to ask her.

I tucked the box into my jacket pocket and gathered my things, finally shutting off the light to my office.

The drive home was quick, and I took the elevator up to the condo. When I opened the door, soft music filled the apartment, the lights were dimmed in the living room, and a candle was burning on the coffee table.

I dropped my briefcase just inside the door and put my keys on the table. Mia had already begun to make changes, adding her feminine touch to things in the short time she had lived with me.

I could hear the shower running and quietly walked toward our bedroom, but first I slipped into my office and placed the little black velvet box at the back of the center drawer where Mia wouldn't find it.

I undressed and slipped into the bathroom. Steam filled

the room, but I could see the outline of Mia standing in the shower, her back turned to me.

"Hey, sexy. I'm home." I pulled the shower door open and stepped inside, Mia turning to face me, my eyes washing over her perfect, full breasts, my cock instantly going hard at the sight. I hadn't been able to keep my hands off her, especially when she stood there looking at me so innocently. I pulled her warm body against mine and kissed the side of her neck, breathing in her clean scent.

"I'm so glad to see you." She wrapped her arms around my neck, meeting my lips.

"Did you get everything done at the house with Autumn?" I asked.

"Yep, it's all done and ready for the real estate agent tomorrow. He's hoping for a fast sale."

"Good, then we don't have to go back tonight?" I grabbed her under the ass and picked her up, she wrapped her legs around my waist, and I backed her up until she was resting against the tile, attacking her mouth again.

"Bryce, put me down." She laughed as I kissed my way down her neck and across her collarbone.

"No way. You're mine!" I buried my face in the side of her neck, causing her to laugh out loud. I slowly put her down and smacked her ass and pulled her in for a long kiss.

"Are you hungry?" she asked as she pulled those beautiful soft lips from mine, the look in her eyes screaming for me to take her right there.

"Starving."

"Well, clean yourself up. I'll go and make us something to eat."

She let go of my hand and went to open the shower

door, but I pulled her back against my chest, my arm instantly securing around her waist, the other hand grasping her breast. As my fingers brushed over her nipple, I heard a little whimper escape her mouth, and I bit her earlobe, causing her to drop her head to my shoulder as my other hand traveled down between her legs, my fingers making contact with her clit.

"You're so bad," she breathed out, parting her legs just a little.

"You love it," I whispered.

Twenty minutes later, Mia left the shower fully sated and wrapped in a large black towel, leaving me to quickly shower. "I'll go make us something to eat," she called out, leaving the bathroom.

I had changed into my lounge pants and T-shirt and wandered into my office. I pulled open the center drawer and reached to the back, pulling out the little black box and putting it into my pocket. I heard Mia banging around in the kitchen, and my stomach let out a loud grumble at the thought of food.

I rounded the corner and noticed she had turned the fireplace on. A bottle of wine sat in the chiller in the living room beside two empty glasses, and a plate of cheese and crackers sat beside it.

"It will just be a minute. I have brie in the oven," she said, smiling over at me.

"No problem." I walked over, poured the wine, and then went to look out the window. I wrapped my hand around the little black velvet box that sat in my pocket as I watched Mia's reflection in the glass. Just when I thought I had enough courage to turn and ask her, she walked into the room carrying the plate of hot brie.

"Did you want to watch a movie or something?" she asked, sitting down on the edge of the couch.

I shook my head. I just wanted to ask her. I wouldn't be able to eat if I didn't, my nerves getting the better of me.

"Are you going to come and sit down?" she asked, looking up at me, a worried expression coming over her face.

"Can you come here?" I asked.

"Bryce, what is the matter with you?" she asked. Concern now lined her face as she stood up and came over to me. "Is everything okay?" she asked as she got close enough to run her hand over my shoulder.

I didn't answer her. Instead I dropped to my knee.

"Bryce, what are you..."

Her words stopped as soon as she saw what I held in my hand, her eyes growing wide. The last thing I wanted to do was scare her. We had been in such a great place over the last eight months, I didn't want her to start pushing me away again.

My hands shook as I lifted the lid on that tiny box to produce the custom designed ring I had ordered from the local jeweler. Her hands shook as they covered her mouth.

"Mia, these last few months with you have been amazing." She held her hand up to stop me, but I kept going. "I can't ever imagine my life without you in it again. I want you to be my wife." I looked up into her eyes as they filled with tears and instantly, I became afraid she was going to curl back up into the person she used to be.

She surprised me, and instead she slowly reached down and took my hand in hers and nodded her head. I had never ripped anything from a package so fast as I did that ring and placed it on her finger.

Forgetting about the food or how hungry I was, I picked her up, her legs instantly wrapping around my waist, and I carried her down the hall.

"I want to see you in nothing but that ring, moaning my fucking name," I murmured into her ear as I lowered her to the floor.

Chapter Twenty-Four

I watched from the front window as Bryce and the real estate agent walked down to the edge of the lawn and hung the sold sign. At first, we were going to keep my little bungalow, but then we decided we didn't want to have to deal with renters.

I looked around the little bungalow where I had spent the better part of my life, reminiscing about all the events that had taken place while I had lived here. This house held so many memories for me, all of them flashing before my eyes like an old movie.

I heard the backdoor slam and ran my fingers under my eyes to remove any tears that may have fallen. I didn't want Bryce to think I wasn't happy with our decision. The truth was I couldn't be happier. It was just hard to let go of certain things.

"Mia?" I heard him call out.

"Yeah, I'm in here," I called back from the front room, still looking out the front window.

"There you are. You just about ready? We are supposed to meet everyone down at the little cafe by the water."

I bit my lower lip and looked around the room one last time. "I think so." I couldn't help a twinge of sadness hitting my voice. It was harder to say good-bye to these memories than I thought it was going to be, but my future held so many more in store for me, and I couldn't wait to embark on the journey with Bryce.

"How about we go and take a walk down by the water?" he said, wrapping his arms around me from behind and kissing me gently on the cheek. "Just us, before we meet up with everyone. I'll call and tell them we're running late and bump the time up to eight."

"That would be nice. I would like that," I said, leaning back into him, letting his warmth and strong embrace envelop me for a second.

"All right then, let's go." Placing another kiss on my cheek, he grabbed my hand, but I was hesitant and didn't move.

"Could you maybe give me a minute?" I asked, looking into his eyes and swallowing hard. "I just need a minute or two."

"Of course. I will be out in the car, okay? Come out when you're ready." He leaned in and kissed me before opening the front door.

I watched him walk down the walkway and get into the car. I didn't think saying good-bye to this house would be this hard. I took my time going through each room of the house, reflecting over the last fifteen years of my life once more. I remembered the first night I had gotten the key. I had come over and just sat in the living room on the floor for hours, so excited about what the future held for me here. But now I had such bigger and better things to look forward to.

I glanced at my watch, realizing that Bryce had been sitting waiting for me for close to twenty minutes, and walked to the front door and pulled it open. Taking one final look around, I walked out the door, locking it behind me. I handed the key to the real estate agent who stood beside his car, thanked him for everything, and climbed into Bryce's car.

"You okay?" he asked, putting his phone down on the console between the seats.

"Yep. Let's go," I whispered. He backed out of the driveway, and for the final time, I looked back at the dark house.

It was a quiet ride as Bryce drove down to the waterfront. I looked out the window, watching the trees pass by, listening to the soft music Bryce had playing in the car. I was lost in my thoughts when I felt his hand on mine. He didn't say anything. He just held it tight for the remainder of the drive.

Once we arrived downtown, it was a matter of seconds before we found a parking spot. He came around the car and pulled my door open, offering me his hand. "Did you want a coffee first?"

"That would be great. Was everyone okay with waiting until eight?" I asked as I climbed out of the car.

"Of course. It's all good." He winked at me.

Once we had our coffee, we started walking around the

water. It was a gorgeous night, a cool breeze off the lake blowing around us. It was only the end of September, and a few boats from the marina were out on the water, the people enjoying one of the last boat rides of the season.

We continued to walk for a bit, finally sitting down on a little bench halfway around the lake.

"I was thinking, with the money from the sale of the house and my settlement, what if we put that towards a down payment on a house?"

Bryce was quiet, looking off in the distance of the water. I was a little scared when he didn't answer me right away.

"Bryce? Did you hear me?"

"Yeah."

He seemed so far away, I could sense my insecurities rising again and the absolute fear to push away and I had to ask him. "Bryce, have we...have we made a mistake?"

"What?" That had gotten his attention. "No, love, what would make you think that? I was just thinking about where we would move to and about the wedding. You are the furthest thing from a mistake. Don't ever think that." He looked into my eyes and wrapped his arm around me, pulling me in closer. "I seriously cannot wait until I see you walk down that aisle in a white dress, looking all perfect, just so I can rip it off you later and make you scream my name."

We both laughed, my nerves instantly calming.

"And I think it's a great idea to do with the money, but I don't want to rush into something. Let's wait until we find the perfect place."

We finished our coffees, watching the boats out on the water, and then made our way over to the cafe. We had yet to tell anyone about the engagement and really wanted everyone in one place all together.

As we approached the cafe, we both noticed Hunter and Carter's cars parked out front.

"Looks like everyone is here already," Bryce said, pulling the door open for me and guiding me in, his hand resting on my lower back.

As soon as I walked in, I was met with a huge congratulations sign and balloons everywhere. Hope and Autumn came rushing over to me and reached for my hand. "Let us see," they squealed in delight.

I glanced over my shoulder at Bryce who held his hands up in an innocent gesture. "My brothers knew. I had to tell them what your answer was." He shrugged his shoulders and chuckled.

Soon Bryce was seated over with Carter, Hunter, and Chase discussing work, while I sat with Autumn and Hope looking over wedding dress designs on our phones. The plans were already starting, and I couldn't think of two better people to help me plan my wedding.

I felt a puff of air against my legs as someone entered the cafe, and as I went to turn, Autumn grabbed my attention to share with me a dress she thought would look perfect on me, when suddenly I felt someone's hands over my eyes, the room going dark.

"All right, very funny, Bryce. What other kinds of surprises do you have up your sleeve now?" I said, pulling at his hands.

I blinked, letting my eyes adjust once again to the light, and turned around, expecting to see Bryce standing there with some goofy smile on his face, only it wasn't Bryce, and I kind of felt lightheaded at who was standing in front of me.

"You look like you've seen a ghost, Mia. What the hell. Aren't you excited to see your own brother?" Grant asked, standing in front of me, June and the kids standing behind him.

My eyes got blurry as the tears built up in them, and I wrapped my arms around my brother. I had never thought I meant that much to Grant until he stood here in front of me. He had carted the whole family across the states just to be here to celebrate our engagement.

Everyone was quiet as we stood there, me crying into my brother's chest, him hugging me tighter than I ever remembered.

"I wouldn't have missed this for the world. When Bryce called and asked us to be here tonight, we couldn't say no. You mean more to me than you will ever know," he whispered in my ear.

A deep sob escaped my chest as I held him tighter. "Thank you so much for coming."

"All right, you two, break it up. If you weren't related, I'd swear you were trying to steal my woman," Bryce said, getting up and shaking his hand, everyone laughing.

I finally grew quiet, looking around the table at everyone. It was the first time we had all been together in years, and it finally truly felt like home. I had found my place. I had just been lost for the past fifteen years, trying to find my way back to where I belonged.

I quietly excused myself from the table and headed toward the washroom. When I was on my way back to the table, I felt someone grab me from behind and pull me back into them.

Bryce wrapped his arms around me and kissed my cheek. "Were you surprised?"

I looked over to where everyone sat and nodded my head. "You did this?" I asked.

"I did. We've been talking for a bit now. We have been planning this since the night I called and asked him for your hand," he whispered, kissing the edge of my ear.

"You asked my brother?" I asked.

"I did. I figured it was only the proper thing to do. I mean, you don't know where your father is, and your mother, God rest her soul, is gone. He was the next logical choice. I told him when I was planning it, and he promised me he would be here to celebrate."

I looked up into my future husband's eyes, and for the first time in my life, I had never been so sure of anything.

Epilogue

We lay together on the couch, the fire burning and soft music filling the room. Outside, the winter storm raged on, covering everything with snow.

I giggled. "Doesn't this remind you of the first time we were here?" I asked. We had decided to spend our two-week honeymoon at the lake house, and just like the first time, the day before we were to leave to return home, snow decided to fall, trapping us here.

"Yeah, it does. I guess that is fate's way of telling us our honeymoon isn't quite over yet." He laughed, kissing me. He pulled away when we heard a gust of wind outside. "It's getting pretty wild out. I should probably bring in a bit more wood, sweetie," Bryce said, removing his arm from under me and sitting up. "I'll be right back. I don't want to have to fight my way through all that later." He grabbed his hoodie from the couch and threw it over his head.

I watched him go and pulled the blanket around my body. Even though it was warm inside, I was cold without him. He brought in three armfuls of wood and dropped them in the wood box, filling it, and threw another log on the fire before returning to my side.

"You barely touched your wine. You all right?"

"Yeah. My stomach is a little upset tonight," I answered, getting comfortable again as he slid in beside me. "Cold out there?"

"It's more than cold. I would suggest the hot tub, but I think we might freeze," he said, kissing my forehead.

"It's okay, I'm exhausted," I said, yawning. "Did you want to go to bed."

Bryce laughed out loud. "Babe you don't need to ask me twice," he said, wiggling his eyebrows at me. "I could use a little stress relief."

"You can always use stress relief." I laughed, kicking the blankets off me.

We had barely made it down the hall and he had already stripped my T-shirt off, leaving it in a pile on the floor in the hallway as he held me in his arms, kissing me hard.

"Fuck me, you are going to be the death of me, woman," he whispered between kisses.

I could already feel him hard against me. He threw open the bedroom door and held me as I walked backward to the bed. He pulled the drawstring on his lounge pants, allowing them to fall to the floor, his hard cock saluting me.

I sat up on the bed, teasing his cock with my tongue as he stood before me. He fisted his hand in my hair as I continued to deliver little licks to the head of his cock, licking the bead of precum off him.

"Fuck. Don't tease me. Take it in your mouth," he hissed.

I looked up at him, my eyes teasing him as I continued with the torturous little licks.

With his free hand, he held onto my breast, rubbing his thumb over my nipple, his touch running a chill through my body. He gently pinched my nipple through the fabric of my bra, causing me to jump. He stopped immediately. "Did I hurt you?"

I shook my head. "Just a little sensitive is all. Slow down," I whispered. Everything about me felt sensitive tonight.

He pushed me gently back, gripping the waist of my silk pajama pants and pulling them off me, and he crawled in beside me, shutting off the bedside light and pulling the blankets around us. I straddled his waist and felt his hands run up my back and flick the clasp on the back of my bra, his fingers grazing my shoulders as he pulled my bra down and off me, my nipples instantly hardening at the coolness of the room.

Bryce sat up and took one of them in his mouth, sucking and licking. Again, a sharp intake of breath and a jump stopped him. "Baby are you sure you are okay?"

"Yeah, just slow down."

"Come then, lay down." He guided me off him and I lay back into the mattress. He propped himself up on his elbow and met my lips, kissing me slow and positioning himself in between my legs. Kissing me deeply, he slid his way inside of me and started thrusting slow and deep.

Everything about me felt heightened, and within minutes, I could already feel myself getting tighter around him, finally screaming out my orgasm as he emptied himself inside of me.

I lay wrapped in his arms. "You sure you're okay?" he whispered, kissing the side of my neck.

"Yeah, I'm okay." I closed my eyes. We had just gotten married. I wasn't sure how he would react to the news I had to deliver, but I didn't want to wait any longer.

"You remember how I went to see Dr. Price just before we left? I wanted him to renew my birth control."

"Yep, did you remember to pick up your prescription before we left?" he murmured sleepily.

"No."

"No, sweetie, you know how I hate wearing condoms now. Both Hunter and Carter warned me once I went bare, I wouldn't go back." He chuckled.

"Sounds like your brothers." I laughed.

"Well, I don't want to go back," he whined, tickling my side and causing me to wiggle away and scream. "You feel way too good."

"You don't have to," I murmured.

He went quiet, releasing the hold he had on my side. "Mia? What do you mean?" He questioned, raising up on his elbow and turning on the bedside light so he could see me.

I looked up at him, a smile falling on my lips at the questioning look on his face.

"Really? I'm going to be a dad," he whispered.

I was sure I saw a tear in his eye as the words fell from his lips.

I nodded my head without saying anything and bit my lower lip. "I know we talked about it and everything. I know you wanted to wait and travel..."

He placed a single finger up to my lips. "It doesn't matter, baby. Now, next year, never...it doesn't matter. It's going to be an amazing journey, fun and exciting. Get excited, sweetie, we are going to have an amazing adventure together."

The End

Finding Forever
With You

Finding Forever with You

Copyright © 2020 by S.L. Sterling

ISBN: 978-1-989566-07-7

Editor: Brandi Aquino, Editing Done Write

Cover Design: Thunderstruck Cover Designs

Chapter One

Sophie

The heat from the morning sun was hot as I made my way down the street to Aroma Mocha. I was on my way to meet Jenna for our usual Saturday morning coffee date." Normally, we walked to Aroma Mocha together after our yoga class, but she couldn't make it this morning. Instead, I made my way to the local cafe and flung my mat under my arm as I pulled the door open and stepped into the amazing smell of roasted coffee beans and freshly baked cinnamon buns. I looked around the dining area for Jenna, and when I didn't see her, I made my way to the counter and placed our usual order, then took a seat in our usual booth. I pulled my cell phone from my yoga bag and quickly checked my messages. I had just finished replying to someone at work when I spotted Jenna entering the small cafe. She spotted me right away and waved as she made her way through the crowd, her cell phone pressed up against her ear.

"I'm sorry, just a second. It's Matt," she mouthed as she pointed to her phone.

I smiled and slid out of my jacket while waiting for my vanilla latte and blueberry muffin to be delivered. I tried not to pay attention to Jenna while she spoke to Matt, but it was impossible. My best friend looked so happy, and I loved how her face lit up as she listened to whatever it was Matt was saying. The excitement in her voice was almost contagious when she responded to him. I wondered what it was like to be as happy as Jenna was. I hadn't had a decent relationship in years—well, honestly, never, but who was counting.

Jenna beamed as she hung up the phone and tucked it into her purse and turned her attention towards me. "Good morning," she sang. "How was yoga?"

"It was yoga. You know, the usual—downward dogs and tree poses. It would have been so much better with you there."

"Yeah, I know. I'm sorry about that. It was a crazy week, and I needed this morning just to lounge around with Matt."

"Yeah, sure, whatever. You know, I recall someone who so desperately wanted me to join yoga she spouted about how it does a body and mind good to de-stress. Now I go more than her."

"You are right, I did say that, but let's just say that Matt does his best to make sure I stay good and de-stressed." I couldn't help but roll my eyes as she giggled.

"How's Matt?" I questioned, doing my best to change the subject.

"He's good." She got quiet for a moment, a soft smile

coming to her lips. "I should probably tell you that I think I might be in love." Jenna swooned. "He is just everything I have ever wanted. I seriously have to ask myself what made me wait so long."

I let out a laugh, leaned across the table, and whispered, "You waited because you were convinced that he was a player."

"I did not. That was what you said."

"You are such a liar! I told you to take the chance."

Jenna laughed as she stirred her coffee with her biscotti. "So tell me, how's everything going with Ralph?" Jenna asked, taking a bite of her coffee-soaked treat.

I looked around the cafe and laughed. "Ha, don't ask. The man is all tongue. I can't even fathom what he'd be like in bed because I can barely get past a kiss."

Jenna began laughing uncontrollably. "Oh God, that reminds me of that guy I dated in university. Do you remember? What was his name?"

"Scott. Who wouldn't remember? But now look who you have," I said, raising my eyebrows suggestively. Jenna had started dating Matt, one of our close friends, not too long ago. I'd always thought that they would be perfect for one another and was so glad that they had finally taken the plunge.

"And look how long it took to find him."

"At least you found him. I'm just stuck with tongue," I murmured, crossing my eyes and sticking out my tongue. We both laughed.

Truth was, I had struggled in every relationship I'd had, the longest lasting just over a year and ending just as I had come off the hardest year of my life. I was convinced now more than ever that I was destined to be alone. I had just celebrated my thirtieth birthday and felt that lately my biological clock was ticking, but without a serious relationship, there wasn't much I could do about it.

"What about one of our circle?" Jenna asked, snapping me back to our conversation.

"What about them?" I questioned.

"Well, you say that ultimately you want a baby, right? You don't sound super keen on staying with Roger, or the Tongue as you call him, so, what about one of our circle? It takes all the risk out of it. I mean, you at least know who the guy is, what he looks like, what he is like."

"And we are going to kill that idea right now."

"What? Why?" Jenna asked innocently.

"Because you are being ridiculous." I shook my head. "The whole idea of that is just not going to happen."

"No, I'm not. What about Brent? I think you two would make a lovely couple. Or Shawn. Oooh, or Dave. He has an eight-pack most girls would kill to touch," she said, raising her eyebrows.

"Oh my God, just stop." I laughed, hiding my face in my hands.

The door to the cafe opened, grabbing Jenna's attention, her eyes lighting up at whatever idea she had now.

"What?" I asked, taking a bite of the still-warm blueberry muffin that I'd been craving all week. Jenna's eyes were still trained on whoever had walked through the door and was at the counter. I turned just in time to see the sexy Chase Malone leaning against the counter ordering his morning coffee, and I looked back towards Jenna, seeing a silly grin on her face.

"Why not?" She shrugged, her eyes lighting up like a Christmas tree.

"Why not what?"

"Why not Chase?"

"Why not Chase what?" I could feel my heart start to beat faster at what I hoped she wasn't trying to suggest.

"O.M.G! Pull your head out of the sand. He is as single as they come, and he is not looking to settle down anytime soon. He's hot, sexy, smart... Borrow some of his best swimmers and be done with it."

I almost spit my coffee all over Jenna at her suggestion. "Oh my God, no!" I said, balling my napkin up and throwing it at her.

"What is wrong with that idea?? What girl on the face of this earth wouldn't want a night, or hell better yet, a few nights with Chase Malone. Seriously, out of all the guys, he'd be your best bet. I've heard he is dynamite in the sack."

I looked up towards the counter and saw Chase give us an innocent wave.

"Seriously, Sophie, come on, just do it."

"Seriously, Jenna, just shut up already! He's my best friend," I gritted out in embarrassment just in time for Chase to slide into the booth beside me.

"Good morning, ladies," he greeted, reaching across the table for the sugar. "What are you beauties up to on this beautiful day?"

"Trying to help Sophie solve her relationship crisis."

"Oh my God, shut up!" I said, burying my face in my hands.

Chase looked at me, smiling. "Oh, Soph, you are too cute. You think you have a relationship problem?"

I looked to Jenna for help, since she was the one who'd started this whole conversation. "Go ahead, Sophie, share with Chase." She grinned.

I shrugged and looked at him. "Perhaps."

"Perhaps, Sophie, it's more of an asshole problem," he said, winking and pinching my outer arm, trying to lighten the mood just as his cell phone went off.

"What's that supposed to mean?" I questioned.

"It means that you need to find a nice boy." He winked, "Well, ladies, I have to run," he announced, "the world of law is awaiting me. See you ladies next week."

"Absolutely, we wouldn't miss it." Jenna grinned.

I glared at Jenna as she watched Chase leave the cafe. When she finally turned her attention back to me, I didn't know whether to laugh or cry. "Seriously? You think this is funny?"

"Oh come on, lighten up. I'm trying to help."

"Okay, okay," I said, laughing and squirming at the same time. "Perhaps you are right. Maybe I just need to find myself a nice man, but not Chase."

"Okay, not Chase. But I'm not going to sleep until we find you someone!" She giggled, shoving the last piece of biscotti in her mouth.

We sat and talked for a good hour after Chase had left, and finally, after parting ways, I decided to take a walk through the park near my house. I loved walking in early spring, listening to the birds chirp and smelling the crisp air. As I walked, I could still hear Jenna's suggestion at the forefront of my mind. As much as I hated to admit it, she did have a point. I was comfortable with my male friends, and I knew them all well, and perhaps Chase wasn't such a bad choice.

I shook the absurd thought from my head, crossed the street, and entered my apartment building. I took the elevator up to the twentieth floor and opened my door. I dropped my purse on the floor just inside the door and slipped my shoes off. I went into the kitchen and poured myself a glass of orange juice and immediately saw the flashing light on my phone. I dialed into my voicemail while taking a drink of the sweet liquid. The first message was from my boss reminding me of a meeting on Monday morning; the second was Ralph.

I drank down the rest of my orange juice and was just about to call Ralph back when my cell phone vibrated in my pocket. Looking down at the screen, I saw Chase had left me a message.

CHASE: WHAT ABOUT RALPH? HE SEEMS LIKE A STANDUP GUY.

I rolled my eyes. Not him now too. I laughed out loud and texted him back.

ME: HE KISSES LIKE A LIZARD!

I smiled, closed the chat window, and dialed Ralph's number. Within twenty minutes, I had gone from being in a lizard kissing relationship to being very single once again. I threw my phone down on the dining room table and rested my head on my arm. I lay there listening to the silence of my apartment, debating on crying or getting up and carrying on with my life. When my phone vibrated against the tabletop, I grabbed it and saw a message from Chase.

CHASE: EWWW THAT IS GROSS. BET THAT SORT OF MAKES YOU WISH YOU COULD GO BACK A FEW YEARS AGO AND PICK ME DOESN'T IT. HAHA JUST KIDDING.

I let out a silent laugh, silently wondering about the exact same thing, and plugged my phone into the charging port, made my way down to my bedroom, and got ready for the rest of my day.

Chapter Two

CHASE - THREE MONTHS LATER

My cell phone let out a shrill ring just as I grabbed my keys from the entryway table. I pocketed my wallet and threw my jacket on just as the phone rang again. I had half a mind to ignore the fucking thing after the day I'd had. I was stressed to the nines about a case I was working on, and then during court this morning I had received a message from Sophie.

As soon as court broke for recess, I listened to her message. She sounded off, and her message was just strange and out of sorts for her, and it left me feeling concerned. I had attempted to call her back, but court had been called back into session, and unfortunately all I could do was quickly message her back and ask her to contact me in a bit. I had yet to hear back from her. The phone rang out again, and this time I pulled it from my pocket and quickly answered it.

"Hello," I barked. I was rushed for time, and even though I was hoping that it was Sophie, I was also hoping this call would be quick.

"You on your way?" my brother, Bryce, questioned.

"Yep, be there in five minutes," I said, grabbing my comfortable old running shoes from the hall closet, slipping my feet into them, and heading out to meet my brothers for our monthly boys' night. I was looking forward to a night of relaxation, beer, and conversation.

By the time I pulled into the parking lot of Ducky's it was pretty full. I found a spot around back of the restaurant, pulled into it, shut the engine off, and went inside. As soon as I opened the doors, I immediately spotted my three brothers sitting in our usual booth in the back. I was just about to walk over when I heard two familiar voices call out to me. I glanced over at the bar and saw both Carly and Delilah waving at me. I flashed them my sexy grin. "Afternoon, ladies."

"What can we get for you today, Chase?" they both called out in unison.

"How about a cold beer, ladies."

"You got it, sexy," Delilah called back, while Carly winked at me.

My brothers sat watching intently as I waved and smiled to half of the women in the bar before I slid into the booth. Within seconds, our usual waitress, Trinity, set my beer down in front of me. She ran her hand over my shoulder and winked. "Wish you would call sometimes. I would love to see you again. It gets pretty lonely at night," she whispered to me.

I glanced at my brothers, praying that none of them had

heard her comment, but I knew they had just from the way they were watching me. I smiled at her and took a swig of my beer, trying to ignore what she had said, but instead of walking away, she left her hand on my shoulder.

"I might give you a call, but honestly, I'm really enjoying my alone time right now, Trin." I could tell from the look on her face that I had pretty much crushed her, but I wasn't going to lie; it wasn't my style. It also wasn't my style to get re-involved with a woman if I had no interest in developing it any further. Trinity had been fun during the time we had been involved, but I wasn't interested in anything more with her. I looked to my brothers, each of them staring back at me.

"What the hell, Chase. You've been with all these women in here and you still have the balls to come in here and flirt that way? Do you have a death wish?" Hunter asked.

"Hey, each one of these ladies were and are well aware that I don't want a relationship. I'm upfront about it with them. I'm also upfront and honest in regards to when it ends, it ends. Trinity is just lonely, and besides, no one picked on you when you had your cock in everything that moved in this town."

"First, I didn't have my cock in everything in this town..."

Carter let out a loud laugh. "Oh please, give it a break, would you." He grabbed his scotch and took a drink. "You had your fair share of this town too."

Hunter flipped Carter the finger as we all laughed, then they both shook their heads and took a drink. Bryce looked at me with a shit-eating grin. "It's all right, guys. One of these days, he'll turn around, meet a woman, and his world will spin upside down. You know how it is."

"Yep, and the Chase Malone we all know and love will forever be changed by one pussy." Hunter let out a laugh loud enough to call attention to our table.

"Fuck you all! I'm not like you guys. No way am I settling down. I'm having way too much fun." I grinned.

"Yep, that sounds familiar. I think I said those exact same words right before I meant Autumn," Hunter murmured. "I also believe I said them right to the both of you."

"But then you meet someone, fall in love, and none of these girls will even enter your mind," Carter chimed in, setting his glass down.

"What the hell would you know about it? You married pretty much the first women you were ever serious about," Bryce smugly replied.

I shook my head, while Carter and Bryce continued to banter back and forth. I opened the menu and looked it over, even though I already knew what I was going to order: two pounds of hot wings—the same thing I ordered every single time we came here. "You fucks don't know what you are missing," I barked out as the three of them were now involved in one of our usual bickering matches.

"Same could be said for you, you know," Carter bit out, seemingly agitated with me.

Trinity approached our table and was halfway through taking our orders when my phone rang. I glanced down and saw Sophie's number sitting on the screen. "And for you, Chase?" she asked, pulling my attention away.

"A pound of hot wings please, Trin," I murmured as my attention quickly focused back on Sophie's number.

"Only a pound?" Carter asked, dumbfounded. "Normally, you're good for at least two."

"Yeah, watching my waistline." I ran my hand over my eight-pack and glanced once again at my phone that was still ringing. "Excuse me, guys, I have to take this," I said, ignoring the murmurs from my brothers. I got up from my seat and headed out the front door.

"Hello," I said as I pushed the door to Ducky's open and stepped outside into the parking lot, avoiding the group of people heading inside.

"Chase. Sorry to bother you. I know you're probably with your brothers, but my day got kind of crazy after I had called you this morning."

"Hey, yeah it's our usual night out, but it's no bother, Sophie. Sorry I wasn't able to talk earlier. I was in court. I'm glad you called me back. You seemed off in your message. What's up? What's going on?"

Sophie was quiet for a few moments before she cleared her throat. "Do you think you could meet me for dinner tomorrow night? I have something I want to run by you?"

"Is everything okay? It's nothing serious is it?" I could tell from the slight tremor in her voice that whatever she wanted to speak to me about, it was important.

"No, it's nothing bad. I just want to talk to you about something," she assured me.

"Sure, just name the time and place and I will be there." I opened my calendar on my phone to check and make sure I was free.

"The Manor House, tomorrow night at, say, seven."

The Manor House was one of Kings Cove's higher-end steak houses, which made me wonder if everything was indeed okay. "Are you sure everything is okay?" I questioned, wanting to make sure before I got off the phone with her.

"Yeah, I promise you everything is okay. We will talk tomorrow night. I have to run and finish up a meeting with one of my clients. I'll see you tomorrow at seven."

I could still hear the shake in her voice, but before I had the chance to ask her in a different way if everything was okay, the phone had gone dead. I looked down at my cell phone, wondering what could possibly be so important that she just couldn't tell me over the phone, but a few seconds later, I had shrugged it off and headed back inside. I was quiet as I walked back to our table. Once there, I slid into the booth, checked my watch again, and pocketed my cell phone.

"Was that your hot date for tonight?" Hunter questioned, nodding towards my phone.

"Something like that," I answered, still rather distracted and bothered. "It was Sophie. She wants to meet for dinner tomorrow night. She says she has something she wants to talk to me about. I can't recall a time that she didn't just come out and tell me what was up."

"Oh, *the Sophie*?" Bryce asked.

"Not the unattainable Sophie?" Carter joined in, smirking at Hunter.

I rolled my eyes and took another pull on my beer, doing my best to ignore his comment, and glanced at Hunter who sat there smirking at me. My brothers had always bugged me about Sophie, especially when we had been younger and she had turned me down. Although, unlike those times, this time I didn't laugh or answer any of their questions. When Hunter noticed, he looked at them both and cleared his throat just like our father used to when he wanted us to stop bugging one another.

"What time are you supposed to be meeting her?" he questioned.

"Tomorrow night at seven at The Manor House."

"The Manor House?"

"That is what she said."

"Must be something special. That place isn't cheap." Carter said, "I took Hope there not too long ago. Three hundred and fifty dollars later..."

"Yeah, Autumn's been bugging me to take her there since Hope told her about it. My wallet isn't looking forward to that bill." Hunter and Carter both laughed.

"Well, if you care about me, tell Autumn and Hope not to mention it to Mia." All three of my brothers laughed.

My phone vibrated in my pocket as Carter and Hunter went on discussing dinner prices. I looked down at my phone to see a message from Sophie and glanced at my watch. I feverishly typed out a response to her. I put my phone down and immediately it vibrated, causing me to pick it up again.

"What is it now?" Bryce questioned, as I continued to type out my third response.

"Six-thirty. She wants to meet me a half hour earlier. Something has got to be wrong."

"What the hell is the rush? I mean, she's kept you waiting all these years." Bryce laughed, looking over to Carter and Hunter.

"Man, she hasn't kept me waiting. We are friends. It is possible for me to be friends with a woman," I bit out.

"Sure..." Hunter said before all three of my brothers burst into laughter.

Shortly after I had sent my last text to Sophie, our dinner

was dropped onto the table. My mind was so distracted I could barely eat, which was just another thing that my brothers decided to bug me about. I had never been so happy to have my favorite night of the week end.

I drove home in silence, had a hot shower, and crawled into bed, turning the TV on. I was surprised when my phone vibrated and Sophie's name popped up on my screen. As I read her message asking me to meet her yet another half an hour earlier than previously agreed upon, I knew that whatever it was she wanted to talk to me about was important. However, when I asked her once again, she wouldn't even hint at what the issue was.

I shut the light off, shut my phone off, and rolled onto my side and fought to fall asleep.

Chapter Three

SOPHIE

"I Will Wait" by Mumford and Sons played in my ear as I ran up the last flight of stairs back to my condo. I had completed my nine-mile run in record time today. Out of breath, I leaned against the wall and fumbled with my key, finally inserted it into the lock, and opened the door to my place. I walked in, kicked off my sneakers, removed my headband from my hair, and grabbed a bottle of water from the fridge. I pulled the earbuds from my ears and dropped my iPod onto the table before I made my way down the hall to the washroom. I turned on the shower, making sure the water was the right temperature before I pealed myself out of my workout gear. I'd spent the morning working, and after dealing with a rather testy client, going over his corporate year end, I had decided that I need to get into the gym and work off my stress.

The client wasn't the only reason I needed to work off some steam. Dinner with Chase tonight was the other reason.

I stepped into the shower and let the hot water run over my body. As the water beat down on my aching muscles, I tried my best to clear my mind and relax. I dropped two drops of lavender essential oil onto the floor of the shower and took in a deep breath. By the time the water had run cold, I hoped out of the shower and stood in front of the mirror wrapped in a towel. All the hard work of trying to quiet my mind and find my calm had been useless; my mind was more active now than it had been before I had gotten into the shower.

I glanced at my reflection and let out a deep sigh. My mind was busy going over everything that I wanted to talk to Chase about. I had spent the better part of the past week trying to figure out what would be the best way to pitch my idea to him, and after the list of ideas I had made, I still had nothing. I must have gone over fifty or sixty ways today alone on how to even begin the conversation with him tonight before I began to get frustrated.

"Accountants don't pitch people, Sophie," I said aloud to my reflection. The more I thought about it, the more I was beginning to wonder if I wasn't about to make some colossal mistake.

Frustrated with myself, I left the bathroom, walked across the plush carpet in my bedroom, and began sifting through my closet. I needed something conservative yet sexy to wear tonight. I laughed to myself as I started going through my dresses. This is not a date, I thought to myself as I continued going through the dresses that hung in the back of my closet. I was growing frustrated. Accountants *did* have sexy outfits; mine just seemed to be conservative or boring.

I let out a sigh, flipping to the next dress. "Whoa, way too sexy, too sexy, way too conservative, funeral, funeral," I mumbled as I flipped through the dresses that hung in my closet. "Finally...this is perfect!"

I squealed as I pulled out my favorite black cocktail dress and placed it on the bed. I stood back and looked it over. I had only purchased it because it had reminded me of the dress Julia Roberts wore in *Pretty Woman*. I seriously couldn't even remember if I had worn it, but it was perfect for tonight, and I smiled to myself, wandered over to my dresser, and pulled out my only matching black bra and pantie set.

"May as well know I am wearing something sexy underneath..." I mumbled as I slipped into them and then went back to the bathroom and pulled out my makeup bag.

I sat down and brushed my hair, quickly sweeping it up into a clip on my head and looked at my reflection in the mirror.

"You better be prepared. He is a lawyer, after all," I murmured to myself. "You can't just go in there on a whim. Chase thinks twelve steps ahead of everyone and on everything."

How true that statement was. He would have every single argument against why this was a bad idea, if I knew him, which I did, and he would have them ready within sixty seconds of me spilling the beans. That reason alone was why I needed to have a solid pitch ready and have every answer to every reason why he was going to come up with as to why this was a bad idea.

I looked at myself in the mirror, blew out a breath, and smoothed moisturizer into my skin, then I grabbed the bottle of foundation. "Plus, he specializes in contract law. It's going to be a nightmare, if you aren't prepared," I murmured.

I pumped out a squirt of foundation into the palm of my shaky hand and quickly smoothed that onto my skin, then I reached for my powder compact. Carefully, I smoothed out my foundation, making sure there were no bare spots, and reached for my eyeshadow. My stomach rolled in anticipation of our date, and my hands shook.

This whole meeting in public had been my bright idea. I could have just as easily invited him over for coffee and spoken to him in private about all of this, but no, I was the one who wanted to do this over dinner. I was the one who wanted to do it over dinner in a crowded restaurant. I had never even contemplated what would happen if he flat out refused on the spot, got up and walked out of the restaurant leaving me looking foolish sitting there all alone. How humiliating that would be, I thought. Within seconds of that realization, my stomach rolled. I was so nervous, I seriously wondered if I would even be able to eat anything. Another reason why a public meeting was probably not such a bright idea. I quickly lined my eyes with eyeliner and grabbed my mascara.

"What do I have to offer him?" I wondered out loud. "Nothing about my job is even remotely sexy. I'm a freaking accountant for goodness sakes. I guess I could help him from having to pay too much in tax, and I could definitely keep him out of jail for anything tax related." I looked at my reflection in the mirror, nervously smiled, and then dropped my head in my hands thinking how pathetic I sounded, even to myself.

Perhaps a drink, I thought. Maybe that would make it easier and take the edge off. I got up from my vanity and wandered into the kitchen. I pulled open my liquor cabinet and pulled out the bottle of gin, dropped two ice cubes into my glass, and poured myself a gin and soda. I took a sip of the cool liquid and went back to my vanity and began drying my hair.

Where would we meet, I thought to myself as I continued to dry my hair. *I guess we could meet here, or perhaps somewhere between our condos would be better.* Perhaps I could pay for a hotel. No, there was no way Chase would meet at a hotel. He was too well-known around town. Okay, so here. He'd have to come here. I didn't even know why I was so concerned about where we would meet. It wasn't as if we had to hide from anyone.

I ran my fingers through my hair, and as soon as it was dry, I shut the switch off on my hairdryer. I ran my brush through it, styling my strands with my fingers, and once I was satisfied, I grabbed the hairspray. As I stood in front of the mirror, looking myself over, I couldn't stop ringing my hands. My stomach still felt uneasy, and the anxiety was building in my chest, making it harder to breathe. I took another sip of gin and soda, praying that the alcohol would kick in and calm some of this anxiety I was feeling. I slipped my dress on and checked the time.

I still had forty-five minutes. I grabbed my glass and went out to the living room, sitting down on the couch. I grabbed my phone and called the restaurant to confirm the reservation time. I felt like I was going crazy. I had just booked the reservation not even twenty-four hours ago, and here I was, paranoid that perhaps I had made it for the wrong date, or the wrong time, or perhaps they didn't mark it down in their book.

I hung up the phone and glanced at my watch. I could get going but didn't really want to arrive too early. I didn't want to seem too eager. I'd rather walk into the restaurant late than be there before him.

I sat back, grabbed my drink and my notepad and pen, took a sip of my drink, and tried my best to come up with some sort of proposal.

Chapter Four

CHASE

The sun was directly in my eyes, making it hard to concentrate on the cars in front of me. Twice I had almost rear-ended the car in front of me. I tapped my thumb on the steering wheel to the beat of the music that was blaring through my speakers. I pulled into the parking lot and found a spot, quickly cutting the engine.

I pocketed my keys as I walked up the steps to the doors of the The Manor House and entered in behind the couple in front of me. While I stood waiting to speak with the hostess, I still couldn't help but wonder what the hell Sophie needed. I had not been able to figure out what could be so important that she needed to tell me in person. The urgency in her voice had me worried that something was wrong. Was she sick? Was she in legal trouble? It had driven me crazy most of last night and well into this morning, until I had no choice but to head to the gym and blow off some steam.

"Can I help you?" the young hostess behind the counter asked.

"Reservations for two. Should be under Sophie Lancaster." I watched as she ran her finger down the list of names in front of her, finally stopping and crossing our name off.

"Your table isn't quite ready yet, sir. If you would like, you can have a seat in the bar area, and I'll come and get you once it's ready. Should only be about ten to fifteen minutes."

"Sounds good, thank you." I made my way towards the bar, sitting in the first empty seat I found. I ordered myself a crown and cola and Sophie a gin and soda. The bartender set the drinks down in front of me, and I was passing him a twenty when I felt a hand on my shoulder. I turned to see Sophie standing behind me.

I couldn't help but allow my eyes to run over her. I had never seen her in the dress that she wore, but it hugged her curves perfectly. She smiled at me, and I cleared my throat and stood up. "Here, take a seat," I said, offering her my bar chair.

"Thank you."

"This is for you. Your favorite: gin and soda," I said, moving the glass in front of her and leaning in to kiss her cheek.

Sophie looked up at me, quickly kissed my cheek, and smiled. "You remembered!"

"How could I ever forget? It was the only drink that didn't end up making you hang your head out of my car window every weekend when we were in college," I said, winking at her as we both laughed. Even though we still got out with our college friends once a month, Sophie never drank gin and sodas when we were out anymore and hadn't in years. It had strictly been a college thing.

"That is sadly very true. Although I don't think it's a secret that I still can't hold my liquor very well." She smiled and looked up at me. As soon as I met her eyes, we both took a sip of our drinks. I placed my glass back down on the bar and looked back down to see the smile she had worn was now replaced with a look of nervousness. She was fidgeting with the strap of her clutch that sat neatly tucked in her lap.

"What's up, Soph?" I questioned, downing the rest of my crown and cola and signaling the bartender for another.

"Nothing, why?" she let out a nervous laugh.

"Look at you. You're a nervous mess. You never fidget, and you've just about broken the strap on your clutch."

"I'll be right back. I need to use the ladies' room." Before I could say anything, she had jumped up and dashed through the crowd over to the washrooms. Minutes passed, and I was beginning to get worried.

I glanced down at my watch to try and determine how long she had been gone when the hostess came to tell me that our table was ready. I was about to ask her to hold the table when Sophie finally reappeared. Something was up. She didn't have her usual glow. The look on her face reminded me of the time we had been hanging at her parents' house and we had accidentally broken her mother's antique lamp. It had been a present from her father. I smiled inwardly to myself as I remembered her standing with her hands behind her back trying to tell her parents what had happened.

"Our table is ready," I said as she got closer.

"Awesome. Just awesome," she mumbled. I frowned as I watched as she picked up her glass and waved for me to go first, but I refused and instead waved my hand, signaling for her to go first. Once she was in front of me, I placed my hand on the small of her back and together we walked to the table.

I was hoping to find out immediately what was going on, but once we were seated and the hostess had left, Sophie had conveniently buried her face in her menu. I frowned, and even though it was killing me, I didn't say anything while we looked over the menu. We had both settled on our choices by the time the waitress had returned to drop a fresh basket of bread onto the center of our table. We ordered quickly, and I reached in and cut a piece of bread for Sophie, passing it to her. She barely made eye contact with me as she reached over and took it from my hand. Her odd behavior was seriously beginning to get to me.

I sat forward, crossed my arms in front of me, and leaned on the table. "The suspense is killing me here, Soph. What was it you needed to talk to me about?" I asked, taking a sip of my Crown and Coke, while she buttered her bread and took a bite.

She looked around the room, ignoring me. I let out a breath and started slicing the loaf of bread again. "You know I adore you, right?" her soft voice questioned.

I looked up at her, pausing from cutting the loaf of bread. "Yes, of course, and I you." I winked, trying to lighten the mood, but she completely ignored me.

"And you know I'm not getting any younger, right?"

I frowned. "Neither am I."

"And historically you've always come through for me."

She swallowed hard, setting her bread down on the side plate. "No matter what."

"Okay, let's cut to the goods here, Soph. What's going on? Are you okay? Are you sick? In legal trouble?" The way she was carrying on, I feared she had some sort of terminal illness.

I proceeded to cut more slices off the loaf of bread.

"Well, it's just I want a baby, and I want you to be the father," she blurted out.

My head shot up. I looked at Sophie, who sat across from me still chewing on her bread as if she had just told me who won the hockey game on Friday night. I swallowed hard, not sure I believed what I had just heard.

"Did you hear me?" she asked, waving her hand in front of my face.

"You—you aren't getting any younger, and you...you want my swimmers?" That was all I could get out before I felt a searing hot pain in the hand that was holding onto the loaf of bread. I glanced down and saw blood starting to soak into the white napkin I was using to hold onto the bread with.

"Shit," I mumbled, pulling my hand towards me.

"Oh my God, Chase." Sophie jumped up and grabbed her napkin and my hand and quickly pressed the napkin against the cut, gently but firmly squeezing. She held it for a couple of seconds, and then pulled the napkin away to inspect the cut. I sat there not knowing what to say or do, completely shocked at what she had just blurted out. "It's okay. I don't think you need stitches or anything. Just hold the napkin tight, and the bleeding should stop," she said, continuing to examine my hand.

"You want my swimmers?" I mumbled, completely forgetting about the cut on my hand.

As the waitress approached our table, Sophie asked for a band-aid, and I raised my glass, signaling for another Crown and Coke. Hell, at this point, they could just bring me the entire bottle of Crown. My appetite had fled after what Sophie had asked, but I sure as hell needed to get loaded.

I couldn't believe my ears. Sophie, the girl who had told me no all those years ago, now wanted...a baby...my baby. I felt like I was going to faint. I swallowed hard. "Why me?"

"Well, honestly, I'm thirty, and there is absolutely no one on the horizon for even a date, never mind a relationship that would lead to a baby anytime soon. Second, I've known you all my life. I'm comfortable with you. You have a good work ethic, you're smart, not to mention attractive. You are caring, kind, and considerate, and I seriously can't think of a better father for my child." She let out a deep breath and brought her glass to her lips.

"I see."

The waitress appeared carrying our food and set our meals down in front of us. The craving I'd had all day for bacon-wrapped filet mignon smothered in onions and mushrooms was now long gone. I stared down at the perfectly cooked steak, my mind spinning in circles, while Sophie was busy cutting a piece of steak into bite-sized pieces. She popped a piece into her mouth, the nervous look now gone as she chewed. I didn't know what to say. I felt as if I were in the middle of a very bad dream.

I had no idea how long I had sat there watching her eat, but the next thing I knew, she had cleared her plate while mine was still full and getting cold.

"Are you okay? Aren't you going to eat?" she asked, looking a bit worried.

I picked up my glass of Crown and Cola and took a large drink. I shook my head and set the glass back down. "I'm not really all that hungry," I mumbled.

She nodded and pulled the napkin from her lap, moved her plate to the side, and placed her arms on the table. "Well, now that I have laid everything out, do you have an answer for me?" Her eyes filled with hope.

I looked at her. She was expecting an answer right now? It was as if she had asked me to pick something up from the store for her, not give her a baby. I let out a breath, looking down at my plate, and then at my napkin-swaddled hand.

"I'll have to think about it, Sophie. This is a big decision, and one I am not going to take lightly."

The excitement in her eyes had disappeared and was now replaced with disappointment, and I certainly didn't like seeing it; however, there was no way I could just commit to something like this.

"Sir, was there something wrong with your meal?" our waitress asked as she picked up Sophie's plate.

I shook my head, afraid to speak.

"Would you like that plate boxed up?" the waitress asked as she dropped our bill on the table.

I nodded. As soon as she had cleared our plates away, I reached for the check folder, but Sophie grabbed it first. "I'll get this," she said and opened the folder.

"No, give it to me please," I insisted, holding my hand out, but she shook her head and slid her credit card into the slot and set it beside her at the edge of the table. She kept her head down, ignoring me, and sifted through her purse.

We sat in silence, Sophie going through her purse, and me thinking about how I could have done things differently. It seemed to take forever, but finally the bill had been paid, and I now sat with my takeover package in front of me. Sophie quickly put her credit card back into her wallet and stood. "When can I expect to hear from you?" she questioned.

I thought for a second. I didn't want to jeopardize our friendship, so I answered with the first thing that came to my mind. "Next week?"

She leaned in and kissed me on the cheek, smiled shyly at me, and turned and walked away. I sat back down at the table, trying to grasp what the hell had just happened. I was at a loss for words and really wasn't sure I should get behind the wheel.

I pulled my phone from my pocket and dialed Hunter's number. It was almost eight. I knew he was probably putting the kids to bed, but I needed my brother. The phone rang five times before an out-of-breath Hunter answered. "Hey, man, what's going on?"

"Hey, listen, can you come pick me up?"

"Ah, why? Is everything okay?"

"I'll explain when you get here."

"Where is here?"

"The Manor House," I choked out and hung up the phone before he could refuse.

Chapter Five

Sophie

I left the restaurant and walked across the parking lot, feeling completely and utterly defeated. The whole night had been an utter disaster. Not only did I make a complete ass of myself, but I also injured my best friend. That cut looked pretty bad. I crawled into the driver's seat of my car, threw my purse on the floor, and started the engine. I sat there for a few moments trying to center myself and finally pulled out of the spot.

I blew out a breath as I pulled up to a stoplight. The feeling of humiliation continued to sink in. There was no coming back from this now. Why hadn't I really thought through the entire conversation? I slammed my hand down on the steering wheel, annoyed with myself. I really didn't know what I was expecting. Had I expected him to be like he had always been: eager to help me with whatever dilemma I had been facing? Perhaps that was just it. Perhaps I had expected him to turn around and instantly agree. Instead, he had cut his hand, hadn't eaten dinner, and barely said two words to me the entire time we had been at the restaurant. He also had drank one too many Crown and Cokes, and I just left him there to fend for himself.

I should have turned around and went back to get him, make sure he got home safe, but instead I turned the radio on and proceeded through the green light, the guilt of the night sinking farther into me. What if I had just ruined our lifetime friendship? My stomach sank at the thought of no longer having Chase around. The thought of not having him in my life nearly made me sick.

A blaring horn pulled me from the thought, and I immediately noticed I was driving into the oncoming lane. I quickly righted my vehicle and drove a ways down the road to my apartment.

I locked the door behind me, turning on lights as I entered my condo. I kicked off my shoes, dropped my purse on the floor, and slipped out of my coat, hanging it in the small closet. My mind was still racing a mile a minute over how I could have done things so differently.

I grabbed the remote from the table and turned the TV on, drowning out the quiet of my apartment, and wandered down the hall to my bedroom. I looked at myself in the full-length mirror, my makeup slightly smudged now from the few tears that I hadn't even realized had fallen on my way home. I turned away from my reflection and unzipped my dress, letting it fall to a pile in the middle of the room. I slipped out of my bra and panties and put on my sweats that were lying on the bottom of my bed. I needed to relax. I quickly washed my face, put my hair up in a messy bun, and shut the light off.

Time had passed once I had found something on TV, and I now lay on the couch trying to get lost in an episode of *Friends*; however, the only thing on my mind was how I had foolishly proposed my bright idea to Chase. Over and over, the words I had so casually dropped ran through my mind like a bad nightmare. Perhaps I should have been more prepared than I was. Perhaps I should have written them all down to present to him in a more business-like way. He may have been more receptive if I'd had everything in a nice presentation folder, like one of his legal briefs he had shown me numerous times. Nevertheless, the damage was done, and it was out in the open now, and all I could do was wait. Wait for his answer, either yes or no, or perhaps he would say "Get away from me, Sophie, and don't bother coming around again." Honestly, I wasn't even sure what it was I expected him to say. Was I really expecting him to drop everything and say yes? Or was the answer he gave me more the one I was expecting?

I reached for the phone and relaxed back against the pillow behind me and debated calling Chase and apologizing. I dropped my head back against the pillow and pinched the bridge of my nose, trying to gather up the courage to dial Chase's number. Instead, I let out a sigh and called Jenna. I needed to talk to her, but the phone just rang and rang. I was just about to give up when I heard her answer completely out of breath.

"It's about time you called me!" Jenna blurted into the phone. "You said you would call by seven."

"Yeah, sorry, I lost track of time. What were you doing?

You're all out of breath. Oh my God, I didn't...I didn't interrupt anything, did I?" I questioned, my face heating.

Jenna broke out in laughter. "Good Lord, girl, Matt isn't even home from the office yet. Besides, if you think I would answer the phone in the middle of that, you are crazier than I originally thought. If you must know, I was running on the treadmill. Get your head out of the gutter. I'm trying to be good this month. I fell off the wagon last month going to Aroma Mocha almost every weekend, and my waistline is showing it."

"Girl you are crazy. You're perfect!" I glanced at my watch. "Besides, it's almost ten. You should be in your sweats relaxing."

"Ha, tell that to my jeans, and I'm in my sweats. Also, running is a form of relaxation I guess." She giggled. "So what took you so long to call me? You could have saved me from all this torture tonight, and we could have gone and gotten ice cream."

I let out a small laugh. "I had somewhere I needed to be after work."

"You had somewhere you needed to be? Where? You basically live at the office, and when you aren't there you are at home."

"Well, I had something to do after work. I just got home about a half an hour ago."

"You had something to do after work. Why are you being so vague? You tell me everything. So, do you care to share with your good ol' friend? Stop making me have to try and guess."

I giggled. This was just like Jenna; she always had to know where I was. "I had dinner plans."

"Oooh, anyone I know?"

I let out a deep breath. "If you must know, I had dinner with Chase." We both grew quiet until I cleared my throat. "I did it." I couldn't hold back any longer.

"You did what?" she asked curiously.

After that afternoon at the coffee shop, and after my breakup with Roger, we had talked at great lengths about me asking one of our close friends to be the father of my child. I had been adamant at first, but she had been totally supportive and kept telling me to just go for it.

"I asked Chase to be the father of my child."

I heard a gurgle and a cough on the other end of the phone as Jenna choked on whatever it was she was drinking. "You did what?"

"You heard me."

"Well, what did he say?"

I let out a little laugh, remembering his face as I had asked him. "Well, it didn't go as smoothly as I thought it would. First, he sliced his hand open."

"What? No, I mean, what did he say to your question?"

"He said he would think about it."

"Oh my! And you told him everything, right?"

I let out a sigh. Perhaps if had I told him everything, his answer might have been different. "Well, if he hadn't been bleeding all over the place I might have, but no, I didn't. Do you think I should have told him everything?"

Jenna started to laugh. "Sophie, it may have helped your case if you had. Don't you think?"

"Perhaps. I don't know, maybe this really is a bad idea."

"Why do you say that?"

I laughed. "If you had seen his face, you'd be thinking

the same thing. I can only imagine what the other guys would have said if I had asked one of them."

"Girl, you are crazy."

"No, I'm serious. I also keep thinking that if I had just gone in there with everything written down and in a true proposal style, he may have looked at the entire situation differently. Maybe more like a business deal."

"Perhaps if you had delivered all the goods, then he might have jumped at the chance. Listen, I've got to go. Matt just walked through the door. Call me later and we will talk, okay?"

"All right, night."

"Seriously, Soph, talk to him, give him all the goods."

"Good night, Jenna!"

I hung up the phone and turned the TV off. Shutting the lights off, I grabbed my cell phone and headed to the bedroom. I crawled into bed and lay facing the floor-to-ceiling window, looking at the lights of the city like I did every night. My mind was still running over everything that had happened tonight. Jenna was right. If I had given him all the details up front, perhaps his answer might have been yes. However, I was glad I had held back because he might have cut his hand off too. I giggled at the thought. I grabbed my cell phone from the side table and quickly opened a text message to Chase.

I typed feverishly at first, then decided to delete everything and began again. I couldn't just come out and say it like I was planning to. I had no clue where he was. He could have been behind the wheel of his car, God forbid. Besides, I didn't want him to get the information through a text either.

ME: Would you be able to meet me tomorrow for lunch.

At the risk of sounding like those infomercials we used to watch as kids...but wait! There's more...but wait, there is more, and I want another chance to discuss this with you.

I blew out a breath and placed my cell phone on the table, closed my eyes, and tried to fall into a deep sleep.

Chapter Six

Chase

I sat on the hood of my car and looked up at the dark sky in utter shock. I still couldn't believe what had transpired tonight. My best friend had asked me to be the father of her child. I shook my head and ran my hand through my hair. I glanced down to the bag of cold food that sat beside me, my stomach letting out a loud grumble. I wasn't sure if I was hungry or if I was going to be sick.

I let out a huff and pulled my phone from my pocket. I checked the last text I had received from Hunter and saw it was over an hour ago. I was just about to message him to find out where he was when a car I recognized pulled into the parking lot and in beside mine. I hopped off the hood of my car, grabbed the bag of food, and pulled the passenger door open on Hunter's car.

"It's about damn time!" I said, crawling into the front seat and pulling my seatbelt across my body.

"Yeah, well, Autumn needed help getting the kids to bed. It was bath night. It's not like I can expect her to deal with them all on her own. What the hell happened to your hand?" Hunter questioned, staring down at my napkin-wrapped hand. "And what's wrong with your car?" he asked and nodded towards my vehicle.

"Nothing."

"You called me out here for nothing? What the hell you do to your hand?"

"Not for nothing. I had a little too much to drink, and this..." I said, raising my hand. "I cut myself while slicing a loaf of bread." I shrugged.

"Jesus," he muttered under his breath as he watched me place my leftovers bag between us.

"What?" I questioned.

"Leftovers? From the sounds of things, the portions are small there. Carter said he was still hungry when he left, and you come out with leftovers? Was it at least a good meal?"

I shrugged. "Honestly, I have no idea!"

"What do you mean you have no idea? You were just there for dinner."

"If you must know, the bag contains my meal. I couldn't eat. I totally lost my appetite after I cut my hand. Here, if you want you can take it home and share it with Autumn. She'd probably enjoy it," I said holding the bag out to him. I glanced over at my car and locked my doors with my remote fob.

I didn't even need to look at my brother because I could

feel him staring at me as if I had lost my mind. "Are you feeling all right? You're acting strange."

"Can we just go?" Hunter continued watching me for a second, not saying anything. "Please?"

Hunter didn't argue. Instead, he revved the engine and put the car into reverse and sped out of the parking lot. We had driven about two blocks and were stopped at a stoplight. He was tapping his thumb on the steering wheel and watching a lady walk across the street when he cleared his throat. "Care to talk about it?" he asked once the light turned green and he started driving through the intersection.

I threw my head back against the headrest, and with my eyes closed I mumbled, "Sophie wants to borrow my sperm." I blew out a breath and tried to calm myself down, but the car came to an abrupt stop, and a horn blared out from behind us. "Hunter, what the hell!"

"Sorry about that, but did I hear you right?"

"Yeah, you heard me. Sophie, she wants a baby, and she asked me to father the child." I still couldn't get her voice out of my mind—or the look on her face as she had asked me. The beginning of the night she had been so distraught, but once she asked me, she had appeared to be confident yet completely hopeful that I would do it.

"So like you'd whack off in a cup and pass it over to her?"

"I guess so. I haven't a clue. I cut my hand, and, well, then I started drinking, and the rest of the night went to shit. I could barely even remember my name let alone have any type of real conversation on the matter."

Hunter let out a loud laugh. "That's fucking awesome. So what did you tell her?"

. . .

I sat there trying to remember exactly what I had said. All I could remember was the look on her face, the look that I had let her down. There had never been another time in my life that I had remembered ever seeing her face look like that when it came to me. It haunted me. I cleared my throat. "I didn't say anything. I couldn't. I was so shocked that, no matter how much time had passed, I could barely put two words together. Once I gathered myself together enough, I told her I'd think about it. She left looking so defeated."

"Well, you could always negotiate. I mean, you do practice contract law. It's a sterile transaction, right? So slap a contract together, have her sign, and be done with it. I mean, seriously, this is simple. You're making it more difficult than it needs to be. Look at it logically."

"Can you pull over?" I mumbled, undoing my seatbelt, and reaching for the door handle.

"Pull over? What the hell for?"

I couldn't wait. Instead, I rolled down the window and stuck my head out, throwing up right down the side of Hunter's new BMW. My stomach was still swirling as I pulled my head back in the car and put the window up. "Sorry about that. You might want to drive through that car wash over there," I said, pointing to the one across the street. "I'll pay."

"Damn right you'll pay. Jesus, Chase, this is a brand new car."

"Sorry, man."

Hunter began laughing. "It reminds me of when we were younger."

Hunter pulled into the car wash, and we sat in utter silence as we drove through. I sat facing straight ahead, focusing on the movement of the brushes as the whole night played out again in my mind. "Perhaps you should eat something?" Hunter said, pulling back out onto the street and continuing to make his way towards my condo.

"I'm really not hungry."

"All right, so, what did she say exactly? I need all the details."

My phone vibrated in my pocket. I let out a breath, pulling my phone out and looking at the screen.

"Fuck me," I murmured, shoving my phone back in my pocket.

"What?" Hunter asked, pulling into the parking lot of my condo and putting the car into park.

"That was Sophie."

"And?"

"She wants to have lunch with me tomorrow. She says there is more, and she wants to discuss it with me in person, and I think I'm gonna be sick again," I said, opening the car door and crawling out just in time to toss my cookies on the edge of the parking lot.

Hunter chuckled and rolled down the car's window. "Here, don't forget your food," he said, holding up the bag.

"Keep it. Thanks for picking me up." I held my hand over my stomach and waved. Once he pulled from the parking lot, I walked to the main entrance, punched in the security code, and headed up to my condo.

Chapter Seven

I'd woken early after a rather restless night of sleep. I had tossed and turned, constantly checking to see if Chase had answered my text – he hadn't. I'd rolled out of bed before my alarm with a bad headache, a bad case of bed head, and practically everything in my body aching. I took a hot shower, popped two pain pills, and got ready for work, leaving the condo with bagel and coffee in hand.

I took my usual route to my office and decided to make a pit stop down by the waterfront. I parked the car, grabbed my coffee, and took a walk down the pier. I needed to try and forget what had happened last night before I got into the office. I would never be able to get through my day, if my mind wasn't clear.

I sat down on a bench, sipped my coffee, and watched the boats leaving the harbor. It was a beautiful day, the sun was shining, the birds chirping, and I took in a deep breath of fresh morning air. While I sipped on my coffee, I watched couples walk along the water's edge, holding hands. I smiled to myself, and once my cup was empty, I got up and made my way back to my car, glancing at my watch.

I pushed the heavy door open and walked into the lobby of my office. I was surprised to see the waiting room as full as it was. I had figured it would still be quiet at this time, and that was when I saw one of my clients was sitting waiting for me. I glanced at my watch as I made my way to my office, and then up to the clock on the wall, and realized my watch had stopped. The place was packed because *I* was the one who was running late. Almost forty minutes late, to be exact. Certainly not the way I wanted to start my day.

I set up my computer in record time and pulled the client file and immediately called them in, apologizing profusely.

A lot of conversation and two hours later, I walked back into my office and picked up the client file that still remained on my desk. That made two appointments down, and even though the day started out rocky, I was feeling surprisingly good, and then I looked to the stack of files that sat on my to-be-done pile. A surge of stress ran through me, and I shuddered at the thought of all I still had left in front of me for today.

"Hey, girl. I'm on my way to refill my cup. Did you want a coffee?" I heard Carol ask as she stopped just inside of my door. She leaned against my door, looking over to the corner of my desk where my work sat. "Looks like you might need one, considering your workload today."

"That would be wonderful, and I have a feeling that I

will be taking half this stack home. I just spent an hour with Mr. Leeman and Mr. Sage. Oh, and did you know that Mr. Sage does not like it if you are late," I said, rolling my eyes.

"Ah, yes, Mr. Sage. Say no more, my dear. That alone calls for one *strong* cup of coffee that you should have had prior to the next appointment." We both laughed as she reached for my cup, and then carried on down the hall.

I walked around and sat back down in my chair and opened up the next file that sat on top of the pile. I was going over the notes from our last meeting when Carol set the cup of coffee on my desk. "Thank you! You're a saint," I said, letting out a breath and smiling up at her.

"No worries. Good luck with the rest of your day. I have a boardroom meeting I have to get to."

"Have fun with that."

"You betcha." Carol winked and disappeared from my office.

I glanced at the clock on my desk and went back to reading over the file. I was glad to see I had a few hours before my next meeting, which meant I had plenty of time to get prepared, I thought to myself. I took a sip of coffee and began reading over the client file in front of me.

A good twenty minutes had passed, and I had just gotten deep into file when my cell phone vibrated across my desk, causing me to jump. My heart sped up a little when I saw Chase's name on my screen. As I answered, my stomach did one of those excited but nervous little flips.

"Good morning." I did my best to keep my voice upbeat. I didn't want Chase to think I was nervous to talk with him, but the truth was, my heart was pounding out of my chest.

"Morning. I'm sorry to bother you at work, but I got

your message and was hoping that perhaps you still wanted to meet for lunch today."

I glanced down at my watch, and then to my schedule, noting I had time between eleven and one free. "Yep, how is eleven?" I questioned.

"Eleven works fine."

"Where did you want to meet?"

"How about The Manor House, and would you be able to do me a favor and pick me up on your way?" He chuckled.

I frowned. He'd had his car last night. I'd seen it. "Sure. Your car in the shop?"

Chase let out a breath. "No, it's still at the restaurant. Hunter came and picked me up last night. I was in a little bit of shock, not to mention I'd had too much to drink, and my best friend left me high and dry."

I let out a little giggle. "Yeah, I'm sorry about that. Guess I will see you in an hour or so."

"Sounds good. Oh, and, Soph, I'm looking forward to finishing our little talk today."

"Yes, of course. I'll see you soon." I hung up the phone and did my best to ignore the funny feeling in the pit of my stomach as I tried to dive back into the file in front of me. My stomach rolled in anticipation of talking to Chase, and I found it harder to concentrate the more I tried. After ten minutes, I grabbed my legal pad and jotted down some things I wanted to make sure I brought up to Chase. I wasn't about to blow another chance with him. I needed him to realize that I was serious about this.

I saw a few drops of rain on my windshield as I pulled up outside of Malone Law. Chase stood on the sidewalk and waved when he saw my car pull up. He looked just as tired and worn down as I felt. I waved as he approached my car, my stomach doing that anxious little flip again. To say I was nervous was an understatement. Since he had called, I had been absolutely useless at work, and even working on the list of things I wanted to mention to him had been of no help. I quickly tucked the legal pad between my seat and console so that he couldn't see it when he climbed in.

He opened the car door and climbed in, doing up his seat belt before he turned and looked at me. "Hey! How are you?" he mumbled, giving me a nervous smile.

"I'm okay. How are you?"

"Okay." I swallowed hard and pulled away from the curb and headed towards The Manor House. Chase was oddly quiet on the drive, looking out the window as we made our way the five city blocks to the restaurant. I pulled into the parking lot and right up beside Chase's car and cut the engine.

We walked side by side into the restaurant, neither of us saying anything. The tension between us was unbearable, and all I kept thinking to myself was that I was the one who had created this tension. Me and my silly ideas.

Within ten minutes, we were seated at the back of the restaurant, bread basket sitting between us on the table, while the waitress was waiting to take our drink orders.

"I'll have a soda water with lemon," I said, looking to Chase.

"Crown and Coke." He coughed into his hand.

"Um, how about just a coke? I don't want a repeat of last night." I giggled.

Chase rolled his eyes and dismissed the waitress. As soon

as she had walked away, he looked over to me. "I'm fine, you know. I'll be fine." He opened the menu in front of him.

I stuck my head into my menu and sat staring at the page, the names of the dishes eventually all blurring together. I was beginning to doubt if I could indeed go through with this whole thing again, after what had happened last night. I sat there trying hard to find something that I wanted to eat, and that was when my worst fear entered my mind. What if he said no? I really didn't know how I would react to that answer.

Chase slapped his menu shut, causing me to jump and draw my attention to him. He reached for the bread, but I quickly swatted his hand away. "Let me." I grabbed the knife from the table and took the bread, cutting it into pieces.

"How is your hand anyways?" I asked.

"It's okay," he said, looking down at his bandaged hand and reached for a piece of bread.

"I felt awful that you cut yourself."

Chase shrugged as he buttered his bread and took a bite.

"All right, so back to what we were talking of last night," I said, finally putting the knife down and grabbing a piece of bread for myself.

"Yes, about that. I have a few things that I want to say," he said, clearing his throat, but I put my hands up to stop him.

"Before you say anything, you should know I want to do this natural," I bit out as he buttered his second piece of bread, fearing he may stab himself with the butter knife.

"What? Childbirth? Of course, both Carter and Hunter have said that Heather and Hope have said they wouldn't have done it any other way, so I can totally understand that."

I shook my head and took a drink of my soda water before continuing. "Um, no, not childbirth. Well, no, yes childbirth, but making the baby. Thought perhaps we should start here first. I also don't want you to worry. I won't hold you accountable for anything."

Chase looked around the restaurant and then back to me. So far so good, I thought to myself. *He hasn't cut himself or passed out yet.*

"Okay. Go on." He swallowed hard.

"Okay, so this is what I was thinking. You'd spend the week at my place. Now if you stay in October, which is next week, I've counted everything out, and if everything goes according to my plan, then I will be good to work right through tax season before the baby comes. However, it has to be the first week of the month. One week earlier or later, and it will mess everything up."

Chase finished chewing and took a drink, placing his glass down on the table. "I see you've really thought this out."

I nodded. "I have. I'm very serious about this, and that also is exactly the right time. I've been tracking my cycle, and next week is the most optimal time for me to get pregnant."

Chase was just about to say something when our food was placed in front of us. His eyes met mine as the waitress announced each dish and finally walked away. We both dug into our plates and ate in silence. Once our plates were cleared and the bill was delivered to the table, Chase sat forward.

"Listen, Sophie, I'm still going to think about this. I will have a decision to you in a couple of days. Does that sound okay?"

I nodded. I felt confident that I had laid everything out on the table. Chase hadn't fainted or cut himself, and I felt satisfied and hopeful with his answer. I went to reach for the bill, but Chase grabbed it first. "You got last night. The least I can do is get lunch." He winked.

"All right, I've got to go," I said, glancing down at my watch. "I have a client in a half hour. I'll talk to you soon."

Chase stood as I stood, and unlike last night, this time he kissed me on the cheek before I walked away.

Chapter Eight

Chase

I had been trying to type out this damn email for the past hour and still had yet to get the tone of it correct. I hit delete, wiping the entire contents of my email, and slammed my fists on my desktop and began typing again. The sooner I could get this finished, the quicker I could get home and unwind, and unwinding was exactly what I needed. I was about three sentences into the email when I once again hit delete and began all over again.

"Hey, man, you all set?" Hunter appeared in my doorway, leaning against the doorjamb, shoving the last of what looked like a muffin into his mouth.

"Yep, all the loose ends are tied finally. I was just trying to get out one last email for the day, but I can't seem to get the wording correct."

Hunter pulled the chair out on the other side of my desk

and sat down across from me with a smug smile. "Things still bothering you, are they?" He grinned.

I nodded. That was an understatement. I'd barely slept in two days. "How are Autumn and the girls? Did she enjoy my dinner the other night?"

"She did, and everyone is good."

"Great! I really miss those angels. I should drop by and visit soon." I shut my laptop in frustration and placed it in the bottom drawer of my desk and looked to Hunter who was still smiling away. "I'll just write the damn email tomorrow morning," I said more out of frustration than anything else.

"What's up? Did you need something before I leave?"

"Just wondering how you made out with your dilemma? Bryce said you went to see her for lunch."

I was just about to answer when Carter and Bryce walked into my office and each took a seat on the couch. I paused. I wasn't sure if I wanted to share this entire situation with everyone. Hunter already knew, so it was a little different sharing it with him. However, I had to remember these were my brothers, and there wasn't much that any of us didn't share with one another. I swallowed hard, trying to decide if I should tell everyone or keep my mouth shut.

"What dilemma are you facing now?" Carter asked, squeezing the spot between his eyes.

"Perhaps he's been mesmerized by that pussy we were talking about two weeks ago." Bryce and Carter both chuckled.

I glanced at Bryce and Carter and back to Hunter who knew the truth. As Carter and Bryce sat there laughing, I was getting more and more irritated, and before I could stop them, the words just fell from my mouth without a care as to what they thought. "Sophie wants to borrow my sperm."

Bryce and Carter both looked at me as if I had spoken another language. "What?" Carter sat forward, resting his forearms on his knees, totally interested in what I had to say next.

"Sophie, she wants a baby and she asked me to um..."

"So like you'd whack off in a cup and pass it over to her. That sounds fucking exciting." Bryce laughed, elbowing Carter, who also began laughing.

I laughed more to myself. "No, not exactly. At first, I thought she was kidding, but now she has proposed seven days of no-strings-attached sex." I ran my hands through my hair.

"Fuck me. You may just be the luckiest bastard alive," Bryce commented. "Sophie is hot as fuck, a little uptight, but I bet once you get her going, she is kinky as fuck too," he said, raising his eyebrows.

"That's enough," I bit back, glaring at my brother. It wasn't that the thought hadn't crossed my mind. Actually, it had crossed my mind many times. My tone was more because he, too, was thinking that exact same thing, or perhaps had in the past.

"What did you tell her?" Hunter asked, trying to pull my attention away from Bryce.

"To be honest, I still haven't answered yet. I was once again so shocked, I didn't know what to say, so I told her I'd think about it."

Each one of my brothers looked at me as if I had lost my mind. "Whoa, hold on a second. A girl gives you permission to screw her, no strings, and you don't jump at the chance?"

Bryce questioned. "Are you feeling all right? I think you might be sick."

"Yes, I'm feeling fine," I said, getting up out of my chair and pacing across my office. "Oh, I know you don't believe this, but I do have a conscience. I do respect women, and I don't want to do anything that will jeopardize our friendship."

Bryce roared with laughter. "Jesus, that is the funniest thing I have heard all day."

Carter chuckled and stood up and walked towards the door. "I've got to get home to Hope and the kids. We're headed to the zoo tomorrow, and I promised them we'd go and stay overnight and make a weekend of it. Hunter, Bryce, I'll see you later. Chase, good luck." He chuckled again and walked out the door.

"See you Monday," Hunter said and turned back to face me. As soon as Carter was gone, Bryce came and sat in the empty chair on the other side of my desk.

"So, you have a conscience. Could have fooled us." Bryce laughed, bringing us all back to our conversation.

"Shut up. She's one of my best friends. What would you do?"

"Oh, so that makes it different than every other woman out there? And what would I do? I jump at the fucking chance."

"Yes, it does make a difference," I mumbled, ignoring his other comment.

"What are you afraid of, that she may not like your piggish ass afterward?" Bryce bit out. Bryce had stayed with me for a bit last year before he met Mia. He, of all of my brothers, knew exactly how I was.

I stopped pacing and looked over at Bryce. He had pretty much hit it on the head. What if, by doing this, we totally ruined the relationship we already had with each other? We basically spoke every day in one way or another, we hung out on weekends, vacationed with the same group of people in the summer, and I already knew that not having her in my life or her not speaking to me would probably kill me.

"That's exactly it." Bryce laughed when I didn't respond immediately. "You're afraid."

"Can I not share anything with you asses? I don't know what the hell to do. I've never been in this position before."

"Do whatever you think you should." Bryce shrugged, looking at his watch. "I've got to run too. We are expecting Mia's brother and his family this weekend. She'll kill me if I'm not home on time tonight, and since I'm already late, I'm gonna have to make it up to her. See you next week." He waved as he walked out of my office and soon he, too, was gone.

"Hunter, what would you do?" I asked, trying to get some kind of feedback from someone older and wiser—and perhaps a little more mature.

"Honestly?"

"Yes."

He blew out a breath and placed his hands behind his head. He took a few minutes and thought, and then took a deep breath. "Well, I'd have to consider a lot of things."

"Like?"

"What my relationship with said person is and what it might become afterward. So I get where you are coming from on that front. I mean things are going to work out one of two ways: either everything will go back to the way it is now, or the worst, this will drive a rift right between you. You need to figure out how comfortable you would be with that last aspect. You also need to think about protecting yourself. I mean we as a company have a shit-tonne to lose if you go through with this, and then she wants to come after you financially."

"I'm not worried about that. Sophie is in a good place, and I've known her my entire life. Hell, we've all known her. I don't think she is doing this in any way to be vindictive."

"Neither do I, but the stress of dealing with a child alone can do a lot of funny things to people. What happens if she falls in love with you and you don't return the feelings, or you get married and she resents you forever and comes after you. You need to think of all of these things. I mean, you are right, we have known her all her life. Now, on the other hand, you also need to figure out what would happen if you end up wanting more."

"I won't," I immediately replied.

Hunter chuckled at my quick and immediate answer and rubbed the back of his neck. "Listen, I know I'm in a way different place than you are currently, but when I found out Autumn was pregnant, something in me changed. It was like a switch. Suddenly, I wanted to see my baby be born and grow up, and it killed me when she pushed me away. What if you feel the same way and she wants nothing to do with you?"

"Seriously? I'm a donor, nothing more," I bit out.

"So, then you're telling me you're going to do it?"

I looked at my brother. Hunter had brought up great points, and I'd given zero thought to how I might feel about the entire process, especially how I might feel afterward. I'd also given zero thought to what would happen if she wanted more. I blew out a breath and dropped my head back and stopped and thought for a second. I hadn't really thought about any of the things he'd brought up. All I'd seen was the hurt in her eyes when she walked away from me. I'd seen it before caused by others, and I'd seen happiness, and honestly, I liked seeing the second better. I just wanted to do whatever it took to see that happiness in her eyes again.

"All I'm saying is be careful and be prepared for what you might not expect. Sophie has lived in Kings Cove her entire life, and she isn't going anywhere."

"What is that supposed to mean, she isn't going anywhere?"

"Well, it means that one day, after all this is done with, you will probably run into her on the street. Your son or daughter will be with her. The part that will hurt the most will be the fact that they won't even know who you are when you run into them, but you will. He or she will just think you are nothing more than an acquaintance that their mother knows, but you're going to know. I just want you to think and be fully prepared for how that might feel."

I sat there considering what he had just said. I knew there was a lot of truth in what he was saying. I had seen what a mess he had been over the whole Autumn situation. I blew out a breath.

"Oh, and what if she ends up wanting child support? That can end up being an entirely different can of worms. We work in the law field. Ask Carter the shit he's seen people pull. It will definitely open your eyes."

I nodded. He was right. "What do you think I should do?"

"If you are absolutely sure that you're really going to be finished with this situation after the deed is done, then form a contract and make her sign an NDA," Hunter said, crossing his arms and sitting back in the chair. "If you aren't totally sure, then make sure you do a little soul searching yourself before you enter into anything with her."

"Thanks, man. I'll be working on that tonight."

"So I guess that is your answer then?"

"Yeah, I think so. I told her I'd have an answer to her by this weekend."

"Well, just be careful. Make sure it's the right thing for you, and if you need anything, just call me, okay?"

Hunter got up and walked to the door, turning the handle, and was just about to leave when I cleared my throat.

"Hunter?"

"Yeah?"

"She wants it to be natural and fun. How the hell am I going to do that?"

"Treat her no different than the way you've treated the other women you have been with." He shrugged.

"No. I just mean she's my friend. It's going to awkward enough. I don't want to fuck this up."

"Fuck, do you need me to teach you how to use your fucking cock too?" He chuckled. "I dunno, get her some toys, have fun with it. Get her worked up, just relax, and have a good time. Remember, it's only a week, and since there is no relationship going to be formed, you really can't possibly fuck anything up."

That was Hunter's advice. Before I could tell him I was more worried about fucking up my friendship with her, he had already left my office and was on his way.

I stepped out of the shower and wrapped a towel around my waist. I dripped dry while I shaved, and then I walked to the kitchen with a renewed sense of who I was. The weight of having the decision lifted off me had made me feel much lighter than I had in days.

I pulled the fridge open and grabbed a beer and wandered into the living room. Flopping down onto the couch, I turned on the TV to catch some late-night news.

I needed to unwind. The tension I'd been carrying in my upper back and neck all week was now killing me. As I had driven home, I'd been happy with my decision, but now I realized that I wasn't proud of most of the things I had done when it came to women. I let out a breath. I didn't want Sophie to become just another woman on that already long list.

I thought back to the afternoon. All I had gotten from Bryce were wisecracks about my sex life. Hunter had been the one who had made the most sense. He had spoken to me from his heart. He genuinely wanted me to be prepared.

I picked up my cell phone, checking again to see if she had messaged me while I had been in the shower, but the only message that sat there was mine. "Fuck," I mumbled under my breath.

I threw my cell phone down on the couch beside me and reached for the documents I had printed earlier and started reading them over once again, making sure everything I wanted to be included was there. I was about halfway through them when my phone started to vibrate, and when I looked down at my screen, I saw Sophie was calling.

"Moment of truth," I murmured before taking a deep breath. I hesitated for a moment and stared at her name, and then I picked up my phone and answered.

Chapter Nine

SOPHIE

"I heard from Chase," I practically shouted into the phone. "He said yes." My stomach flopped at the thought. I lay in bed staring up at the ceiling, twirling a strand of my hair around my finger as I waited for a response from Jenna.

"EEEK! All right, girl, this calls for a day of shopping. We need to get your primped and primed and ready. We need to shop. We need to go to the spa and get things waxed. Oh, I am so excited. When is he coming? No pun intended." She laughed.

"Tomorrow, for one week."

"You guys live two blocks away from one another and you're taking him hostage?"

I was giddy with excitement and began laughing. "No. It's part of my plan. I have to maximize my time."

"Maximize your time?"

"Yes, that way we can get in as many sessions as possible."

"You make it sound as if this is a therapy appointment."

I let out a laugh. "I guess you are right."

"Okay, if you say so. Well, this calls for a girls' day, so get dressed. We are going out."

"What? I can't. I have so much to do," I said, looking around my already spotless apartment.

"Yeah, sure, I know you. You are laying there thinking your apartment is such a disaster when in fact you could eat right off your floor because you can't even find a piece of lint. So whatever you need to do, we will do it together. Get ready. I'm coming to pick you up."

Before I could say anything, Jenna was gone, and I threw my phone down on the bed and let out a breath. Twenty minutes had gone by before I had gotten up and showered, and now I sat beside Jenna at Kings Cove's only day spa, Pampered Soul, with my feet propped up on the footrest while some woman went to town filing the soul of my foot.

"What color polish would you like?" she asked me, handing me a color selection to choose from.

I looked over at Jenna, who was rooting through her purse for something and let out a breath. I had just begun flipping through the colors when Jenna suddenly ripped them from my hand.

"Oh no, no, no, no, no, no, you don't. I will choose. You need something hot and sexy. She needs something hot and sexy for her date," she said, smiling at the girl.

"I'm capable of choosing hot and sexy," I said, trying to reach for the color selection and failing as Jenna pulled them farther away from my reach.

"Oh no, the last time you needed to select hot and sexy,

you ended up choosing clear coat. No, no, we need something more like this." She held out a deep, dark-red color.

I looked at her as if she had lost her mind. There was no way I could wear a color like that. "Jenna, no way. Bogota Blackberry is not going on my toes."

"Oh yes, it is. She will take this one please," Jenna said, handing the colors back to the pedicurist. "Actually, make it two please. You'll see, clear coat is something my grandmother wears, and she hasn't had a date in years," Jenna said, smiling and looking immensely proud of herself.

"Jenna," I bit out, trying hard not to laugh at the face she was making.

"Girl, you need to chill out. Now sit back, relax, and don't worry. Just trust me." Jenna sat back and closed her eyes, urging me to do the same.

I finally sat back and did my best to enjoy my time with Jenna. It took an hour, and now we finally sat waiting while our toes dried. Jenna had just put her phone back into her purse and looked to me. "Okay, so what is next?"

"Well, I need to shop for food, wine, flowers, and candles."

She glanced down at her phone and then over at me. "That's all? What about lingerie? Sheets? Perhaps a scented bubble bath? Give me your list." She held out her hand, and I reluctantly placed my folded list in it. She opened the paper and read over what I had written, and without a word, she pulled a pen from her purse.

"What are you doing?" I frowned as she circled some things, crossed others out, and chewed on the end of her pen, lost in thought.

"I'm making some...ah...shall we say, minor adjustments. Do you trust me?"

"Ha, yeah, look at my toes. Do I trust you. Clear coat would have been more...me."

"Yeah, and the next thing I know, you will be going to the old-age residence over on Madison and partaking in bingo night. All right, girl, let's go, we have lots to do." Jenna said, dropping my list and the pen into her purse.

Twenty minutes later, we walked through Bed Bath and Beyond, making our way to the bedding department. I stopped at the first sheet display I came to, the one I always purchased from, while Jenna continued to make her way deeper into the department. I had decided on my usual sheets in a different color and was about to make my way over to the candles when I heard Jenna call my name. I turned around to see her walking towards me holding a package of sheets over her head. I wandered over to meet her, afraid of what she was going to present me with.

"These. These are the best sheets in the world. These are what you need." She shoved the package into my hands and took the sheets I had chosen and threw them on top of the nearest display.

"But I like what I had."

"Sophie, my love, trust me. Matt loves these sheets. They were the sheets I had on my bed the first time we...you know."

I held my hand up to stop her from divulging anything else. I knew I wasn't going to get away with anything different, so I succumbed. "Fine, but I'm taking these too," I said, grabbing the other package.

"But those ones are not going on your bed. These ones

are," she said, grinning at me while she shook the package.

"I don't see what it matters, honestly. Sheets are sheets."

"Girl, trust me, it matters!"

"I'm not trying to seduce him. We are having sex for one purpose, that is all."

Jenna burst out laughing. "Girl, there is nothing wrong with a little seduction. This is Chase Malone! You need to have some fun. I'm sure he'd appreciate a little seduction! Plus, the remaining women in this town that have yet to sleep with him would kill for this opportunity. Are you blind? Do you not see them looking at him everywhere we go?"

"To be honest, I've never really paid attention. Besides, I wouldn't know how to seduce him anyways." I shrugged and continue following Jenna through the store. Just as we approached the cash register, she stopped and turned to me, grabbing me by the shoulders. "You need to have fun with this, Sophie. Relax and have fun. I know it's a new concept for you."

I ignored her words, made my way to the checkout, and paid for my purchase. As soon as we were out of the store, Jenna was pulling me over to Forever His, a small lingerie store. I walked over to my usual table—cotton bras and panties—and glanced over to where Jenna stood. I could feel my face heating at the items she was sifting through. I stood there blushing just from watching her. It wasn't a wonder I had never made my way over to that table, those things totally intimidated me. Ignoring Jenna, I turned back to the table I was looking at and picked up a couple of pairs of panties when I heard her call my name.

"Oh, Sophie, this would great on you!" She held up a

black lacy bra.

I swallowed hard and nodded. I guessed I could pull it off, until she held up the matching panties. "Are they....are they crotchless?" I whispered, ripping them out of her hand before anyone saw what she was holding up.

Jenna let out a loud laugh. "Yes! You need these."

"Jenna, no. There is no way I am going to wear those," I said, turning my back on her and sifting through the pile of cotton panties that were way more my speed.

"Come on, Soph. Come on, lighten up. These are fun!" She giggled, "Matt loves..."

I held up my hand to stop her, "SHHH...I don't even know who I am shopping with right now," I said, throwing down the panties I had picked out and went to walk away.

"It's your best friend, who is making sure you are going to have the time of your life this week." She shoved the bra and panties into my hand, looking me in the eyes. "Trust me. One week, Sophie. One short week, and then you are going to have a bun in the oven, and your sex life will be over."

I burst out laughing. That was the funniest thing I'd ever heard—my sex life. My sex life in the last five years had consisted of two men. That was it. One who never made me orgasm, and one who kissed like a lizard and had never gotten past third base. So if it was my sex life she was truly worried about, I hated to tell her it was already non-existent.

"What's so funny?"

"My sex life, that is what is funny. It's been so long since I've had sex, I'm pretty sure I almost forget how to do it."

"Well, girl, you better figure it out fast because you have picked the one man in this city who hasn't forgotten how to. You'll be in good hands," she said, raising her eyebrows.

"Very, very good hands. Now relax. Come on, let's go over there and look some more, but you are getting these." She closed my hand around the black bra and panties and smiled at me, pulling me with her.

I ended up walking out of Forever His with a bag full of lingerie I'd probably never wear, a much lighter pocketbook, but a very happy Jenna. The rest of the afternoon was spent shopping for food, flowers, and candles. Once I had everything that had been on my list, we headed back to my condo.

Jenna stopped the car outside of my condo and put the car into park. "So you're good? You have everything you need?"

"I think so," I said, grabbing the two bags that sat at my feet. "Can you pop the trunk so I can grab the rest of the bags?"

"Sure thing. Remember, if you need me, call."

I nodded, hugged my best friend, and then climbed out of her car, grabbing the rest of my bags. I smiled and waved and watched as she pulled away from the curb.

It was almost eleven by the time I finally sat down on the couch with my glass of wine. I had spent the rest of the afternoon making sure that everything had been washed, dried, and put away. I even had the new sheets washed, and they were already on the bed. Jenna was right, they were wonderful, I'd thought as I ran my hands over the high thread count sheets.

I flipped the TV on, pulled the blanket off the back of the couch and over my legs, and sipped on my wine. Tomorrow, Chase would be here, and hopefully by this time, we would be deep in one another. I just prayed that I was truly ready for this...and that I wasn't making a huge mistake.

Chapter Ten

Chase

I stared down at the mess of papers in front of me and let out a deep sigh. I had been going over and over them, and I was still unsure if this was how I should proceed. I ran my hands through my already disheveled hair and took a sip of my first cup of coffee of the morning. I flipped on the stereo, and light jazz poured through the speakers. I took another sip of coffee and looked back down at the mess of words that sat in front of me. What would she think when it was time for me to present this agreement to her? Was she going to hate me? Would she be fine with it?

I grouped the papers together, straightened them, and then reread them for the thousandth time. What the fuck had I agreed to do? I thought to myself, and threw the documents down on the table. I sat back and ran my hand over my face.

I drank down the remainder of my coffee and glanced at the clock. I had to get moving if I was going to be on time. I had slept in this morning, like I normally did every Sunday. Today, though, I had brunch planned with my brothers, and I knew they would be waiting for me.

I grabbed the papers off the table, dropped my mug in the kitchen sink, and headed down to my bedroom. An hour later, I was showered, packed, and the kitchen was tidied, and I was on my way out the door to meet the boys for brunch before heading to Sophie's for the week.

I walked into Deb's Place and nodded to our usual waitress before walking into the dining area. Hunter sat over in the corner alone and waved once he saw me.

"Hey, man, where is everyone?" I asked, taking a seat across from him.

"Carter isn't back from his weekend ventures yet, and Mia's brother decided to extend his family's visit. So, it's just us this morning. How you doing?"

Honestly, I felt as if I were going to be sick. The coffee I had this morning kept repeating on me, and my stomach hurt too much for food. I was nervous, afraid I was making a mistake, but I ignored all those feelings and smiled at my brother. "I'm great!"

I signaled to Andrea to fill my cup with coffee. "Bullshit, you're great." Hunter said chuckling, "Is that why you look like you're going to throw up?"

I ran both hands through my hair and looked at my much-older brother, ignoring what he had just said and thinking about what needed to be done before I could go to Sophie's. "I guess I'll feel better once I am at her place and everything is out in the open and done." I shrugged.

Hunter chuckled. "Yeah, once your balls deep in her, eh."

"What can I get for my favorite men this morning?" Natasha asked, stepping up to the side of the table.

"Our usual: poached on toast," Hunter said, handing over the menu.

"Sure thing," she said, taking the menus and winking at me as she walked away.

"So, did you get that paperwork finished?"

I nodded. "Yeah it's done."

"Good." Hunter picked up his coffee cup and took a mouthful.

"Yeah, it is good. There is only one problem."

"What is that?"

"Well, the more I read it, the more worried I'm getting. I just don't want to come across as being an asshole, you know?"

"Dude, what is wrong with you? You are protecting yourself. You're being smart. That's it. Just look at it that way. People get fucking crazy when things go wrong or when they are faced with a situation that they can't handle. You know that, or you should. We all deal with it all the time. I can look it over, if you want, and make sure you haven't missed anything?"

I nodded, drinking down the rest of my coffee just in time for Andrea to come around for refills. "I know they do. It's just I feel that I should be able to trust her."

"You should, but it doesn't mean that you can't put extra precautions in place. Just relax."

My brother was right; there was nothing wrong with a form of protection. It would be something I would suggest to any of my clients. An hour later, fully caffeinated and with full bellies, we stood in the parking lot by our cars while Hunter went over the papers I had drafted. "Good news is everything looks good. I'll witness it once they are signed," he said, handing me the folder. "Where you headed now?" Hunter asked, pulling his car door open.

"The market. I need to pick up a bottle or two of wine and some flowers or something."

"You don't think she has thought of that?"

"I'm sure she has, but I don't want to come off as a total asshole." I laughed. "Just because this is an agreement doesn't mean she doesn't deserve to be treated like a lady."

"All right, man, talk to you later. I have to get home to Autumn and the kids."

I waved as he pulled from his parking spot and climbed into my car. The market was jammed as I maneuvered myself through the aisle looking for Sophie's favorite bottle of wine. Finally spotting it, I grabbed two bottles and made my way to the front of the store, but not before I stopped at the flower stand and grabbed a dozen red roses and got in line to pay for my purchase. While waiting, I grabbed my phone from my back pocket and typed out a message to Sophie, letting her know I would be there shortly. She responded quickly, giving me a simple thumbs-up emoji, the same as always.

A half hour later, I stood outside her door listening to her bang dishes around in the kitchen. I set my bag down on the ground, took a deep breath, and lifted my hand to knock.

"Coming," I heard her call from inside, and suddenly I felt nervous, my stomach flipping. I ran my hand through my hair, picked up my duffel bag off the floor, and flung it over my shoulder. The door opened, and Sophie stood inside, a nervous look on her face, even though she was doing her best to hide it behind a smile.

"Here, these are for you," I said, holding out the wrapped flowers and a brown bag containing the two bottles of wine.

Her face lit up with a smile as she reached out and took the flowers. "Thank you. I guess you should come in," she said nervously and stepped off to the side to let me in.

I followed her into the familiar apartment and shut the door behind me, while she busied herself in the kitchen putting the flowers in a vase.

"Where should I put my bag?" I called.

"In the bedroom." She smiled, carrying the flowers and setting them on the table.

I made my way down the hall to her bedroom and looked inside. Everything had its place. The bed was made perfectly, not a wrinkle in sight. I stepped inside the door and set my bag on the floor by the bed, which immediately looked out of place in the picture-perfect room. I bent down and pulled the documents from inside the bag, holding them tightly, thinking it might be better to get this over and done with first than to wait until later. I didn't want to get in the moment with her and then decide to spring this on her tomorrow or later in the week.

I pushed my sleeves up and headed back out to the front room to find Sophie sitting on the couch, two glasses of wine in front of her. She patted the spot beside her for me to sit down, but not before she noticed the folder that I carried with me. I blew out a breath and took a seat as I watched the unsure look in her eyes.

I took a sip of wine, set the glass down, and then cleared my throat. "Sophie, listen, before we get started here, I think we need to go over a few things."

Her eyes met mine in question. "Okay," she said hesitantly, unsure of where I might be going with this.

There was no easy way to bring this up, so I set the documents on the table in front of her. "Okay, so don't be angry with me, but I need you to sign these."

"What is it?" she asked, picking the documents up off the table, reading the top page, a frown settling on her face as she glanced at the document. "An NDA? You want me to sign an NDA? Why?"

"It's not only an NDA but also a contract. It just states that I am only responsible for providing you with sperm, that is it. That you won't come after me for things such as child support. It also states that I don't want visitation, and that I won't come after you for custody in the future. The NDA is just to ensure that this...transaction, if you will, will remain solely between us. That it won't get out that I am the father of the baby."

I watched as she read through the documents silently. "Chase, I don't understand." She swallowed hard as she flipped through them again. As I watched her, I could see her cheeks getting flush, and she was breathing rapidly as her eyes began to get glassy. I could tell she was struggling with this, and that was exactly what I didn't want.

I reached out and placed my hand on her arm. "Don't worry. It's just to protect us both." I thought I was going to have to keep explaining, but she reached for the pen that was sitting on the table and quickly scribbled her name on the bottom line of both documents. Then she passed me the pen without making eye contact, and I too signed the agreement.

I set the folder off to the side and picked up the glass of wine that sat in front of me and held it out. "I'd like to propose a toast," I said, waiting for her to pick up her glass. She let out a little huff and looked at me, and with a little shake in her hand, she picked up her glass and held it out towards me.

"Here's to one week. Let's hope my swimmers travel far and everything goes well to give you what you want," I said, clinking my glass against hers. I brought my glass up to my lips and sipped the cool liquid. Instead of drinking from hers, Sophie set the glass down on the table and jumped up off the couch. I watched as she walked across the room without saying anything, and then she stopped and lifted her hand to her eyes before turning around to look at me.

"Can you please excuse me for a moment. I, um, I need a minute." Before I could stop her, she had walked down the hall, leaving me alone in the living.

Chapter Eleven

The panic had started way before Chase had even arrived. It had started with shopping and had gotten worse by the time he had knocked on the door. The contract was what had literally sealed the deal. I did everything in my power not to shake as I signed my name on that very solid black line, and I had held it all together perfectly, until he had raised his glass and made that toast. As our glasses clinked together, I knew there was no way I would be able to take a sip of wine.

I had managed to walk away, my chest heavy, tears burning in my eyes. I had gotten out the words in time before that solid lump settled right in the middle of my throat, constricting my voice.

He, of course, agreed, letting me know he would be right there waiting for me when I returned. I practically ran across the plush carpet and into the bathroom, every step of the way fighting back the tears that threatened to fall. I closed the door behind me and leaned up against it, closing my eyes tightly.

I needed somewhere private and quiet, just in case I started to cry. I didn't want Chase to hear me. I didn't want him to know that it was his contract that had upset me. I also didn't want him to know that, right at this moment, I wasn't sure I wanted him to be out there when I returned. I tried to fight back the tears, but before I knew it, a single tear fell from the corner of my right eye, making a path for more to follow. What the hell was I even doing?

I tried to calm myself, but the more I thought about this entire situation, the more upset I became. I stepped in front of the mirror and wiped the tears from my cheeks and looked at my reflection. I was the one who had proposed everything like a business deal. I was the one who had mapped it all out. He was right, this was a transaction, nothing more. A simple exchange, if you will.

What had I really expected him to do? He's a lawyer—a very smart and successful one at that. Of course, he was going to want to protect himself; he would be stupid not to. I would be stupid not to protect myself too, but this was Chase, a man I had known my entire life and one I trusted very much. I didn't think I needed to protect myself against him.

I picked up my pressed powder compact and smoothed some on my skin, trying to get rid of the tear lines. I checked my reflection in the mirror.

Perhaps he was right and a contract would be for the best. Even though Chase was my best friend, I couldn't imagine raising a child with him. The man was a successful lawyer, but his personal life was a complete disaster. With him not wanting to be in the picture, I didn't need to worry about co-parenting. I wouldn't have to worry about someone spending their time undermining what rules I had put into place. Besides, I couldn't even begin to imagine Chase raising a child. I had seen him with his brothers' kids; he was a nightmare.

The last time he had watched Hunter and Autumn's little girls I was called to the rescue because one of them had gotten gum in her hair and he panicked. A little ice and it came right out. I laughed at the memory. I remembered walking in the door and finding Chase with a pair of scissors and a screaming child begging Uncle Chase not to cut her hair. I smiled to myself and the memory, swallowed hard, checked over my makeup, and let out a breath. This was the right choice. He was right.

I ran my brush through my hair and shut the light off. I made my way back down the hall and walked back out into the living room. Chase was still sitting on the couch in the same place I'd left him. I walked around and sat down beside him, picking up my glass and drinking down my wine. I glanced to Chase, and the more I looked into his trusting blue eyes, the more I felt I needed to drink. I grabbed the bottle I had left on the table and poured myself another full glass, drinking that one down just as fast—if not faster than the first one. The tension in the room was so thick that I was having a hard time breathing.

He watched me as I poured my third glass of wine, emptying the remainder of the bottle into my glass. "Whoa, Soph, slow down," he said, taking my glass from me. "We have all night, sweets." He placed his hand on my thigh, giving me a squeeze.

I smiled at the nickname "sweets," a name he had given me when we were fifteen, and one he had never let go of. I swallowed hard. My eyes burned, and the jumbled ball that sat in the pit of my stomach was making me uncomfortable. I was beyond nervous, and I suddenly wondered how on earth we were going to do this, especially if I felt this way just sitting here beside him fully dressed.

"Everything okay?" he asked. I nodded as he took my hand in his. "So how did you want to go about this?" he whispered.

I thought for a moment. How *did* I want to go about this? I had no clue. I figured he would have had it all figured out; he was far more experienced than I was in this department. I let out the breath I was holding and shook my head. "I dunno. Perhaps...perhaps, maybe we should kiss first." I shrugged.

"Okay, we can do that."

He stood from the couch and reached for my hands, pulling me to my feet. He pulled me closer to him. The smell of his cologne and the touch of his hand on my waist sent a chill through my body. His hand didn't remain on my waist for long because, as quickly as he touched me, he pulled his hand away as if he had been burned. Instead, he gripped my hand with his and pulled our hands between us. He leaned in, turning his head in the same direction I had turned mine. We were as awkward as we had been the first time he had kissed me, only that time he had succeeded.

"This isn't going to work," I mumbled, frustrated, placing my hand on his broad chest and pushing him away.

"Whoa, whoa, what isn't?"

"All of this...It's pointless. I mean, we can't even share a simple kiss. How are we supposed to sleep together?"

Chase stood there staring at me. I could tell he didn't know what to say, and I didn't blame him. Finally, completely frustrated, I stepped away from Chase and walked over to the window. I looked out over the city and did my best to concentrate on anything else than the problem at hand. I heard Chase clear his throat, and I turned around in time to see Chase pull his phone from his pocket and begin dialing.

"What are you doing?"

"We, Sophie Lancaster, have a date. We are going out. Chase Malone doesn't give up this easily. You of all people should know that," he said as he typed something into his phone.

I looked at him wide-eyed. "Going out? Where are we going?"

"You'll see. Grab your jacket. Let's go," he said, making his way to the door, slipping on his coat and shoes.

We had walked over to Kings Cove Park as the sun began to set. "Where are we going? Are you going to tell me?" I asked again, running to catch up to him for the third time.

"We are going on a horse-drawn carriage ride through the park. I want to just chill a little. I know the guy who runs the carriages, so I messaged him and he said the guy would be waiting for us at the east entrance."

I slowed down and was just about to protest when the east gate came into view, and just as Chase had said, a horse-drawn carriage was already sitting there waiting for us.

"Come on, Soph, pick it up a little," Chase called and

approached the driver, introduced himself, and slipped the man some money.

"Where to, sir?"

Chase looked in both directions before answering. "Through the park down to the water?"

"Sounds good, sir."

Before Chase returned to my side, he leaned in and whispered something into the man's ear. He nodded and turned to smile at me. "Climb in, miss."

Chase stepped up beside me and placed his arm around me, his cologne invading my senses. "Climb in," he whispered, staring into my eyes, taking hold of my hand and helping me up into the carriage.

I had just sat down when he climbed in beside me and reached for one of the blankets that was folded neatly beside me and threw it over our legs just as the carriage pulled away from the sidewalk.

I sat back and breathed deeply, trying to relax as I listened to horses' hooves clapping along the pavement. I watched the birds flit through the trees. As the gentle breeze blew, I closed my eyes and just sat listening to the sounds around me.

"How did you know I've always wanted to do this?" I whispered more to myself than Chase, even though it was directed at him.

"You've never done this before?"

I shook my head. "Never." I looked over to him, and a soft smile sat on his lips.

"I guess you could say it was a lucky guess then." Chase placed his arm behind me and sat back, encouraging me to do the same, finally pulling me against his body.

I finally felt myself starting to relax as I listened once again to the sounds around me. It was almost therapeutic, and once we turned into the tree-lined lane heading towards the water, the thousands of tiny lights the city always put up at this time of year had come on, lighting our way.

I felt Chase kiss the top of my head. "Are you enjoying this?" he whispered.

I nodded and smiled to myself. I closed my eyes and enjoyed the breeze across my face when I felt the carriage finally came to a halt.

"Sir, I believe this is the stop you requested."

I opened my eyes in time to see the driver turn and nod to Chase.

"Thank you. Oh, and there is no need to wait. We can walk back," Chase said, throwing the blanket off us and climbing out of the carriage. He held his hand out for me to take. I let out a little squeal of surprise when he grabbed me around the waist instead and lifted me down.

Once I was on the ground, he grabbed my hand, and together we walked for a bit, coming to a clearing at the edge of the lake. Chase stopped at the first bench we came to and looked around but then shook his head. "Nope, not this one," he mumbled under his breath as he looked out over the water.

I frowned. "What is it? What are you looking for?" I questioned, but he held his hand up, ignoring me and walking ahead to the next bench, then to the next bench, until finally he stopped and sat down.

"Have a seat," he said, patting the bench beside him and smiling up at me.

I laughed and took a seat, looking out over the calm water. "So what is so special about this exact spot?"

Chase looked at me and put his hand over his heart, acting as if I had fatally wounded him. "Sweets, I'm shocked. You don't remember?"

I shook my head, laughing at his actions. "No, I'm sorry, I don't."

"Come here." He got up off the bench and moved a few steps ahead. When I didn't jump right up, he waved his hand impatiently, signaling for me to join him. "Come on."

I rolled my eyes, let out a breath, and stood, taking a step forward and stopping beside him.

"No, it was more like here," he said more to himself as he grabbed me and positioned me where he wanted me to stand. "What about now?"

"I'm sorry, but I've got nothing." I giggled, shrugging my shoulders.

"Trust me?" he asked as he stepped closer to me yet. I could feel the heat from his body and smell his cologne as he stepped in even closer to me. My heartbeat accelerated, and I let out a breath as Chase stepped up against me, his chest lightly brushing against me.

"Yes," I answered, my voice shaking, swallowing hard.

"Close your eyes," he whispered. I could feel his breath on my cheek as he leaned in and tenderly brushed his lips across mine. My eyes opened instantly, and Chase pulled his head back to watch my reaction. The first thought I had was to pull away, but that thought was soon replaced by curiosity. Instead I leaned in closer toward him, and he bent in again, this time pressing his lips hard into mine. His arms slowly and gently wrapped around my body and pulled me even tighter against him, his tongue brushing against mine.

It didn't take long before I was lost—lost in his kiss, lost in his arms, lost in the moment between us. I heard nothing around us, and I had forgotten everything. When his tongue brushed through my mouth again, I pressed my body harder into him. His hand rested on my cheek as he sucked my bottom lip into his mouth, finally pulling away, leaving my lips feeling empty.

"Open your eyes. Now do you remember?" he whispered.

I opened my eyes and looked into his and gently smiled. In an instant it all came rushing back to me. The old courthouse now turned into the Whisper Wind Restaurant off in the distance behind him. "I do, I so do. This was the place of our very first kiss."

"Hopefully, this one was a little better than that first kiss so long ago." He chuckled and brushed a strand of hair off my face, studied my gaze, and then leaned in and met my lips again.

"A little," I mumbled and met his lips again.

Chase Malone knew how to kiss—gentle yet firm, with just enough tongue, and like everything else he did, he put his whole self into it. I was now afraid of what it would be like to sleep with him if he put that much effort into kissing. I was scared that he would ruin me completely for anyone else.

Chapter Twelve

I hadn't wanted to stop kissing her. I had wanted to get lost forever in those lips of hers. She tasted so good, and I almost lost it when I heard that gentle moan escape from her as I pulled her body into mine and ran my hands through her long, soft hair. I couldn't remember the last time that a kiss had been so good that I didn't want it to end. I sadly realized that it had to end when I felt Sophie shiver in my arms. The wind had picked up, and I knew I needed to get her back to her apartment, back to warmth and safety and privacy.

A light rain shower had started coming down about a block away from her condo. We had picked up our pace but still got stuck in a sudden downpour that stopped as soon as we hit the front door. We had both taken a hot shower, changed, and now we sat in front of the fireplace on the floor, TV on in the background. A small buffet of Thai food was spread all over the coffee table in front of us.

"Oh my, that was delicious," Sophie said, placing her plate on the table and sitting back against the couch.

"I'm glad you enjoyed." I brushed a strand of hair from her eyes. "How about you find something to watch, and I'll clean up."

"Oh no, that's not necessary. I got it," Sophie said, getting ready to get up, but I took her hand off the plates and shook my head.

"I got it," I said sternly and grabbed our plates while she flipped through the channels and piled some of the takeout containers on top of them and carried them into the kitchen. I cleaned out the leftovers and put them in the fridge. I put the dishes into the dishwasher, and then grabbed one of the chilled bottles of wine from the fridge and two wine glasses. Since we had shared our first kiss, something had changed between us. Not only was I more at ease, but Sophie was as well. The only thing I was worried about now was how she might react if something happened between us tonight.

When I re-entered the living room, Sophie was curled up at the opposite end of the couch from where I normally sat. As soon as I sat down, Sophie grabbed the blanket from the back of the couch and wrapped herself in it, using it almost as a shield.

"Is *The Wedding Singer* okay?" she asked.

"Sure." I shrugged and poured us both a glass of wine, handing her a glass.

"What's with you?" I questioned.

"Nothing." Sophie couldn't fool me; something was bothering her.

"Please, Sophie, I'm not a brand-new guy in your life. Normally, you have your feet in my lap, and you're sprawled out hogging the couch. Instead, you are curled up in the corner hiding under a blanket. What's going on?"

She let out a sigh, looking at me out the side of her eye. "You said you wanted this to happen naturally, but how does that even happen?"

"Believe me, please, it does, but you kind of have to trust me enough to actually touch me, and to let me touch you. It would help if you were being somewhat normal and not worrying your pretty little head. Put your trust in me and fucking relax because you're freaking me out."

Sophie burst out laughing. "I'm sorry." She giggled and threw the blanket off her, sitting up.

"Get over here," I said, holding out her glass of wine and adjusting so that she could sit up against me. She took the wine and edged her way closer.

An hour later things were more normal. Sophie was now curled up at my side, her head resting on my upper abs, her arm wrapped around my waist. My arm was resting around her waist and we lay lazily watching the ending of *The Wedding Singer*.

"You know, I give him props for the public proposal, but how the hell can you take a guy seriously without a ring?"

"What makes a public proposal so special?" I questioned, kissing the top of her head.

"Well, look at him. He is up there risking it all. In front of all those people, he risks the humiliation of her possibly saying no."

"Oh, Sophie, come on. It's totally predictable. I mean, if

he thought she would say no, then he would never propose in front of everyone."

"No, I don't agree. I think it totally shows how confident he is and that he fully believes that she will say yes."

"I see. So, do you think that if he proposed in private he wouldn't be risking it all?"

She thought for a second and looked up at me. "I never said that."

"And the ring, what if he forgot it and packed it in his checked luggage?" I shrugged. "You know guys get nervous too and forget things."

Sophie let out a laugh and covered her face, and I took that opportunity to shimmy my body down a bit to lie beside her.

"That is exactly something you would say," Sophie mumbled behind her hands.

"What is?" I whispered as my one hand softly stroked her hair as the ending credits started to roll. It was silky and soft and smelled good, and I suddenly began to question why we had never decided to be friends with benefits. I mean, sure, she had put an end to my fantasy of dating her quickly when we were young, but we had never explored that aspect of our relationship. She looked up at me and grew serious while I stared into her eyes.

"What are you thinking about?" she mumbled, closing her eyes and resting her head on my chest.

I breathed in her scent and closed my eyes, debating asking her what had been on my mind for the last half an hour. I had run over the words in my mind repeatedly. I cleared my throat. "Why didn't we ever do this sooner?"

"Do what sooner?"

"Why were we never friends with benefits?" My cock instantly jumped at the idea.

Sophie lifted her head and looked me in the eyes and shrugged.

"I've always found you attractive, Sophie. I won't lie, and honestly, I don't think I've ever hid that from you either." I leaned in slowly and allowed my lips to graze over hers, my cock hardening instantly behind my zipper.

"Chase, I know who you are. It's not like it's a state secret. You've been with so many women, and I never wanted to be one of many."

"That makes sense I guess," I said, brushing away the loose strand of hair that had again fallen into her eyes, "but if those are your reasons for why you and I never hooked up, then why did you choose me for this?"

Sophie let out a sigh and rested her hand on my chest and her chin on top of her hand. She was silent for a few moments, and then looked me in the eyes. "This is probably going to sound really stupid, but I know who you are. I also wanted this to be special for me, and I know how you treat women. I've watched you. No matter the state of your relationship, you've never treated one of them badly."

I slowly brought my lips to hers and kissed her softly. It was that moment that I decided I would do whatever it took to make sure that our time together was special for her. When our lips parted and she looked into my eyes, I placed my hand on her cheek and slowly brought my lips to hers again. I gripped her ass with my hand and ground myself into her so she could feel exactly how excited I was for this to begin.

Chapter Thirteen

I didn't think I would ever forget the look in his eyes when he placed his hand on my cheek and slowly brought his lips to mine. I would also never forget the first kiss that happened tonight; it was so soft and gentle, how he was nipping at my bottom lip as if he were unsure of himself, unsure of how I would react at my best friend kissing me. He lay beneath me and as we kissed, he gripped my ass, grinding into me so I could feel how hard he was for me. I'd be lying if I said I wasn't hot for him, and if he slipped his hand in my pants, he would see just how true that was.

We now lay side by side, my head resting on his arm as we continued to kiss on the couch. He pulled me into his arms, squeezing part of my body and pulling me closer to him. My hands shook as I shyly began to explore his body. When my fingers touched the button of his jeans, he gripped my hand and placed it on the bulge behind his zipper and he let out a moan as I gripped him through his jeans.

"Let's go," he murmured. He slipped off the couch and, pulling me with him, we wandered down the hall to my bedroom. We hadn't even made it halfway down the hall when he grabbed me and pushed me up against the wall, kissing me hard while his hands roughly explored my body. A shiver ran through me as his hands brushed over my breasts, my nipples already hard and seeking his attention.

He kicked the bedroom door open, grabbed me and kissed me hard as he guided me over to the bed. Our lips parted and we stood before one another, breathless, his eyes trailing from my face down my body. He gripped the edge of my T-shirt and lifted it over my head, dropping it onto the floor. His eyes wandered over my body and suddenly, I remembered I wasn't wearing any of the pretty lingerie I had bought on my shopping trip this afternoon. I had spent a small fortune on all that frilly lace attire, and here I was wearing one of my normal cotton bras and plain old cotton granny panties, as Jenna so appropriately called them.

I started to cover myself up when I was pulled back into the moment when I heard Chase groan, "You look fucking amazing."

I had no time to react because his mouth crashed hard into mine and his tongue brushed through my mouth, bringing me right back to the moment, and I forgot all about what I was wearing. His hand found my breast, and he brushed his thumb over my nipple as he kissed down the side of my neck. I felt his hands reach around to my back and begin to fiddle with the clasp on my bra when I froze.

"What is it?" he whispered, fighting to take my lips again.

"What if...what if you don't like me?" I questioned. I felt like I was in my teens again. It had been so long since a man had seen me, I was feeling super insecure.

He stopped what he was doing and, still holding me in his arms, looked down into my face. I felt the clasp of my bra go and the material became loose on me. "Impossible," he whispered, smiling at the fact that I hadn't even noticed he had flicked the clasp of my bra.

"You say that...but..."

His lips pressed hard into mine, stopping me from speaking any more than I already had, and he backed me up to the bed. The back of my knees finally met the edge of the mattress, and I fell backward onto my soft bed. He wasted no time. His hands gripped the waistband of my yoga pants, quickly ripping them and my panties off me.

I looked up at him as he stood there between my legs, still fully clothed. I could see his cock painfully straining against the zipper of his jeans as his eyes took in my body. He bent over top of me and took the straps of my bra, the tips of his fingers grazing over my arms as he pulled it away from my body. He kneeled down between my legs onto the bed, one arm supporting the weight of his body, the other hand gently rolling my nipple between his fingers. I moaned into his mouth as his met mine.

"You're beautiful," he murmured as I let out a soft moan as he gently pinched my other nipple between his fingers. He kissed down my neck, pressing tiny kisses along my collarbone, and then running his tongue from my neck down between my breasts. He trailed his tongue up my left breast, rolling his tongue around my nipple, and then sucking it into his mouth. Then he repeated the same action over to the other one. I could feel the heat and throbbing between my legs intensify as he trailed his tongue down my belly, stopping and lightly blowing over my skin.

I felt him slide off the bed onto the floor, and he kissed my lower belly, which caused me to jump. I lifted myself up, resting on my elbows, and watched as he grabbed my legs, placing his hands on the inside of my thighs and forcing my legs open. "You're so fucking wet," he muttered as he blew his warm breath on my already throbbing center.

I watched him as he looked up at me, and I had just about come on the spot listening to his words. I bit my lower lip. He had barely even touched me yet, and my body was already begging for him to make me come undone. I arched my back and bit my bottom lip as he blew over me again. He had me hooked around him, and I felt his hands grip my waist, holding me in place, and then I felt his hot tongue connect with my center, causing my head to fall back in pleasure. His tongue ran through my wet folds once, and I was thriving and panting and fighting from screaming his name as my hands gripped his. The harder I gripped, the harder he gripped back, my body straining as he continued this wonderful torture that was almost too much for me to endure. I couldn't hold back any longer, and I let out a thunderous moan as my release came.

I was completely spent as I rested on the mattress, my eyes closed, trying hard to regain control over my breathing. My heart was beating so hard it felt like it would beat right out of my chest. I lay there in the quietness of my room and heard him chuckle as I felt the bed move, and I opened my eyes to look in his direction. He now stood between my legs. His jeans had fallen to the floor, his hard, thick cock sat in his hand, and his eyes washed over me as he stood there stroking himself.

Before I could say anything, even beg for a moment to regain control over myself, he dropped his cock and gripped my legs, pulling me down to the edge of the bed. He was definitely in control of this situation, and I secretly loved every second of it. Once he had me where he wanted me, he ran his cock through my wet center, placing himself snuggly against my entrance. Bending down, he met my lips as he slowly inched himself inside of me, stretching me, his hands running over me, gripping my body as he pumped deeply into me. I cried out his name and dug my fingers into his back as he pressed his way into me, until he was fully seated in me.

"Soph..." he breathed out as he continued to pump into me, slow and deep. I gripped his back, feeling his tense muscles, his breathing ragged, and thought for a second that I felt his body quiver. He hands gripped my body tightly, stiffening as he poured himself into me. He collapsed against me, catching his breath.

We now lay in the dark, my head resting on Chase's chest, listening to his heart beating. His fingers danced in tiny circles on my shoulder, occasionally kissing the top of my head. "What are you thinking about?" I asked.

"I just don't want you to think that I am always that weak. I can normally go for hours."

I blushed at his words, not sure what to say.

He chuckled a little. "I'm also really curious as to why we waited so fucking long to do this?" he said, pulling me closer to him.

I thought for a minute. I searched my mind to try and

find some reason that actually made sense for me to answer his question. The longer I thought about it, I quickly realized that I could not come up with anything that made sense. I didn't know if it was because he had just totally blown my mind or because part of me had always secretly wanted him. Whatever the reason, I was glad we finally had, and I was looking forward to the rest of the week. I shrugged and, looking off into the distance, I whispered, "Honestly, I don't really know why."

"Well, that calms me a bit. It must have been good if you're actually answering that question with that answer." He chuckled, placing his arm behind his head, pulling me closer.

I lifted my head and kissed his lips. "I really can't think of a way that it could have been any better. Thank you."

Chase chuckled. "Well, I can." He rolled up onto his shoulder and pulled the blankets up over our head and kissed me hard, his hands roaming over me again, leading us both back down that path of no return.

Chapter Fourteen

CHASE

I woke to the shower running. Other than that, the apartment was silent, and the sun was starting to rise over the neighboring apartment buildings. I rolled onto my back, put my arm behind my head, and lay there staring at the ceiling, trying not to think of Sophie naked in the shower, but it was proving to be impossible.

I had laid awake long after Sophie had fallen asleep. I lay there watching her, watching the calmness on her face that I so rarely saw from my best friend. The evening had started off somewhat rough but had ended in mind-blowing sex. I loved my best friend, but at times she was so uptight and worried about everything that it drove me crazy. Especially now she was so worried about how things would end up progressing between us that it had pretty much forced me to pick up my game. That was one thing that was different about her than all the others I dated, I rarely had to work at it, which had made me lazy. Images flashed through my mind of her earlier in the evening. The look on her face when I had taken her on the carriage ride down to the lake, then the look in her eyes at the end of our first kiss. I softly smiled to myself thinking about it. The more I had watched her while she slept the more I realized just how beautiful she truly was. Suddenly, the need to place my lips on hers was overwhelming, and I'd had to force myself to roll over to keep from kissing her again.

I'd had no idea where it had come from, but that same need that I had fought off last night while watching her sleep was starting all over again. My cock was starting to ache at the thought of kissing those perfectly bowed lips. I reached under the sheets and gripped the base of my cock, squeezing it, trying to get the throbbing to stop, but it did little good. "Fuck it," I said aloud to myself and got up from the bed.

I was just about to the bathroom door when I heard the shower shut off. A huge surge of disappointment ran through my body, but I decided to go ahead and open the door anyways. We could always just jump right back into that hot shower.

My hand was just about on the door handle when the door was suddenly ripped away from me and a towel-wrapped Sophie came bursting into the room. Her eyes wandered over my naked body, stopping on my hardened cock. Her cheeks flushed and a small smile came to her lips, which quickly vanished when she saw me looking at her. "Good morning," she murmured.

"Good morning. You're up early this morning."

"Every morning. Where were you going?"

I smiled. "Well, since I woke up in a cold empty bed, I thought I would come in and surprise you, maybe have a little fun in the shower," I said, raising my eyebrows at her and tugging at the knot in the front of the towel, trying to pull her closer, or better yet make her lose that towel she was now clutching tightly.

She stepped back out of my reach. "In the shower?" She scrunched up her nose in this cute way I had never seen her do before, or perhaps had never noticed, at my suggestion.

I did my best to suppress the laugh that threatened to erupt at her comment. "Come on, have you seriously never done it in the shower before? Shower sex is fantastic."

She shook her head as her cheeks flushed and her gaze hit the floor in embarrassment. She let out a sigh and walked over to her closet and began sifting through the clothes that hung there.

"Wait, you're serious? You've never done it in the shower?"

"You should get dressed, in case you forgot today is Jenna's birthday. We have plans with her and Matt tonight, and I still need to grab a gift for her."

"Come on, Soph, I didn't mean to upset you." I frowned and watched as Sophie clutched the towel tighter to her body. She ignored me by starting to search through her closet. I hadn't meant to upset her. Hell, I wanted to throw her over my shoulder, take her in that bathroom, and make her forget about anything and everything she felt she needed to do today. I was about to grab her waist and pull her into me when she looked over her shoulder in my direction.

"Didn't you hear me? Are you going to get ready or are you going to stand there all day and stare at me?"

The smile fell from my face when I realized she was serious and I made no further attempts to talk about the subject. Instead, I grabbed my bag that sat on the floor at the bottom of the bed and went into the bathroom, shutting the door behind me.

We had spent most of the afternoon at the mall looking for a gift for Jenna. No matter what I had suggested, Sophie flat out turned it down. I was beginning to get very irritated when she finally decided on a gift basket from one of Jenna's favorite stores and a couple movie passes. As the day had gone on, the tension between us mounted, and Sophie seemed to be more on edge than she had been earlier that morning.

I had been instructed to be ready by five, and I stood looking over my reflection in the hallway mirror fifteen minutes early while I waited on Sophie. I rolled up the sleeves of my shirt and straightened my collar as Sophie came out from the bedroom. "You just about ready?" I questioned, glancing at my watch.

"Are you sure we shouldn't just drive our own separate vehicles?" Sophie asked as she grabbed her shoes from the closet and slipped them onto her feet.

"It's fine. If they ask, which I'm sure they won't, but if they do, I picked you up because your car wouldn't start." I shrugged. "They won't think anything of it because I am closer to you than they are. It would make perfect sense that you called me and not them."

"All right, if you say so, but I think it would just be easier to go separately," she bit out, slipping into her coat.

"Why? I'm just coming back here tonight anyways."

You could cut the tension with a knife as we drove in silence to the restaurant. Sophie sat fiddling with the ribbon on the gift bag, as she looked out the window, completely ignoring me. I knew those two things combined meant she was pissed off with me, but I still tried to calm the situation. "You can put the radio on if you like," I offered, pulling out onto the main road. I'd had all the silence I could handle.

"No, it's okay." Sophie shrugged, not once looking my way. "I have a headache."

"Sure, okay a headache, right," I mumbled under my breath. That comment had gotten me a stern look from Sophie, who went right back to looking out the window when I'd glanced at her.

She had been acting like this all day for absolutely no reason, and I was beyond irritated by her cold shoulder. We had never treated one another this way. I pulled up to the stoplight and turned to watch her. She sat there still twirling that stupid ribbon around her finger, ignoring me as if I weren't even there. "Is everything all right?"

"Yes, of course. Why would you ask that?"

I let out a deep breath and prayed I wasn't starting a major argument with my best friend before heading into a birthday celebration for another one of our friends. "Soph, you've barely looked at me since this morning. So you can say what you want, but I'm not an idiot."

"Let me guess, you've been with enough women to know when one is upset with you." She let out a breath, rolled her eyes, and pointed to the sign coming up on our right to show me that we were almost there. I pulled into the parking lot and into the first spot and cut the engine.

"What exactly is that supposed to mean?"

"Just drop it. We are late. Now are you sure you don't want me to go in first? You know how I always arrive before you. If they ask, I'll just tell them that I parked around back."

I blew out a frustrated breath. "Sophie, it's fine," I said as I unbuckled my belt. This was exactly like Sophie, worried about everything. At this point, I didn't care what Matt or Jenna thought. What I cared about and was more concerned with was what she had meant by that snarky little comment. I took one look at her worried face, rolled my eyes, and took her hand in mine. "They aren't going to think anything of it. Just relax," I said, bringing the back of her hand to my lips and kissing her. "Why are you so worried?"

"I'm not worried about anything," she murmured, hiding her eyes from me. Instead of taking two minutes to talk to me, she grabbed the gift bag and her purse from the floor and got out of the car.

I frowned and followed her lead. By the time I had locked the doors and walked around the car, Sophie was already halfway across the parking lot, so I picked up the pace to catch up to her.

We were barely through the door when I saw Jenna wave from the table in the back. Placing my hand on Sophie's back, I leaned in to whisper in her ear when she suddenly called out to Jenna and went running into the restaurant, leaving me standing there.

I stared down at the half-eaten piece of apple pie that sat on my plate and ran my fork through the sweet, sticky filling. Sophie and Jenna were now out on the dance floor, while I sat with Matt in the booth. I sipped on my Crown and Coke, while Matt told me about one of the cases he was working on at the firm. I knew he was telling me something important, I could tell from the look on his face, but my mind was on one thing and only one thing—Sophie. I couldn't tear my eyes away as I watched how her hips swayed as she danced. She had me entranced, and I couldn't help but allow my eyes to wander her body.

"Did you hear what I said?" Matt snapped his fingers in front of my face as he waited for a response to whatever question he had apparently asked.

"Huh, what?"

"You feeling okay? You barely ate anything, and you're not paying attention to anything I have said."

"Yeah. I'm sorry. My mind is on other things right now."

"I can see that. Care to talk about it?"

I shook my head and looked over his shoulder at Sophie.

"What the hell are you looking at?" he asked as he turned around and looked in the direction of the girls.

"Nothing, it's nothing. So back to what you were saying," I said, trying to pull his attention back to me, but it did little good. In full view, Sophie and Jenna were both dancing and laughing. My eyes were trained on the curves of her hips as she danced on the dance floor with Jenna. I took another sip of my Crown and Coke, trying to calm the ache in my pants, when I noticed Matt staring at me.

"Sophie, huh?" Matt asked, smiling at me. He had seen me staring at her; there was no hiding it now. I fought internally for a few minutes about spilling everything to Matt.

"Sophie what?" I heard Jenna ask, and I looked up in time to see that both Jenna and Sophie stood beside the table out of breath and with smiles on their faces.

I swallowed hard, thinking fast. "Sophie and I should get going," I said, looking at my watch and downing my drink.

"Already?" Jenna and Sophie cried out at the same time.

"Yeah, I have an early morning tomorrow, and I need to drop Sophie off before I head home," I lied. Sophie met my eyes, and I hoped she could read the want in them. I didn't want to fight with her. I just wanted to pin her up against the wall in her bedroom and have my way with her.

"We can take her," Matt announced.

"Yeah, stay," Jenna urged, wrapping her arm around Sophie. "Dance the night away with me."

Sophie looked at me and bit her bottom lip. "No, it's okay. I'm tired anyways," Sophie said, hugging Jenna and whispering something in her ear at which Jenna nodded and smiled.

As we were on our way out of the restaurant, I stopped and took care of the bill for the four of us. I figured it was the least I could do for bailing early. Sophie had wanted to pay, but I insisted.

We drove back to Sophie's condo in uncomfortable silence again. She still would barely make eye contact with me. We had ridden the elevator in silence and were now standing outside the door to her condo. I leaned up against the wall, watching while she fumbled through her purse for the key. If she knew the thoughts that were running through my mind, she might start looking at me a little nicer. "You planning on talking to me tonight?" I asked quietly so we didn't disturb the other tenants.

She continued rooting through her bag and finally pulled her keys, quickly inserting it into the lock and opening the door. She dropped her purse to the floor, kicked off her shoes, and turned to look my way. "What would you like to talk about? My lack of sexual experience for one?"

"Are you serious?"

"Yes, I'm serious." She turned and marched down the hall toward her bedroom. I followed. There was no way I was going to spend the night fighting with her because she was hung up on the stupid idea that I had been making fun of her this morning.

I walked into the bedroom to see her digging through her top dresser drawer and shoving handfuls of what looked like lingerie into a bag. "I take it you told Matt all about how inexperienced I am. Bet the pair of you had a really good laugh over it too."

"What on earth are you talking about? No, I didn't tell Matt anything. What are you doing?"

"I'm getting rid of all this stuff. All the stuff I bought that I am too inexperienced to wear. Not only that, but I'd feel like an utter ass wearing them for you anyways," she barked, continuing to stuff things into the bag.

I walked over and grabbed her hands, stopping her from shoving yet another handful of lacy and silky things into the bag. "Just stop."

"No, I bought this so you'd like being with me. So, I compared to all the others you've been with. Figured you might as well have something that you like to look at if you had to do this." She held out a black lacy bra and panties, which I took from her and looked at. I couldn't help the smile that sat on my lips. They were hot as hell, and I'd probably kill to see some woman in them, but they sure as hell weren't Sophie.

"What? What is so funny?"

"Crotchless panties, Soph, really?"

I met her eyes, her cheeks flushing from embarrassment, which made her look so sexy. "See, you've seen these before. I'd only ever heard of them." She turned away to hide from me.

I looked down at the bra and panties in my hand and dropped them to the floor. I could tell from behind that Sophie was crying; she wiped at her eyes. I walked over and placed both my hands on her arms. "Sophie, this isn't you. These things aren't you."

"What isn't?"

"All this stuff you bought. This isn't you. Guys want to be with the real you, inexperienced or not."

"Well, believe me, I am as unexperienced as they come. You hit the jackpot with that, and if you think different, you're fooling yourself."

"Look, I'm sorry, okay, for however you took my comment, but it wasn't meant to be insulting to you. I also didn't think you would take it the way you did. I don't really care how experienced or inexperienced you are. That's all part of the fun, if you know what I mean," I said, grabbing her and pulling her into me.

Sophie let out a loud laugh and pushed me away. "Sure it is," she said, ripping the undergarments that I still held in my hand and shoved them deep into the bag. "I must have been a damn fool buying all these. I'm sure you got a kick out of this. Glad I didn't put them on and parade around for you. You probably would have died with laughter."

I grabbed the bag from her hand and threw it over on the bed. "That's enough. That shit in that bag isn't you, and it never will be you, no matter if you'd been with two or twenty men. I've apologized and I meant it. Forgive me or don't."

Sophie stood across from me, not knowing what to say. I wasn't kidding, I wasn't joking. I was done if this was how she was going to act. Within seconds she went from staring at me, wondering if I were being truthful, to being wrapped in my arms, kissing me hard. It had caught me by surprise, but with little hesitation, I wrapped my arms under her ass and lifted her as she wrapped her legs around my waist, and I carried her over to the bed.

Chapter Fifteen

Sophie

I woke with a start, my breathing heavy. The room was dark, and I rolled over to see the other side of the bed was empty. I ran my hand over the sheets, but they were already cold, letting me know that Chase had been up for a while. I rolled over and stretched, my body aching in places I hadn't thought possible. My body relaxed into the mattress, and I thought back to last night.

After we had talked and cleared the air, and made up, we'd decided to catch a movie before bed. I'd changed while Chase made popcorn and found something on. When I walked into the living room, I was surprised to find a blanket sprawled out onto the floor in front of the TV, pillows thrown down and the fireplace on. I'd frowned at the mess on the floor and was about to ask what was going on when I heard the clink of two glasses. I turned to find a shirtless Chase standing holding two glasses and a bottle of wine.

"Thought we could curl up on the floor, watch a little TV," he said, setting the glasses down on the table and opening the bottle of wine. "Sound okay?"

"Sure, what did you want to watch?" I questioned, grabbing the remote and flipping through the channels. Before I had gotten far, Chase slipped the remote from my hand and replaced it with my wine glass and put the remote onto the dining room table.

"Come, sit down."

I looked at him questioningly but did as he asked anyways and relaxed back into the pile of pillows. Chase grabbed the blanket that sat on the back of the couch and spread it out over top of us, then he, too, sat back and relaxed. "We will watch this," he said, nodding to the TV.

I looked at the screen and giggled. "It's not even in English, and it has no subtitles. How on earth are we going to understand it?"

Chase shrugged and lay down beside me. "Well, the remote is over on the table, so I guess we will have to make do."

"You are crazy," I said, kicking the blanket off me before trying to stand up, but Chase grabbed my arm stopping me and pulled me down beside him.

"Perhaps, perhaps not." He leaned in and kissed me.

An hour later, we both lay on our sides, Chase spooned up against me as we continued to watch this foreign film. I was about to ask him a question and jumped as I felt Chase grind into me. The ridge in his pants proved that he wasn't paying attention to the movie and wouldn't be able to answer what I was going to ask because he clearly only had one thing on his mind. His lips moved against the back of my neck, kissing me.

"Fuck, I want you," he murmured between kisses as he ground himself into me again. He sucked my earlobe into his mouth before rolling me over and attacking my lips. His kiss felt different this time. It was deeper and slower. His hands moved over my body, and his touch was different as well. It wasn't as firm and cold; instead it was softer, gentler, almost like a caress. When he pulled away from my lips and looked into my eyes, even his look was different. It was as if he were looking into my soul. I closed my eyes, kissing him back.

I remembered last night, how we had gone from making out to having sex on the floor in front of the fire. Afterwards, he had carried me back to the bedroom where we had made love until the wee hours of the morning. It had been the most perfect night, I thought to myself as I lie in the warmth of my blankets, but then reality kicked in, and I looked around the bedroom.

"Sophie, you are imagining things," I said aloud to myself. We hadn't made love. *After all, you have to be in love to make it, don't you?*

I thought back to his tender touch and kiss and how he slowly drove himself into me, and I squeezed my legs together, my center throbbing and driving me crazy. I tried to chase the thoughts of last night through my mind, but it did little good. I closed my eyes and dipped my fingers between my legs, running them through my soaked center, my other hand traveling up to my bare breast, pinching, and rolling my nipple between my fingers. I could feel my orgasm building, and I tipped my head back.

"There is always something so fucking sexy about watching a woman get herself off."

I jumped at the deep voice and pulled the blanket up around my neck and glanced toward the door of my bedroom. Chase stood there leaning against the doorway. He was dressed in light-colored jeans and a white T-shirt that hugged his muscles. He held a glass of juice in one hand and a small pink bag in the other.

"I...oh my God..." I sank down and pulled the blankets over my head. If I had ever wanted to die, now was the time. Not only had he been watching me, but the images going through my mind were of him.

I heard Chase start to chuckle, and then felt the side of the bed dip down and hands prying the covers off my head.

"I didn't think you were here," I mumbled, still trying to hide my face.

"Well, I wasn't, but I certainly am now."

"Yeah I see that. My God. I want to die. I am so embarrassed."

"Fuck, I'm not. That was damn hot."

My heart was pounding in my chest so hard I was sure Chase could hear it. I was also glad I was lying down because I thought I might pass out. Trying to calm myself down, I then heard the rustle of that little bag he had been holding.

"Which leads me to this," he stated, his voice deep.

I opened my eyes and watched as Chase pulled a little box out of that pink bag and opened it.

"What is that?"

"Just a little something I picked up for you." He smiled and held up a small pink object.

I could feel my cheeks heating as he held it out for me to take. "Take it," he urged.

I shook my head, but he pulled my hand forward and set it in my palm. "What is it?"

"It's a vibrator."

"This is a vibrator?"

"Yes, you wear it on your finger and press it against your clit."

I rolled it around in my hand, the heat in my cheeks still present as he watched me. I didn't know what to say or do for that matter. Did he want me to try it now, when I was alone, or while we were having sex?

"Did you want to try it?" he asked, placing his finger under my chin and lifting my head so I could meet his eyes.

I instantly shook my head no. I'd had enough embarrassment for one day. I couldn't possibly let him watch any more.

"Why not?"

I shrugged. Instead of waiting for me to take the lead, he slipped his hand into mine and flicked the vibrator on. It tickled the palm of my hand. I sat there looking down at this little toy when he took my hand in his. "You're curious, I can tell." He gripped my hand and pulled my hand down between my legs. "Lay back. Let's have some fun," he whispered.

Chapter Sixteen

I was furious and swore under my breath as I walked down the hall towards my office. I threw the file I'd been holding down on my desk and shut the door. As soon as I was behind my computer, I began typing notes into the electronic client file. How the hell I had allowed myself to be pulled away from Sophie for this type of shit was beyond me.

Sophie and I had spent the morning in bed together. I was absolutely fascinated watching her come undone while playing with that little pink vibrator I had gotten her. I was content and happy, until my phone had rung. I'd ignored the first call, quickly distracting Sophie to focus back on herself. However, when the phone rang for the second and then third time, she huffed out loud and told me just to answer it.

I feverishly typed my notes, completely pissed off that

what my client had considered an emergency was nothing that couldn't have waited until Monday. Not that my clients weren't important, but this was something that I could have easily handled over the phone in about twenty minutes and did not require a face-to-face meeting.

"Well, well, look who it is," I heard from the doorway and looked up to see Hunter standing there.

"Hey, man."

"What's got you in here?" he asked, sitting down across from me.

"Apparently, a non-emergency, emergency." I let out a laugh, completing my notes and closing my laptop.

"I see. How's it going with Sophie?"

"Good, I guess." I shrugged. I wasn't really sure how I was supposed to answer that question. After all, my only job was to get her pregnant.

"Good, you guess?"

"Yeah, I mean, it isn't that hard to have sex all the time and get someone pregnant is it?" I chuckled.

"True."

"Listen, I really can't stay and talk. It's Friday night, and I promised Sophie I would bring pizza back with me. Which it's nearing seven already," I said, glancing down at my watch, picking up the client file and filing it away.

"All right, well, I guess I will see you Sunday night for dinner?"

Good thing I was facing away from Hunter because the mention of Sunday night family dinner had me closing my eyes. I'd totally forgotten because I had promised that I would spend the remainder of the weekend with Sophie and return home Sunday night. It was two more days than we had originally agreed to, but not only did I want to make sure that I had given myself optimal chances of fulfilling my end of the agreement, I didn't really want to leave her.

"You can always bring her along, you know. It's probably just going to be the four of us. Carter and Hope are taking the girls to a dance competition, and Bryce and Mia are up at the cottage."

"I'll think about it, okay." I grabbed my coat off the back of my chair, said good night to Hunter, and made my way down to the lobby.

I walked out the front of the building and to the car. Before I pulled away, I called and ordered the pizza. As I drove down the street, I thought about what Hunter had asked. I had spent the entire week with Sophie, much of the time in her bed, and truth was, I was sad that our time together was coming to an end. I couldn't seem to get enough of her. The little time that we had spent apart today had me missing her more than I really should have, for just being friends. Truthfully, my concentration on the issue at hand had been horrible—not because I didn't consider the clients concerns that this wasn't really an emergency, but because Sophie was the only thing that was on my mind. I was so eager to get back to her condo and to her, that I ran two red lights on my way to the pizza place and another two on the way back to the condo.

I stood in the elevator, pizza box in hand, counting the floors as the elevator climbed. It felt like forever until I hit my stop. The smell of pizza nearly drove me crazy as I made my way down the hall, slid the key in the lock, and walked in. "Hey, I'm back. I got the pizza."

"Perfect, you remembered. I'll grab the plates. I'm starving," she said, popping her head around the corner and smiling. "Oh, and I won't kill you with wine tonight. I grabbed a bottle of Coke when I was at the grocery store this afternoon." She smiled.

"Awesome!" I yelled out, dropping the pizza box on the small dining room table. I opened the lid as Sophie set the plates and bottle of Coke on the table.

"Half extra cheese, half double pepperoni and cheese." I smiled as I looked down at the steaming pie, my stomach letting out a loud grumble.

"Chase, seriously, you taint my extra cheese with the taste of your pepperoni?"

"You certainly haven't complained about my pepperoni all week," I said, smiling. When she didn't laugh, I bumped her arm. "Come on, I have suffered through wine with pizza for you. The least you can do is suffer through pepperoni." I chuckled, pulling her in closer. She rolled her eyes and grabbed a slice from the box.

"So is Friday night always pizza night?" I questioned, grabbing two slices and joining Sophie on the couch.

She nodded as she bit into her slice. "I count it as my one and only treat during the week. Something I can look forward to and not feel guilty about."

"And you're really serious about pepperoni? Seriously, it's so good. You really should try it. Live a little," I said, laughing as I took a bite.

With her mouth full, she shook her head and smiled. "Uh-huh."

She was adorably cute as she sat there shoving food in her face. "What is it about it? I really couldn't imagine ever having pizza without it."

"It's the taste. The whole entire pizza ends up tasting like it. Not to mention the pool of grease that sits in your stomach afterward, along with all the extra calories that I don't need added to an already high-calorie meal."

"So, are you telling me you won't kiss me tonight because of pepperoni?" I leaned forward, blowing kisses her way. She shoved me away as she laughed out loud.

"I never said that."

"Well, that's a good thing, because I don't know how the hell I would help you work off all those extra calories you just consumed if you won't kiss me." I winked at her, leaned in, and met her lips.

Once I was finished, I set my plate on the small table in front of us and leaned back, kicking my feet up on the coffee table. I dropped my head back and closed my eyes for a moment, then I looked over to Sophie to see her face had grown serious.

"Is something wrong?"

Sophie shook her head and cleared her throat. "I have something I want to ask you," she bit out.

"Okay."

I studied her face as the difficulty of whatever it was that she was going to ask etched over it. "Don't feel pressured to say it's okay. If you are pissed off and upset with me, just tell me okay."

I frowned. I had no clue what she was talking about. I had literally left her in bed naked, writhing from a third orgasm this morning, when that call had come in, and I had spent the afternoon at the office. "Sophie, what is it?"

"Before all this started, before I had signed the agreement and the NDA, I sort of told Jenna about this. It's been eating at me since the other night. That was why I was so stuck on taking our own vehicles and why I was somewhat upset when we had gotten home."

I tipped my head back and closed my eyes tightly as she spoke. It certainly wasn't what I wanted to hear, to know that someone knew what was going on between us.

"I'm sorry. I needed her help to shop and things. I was so nervous, and I never really thought that you would make me sign anything, but now I'm afraid that if you were to find out any other way, you'll be even more pissed off with me than you probably are right now. Please, Chase, don't hate me."

I sat there with my eyes closed trying to contemplate why I wasn't severely pissed off with her at this moment. I wasn't angry that her best friend knew. I also wasn't pissed that Matt probably knew too. I was shocked that with that revelation there was still nothing more that I wanted to do than to still be here with her. I let out the breath I was holding and looked over to her. She sat there, completely unsure of herself, biting on her thumb as I considered what I should tell her. When I saw the tear leave her eye, I quickly decided I needed to say something to her to calm her nerves.

I sat forward and placed my hand on her knee. "It's okay. Don't worry about it. I am sure that the information isn't going to go anywhere." I shrugged.

"So you aren't going to sue me?"

I let out a loud laugh. "No, Sophie, I'm not. However, you are going to owe me."

Her eyes lit up with surprise, catching me off guard. "What...what do you want?" she asked, biting her lower lip.

"I have a little bit of money in investments. You can have that."

I let out a laugh at her suggestion. "I don't want money." I laughed. "Instead, I'd like it if you join me Sunday night."

"What for?"

"Sunday night is family dinner night. You, my dear, are going to join me."

She let out a laugh as she shook her head. "I don't think so, Chase."

"You don't think so?"

She shook her head. "I don't want to give your brothers the wrong idea."

"The wrong idea? Hell. But it's okay you told Jenna?"

She thought for a few moments, every once in a while glancing at me. "Okay, you might be able to sway me."

"What might you want?" I questioned, studying the playful look in her eyes.

She didn't say anything. Instead, she got up off the couch, turned the TV off, peeled off her shirt, throwing it to the floor, and started walking down the hall to the bedroom, stopping to turn and look back at me as she reached behind her and unclasped her bra. Instantly, my cock hardened and I reached for the lamp, shutting it off, and ran down the hall after her.

Chapter Seventeen

I trailed behind Chase as he climbed up the front steps of Hunter's home and rang the bell. We heard a loud commotion inside, and then the door opened and Kaylee and Paige came bounding out the front door. They grabbed Chase by the legs, hugging him. I couldn't help but laugh at the excitement in their faces as they hugged their uncle. My heart warmed as he bent down and wrapped his arms around them both, tickling them. They squealed with laughter, and once he had let them go, they both looked up at me.

"Who's that, Uncle Chase?"

"This, girls, is my friend Sophie. Do you remember her? She came and helped me get the gum out of your hair?" Both of the girls laughed and laughed, and then they went running into the house calling out that we had arrived.

"Come on, in you go," Chase said, as he walked down

the stairs, placed his hand on my lower back, and guided me in.

"Hey, Chase," Autumn called and came over to greet us. On her hip she carried the newest addition to the family.

Chase leaned in for a hug, kissing her on the cheek. "How is Jessica feeling?" he asked, leaning down, and kissing the forehead of the baby she was carrying.

"A little better. No fever today," she said, brushing the baby's hair off her forehead.

"That's good."

"You must be Sophie," she greeted me with a smile, and then looked between Chase and me. "Would you mind holding Jessica while I get dinner on the table?"

"Oh no, I'm completely—" I couldn't even get the words out of my mouth before Jessica was plopped into my arms. I looked to Chase and then to the baby, and then to the back of Autumn who was already disappearing into the kitchen.

"Chase, I—I don't know...Here, you take her," I begged, holding Jessica out to him.

"No way. It will be good practice for you. You've got this." He grinned.

I could feel the panic starting to climb inside of me when we heard a booming hello from behind us. I turned in time to see Hunter come around the corner and shake hands with his brother. They exchanged a few words, while I stood paralyzed looking down at Jessica.

"Hey, Sophie, how you doing?" Hunter asked.

"I'm good, and you?"

"Good. Sorry, it's pretty crazy around here today. Are you ready to eat? Autumn has been cooking all day."

"Starved," I said, repositioning a wiggling Jessica in my

arms just in time for her to throw up right down the front of my shirt.

"Oh, God, so sorry about that," Hunter said, stepping in and taking her from me as I fought back puking myself.

Autumn came out of the kitchen carrying two bowls and took one look at me. "Oh, dear...come with me. I will get you another shirt." Autumn set the bowls down on the table and signaled for me to follow her as she started climbing the stairs.

Chase smiled at me and nodded as I followed Autumn upstairs. By the time I had gotten to the top of the landing, she had already found me a T-shirt, grabbed a towel from the hall closet, and showed me to the washroom. "Come on down when you are ready. I am so sorry about that. She has been feeling unwell for a few days."

"It's okay, no worries."

Autumn smiled at me and went back downstairs. I walked into the washroom and shut the door behind me and turned to look at myself in the mirror. My hands shook as I undid the buttons of my blouse. I ran the cloth under the water and cleaned my chest, then I filled the sink with warm water and soaked the blouse, working at the spot to get it clean. I slipped the T-shirt Autumn had loaned me on, rang the blouse out, and looked at my reflection in the mirror.

Who the hell was I kidding? I had no clue what the hell I was going to do with a baby. I was completely uncomfortable even holding her, and if I couldn't even hold a baby, what the hell was I going to do with my own. I slammed my hands down on the counter and without warning the tears began to fall. I closed my eyes, and for the first time ever I began silently praying that I didn't end up getting pregnant.

A knock on the door startled me. I swallowed hard and turned the tap on, filling my hand with water and taking a sip. "Be out in a minute," I called, wiping the tears from my cheeks.

"Sophie, it's just me. Everything okay?" Chase called out. "You've been up here a while. Everyone was getting concerned."

I took a deep breath and opened the door. Chase stood there, smiling, looking sexy as hell. As soon as he took a look at me and saw I'd been crying, the smile disappeared from his face. "What is wrong?"

He pushed me back and stepped into the bathroom, shutting the door behind him to give us privacy. As soon as he turned back to face me, I lunged forward, wrapping my arms around him and burying my face in his neck.

"Hey...hey...what is it?" he soothed as he wrapped his arms around me and pulled me against him, trying his best to comfort me.

I couldn't answer him. My throat was tight, and all I could do was cry. I cried because, no matter what anyone said, I was going to miss having Chase around the house. I was going to miss our nights together, our days together. I couldn't truthfully say I'd miss him because he was my best friend and he would always play a strong part in my life. I was more upset with myself, that I had allowed my feelings to take hold, and that in some strange way, I had fallen for him, and somewhere in those few minutes that I had held that baby, the realization came to me: I had decided to have a baby and deny that baby his father. Even though he said he wanted no part of it, I still didn't feel that it was fair. Regardless, Chase held me while I cried, and when I finally pulled away, he looked down into my eyes.

"Are you okay?"

"I will be. Sorry, I guess I was just feeling a little panicked. I was embarrassed," I lied.

"Hey, no problem. I get it. Hunter and Autumn get it. But I came up to tell you dinner is ready. So come on. You can leave your blouse soaking and come up and get it afterward."

"No, no, it's okay. I will just fold it up and ask Autumn for a bag. You'll have to return her shirt to her."

"No worries. Come on." He waited until I folded my wet blouse, took my hand, and together we walked downstairs.

We drove back from Hunter and Autumn's in silence. We had enjoyed a great meal and talked for hours afterward, ending the evening with a game of cards. Chase pulled into the parking lot and cut the engine. He climbed out of the car and came around to open my door.

"Come, I'll walk you to the door," he said, holding his hand out for me to take. We walked hand in hand, and when we stopped outside the main door, I leaned in and kissed his cheek.

As soon as I backed away, he quickly stepped in and met my lips, kissing me hard. He was supposed to be going home tonight, but instead it only took me a few moments before I invited him up for a good-bye drink. As soon as the elevator opened on my floor, I found myself pressed up against the wall and Chase pressed into me. With his hands in my hair, his lips on mine, I eventually guided him down the hall and into my condo. The minute the door was shut, he took over, pulling my shirt over my head, picking me up, and wrapping my legs around his waist and carrying me to the bedroom.

I lay on my left side staring out at the lights of the city. We had made love long into the wee hours of the morning. I still hadn't slept—I couldn't—and I glanced at the clock to see that it was almost five. I would have to get up soon.

Chase lay beside me snoring gently, his one arm under my neck, his other resting gently across my waist. I hadn't been able to stop thinking about the feel of his hands as they caressed my body, or the way he gripped me tighter as he sank himself deeply into me. I couldn't forget the way he looked at me, the words he had whispered or the way he called my name as his muscles tightened, for the first time, as he came.

I smiled to myself at the memory and laced my fingers between his, bringing his hand up to my lips, kissing him. He stirred and pulled me closer to him. "What is it? Everything okay?" he whispered, placing a kiss on my bare shoulder, pulling me back tighter against him.

"Yes. Go back to sleep," I whispered, snuggling against him. Within seconds, he was breathing against my shoulder, lightly snoring again. As soon as I said those words, it hit me like a train.

In a few short hours, we would be over. Even though I knew the single Chase, I also knew that no matter what type of relationship he was in at the time, he was totally committed. I started wondering what it would be like to be with him like this forever. Every night coming home after a long day and curling against him. I couldn't help but watch him with his nieces tonight, how much they loved him, and how much he loved them. He had gotten down on the floor with them after dinner and allowed them to crawl all over him until Hunter had finally called them off.

I wondered what he would be like as a father, wondered if he would change and be like his brothers if someone really caught his eye. I let out a deep breath. There was no point in wishing it were me who caught his eye because it would never become reality. We had made the agreement. There was no going back on it now.

In the morning, Chase would be gone and our lives would return to normal. He would go back home, back to his single life, and to the women who waited for him. I would go back to tax returns and boring dates, and perhaps in nine months the pitter-patter of tiny feet. I had no right to be sad; this was what I had wanted. Yet when I closed my eyes, I had to fight all the thoughts out of my mind and try to get at least a half hour of sleep before I had to get up and start my day.

Chapter Eighteen

CHASE

It had been six weeks since I had left Sophie's. Life had returned to a new normal for me. I sat in my office, files sprawled all over my desktop. I was trying to work my way through the pile before I left for the afternoon. I had been busy and had spent the better part of the last few weeks in client meetings. I had been in contract negotiations with two clients who seemed to take joy in not being able to agree on anything.

"Fuck," I said out loud with a huff as I slapped the file down on my desk, hung up my phone, and checked my watch. I'd have loved to blame my clients for all of my stress, but that wouldn't have been fair because they weren't the reason I was stressing. As a matter of fact, I should be thanking them because they had kept me busy enough to keep my mind off the true stressor: Sophie. I had been thankful at first, but now it seemed both were getting on my nerves.

I got up and shut the door to my office. It was loud in the hall, and I was just about to make a call to my three o'clock appointment to reschedule, since I still didn't have all of the information from them that I had requested. I had just begun to dial when someone knocked on my door.

"Come in," I called, sitting the phone back into the cradle.

"Hey, man. How are things?" Hunter asked as he sat down across from me.

"They're fine, I guess," I answered, letting out an irritated huff.

"What's wrong? Is it the case you're working on?" he asked, spinning the file around and taking a look.

"That and a few other things. I swear these clients just revel in agreeing to disagree, and the other ones haven't provided me with all the information I asked for over a week ago."

"Come on, you aren't new. You know what people are like. If everyone agreed, we wouldn't have a job. As for the information, just keep billing them for every hour that they waste. They will eventually get tired of paying your fee and get you what you need. However, I don't think that is the only thing that is bothering you." He spun the file back around and sat back in his chair.

"It's not."

"Well, what is it?"

I let out a breath and put my hands behind my head. "How long does it normally take to find out if you're pregnant?"

Hunter let out a laugh. "It's not something you should be worrying about, Chase. You won't ever be pregnant."

I looked at Hunter as he continued to laugh at his own poor excuse of a joke. "You know what I mean. Shouldn't Sophie know by now? I mean her medical appointment was this morning, and it's been almost four weeks."

"She might know, she may not. Have you asked her?"

I shook my head, running my hand over my face. "No."

"Well, instead of sitting here torturing yourself, you should try that. In my experience, that is the best way to get an answer. What are you doing for lunch?"

"I already ate. I ordered in."

"All right, man, I'll talk with you later. Call her, ask her, and put an end to your suffering."

"Yep, I'm calling," I said, picking up the phone.

Hunter waved at me and shut the door behind him, leaving me with a quiet office and my own thoughts. I dialed her cell phone and sat there listening to it ring. "Come on, pick up," I whispered. I jumped when I heard her voice, but the excitement eased when I realized it was her voice mail requesting that I leave a message and she would return my call within a day. I threw my cell phone down on the desk and ran my hand over my face. Fuck, I couldn't wait a day. I dialed her home line instead, only to arrive to the same conclusion—a damn voice mail.

I let out a huff, picked up my coffee cup, and made my way down the hall to the employee lounge. A fresh pot of coffee had just finished brewing, thanks to my wonderful assistant, and I poured myself a fresh cup.

"Hey, Chase. How have you been?" I heard a familiar voice ask.

I turned in time to see Chelsea walk into the lounge and sit down at the table. Chelsea and I had dated once or twice over the past year—nothing serious, just a fun romp or two when we were both lonely. Not one of my wisest moves, since we had a rule at our firm that we didn't mix business with pleasure.

"Good, thanks. Yourself?"

"I'm good. Listen, Chase, I have a family event to go to in a couple of weeks. I just broke up with my boyfriend. My mom and dad are expecting a plus one, and I was wondering if you would be interested in accompanying me? I promise I will make it worth your while."

I turned and met her eyes, but the only person who ran through my mind was Sophie. "Um, I, ah... I can't. I have a prior engagement," I lied.

"But you don't even know what weekend it is," she laughed.

"I said I am busy." I picked up my coffee cup, pushed by her, and left the room, walking back to my office.

I walked into my office to find my cell phone vibrating on my desk. I set the mug down and picked up the phone. I saw a message from Sophie was waiting for me. She had texted to tell me that she was just now getting to the doctor. I'd gotten the appointment time wrong.

I blew out a breath and instantly the need to know calmed. I was just about to text her back when reception buzzed my office to let me know my next appointment was waiting for me. I dropped my phone and left my office to go meet my clients. Sophie would have to wait, and this would help me pass enough time to hopefully keep my mind off the news.

Soon one appointment turned into two, and the next thing I knew, it was almost six. I had shut off my laptop and grabbed my cell and checked the last messages exchanged between Sophie and me. It was still the same: she hadn't said anything more, but I was sure she should know by now.

I grabbed my jacket from the back of the door, shut the lights off, and made my way down to the parking lot. I pulled out of the parking lot, my wheels spinning, and began the drive across town to Sophie's office.

Chapter Nineteen

Sophie

It was a little after four-thirty, and I sat in the waiting room flipping through one of the parenting magazines that sat on the table. I was still waiting for the doctor to call me in for my results. I glanced at the clock. I was glad that I had canceled my appointments for this afternoon. This was taking far longer than I had originally thought it would.

I shifted in my seat, trying to get comfortable again. I picked up my cell phone, glancing at the messages Chase and I had exchanged, trying to figure out what I could say to him to ease his mind.

"Sophie," I heard my name being called and looked up to see the same nurse who had taken my blood work earlier standing waiting for me.

I smiled. I could barely contain my excitement. I already knew that the answer was going to be yes. I could feel it. My period was two weeks late, I was bloated, and call me crazy, but I could already feel the life of my unborn baby boy or girl living inside of me. I hadn't told Chase, but I'd taken a drugstore pregnancy test and gotten a positive result and figured I should see the doctor just to be sure. I quickly folded the magazine and placed my cell phone in my purse, zipping it closed.

I followed her as she led me down the hall. I stopped abruptly when she stopped outside of one of the exam rooms and opened the door. "Just have a seat. The doctor will be with you shortly."

"Thank you." I walked in and took a seat, once again pulling out my cell phone to figure out what to message to Chase. I read over his last few messages and was just about to let him know I would call him as soon as I got home when the door flew open and the doctor came flying into the room.

She smiled and took a seat across from me, quickly signing into the computer. "Sorry to keep you so long, Sophie. The lab was behind. It's been a crazy day here today," she said, blowing out a breath and typing yet another password into the computer.

"It's not a problem, really. I booked this appointment more as a formality than anything. I'm pretty sure I already know the answer anyways."

"You do?" she said, looking over at me. "Well, why don't you tell me then, and we will see if the power of intuition is right," she said, leaning forward and placing her arms on her knees.

I smiled. "Well, my period is a week late. I am so bloated and tired all the time. I finally broke down and took one of those drugstore tests and it came back positive. I mean, I didn't really need to because I already know I am pregnant. I can already feel him or her inside of me," I said smiling, resting my hand on my belly.

"I see. Well, I always tell my patients that those tests at the drugstore aren't always accurate, and that is why I suggest popping in for a visit too. I am glad to see you took my advice." She sat back and flipped across a couple of screens, reading over what I guessed were my test results. She looked over to me and back to the screen before saying anything.

"Yes, I'll agree with you, all the symptoms line up, so I wasn't really surprised when I got a positive response on the test."

I smiled.

"Sophie, hon, I'm afraid your test results have come back negative."

The room spun as her words hit me like a punch to the stomach. "That's...that's impossible. I mean, I have symptoms. I have all the symptoms."

"Sophie, you have symptoms of many things, not just pregnancy. You said on the intake form you have been feeling very stressed, your diet has been off, and you haven't been sleeping well. Those three things right there will make your period late."

"No." I sat there biting my bottom lip. "No, are you sure you have the right results? Dammit." I closed my eyes tightly, trying to fight off tears.

"Sophie. It's okay to be upset." She placed her hand on my knee.

"Dammit, just tell me, are you sure?"

She nodded. "Yes, Sophie, I'm sorry. There is no baby." She was silent for a couple of minutes. "You know, sometimes, when we want something so bad that we—"

I held out my hand up to stop her. I didn't want to hear any more. "Well, then, I guess there is no reason for me to take up..." I swallowed hard. "Any more of your time." I grabbed my coat and purse and was just about to head out the door when my eyes began blurring and my head began throbbing. I stopped and pinched the bridge of my nose.

"Sophie."

I inhaled deeply, turning and looking towards her, nodding through tear-filled eyes, and took off down the hall. I rushed out of the office and down to the parking lot, taking the stairwell so that I didn't have to be in the elevator at the same time with anyone for fear I couldn't hold back the flood of tears that I felt coming on. There was no way I would be able to look at anyone. I ran across the parking lot to my car, quickly unlocked the door, and climbed in.

I slammed my door shut, threw my purse into the passenger seat and buried my face in my hands and let it all out. The final nail had been hammered in. I wasn't pregnant. I had slept with my best friend at first in hopes of becoming a mother, and it had been all for nothing. Instead, I had fallen in love with him and couldn't even tell him. I didn't even have him to hold me through all this heartache, because that was what it was, pure and total heartache. I felt as if a part of me had died and that no amount of time would fix me.

I had taken my time after my appointment to drive back to the office. It was now a little after seven, and I sat in my office with my door closed. I had struggled my way through the last appointment of the day that had been waiting for me when I had gotten back. My work day was over and now I sat with a hot cup of chamomile tea trying hard to concentrate enough to be able to go over the client file for my appointment tomorrow morning. All I really wanted was to go home and curl up in bed, put the heating pad on, and zone out in front of the TV.

I looked to my cell phone that sat on the corner of my desk, the little blinking red light reminding me that I still hadn't contacted Chase after I received the news. I really didn't have any desire to talk to him or anyone. I reached for a scrap piece of paper to make a quick note when I heard a loud, deep voice out in the hall. As the voice crept closer and my anxiety built, I was about to get up and see what was going on when my door opened and Chase strode in, Marie following behind him.

"Sir, I can't let you interrupt her...I told you, she asked for privacy. I'm sorry, Sophie, he came barging in and wouldn't stop, even after I told him you weren't taking any more clients tonight. I didn't mean to have him interrupt you. I know you said you wanted not to be bothered."

I looked into Chase's blue eyes and instantly felt a fire deep in the pit of my stomach. I glanced to Marie who stood there ringing her hands. "It's fine, Marie." I smiled weakly. I met his blue eyes again and sat back down behind my desk. Marie nodded and pulled the door closed behind her, leaving us alone.

"What the hell? Is she your own private security or something?" Chase chuckled.

"Chase, I had asked not to be bothered. She was simply doing her job," I bit out, closing the file on my desk and shutting down my laptop, then shoving both into the bag that sat at my feet.

"Do you have a minute?"

"Not really. I need to get home and get this work completed. I have an early morning tomorrow, and I am really very unprepared for it." I grabbed my coat and threw it around my shoulders.

"Listen, just give me a minute. I sent you a message today, and you didn't respond, but I've been thinking. I want to be a part of this pregnancy. I want to help you in whatever way you need. I know I said I didn't, but I do. I want to help you decorate the nursery, buy supplies, change diapers, and have my allotment of baby time."

I looked into his blue eyes, which were now filled with so much hope, want, and excitement that I didn't know what to say. It was enough that I was crushed, but now to have to face that crushing look in his eyes, an indescribable feeling came over me. I had no words. Nothing I could say would make it less painful, so instead I just stood there staring back at him.

"I want to be there for the next doctor appointment, for all the appointments, especially the ultrasound. I want to be there to hear the baby's heartbeat for the first time. I just need you to tell me when and where to be, and I'll make it happen. I want to be there for all the firsts. I want to be there for you when you deliver, when you go home. I want to be there to see his or her first steps." He pulled his phone from his pocket and flipped until he found what he was looking for. "First, we will start with the next appointment. Tell me when and where." When I didn't say anything to that, he looked up and met my eyes.

"Why the sad face? I thought you would be happy to have some sort of support system. Some help..."

I let out a sigh. "I would be grateful for the support system, but it doesn't matter, Chase." Those were the only words I could get out. I swallowed hard, continuing to pack my bag so that I could avoid what I knew was coming, what I knew had to come. I had to tell him, but honestly, I didn't even know how.

"Sure it does. Why would you say that?" He set his phone on the desk and approached me. He placed his hands on my arms, stopping me from what I was doing. He placed his finger under my chin and raised my head so he could look into my eyes.

The longer he looked into my eyes, the more my eyes burned, and I tried so hard to muster up the courage not to cry, but as soon as I blinked, a tear slipped from the corner, giving me away. "It doesn't matter, because there isn't a baby. It didn't work. I'm not pregnant."

I could see the stunned look in Chase's eyes, and then I slowly felt his hands slip down my arms as the words hit him full force. "But...that's impossible."

"But nothing. It's not impossible. There is no baby. So you're off the hook. You don't need to pretend to want to be here for me, Chase. You don't need a baby. You're a hot, single guy with your life in front of you. My little experiment, all the planning, didn't work, so things will go back to the way they were. You can go back to dating all those gorgeous women, and I will go back to my boring old life of lonely weekends, taxes, and the occasional shitty date. Thank you for trying. I've got to go though."

I turned away from his stare, zipped my bag closed,

picked up my purse, and left my office, leaving Chase standing there against my desk. There was nothing more to say. I didn't look back. I couldn't. I didn't want to see the joy of him being off the hook, and I didn't want him to know any more than he already did that I was completely crushed.

I took my time walking down the hall and into the lobby where Marie sat. I approached her desk and stopped to hand her a few important documents. "Can you please make sure these get faxed tonight before you leave, and just so you know, Chase is still in my office. He is welcome to stay as long as he needs. Just let him have some time okay."

"Sure thing, Sophie. Have a good night, and I will see you tomorrow."

"You as well."

I drove slowly on my way home, a drive that would normally take me ten minutes taking me twenty. I had never been so happy to walk into the quietness of my condo. Not caring, I left a trail of my belongings all over the floor and grabbed a bottle of water from the fridge. My heart had been heavy and my head hurt, and now I felt worse because I had walked out on Chase, but I hadn't had a choice. I didn't even know how to handle what I was feeling. I took my water, shut off the light, and made my way to my bedroom.

I shut my bedroom door, turned on the heated mattress pad so it could warm up, and put the TV on. I washed my face, tied my hair back into a messy ponytail, and changed into my favorite flannel pajama pants and T-shirt. I pulled the large blinds across the floor-to-ceiling windows, something I never did, and pulled the duvet down and crawled into bed. I fell into the large pile of pillows and pulled an extra one into my body. As I inhaled, all I could smell was

Chase. The longer I lay there inhaling his scent, the longer I had to hold onto the sob that was threatening to escape my throat.

When my chest felt like it was going to explode, I finally succumbed, and a loud sob escaped me, echoing through the room. I held onto that pillow, inhaling his scent, and cried, wishing that Chase's arms were wrapped around me, trying to comfort me. I not only cried for the loss of something that could have been but for the loss of Chase as well, because no matter what, I couldn't have him as a lover or a friend. That was when the full realization hit me. I had lost both him and a baby this afternoon.

Chapter Twenty

I drove around the city aimlessly for three hours, after I had left the quietness of Sophie's office. I'd waited at least a half hour after she had left before I got behind the wheel of my car. I was now down at the waterfront.

I shut the engine off and began walking through the park back to the spot where Sophie and I had shared our second first kiss only a few weeks earlier. I sat down on an empty bench and looked out over the water. Memories flashed through my mind. I smiled at the memory of the look on her face as our lips had parted the first time.

My phone vibrated in my pocket, pulling me out of my memories. I checked my messages to see that my brothers were waiting for me at our normal restaurant location. I was about to message them to let them know I wasn't coming but decided getting out with them would do me good. I needed to pull myself out of this funk.

Twenty minutes later, I pulled into the parking lot of Wings and Things. I immediately saw that all of my brothers' vehicles were parked. I cut the engine and checked my phone once again for any message from Sophie. I was hoping for anything, a hello, fuck you, die bastard die, whatever she wanted to send, but there was nothing.

I removed my seatbelt and shoved my phone back into my jacket pocket. Walking into the restaurant I was greeted with an onslaught of waving women, most of whom I had slept with at one time or another over the years. We apparently needed to change up our location, I thought to myself, but I was polite, greeted them, even making small talk with some. I approached the bar, ordered a beer, and made my way back to where my brothers were waiting.

I slid into the booth beside Hunter and shoved my face into the menu that sat waiting for me. Carly dropped a beer in front of me, flashing me one of her smiles. When I didn't make eye contact and only mumbled a thank you, she walked away with a look of disappointment.

"What the fuck is up with you?" Bryce questioned, looking between Carter and Hunter.

"Nothing?"

"Nothing? What the fuck? Four months ago you and Carly were all over one another. You'd take her home, screw her brains out, and now you barely acknowledge her?" Bryce seemed a little pissed off and picked up his beer and took a swig.

"Mom would be so disappointed with you," Hunter said facetiously, trying to get under my skin. I knew he was doing it on purpose, since he was the only one who I'd really confided in, yet he still didn't know the outcome.

I did my best to ignore them, letting them carry on with whatever conversation they had been in the middle of before I'd arrived. I wasn't really all that hungry, and I finally shut the menu, downed the remainder of my beer, and was well into my second one before I heard my name mentioned.

I looked to Carter who sat there staring at me. "You sure you're all right?"

I nodded, downed the remainder of my second beer, and signaled for another one.

"Jesus, you should slow down there, bro. You have a car to drive home," Carter said, nodding towards the empty beer bottle.

Hunter turned to look at me. "Did you finally hear anything?"

I nodded. For the past couple of weeks, I had let my brothers believe that everything was back to normal with me and that I was back to my old dating ways. I had made up dates with numerous women to avoid our nights out. I'd made up stories of the girls I had taken home, but the truth was that, since I had left Sophie's apartment that Monday morning a few weeks ago, I hadn't been able to look at another woman, because the only one that was on my mind was Sophie. I'd spent my nights at home, watching movies, texting or chatting with Sophie on the phone, even spending one more night in her bed, but now I feared my lies were about to surface, because telling them all one thing via text was different than sitting in front of them.

"Well? Is she pregnant? Did you fulfill her need? Did

your super sperm win?" Hunter and Carter chuckled at Bryce's insinuation. I, on the other hand, did not.

"When is the big day? With any luck, Mia will be expecting at the same time," Bryce said.

"What big day?" I asked, picking at the label on my beer.

"Really, Chase? You have to ask? When is the due date?"

I let out a deep breath, continuing to pick at the already mangled label on my beer bottle. I could feel them watching me as I sat there trying to decide to tell them. "All right, let me level with you guys. There is no baby. She isn't pregnant, and honestly, I'm devastated."

The silence at the table was deafening. I watched them as they looked between one another, not really sure what they should or could say. "Don't you guys have anything to say at all?" I asked.

"Why are you so devastated? I mean, you made her sign the contract, remember?" Hunter said quietly.

"I remember," I said, flinching at the memory.

"We're a little lost here, Chase," Bryce said, setting his bottle down and looking at the others. "You wanted nothing to do with everything after the deed was done. Your words, bro."

"Look, I haven't exactly been truthful with you guys." I looked to my three brothers. "I haven't been with a woman since Sophie. There have been no dates. I've been hanging out at home watching TV, playing video games, and talking or texting with Sophie. So when I've told you I couldn't do something because I had a date, I was lying."

The three of them exchanged a knowing glance, then looked back at me. "So, you want her because of the baby?" Hunter questioned.

"No. I want her no matter what. I can't get her out of my fucking mind. She's everything. Everything about her is fucking amazing."

There was the truth. It had finally moved past my lips and was now out in the open. I felt a ton of weight lifted from my shoulders for finally speaking the actual truth. I'd had a taste of her, and I didn't want to be without her, regardless of a baby. I wanted Sophie.

"Have you told her?" Carter questioned.

I shook my head. "Look, I saw the look in her eyes, that look of disappointment. I saw the look, and I know what that look means. She wants nothing more to do with me."

"Yeah, well, you don't know that until you tell her how you feel. Give her a chance to respond to your feelings."

All through dinner, I listened to each of my brothers do their best to convince me that I should talk with her and share my feelings. I also came up with every single excuse that I could think of as to why this was a very bad idea. Although, no matter what my excuses, they combated them with a reason why I was just being a coward. At the end of the night, accepting what I'd been telling myself, I'd come to the conclusion that there was no way I could tell her. I sat in the parking lot and watched as each of my brothers left.

I sat in my car, alone, rethinking each of their advice while I waited for the engine to warm, my mind constantly racing back to her face this afternoon as she stood there telling me that there was no baby. I looked at the clock; it was close to midnight. I knew she would still be up. At least I hoped she would be as I put my car into drive and pulled out of the parking lot. My brothers were right; I would regret not telling her how I felt for the rest of my life, and living with that would be harder than coming clean and telling her how I felt.

I drove through the city thinking of what I was going to say to her when I finally saw her. Should I just swoop in, grab her in my arms, kiss her, and confess everything? I stood in the elevator of her building tapping my foot impatiently as I was lifted to her floor. I ran down the hall and stopped outside of her door, then I inhaled deeply and banged on it. I wasn't going to give her the chance not to answer. I banged again, and finally the door was abruptly opened and a red-nosed, tear-stained face stood before me.

"Chase? What on earth?"

I pushed my way into her apartment, grabbing her and pulling her into me. "You, you're what I want." I pressed my lips to hers and pulled away. "Marry me?"

"Chase." She pushed her hands on my chest, trying to push me away. "Let me go."

"Not until you promise me you'll marry me."

"Let go of me!" she barked, finally pushing me hard enough that I stumbled. "You've been drinking! I don't want you to only want me when you are drunk. I want you to want me sober."

"I've had a couple beers, but I'm not drunk."

"You are. I can taste it on you."

"Sophie, I'm not. Fuck, I love you." Sure, I'd probably had too much to drink. I probably shouldn't have driven, and this was far from my smoothest performance to date, but what I was saying was the truth. It was how I felt.

"I can't do this, Chase. Please." Her hand covered her mouth and a tear escaped her eye. "Please, just go."

She turned away from me, and her shoulders started to

shake. I reached out to her to pull her into my arms to comfort her, but she was too quick and stepped out of my reach. I wanted her. I wanted her so damn bad, and I stepped forward and placed my hand on her arm, but she ripped herself away from me.

"I told you to go."

I didn't say anything. I just stood there looking at her. Looking at the curves I wished to touch, the hair I longed to run my fingers through, and the body I wished to hold and worship while she lay beneath me. I had committed those feelings to memory. I'd committed those memories to mine. There was no winning. She wasn't going to change her mind, so, without a word, I walked out of her condo, shutting the door behind me. Behind us.

Chapter Twenty-One

It was cold and blustery out. I glanced out my office window to see the mess of snow falling. I dug into my dish of Moo Shu Pork that Jenna had so kindly brought to me. She sat across from me rooting through her purse for her dental floss, finally finding the little blue container.

"I should have had you bring me two of these—one for now and one for tomorrow night." I giggled.

"I have no problem doing this again tomorrow night. I'll even grab two of those to-die-for cinnamon rolls from Aroma Mocha," Sophie said as she shoved the remainder of her egg roll in her mouth.

"Well that sounds like a date that I'm not going to pass up!"

"Have you heard from..."

I was about to hold my hand up to stop her from asking when Carol popped her head into my office.

"You lovelies have any hot plans for tonight?"

"Hey, Carol!" Jenna said, waving, a big smile on her face. "How are you doing?"

"I'm well, Jenna. It's so nice to see you. Please tell me that you are trying to get this girl out of here for Valentine's Day?" she said, nodding towards me.

"Well, yes, she doesn't know it yet, but I have a date lined up for her. It's getting Miss Stubborn to agree to at least meet us at the restaurant," Jenna said, pointing at me.

"Listen, the both of you. For you it may be Valentine's Day, but for me it's Singles Awareness Day. I plan to work until seven, maybe eight, then head home and have a love affair with a bottle of wine and a pizza. Perhaps a chocolate cupcake."

They both let out a loud laugh, but I was serious. I spent most of my days at the office, including the weekends. I had stopped going out for our monthly get-together. As a matter of fact, I had stopped going anywhere and everywhere that I could possibly run into Chase. I still went to Saturday-morning yoga, but afterward we either went to my place or Jenna's for coffee.

"I'll do my best, Carol, but she is a tough one."

"That she is."

"Would the two of you please stop talking about me as if I am not sitting right here."

"All right, I have to get out of here. I promised John I'd be home. He's taking me to a play. Good night, ladies."

"Night, Carol," we both shouted in unison.

I turned back to Jenna, who now sat staring at the

engagement ring on her finger. Matt had finally proposed, and she was over the moon excited. I didn't blame her; they made the cutest couple, and I was so happy to see that they were finally taking the next step. I let out a loud sigh and set my fork onto the side of the container.

"Are you sure you won't join us tonight?" Jenna pleaded. "It will only be Matt and I, I swear. We miss you and really want you to join us. Plus, we are gonna talk wedding details, and you need to be there if you are going to take me up on my offer and be my maid of honor." She had invited me to join them for dinner, but I really didn't want to feel like a third wheel.

I nodded. "I'm sure. Did you see that waiting room full of people out there? Someone must help them. Besides, it's Valentine's Day. You guys should be alone. There is plenty of time to go over wedding details."

"It's just another day, Sophie. It's fine. Matt told me when he made the reservation he had already asked for a table for three."

"Well then you will have lots of room then. Really, it's fine. I chose to work tonight so everyone else could be home. Go enjoy yourself. Maybe we can do coffee at my place this weekend. I will cook brunch or something." I shrugged. If I knew Matt and Jenna, I knew that the table for three they were claiming to have would really be a table of four and Chase would probably be the other guest. "Seriously, I'm fine. Go."

"Sophie, it's been five months. You can't keep ignoring the outside world. How will you ever meet someone?"

"Ha, Jenna, don't even start that. I'm perfectly good with staying single, okay." I turned my attention to the file that sat on top of the pile. I didn't want to be hounded. I wanted my friend to leave me in my misery and go and be with her fiancé.

"All right then, on that note, I guess I will be going. I've taken up enough of your time."

I hugged Jenna, and as she left, I wandered down the hall and grabbed another cup of coffee and went out to call in my next client. I'd been in the meeting going over the client's tax return for twenty minutes when I heard Marie raise her voice. I did my best not to pay attention to it, but when I heard her raise her voice again, I quickly excused myself.

I opened my office door and was smacked in the face with the aroma of a freshly cooked pizza. My stomach let out a loud groan, even though I'd already eaten.

"Marie? What is going on? Who ordered pizza?" I called as I walked around the corner to see a room full of people and Marie guarding the entrance of the hallway with her life from Chase. I stopped in my tracks at the sight.

"There she is. I told you I knew she was here. Now let me in," he bit out, trying to push his way past Marie. When she blocked him again, he stepped into the first boardroom and threw the pizza box down on the table. "It's okay, you don't want to let me in to see her. It's no problem. The meeting can be done in here as well. It doesn't need to be held in her office. Oh, and it's not a problem. I have nowhere to be, so I'll wait," he said, setting my favorite bottle of wine down beside the box and turning to hand me a dozen long-stemmed red roses.

"Chase, what are you doing?" I whispered, shocked, but took the flowers from his hand, bringing them to my nose.

"I have brought you your Valentine's Day dinner." He

flipped open the pizza box, exposing a heart-shaped pizza. "Double cheese. No pepperoni. And wine because I know you love wine with your pizza."

My eyes began to burn, and within seconds, they were filled with tears that I tried hard to blink away, but they spilled over the edge of my eye and ran down my cheek. I wiped at them instantly to hide them, but it was too late. Chase had already seen.

"My God, I am always making you cry," he said, taking a step closer, reaching out and cupping my cheek, wiping away another tear with his thumb. "I've got to work on that," he mumbled.

"Chase, people are watching," I whispered. I knew the door to the boardroom stood wide open and many sets of eyes were watching from the waiting room. "Let me close the door, okay," I said, trying to step around him, but he blocked me.

"So, let them watch. Let them all watch." That was all he said before he dropped to one knee and pulled from his pocket a little box. "Sophie, I can't stop thinking of you. You're actually all I think about."

"Chase, what are you doing?"

"Shhhh..."

I watched through blurry eyes as Chase cracked open the little box he held to reveal a diamond solitaire surrounded with tiny blue sapphires.

"Chase..." I mumbled through tears.

"No, you are going to listen. I want to be with you. I want to make babies with you—many, many babies. If we can't make them, then we will adopt. I even know someone who might be able to help us out with that. Even if we don't,

I honestly don't care, as long as you will walk through the rest of my life by my side."

He reached behind him and pulled from his pocket an envelope. "What is that?" I asked.

"This," he said, looking to the envelope in his hand, "is that stupid NDA and contract that I made you sign. I was very stupid to even think about bringing it to the table. Stupid and naive to think that I would have been able to be with you and not fall head over heels in love with you. I want to be with you forever, Sophie, and if I have to I will spend the rest of my life trying to prove it to you."

He ripped the envelope in half, and then those halves in half, throwing them to the ground. "It's done, it's over, they are gone," he said, smiling up at me. "Besides, they were never legal anyways. I didn't have the heart to have them notarized." He chuckled.

"You do know I have a shredder in my office, right? It might be easier." I smiled down at him.

"Well, what do you say?"

"I say you should pick yourself and that paper up off my office floor," I said, not giving away exactly how excited I was. His face dropped, and he reached for the ripped pieces and stood up. He lifted his head and met my eyes. "Now I think you should kiss me."

Chase smiled and pulled me into his arms, kissing me deeply. As soon as we parted, he took the ring and slipped it onto my finger. I looked down at my hand and back to Chase.

"I love you too," I whispered.

The people waiting in the waiting room broke out into a loud applause, some yelling words of congratulations. I had completely forgotten they were standing there behind me watching us. I buried my face into Chase's shoulder to hide my embarrassment.

"Give us a few minutes, folks," Chase called out before closing the door to the boardroom. His lips met mine as he pushed me up against the door, kissing me hard. "I say you close up shop, come home with me, and let me worship you all night long."

"I think that sounds perfect."

Chapter Twenty-Two

Chase

The second that boardroom door clicked closed, I shoved Sophie up against the wall. I kissed her deeply, but it wasn't nearly enough. I wanted to rip her clothes off and screw her right there on the boardroom table. It had always been a fantasy of mine, one I'd not fulfilled but knew that within time we would celebrate a first for both of us. I tried, but she begged me not to, insisting that she needed to get back to the clients, especially the one she had forgotten about in her office. So, reluctantly, I let her go, and I sat waiting in the lobby of her office, my cock straining against the zipper of my jeans for an hour while she dealt with the remaining people who had insisted on seeing her before we left for the night.

I had never been so happy to see the last person leave, and shortly after Sophie came walking out of her office, her briefcase in hand, and her coat flung over her arm. She gave me a sexy smile as she walked across the lobby to where I was waiting.

"It's about time," I kidded, knowing just how important her business was to her.

We stepped out into the cold night air and I took her hand in mine as we walked across the parking lot. I stopped at my car and opened the passenger door, looked behind me and saw Sophie walked towards hers. "Where are you going?" I questioned.

"To my place," she stated.

"No, you are coming with me." I walked over, guiding her back to my car.

"Okay, but I need to stop and get a few things first then."

"Like?"

"Well, I need a toothbrush, hair care products, shower products, clothes." She looked up at me innocently.

"I have an extra toothbrush, I do have a hairdryer, and I do shower, so I have products, and there is nothing that I plan on doing with you this weekend that will require a tremendous amount of clothes. I promise." I smiled.

"Chase, don't be ridiculous."

"I'm not, trust me. What I plan on doing with you over the next twenty-four to forty-eight hours does not require clothes."

She covered her mouth as she laughed and climbed into my car. I raced through the city, and twenty minutes later, her briefcase and coat were in a pile on my floor by the doorway and a trail of clothes led the way to my bedroom.

My cock ached as I sank into her tightness. Sweat poured off my body as I pounded into her. Her cries were loud and echoing through the room. I loved the sounds she made because of me. My one hand gripped her hip and the other gripped her shoulder, holding her close to me. The harder I thrusted, the deeper I went, and the louder she became. I could already feel her tightening with every thrust and knew she was on the boarder of her release. I stopped and pulled out of her. I watched as her head dropped to the mattress, breathless.

"Why...why did you stop?" she asked breathlessly.

"I want to be able to see your face as you come." I leaned over, whispering in her ear, "Roll onto your back."

When she didn't move right away, I quickly flipped her over. She let out a laugh. I pulled her closer to the edge of the bed and quickly sank back into the heat and tightness I so loved. Her moans sent chills through me as I knew I was the one causing her to make them. It only took a second to get her right back where she had been, and I stroked her clit to help her along.

She forced her head back, lifting herself off the mattress, and let go. Her cries were louder than before, and I began to worry if my neighbors were going to hear. That worry went away quickly as I felt my balls tighten and I gritted out her name, pouring myself into her.

Minutes after cleaning her up, she lay cradled in my arms, staring down at the ring that she now wore. "What are you thinking about?" I asked as I ran my fingers through her hair.

"Just the answer to that question you asked me so long ago."

"What question?"

"Why we waited?"

I looked into her eyes. There was a seriousness behind them that, in all the years that I had known her, I had never seen before. "And what is your answer?" I asked as my heart began to pump a little faster, hoping that perhaps her answer was the same as mine.

"Honestly, I think every relationship has failed me in one way or another because of one reason. You. I think that without knowing it, in some way I have been in love with you from the start. I never really knew how to express it or how to show it, and at the risk of losing our friendship, I never was brave enough to do anything about it."

I laced my fingers through hers and pulled her into me. I had done a lot of soul searching over the last five months, and I knew that was exactly how I felt as well. "I think you might be right," I whispered as I placed my hand on her cheek and gently met her mouth, kissing her deeply.

Monday morning I walked on air as I made my way into the boardroom. Carter, Hunter, and Bryce all sat in their usual spots, a coffee in front of them, going over whatever documents were being brought to the table. I sauntered in, dropping my suit jacket on the chair behind me, and sat down.

"Jesus, it's about time you got here," Carter complained, glancing at his watch.

"We weren't sure if we should start without you or send out reinforcements to find you," Bryce stated.

"However, we guessed we should just start without you,

since we figured you were probably balls deep in your fiancée this morning." Hunter grinned.

These fuckers, I thought to myself, and I hung my head low and sat in my usual spot. I hadn't bothered to call any of them after telling them what my plan had been, so none of them knew how it had gone. I let out a breath. "She said no. No, I don't want to talk about it, so let's get down to business," I stated with no emotion.

I almost burst out laughing at the looks on their faces as they quickly averted their eyes from me and to one another, and suddenly the mood in the room shifted.

"Jesus, man, I am so sorry," they all said in unison.

The room went quiet as I opened up the file that sat in front of my spot. I fought off the urge to smile.

"Did she give you a reason?" Hunter questioned.

I shook my head. I knew if I looked up at any one of my brothers, I would burst out laughing.

"She can't just say no without a reason," Bryce stated.

"Sure she can. Why can't she?" Carter questioned.

"Fuck that. If it were me, I'd demand an answer. Look at him. The poor ass has been through enough. He at least deserves an answer. Get her on the phone. Let's break her true Malone style."

Pretty soon, even Hunter was involved in the conversation, and my three brothers soon forgot I was sitting there. They spent ten minutes arguing amongst themselves about my problems, before I cleared my throat to remind them that I was still there and that I could hear everything they were saying.

"Hey, we're sorry, man. Totally inappropriate behavior," Carter said, shaking his head.

I chuckled to myself. "It's all good. She said yes."

"You ass." Bryce smiled. "Congrats, brother."

"So, when is the big date? You know the girls will want to know right away."

"We haven't set one yet but will soon."

"Better get to it, because as soon as we tell Mia, Autumn, and Hope, you know they are going to want to start planning everything," Bryce said, pulling me in for a hug. "Congrats, bro."

Our weekly Monday-morning meeting quickly turned into a celebratory one, which turned into a celebratory lunch.

Chapter Twenty-Three

SOPHIE

Chase and I had spent the better part of the week at his place discussing at great length how we were going to move forward. We had decided that I would sell my condo and move into his, which was bigger, and ultimately had the best view of not only the city but of the harbor as well. Hunter had recommended their realtor, and I found myself running through my condo a week later, cleaning like a mad woman for an appointment with her Sunday morning.

I'd just gotten out of the shower and was sitting in the living room with the paper and a hot cup of coffee in hand while waiting for her to arrive. I was reading through an article when my cell phone vibrated on the table. I glanced at my phone and laughed when I saw Jenna's name. Her message of "are you okay" caused me to giggle, and I glanced to the sparkling diamond that I now wore on my left hand. I quickly began typing a message but stopped and called her instead.

"Hello," she sang into the phone. "It's about time you called. I was beginning to wonder if this past Valentine's Day didn't do you in."

"I know. I'm sorry."

"Don't be sorry. Just tell me if you are okay."

"Listen, do you think you could meet me in a little bit?" I asked, using the same depressed voice I'd been using for the past five months, even though I was so far from that state of mind I now had whiplash.

"Of course, I can meet you. Just say where and when and I will be there. Is everything okay?" I heard her whisper something to Matt. It didn't surprise me as much as it bothered me that I had been their topic of discussion lately.

"Um, how about four at Aroma Mocha? The cafe should be pretty quiet by then."

"Oh, Sophie, at four? Come on, you need to start getting out again with humans."

"I know, I know, and I do get out with humans. I do still work, you know. Come on, please," I begged.

"Fine. I will see you at four, but only if you promise to come out with us on Friday night."

"I won't promise, but I will try, okay," I lied. I already knew we were meeting them Friday night. Chase just hadn't said anything to Matt yet.

"All right, I'll take that answer, since it's better than the last few I've been given. I'll see you in a little bit."

We both hung up the phone. Just as I set my phone down, the realtor knocked on the door.

Two hours later, I shut the door to my condo and called Chase. "All the paperwork is signed," I sang into the phone.

"Awesome. Everything go okay?"

"Yep. I'll be over in a little bit, okay? Jenna wants to have a coffee. See you tonight?"

"You know it. I'll come to your place that way we can bring some of your things here tomorrow. Sound good?"

"Sounds great. See you soon."

I slipped my cell into my purse and left my condo. I walked down to Aroma Mocha. It was a beautiful, sunny day, and I couldn't wait to share the news with Jenna. I felt like I'd been holding this secret long enough. I walked in and placed our order—coffee and muffins as always—and took a seat over in the back corner.

I'd been waiting for ten minutes when I finally saw Jenna pull the door open and walk in. She looked around the fairly empty diner and finally saw me. I had to keep my head down to contain the smile that I had hidden on my face.

"Sophie, look at you. You're an utter mess," she bit out as she slid into the seat across from me. It was true. After the realtor left, I had thrown my hair up in a messy ponytail and put on an old T-shirt and jeans. If I was going to be packing later, I didn't want to wear good clothes.

I shrugged. "I guess, but I didn't think I looked that bad," I mumbled.

"Honey. You can't keep doing this to yourself. You can't keep hiding in your condo. We all miss you, and we are all very worried about you. I figured that after last weekend you would be good to go, but you've now been avoiding me. You didn't show up for yoga on Saturday either."

Shit, I had forgotten all about yoga, and I had promised Jenna I would be there too. I was about to explain when our coffee and muffins were placed down in front of us, and as Jenna thanked the waitress, I pulled my hand from below the table and grabbed my coffee mug.

As the waitress walked away from our table, Jenna turned towards me and was just about to say something else that would either be in the form of yelling and giving me shit or trying to comfort me, when her eyes spotted the ring I wore.

"What on earth..."

"He asked me to marry him. Obviously, I said yes," I said, wiggling my fingers.

Jenna reached for my hand, gripping it tightly and pulling it towards her.

"My God, girl, that is gorgeous," she said as she continued looking it over. Then she raised her eyes to mine and smiled. "Are you happy?"

"Jenna, seriously, I couldn't be happier. He's everything to me. I mean, there aren't many people who can say they are lucky enough to marry their best friend."

"My God, I have to call Matt," Jenna said, rifling through her purse for her cell phone. "We need to celebrate."

"Hold up. I know Chase wanted to tell Matt, so don't ruin it for him." I giggled.

"Okay, fine." Jenna pouted, putting her purse down.

"We have lots to talk about. I need a dress, and you need a dress," I said.

"We get to shop together for our wedding dresses," we sang in unison.

I could feel the excitement building, and before I knew

it, we had been sitting in the coffee shop for over three hours. We had gotten lost in plans and locations and flower choices and honeymoon spots.

"This is going to be so amazing. I seriously cannot wait," Jenna said, laughing.

Suddenly, I felt a hand on my shoulder and looked up to see Chase standing beside me, and Matt trailing behind with a tray of coffees. We had been so wrapped up that we hadn't noticed the time.

"Congratulations, guys!" Matt said, setting the tray down on the edge of the table and passing each of us our coffees.

Chase slid in beside me, putting his arm around me and pulling me into him. "I was getting worried. I called Matt to see if you were over there, and he was the one who led us here." He leaned in and kissed me.

"Sorry about that. We got caught up in wedding plans," I said, kissing him.

"And so, it starts!" Matt laughed.

"We were both afraid of that." Chase chuckled, fist bumping Matt.

We spent the better part of the night talking, laughing, and throwing around ideas. It had been one of the best days the four of us had shared together, and only the beginning of many more to come.

Chapter Twenty-Four

I stood at the altar with my brothers and Matt. The girls had already come down the aisle and had taken their places across from us. The doors opened at the back of the church, and the second I set my eyes on Sophie, I could feel the tears start to form. I swallowed back the lump in my throat and watched as Sophie walked down that aisle, leaving me weak in the knees. She looked absolutely stunning. Once she stood before me, I leaned in and kissed her cheek. I couldn't wait for her to be mine.

After the ceremony, we had partied the night away with our friends and family. It was midnight, and we had just finished sharing another dance when I pulled her into me and whispered that I thought it was a good time to get going. I watched the look in her eyes as she silently agreed with me. We said our good-byes and left the venue.

I rolled over and looked at my sleeping wife. Glancing at the clock, I saw it was only five; the sun was barely up. I slid my arm under her and pulled her against me, listening to the soft moan that escaped her lips. We were leaving for our honeymoon in six hours. Two weeks in Hawaii, just us, no distractions.

"Baby, good morning," I whispered, sucking her earlobe into my mouth.

"Morning," she mumbled sleepily and stretched.

"Are you ready for our next adventure?"

She opened her sleep-filled eyes and looked at me. "What time is it?" I could hear the panic in her voice at the thought we had slept in.

"It's only five. We have lots of time."

Sophie raised herself up onto her elbows and looked around the hotel room. "I almost forgot where we were." She mumbled, laughing, "Guess we should get up then and have some breakfast."

I grabbed her, pulling her back down. "No way, not yet. I haven't made love to my wife yet this morning," I mumbled, kissing the side of her neck and rolling her so I was on top.

"We can't be late." Sophie laughed and then sucked in her breath as I sucked her nipple into my mouth.

"Are you already making up excuses? My brothers did warn me of this you know." I chuckled. "Calm down. We won't be late, no worries. Just relax and let me work my magic."

Sophie let out a laugh as I squeezed her sides before kissing my way down her body. I loved watching my wife come undone, and make her come undone I did.

Three hours later, we walked hand in hand through the airport to our gate. We had lots of time, so as we wandered, we stopped in some of the shops along the way. We browsed around, each of us grabbing a couple of books and magazines for the beach. We grabbed a couple coffees and bagels along the way, too, since we hadn't had time for breakfast at the hotel.

We were now seated at the gate, both reading, both eating breakfast and sipping on hot coffee.

I looked up from my book and watched her. The soft smile on her lips as she read what must have been a funny part in her favorite author's newest rom-com. It was in those few moments that I realized I couldn't have been happier. I had married my best friend. Someone who had always understood me, always listened when I needed her to. I was only sad for a second when I realized that I had wasted all this time. She had been right in front of me all along. What mattered now was that we start our lives together.

"What's got you so serious?" she questioned, pulling me out of my thoughts.

"Nothing." I smiled and shoved my head back into my book. When I looked up again a few minutes later, I caught her watching me.

"What were you thinking about, Chase?" she asked.

"Just how much I love you," I answered, grabbing her hand and lacing my fingers through hers.

Her cheeks lit with color and she smiled. "I love you too."

The overhead speaker called out our flight number. We gathered our stuff, grabbed our bags, and made our way over to the boarding gate. I was beyond blessed, and I couldn't wait to start forever with Sophie.

About the Author

S.L. Sterling had been an avid reader since she was a child, often found getting lost in books. Today if she isn't writing or plotting, she can be found buried in a romance novel. S.L. Sterling lives with her husband and dog in Northern Ontario.

Sign up for my
Newsletter and get Forbidden for FREE

Visit My Website

Join my Street Team
Sterlings Silver Sapphires

Titles by S.L. Sterling

It Was Always You
On A Silent Night
Bad Company
Back to You this Christmas
Fireside Love
Holiday Wishes
All I Want for Christmas
The Greatest Gift
Office Misconduct
Into the Sunset

All American Boys Series

Saviour Boy
The Boy Under the Gazebo

The Malone Brother Series
A Kiss Beneath the Stars

In Your Arms
His to Hold
Finding Forever with You

Vegas MMA
Dagger

KB Worlds Everyday Heroes

Constraint

Coming Soon from S.L. Sterling

Our Little Secret - June 2022
Our Little Surprise - August 2022

Preorder Here